Sleepers

Book Three of Cat's Tales

Sandie Bergen

To Lynene

Ria Cho

Sandie

Mature Content Disclaimer:
This book contains mature content,
including some sex and violence.

Other books by Sandie Bergen

The Jada Trilogy

The Jada-Drau
Tyrsa's Choice
The Angry Sword

Cat's Tales

Arvanion's Gift
Silver Cat Black Fox

Dedication

I'd like to dedicate this book to Diana Cacy Hawkins. I sincerely don't know where I'd be without her continued support and dedication. Your friendship means so much to me.

SLEEPERS

Copyright©2014 Sandie Bergen

Edited by Sandy Fetchko
Cover art, design, map and layout by Ilsie Om.

Published November, 2014 in print and Ebook

Print ISBN: 978-1-940510-19-4

Marion Margaret Press
Headquarters:
PO Box 245
Hebron, NE 68370

email: publisher@marionmargaretpress.com

www.marionmargaretpress.com

Acknowledgements

It is a known fact that hugs can lift serotonin levels, elevating mood and creating happiness. They can instantly boost oxytocin levels which heal feelings of isolation, loneliness and anger. Hugs can strengthen the immune system, relax muscles and balance out the nervous system. Hugging someone is not only good for your health, it's good for the ones you care about. The Elves, of course, know this so...

Hugs to Steve Shumka, massage therapist and kilted warrior in a past life. Here is another book that has benefited from his willingness to share his knowledge and experience.

More hugs to Sandy Fetchko for keeping my wandering grammar in check.

As always a big thank you and lots of hugs to my family, Charlie, Amanda and Aaron, for putting up with my foibles, the least of which is staring off into time and space as I listen to what my characters have to tell me.

Hug someone you love today!

Prologue

In the grey place between Arvanion's beloved worlds, the place that shouldn't exist, on a plain of nothing, stood a castle. Walls, a mile long and seventy-five feet high, surrounded a castle of towers, seven in all. Six of the structures stretched up ninety feet to the grey sky, encircling the seventh, an unbelievable monstrosity of dark stone, one hundred and fifty feet high, studded with horrifying stone figures.

Carved faces—some Elven, some Tiranen, some Human, all twisted in agony—surrounded the arched doors, decorated the few windows and peered out from crags and crannies in the tortured building. Statues of demons from seven of the nine hells perched on balconies and cornices all up and down the hundred and fifty foot tower.

Khadag ignored it all. He ran up the long stairs of the central tower to Balphegor's throne room, his heart racing in expectation, the hair lock hanging from the top of his head swishing against his neck. He'd arranged to have the vaurok bodies on Crescent Island taken to Fornoss for ceremonial burning before coming here. He'd also asked another First to find a suitable home for the white egg, the last survivor of the disaster on Crescent Island. *Once the master hears my plan he'll make me Fleet Commander and Delcarion can lick my nose slits.* In his excitement, he almost forgot to knock.

"Enter."

The unspoken word slid through Khadag's head, lingering like pond scum on skin. His brow ridge dipped at the figure on the throne. Balphegor had shunned the form he'd worn for as long as Khadag remembered, that of a Human male child. A youth now sat there, a male and not quite Human. Cat-like ears perked up from the top of his head, a golden lion's mane surrounded his face, flowed down his bare back. A tawny tail flipped back and forth. Fur hid the skin of his lower body, the same shade as the tail. Clawed feet, too long to be called paws, rested on the stone dais at the foot of the throne.

The rest of the room remained the same. The blue marble throne, the only other hint of colour in the long, grey room, perched at the far wall. Khadag strode towards his master, passing the stone table and the fire pit in the centre of the room, avoiding the heated swords and pokers protruding from the pit. He didn't bother acknowledging Delcarion, who stood by the fire pit, arms crossed, head tilted at an angle that left no doubt as to his state of mind. Angry, definitely angry, and that pleased Khadag. His mouth curved in a smile as he prostrated himself before Balphegor. "My master, I await your command."

"Go to the table. Lay your left arm on it."

Khadag lost his smile. Jaws clenched, he glared at Delcarion, hiding behind cowl and cloak as always, then strode to the stone table. *That dung-eater didn't tell him I had a plan! Now the master's punishing me for something not my fault.* He couldn't argue his case, however, not unless the master allowed it. Delcarion visibly relaxed. Though a spell hid the slug's face, Khadag could imagine his grin. He clenched his right fist and placed his left arm on the table.

"Delcarion, please remove his hand at the wrist."

"With pleasure, my master." Delcarion's voice rasped with a harshness not found in Human or Elf and Khadag briefly wondered once again what kind of creature he was—until the master's words sunk in.

Remove my...! Khadag's blood turned cold. Rather than dwell on the inevitable, he clenched his teeth tighter and spread his legs, readying himself for the blow.

With a swirl of his black cloak, Delcarion turned to the fire pit. Three dark iron swords lay with their blades in the coals. He took a moment to choose one.

"Just get on with it, goblin-turd," Khadag muttered.

Delcarion finally made his choice and with a swift, solid swing of the red-hot blade, removed Khadag's left hand. His vision blurred and he almost passed out. He prided himself on the fact that he remained standing, though he had to lean on the table to do it. Pain throbbed through his truncated arm to his entire body until he thought he'd burst.

Khadag shook with the effort to hold himself upright and deal

12

with the agony. Long, blinding minutes passed before he could think of something other than his pain. He raised his head to the grey, unseen sky above and bellowed; not from the injury, his master hadn't allowed it, but in triumph at his success in keeping Delcarion from seeing him cowed.

When he could see again, Khadag examined his stump. He had to admit, Delcarion had done a good job. The blistering hot sword had cut clean, leaving the wound cauterized. Not a drop of blood had been spilled, though the stink of seared flesh filled his nostril slits. Khadag took greater pride in that he'd still shed none of his blood on that thrice-damned table. Delcarion couldn't say the same. Khadag's hand now lay on the stone slab, a dead thing, no longer useful.

"*Come to me.*" Balphegor's slippery voice dripped in his mind.

Khadag took control of shaking legs and made his way to the throne. He prostrated himself, a clumsy effort due to the injury. "My master, I am at your command." His voice came out rougher than usual.

"*Delcarion told me of the loss of the ships. Though Mectan was responsible, someone had to be punished and since you were the only survivor…*" Balphegor shrugged. "*I would have taken your life, but I need you. He also mentioned some sort of plan?*"

That surprised Khadag. "Yes, my master. I believe if we'd had the proper modifications to our ship, the ramming would have been successful. If we put metal, perhaps with something like a spiked iron fist at the bow, we could…"

The cat-man on the throne waved his hand. "*Spare me the details. Take who and what you need. Go to Fornoss to make your preparations.*"

Despite his pain, Khadag smiled. "Thank you, Master."

"*Now go.*"

Khadag rose, clumsier than he wished. When he strode past Delcarion, he bared his teeth in a wide grin. *Interfere with my plans, will you? It will get you nowhere. I don't need two hands to draw plans or command my workers.* He did need rest to recover from the loss of his hand. Rest, however, had to wait until he'd organized his workers and had them transporting supplies to the spot on Fornoss he'd chosen, a long peninsula on a small continent bordering the one remaining ocean.

13

Delcarion tapped his fingers against his thigh while he watched Khadag exit the throne room. All had not gone as planned. The vaurok should have been stranded on that island for six months. *Mind you, chopping off his hand was exhilarating.* Not enough punishment, though, and now the master wanted him to play with his toy boats. *Most irritating. At least he'll be out from under foot for awhile.* There were advantages to everything, if one knew where to look.

"Delcarion."

"Yes, my master?" He strode to the throne, prostrating himself before the unusual creature.

"Have you made any progress on your…little project?"

Delcarion kept his groan to himself. *No, not much.* "Some, Master. I have been able to expand the portal time to twelve minutes."

"It must be longer. The portal bigger." The youth's eyes, one a maelstrom of corruption, the other milky-white in death, burned straight to Delcarion's soul. *"We must get an army through."*

…in case of a defeat, Delcarion finished. It also made raids easier. Once the band had struck, they could escape before help arrived—which had been a problem in the past. The vauroks would be tracked and caught before they could make it back to one of the hidden, stationary portals. "I will continue to work on it."

"See that you do." A careless wave of his hand dismissed Delcarion.

℘   •   ℭ

Naron traced the words on the new gravestone —'Rayson, Son of Carle. Died with Honour in the Protection of our Lord Gethyn. In the Year of Ar, 824'. A fancy emblem, a wolf's head with a garland of ivy underneath, sat at the top of the stone, letting everyone know this man had received the Gold Wolf, Kitring-Tor's medal of valour. Too bad it was posthumous. Rayson would have worn it with pride.

It was an expensive stone. His family could never have paid for it. The new baron, Gethyn's son Edan, had it made for Rayson and for five others who'd died defending their lord. Naron was grateful to the baron,

14

but still resented the fact that Rayson had to die. If only that Elf girl…

A month and a half had passed since his brother's death. Naron had been sent home to his family's farm, in the northeast corner of the barony, to spend time with his family—and to grieve. Now he had to return to his unit. He brushed snow off the top of the stone and where it stuck to the words.

"You didn't have to die. Why did you do something so foolish! Gethyn was an old man, he'd have died soon anyway." A tear moistened his cheek. Despite Rayson's efforts, the old lord had perished.

Naron plunked himself on the ground and pulled the hood of his cloak over his sandy-blond hair. The graveyard sat on a hill and even though the sun shone, the wind blew cold. *If only that Elf girl had healed him. Lindren said she couldn't, but that soldier, the one from Kerend, said she could. How would he know?* Naron couldn't see…

"Well, hello stranger."

Naron glanced up. A man stood there, in plain brown trousers and jerkin, a cloak of the same colour wrapped around him. He looked familiar. "Hello. Have we met?" He stood, the better to see the man's face under the hood of the cloak.

"Yes, I'm the one who, ah, accidently overheard your conversation with Lindren. The name is Atax." The man smiled and lowered his hood. He had an ordinary looking face, youthful though he didn't seem young. Dark brown eyes, set in winter pale skin, sat under a neatly trimmed thatch of black hair, cut short, yet stylish. Naron could easily look him in the eyes.

"That's a coincidence." A strange one. "I was thinking about you."

Atax smiled. "Were you also thinking about our conversation?"

"Ah…yes, but, what are you doing here? And why are you out of uniform?" The man had worn the badge of Kerend, not Gethyn. The hairs rose on the back of Naron's neck.

"I quit the army. Had enough of cold beds, bad food and danger every time you turn around. I'm on my way to Tezerain, I have relatives there. I took a small detour to visit a cousin of mine who, I just found out, passed away. I'm here to pay my respects."

Naron's eyes narrowed. "What is your cousin doing here?"

15

The smile increased, ever so slightly. "He married a girl from a village not far from here. Her parents had no other children, so he took over the farm when they died."

It sounded plausible. Kerend lay next door to Gethyn and here the border was quite close. "What was the name? I might know them."

Atax chuckled. "You're full of questions today." He fished around the pockets of his cloak. "Ah, here we are." He pulled out a small flask. "I was given this as a going away gift from my brother. It's brandy from Thallan-Mar. Share some with me? For old times' sake."

What old times? Naron said nothing, though. Thallan-Mar brandy was rare in the northern baronies. He'd tasted some once and that had been a sip. "I suppose so."

With a flourish, the stranger indicated they should sit. He passed the flask to Naron. "First drink to a brave warrior."

Naron snorted, but took the flask, drinking more than a sip. It burned on the way down and tasted so good…light, with a hint of sweet fruit. It slid down like silk. He stole another mouthful before handing it back.

Atax held the flask to his lips, then lowered it. "How' s your family handling the loss of your brother?"

Naron dropped his gaze to his boots. "Not well. He was the oldest and I only have one other brother. He's eight and barely able to help out on the farm. When summer comes, I'm quitting the army so I can help my parents."

"That's very decent of you." He passed the flask back. "Have another drink. Nothing like good brandy to warm you on a cold day."

"Thanks, I think I will." If the man offered, how could he refuse?

Atax shook his head. "Bad business that."

Naron gulped down the mouthful he'd taken. It still burned as it slipped down his throat. "What business?"

"Your brother. And the others who died needlessly."

A month and a half and it still hurt. Naron said nothing as he tipped the flask once more.

A sigh escaped Atax's thin lips. "Such a waste. Especially since the Elves could have helped, if they really wanted to."

16

"You said that the last time we met." Naron passed the flask back. "Lindren said otherwise. I doubt he'd lie."

"How do you know he would or wouldn't?"

"Baron Gethyn…he always trusted Lindren. He'd know." *Wouldn't he?* Naron's head spun a little, from the brandy he supposed. When Atax returned the flask to him he didn't refuse it.

Atax chuckled again. "Your Baron Gethyn was an excellent warrior. He also knew how to manage his lands." He spread his arms. "Look at what he's done and in such a short time, too. Just thirty-nine years. An amazing man."

"Yes, he was. To Baron Gethyn." Naron raised the flask, took a drink, then passed it back to Atax.

He also raised the flask. "To Baron Gethyn." Atax gave it back. "Even so, I think he was blinded by all that Lindren did, supplying money and Elves until the army had grown big enough. I've seen a few battles, my friend, most of them with Elves fighting alongside. More humans die than Elves every time. Don't you think its a little suspicious?"

Naron frowned. Atax's face blurred, then straightened out again. "But, isn't that because more Humans fight than Elves? There's usually only one or two companies, while there's hundreds of us."

"And that's another point. Why send so few? If they sent more, we'd have a better chance of cutting our losses. Besides, I'm talking percentages. Less Elves are killed than Humans."

"Isn't that because they have better armour? And I think I heard their mail is better too. Wouldn't that help?"

Another smile slid up Atax's face. "Of course it's true. Thank you for bringing that up." He waved a finger in Naron's face. "Why don't they share their mail and armour with us? It's all a plot I tell you."

"A plot? To do what?" None of it made sense, and yet, when he thought about it, Atax had some very good points.

"Have the Black Lord's forces kill us and we kill them, leaving the world to the Elves…all by themselves. They'd have the whole thing."

Naron hiccupped. He took another drink. "Wouldn't that be a little difficult to pull off? I doubt the Elves know exactly how many vauroks and goblins there are, let alone trolls, wyverns and…*hic*…hell wolves." Naron frowned again and looked at the flask. *Maybe I've had too much.* He shook it—it was over half gone—then passed it to Atax. The strange man slipped it back into his cloak. "There's not just us either, there's the rest of Kitring-Tor, Thallan-Mar to the south, The Denfold to the east, and...and...all those other places. I don't see how they could possibly plan for everyone to kill each other at the same time."

"Ah!" Atax held up a finger. "But that's just it, it wouldn't be at the same time. Elves live forever, they have all the time in the world to bring their plans to fruition. Just think about it. Why else would they not send in more troops? Why else would they not heal us or make us armour like theirs? And trust me, they can heal us."

Naron had no answer for that, not with the brandy-fog clouding his brain. Maybe Atax was right. "Their armour makes them hard to kill." Didn't he say that already? It was difficult to remember.

"Not if you know where to put your dagger. Come from behind and go for the face. A quick stab to the eye and there you are. They never wear full helms. And coming from you, they'd never suspect it either."

"Me? But...why would I want to kill an Elf? They help us, even if what you say is true, they're still helping us, aren't they?" *Or are they? If what Atax says is the truth, then that Elf girl really did let Rayson die. For nothing. Just so they can have the world to themselves.* Naron's hands tightened into fists.

Atax stood. "They're pretending to help us. They really want us gone from their land. They never wanted us here in the first place. Ar brought us to Urdran to live in peace and harmony, but the Elves resented it. And now we're paying for it."

Naron looked up into his eyes. He seemed so tall, standing over him like that, his brown eyes alight with the fire of conviction. He truly believed what he said. Could it be true? Naron thought about Rayson, about the Elves that fought and died compared to the Humans, about the armour and how to kill an Elf. *He must be right. Rayson died for nothing.*

Atax nodded. "Rayson died for nothing."

How did he know what I was thinking? Naron tried to stand and almost made it. Atax held out his hand. Naron used it to stagger to his feet.

18

"Remember what I said. It's very important." Dark brown eyes bored into Naron's, imprinting his words on his brain. Then he was gone.

Naron struggled to keep upright while he searched for the stranger, but he'd vanished. Somewhere in the back of his clouded brain he didn't remember Atax taking a drink of the brandy, but, somehow, it didn't really seem to be important. There were more serious issues to think about.

Chapter One

Cat stared at the hustle and bustle of the docks of Tezerain, the noonday sun sparkling off the wide waters of the Dorrin River. The single dock of Meat Town couldn't begin to compare. So many boats of various shapes and sizes floated in the harbor that the water could hardly be seen. The gulls, crying their hunger, had multiplied tenfold from those at the mercenary village. She glanced back at the big Human following her down the gangplank of the Elven ship and smiled.

"As much I enjoy your smile," Rhone Arden said. "I'm supposed to be your bodyguard. A proper lady pays little attention to servants."

Apparently a proper lady doesn't wear trousers, shirt and tunic, or pack a bow either. Humans had so many rules about what they could and couldn't do…all terribly confusing, but with Rhone Arden as her bodyguard, it meant she could be near him. Especially at night. Cat smiled again, this time to herself. Rescuing him from Crescent Island was the best part of the whole excursion to find Jeral's crystals.

A ship about the same size as theirs floated nearby, the single, brightly coloured sail folded neatly against the yardarm. Men swarmed the deck, which wasn't unusual except for the colour of their skin. They varied from a light to a very dark brown, a vast difference from her own pale golden shade. She stopped at the bottom of the gangplank. The dark sailors stared back. Rhone almost bumped into her. He carried her saddlebags, as well as his pack, and shifted them to a better position on his shoulder.

"Am I allowed to ask you questions?" Cat asked.

Rhone's eyes studied her a moment; it was all she could see of his face. He wore a black cloth mask to conceal his features. If anyone recognized him, it would mean his death, despite the fact he was a baron's son. A cloak, pulled close around him, hid a leather jerkin and most of his trousers, all in black. They made him similar in appearance to the assassins belonging to the Brotherhood of Ar.

20

"I suppose so," he said, "but try to keep them to a minimum. We're expected at the castle."

Cat wrinkled her nose. "Those men over there."

Rhone's unusual sea green eyes followed where she indicated.

"I've never seen men with that coloured skin before," she said.

"They're from a country far south of here, where the sun shines much hotter. I'd imagine they're traders, though they're early this year. They don't usually arrive for another month or so. Can we continue? You're holding up the line."

She glanced back at the Elves—her adopted father Lindren, his sons Darsha and Shain, and her friend Kelwyn—all standing on the gangplank, looking annoyed. Captain Mathyn and his soulmate Yira leaned on the railing, both wearing smirks.

"Can the questions please wait, Cat?" Linden said. "I really want a bath."

His appearance bothered her; he looked so tired and the dark circles under his eyes hadn't gone away. She slipped her eyes out of focus so she could see the colour of the light surrounding his body. The normal bright blue was washed out and blended with pale yellow, indicating pain. He had no injuries, so it had to be a headache. The sea battle had affected him more than he let on, but when she tried to talk to him about it he shushed her.

Cat moved to the side, Rhone sliding around behind her, and the Elves made their way down to the dock, burdened with their packs and saddlebags. While she waited for them to pass, she smoothed down her unbound silver-blonde hair, ensuring her ears were covered, and pulled up her hood. She usually wore it in a braid, but Lindren still wanted her to pretend she was an Elf and she couldn't do that with her ears exposed.

Lindren took the lead. "Follow me and don't wander off."

"I'll make sure she stays in line," Rhone said, his eyes scanning every direction.

Cat grimaced. She resigned herself to taking in the sights and storing up her questions for later. They left the docks and walked up a street lined with large buildings. Most of the snow on the ground had melted, leaving a layer of muddy slush, thick in some places, thin or gone in others. Men worked with horses, carts, pulleys and ropes, moving large boxes, sacks and other containers in and out of the buildings.

"Lindren!" Rhone hissed.

The Elf stopped and turned to look where Rhone discreetly pointed. Several men unloaded sacks off a wagon and hauled them over their shoulders into the long building.

"I don't believe it. That man who just went into the warehouse is Jonlan, the one with the black hair and beard." Rhone kept his voice low.

Lindren moved beside him. "Are you sure?"

"I spent enough nights tossing back ale with him. A mere beard can't fool me."

A moment later, the man came back out, his black hair tinged blue in the sun.

"What do you want to do?" Darsha asked.

Rhone gave him Cat's saddlebags and slipped his pack off his shoulder, passing it to Shain. "I don't think I can sneak up on him, not dressed like this. I don't want to attract any more attention than I have to. But I need to talk to him."

Lindren frowned. "Do you want to reveal yourself so soon? He might alert the guards and then you'll be in for it. Mind you, we're not far from the ship. How fast can you run?"

"If he's guilty, the last thing he'd want to do is call the guards. I know him. He'll either be very glad to see me or run like hell. Walk on to the end of the building. Wait for me there. Kelwyn, can you watch the back for me in case he runs?"

Kelwyn nodded and shed his belongings, distributing them amongst the other Elves, then sauntered to the end of the warehouse and around the corner. Lindren, Darsha and Shain were now piled high with packs and saddlebags. Cat took pity on poor tired Lindren and hoisted Kelwyn's pack over a shoulder.

Rhone took a deep breath. "Wish me luck."

Cat's breath caught in her throat. She wished with all her heart that Arvanion would send him the best luck he could.

Rhone walked casually towards the workers, ignoring their suspicious glances. With the number of men and carts in motion, he came within ten feet before Jonlan spotted him. "Jonlan?"

The man took a step back, a Y-shaped scar visible above his right eye.

It is him!

Light brown eyes widened and Jonlan dropped the sack he'd been carrying. "Ar's lights! It's the Brotherhood!" He turned and ran back into the warehouse.

"Wait!" Rhone dashed after him.

One of the workers threw a sack at Rhone's feet. He stumbled, cursing. Another man took a swing at him.

Rhone dodged it. *Brave man, throwing a punch at someone he thinks belongs to the Brotherhood.*

Now in the dim warehouse, Rhone had to let his eyes adjust. Men bumped into him, apologizing though it was deliberate. More blocked his path. When he could see better, Rhone dodged around barrels and crates, jumped over sacks. Around and over the warehouse contents, Rhone searched. No sign.

Kelwyn appeared at the rear doors.

"Did you see him come out?" Rhone asked.

"No, but there's a lot of people and stuff back here. He might have slipped past me."

Rhone doubted it. Jonlan had to be hiding inside.

Three burly men, one with a crowbar, strode through the open double doors. The two on the ends searched the area, high and low, while they walked. Ar's Brotherhood rarely worked alone. Rhone set his hand on his sword; so did Kelwyn.

The middle one, the oldest and baldest, spat at Rhone's feet. "We don't want yer kind round here. Yer nothin' but trouble."

"I don't want trouble. I only wish to speak with Jonlan. I have no intention of hurting him."

The oaf on the right grinned, despite the fear in his eyes. "Who?"

23

Rhone clenched his fist. "The man with the black hair and beard who ran when I called his name."

"Still don't know who you mean," drawled the man on the left. His fear released itself as sweat. "Ain't no one here with that name or description. You must be confused."

"We saw him," Kelwyn said, his eyes dark. "Are you calling us liars?"

"Never called no Elf a liar before this." The man in the middle slapped his crowbar on the palm of his hand. "Never tried to hurt one either. There's always a first time."

More men gathered, all obviously on the brutes' side. Cat and the other Elves came in the front doors and moved in behind Rhone.

"I'd appreciate it if you'd move on, dark man," the one slapping the crowbar said. "But you can leave the pretty one behind." A chorus of laughter bounced off the walls of the warehouse. "We ain't seen the man you want and we don't know anyone called Jonlan."

"He's lying," Cat said. She appeared confused.

"I know." A blind man could see it. Rhone clenched his fists. He'd come so close. "Let's leave for now."

"I agree." Lindren's voice sounded hard. Not surprising, he'd be worried about Cat.

"Tell Jonlan I mean him no harm. If he wishes to talk, I'll be at the castle. He can send a messenger. Tell him to ask for Fox." It was worth a try.

The man on the left hadn't lost his forced grin. "Ain't no one to tell."

Or not. Rhone backed away, the Elves and Cat with him, until they turned the corner of the warehouse. He leaned against the grey wood. "That didn't go well."

"It was strange," Cat said, her brows dipping in confusion. "That man lied when he said he didn't see the man you wanted, but he didn't lie when he said he didn't know Jonlan." She set her things on the ground and rolled her shoulders.

How would she know whether the man lied or not?

"Could he have changed his name?" Kelwyn asked.

24

"Very possible." Lindren dropped his burden. "If he's guilty of Jornel's murder, it would be a smart move."

Rhone hadn't thought of it. "Well," he sighed. "I'm not going to hold my breath waiting for a messenger. We'll have to find some other way to flush him out." *And another way to prove I'm innocent of that murder.*

Lindren rubbed his eyes. "Regardless, we can't deal with it now. Let's sort out our belongings and head for the castle. I really need a bath."

"You don't look good," Cat said, shouldering her pack, bow and quivers. Rhone picked up her saddlebags and took his pack from Shain.

"I'm fine, Cat. Let's just go."

Rhone didn't think Lindren looked fine. It wasn't his place to say anything, though. Darsha and Shain must have felt the same way—they distributed their father's belongings between them, refusing to let him carry anything. Lindren didn't put up much of a fight.

When they reached the street, Rhone glanced back at the doors where he'd spotted Jonlan. Normal activity had resumed. Jonlan was nowhere in sight.

℘   •   ℆

Cat didn't think much of this part of town. Other than the boats, the rest of the dock area was boring, merely a crowd of people, big buildings, a lot of stuff in boxes, barrels and sacks, and one horrible smell; a far cry from the peaceful forest enclave where she lived. As they walked up Wharf Street—Kelwyn beside her, Rhone behind—they passed rundown homes, fish shops, taverns and inns, interspersed with the odd armoury, weapon or food shop. Alleys littered with smelly garbage broke up the rows of shabby structures. Shain pointed to one sitting between a tavern and a fish shop.

"This is where the Hrulka found you the night you disappeared," he said.

It was wider than the other alleys she'd seen. Two of the magical horses could fit, though there wouldn't be much room left over. She stared at it, trying to dredge up some memory from that night. Kelwyn set a hand on her shoulder.

"Do you remember any of it?" Lindren asked.

She shook her head. "Nothing."

"I wonder if Rodrin has been able to discover who was behind it?" Darsha asked.

"We'll find out when we get to the castle." Lindren motioned them on.

At the next corner, a man in old clothes and a ragged cloak sat hunched up on a blanket. He had a metal cup in front of him. Cat couldn't figure why he looked so strange, until she realized he had no legs. *I wonder how he lost his legs?* "Why does he have a cup out like that?"

Shain answered. "He's a cripple and can't work, so he begs for money."

Several people walked by, ignoring him. As Cat watched, five more passed without even looking at the poor man. She pulled out her small leather purse.

"What are you doing, my lady?" Rhone asked.

Cat blinked at use of the honorific. He'd never used it before, then she realized it was part of his disguise as her bodyguard. "Giving him some money."

Rhone sighed and handed his pack and her saddlebags to Kelwyn. "Don't bother." He picked the man up by his collar; at six inches over six feet and with a build that resembled the males of her own race, he had no difficulty handling the smaller man.

"Hey, mate! I'll call the watch if'n you don't let me go!" Two legs unfolded from somewhere under his cloak.

"Go right ahead. We can tell them how you're cheating people out of their hard earned money." Rhone set him on his feet. "Pick up your ill-gotten gains and scram."

The man grabbed his cup and blanket, and scampered down the street on two perfectly good legs. The cup rattled as he ran.

"Well that...!" Cat held her tongue in check while she glared after the man, then turned to Rhone. "How did you know?"

Rhone retrieved the pack and saddlebags. "I remember him. He hasn't changed."

Cat glanced down at the coin in her hand and, on impulse, gave

26

the silver crown to a passing boy who wore little more than rags, despite the cold weather.

Once he'd put his eyes back in his head, the boy skipped away."Thanks, lady!"

"Why did you do that?" Kelwyn asked.

"He looked like he needed it."

Kelwyn smiled and kissed her cheek.

"Cat," Lindren said, exasperated.. "If you're finished passing out money, could we please go to the castle?"

Rhone chuckled. She stuck her tongue out.

Chapter Two

When Cat, Rhone and the Elves rounded the corner of Wharf and Dolphin Streets, they almost ran into Arnir. He rode Pian and carried the reins of the other Hrulka. Two men stopped in the crowded street to stare at them. One glare from Kelwyn sent the curious pair on their way.

"Where were you half an hour ago?" Cat complained to her brother, in Torian rather than Elven. She rubbed Krir's nose, glad to see him again. "We're carrying a lot of stuff."

"Some more than others, I see. I came as soon as I received word." Arnir took the hint and spoke in the same language. He dismounted and Cat gave him a hug.

"Lindren isn't feeling well," she whispered in his ear. "We had a big fight and he used too much magic."

Arnir frowned, studying his father. "What kind of fight?"

Lindren sighed. "Cat, sometimes I wish you'd just be quiet for once." He hauled himself up on Auri. Shain, snickering, settled his father's saddlebags behind him while Lindren took his pack back from Darsha.

"Why shouldn't I tell him? It was a really bad fight and you are still not..." Cat snapped her mouth shut at Lindren's glare, then, scowling, took her saddlebags from Rhone and placed them over Krir's back. She tied on her bow and quivers. If it was the other way around, he'd want to know.

"Should I be concerned?" Arnir rested his hand on Lindren's leg. His father moved Auri away. Now Arnir frowned.

"We'll tell you about it later. At the castle. After I've had a bath and a rest." Lindren pointed his Hrulka's head in that direction. "Now mount up."

While Darsha, Shain and Kelwyn loaded their belongings and settled into their saddles, Arnir looked askance at Rhone. "Is he with us?"

Cat's mood jumped up a notch. "He's my new bodyguard. He

28

says to call him Fox. We'll tell you that story at the castle too." She turned to Rhone. "This is my brother, Arnir."

"I suspected it." Rhone nodded a greeting. "Pleased to meet you, my lord."

Arnir cast Lindren a skeptical glance. Lindren shrugged.

"Sorry I didn't bring an extra mount," Arnir said to Rhone.

Before the man could answer, Cat said, "It's all right, he can ride with me." She almost bounced into Krir's saddle, then slid forward, talking to the Hrulka as she did, making sure he understood it was all right for Rhone to ride him. Krir, though unsure, agreed. "Is it acceptable for you to ride with me?"

Rhone shrugged. "Since I don't relish the long walk uphill to the castle, it's fine by me." He passed his pack to Darsha. It took a moment or two to climb onto the big horse. "Sorry about the clumsy mount, it's been a while since I've sat on a horse and never one this big."

Arnir took the pack from his brother and passed it up. "I believe you just might be the first Human who's ever ridden a Hrulka." Cat's brother still gave Rhone strange looks.

"Another first," the man muttered.

If Cat had her way, he'd be the first Human to make love with a Tiranen. She smiled all the way to the castle.

ဆ · ෙ

Not only Rodrin waited to greet Lindren and his family. Queen Lisha, Prince Gailen and Lady Selesa flanked him while Talifir and the twenty-nine other Elves Lindren had sent as escort for Arnir stood in the Throne room. As soon as they entered, Rodrin's eyes shifted straight to Rhone. Lindren hadn't had the opportunity to do much thinking about what he'd tell the Kitring-Tor king. One thing he did know, he couldn't tell the truth. Rodrin would have to arrest him.

"Nice to have you back," Rodrin said, his eyes straying once more to Rhone, who stood behind Cat with his arms folded, looking every bit the mercenary he pretended to be. "Though I must say, you don't look like you've slept much."

Lindren nodded a greeting to Rodrin's wife, son and future daughter-in-law. "We ran into some trouble. There's much to discuss. Would you mind if it waited though? We're all in desperate need of a bath." *And I need to get rid of this headache.*

"And a rest by the looks of it. You've just missed lunch. I'll have some food delivered to your rooms along with tubs and water for all." Rodrin deliberately turned his gaze to Rhone again.

Much to Lindren's chagrin, Cat piped up. "He's my bodyguard, so I don't get…kidnapped…again." She wore her smile all over her face.

Rodrin blinked. "I thought you Elves were planning to do that."

"The situation changed." Lindren wished they could pass on the questions and go to their rooms.

Gailen pointed a finger in Rhone's general direction. "Why does he wear that mask? He looks like one of Ar's Brotherhood."

"He isn't…" Cat started.

"The Brotherhood don't wear cloaks," Kelwyn interrupted. "I've seen a few."

Cat leaned slightly towards the prince. "He has a lot of scars."

Lindren almost laughed. It was the truth, though most of the scars were on his back.

Cat wasn't finished. "Would it be possible to have a bed set up in my sitting room? He'll need a bath too."

Lindren wished she wasn't so forward about it all.

Rodrin frowned. "Are you sure you can trust this man? Where did you find him?"

Darsha spoke before Cat could open her mouth. "We hired Fox in Meat Town."

"Fox?" Rodrin's frown deepened.

"He comes with a good reputation."

Smart thinking, son, Lindren thought, wishing he could lie down.

"Sorry to sound like I'm grilling you," Rodrin said. "But why were you in Meat Town?"

Lindren sighed. "We ran into two vaurok ships and were beat up pretty bad."

Rodrin's eyebrows rose and he opened his mouth to speak.

30

Lisha stepped forward. "Please, my lord. Lindren looks so tired. Can this wait until later?"

Bless you!

Rodrin's smile returned. "Of course. Get cleaned up, have a bite to eat and a rest, and we'll discuss all this after dinner."

They took their leave of the king and his family, Lindren thanking Arvanion Rodrin didn't throw Rhone out on his ear; though he still might.

ॐ • ॐ

When Cat arrived at her suite, Jewel waited for her. The little maid frowned when she saw Rhone, who positioned himself by the door. *Here we go again.* Cat set her bow, quivers and pack near him, next to the two quivers already leaning against the wall. Rhone put her saddlebags and his pack near the small table.

Jewel stiffened and stuck her nose in the air. "My lady, who is this strange man? He shouldn't be in your rooms. Where is Lord Kelwyn?"

"Kelwyn is having a bath. This is my bodyguard. He says to call him Fox." She stepped closer to Jewel. "Please be nice to him. The king is having a bed brought up…"

"A bed! My lady! Lord Kelwyn staying you with is bad enough, but at least he's your cousin. This…this…*mercenary*…is dangerous! He might just kidnap you himself. Or worse!"

Rhone took a step forward. "Look, miss. I've got ten gold royals riding on this job. My mother didn't raise me to be stupid."

Jewel's jaw dropped. "Ten gold royals!"

"Yes, now if you've finished insulting me, it sounds like my lady's bathtub has arrived."

Sure enough, a knock sounded on the door. Rhone opened it. Judging by the hustle and bustle out in the hall, the Elves' tubs had arrived as well. In no time, her bath was ready.

Jewel tested it. "More hot water. My lady likes it hot."

One of the men bowed and they all left.

"Why does he wear a mask?" Jewel demanded. "Too afraid to

31

show his face?"

"He has a lot of scars." It seemed to work for Rodrin.

"Hmmph! I'll just unpack your things, my lady," Jewel said, with a scathing glance at Rhone.

While the maid had her back to her, Cat shrugged her helplessness. Rhone's eyes crinkled and she could picture his wonderful smile. It took a long time for him to show it, but when he did it had been worth the wait.

"Don't bother putting my shirts and trousers away," Cat said to the maid. "They all need to be washed. But there's another outfit at the bottom of the pack that needs to be hung."

Jewel picked up the shirt Cat had worn in the battle. "You weren't kidding. What's all over this? Is that blood? And it's torn!" Tsking, she picked up something else. "What's this for, my lady?"

"Oh! My shells and things. I forgot about those." She helped Jewel pick her treasures out of the clothes, gathering them all in her arms. "Where can I put them so they're safe?"

"Why do you want to keep that junk?" the maid asked.

Cat clutched them tighter. "I've never seen things like this before. My brother at home hasn't either, so I thought I'd bring some for him."

"Another brother, my lady? You have four brothers?"

The small drawer in the table near the door looked like a good place to store the shells and driftwood she'd collected from her first visit to the ocean. "Yes. He's younger than me. His name is Robilan, but we call him Robbi."

"That's a nice name." Jewel finished pulling the rest of Cat's dirty clothes out of the pack, then picked up the torn and bloody one. "I don't think we're going to be able to get this blood out, my lady."

If it didn't come out, Cat would be down to two sets of every day clothes. "Can someone try?"

Jewel put the clothes in a pile. "Yes, but don't expect miracles. You do have two other outfits in the wardrobe, you could wear those until we have something made."

"They're supposed to be for special times." Cat hadn't thought about someone here making her clothes. Since her people died, Lindren's soulmate, Rhianna, sewed all her outfits.

A knock sounded on the door. Jewel opened it this time. Two men came in with steaming buckets and filled the tub almost to the brim.

Jewel shooshed them out. "Time for your bath, my lady." She glared at Rhone. "That means you leave." She pointed at the door.

Rhone folded his arms. "It means I stay. I have to guard the lady and I can't do it if I'm not here." He turned and faced the wall.

Jewel's mouth dropped open. Cat put her hand over it. "It's all right. Lindren expects him to stay with me. He really is a nice man, he only looks mean."

"My lady," Rhone said. "I thank you for the compliment, but I would prefer people to think I'm mean and nasty. There's a better chance they'll behave."

"Oh. All right." *I suppose that makes sense.*

Jewel threw up her arms. "I simply don't know what to say!"

Cat shrugged out of her long leather tunic and sat so she could pull off her boots. "You could take my things to be washed while I have my bath." She undid her trousers, letting them drop to the floor, took off her shirt, then handed them and her long tunic to Jewel.

"My lady! Honestly!" Despite the clothes, the maid managed to put her hands on her hips. "I am *not* going to leave you alone with that...that brute!"

Cat heaved a mental sigh and tested the water. It was perfect. "Then just ignore him. Please."

She slid into the water and let the heat caress her skin. There was nothing like a hot bath to soothe frayed nerves...and Jewel could certainly fray a lot of nerves.

While Cat washed, Jewel hung up the gold and silver outfit, then fussed with her belongings. When she was done, the maid washed her hair for her.

"What's this, my lady? It's green."

"It's vaurok blood. I thought I'd brushed it all out. I guess I missed some. We were in a fight. Two vaurok ships attacked ours."

Jewel gasped. "And you fought? I thought you only used a bow."

"No, I fight too."

The maid shook her head. "Well, at least you managed to escape injury. I just don't know about you Elves. You're all so strange."

Cat could say the same about Humans. She glanced at Rhone. He'd hardly moved. "Can someone bring more hot water up for his bath?"

"Of course not. If he wants to wash, he can use this water. We don't cater to *mercenaries*." Jewel made the word sound bad.

Poor Rhone. This water isn't going to be very warm by the time I get out. At least she didn't put any of those stinky bubbles in it.

Jewel rinsed her hair and Cat stood up, glad to be clean again.

"If he's going to have a bath, you'd better come into your bedroom and dry off there." Jewel almost pushed her into the room and slammed the door.

Another knock sounded on the outer door. Rhone answered it. "My lady," he called. "Your food is here."

"I'll eat it after you've had your bath," Cat said.

Jewel now scowled at her.

"As you wish, my lady," Rhone responded.

The maid toweled Cat dry then wrapped her hair in the towel. She opened the wardrobe doors. "Since all your other clothes are dirty, you'll have to wear one of these." She pulled out the black and silver outfit.

"I don't really need anything, Jewel. I want to lie down for a while." As soon as Rhone finished his bath, she had plans for him.

"You need to eat and you're certainly not going to do it wrapped in a towel. Not with *him* out there."

"Oh. Right." Rhone would have to wait a little longer. The odd splash came from the other room and Cat tried hard not to picture him in the tub; her eyes might start glowing.

Jewel helped her dress. Cat had worn the outfit a few times at Mid-Winter festivals. Made of black material with a soft nap, it shimmered with muted rainbow colours when the light caught it. The tunic had long sleeves, a high back, and dipped in the front, showing off the tops of her breasts. Dainty silver leaves adorned the hem, neckline, and sleeves of the tunic. The black trousers hung loose and were gathered at the ankle, Tiranen style.

Cat sat in the small chair by the window, staring out at the practice grounds while the maid brushed her hair. When finished that chore, Jewel fussed with things in the room. Finally, Rhone announced he was done.

"Well that took long enough," Jewel said, her voice snippy. "Please come and have a bite to eat, my lady."

Cat had to admit, she was hungry. She snuggled down into one of the comfortable chairs by the crackling fire.

Jewel gasped, then glared at Rhone, who stood by the door once more looking quite formidable. "Did you eat some of my lady's food?"

"Yes, there's plenty there."

At five feet, Jewel had to look up a long way to scold him. She wagged her finger. "You are a servant! Servants do *not* eat their lady's food! You filthy, stinking…."

"No, I'm not. I just had a bath."

Cat jumped out of her chair. "Jewel! Please!" She remembered what Lindren said about taking a firm stand with servants. "He's here to guard me. He needs to eat too. And there's lots here."

"But, my lady…"

"I didn't want to offend my lady by removing my mask to eat," Rhone said. "I have scars, remember."

That shut Jewel up, until she found Rhone's dirty clothes in the same pile as Cat's.

"You go too far!"

"Jewel, if he's guarding me, how is he supposed to wash his clothes?"

The girl scowled, then picked up the pile of laundry. "I should have someone else take this, then I can sit with you while you rest."

Cat's heart leapt to her throat. Jewel's presence would ruin her plans for Rhone. "Please don't. Remember what I said before? I can't sleep if someone is watching."

Jewel eyed up Rhone. "Well, make sure you lock your door and call for the guards if there's any problem."

"I insist she lock her door," Rhone said, his voice gruff.

Cat sat in the chair once more and bit into a piece of cheese.

Jewel harrumphed. Rhone opened the door and she stomped out. He slid the bolt closed. "She didn't say which door, now did she?"

Cat laughed and joined Rhone. She pulled his mask down and kissed him, slow and sweet. When they broke off, he stared into her eyes, running a finger down her cheek. By the look in his eyes, hers were glowing.

"Eat," he said. "I don't want you fainting from hunger half way through."

She'd just finished eating when a curt rap sounded at the door. Rhone pulled his mask up. Cat almost groaned when she saw the face behind the door.

Jewel flounced her way into the room. "The laundry women have your clothes. They say there's no chance the blood will come out, it's set. So I've arranged for the seamstress to come see you tomorrow morning to make you some new clothes."

"That's fine, thank you. I'm going to go lie down," Cat said, hoping she'd take the hint.

"Are you sure you don't want me to stay?" The maid gave Rhone another suspicious glance.

"No, thank you. I'll be fine."

Without taking her eyes off Rhone, Jewel scooped up Cat's boots. "I forgot these. They need a good brushing." She put her hand on the doorknob. "Now you make sure your bedroom door is locked and remember the guards are just outside."

Cat tried not to let her impatience come out in her voice. "I will."

Rhone locked the door and reached her side in two long strides. He pulled down his mask and threw back his hood. "That woman takes annoying to all new levels."

He didn't let Cat respond. After a long, passionate, demanding kiss he leaned back. "That's better."

Cat blinked. "What?"

"The glow left while you ate. That's a beautiful outfit, by the way. I wish our women wore clothes like that. How do I get you out of it?"

Rhone drew her close once more, his lips on hers, then moved to her neck, nuzzling his way down to her breasts. One hand pushed her

36

tunic up and he teased one of her nipples. The other slid down to caress her bottom.

Another knock, and Rhone groaned. "Who now?"

He pulled up his mask and hood before opening the door.

It was Kelwyn. "I just wanted to see if Cat…Oh. Never mind."

Cat tilted her head. "What's wrong?"

"Nothing, it's just…" Kelwyn looked at Rhone and back at her. "I'm interrupting. I'll talk to you later." He smiled, though it seemed sad.

His words from their time on the ship came to her. 'He's the one'. Kelwyn had been her only friend for many years, then a sometimes lover. Cat couldn't let herself love him the way she wanted, he'd find his soulmate one day. She had to take other lovemates, though it broke her heart to see him there with that look in his eyes.

She gently tugged the black forlock that always seemed to find a way to hang in his face, then gave him a hug and a light kiss on the lips. "I'll see you later."

"Later, then." Kelwyn stepped out the door.

Rhone closed it. "Maybe now we'll have some peace." Off came the mask and hood.

Cat slipped into his embrace, lifting her lips for a kiss.

Another rap sounded. Rhone clenched his teeth. "What now?" Up went the mask and hood.

It was Darsha. "Now that Father's had a bath and a bite to eat, he wants to tell Arnir about everything that happened before he has a rest. Do you want to come?"

Rhone looked at Cat. So did Darsha.

"If he doesn't mind, I'd rather stay here."

Darsha smiled and Cat suspected he knew exactly how she intended to spend the rest of the afternoon. Then she remembered her glowing eyes and groaned inside.

"No problem. I'm sure he'll understand." Darsha gave them both a nod and headed for Lindren's quarters.

Rhone closed the door and leaned against it as if he could keep intruders out. "This is as bad as the mercenaries at the tavern in Meat Town." He opened the door again.

"My lady wishes not to be disturbed," he said to the guard. "Especially by Jewel. And if the men come with my bed, tell them to leave it here and set it up while my lady's at dinner."

Cat couldn't see the guard, but she could hear him. "I don't take orders from you. I don't know who you are."

This is ridiculous. It's going to be dinner and I won't have spent any time with Rhone. "Please do as he asks. He's my new bodyguard," she said, keeping hidden.

"As you wish, my lady."

Rhone slammed the door. He locked it, almost pushed her into the bedroom, then locked that door as well. Off came the mask and the entire cloak this time. He tossed them both onto the bed. "Now then. There will be no more interruptions. You are mine."

Cat smiled.

Chapter Three

Lindren sat in his chair by the fire, trying to act normal. Arnir perched on the edge of the other stuffed chair, waiting for an explanation Lindren didn't want to give. Kelwyn and Shain sat cross-legged on the floor, helping themselves from the large tray on the table between the chairs. Lindren had eaten some of the bread, cheese, fruit and pastries Rodrin provided, enough to keep his sons happy. The food sat like rock in his gut. The headache had worsened and try as he might he still couldn't access his power, and it worried him. He wanted to rest; his throbbing head wouldn't let him.

Darsha knocked, then entered. "Cat says she'd rather not come. It looks like she and Rhone have other plans."

Lindren watched Kelwyn's face for any sign of the anguish he'd shown on the ship. His nephew's expression remained impassive, perhaps too much. He still didn't understand how Kelwyn could love Cat like he did.

Kelwyn swallowed whatever he had in his mouth. "Her eyes were glowing when I was there."

"Same here." Darsha folded his long legs before joining Shain and Kelwyn on the floor. He helped himself to a thick apple pastry.

Arnir's brows dipped in a frown. "Glowing?"

"There's so much to tell," Lindren said, with a sigh.

"So out with it," Arnir said. "I'd like to hear it all, the battle, Fox, the crystals, why you're so tired...and Cat's glowing eyes."

Lindren wished he could have some wine, but it would only make his headache worse. "Cat's eyes. It seems every time she's kissed, really kissed, her eyes glow. Before Cat, I only saw it once. I accidently caught her parents kissing. Both their eyes were glowing. I have to assume it's a normal reaction for the Tiranen, perhaps to show their desire. If so, they never bothered to tell Cat. It's caused the odd problem in the past."

"So I'm to take it Fox is more than simply a bodyguard for Cat?"

Arnir asked.

Shain chuckled. "He is. You should have seen her trying to get his attention. Subtle our little sister is not."

Lindren decided it was time to put an end to Shain's fun. He could go on about Cat for hours. "As far as the trip is concerned, everything went well until we hit Crescent Island."

"And Cat's amazing ability to find trouble kicked in," Shain said, his grin firmly in place.

Lindren gladly let Kelwyn and his sons tell most of the tale. By the time it was done, the boys had polished off one bottle of wine and started another, and Lindren's headache was so bad he had to struggle not to throw up. He kept his head resting against the back of the chair. It didn't help much.

"So after the dolphins found Charyn, much farther away than Mathyn thought, we headed for Meat Town," Darsha said. "She'd constructed some kind of sail that has Mathyn excited. He wants to spend some time here playing with it."

Shain snorted. "Then Cat latched her claws into Rhone by suggesting he be her bodyguard."

"I can see why he'd want to clear his name, but it's going to be hard. Four years have passed." Arnir drained his cup and set it on the table.

"Well, " Lindren said. "We know Jonlan's in town. It's just a matter of finding him again and I think that's where my Elves and Mathyn's will be useful. We can have them look for him, not approach him mind, we don't want to scare him off. Just keep track of where he goes and when. We'll let Rhone decide what to do."

Arnir nodded. "And the crystals?"

"I'm planning on seeing Jeral tomorrow afternoon about those. We only brought two, Mathyn has the other two. I'd like to keep them secret. I'm hoping our mages can use them." Lindren pinched the bridge of his nose, forcing back the pain and waves of nausea.

"I think it's time you had a rest, Father." Arnir leaned forward, his grey eyes intent. "I was hoping to discuss Dayn with you this afternoon, but it can wait."

40

"You do look worse." Darsha stood and brushed crumbs off his trousers. He glanced out the window. "It's not long until dinner. We should all rest."

Kelwyn and Shain joined Darsha as he headed out the door, leaving only Arnir, who hadn't left his seat.

"Tell me what's wrong, Father. You're more than just tired."

"It's as Cat said, I overextended myself. I put far more of my power into holding Vron's shield than prudent. When it shattered, both Vron and I passed out and I stayed that way until the following afternoon."

Arnir frowned. "I've never heard of it lasting that long."

"Neither have I. When I woke, the ship was slowly sinking, so I fixed the hole that was causing most of the problem...and passed out again."

"Father, I don't like this. Let me check you over." Arnir made to stand.

Lindren waved him down. "Not just yet, I'm not finished." He took a deep breath. "When I awoke, I'd lost another day. At first I felt almost normal. I didn't do anything about the other breach until the next day, just to be sure. I asked the help of two other mages. The headache came back anyway. I fixed the breach, though I swear I crawled through all nine hells to do it. And the headache didn't go away, even after I'd slept." Lindren sat forward. Perhaps a change in position would help. "It bothered me not fixing the rest of the damage, but there was nothing I could do. I'll ask Talifir to finish."

"Wise idea. I don't think you should push yourself right now."

"By the time we reached Meat Town, I felt much better." Lindren continued. "Mathyn asked me to spell a pair of shoes to fit Rhone. A simple little spell. The block came back. I pushed harder and it finally broke. It took a lot out of me and I haven't been able to access my magic since. I finally asked Hanrish to ease my headaches." Lindren rested his aching head against the back of the chair again. Nothing seemed to ease the pain. "I have no idea why this is happening."

Arnir placed the small chair by the desk in front of Lindren and sat down. "Lean forward." He set his splayed hands on either side of

41

Lindren's head and began the sing-song chant, the ages old words that would focus his power. Lindren longed to join him, to feel the pulse and surge, the familiarity of the enchantment Arvanion had granted some of his Elves. His power was there, beyond his reach, like a leaf floating in a pond an inch from his touch.

Lindren closed his eyes, giving himself over to his healer son. Arnir's magic, a soothing warmth, slowly pushed back the pain in his head to a point where it didn't matter.

Arnir didn't stop there. He kept pushing, probing, his touch like a thousand little finger brushes along the edges of his nerves. There was no pain, though it sent a shiver down his spine. Lindren had never felt that level of probing before.

After a concerted push, a pop sounded in his head and the pain vanished. His own magic rushed to the surface. Lindren reveled in its familiar glow, gentle and so completely fulfilling, like the touch of his beloved soulmate, Rhianna. He felt whole again. Arnir removed his hands.

Despite his exhaustion, Lindren smiled and opened his eyes. He lost the smile when he saw Arnir's white face. "Arnir!" His son almost fell over on top of him. Lindren set him gently back into the chair.

"I'm all right, Father. It just took a lot more out of me than I thought it would."

Lindren sat down, worry over himself now turned to worry for his son. "What happened? I thought you were only going to fix my headache."

Arnir closed his eyes. "I thought so as well. But then I felt something else...the same thing I felt when I probed Dayn." He opened his now dark grey eyes. "You have black magic in you."

"Black magic! How?" His thoughts drifted back to the world of Morata and the spell that had allowed Balphegor to capture his mind. "When Cat checked me at the battle of the Wall she said the black was gone. I wonder if she missed something."

"Possible." Arnir sat up and rested his head in his hands. "It's strange though. Dayn's little black spell is resting at the base of his skull. Yours is centered in the palm of your right hand."

Lindren turned his hand over and stared at it, trying to see if anything was there. There wasn't. *My hand...there's something...* He gave up, too tired to think straight.

Arnir rubbed his forehead. Colour slowly returned to his face. "I couldn't remove Dayn's spell completely and I can't remove that one either. I only had Talifir with me, so I'd decided to wait until you arrived. With the three of us, I thought we could handle it. But with that..." He pointed to Lindren's hand. "I don't think we should chance it without another healer."

"There's sixteen mages aboard Mathyn's ship, including two healers. We've got all the help we need. It'll have to wait until tomorrow, though. I need rest. And so do you."

Arnir nodded.

"My bed's big enough for two. I don't think you'll make it to your room."

Lindren helped his son to the bedroom, then laid down beside him. He almost passed out.

⅝ • ↄ

Rhone undid the ties on Cat's trousers. They slid to the floor, joining the tunic he'd already removed. He pressed her against him, his lips devouring hers, his hands never stopping as they sought to explore every wonderful inch of her. Her musky woman-scent shot straight to his head and set it spinning, as if he'd drunk too much wine.

When he broke off the kiss, he pushed her back enough to have a good look. Before him stood the woman of his dreams. Her still damp, silver-gold hair floated around a face sculpted by the goddess Vania. Her perfect full breasts perched high on her chest. His hands rested on a narrow waist that blossomed out to full hips. Long legs finished her off.

Rhone planned to spend the rest of the afternoon with those legs wrapped around him. "Nothing's going to stop me making love to you now." He pulled her close for another kiss.

Cat put a finger against his lips. "I can think of one thing."

Rhone frowned. "What?"

43

"You have too many clothes on."

"That's easy to fix."

With her help, it didn't take long. Nor did it take long to find the bed. He stretched out on top of her, aware of every touch of her skin as it sent delightful shudders through his body.

"It's been four years since I've been with a woman," he said between kisses to her lips, neck and breasts. Rhone slid into her. She fit so well. "I'm not going to last long."

"That's all right."

Thank Ar for an understanding woman. He was right. It seemed mere seconds and lighting explosions ripped through his body, pulsing, darkening his vision. He savoured every moment as if it was his last. *You wonderful girl. Thank you, Vania. Thank Ar!* "Thank you."

Rhone rolled off Cat, breathing deep, relishing the last tingling moments of ecstasy. A rush of cold air and a thump brought him back to his senses. He opened his eyes, reaching for Cat. She wasn't there. "Where did you go?"

He blinked to clear his vision and rolled onto his side. Cat sat on the floor, her arms behind her, holding herself up, one leg caught in the sheet. She looked delicious with her breasts thrust out like that, until he saw her face. Two tears wound their way down her golden cheeks. She stared at him out of eyes filled with horror.

"What's the matter?"

She said nothing. He remembered Lindren telling him she didn't like to talk about previous lovers. There was only one thing it could be.

Rhone freed her foot. "Let me guess. Some pig of a man, or Elf, took what he wanted and left you." By the expression on her face, he'd guessed right. He helped her off the floor and held her tight, reveling once again in the touch of her skin on his. "I won't do that to you, Cat. I've never left any woman wanting." A kiss calmed her and she relaxed into him.

Another kiss coaxed a smile out of her.

"Why don't you clean up?" he said, wiping her tears. "I'll be waiting right here. I'm not finished with you yet, not for quite a while."

Her smile grew and she walked to the garderobe, her hips

swaying in a most enticing manner. It wouldn't be long before he'd be ready for another, longer, round. When she returned, he kept his promise. Only the setting sun, and fear that Jewel might pound on the door, put an end to the session.

ᏚᎧ • ᏣᎡ

Cat sat at the dinner table, a song in her heart and a smile on her lips. She didn't think anyone could beat Kelwyn for enthusiasm in love making. Rhone managed it more than once. Her dream on the ship had come true; he was every bit what she'd imagined one of her people would have been like.

No sooner had Rhone let the guard know visitors were welcome again when Jewel arrived with his dinner. It made sense since he wouldn't be allowed to sit with her or eat in front of other people. Rhone ate, facing the wall, while Jewel fussed over Cat's hair and slightly wrinkled outfit.

He now stood behind her chair, a mercenary once more. Kelwyn sat next to her. Cat realized she'd missed his company, despite the enjoyable time with Rhone. She and her friend had spent most of the last two months together. Not since before the death of her people had she spent that much time with Kelwyn, at least that she remembered. She'd have to make a point of seeing him tomorrow.

The long fireplace crackled merrily, hundreds of candles in the chandeliers and lanterns gave off a light scent, and the murmur of the Elves provided an almost musical background.

"You're happy tonight, Cat," Darsha said, a twinkle highlighting his silver-grey eyes.

"I am. It's nice to be clean again."

Darsha and Shain laughed. Cat's cheeks warmed. They knew how she and Rhone had spent the afternoon.

With thirty-six Elves to feed, as well as his normal retinue, Rodrin also housed the wounded soldiers from the battle north of Kitring-Tor. He set up the Elves in the throne room instead of the dining hall, so they could eat without smelling the meat Humans preferred. Cat joined them,

45

not wishing to put up with the disapproving stares and comments she'd attracted from Rodrin's people, both male and female. She'd have meat another day.

"How are Baron Rais and the others?" she asked Arnir, who sat across from her.

"Very well, I checked on them myself. You did an excellent job." His smile told her all she needed to know.

Pride filled her heart. She'd been a useless nuisance and a pest for much of her life; it felt good to hear honest praise for the way she'd cared for the wounded men.

"You look better, Lindren." Cat thought Arnir appeared tired.

"I've rested and I do feel better." He spooned up some of the creamed vegetable soup. It was lightly spiced and Cat wished there was more than one bowl.

"How's Dayn?" Kelwyn asked, finishing off his soup.

Lindren spoke instead of Arnir. "After dinner, I'll update everyone, so please don't go anywhere when you've finished eating."

Cat had forgotten about the king's second son and the black in his light. Merely thinking of him gave her shivers. When the meal was done and the dishes cleared, Lindren raised his hand for attention. He sat at the head of the table and the Elves turned their eyes to him.

He spoke first to Rhone. "Fox, do you mind if we speak in Elven? There are matters we need to discuss that cannot be overheard by wandering staff. Cat can fill you in later."

"Of course."

First topic was Rhone himself. Lindren explained who he was and that he'd been unjustly accused of murder, hence the name Fox. He gave them Jonlan's description with orders not to approach him, only report, and told them Rhone was also Cat's lovemate and was to be treated accordingly. Next came Dayn. The Elves who'd escorted Arnir knew only that the prince had been touched by black magic, not how.

"It seems Dayn wishes to be a wizard," Lindren told them. "When Jeral refused to take him as an apprentice, he went to someone else. That someone turned out to be a sorcerer, in league with Udath Kor. He put a spell on Dayn that, thanks to Cat's truth-seeing, we were able to discover,

46

and with Arnir's healing it has been contained.

"Unfortunately," he continued, "it's still there and will require a great deal of magic to remove. I'm planning to ask Mathyn's healers to join Arnir and myself to try to get rid of it. Talifir, I need you to finish the repairs on the ship. Their plant mage was lost in the battle and I...don't have the time." It wasn't often Cat heard Lindren tell a lie, though she understood why.

Talifir, who sat beside Arnir, nodded his agreement.

"As for the rest of you, you're free to do what you wish unless otherwise ordered. If you're out and about in the city, please keep an eye open for Jonlan and don't let him know you're following. Understood?"

All the Elves nodded and Lindren dismissed them. He motioned for Cat, Kelwyn and his sons to remain behind. "Let's go back to my room. We have things to discuss."

Now Cat's curiosity was up. She beat everyone there. Quint, Lindren's servant, was inside awaiting Lindren's return. After her father dismissed the man, he sat in his chair by the fire. He offered the other to Cat. Kelwyn and his sons arranged themselves on the floor while Rhone took up a position behind Cat.

"Rhone," Lindren said. "I don't mean to be rude, but we have family things to discuss. Would you mind waiting outside?"

"Not at all." He closed the door quietly behind him.

"What's up?" Shain asked, speaking in Elven. "I thought you were going to spend this evening with Rodrin, catching up on events."

"I will later, right now we have something more important to discuss." Lindren turned towards Cat. "I want you to check my light."

"Are you still not feeling well?" If he wasn't, why wouldn't he talk to Arnir?

"Just do it, please." Lindren stood up.

Cat unfocused her eyes. Though the blue surrounding his body looked paler than it should, he wasn't in pain anymore. Arnir must have taken care of it. "Other than a little pale, your light looks fine."

Lindren sat back down. "Now check my hand." He put out his right hand, palm down.

"It looks fine too," Cat said, puzzled.

He turned his palm up and Cat gasped. A small black dot sat right in the middle of it. She flipped his hand over. It was gone. It only showed on Lindren's palm and only when his fingers didn't block it. "How did that get there?"

"Father had a headache earlier. I fixed it for him and found this." Arnir indicated Lindren's hand. "What do you see, Cat?"

When she told him, Darsha asked, "How did it happen?

Kelwyn's brows furrowed. "Could it be left over from that spell on Morata?"

"It's possible," Lindren sat back in his chair. "but why wouldn't Cat have seen it?"

Cat thought back on that day and how worried she'd been for him. "I'd had my eyes unfocused for a long time and my head hurt. I might have missed it. And I don't think I've checked your light much since." She frowned. "I checked you this morning because you didn't look well. I saw the pain from your headache, but that was all. I didn't think to look at your hand. Your other spell showed all over."

"Did you recognize the spell, Arnir?" Darsha asked.

"No, other than it had to have been put there by a sorcerer, or Udath Kor himself. Perhaps when we remove it I can dig deeper. With Mathyn's healers, we might be able to find out something."

"I want it gone as soon as possible." Lindren's eyes had turned dark and Cat didn't blame him for his anger.

"I'll send word down to Mathyn's ship tonight," Darsha said. "Would tomorrow morning be all right?"

Lindren nodded. "Then we'll see Jeral in the afternoon. Cat, are the crystals safe?"

"Yes. They're in my saddlebag so Jewel hasn't seen them."

"Good." Lindren stood. "It's time I met with Rodrin. You all can do what you want tonight."

"After I send word to Mathyn," Darsha put in.

Cat's heart bounced between worry for Lindren and happiness over time with Rhone.

Talon whistled a tune as he strolled up Tanner Row. This late at night few people were abroad and the sound of it echoed off the stone walls of the deserted tanneries. Over eighty years before, the townspeople had complained about the smell those businesses produced and the king paid to have the tanneries moved out of town. Now they stood empty, home to rats, cockroaches and those brave enough to use them for shelter.

News had come from the castle that the silver-haired Elf had returned. He needed to check to make sure she was in the same suite. His plans hadn't come together as quick as he'd hoped; the solution to the problem of thirty-six devil horses continued to elude him. The plan for kidnapping the girl was all set, though. The sack with his tools sat ready and waiting in his room; rope, gag, darts and the tiny bottle of No-Kill. If only he could procure enough of the drug to knock the horses out as well. Unfortunately, it would take a great deal more money than he had.

Talon turned the corner onto Wharf Street and kicked a stone out of his path. His friend Rat had been acting strange lately, more worried than he was about whether the girl would show up or not. He'd finally told the kid he could come with him next time, though he'd probably have to muzzle him to be sure he kept quiet. Excited, Rat ran off to the Pit, the poorest part of town, to find a girl to sell.

Near the river, Talon ducked into an open-ended alley leading to a little used, brush-lined path meandering down to the entrance to the old sewers. He reached three fingers into a well-hidden hole in the stone sealing the unused tunnels. A secret door swung inwards. He ducked in and lit the torch that always sat there.

After closing the door, he made his way to the garderobe of an unused room in the southern wing of the castle. Once inside, he walked the secret tunnels to the girl's room. Talon hoped her lover lay with her tonight; he'd enjoyed the last show considerably. It wasn't long before he stood in the tunnel in the wall between her rooms, his eye plastered to the peep hole.

Moonlight caressed Rhone's chest, highlighting the fine pelt of hair begging for Cat's touch. Once Jewel finally left, they'd spent a most enjoyable evening together.

He lay on his back, taking up an incredible amount of the oversized bed. Cat rested on her side, watching him. Rhone made the most ridiculous noises. They'd started a few moments before and she was sure she couldn't sleep with him doing that. Cat wondered if she should wake him. Maybe there was something wrong. He snorted and she jerked back. Then it stopped. One eye cracked open.

"What are you doing?" he asked, his voice as sleepy as his eyes.

"You're making funny noises and I thought there might be something wrong."

"Funny noises?"

"I don't know the words for them."

"I guess I was snoring, though I didn't realize I did." He pulled her close.

"Snoring? Why do you do it?"

Rhone kissed her nose. "I don't do it on purpose and I don't know why it happens. Some men do, some men don't and some are louder than others. I swear my father could shake the windows. I hear some women snore as well. I gather Elves don't?"

"Not that I know of." Cat hadn't heard her real father make noises like that either. "How am I supposed to sleep?"

"Try harder." A smile teased the corner of his mouth. "I don't suppose if I made love to you again it would wear you out enough to fall asleep, would it?"

"You could always try."

He pulled her on top of him and buried his hands in her hair, kissing her slow and sweet. Now that his initial needs had been met, he took more time and care with his kisses. He was quite the expert. Then a tingling sensation started at the base of her neck. It crept down her spine and Cat sat up. An all too familiar itch formed at the back of her head.

"What's the matter?" Rhone asked.

50

"Someone is watching me," she whispered.

The sleepiness left Rhone in an instant. He rolled out from underneath her and off the bed. In no time, he had his trousers on and sword in hand. "Where's it coming from?"

"You're not going to believe me," she said. "It happened the last time I was here." No one had believed her then.

"Just tell me, Cat."

She sighed. "It...it's coming from the wall, by the fireplace."

Rhone searched the room, peered out the window, then unlocked the door and checked the sitting room, including the balcony, the same as Kelwyn had done a month and a half before. He came back in and sat on the bed. "There's no one out there. There's no one in here. Are you sure you're being watched?"

She nodded. "It's not a feeling I can ignore. It's happened a lot lately and nothing is found, but it makes me feel...strange."

"And it's coming from the wall?"

Cat nodded again.

Rhone stood once more and pulled the bed curtains. "Do you feel it now?"

The tingling and the itch at the back of her head disappeared. "No. It's gone."

He opened them again. "Now?"

"Yes."

"Strange is right." Rhone tugged the curtains closed. "Leave them this way, then." He waved her back into bed. "I'll discuss it with Lindren in the morning and see what he wants to do." Rhone spent the next hour easing Cat's fears in a most delightful manner.

Chapter Four

Rat pounded his fist on Talon's wall. "But you said I could come!"

"That was before I found out she can sense me. Rat, be reasonable!" Twice before searches had been done of her room. Talon had thought he'd made a noise. This time he was sure he hadn't and, with the girl talking in Torian, it confirmed she'd sensed him.

Talon grabbed the boy's boney shoulders. Though thirteen, he looked nine. Ragged, thin, with a perpetually runny nose, Rat was no different than any other waif working for Yait. "If we're discovered," Talon said, "it's not only the end of our dreams, it'll be the death of us."

"But you promised!"

"Sometimes promises can't be kept. You know that as well as I."

Rat hung his head and Talon released him.

"Don't you think it's more important we get the money than see the girl futter her lover?" Talon sat on his clothes chest, the only piece of real furniture in the room. His bed lay in the corner, a simple pallet with a straw mattress and some old blankets he'd scrounged. "Besides, I told you, once we have her I'm going take her before selling her to Tozer. I said you can watch, and I mean it. Really mean it."

Rat's lower lip stuck out a mile. "Blood and bones promise?"

"Blood and bones." If Talon reneged now, Rat was owed some of Talon's blood and one of his bones. Usually a finger or toe was taken, but sometimes a man had gone for something more vital.

"We can't take the chance that those tunnels will be discovered," Talon said. "I need them to kidnap the girl, there's no other way to nab her. Especially with that big lug hanging around. I hope he's not going to be in her bed every night or I'll have to drug him too."

Rat perked up. Talking about sex always warmed the little pervert's blood. "What happened to her Elf lover?"

Talon shrugged. "After I left the girl's room, I checked his. He was there, lying on his bed, though he wasn't asleep. He just stared at the ceiling. I wonder if they had a fight?"

"Anythin's possible. 'Specially with Elves." Rat jammed his hands into his pockets. "At least she don't mind doin' a Human. That'll be a good selling point in our favour." A nasty gleam lit up Rat's eyes. "When are you going to take her?"

"Everything's ready, except for those damn horses. Thirty-six of the bloody things. I've hung around the stables, offering to do odd jobs for a couple of pennies, so I know the routine. I just don't know how to stop those demons from coming after her like last time." Talon sighed, racking his brain for anything that might work. "If only I had enough No-Kill. I could knock the lot of them out."

A greasy smile crept up Rat's face. "How much do you need?"

"More than I have money for." Yait made it quite clear this job was on Rat's head, and now Talon's, and wouldn't fork over any money for taking the girl, only reap in the benefits.

"I have money." Rat's words took a moment to sink in.

Talon's eyes narrowed. "I need more money than your share of selling girls to brothels."

"I didn't get this money that way and it's a lot more'n a handful of coppers." Rat dug around his filthy pockets. "Here it is." He held up a bright, shiny, gold royal.

Talon's eyes almost fell out of his head. "Where did you get that? Did you steal it from Yait?"

"Course not! Nobody steals from Yait and lives." Rat tossed the coin in the air. It glittered in the candlelight as it fell.

Talon couldn't take his eyes off it. One of their kind didn't see too many gold royals and when they did, they weren't allowed to keep them. They had to go to Yait. It disappeared back into Rat's pocket. "Where Rat. Tell me now."

Excitement lit up the kid's plain features. "Tozer gave it to me."

Talon grabbed the front of Rat's coat. "Tozer! Why would that slimy slug give you a gold royal?"

"I asked him for it, so I could steal the girl." Rat tried to squirm out of his grip.

"You went to him? Why? We're doing this job for Yait and were supposed to wait until we have the girl before we contact Tozer. What if Yait finds out? We'll be skinned alive!" It was all part of Yait's plan to bring down Tozer, the Pit Lord's main competition.

"He won't find out. And we need the money. When I saw all those demon horses, I knew we couldn't do it alone. You just said so. With this, you can buy all the No-Kill you need."

Despite the look of hope on Rat's face, Talon wanted nothing more than to punch the little turd. The kidnapping was supposed to be a way of getting rid of Tozer and make Talon enough money to get out of Tezerain to start a new life. Now Rat may have ruined his dreams. Talon let him go and sank back onto his bed. "I hope you haven't made a mistake, Rat."

"I haven't! You'll see! Here." Rat fished the coin out of his pocket again. "You take it. Buy the No-Kill. Then we can get the girl, frame Tozer and get our money." The hopeful look on his face almost made Talon laugh.

He stared at the coin in his hand, far more than what he needed. It would take some time to gather the No-Kill, maybe a week. With Rat's help, he could feed it to the demon horses in their evening mash. He'd have to keep going to the stables though, to keep up appearances. Maybe it might work out after all. Talon closed his hand around the large coin, enjoying the feel of it. He anticipated running his hands through a whole lot more of them. "We have to stay away from her, Rat. You hear me? We need this money."

Rat nodded solemnly. "I did good?"

Talon glanced at him before returning his eyes to the shiny piece of metal. Dealing with Tozer was a complete unknown. "I don't know. We'll see when it's all over."

৵ • ৫

Cat lay on her bed, missing Rhone's warmth. He'd risen at the break of dawn to sleep in the cot the servants had set up for him in the sitting room; he said it needed to look slept in or Jewel would have a fit. When the maid arrived, he also needed to be dressed so he could answer

54

the door right away.

The anticipated knock came and Cat slipped into the black and silver outfit, unlocked her door—which Rhone insisted needed to be locked to keep up appearances—and stepped into a room full of people, mostly women. Jewel set Rhone's breakfast on the desk. Cat counted heads. Besides Rhone and the maid, there were only four extra women, but they all had their arms full of baskets or bolts of cloth.

"All right, ladies," Jewel said, her hands decorating her hips. It seemed her favourite position these days. "Lady Cat needs some new clothes. While *he*..." she pointed to Rhone, "...is eating, we'll take care of my lady in the bedroom."

Jewel shooshed everyone in, including Cat, and for the next half hour two ladies poked, prodded and measured while the others held up different materials, clucking and tsking. Cat tried to make a suggestion or two and was immediately hushed.

"These women have been caring for the castle's ladies for years,' Jewel told her. "They know what they're doing."

"May I at least ask that they make me a shirt and trousers? I don't like wearing dresses." Not a one of the bolts of cloth looked like trouser material. Perhaps they did things different here.

"Of course you may, my lady." With that inconclusive statement, Jewel whisked the women out the door. Unfortunately, she didn't leave.

Another knock announced Cat's and Rhone's laundry. Jewel wouldn't let Cat out of her room until she was dressed in clean shirt and trousers, and her hair brushed. By the time they were done, Rhone had long finished eating.

"You will be breakfasting with the King and Queen in Prince Dayn's rooms, my lady."

Cat groaned inside. She'd been hoping to avoid him.

"Unless I'm told otherwise," Jewel continued, inspecting the mantle for dust, "lunch will be here, in your rooms. After that, I believe you are scheduled for a visit with Master Jeral. Dinner will be back in Prince Dayn's chambers. Since you're going to be staying with us for a while, you might want to find something to amuse yourself." She fluffed the cushions in the big chairs. "I could show you the library or you could join Queen Lisha for the sewing sessions."

Sewing sessions? If that meant sitting with the other ladies while they stitched things and talked about Cat's clothing and habits, maybe the library might be a better choice. "How long are we staying?" Long enough to find Jonlan and solve Rhone's problem, she hoped.

"At least until Prince Gailen and Lady Selesa's wedding. Apparently it was all decided last night between His Majesty and Lord Lindren." The maid added wood to the fire.

"What is…what's a wedding?" It sounded like a big event.

"My lady, honestly." Jewel's hands returned to her hips. "How can you not know what a wedding is?"

"I'm sure she knows," Rhone said, his voice gruff. "She simply doesn't know our word for it." He ducked his head to Cat in a brief bow, his face shrouded in the mask and hood. "My lady, it's the ceremony where Prince Gailen and Lady Selesa will be officially married, joined to one another for life, with the blessing of Ar and Vania."

Jewel flashed him a glare that would make a snake hide its head.

"Oh! That sounds like it might be fun." Cat had never seen a Human bonding ceremony. *I wonder how different they are?* "How long until the wedding?"

"The first day of spring." The maid flounced off to the bedroom.

Over a month away. Time to search for Jonlan and plenty of time to do nothing. "What will I do until then?" she whispered to Rhone.

He shrugged. A double rap on the door put a halt to the conversation. It was Lindren. He appeared much better than yesterday and wore his usual smile.

"Ready for breakfast?"

The other Elves waited in the hall. After greeting each with a kiss, she latched onto Kelwyn for the walk to Dayn's rooms.

ᛋᛟ • ᚳᛦ

Breakfast turned out different than Cat had planned. She wanted to discuss the upcoming wedding. Dayn had other ideas. He sat beside her talking her ear off. He commented on everything from her clothes

56

and hair to the care she'd given the wounded men from the northern baronies, interspersed with apologies for his behavior during her last visit. Cat thanked Arvanion when the meal finally ended.

Then it was time to do something about the mysterious black dot on Lindren's hand. Mathyn, Hanrish and Ardamin stood near Lindren's room when they arrived.

"Would you mind waiting outside the room again?" Lindren said to Rhone.

The big Human chuckled. "Of course not, my lord."

Once the door was closed, the questions started—in Elven.

"What's this about you having a black spell on you?" Mathyn asked. "Would it have anything to do with how you've been feeling since the battle?"

Lindren motioned for him to take a chair. He took his usual spot. Everyone else either sat near the fireplace or stood close by. Cat cuddled up to Kelwyn. She still felt guilty for not spending more time with him.

"Arnir discovered it when removing my headache yesterday," Lindren said. "Hanrish, did you feel anything when you worked on me?"

The Ringwood healer shook his head, then directed a question to Arnir. "Did you do anything other than deal with his headache?"

"Yes. I was concerned over the way he'd been feeling so I did a full probe. That's when I felt it." He glanced from Hanrish to Lindren and back again. "It took me a lot longer to contain it than Dayn's, so I think it's been there for a while."

"Which puts out the battle," Ardamin said.

Arnir nodded. "I got the impression it was a lot older than that." He turned his gaze to Lindren. "Have you been able to remember anything, Father?"

Lindren leaned forward. "Kelwyn, the year Cat came back to us, do you remember the vauroks she spotted on the Wastelands?"

Cat remembered the incident quite well; one of the many times she was a nuisance.

"Yes, I do." Kelwyn's frown matched Darsha's and Shain's.

"Though I didn't accompany you, I remember it," Darsha said.

"When we checked the site where we found the bodies, there was

57

no black magic. It was only on the second trip that we discovered where the border patrol were actually killed."

Kelwyn nodded, his expression somber.

Lindren scanned every face in the room. "While I was investigating, I felt something hit my palm." He lifted his right hand. "This one. It was the middle of winter with snow on the ground. It couldn't have been an insect."

Mathyn's frown deepened. "You think it was a spell?"

"It had to be. The whole incident was strange. It seemed pointless. A waste of lives on both sides. But if it was meant to plant a spell…"

"What exactly happened?" Hanrish asked.

"Cat spotted vauroks in the Wasteland, so I took a band up to investigate. We killed them, but there was no sign of my border patrol." Lindren sat back and folded his hands on his lap. "We finally found them, all dead, but there wasn't enough blood for the amount of damage done. Further searching led us to a spot a mile away. It reeked of black magic. That's where…I think…I picked up this." He rubbed the spot, as if he could make it go away.

Cat shifted her eyes out of focus. She couldn't see it; he had his palm turned away. Strange, how she could see Dayn's spell but not Lindren's.

"So." Shain cracked his knuckles. "How do we get rid of it?"

The corner of Lindren's mouth turned up. "Thank you for the offer, son, but I think you'll have to sit this one out."

"Not quite." Shain jumped to his feet. "I can order the wine. I think we're all going to need a drink when this over." He sauntered to the door and spoke to someone outside; Rhone, or more likely, the guard.

Lindren stood. "I think it might be best if I lay down."

Hanrish agreed and they all gathered in the bedroom.

Darsha and Kelwyn retrieved wooden chairs from their rooms so all three mages could be seated. They decided Arnir would do the actual working with Hanrish and Ardamin helping as needed.

Lindren settled himself on the bed. "Cat, would you mind monitoring for us?"

She nodded and sat cross-legged on the bed beside him, to his right. "Give me your hand." Cat placed it on her lap, palm up. When she unfocused her eyes, the black spot stood out like an evil stain. "Please get rid of it."

Arnir took off his tunic and rolled up the sleeve on his left arm. "We will."

℘ · ℭ

"Alanadril amorathan shoen doramira…" Arnir whispered the ancient words, centering his magic. Beside him, with his hand gently resting on Arnir's bare arm, Hanrish echoed his words, as did Ardamin next to him, like a chain of power flowing into Arnir's soul. Those around him, Shain, Darsha, Kelwyn, Mathyn and Cat, faded as he concentrated on his power and that of the two Ringwood mages.

First he touched his father's heart, strong and steady in its rhythm of life, then spread to his other organs, ensuring everything was as it should be. A quick check confirmed the spell hadn't escaped the magical confines Arnir had built for it. Nausea rose up to greet him. He forced it down. Another check confirmed Hanrish and Ardamin, though nauseous as well, were focused and ready to lend their power.

To the best of his knowledge, what Arnir was about to do had never been attempted before, not even by Taurin when he lent his strength to Lindren so he could escape Udath Kor's place between worlds. As with Dayn, the black spell sat in its containment, refusing to budge. The first thing Arnir had to do was release it. Piece by piece, he broke down the wall he'd built. The black flared, sending his senses reeling with sickly rot. He'd been expecting it. Hanrish and Ardamin had not and they both had to suppress their initial reaction to vomit.

Arnir gathered his power and blended it with that of the other mages, stronger and more powerful than he could ever hope to be on his own. He pushed from all sides, squeezing the dark blot smaller and smaller. It fought back, trying to claw its way through any crack or crevasse in Arnir's weaving.

He tightened the spell. Sweat formed on his brow and he drew more power from the two mages beside him. Arnir squeezed. It shrunk, then shrunk again. Harder and harder, Arnir pushed his will. When it finally gave, he swore he heard a scream and then it was gone, a few wisps clinging to the edges of Arnir's spell. He dissected them, taking each remnant apart. As he did, he discovered how, and why, it had been made.

"Cat," Arnir whispered, his breath ragged. "Do you see it?"

"No. I think it's gone." She smiled.

He tried to return it. Once he recovered, he went back in, checking every artery, vein, muscle, tissue and bone. Arnir could find no sign of the sickly black rot. Gently, he released the two healers' power back into their care.

"That was a lot harder than I expected," Hanrish said, his face pale. Ardamin seemed no better. "I've never felt nausea like that."

Arnir attempted a smile. "Just think. We get to try it again with Dayn."

Ardamin groaned. "Not for a few days, I hope."

Lindren sat up and Cat gave him a hug. "Thank you, son," he said. "And thanks to you two as well. I know it cost you a great deal and I do appreciate it."

Both Ringwood healers nodded. Shain poured wine for all.

"Hmmm." Mathyn studied the pair. "I don't think either of you are capable of walking back to the ship."

"They can rest here," Lindren offered, taking a sip of the fruity white. "I'm a little tired, but nothing compared to them." He shifted his attention to Arnir. "Were you able to discover what it was?"

Arnir nodded. "A spell of finding, an extremely powerful one to have remained secret that long."

Lindren stiffened. "Udath Kor. It had to be. He's been tracking me all these years."

"Isn't it odd for him to do it?" Darsha asked. "I thought he always left the dirty work to his cronies."

"If he'd had someone else place the spell, only that sorcerer would have been able to track me." Lindren shook his head. "No, this he needed to do himself."

Shain poured everyone a glass of wine. When he handed Lindren one, he said. "I think you really need this, Father. I can't imagine living with that for so long."

"Thing is…" Lindren took a sip. "I didn't even know it was there." He chewed the inside of his cheek. A habit he had when thinking for as long as Arnir could remember. "Cat, those times you felt you were watched, the times that couldn't be explained, you were always with me, out of Silverwood."

"Yes. The first time was on Morata, then on the ruined farm, the way here before the Old Forest and again on the ship. Except for the times in my room here. I felt it again last night, but not when the bed curtains were drawn."

"Another puzzle for another day," Lindren said. "I think what you were feeling, when you were with me, was Udath Kor using his spell. He was watching me and you felt it."

Cat's eyes widened. Mathyn whistled. Shain's jaw dropped while both Darsha and Kelwyn wore dark expressions.

Arnir didn't like it one bit. "How many other people are under surveillance and don't know it?"

"It's a good thing all the enclaves have scry-shroud spells," Mathyn said.

Hanrish rubbed his eyes. "When we get back, we're going to have to alert every healer on every world to watch for this spell. The three of us know what to look for, we'll pass it on."

"Good idea," Lindren said. He drained his glass. "Time for you two to rest. Arnir, you as well." He motioned Cat off the bed, then stood up and helped Hanrish lay down. Mathyn assisted Ardamin.

Arnir wanted to stand up; trying to find the energy proved difficult. Darsha and Shain helped him back to his room. He sat on his bed. "I don't think I'll be able to visit with Jeral this afternoon."

Darsha forced him to lie down. "I doubt Father will expect it. We'll fill you in."

Arnir closed his eyes, trying not to shudder at the remnants of nausea still plaguing his stomach.

Chapter Five

Cat and Rhone spent the time before lunch locked in the bedroom. He'd barely finished dressing when Jewel knocked on the door. She carried a tray while a young girl followed her with another. Cat thought the girl might be around twelve; with Humans it was difficult to tell.

"Just put his tray on the desk, Rya, thank you." Jewel set hers on the table between the two stuffed chairs. The girl did as told and, without a word, curtsied to Cat and left.

The delicious aroma of cinnamon filled the room. Jewel lifted the cloth from the tray. Two thick slices of roast pork, drenched in gravy, lay on one plate. Another held a small loaf of fresh white bread. Steamed carrots sat in one shallow bowl, while a slice of thick apple pie rested in another. A small pot and cup sat in the upper right hand corner of the tray. Cat's mouth watered.

Rhone removed the cloth covering his food, the same as Cat's. *At least they're feeding him well.* He pulled the small wooden chair close to the desk, facing away from them, and dug into his food. Cat didn't blame him, all he'd had to eat while stranded on Crescent Island was fish, more fish, a few berries, roots and nuts; and still more fish.

"Sit here, my lady," Jewel said, picking up a napkin lying next to the cutlery. She motioned to the stuffed chair and Cat sat down. The maid laid the napkin on the arm of the chair and moved the table closer. "Which would you like first?"

"The pork, please."

Jewel placed the plate on her lap, then picked up the knife and fork. Cat thought she planned on cutting the meat and feeding her, but she passed them to Cat before sitting in the other chair.

"Have you thought about ways to occupy your time, my lady?"

Cat had a mouthful of warm, juicy pork. She shook her head.

"Well, as I said before, there's always the library." Jewel fidgeted with her apron, crinkling it, then smoothing out the wrinkles. "King

62

Rodrin has hundreds of books and scrolls of all kinds. There's poetry, histories, even some romance stories, I think." She giggled. "If you don't mind my asking, my lady, do you have...someone special?"

Cat almost choked on her pork. *Yes, and he's sitting right behind you. What do I say now?*

When Cat didn't answer right away, Jewel blushed. It was the first time Cat had seen the girl with red cheeks. "I'm sorry, my lady. I shouldn't pry. Do you like reading books?"

Cat swallowed the meat. "Not really. Lindren does. He once borrowed a book of poetry from Rodrin's father. He said it was very good." She cut another piece of the delicious pork, wishing there was more.

"She's just learned the language," Rhone put in. "I doubt she knows how to read Torian."

Jewel shot him a glare. "So maybe the library's not such a good idea. Sewing then?"

"Lindren's...wife...makes all my clothes. I don't like to sew." She'd attempted a few things, including a tunic for Kelwyn. Rhianna had helped with it, the only reason it turned out as well as it did. Cat finished her pork, Jewel took her plate and passed her the carrots.

"Hmm, some of the ladies play musical instruments, like the lute. Do you know how to play?"

"I don't know what a lute is."

Jewel turned slightly in the chair. "You make music with it, my lady. It's sort of shaped like a large gourd with a long neck." She used her hands to demonstrate. "It has strings that you pluck to make sound."

"Elves have those," Cat said. *And a lot of other instruments as well.* "I can play the ones Elves have and other things too." She finished her carrots and Jewel passed her the bread.

Cat wished she could have the pork plate back again; she'd have liked to sop up the last of the gravy with it. She also wished she had butter.

"Maybe there might be some that you don't know. I could find a teacher for you."

"Perhaps."

63

The bread disappeared and Jewel put the bowl with the pie in it on her lap. "Some ladies like to play games, like Kings and Knights, or go falconing." The little maid sighed. "I suppose you could always go outside and practice with...that thing." She waved her hand in the direction of Cat's bow case.

Rhone slid his chair back, his mask in place once more. "I've seen my lady shoot." He took up his place by the door. "She doesn't need practice."

Jewel threw her hands in the air. "There must be *something* you want to do, my lady."

A knock sounded on the door. Rhone opened it to reveal Lindren. "Are you ready to visit Jeral?"

"Just about." Cat poured her own tea, gulped it down, then swallowed the last two mouthfuls of pie. "Now I am. Is he coming, too?" She indicated Rhone.

Lindren smiled. "Yes, he is."

Rhone picked up her saddlebags and bowed to Cat, motioning her out the door. Never had she been so glad to leave a room.

ℰ • ℛ

Jeral's tower hadn't changed much. The skull was gone and for that Cat was grateful. The only other noticeable change was the fire burning in the fireplace; it had been cold the last time they came. The wizard hadn't changed either, including his robe. He still looked like a funny old man with scraggly hair and beard, and a lump on the side of his nose. Kelwyn said it was a wart and that some Humans got them while others didn't. She wondered if Rhone might get one. It could be interesting to watch it form.

"Welcome back, my friends." Jeral picked up some books off one of the chairs and placed them on a shelf.

Once again the Elves had to clear places to sit. Cat settled herself beside Kelwyn, giving his hand a squeeze under the table. Maybe she could play one of those games Jewel mentioned with him.

Rhone placed her saddlebags on the table and stood behind her.

64

Jeral flashed him a peculiar look. "And who is he?"

"This is Fox, Cat's new bodyguard," Lindren said.

The wizard's odd expression changed into another, this one accompanied by a small frown. "Strange and stranger still."

"What do you mean?" Darsha placed a scroll on a shelf and sat down next to Shain.

Jeral shook his head. "In a moment. Where is Arnir? I thought he'd be here as well."

Lindren took his seat next to the wizard. "He's resting. We've had another incident with black magic." He explained the spell of finding, how it was discovered and that the mages removed it, though it tired all three of them.

If any of it surprised Rhone, he made no indication; he stood as still as a statue.

"We plan on talking to all the healers and check our warriors and Elders for spells," Lindren finished.

"A wise idea." Jeral stroked his beard. "Do you think they'll be able to get rid of Dayn's problem the same way?"

"That's the plan, only I'll be joining them as well."

"Father," Darsha said. "Are you up to it? You've been through a lot."

"Actually, I feel fine. I had a good sleep last night and this morning's working wore the healers out, not me."

"So, what is this 'lot' you've been through lately?" the wizard asked.

Lindren described their trip, how they found the crystals and the battle that occurred several days later. He said nothing about Rhone.

Between the warm room, boring conversation, and her time with Rhone, Cat tried hard not to fall asleep.

Once finished, Lindren said, "To be honest, I'm quite tired of relating the tale. Cat, could I have those crystals, please?"

She pulled them from her saddlebag. Lindren passed them, one at a time, to Jeral. Six inches in length and three wide, the crystals gleamed with a soft inner glow. No sun shone today to scatter tiny rainbows everywhere.

65

"Ahh, beautiful. Two of them and here I'd have been happy with one." He set the first on the table. 'While you were gone, I practiced with the other. It's completely burned out now, but it served its purpose." Jeral patted the crystal he held. "I've made some notes in case something happens to me. We wizards tend to guard our discoveries like a dragon with its hoard. This, however, is knowledge that cannot be lost. It's too valuable."

Lindren nodded his head. "A wise idea. Now then." He leaned forward. "Were you successful in finding any prophecies?"

Finally! The reason they'd come to Kitring-Tor weeks ago.

"I have and in the most unusual places." Jeral set the crystal he held on a shelf, then resumed his seat.

"What do you mean?" Shain asked.

Jeral reached down and brought up a large book, its leather bound covers frayed and worn. He moved the crystal to make room. When the wizard opened it, he gently turned the yellowed pages. "I found this one while researching a spell for levitation. Never did find what I wanted, but this stuck out like the wart on my nose." He pointed to some words in the middle of a page. "Not only do these words not belong here, they're not even written in the same language." He cleared his throat.

'Silver Cat, Black Fox, Dark Elf,
All will ride, all will fall,
Under the gaze of the Bashful Lady,
All will bring the Sleepers home.'

Jeral looked up from the book. "I'd read this page many times before and never saw these words. As far as I can guess, they just appeared sometime in the last forty years. I'll be honest with you, Lindren. I've known about this one for a while." He tapped the page with a thin, bent finger. "When you walked in here last month, I discovered who the Silver Cat and Dark Elf had to be. Today..." He looked straight at Rhone. "Today I have found the Black Fox."

"Now wait a minute." Rhone unfolded his arms. "I'm not part of any prophecy. I'm just getting paid to protect the lady."

Jeral stabbed the page. "This tells me you're a little more than that." He turned to Lindren. "You were right when you said there's something going on up in the Barriers. Come nightfall, if you look north, you'll see the constellation we call the Bashful Lady. In two and a half months, she'll be sitting right over Broken Man Pass as viewed from Tezerain."

"Arvanion!" Shain exclaimed.

"I suppose I'm the Dark Elf," Kelwyn said, picking up the thick strand of black hair hanging over his forehead. He didn't seem too happy.

Neither was Cat. It felt creepy to have something like that written about her.

Jeral nodded. "I don't see who else it could be. It might be the powers Ar gave me, but it feels right." He returned his gaze to Rhone. "And so do you."

Rhone radiated anger.

"So what does it mean?" Darsha asked. "'All will ride, all will fall?' That doesn't sound good."

Jeral shrugged. "That's the thing with prophecies. Quite often you don't know what they mean until it's happened. The way I read it, the three of you need to go to Broken Man Pass so you can wake the Sleepers."

"And they need to be there in two and a half months time." Lindren didn't seem happy either.

"Who are these Sleepers?" Rhone's voice still sounded tight with anger.

Lindren turned his grey eyes on him. "I think they're dragons." Jeral nodded.

Rhone frowned. "Why do you think that? The dragons disappeared centuries ago."

"Because," Lindren informed him, "a dead dragon spoke to Cat and told her to wake the Sleepers."

Rhone didn't move, he didn't even blink. He simply stared at Cat.

"It's true," she said. "It happened forty years ago."

"And the prophecy showed up sometime after that." Rhone shifted his stance. "I don't believe it. It's impossible."

"And yet, it's true." Jeral glanced down at the book again. "Great Ar!"

Lindren leaned over to see. His eyes widened in surprise. "The prophecy! It's gone!"

Stunned silence greeted his words. After a moment, Rhone said, "I think I need to sit."

Shain jumped up and offered him his chair. Rhone almost fell into it.

"Ar's telling us something." Jeral fixed each of them with his stern gaze. "I think we should listen."

Lindren nodded. "I agree. The three of you need to be at Broken Man Pass by the end of Marand month."

Cat's emotions ran from one end of the scale to the other. She had no idea what was expected of her and that was frightening. On the other hand, if it meant meeting dragons it could be something good. Even better, it meant Rhone would be around for awhile. Then she thought of the 'All will ride, All will fall' line, and worry set in, for Rhone and for Kelwyn.

Shain leaned against a shelf next to the fireplace. "'Silver Cat, Black Fox, Dark Elf. All will ride, All will fall. Under the gaze of the Bashful Lady, All will bring the Sleepers home.'" He snorted. "It's a terrible prophecy. In all the stories I've read, the prophecies rhymed."

Darsha gave him a wry smile. "Stories are just that, Shain. Stories."

"Don't be so sure," Jeral said. "I translated it for you. It was written in Old Talerian."

Shain thought a moment. "Huh. I guess it does rhyme after all."

Lindren looked at Rhone. "Have you recovered yet?"

"No. I've always followed my own path. Or tried to. I don't like having my life dictated to me by a prophecy."

"You will come, won't you?" Cat asked. If he didn't, the prophecy might not come true and the dragons wouldn't be woken.

"I'll think about it."

At least it isn't a 'no'. She turned to Kelwyn. "What about you?"

"If you go, I go."

Cat smiled.

"If you've all absorbed that one, there's more." Jeral reached down one more time. The book he laid on the table was smaller, thicker than the last and just as old.

Lindren stared at the book. "More?"

Jeral opened the front cover. "Two more."

"About me?" Cat's heart skipped a beat.

"Yes. I find this one quite intriguing." The wizard tapped the inside cover. Lines comprising of squiggles covered most of it.

'Daughter of silver, daughter of gold,
Shining hope of all foretold.
A dead man, his heart she thieves.
In return, a child he leaves.
A son, both brave and bold.

Daughter of silver, daughter of gold,
Demon-spawn her love will hold.
Heart of dark, with soul of light,
Their children, with eyes so bright,
Will right this wrong of old.'

"This one rhymes," Shain said. "Other than that, what does it mean?"

Jeral cocked his head to look at him. "Now that I know who it pertains to, it means much."

"It does indeed." Lindren stared at the words, a strange smile on his face.

"What?" Cat couldn't read it. "What does it mean?"

Lindren turned his smile on her. "I think it means you might have children one day."

Cat's mouth dropped open. "How?"

Darsha leaned over, reading the words. "How can you be happy about this, Father? It sounds like she'll have a son by a dead man and more children by demon-spawn."

"What?" Cat almost jumped out of her chair. Kelwyn set his hand on her shoulder.

"It says right here." Darsha set a finger to the passage. "'A dead man, his heart she thieves. In return, a child he leaves. A son, both brave and bold.'" He looked up. "The way I understand it, you'll have a son by a dead man. Father, how is that even possible?"

Lindren shook his head, his smile still firmly in place. "It doesn't actually say the dead man is the sire. It just says he'll leave a child. Perhaps it means Cat will adopt a son."

"Possible, but this one leaves no doubt," Darsha went on. "'Demon-spawn her love will hold. Heart of dark, with soul of light, Their children, with eyes so bright, Will right this wrong of old.'"

"Demon-spawn!" Cat clung to Kelwyn, who held her tight.

"I think this is the important line, here." Lindren's finger replaced Darsha's. "'Heart of dark, with soul of light.' No true demon would have a soul of light. There's more going on here than is immediately discernable." He sat back.

Jeral nodded his agreement. "Hm. These words just vanished as well. It's a good thing I wrote all these down."

Kelwyn still held Cat tight. Her eyes now leaked tears. *Dear Arvanion! I don't want to be with a demon!* She sniffled and Kelwyn dried her face with his shirt sleeve. Cat wanted children, but what would she have to go through to get them? Adopting sounded much safer.

Rhone stood up, taking his position behind Cat once more, echoing her thoughts. "Children…at what price?"

Lindren leaned past Kelwyn and took Cat's hand. In Elven, he said, "Trust Arvanion, Cat. I'm sure he's the one who sent these prophecies. If he intends for you to have children, I doubt it will be as bad as it sounds. Now, Jeral says there's one more. Shall we hear what it says?"

Cat sniffled again and nodded. *I hope this one has better news.*

Lindren leaned back, looking to Jeral. "What's the third one?"

Jeral picked up a third book off the floor. It appeared newer, not so worn. "This one showed up seventeen years ago." He flipped through the pages, stopping at one somewhere in the middle. "Like the first, it

70

replaced what was there. And it's written in Galashian, so don't expect it to rhyme, Shain."

'Love is as love shall be,
Soulmates for Elven blood,
Bondmates for Tiranen,
Truemates for the moon lady.
One shall be a knight so strong,
A lion to give her strength.
Second a mage, with powers great.
His aid will help her more.
Third a warrior, courage is his,
A life of light and happiness.
The fourth, a son born of hell-fire.
Bane of all that is wrong.
For her a love, to hold, to share,
For her a friend, who's help she'll need.'

Cat blinked the last of her tears away and sat up. "Is this really for me? I didn't hear silver in there."

"No," Jeral said. "But the moon is often described as silver and since it just appeared out of nowhere I have to assume it applies to you as well."

She stared at the bold letters, more like runes than the other two. "So what does this one mean?"

Darsha gave her a smile. "It talks about love. Soulmates, bondmates and something called truemates. I think you'll be falling in love with these fellows."

"A knight, a warrior, a mage and a...son born of hell-fire?" Shain raised an eyebrow. "I wonder if he's the demon-spawn."

"Could be,' Lindren said. "If he is, there's more hope here. It says he's the bane of all that is wrong."

"What is wrong?" Rhone's voice still held a hint of anger. "To us, the Black Lord and all he stands for is wrong, but so is thievery and murder. To the vauroks, what we do to fight them is wrong."

71

"This prophecy is all positive," Lindren pointed out. "I don't see how it could relate to anything other than our side."

A son of hell-fire is positive? Cat couldn't see it. She leaned against Kelwyn and he held her once more. She stared at the funny words, wishing it all would go away—and they did.

"Hmph." Jeral rifled through some papers. "I made a copy of these for you." He passed them to Lindren.

"Thank you, I appreciate it. I'd like to study these more. As time passes, something might give us a further clue."

"I have a question," Rhone said. "Cat explained what a soulmate is. What's a bondmate?"

Lindren answered. "The Tiranen form of marriage."

"What's the difference?"

Darsha took over. "Soulmates are for life, bondmates aren't. The Tiranen changed mates frequently, for them anyway. A bonding might last a few hundred years or a thousand, but not for life."

Rhone had another question. "What is a truemate, then?"

"That," Lindren said. "We'll have to wait and see." He stood up. "It will be dinner soon and I'd like to try to absorb some of this." He rolled the papers into scrolls.

"Just a moment more, if you don't mind." Jeral fixed his watery blue eyes on Rhone. "I've been trying to figure out what's odd about you."

Cat's heart caught in her throat. Rhone gripped his sword hilt.

The wizard stood, his hand on the crystal in front of him. "Your speech is much too educated for a typical mercenary. You don't use Cat's honorific. Your voice…it niggled at me. I've heard it before. And when you sat down, I saw your eyes, Rhone Arden."

Cat leapt out of her seat and stood in front of Rhone, her arms wide, trying to protect him. "He's innocent! He didn't kill that man!"

Jeral studied them both a moment, then a small smile crinkled one corner of his mouth. "That would be your truth-seeing I take it?" He chuckled. "In that case, your secret is safe with me."

Cat hugged Rhone, her heart beating faster than a hummingbird's wings. Thank Arvanion the wizard knew about her truth-seeing.

"So that's the way of it." A gleam highlighted Jeral's eyes. "I won't take your man from you, Cat, but you'd both better be careful. I'd hate to see someone else figure it out. Not that those foolish nobles have a brain between them."

Rhone pulled down his mask and put his arm around Cat. "Thank you, Master Jeral. I appreciate it. I'm hoping I can find some clue to the truth. Now…" He pushed Cat away from him. "What's this about truth-seeing? More Elven secrets?"

All eyes turned to Lindren. "It's something we prefer to keep quiet. It's more effective. Cat can tell when someone is lying. It's a special ability only a few Elves have ever had. Why she has it, we don't know."

"That would explain why you believed me." Rhone guided Cat back to her seat. "You're full of surprises, aren't you."

Kelwyn took her hand and Cat leaned into him, grateful for his comfort.

"I don't know how much help I can be," Jeral said to Rhone. "But if you need anything, come see me. Of all the nobles I've met, you and your family are some of the rare few who were born with a bit of common sense."

"Thank you." Rhone gave him a half bow.

"If we're all done here," Lindren said. "There's much to digest and not long before dinner."

"When we'll have something else to digest," Shain put in.

Everyone rose from their seats, Kelwyn keeping a good grip on Cat's hand. Rhone replaced his mask.

When they reached the bottom of the tower, Kelwyn said, "Do you want to talk, Cat?"

She opened her mouth to say yes.

Rhone interrupted. "Would you mind if it waited until later? We have some things to discuss."

What now? Trying to absorb everything she'd heard would take some time and she'd appreciate Kelwyn's opinion. Perhaps tomorrow. She suspected Rhone would have plans for after dinner.

"Not a problem." Kelwyn's eyes said otherwise.

Cat sighed and they headed down the hall.

Chapter Six

Rhone bolted the door, tossed back his hood, and whipped off his mask. He threw it and the cloak on his cot. After dragging Cat into the bedroom, he locked that door too. "Why didn't you tell me about your truth-seeing? I thought you trusted me. The relationship between a bodyguard and his charge involves more trust than that of a husband and wife."

He gripped her shoulder. "When I say do something, you can't question my decision or we could both end up dead." He kept his voice low; to Cat, he shouted.

Her heart sank. *He's mad at me again.* "Lindren told me not to tell anyone. And I do trust you. That's one of the things my truth-seeing tells me. I know you're not a liar, I'd see it. And you don't have a lot of strange colours in your light."

"My light?" Rhone released her arm.

Cat shrugged. "I don't know what else to call it. It's a light that surrounds a person's body. It's supposed to be blue, but it can have other colours that tell me what that person is feeling, like happiness, anger or sorrow. It also tells me if people lie. That colour is purple. It took me a while to figure out that if someone lies a lot they have purple in their light even if they're not saying a lie at the time. You don't have purple, so it tells me you don't lie, at least, not a lot. Since you don't lie, you're not the type to deceive, so I can trust you."

"I prefer the truth." Rhone leaned against the door, folding his arms, a smirk turning up the corner of his mouth. "Your thinking is a little flawed. A person doesn't have to lie to deceive or betray someone, so don't rely on it. Your comment about my scars proves it."

He continued to stare at her with his half open eyes. Cat tried not to squirm.

"What other colours do you see?" Rhone said, after too long a moment.

74

She let out the breath she held. "Too many. I don't know what they all mean."

"Isn't there someone who can teach you?"

Cat shook her head. "There are no truth-seers still living. Truth-seeing is an Elven talent, not Tiranen. And a rare one at that. No one knows why I have it."

"Ar must have given it to you for a reason."

Arvanion, not Ar. "Lindren says the same thing, but I don't know what it could be." Cat sighed and sat on the bed. Rhone's anger seemed to have dissipated somewhat. "I detested it for a long time. My brother hated me because of it." At Rhone's questioning look, she added, "I caught him in a lie and told our parents. I was ten."

Rhone snorted. "With some, that's all it would take. What did he do?"

"He said he was going to a friend's place. The purple in his light said otherwise."

"That doesn't sound terribly bad. What was he really going to do?"

Cat shrugged again. "My parents were so shocked by my truth-seeing they never asked him." She hung her head, a too familiar hurt clenching her heart. "Mordru tormented me for forty-two years. Two days before he died, he apologized and meant it. I checked his light." *I miss him. Arvanion, I miss him!*

Rhone sat beside her and held her close. After a few moments, he kissed the top of her head. "You said I don't have a lot of colours in my light. Which ones do I have?" He pushed her back. "You don't have to tell me if it makes you uncomfortable."

She smiled, despite her sorrow. "I don't mind. You have a lot of red. Anger. Which I suppose is understandable since you've had so much bad happen to you."

"Anger." Rhone's eyes took on a distant look. "I feel like I've been angry all my life. If it isn't one thing..."

Cat tilted her head, her smile faded. "What do you mean?"

His eyes snapped back to her. "Nothing. It's not important. Any other colours?"

75

He wants me to tell him everything but he tells me almost nothing. Cat let it go, not wanting to fight. "You worry. That colour is a light blue-green. When you were wounded you had pale yellow, that's pain."

Rhone's brow lifted. "Can you tell if someone's sick?"

Cat nodded. "But not how bad or what's causing it. You have a lot of blue, which means you're a good person, and healthy, though sometimes it's washed out when you're unhappy or sad, though true sorrow is a different colour."

Rhone shook his head. "You are an unusual girl. I've never heard of such a talent." He didn't seem angry or upset anymore. "If I had your gift and I looked at you, what colour would I see the most? Hmmm. So tell me, just what is the colour for curiosity?"

Her cheeks warmed. "Pink."

Rhone chortled. "Figures. I imagine pink overwhelms your blue."

He calls me curious! He's the one asking all the questions. She chuckled to herself. With the return of his good humour, his eyes brightened, once again reminding her of the cool lagoon on the island where they'd met and the first time their eyes made contact. Her heartbeat quickened. "I haven't told you the other colour I see a lot of in you. It's my favourite. Sometimes."

"And that would be?"

"Orange." They were alone, still she leaned close to whisper in his ear. "That means you want…you know."

Rhone laughed. "And I suppose you see that when I look at you?"

"I do." Her smile grew.

He leaned back against the headboard, taking her with him. A sweet kiss followed, too short for Cat's liking.

"I'd kiss you more, but it's almost dinner time and Jewel will insist on helping you dress. I'm sure you don't want her to see your eyes glow."

They'd made love that morning. It would take a much longer kiss than the one he gave her for that urge, and the glow, to start. She shook her head. "Jewel thinks I'm strange enough."

"You're not strange, just…" A knock interrupted Rhone's words. "And that would be Jewel." He sat up, once again taking her with him.

76

"I'd better get my mask and cloak back on. Do you want me to let her in?"

Cat sighed. *I'm just…what?* "No, I will. She'll scowl at you again."

"She'll scowl anyway." Rhone motioned for Cat to lead the way. "I hope she has my dinner."

ℰ﮲ · ℜ

Instead of enduring the bustle and noise of the dining hall, the king invited Cat, Lindren and his family to a quiet meal in Dayn's suite. None of the trays the servants brought included meat. Rhone was glad he'd eaten earlier; the thick slices of roast beef in a dark, rich gravy was a delicious change to the fish he'd eaten for four years.

Prince Dayn placed himself next to Cat and refused to let her alone. More than once Rhone found himself with clenched fists and jaw. As Lord Rhone Arden he wouldn't have been permitted to say much; as Fox, he couldn't even glare at Prince Pimple.

Cat said little, her mood sinking further with every passing moment. Rhone hoped his earlier anger didn't have anything to do with it; she'd seemed fine when they left her rooms. It had to be the prophecies. She played with her food and answered Dayn when forced. Rhone suspected the black in Dayn's light wasn't the only reason she avoided conversation.

After the meal they sat drinking wine and talking…except for Rhone, who kept his position by the door. From what was said, and not said, Rhone realized the rest of King Rodrin's family must not be in on all the goings on. Not a one of the prophecies was mentioned, nor the spell on Prince Dayn.

The evening wore on, until finally Lisha mentioned Cat's lack of interest in any of the topics discussed. Lindren suggested she go to her room. Cat didn't argue and excused herself.

She kept her promise to ignore Rhone while they were in public. He walked two paces behind as she dragged herself up the stairs. When Jewel finished fussing over her, he bolted both doors.

"You were quiet at dinner tonight," he commented, as they

undressed. "You're not still fretting about those prophecies are you?"

"I'm afraid, Rhone. A demon, and possibly a dead man, are supposed to father my children."

He led her to the bed and pulled back the covers. "In." She climbed in, him right after. "Prophecies are funny things," he said, arranging the blankets around them. "They don't always mean what they seem to." Rhone put his arms around her and drew her close. "Let me tell you a story I heard as a child.

"There was a kingdom, long ago, it doesn't matter where. A prophecy came to light that said only one son would be born to each ruler, but that son would always live long enough to rule and have his own son. And that's the way it was for many centuries."

Cat snuggled into him and rested her head on his shoulder.

"The second part of the prophecy said there would come a time when two sons were born and disaster would result," Rhone continued. "Jealousy would cause the downfall of the kingdom. No one worried much about the prophecy until a queen gave birth to a second son. All the king's councilors and mages pondered the situation, each with their own solutions.

"One fellow even suggested killing the second son to solve the problem. The queen wouldn't hear of it and in a fit of temper had the offender hanged." Rhone played with a lock of her hair while he spoke. "The king wasn't pleased about either event, but listened to his queen who suggested they give the second son more love and attention, thereby giving him no reason to be jealous. They doted on him, bought him wonderful things and generally spoiled him rotten.

"When the second son was old enough to marry, a beautiful princess was found for him. The first son, the heir, wasn't neglected as such, but didn't have as much attention lavished on him as his brother. When the time had come for the first son to marry, nothing was done, no bride was found for him. When he confronted his father, the king told him 'There's plenty of time yet, my son. Someone worthy will be found.'

"When his younger brother's bride arrived, the older grew envious. She was beautiful beyond reason and the first son coerced the girl into his chambers where he took her for his own. When the second son found out, they fought and the second son was killed. The law decreed that the surviving heir be banished in disgrace and the king grew depressed, retreating into his chambers. The queen was now too old to bear more children and the king refused to set her aside and take another. He neglected the land, keeping to his chambers and his wine bottle."

"If I ever do have children," Cat said, "I'll be careful not to favour one over the other."

Rhone gave her a reassuring squeeze. "Ten years after the death of the second son, the first came back at the head of a huge army. He tore through the land destroying and killing like an avenging spirit. Crops were burned, peasants killed, women raped and every building set alight. Due to the neglect of ten years, there was very little army left. The soldiers defended their homeland bravely and most of both armies were destroyed during the fight for the capital. The castle guard fought hard, but by the time the battle was over, only the heir was alive. All his men had died, as had the guards. He crashed through the door to the king's chambers and, without a word, cut off his father's head. What was left of the kingdom was his.

"For about two minutes. As he stood gloating, his mother crept up behind him and stabbed him in the back with her dagger. He had enough time to kill her before he died. With no ruler and the land in ruins, the few surviving citizens left and the kingdom was gone."

"That's a sad story," Cat mumbled into his chest. "Is it true?"

Her lifted her chin. "You can't tell?"

She shook her head. "If someone believes something is true, then they're not lying. Besides, I wasn't checking."

Rhone chuckled. "I was told the story by my mother. It could be true. What it does show is that prophecies will find a way to fulfill themselves, despite the efforts of mere humans. The king and queen made the prophecy they were trying to avoid come true."

"So what should I do?"

"Nothing. If it's meant to happen it will and there's very little you can do." Prophecies were a pile of troll dung anyway, stories to pass the time. He felt a warm tear fall on his chest and lifted her head so he could kiss her. "I wouldn't worry, though. As I said, sometimes prophecies don't turn out the way people think they will. A dead man, for instance. Lindren's suggestion is quite valid, and men who are awaiting the hangman's noose are considered dead men, even though they aren't yet. As are those working in the mines of Ordran. It's only a matter of time."

Cat buried her face in the crook between his neck and shoulder, her breath a warm tickle on his skin.

He stroked her hair. "It may even be that you'll save him from impending death."

"And the demon?" she asked, after a moment.

"Demon-spawn, not demon, and I can't imagine what that means, not yet anyway." Rhone rolled her over until she was underneath him, then kissed her, on the lips, the cheek and worked his way down.

"Don't worry about it, Cat," he told her between kisses. "You could stew over it for centuries before anything happens." Taking a nipple in his mouth, he curled his tongue around it and gently sucked. A sigh and a moan escaped Cat's sweet lips.

After a moment's pleasure, he moved back up, placing his hands on either side of her head and kissed her deeply, delighting in her softness, her touch, as she wrapped herself around him.

"By Ar and by Vania, Cat, and by all that's holy, I wish I could spend forever with you and negate that prophecy, but that's just not possible." Rhone smoothed a wisp of hair from her face, her wonderful eyes sad. Odd thing was, he meant it.

"I know," she whispered, and kissed him. "But we can enjoy the time we do have."

Rhone smiled. "That we can," he said, and spent a long time helping her forget her fears.

ဆာ　◆　ௌ

Dayn twisted the ruby ring on the middle finger of his right hand. Twice now he'd had a meal with Lady Cat. Try as he might, she wouldn't respond to him. He refused to give up. Once Lords Lindren and Arnir removed the spell, he'd be free of Tozer. He wouldn't have to turn Lady Cat over to the turd. Perhaps he could take her riding or show her his favourite falcon. Maybe she could sit with him while he sang her songs of love. That might soften her up; if only he could get rid of that brute she'd hired.

Why would she need a Human bodyguard with over thirty Elves in the castle? Surely no one would be foolish enough to try kidnapping her now.

A knock came at the door. Dayn ignored it. It was probably Brion coming to help him get ready for bed. He didn't want to sleep right now. Instead, he picked up his glass of white wine and tossed the last of it back. The knock sounded louder.

"Enter!" Dayn growled. He poured himself another glass of wine.

The face in the doorway wasn't Brion. Dayn almost spilled the wine. He set the bottle down. "Josef. What are you doing here?"

The servant closed the door. His black eyes, two pits leading to nothingness, settled on Dayn's. "My master has a message for you." He pulled a piece of paper from his trouser pocket and passed it to him.

Dayn didn't take it. "I'm not seeing Tozer anymore. He no longer has a hold on me."

Josef clenched his fist and Dayn's head exploded in pain. "No one is free of the master. Now read it."

The man spoke quietly, though it seemed loud to Dayn's ears. He took the paper. There was none of the proper salutation entitled a prince.

'I know an Elf has tampered with my spell. It doesn't matter. I still own you, body and soul. You will bring the girl to me. Once I have finished with her, you can have her back. She will be all yours. The messenger has something for you. Wear it, but keep it hidden. If you don't do as told, you will be dealt with and all the Elves of Urdran won't be able to help you. You cannot hide from me.'

It wasn't even signed. Dayn crumpled the paper, his heart pounding. *How can he get me here? My rooms are warded!* Once he left them, however, it would be another matter. He'd never be able to take Lady Cat riding, or anyone else for that matter, unless he did as Tozer wished. He said he'd give her back after he'd finished with her. What did he want? To bed her? If that's all it was, Dayn could handle it, as long as he could have her after.

He tossed the paper in the fire. "The note says you have something for me. What is it?"

"An amulet." Josef pulled it out of another pocket. "It will…protect you."

Dayn took it. It dangled from a simple leather string. The amulet itself was made of gold, though it had a strange reddish cast to it. Runes of some kind were scratched into one side. The other had a raised face so demonic and evil it turned Dayn's stomach. He looked at Joseph, unsure if he should take it. What if it was found?

"Put it on," Joseph said, his eyes boring into Dayn.

Dayn gulped and slipped it around his neck.

"Hide it."

He slid it inside his shirt, ensuring not even the string could be seen. The amulet felt cold, colder than ice, so cold it burned. Dayn tried to lift it away from his skin, but it seemed stuck. He pulled. It was stuck.

Joseph smiled. Dayn shivered with horror. The man bowed and was gone.

Chapter Seven

Cat crumpled the message Jewel had read to her. In a fit of pique, she threw it in the fire.

"If I might be so forward, my lady, what did it say?" Rhone asked, returning from the garderobe.

Jewel spun to face him. "It's none of your business! Keep your nose to yourself."

"It's very much my business." Rhone took up his usual spot by the door, looking menacing. He did it very well, even with the mask and hood. "That message has upset my lady. What if it's a threat to her?"

Cat sighed and plunked herself in the chair. "It's not threatening, just annoying. Prince Dayn wants me to spend some time with him this morning. He said something about playing games."

Jewel's attitude perked up. "You should, my lady. The Prince is an expert at Kings and Knights. I'm sure he'd be glad to teach you. It would be a wonderful way to pass the time."

Spending the morning with Dayn was the last thing Cat wanted. She couldn't think of any excuse not to, though. It wasn't as if she had a lot to do. She'd like to look through more shops, but it seemed a flimsy excuse. *I also want to spend time with Kelwyn.* The solution smacked her in the face; she could invite Kelwyn along with her.

"Jewel, would you see if Kelwyn's in his room? Maybe he'd like to play Kings and Knights too." At least she wouldn't have to put up with Dayn on her own. Cat doubted Rhone would deter him much, flirting with her in front of his family didn't appear to bother Dayn.

"Yes, my lady." The maid gave her a curtsey and Rhone opened the door for her. She scowled on the way out.

"You really don't like Prince Dayn, do you?" Rhone leaned against the door. Maybe he wanted to keep Jewel out.

"No, I don't. And it's not just the black. I don't like him as a person."

"Then…"

A knock interrupted Rhone's next words. It was Lindren. Cat rose and gave him a kiss.

"Have you found something to do with your days while we're here?"

Cat wrinkled her nose. "Dayn wants to teach me to play Kings and Knights. I'm asking Kelwyn to come too."

Lindren chuckled. "Safety in numbers?"

"Something like that."

"I've spoken to Wendyl Banren, the king's personal healer," Lindren said. "He's quite impressed with the skill you displayed caring for the northern barons' men. He's asked if you could stop by the hospital…"

Cat blinked. "The what?"

"Hospital, the place where he works." Lindren's smile was back to normal. His silver-grey eyes danced with humour. "When he suggested it, I thought perhaps you could spend some of your time there learning how he takes care of people."

"I'd like that." Cat's spirits picked up.

Another knock announced Kelwyn, Jewel right behind.

"I'll go then," Lindren said. "I want to see Arnir."

Cat hadn't seen Arnir at dinner the previous night or breakfast that morning and assumed he was still tired from removing the spell. She gave her father another kiss and hug, then one each for Kelwyn.

Once Lindren closed the door, Cat told Kelwyn about Dayn's message. "I don't want to go, but I don't see how I can get out of it. So I thought you could come, too. We could both learn how to play Kings and Knights."

"I've heard about the game," her friend said. "Never played it though." His smile lit up his face. "I'll come with you."

"Oh, thank you!" Cat gave him another kiss and hug.

As they walked up the stairs to the prince's suite, Rhone following, Cat told Kelwyn about Lindren's suggestion regarding the healer.

"I think it's a great idea." Kelwyn took her hand. "Not only will you learn things you don't know about healing Humans, it'll help keep the boredom away…and you out of trouble."

"Kelwyn!"

When they reached Dayn's door, Cat's good mood vanished. Heaving a sigh, she knocked.

℘ • ℂ℞

Jewel stared at the door the mercenary Fox had closed. *I really don't trust that man. What ever possessed those Elves to hire him? There's definitely something strange about him.* Strange things had happened ever since the Elves arrived. Leaving for awhile hadn't put a stop to it. *I just don't understand those Elves.* They didn't mind Lord Kelwyn sleeping in the same room as Lady Cat, nor did it bother them that Fox slept in her sitting room. The lady herself took peculiarity to a new height, with her strange clothes and habits. Maybe living for all those centuries made them a little crazy.

She sighed and pulled a dusting cloth from a pocket. The mantles in both rooms needed attention. As she worked, Jewel realized there was nothing she could do about any of it, except keep a careful watch out for Talon. The thief hadn't shown his face since the Elves left, which confirmed her suspicions about his intentions. He had to be responsible somehow for Lady Cat's kidnapping.

Jewel needed to play the game right. If Talon put in another appearance, she'd have to find out how he got into the castle. The information could prove very valuable. If she showed everyone that her intentions were honourable, perhaps even if her background was discovered, she could keep her job. *I can't go back there!* She had no family left who'd take her in and her only friend before coming to the castle had died. Jewel was on her own and had to protect not only herself, but Lady Cat as well.

℘ • ℂ℞

Cat had a headache. Lunch was in Lindren's rooms with Kelwyn and her brothers. Lindren and Arnir occupied the chairs, everyone else

85

sat on the floor near the fireplace, their plates balanced on one leg; except for Rhone. He'd eaten in her rooms and now sat behind her, one arm resting on an upraised leg. Her head throbbed and she considered asking Arnir to get rid of it. Though he looked much better today, he still wasn't his usual self. Neither was she.

Dayn hadn't been happy to see Kelwyn, or Rhone who he almost threw out of the room until Cat said she'd go as well if he did. She swore he spent more time trying to touch her hand or arm than teach them how to play the game and all she could feel was the sickening taint.

Once she'd played a game or two, she decided she preferred Rune Stones. Kings and Knights was a war strategy game involving a special board and carved ivory pieces. Kelwyn took to it right away. Cat wished him well with it. She had no desire to play, or visit Dayn. The cheese she held tasted bland and Cat set it back on her plate.

"What's the matter?" Lindren asked.

"Dayn gave me a headache. I can feel the taint on him and he kept wanting to touch my hand." Cat shuddered. "Do I have to go back and visit him?"

Lindren set his empty plate on the table between the two chairs. "You should at least be polite, but I don't think you need to spend every morning with him. Once we remove the black spell, I'm sure things will improve."

Cat put a hand to her right temple and rubbed. It didn't help. "Arnir, would you mind getting rid of it for me?"

"I'll take care of it," Lindren said, motioning her onto his lap.

"Thank you, Father, I appreciate it." Arnir's eyes appeared darker than they should.

Once settled on Lindren's lap, Cat said to Arnir, "You're still not feeling well?"

Her brother smiled. "Just tired. I'll be fine in a day or two."

Cat laid her head on Lindren's shoulder and he whispered the ancient words of power. She closed her eyes and let his soothing touch remove the pain. When it was gone, she sighed.

"Something wrong, Cat?" Lindren asked.

"No." She sat up. "It just feels good to have that headache gone."

Cat gave him a hug and slid off his lap. "It's time to go the healer's. Are you coming too, Lindren?"

"I'd like to visit with Soran Rais for a bit, if you don't mind. See how he's doing. Just remember, sleeproot and utahara only grow in the enclaves, so don't promise them to Wendyl. We don't have enough to trade with everybody."

"I'll remember."

"Still more secrets?" Rhone asked. Cat didn't bother checking his light, she knew it would show red.

"We've used them on Humans in the past and will continue to do so as supply allows. Cat used them both on the injured men recovering in this castle." Lindren leaned forward, resting his arms on his knees. "I understand your anger, but we do try to help when we can." At Rhone's nod, he sat back.

"Kelwyn? Do you want to come?" Cat asked, trying to break the tension.

He shook his head. "I like watching you work, not someone else. Darsha and Shain want to go into town and I thought I'd go with them. Do you mind?"

"No. I guess I'm on my own, then." She turned to Arnir. "Somehow I doubt you'll want to come."

He chuckled. "No, not really. I've spoken with Human healers before. I think I'll go back to my room and lie down."

Darsha, Shain and Kelwyn all rose, placing their plates on one of the trays. "We'll keep an eye out for Jonlan," Darsha said to Rhone.

"I'd appreciate it." Rhone stood and stretched before replacing his mask. Cat checked his light, the red was almost gone. He bowed to her. "Are you ready to go?"

She smiled. "Yes."

Rhone strode to the door and opened it. "After you, my lady."

Cat stepped out into the hall, then stepped back in. "I don't know where I'm going."

Her brothers and father laughed. Rhone rolled his eyes. "I'll show you," he said.

Rhone directed her down the stairs and out the throne room to the long corridor before the outside doors. The Winter Garden lay to the right. They turned left, to the far end of the north wing, and stepped into a large room holding twenty beds. Nine people rested or slept, some tended by women in dark green dresses with long white aprons and black cloths concealing their hair.

A slender man with black hair, shot through with grey, spoke with one of the ladies, his back to them. Cat didn't remember meeting him the last time she was in Tezerain.

The woman nodded her head, then spotted Cat and Rhone. "Lord Wendyl, someone is here to see you."

The healer turned, his smile genuine and warm, dark eyes sparkling. "Ah, Lady Cat." A few strides of his long legs brought him close. He bowed and held his hand out. Cat was used to this custom now and gave him her hand to kiss. "I'm Lord Wendyl Banren. I must compliment you on your skill. The man whose arm had to be amputated is recovering nicely and his stomach wound is healed. Your stitches are the best I've ever seen."

"Thank you," Cat said, trying not to blush. She glanced around the long room. Beside each bed there was a table, each with a candle, cup and metal pitcher. Two windows at the far end allowed in light. A chandelier helped. Two doors lay to her right, one near her, the other half-way down. "Lindren said you could show me some of the ways you heal people."

"Gladly. This way." Wendyl directed her to the first room, a silent Rhone dutifully following. "Let me show you where we store our medicines and herbs."

Lit by only a few candles, the room was lined with shelves. Various sizes of jars, bottles, boxes and bags filled them, each labeled and placed neatly. One jar looked like it had leeches in it. *What would he do with those?* Cat's sensitive nose picked out willow bark, ginger root, mint, valerian, parsley, honey and other items she was familiar with. Some eluded her.

"We keep the light to a minimum in here," Wendyl said. "The herbs keep better in cool, dark places. The more sensitive herbs and roots are stored downstairs."

He lit a candle and directed her to another door, opposite the one they'd entered. It led to a dark room underneath the herb room. Long strings of garlic and mandrake roots hung from the ceiling. Sacks and crates sat on the floor, while more jars and bottles covered the shelves. Between those upstairs, and those below, Wendyl used far more items in his medicine than Cat thought possible. Then she remembered Humans developed conditions and illnesses Elves and Tiranen didn't. She realized there was a great deal to be learned about Human healing, more than could be taught in the five weeks before the royal wedding.

Back upstairs, Wendyl escorted her to the second room—one that sent shivers up and down her spine. A full skeleton stood in one corner, held up by thin leather straps, it's skull set in a permanent grin. Visions of a field of bones flashed through her memory, reminding her all too clearly of how her people had died. She forced herself not to look at the thing, instead concentrating on other objects in the room. *I have to stop letting it bother me if I'm going to be here every day.*

A wooden table sat in the center, a pungent odour she didn't recognize permeating it, though that wasn't what disturbed her. Saws and other sharp metal instruments hung on the walls. Knives and needles of varying sizes lay on cloths on a counter running the length of the far wall.

Cat thought of the Kerend man who'd lost part of one arm and how the soldiers had taken it off. Tarine told her the Humans had nothing like sleeproot. *That poor man. The pain must have been tremendous.*

Wendyl still held his smile. "Here's where we do the surgery, sewing up wounds and curing ailments." He pointed to an iron stove in the corner. "We can even boil our own water."

"Are any of the men from the northern baronies here?" Cat wanted out of that room.

"Just one, the rest have been quartered elsewhere in the castle to continue their recovery." He gestured her out the door. "Harrol, the man who lost his arm, is over here by the window."

Harrol appeared to be in his late twenties, the owner of a plain, yet pleasant, face. She hadn't paid much attention to his features while she cared for him, only his wounds. His brown eyes appeared as desolate

89

as his expression. A thick bandage covered the stump of his left arm, taken off above the elbow.

Wendyl stood at the foot of his bed. "Harrol, this is Lady Cat. She's the Elf who saved your life."

The injured man looked her up and down, then turned away. "You shouldn't have wasted your time, my lady. I'd have preferred to die."

Wendyl frowned. "Harrol, we've discussed your attitude. That's no way to talk."

"No. He should speak how he feels." Cat did a quick check of his light, a nice blue with far too much pale yellow and yellow-green, the colours of physical and emotional pain.

When Cat moved closer to the man, Wendyl motioned to one of the ladies who brought a chair for her. "Why do you want to die?" she asked. "You still have the gift of life and that is very precious." She wished Arnir could heal the man. That was one argument she didn't want to get into again, especially with her brother.

Harrol turned his sad eyes back to her. "I'm a soldier. It's all I know how to do. I can't fight with just one arm."

Her people had fought with missing arms many times. It wouldn't help him, though. Cat thought back to the traumatic days following the battle. "Lord Aris spoke with you. What did he say?"

It took a moment for him to respond. "He told me to come back once I've healed. He'd find a place for me." Harrol lifted the bandaged stump of his arm. "What can I do with this? What woman will want to marry me?"

His voice broke and Cat wondered if that was the real problem. Perhaps he had a girl back in Kerend. "Why would it stop someone from falling in love with you? It says nothing about the person you are inside."

"Would you want me, my lady?" He waved his stump, his voice strained with anger. "Would you want someone who couldn't hold you properly? Couldn't work a farm? Couldn't support you?"

"I want someone who cares for me inside, not what I look like," she replied, speaking a truth she'd only ever voiced to Kelwyn and Taurin. Why she did so now, she couldn't explain. "That's the only thing

90

that truly matters; what's inside, not the way you look outside. Inside is the real you. Don't ask me how I know, but you're a good and brave man. Any woman would be proud to call you husband."

Harrol opened his eyes wide in shock. He could say nothing for a moment. "I...I'll think on your words, my lady."

"You do that," Cat said, with a smile. Then an idea hit her. "Do you know how to read and write?"

"No. No, my lady. There's not much use for reading and writing in the army, unless you're an officer."

"I can't read Torian. If you're up to it, do you want to learn together? You could be more useful to Aris if you could read and write. We could spend a couple of hours in the morning. I'm sure we could find someone to teach us." That would leave her time before lunch to wander around shops, visit with Kelwyn or lock herself in her bedroom with Rhone.

Wendyl's smile grew. "All the Priestesses of Vania who work here are schooled. I'm sure one of them would be pleased."

"I...would like that." Harrol still appeared in shock. "Thank you, my lady, but, why? Don't you have other things to do? Why would you want to spend your time with a broken soldier?"

"My father wants to stay until Gailen and Selesa's wedding, so I have plenty of time. And I think I would enjoy learning with you."

Harrol braved a small, confused, smile. "I look forward to it, my lady."

Wendyl escorted her to a spot near the door before he said a word. "Lady Cat, that was extraordinarily generous of you."

And solves my problem with Dayn. "I think he'll find he has much to live for."

They spent the rest of the afternoon going over the healing properties of some of the medicines in the upper room.

℘ • ℜ

Two days later, Arnir and the Ringwood healers decided it was time to tackle Dayn's spell. Lindren felt better than he had since before

91

the sea battle. Darsha, Shain and Kelwyn insisted on accompanying them and Lindren chuckled to himself over their concern. When he thought about it, if roles were reversed, he'd feel the same way.

Cat came also, Rhone with her, to keep an eye on things from her special point of view. She'd miss her afternoon session with Wendyl, but they needed her.

When they arrived, Jeral was waiting for them with Rodrin and Lisha. Although Dayn's sitting room was quite a bit larger than Lindren's, it made for a crowded room.

The first thing the prince did was latch himself onto Cat. "I hope this works," he said, tucking her arm in his. She didn't quite manage to hide her shudder or her revulsion. "I missed you yesterday. Kelwyn is catching on to the game quite well, but I personally feel you need more practice."

Lindren also hoped the working was successful. If it wasn't, they'd have to sit down and figure out what to do with the boy; they couldn't let him run around with a sorcerer's spell on him.

"I was busy," Cat said. "The Priestesses of Vania who work in the surgery are teaching me to read and write Torian."

Amazing how she maneuvered that. She'd managed to find a way to avoid Dayn without hurting his feelings. *Perhaps she's picking up the concept of diplomacy after all.*

A brief frown dipped Dayn's brows. "If I'd known you wanted to learn, I could have taught you." He simply didn't give up.

"Welcome, everyone. Please be seated." Rodrin gestured to the extra chairs provided. "There's wine if anyone so desires."

Soon they all had a seat, except Rhone who stood by the door.

Kelwyn took Cat from Dayn and placed her beside him. With a smile, he directed Dayn to the healers. "I believe you are the guest of honour today."

Lindren almost laughed at the annoyance on the prince's face.

The king cast a wary eye at Rhone before settling himself on the sofa beside Lisha. "How do you fellows want to proceed?"

Arnir spoke for the healers, since he knew the most about the situation. "Last time I tried to deal with it, I had Dayn lay down on the sofa. It made it easier to work. Father, Hanrish and Ardamin will then form a chain, each touching the other, with Father touching me. That way I can access their power."

"Fascinating," Rodrin said. "I suppose that means you'd like us to get off." He stood and held his hand out to Lisha, helping her to her feet. Chairs were quickly rearranged. Lisha insisted on sitting at the head of the sofa to keep close to her son. Rodrin sat beside her.

Dayn bowed to Cat. "My lady, I must admit I'm quite nervous about the whole thing." A fine sheen of sweat covered his brow. He seemed extra fidgety. "I know it sounds inappropriate, but would you mind holding my hand?"

"Dayn!" Lisha's usual smile vanished. "It *is* inappropriate. You should be ashamed."

The prince appeared unhappy, not ashamed. Though it shocked Lisha, it might not be a bad idea. Cat could check his light easier. Lindren crooked his finger at her. When she'd woven her way through people and chairs, he said, in Elven, "I know the black bothers you, but would you mind doing as he asks? It'll not only make it easier to monitor him, I think he might settle down faster. He's behaving oddly, even for Dayn."

Cat stiffened. "I hope Arnir gets rid of it soon. I don't know how long I'll be able to stand it. It seems stronger."

Lindren smiled. "Thank you."

"If it will help, I'll hold your hand." Cat settled herself in a chair by Dayn's legs and took his hand. Despite his obvious fear, the prince smiled.

Arnir took his place in the chair near Dayn's head, with Lindren and the Ringwood healers in a row behind him. Everyone else found places elsewhere, Jeral near the fireplace.

"What if this doesn't work?" Dayn asked Lindren, his young features radiating a mixture of fear and hope.

He's only eighteen years old; he shouldn't have to deal with something like this. However, he had brought it on himself. "We'll figure that out later."

Arnir closed his eyes and chanted the words that focused his power. Lindren, Hanrish and Ardamin did likewise.

A familiar warmth flowed over Lindren, as did relief that the block was gone. The power spread from the center of his being to the tips of his fingers and toes. He reveled in it a moment before securing the link with Arnir. As he did, the power from the Ringwood healers flowed through him, thrumming like the wings of a hummingbird. This was what he'd been born to do, wield the life giving power of Arvanion, and he loved it.

Arnir reached over to touch his glowing white fingers to the prince's face. A backwash of the taint reached through the line and they all shuddered. Lindren didn't envy his son the job that lay before him. Ancient words as familiar as his own body kept his power focused, yet allowed him to watch the working.

Cat appeared distinctly unhappy. Both Rodrin and Lisha showed signs of worry. Dayn shivered. Arnir hadn't said anything about Dayn's fear during the first working, but then, the prince hadn't known about the spell on him at the time.

Through the link, Lindren could sense Arnir peeling back the layers of his containment spell. The black throbbed and pulsed in counterpoint to that of the Elven magic. The strength of it turned his stomach and he had to force himself not to retch. Both Hanrish and Ardamin rested their heads in their free hands. Arnir pushed harder, delving into their power so as not to deplete his too soon.

When the last of the containment spell fell away, the black exploded, not into tiny slivers, but out and into the rest of Dayn's body. Arnir pushed harder, trying to regain control. Waves of nausea gripped Lindren and the healers. Ardamin gagged. Cat snatched her hand away.

Arnir gasped and jerked back. "There's something wrong!"

Chapter Eight

Sickening black coursed through Dayn's body. Cat almost fell off her chair in her haste to shake off his hand. Somehow, Kelwyn was beside her, steadying her. "Lindren!" She spoke in Elven. "The black is all over and it's a lot stronger. Much worse than before!"

"What's wrong?" Rodrin demanded, on his feet now.

"I don't know." Arnir clasped his hands together. They shook. "Something's made the spell stronger. It escaped and is taking control."

Lisha gasped. Tears formed in her eyes. Rodrin drew her close. Dayn sat up, his face sick with terror. Cat checked his light. Black shadowed half of it. The remainder was a blend of pale blue and the strange, swirling mixture of green, yellow and reddish-blue that she'd identified as the colour of fear.

Lindren crouched beside the prince. "Dayn, has something changed? Have you felt anything different since Arnir last touched you?"

Dayn shook his head. "N…no. I…I haven't done…felt anything."

Purple washed over the part of his light not smothered with black. Still speaking in Elven, Cat said, "He's lying." Her heart pounded and she clung to Kelwyn, keeping her eyes out of focus so she could report to Lindren on Dayn's condition.

Lindren turned back to the young man, anger darkening his eyes. "Tell me the truth, Dayn. Something has changed."

"It wasn't anywhere near this bad before, Father," Arnir said. "This is something new."

"Dayn?" The tone of Rodrin's voice demanded an answer.

Dayn gulped, looking from one face to another. "There's…there's nothing…different."

Lindren leaned close to Cat. He spoke in Elven. "Can you see anything that might be responsible?"

"What's she doing?" Rodrin asked.

"Later." Lindren held up his hand, stopping further questions.

Cat searched, her unfocused eyes scanning the prince's head, arms, chest...*there*! "A large patch of solid black on his chest...over his heart." Her eyes hurt and a headache threatened.

Lindren turned his cold gaze to Dayn. "Take off your tunic and shirt."

Dayn clutched the front of his tunic. "No! I don't have to!"

Rodrin added his glare to Lindren's. "Yes you do, and if you don't, we'll hold you down and do it ourselves."

"You...you wouldn't." Dayn's voice squeaked.

His father leaned towards him. Lisha's tears flooded down her cheeks. Dayn's brown eyes resembled a rabbit's who knew its time had come. He undid the fastenings on his tunic and Rodrin backed off, his face stony in anger. Dayn shrugged out of the tunic. Cat let her eyes shift back into focus. She leaned into Kelwyn and he held her tight.

With trembling hands, Dayn undid the buttons of his shirt. When he finally pulled it apart, an amulet, about the size of the palm of Cat's hand, rested against his sparsely haired chest. A reddish gold, it glimmered in the candlelight, highlighting a nightmare face. Lisha gasped and collapsed into her chair.

Jeral's eyes flew open. "How did that get through my wards?"

The Elves stared, as if unable to believe their eyes. Cat checked Dayn's light again. The amulet pulsed an obsidian black, except it didn't shine the way the stone did. It sucked in what remained of Dayn's light, slowly, yet noticeable.

"Lindren," she whispered, her horror matching that in her father's eyes. "That thing, it's absorbing Dayn's light."

"It's got to go. Now." Lindren touched it and cried out, snatching back his hand. When he spread out his fingers, blisters appeared where he'd made contact with the reddish-gold metal. "It's reacting to my magic!"

Darsha stepped in. "I don't have magic." Still, he touched it tentatively at first. When nothing happened, he grabbed it.

Dayn screamed. "Don't touch it! It's stuck!"

Cat's oldest brother crouched to examine the amulet and Dayn's flesh. "He's right." Darsha tugged, raising the skin of the prince's chest with the amulet. "It seems to be sinking into his skin."

"Don't! It hurts!" Dayn attempted to push him away. "I tried that already!"

"Can...can you remove it with your magic?" Rodrin asked, his face pale.

Lindren shook his head. "Not without more help. We'll have to..."

Darsha's hands shot out like snakes. He had his dagger in one and sliced the leather thong. With the other, he grabbed the amulet and tore it off the prince's chest, taking the skin with it, then threw it on the floor. Dayn screamed, so did Lisha. The amulet landed at Shain's feet. Shadows cast by the flickering fire gave the twisted face life. It seemed to laugh. Shain touched it with the toe of his boot.

Rodrin bent down and tore a large piece off one Lisha's underdresses. He tossed the cloth to Lindren, who pressed it against the prince's wound. Darsha sheathed his dagger and moved out of the way.

"I know it hurts, but it's for the best," Lindren said. "Quick thinking, son." In Elven, he said, "Cat, how's his light now?"

"The black has decreased, but it's still stronger than it was." The pale yellow of physical pain added to the mix.

"Why do you two keep talking in your language?" Rodrin asked.

Lindren glanced at him. "Later. Please."

Shain stared at the disgusting object, Dayn's bloody skin still attached. "What is this thing, Father?"

"Maybe we should ask Dayn."

All eyes turned to the prince. His chest heaved against Lindren's hand. Tears rolled down his cheeks. "I...I..."

"You owe us an explanation and I want it now." The hard edge had returned to Rodrin's voice.

Dayn fell back to lie once more on the couch. Lindren shifted to maintain the pressure. The prince sniffled back tears. "I got a message the other day, from the sorcerer I went to. He demanded I wear this."

Lindren looked at Cat. She nodded. He told the truth.

"Why didn't you just ignore it?" Jeral asked, the only one in the room who'd remained reasonably calm through the ordeal.

"I…I couldn't. The messenger, I think he could use magic too. He made me put it on."

Rodrin sat back in his chair and put a comforting arm around Lisha. "Why? Why does he want you so bad?"

"I don't know."

At another glance from Lindren, Cat shook her head.

"Dayn," Lindren said. "We can't help you if don't tell us. I know you're lying."

The prince's eyes widened. "How?"

"I just do. Now tell us the entire story. The truth, all of it."

Dayn put his arm over his eyes. "The day I…knocked Lady Cat down, I was on my way back from seeing him."

"Him who?" Jeral asked. "I want a name."

"Tozer. His name is Tozer."

"That rapscallion who's set up business in my city?" Rodrin almost roared.

Dayn's voice was the mouse to Rodrin's lion. "Yes."

The king's face turned to stone. Lisha buried hers against his shoulder.

Lindren checked the wound. It still bled and he replaced the cloth. "Continue, please."

"He…he…" Dayn sobbed. "He wanted me to kidnap Lady Cat, bring her to him."

Cat's heart thumped in her chest. *Did he have something to do with my kidnapping?* It would spell disaster, especially for Rodrin and Lisha.

Dayn tried to sit up. Lindren wouldn't let him. His frightened eyes roved everywhere, except to Cat. "I didn't want to!" They settled on Lindren. "You have to believe me!"

Cat nodded. She glanced around the room. Jeral, Rodrin and all her brothers showed red in their lights, so did Kelwyn and Rhone. To her surprise, both Hanrish's and Ardamin's lights also displayed the colour of anger. She had to admit, she wanted to punch Dayn herself.

Rodrin clenched the hand that wasn't holding his wife. "Did…did you have anything to do with Lady Cat's disappearance?"

"No!" Dayn almost leapt from the sofa. Lindren held him down.

"You have to believe me! You have to!"

Once again Cat nodded and she heaved a quiet sigh of relief.

Dayn sobbed out his next words. "I...I didn't have time. I was supposed to make friends with her, then...then Tozer was to tell me where to take her. I didn't want to, but he threatened me and I didn't know what to do!" He laid his arm over his eyes again. "When Lord Arnir found the spell on me, it scared me to death. I thought once it was removed I'd be all right, I wouldn't have to do what he said. Then...the messenger came...with...that." He pointed in the general direction of the amulet.

Lindren's gentle voice broke the ensuing silence. "Tell us his name and he'll bother you no more."

Dayn lowered his arm. "Josef. He's one of the kitchen staff."

Rodrin disentangled himself from Lisha's arms and strode to the door. Rhone stepped aside, giving him a bow. The king spoke to one of the guards outside, then returned to his seat, and his wife. "In a few minutes he'll be manacled and on his way to the dungeon, under constant watch, with orders that if he moves, he dies."

"When we're finished here," Lindren said. "We'll pay him a visit and see how much of a sorcerer he is. If necessary, we can raise wards around the cell to prevent his escape."

Rodrin nodded.

Lindren turned his attention back to Dayn. "I assume you were to resume the original plan to kidnap my daughter?"

Dayn nodded, then covered his eyes again. "He said that he knew an Elf had tampered with his spell...that he only wanted to talk to Lady Cat...and that he'd give her back when he was finished. I was to wear the amulet so Lord Arnir couldn't remove the spell."

"Give her back." Rodrin leaned towards his youngest son. "To whom?"

Dayn shook his head, his sobs racking his body. Cat clung to Kelwyn. She wanted to run, leave the horror in the room, but she couldn't even stand up.

"*To whom?*"

Cat jumped at Rodrin's words. Kelwyn shushed and soothed her in Elven.

"To...me." Dayn rolled away from Lindren, hiding his face in the sofa, his sobs shaking his entire body.

Rodrin sat back. "I thought as much." He turned to his wife, trying to comfort her.

Cat buried her face in her hands. Her eyes hurt, her head hurt. She felt sick. Kelwyn held her close and she leaned into him, wishing she could forget what Dayn said.

Once again, Lindren's voice broke the silence. "Would you have done it?"

Dayn's muffled voice quivered. "I don't know. I really didn't want to, but I was so scared. I'm still scared!"

"And so you should be." Jeral sat back with a sigh. "That amulet is a dangerous item, made of blood gold. Someone died in its making. If I'm not mistaken, it would have burrowed into your chest. You would then be Tozer's puppet, with little will of your own."

Lindren nodded. "Jeral is right. That thing is worse than the spell."

Rhone stepped forward and bowed. "Please excuse me, Your Majesties, my lords, my lady. If this thing is as dangerous as Master Jeral says, then it should be destroyed."

"Yes," Jeral said. "I just don't know how to accomplish it yet."

In one smooth motion, Rhone slid his sword out of its sheath and, with a mighty swing, clove the amulet in two, startling everyone in the room. A loud crack echoed off the walls. Smoke rose from both halves of the amulet and the rank odour of brimstone filled the air.

Rhone examined his blade, sheathed it, bowed once more and resumed his place by the door.

"Thank you, Fox," Lindren said, with a nod in his direction. "That solves the problem."

Jeral's heavy eyebrows lifted. "I hadn't thought of that. Good job."

Shain picked up the pieces by the top edges. "It looks like there's some kind of writing on the back, but the skin would have to be picked off if you want to read it."

"I'll take care of it, Shain, thank you." Jeral pulled out a hankerchief from somewhere in his robes. He held it out to receive the pieces.

"Dayn," Rodrin said, his voice still as hard as his expression. "I need to know exactly what Josef's part in this was."

The prince still had his face buried in the sofa. "He...he delivered messages, to tell me when and where to meet Tozer."

Jeral harrumphed. "So he could teach you magic?"

"Yes."

"Well,' Rodrin said. "It wasn't exactly treason until he gave you that amulet. I don't want anyone who works for sorcerers in my kingdom, let alone in my castle. He'll get his trial by peers, and by the end of next week he'll be hanging by a short rope."

"If only we could get Tozer," Jeral said. "At least now we know who's after Lady Cat."

"Not necessarily." Lindren stared at the bloody cloth in his hands. "Tozer had a plan, using Dayn. Why would he try to kidnap her another way?"

"To ensure he got her?" Shain said.

"Possibly. But I think we might be looking for someone else as well." Lindren rolled Dayn over onto his back and placed the cloth against the still bleeding wound. The prince's sobs had eased, though he kept his arm over his eyes.

And so he should. I knew there was a good reason I didn't like him. A strange sort of relief washed over Cat. Now she wouldn't have to worry about making up excuses not to see him. No one would expect her to spend time with someone who'd planned to kidnap her.

Jeral leaned forward again, his watery blue eyes fixed on Dayn. "So, young man, just what kind of spells have you been learning?"

"Fire spells. Five of them. I was learning how to form fireballs."

"Hmph. Tozer is a terrible teacher. You never start with fire." Jeral tapped his cane on the hearth three times. "Look at me when I'm talking to you!"

Dayn sat up part way, staring at the old man in shock. "How dare you speak to me like that!"

Rodrin gave him a smack on the head. "Because you deserve it.

Why should you be treated like a prince if you don't act like one?"

Jeral's glare matched Rodrin's. "I speak to all my apprentices like that, when I decide to put up with the trouble of having one."

Dayn's eyes flew open. "Apprentices?"

"I can't possibly leave you to run around only partly trained. And a dangerous part at that. You'd hurt somebody, or yourself. I'll give you two days to rest, then you will report to me every morning, right after breakfast." Jeral waved his cane at the prince. "It's going to be difficult learning to control your anger, but if you truly want to be a wizard, then you *will* make more than just an effort. And you *will* do as I say."

Dayn nodded, almost frantic. "Yes, I do...I will!"

"And the first thing you're going to learn," Jeral said. "Is that you won't have time to chase girls. Is that clear?"

"Yes...sir. Does that mean I'll never be able to pay court?"

"I didn't say never. Just not for awhile."

"I'll do my best...sir...Master Jeral."

"But first, we've got to get rid of that spell." Lindren examined his burnt hand. "Arnir, would you mind? It hurts like a demon and will interrupt my focus."

"Of course, Father." Arnir chanted under his breath. His hands glowed white and, in a few moments, the blisters disappeared.

"Fascinating." Rodrin shook his head in wonder.

Even Lisha managed to halt her tears enough to watch. "Can...can you remove that awful spell from Dayn now?" she asked, her pretty brown eyes rimmed with red. "I'm sure he really didn't know what he was getting into. He can be good boy." A mother's hope lit her face.

"When he wants to," Rodrin added, casting a stern gaze at his son.

Dayn hung his head. "I'm truly sorry for what I've done. I had no idea that man was a sorcerer. I thought he was a wizard, one of ours. I only wanted to learn magic."

Cat unfocused her eyes. He wasn't lying. Pale yellow, maroon, and light blue-green washed over the untouched portion of his light...pain, shame, and a colour she had yet to identify.

The prince raised his head. This time he looked straight at Cat, his eyes bright with unshed tears. "I'm very sorry, my lady. I never should

102

have even considered giving you to Tozer. And…if he finds me again, I'll die rather than let him hurt you. I'm not going to ask you to forgive me. I don't deserve it."

Cat shifted her eyes to normal. No lies there either. She smiled, a genuine one. "I've been accused in the past of being too forgiving. I suppose I'll never change. I do forgive you, Dayn…on one condition."

Dayn wiped his eyes. "Anything."

"You study hard and become a strong wizard, so you can fight the Black Lord. He was responsible for the deaths of my family and it would ease my grief if you would kill as many of his followers as you can."

The prince sat up straight. The cloth fell and blood dripped down his chest. "I will do that, my lady, for you and all those who have lost loved ones in this war."

Lindren smiled, his eyes silver-bright, and Cat knew she'd done right. "Then let's get on with it," he said. He motioned for Dayn to lie down and put the cloth back on the wound. "Cat, would you keep pressure on this, please?"

She nodded.

Darsha resumed his seat, while Kelwyn sat cross-legged on the floor beside Cat. "I'm not leaving you." His expression, and his eyes, remained dark. She may have forgiven Dayn; he hadn't. Once again she was reminded of why she loved him so much and wished they could be together forever. For now, she had Rhone and that would suffice.

Seated in a row once more, the mages resumed their magical chant. Dayn closed his eyes. In moments, Arnir's hands glowed white with the power of healing. He laid his hands on either side of Dayn's face and Cat let her eyes slip out of focus. Once again speaking in Elven, she kept Arnir updated on his light. "The black has decreased more since the last time I checked."

"Perhaps the effect of the amulet is wearing off." As her brother worked, the dark taint receded from the prince's body, beginning at the feet. Several minutes later, it retreated to the place at the base of Dayn's skull where it had started. Same as with Lindren, Arnir squeezed until it broke. A few wisps floated free, then they too vanished and Cat's head hurt again.

"It's gone," she said and rested her head on her right hand. Kelwyn still held the other.

"It was a spell of finding." Arnir rubbed his eyes.

"What's that?" Rodrin asked.

"It enabled Tozer to keep track of Dayn. He knew exactly where he was at any given time."

All the mages appeared worn out. They'd most likely spend the rest of the day sleeping. Though her head hurt, Cat couldn't ask any of them to fix it. She'd simply have to lie down for a while.

Arnir probed the wound on Dayn's chest with gentle fingers. "How do you feel?"

The prince opened his eyes and looked down at the mess the amulet left. "Tired and my chest hurts. Thank you. I thank all of you. I don't deserve what you've done for me."

Rodrin snorted. "That's for sure. I'll send for Lord Wendyl to have a look at that wound. You'll stay here at least until tomorrow morning. You need rest as much as the mages do."

Dayn didn't argue.

Arnir and the two Ringwood mages all made it back to the second floor on their own, under the watchful eye of Darsha. Shain accompanied Lindren to the dungeon to check on Tozer's messenger. Kelwyn refused to let go of Cat's hand and led her into her suite.

"Would you mind if I talked with Cat for awhile?" he asked Rhone.

"No, of course not." Rhone rummaged through his pack. "That damnable amulet put a nick in my sword. I'll just sit here and take care of it."

Kelwyn closed the bedroom door. "You have a headache, don't you."

Cat nodded.

"Then come lie on the bed with me and talk."

Headache or not, Cat smiled, glad to spend some quiet time with her best friend.

Chapter Nine

Cat enjoyed her mornings with Harrol and the Priestesses of Vania, though the Kerend man was quiet, speaking only when necessary. She sincerely hoped he thought about the things he could do, not the things he couldn't.

Wendyl had a table set up in the large room he called a hospital and provided the books, paper and quills they needed. Harrol had trouble with the writing part of the lessons; the pain in his stump prevented him from using it to hold the paper still. The second morning, Wendyl put a rock the size of his fist on the table. It made a perfect paperweight.

Afternoons were usually spent in the herb rooms learning the uses of the various items. The reasoning behind some of them eluded Cat completely, especially the leeches. Why would bloodletting make a person better? Wasn't part of the point of staying healthy not to bleed? Wendyl's answer of 'removing bad humours' didn't sound right. Neither did his reasoning for other treatments. He sounded so sincere and secure in his knowledge that Cat didn't want to question him.

No word had come from the Elves about Jonlan. Fortunately plenty of time remained.

Three days after Dayn's healing, late in the evening, Cat lay in bed with Rhone. Another part of her day she enjoyed. If things stayed the same, the next month would pass quickly. Rhone settled himself beside her and she cuddled into him. Her hand wandered to his back and she traced one of the long scars, a result of the whippings on the prison ship.

He chuckled. "And here I was afraid that if I ever did make it back to Tezerain that the ladies would find them horrifying."

"I don't know about the ladies here, but I think they're fascinating. My people never had them."

Rhone chuckled again and shifted so he almost lay on top of her. After nuzzling her neck for a moment, he said. "You haven't mentioned anything about someone watching you since the first night."

"That's because I haven't felt it. I don't miss it either."

He kissed her, slow and sweet. "Maybe you're getting used to castle noises."

"Maybe."

His kisses, now more ardent, put a halt to further conversation.

Sometime later, Rhone rolled off her, sweat and contentment on his face. "A week ago all I wanted was to make love to you all day. Reality has set in. I doubt I could last that long without sleeping in between."

Cat laughed. "I think you're doing just fine."

He pulled her close for another kiss. The hairs on the back of Cat's neck stood up and her brain itched. She jerked back. Quiet breathing came from the wall by the fireplace, then a scuffle like a shoe on stone.

Rhone frowned. "What is it?"

She leaned close to his ear. "I think you spoke too soon. Someone's watching."

"Are you sure?"

"Positive. I heard him."

He studied her face, then whispered in her ear. "I'm going to get dressed and go into your sitting room. Act like everything's normal. I hate to do this to you, but I think it's necessary. Give me a minute or two, then sit up. Make sure the sheet falls to your waist."

Rhone rolled off the bed, then leaned down close to her. "And stretch. If anyone's watching, that should do it."

He slipped into his trousers, shirt and boots, then picked up the cloak and mask from where he'd dropped them on the floor. In a moment, he left the room.

Cat's heart pounded. *He believes me!* Now all he had to do was catch the culprit. She listened. The sound of breathing still came from the walls. She sat up, then stretched her arms above her head and yawned. The stone wall gasped.

Rhone sauntered into the sitting room, doing up the clasp on his cloak. He put on the mask and pulled up the hood. If there was someone hiding, he didn't intend to keep it a secret. He unlocked the outer door and crouched by the fireplace, pretending to warm his hands.

He knew the instant Cat sat up. A sharp intake of breath, with a slight echo, sounded from behind the bookcase. He jumped to his feet and pulled books off the shelves. Another gasp, and footfalls, faded to his right.

Rhone pounded on the book case. "Hey! Get back here, you coward!" More books fell.

The outer door slammed open and first one, then five more guards entered the room.

"Get Lord Lindren!" Rhone told the first. "Lady Cat wasn't just hearing noises. Someone was hiding in the walls."

The guard turned and ran. In a matter of moments, Kelwyn, Lindren and his sons stood in the sitting room. Dressed in only a shirt, Cat appeared in the bedroom doorway. Kelwyn headed straight for her.

"This time I heard it, my lord," Rhone said to Lindren. "He took two short, sharp breaths and then he ran." He knocked on the back panel of the bookcase. "This sounds too hollow to have stone behind it."

Lindren took a closer look. "Darsha, inspect the other side of this wall, about five and a half to six feet from the floor. Look for a hole big enough to see through but not to be easily seen."

Darsha nodded and headed for the bedroom, giving Cat a hug on the way. Rhone bent down to the height Lindren suggested. The Elder spotted it first.

"Here." Lindren pointed to a small hole five feet from the floor. "Look a little lower, Darsha," he called.

"I found it. Five feet up, two feet from the fireplace."

"It's the same here." Lindren stood straight and headed for Cat. He gave her a hug and a kiss on the top of her head. "I seriously thought you were hearing noises and letting your imagination take over. Sorry I doubted you, Cat."

"I don't know whether to be happy, disgusted or scared."

Shain chuckled. He seemed to find humour in the strangest situations. "Disgusted definitely."

"And scared," Lindren added. "This must be how you were taken. While Kelwyn was gone, it would have been a simple matter to just pick you up and take you in there." He nodded his head in the direction of the bookcase. "The open window was to throw us off. There must be a door somewhere and a hidden corridor leading outside the castle."

"What would you like us to do, my lord?" the guard stationed outside Cat's door said.

"Nothing tonight. He's gone." Lindren ran a hand through his tousled hair. "I'll speak to the king in the morning. All of you can go back to your posts."

Arnir shut the door behind them. Rhone removed his mask. It was cloying and stuffy. He hated it. Lindren sat in one chair and motioned Cat into the other. Kelwyn crouched beside her, still holding her hand. Lindren's sons stood near the fireplace.

"It's entirely likely the bookcase is the door," Rhone said, moving in behind Cat.

Lindren agreed. "There has to be a mechanism somewhere in here to open it."

Shain folded his arms and leaned against the left side of the fireplace. "I wonder if Rodrin knows about it."

"I doubt it," Lindren said. "I'm sure he would have suggested it as a possible route for the kidnapper if he did."

Darsha sighed. "I suppose there's nothing else we can do tonight. Whoever he is, he's long gone and now that we've discovered his secret, I doubt he'll be back."

"Which is a good thing in a way." Everyone looked at Shain. "He won't be trying to kidnap Cat. We've ruined his plans."

"These plans," Lindren said, his face grim. "He could find another way, and there's Tozer to deal with."

"You still think they're two separate attempts?" Arnir asked.

"I do. Why would Tozer need to bother with tunnels if he had Dayn doing his bidding? Which means we need to be extra watchful." He turned his now dark eyes to Cat. "I'm glad you'll be spending most of your days in Wendyl's surgery. There's always people there." He looked at each of them, resting his eyes on Rhone. "We'll just have to be very careful at night."

Rhone couldn't agree more.

∞ · ∝

Lindren sipped his cup of tea, quite comfortable in the large stuffed chair in Rodrin's study. Though the trees were long dead, the oak paneling peering from between the bookcases and gaily decorated tapestries warmed him with its faint woody scent.

Rodrin, seated in a matching chair, scowled. "So I have rats in my walls. Big ones."

The fireplace crackled merrily while sunlight streamed through tall glass windows, adding a distinct contrast to Rodrin's dark expression.

"I didn't think you knew about the hidden corridors." Lindren set his cup down on the table between them.

"Part of this castle is a thousand years old, though I don't imagine I have to tell you."

"I remember when the original keep was built. I don't remember hidden tunnels, though."

"Cat's room isn't in the keep. All of you are in one of the dozen or so additions."

A thousand years before, the keep was little more than a northerly outpost of Thallan-Mar and consisted of two floors. The first held the hall that would become the throne room as well as kitchen and storage areas, while the second provided sleeping quarters for the soldiers. The town gradually built up around it as the area attracted farmers, merchants and fishermen. The keep expanded to accommodate a governor.

A hundred years later the north rebelled against a tyrant king and Kitring-Tor was formed. The governor at the time was killed and the general leading the revolt became the new king. As the country grew, so did the castle.

"Someone, somewhere down the line, built those tunnels," Rodrin said. "Which means there must be plans for them buried in the archives. We don't usually throw things like that away." He gulped back his coffee. "I'll have Thomas look them up."

It took Rodrin's chancellor two days to find the plans; someone had hidden them well. When Thomas laid them out on the desk in the king's study late that morning, Lindren was in attendance. The papers had yellowed with age, the edges crumbled and the ink faded, though not enough to obscure the tunnels.

Rodrin bent over the first page. "Let's see now." He examined some writing in the lower left corner. "I believe the date on here is 308. That's over five hundred years ago."

"It is, Your Majesty," Tomis said, with a bow. "That's when the second part of the southern wing was built, during the reign of Tuomas the Bold."

Rodrin snorted. "The Bold. Right. Look how extensive these tunnels are, it's like a rabbit warren. The man had to be cowering in his boots if he needed these built." He perused the other two papers. "Tuomas even added them to existing rooms. I'd always wondered why some rooms are smaller than others."

"Made them to watch over his lords and ladies perhaps?" The corner of Lindren's mouth turned up.

"Or maybe just the ladies." Rodrin grinned, then lost it. "Sorry. Considering someone's been watching Cat, that was in bad taste."

"Perhaps," Lindren said. "But it could be true. Tuomas wasn't as bold as he wanted people to think. He saw assassins in every shadow, though he had several mistresses. Odd thing is, it was one of the ladies who finally did him in. Poison."

Rodrin straightened up. "That's right. You've known all the kings of Kitring-Tor, not just read about them in dusty old history books."

Lindren smiled. "Is that the first floor?"

"It is." Rodrin tugged the chair closer and sat down. "The tunnels are all through the inside walls of the servants' quarters, on both sides of the throne room." He pulled out the next paper. "This is the second floor." His finger trailed across the yellow page. "Here's Cat's room. There are very few tunnels here and they're all short."

Lindren leaned on the edge of the desk. "This looks like stairs. I can see why there's no tunnel along the outer walls, the windows would interfere. It looks like you follow the tunnel on the first floor to the stairs you want and those lead you to the individual rooms."

Rodrin flipped back to the first paper, then to the second. "I see what you mean. It's not very efficient."

Lindren straightened. "No, but how many people would have been using them?"

"Hard to say. I doubt Tuomas would have let many people in on the secret. He might even have had the builders executed."

That thought hardly surprised Lindren. He'd disliked Tuomas and spent very little time in Tezerain during those years. Just as well, he'd established Silverwood about the same time Thallan-Mar built the original keep and he'd had plenty to do at home.

Rodrin flipped to the third plan. "My rooms. Such as they existed at the time. Hmmm. Looks like Tuomas didn't trust his wife or children either." He tapped the paper with his finger. "There are no stairs or tunnel by my rooms. Guess he was afraid someone would spy on him."

Lindren pulled out the first plan. "There is here, in your study. That must be how he gained access to the tunnels."

Rodrin's features darkened. "We hold important, and private, discussions in this room. I'd hate to think someone was listening. When this is done, I'm ordering those tunnels bricked up. For the security of the kingdom, and my family."

"A wise idea."

Further examination of the plans showed where entrances to the passages were located. Not every room had one; Cat's did, as did Lindren's, right behind the bookcase. Hard as they looked, however, Lindren and Rodrin couldn't find any sign of how to open them on the plans. They'd have to go to Cat's room and search. Lindren planned it for that afternoon.

ഐ • ൙

Right after lunch, Lindren, his sons, Kelwyn and King Rodrin met Cat and Rhone in her sitting room.

"The plans indicated the bookcase is the door," Lindren said. "So I'm going to assume the mechanism to open it is somewhere in here. If not, we search the bedroom."

"Darsha gets the garderobe," Shain said.

Darsha shot him a glare. Lindren mentally shook his head. It was best to ignore him. "Everyone pick a section of wall and push, prod, pull, whatever you think might work."

It only took a few minutes.

"Here!" Rhone sat cross-legged on his cot in the northwest corner of the room. He pushed on a block of stone. It sank back, leaving a four inch gap.

"Five stones up from the floor, six from the wall," Lindren said. "It might be the same for all of them." He stepped closer. "Let me see, please."

Rhone stood and Lindren took his place. He reached his hand in to the right, finding a small lever. A quick check to the left revealed another. "There's two levers here."

"One to open, one to close, perhaps?" Rodrin suggested.

"That would be my guess. Only one way to find out which is which." Lindren tugged the lever on the left. The stone moved back into place and Lindren snatched his hand out; not fast enough and he lost the tip off the end of his middle finger. He hissed in pain and held it up. Blood dripped. "Wrong one."

"Give me your hand." Arnir whispered the words of power and, in a moment, the injury was gone. He cleaned up the blood with a clean handkerchief from his pocket.

"Thank you, son. I think I'll try the other one."

Rodrin snorted. "Not much choice left."

A pull of the lever on the right and the bookcase slid open a few inches.

"Amazing how quiet it is for something that old," Rodrin said. He glanced from one face to another. "So, who's going in?"

"I'd like to." Cat wore a hopeful smile.

"Not this time," Lindren said.

Her smile dipped into a frown. "Why not?"

Lindren thought it should be obvious. "Because at least one person is after you and I don't want you running into him. Since this took much less time than planned, I'd rather you went to see Wendyl."

"Oh." She plunked herself in one of the chairs by the fireplace.

Kelwyn set a hand on her shoulder. "I'll come."

"I'm staying with my lady," Rhone said and took up a position by the door.

"I think just Darsha, Arnir and I should go. There's not a lot of room in those tunnels."

The king grimaced. "You're probably right. While you're gone, I'll go back to my study and let Tomis bore me with paperwork." He bid them good hunting and left.

Lindren opened the bookcase further. It didn't squeak. He crouched down to examine a hinge. "This has been freshly greased. Whoever he is, he planned it well."

"Well enough that only the Hrulka saved Cat," Kelwyn said, his eyes dark.

Lighting his handfire, Lindren twisted to examine the inside of the tunnel. The dust of ages coated the interior. Cobwebs hung in the corners and dried out husks of insect bodies littered the floor. Two levers sat against the fireplace wall. "I found how to open and close it from the inside." Recent footprints disturbed the thick dust; some smaller ones very recent. "At least two people have been here. By the size of the footprints, one could be a child."

Darsha bent over him, studying the prints. "The one from the Dolphin fountain?"

Lindren stood. "Could be. Let's see where these footprints lead."

They entered the passage and Lindren moved his handfire in front of him. His hair brushed the ceiling. The passage ended quickly at a set of narrow, steep stairs. As they descended, Lindren kept his handfire near his waist, the better to see what lay ahead. *I really hate tunnels.* It was too easy to lose direction. *Cat's window faces west, which means I'm going south.*

When they reached the bottom, the tunnel widened enough to allow a person to slip past the stairs to head north, though they had to duck. Most of the tracks travelled to and from the south. Two sets of the smaller ones lay to the north, one coming, the other going.

Lindren glanced north, then south. "I'm going to say south is the direction we want, but I'd like to know why the child went north."

"I'll go," Arnir volunteered and his white handfire lit the darkness.

Lindren and Darsha followed the tracks south, then east and north to an unused room in the servants' quarters. The tracks in the dust led out the door and into the corridor.

"We've lost them." Lindren let out an exasperated sigh.

"Perhaps we should leave it to Rodrin's soldiers. They're going to have to check every unused room on the first floor and we don't know which ones those are." Darsha was right, though with the extra bodies Rodrin now housed there couldn't be many.

"I suppose it might be a bit of a shock to find Elves poking around your room," Lindren said. "Let's find Arnir."

They travelled back through the passages, almost to the stairs to Cat's room when they found him.

"I think the child was lost. He climbed up and down several sets of stairs before heading back," Arnir said.

"We drew a dead end as well. I'd hoped to find more, but it's not going to happen today." Lindren waved them up the stairs. "I need to talk to Rodrin."

When they arrived at Cat's room, they found more trouble waiting. Cat sat in her chair, her cheeks wet with tears. Kelwyn stood behind her, rubbing her shoulders.

"Did you find anything?" Shain asked, closing the bookcase door.

Lindren shook his head. "Two dead ends. What happened here? I thought you were going to see Wendyl," he said to Cat.

She sniffled. "Jewel had some women come and measure me for a new set of clothes a few days ago, to replace the ones that were ruined in the battle. She brought them and...they made me *dresses*!"

Lindren tried hard not to laugh.

Rhone grimaced. "They had a big argument and Jewel stormed out in a huff. I must say, though, I really like the red one."

"It was quite traumatic." Shain pulled something out of Lindren's

114

hair. "You've contracted a bad case of cobwebs."

Lindren ignored him and gave Cat a kiss on the top of her head. "Where are the dresses?"

She pointed to her bedroom. "In there."

Lindren, Darsha and Arnir all entered the bedroom to investigate the despised objects. Two dresses lay on the bed—one a deep, dark crimson velvet with a cream silk lining, the other a rich gold brocade decorated with red roses and bright green leaves. Other items lay near them, folded in small piles.

"They'd look good on her," Darsha noted.

"Yes, they would." Lindren ran his hand down the crimson one. "I doubt anyone would ever get her into them, though. I remember her mother trying, and failing. Cat simply doesn't like dresses."

Arnir sighed. "What a waste of time and material."

"I think I'm going to have to have another talk with Jewel," Lindren said. "After I see Rodrin."

Chapter Ten

That evening, Lindren sat down with Jewel while Kelwyn took Cat for a walk in the Winter Garden, Rhone accompanying them.

"I know why you want to talk to me, my lord," Jewel said before Lindren could even open his mouth. "And I just want to say that Lady Cat needed some new clothes. These dresses will be perfect for the prince's wedding. The head seamstress gave me permission and I'm sure Queen Lisha would agree..."

Lindren held up his hand. "You saw an opportunity to force your customs onto my daughter."

Jewel snapped her mouth shut.

"I told you two months ago that Cat doesn't like to wear dresses. What made you think she'd change her mind in that short a time?"

The little maid played with her apron, scrunching it, then letting go. "I thought if Lady Cat would just try one on, she'd see how beautiful she'd look in them. I know she was attracted to Lord Aris. If she just wore a dress a few times someone else might be interested. Personally, I think that mercenary is scaring them away."

"Thank you for your concern, but Cat doesn't appear to have trouble attracting men."

"I just..." She hung her head.

"I hear it was quite the argument." Fortunately, according to Shain, there was no repeat of the inexcusable language Cat had used on Dayn during their first visit to Tezerain.

Jewel nodded. "I didn't realize my lady could be so stubborn. She said she'd rather kiss a vaurok than wear those dresses. They're so beautiful, my lord. I don't understand why she doesn't like them."

Lindren had hoped Cat could learn to use her position to make her wishes known in a manner befitting a lady of the court. Since their return, she'd handled Dayn well. Perhaps this latest incident was too much for her and drastic measures were called for. "I suspect it was more a matter of you trying to force them on her than the dresses themselves. If you and Cat can't get along, then maybe we should find someone else."

The blood drained from Jewel's face. Tears formed in her eyes. "My lord, please let me have another chance. I won't force the dresses on her, or anything else, I promise. And I'll even have the seamstresses make her a shirt and trousers. Please!"

If Lindren told Rodrin and Lisha, it would probably cost the girl her job. He didn't have the heart. "All right. One more chance."

"Thank you, my lord. I'll be good. I swear!"

Lindren headed for the door. "See that you are."

"My lord? What should I do with the dresses?"

Good question. As Arnir said, it was a terrible waste of time and expensive material. "Hang them in the closet and put the other things in a drawer. You never know, she may change her mind." *And all nine hells might turn to ice.* "Just don't push it."

"I won't, my lord." Jewel stood and gave him a curtsy. "And thank you."

"You're welcome."

"My lord…"

Lindren paused with his hand on the door knob. "Yes?"

"Could…may I speak to you about…something else?" The colour had returned to Jewel's face. Instead of fright, she appeared worried.

Lindren removed his hand from the door and directed her back to the chairs. "Of course."

When they were settled, Jewel mauled her apron again. She stared at the fireplace. "I…I might have some information, concerning the kidnapping of Lady Cat."

Lindren sat up straight. "What is it?"

"I think I know…who might have taken her. I don't have any proof, just a suspicion, but…it's strong."

Lindren leaned closer, took her chin in his hand and turned her face towards him. "It's all right, you can tell me."

"I'm afraid," she whispered. Tears shone in her eyes.

He let her go. "You don't have to be afraid of me."

"I know, my lord. That's why I wanted to talk to you, but if

117

anyone else finds out, I'll probably get tossed out on my ear." Two tears fell, one on each cheek. "I need this job. It's all I have."

"Tell me and we'll figure something out."

She nodded. "I was seeing a boy named Talon. He…he's a thief, and a good one, especially at pickpocket. Two years ago, he stopped coming to the castle. I couldn't find him, though I looked. He just disappeared. Then, the first day you were here, he came to my room. Said he'd been away, had to leave and had just come back. With him a thief, it made sense. He asked about my lady and I…I didn't think anything about it."

Jewel's clenching hands worried her apron. "I told him where her room was. Then he came back the next night too, around the time Lady Cat disappeared, and the following night. I asked him if he was involved. He insisted he wasn't. Talon sounded so innocent, but then he asked about Lady Cat and when I said she was leaving he got upset. He didn't relax until I told him she was coming back. I just know he had something to do with it." Jewel snuffled back her tears.

The girl still hid something. "Why do you think you'll be let go? Is it because you two were lovers? That he'd talk?"

Jewel nodded, her cheeks reddening. "He'll tell everyone where I came from and that…we…" She buried her face in her hands and sobbed.

Lindren wasn't quite sure what to do. If it was Cat, he'd take her in his arms and let her cry it out. Perhaps that's just what Jewel needed, a shoulder to cry on. He drew her into a gentle, awkward hug and held her while she wept.

After a few minutes, she gained control and pulled back. "I…I'm sorry, my lord. I didn't mean to cry and now I've got your tunic damp." She wiped her eyes.

"It'll dry. Why don't you tell me why you're so worried about where you come from?"

Fear flashed through her eyes.

"I won't tell anyone," he said. "It has nothing to do with the kidnapping."

She turned her head, staring once more at the fire. Her shoulders slumped. "I was born in the Pit. I never knew my father."

"Ah. And the castle doesn't hire people from there."

She shook her head.

"You don't sound like you're from the Pit. How did you manage it?"

A little smile made a brief appearance. "A lot of luck, and old Lady Deana Tanrin."

"I'd like to hear the story."

Jewel settled back into the chair, a little more relaxed. "My mother died when I was ten. Since I had no one to protect me, I was thrown out of the hut we lived in."

"I'm surprised you weren't picked up by a procurer."

"Not for lack of them trying, but Mother had warned me about them. I knew all the hiding places and never stayed in one spot long. Then one night, just before it snowed, I was walking the back alleys of upper Dolphin Street searching for scraps of food, when I heard a scream." Jewel made an attempt to smooth the wrinkles out of her apron.

"It was Lady Deana. She lived not far away and had been out visiting a sick friend. A man attacked her and by the time I arrived, he'd taken her necklace and was trying to get a ring off her finger. I didn't think about what I was doing. I just grabbed a nearby piece of wood from an old crate and bashed him over the head."

Another little smile turned up the corner of her mouth. "To tell it short, Lady Deana took me in. She gave me clothes, food, taught me to talk and act properly." Jewel sighed, a lost look on her face. "Four years I lived with her and her maid. I learned to sew and clean, and other things. I helped out and did the shopping for her when she got sick, which she did often. Then, one day she called me to her bedside and said her time had come and that she'd arranged for me to take a position here. Not long after, she died."

"Lady Deana sounds like a wonderful person."

"She was a rare one, that's for sure." Jewel turned her pale blue eyes back to him. "Lady Deana truly was one of Ar's gentle spirits come to earth. So…" Jewel let go a long breath. "That's why I'm afraid."

Lindren nodded. "Talon. Do you know where he lives?"

Jewel shook her head. "I met him just before I left Lady Deana's

119

house. At first I went to the Dolphin fountain to see him, then he came to the castle."

"Why did you decide to tell me? You could have said nothing and you wouldn't have had to risk losing your job."

She stared at the floor. "I just couldn't let anything happen to Lady Cat. I wanted to wait, to see if he came to me again. I'd planned on trying to get him to tell me how he got into the castle. Then I could tell someone. If he told anyone about me, I was hoping they'd think I was brave and loyal and let me keep my job. When the tunnels were discovered, I figured he wouldn't be coming back that way."

"You are brave and loyal, and at this point I see no need to tell anyone how I got this information. You've done the right thing."

Relief washed over her face."Thank you, my lord."

After obtaining a description of Talon from Jewel, Lindren headed straight to Rodrin. The king wasn't happy about his refusal to tell him how he came by his information. Lindren didn't really care. Rodrin sent word out to be on the watch for Talon, a five and a half foot tall man, twenty-one years of age, with sandy brown hair and brown eyes.

₨ • ‘’

Two days later, a guard investigating a room on the first floor of the south wing found several sets of footprints leading to and from a garderobe with a smashed seat. The soldier reported the damage as recent and went so far as to lower himself down to the old sewer tunnels underneath the castle. It took him over two hours to discover the entrance used by the kidnapper.

"Jenrie says he found a mark etched into the stone on the outside, a circle with a barbed slash through it. That's the sign of Yait and the Pit Lords, another pain in my ass," Rodrin told Lindren over a glass of wine in his study. "It explains why items have gone missing over the past several years. Their leader's a smart man. Only a few things were taken every now and then, not enough to bother with an all out search."

"I assume this means Talon works for Yait?" It might be harder rooting him out if that was the case. Gangs tended to protect their own.

120

Rodrin nodded. "It's a safe assumption. Anyone not of the Pit Lords using something of theirs would be castrated, his tongue cut out, hands cut off, then tossed in the street so he couldn't reveal their secret…or get any pleasure out of life."

It was a death sentence. Murder without actually committing murder. "Harsh."

"I suppose you have to be to live like that," Rodrin said.

Lindren swirled the wine in his glass. "You said you planned on taking care of the secret passages."

"I do." Rodrin set his empty glass on the table and settled back into the chair. "I'm ordering the entrance sealed and the tunnel to each room with an entrance will be bricked up so no one in here gets any ideas. In the meantime, I've doubled the guard all over the castle. I don't want any repeat kidnappings."

It should put an end to Cat's noises. Now all they had to do was capture the suspect. One problem almost solved. Another still sat heavy on Lindren's mind. "I don't suppose Raimon Teale is in town, is he?"

Rodrin snorted. "No. As a matter of fact, I've only seen him for a few days while you were gone. Complained about some trouble with a couple of his barons that required his attention. When I asked him who and what, he just said it was nothing and he could take care of it. I expect to see him at Gailen's wedding."

"I'd hoped to speak to him about what happened in Broken Man Pass. I suppose it will have to wait."

"I did hear from the northern barons," Rodrin said. "Except for Soran Rais, not a one of them will make the wedding. Another storm hit, a bad one, and there are too many repairs to oversee for them to come."

"Unfortunate. They'll miss a good party." Lindren stared into the fire, wondering how long it would take to catch the man who may have kidnapped Cat and what really happened in Broken Man Pass.

⃝ • ⃞

Talon crouched in the winter bare bushes near the Dorrin River, praying the guards wouldn't see him. He'd planned to check on the girl one last time before taking her, to see if the big lout was still around.

Three guards stood at the entrance to the sewers, lounging in the torchlight and talking about various aspects of their boring lives. From their talk, they knew about the entrance and that's why they were there, to ensure no one used it before it the king sealed it up permanently. Talon had almost walked straight into them.

He waited until they laughed over some ribald joke, then took a few more steps away, staying in a crouch. When he deemed himself safe, he ran back up the path to Wharf Street. A casual stroll took him to Tanner Row, down Autumn Lane, over to Copper Hill Road and home.

His little room at Yait's, with its single pallet and old clothes chest had never looked so good. He plunked himself down on his bed. *What went wrong? How did they find out?*

A knock interrupted his thoughts. It was Rat, just the person he didn't need to see.

"Talon! Somebody must've talked!" Rat's brown eyes bugged out of his head.

"I know. I went to the old sewers and there were three guards there."

"They found that too?"

Talon frowned. "Too? What do you mean?"

Rat fell to his knees in front of him. "I mean that there's word all over the city that the King's Guard is looking for you. By name and description!"

Talon fell back on his bed, his heart pounding. The one thing he'd prided himself on was his anonymity. No one in the Pit Lords would tell. It could only be one person. "Jewel. It has to be Jewel. But how would they have found the tunnels? She didn't know about them."

Rat lowered his eyes and looked away. Talon sat up.

"You didn't. Please tell me you didn't go there!" He grabbed Rat by his filthy, torn coat. "Tell me you didn't!"

"I just wanted to see for myself! I have an interest in this too." He stuck his jaw out. "It's my money too!"

"And she heard you."

Rat nodded.

Talon threw him backwards and jumped to his feet. "Now it's nobody's money! What's Yait going to say when he finds out the tunnels have been discovered? That was a sure way to some easy loot! I told you to stay away! Do you have any idea what Yait will do to you?"

Rat scrambled up. "Me! Why me? We're in this together!"

"I'm not the one who got the tunnels discovered!" Talon jabbed Rat's chest, forcing him back a step. "That was you!"

Rat stared at the ground, sullen.

Talon paced the short space of his room. "What am I going to do? I'd planned on taking the girl tomorrow night. Everything's ready. I have all the No-Kill I need and then some." He'd planned on four times as much as a person to put one of the devil horses out of commission. "I have everything, except a way to the girl."

"Tozer says to leave it for two or three weeks."

Talon spun on his heel. "Pardon?"

A miserable, dejected expression crossed Rat's face. "One of Tozer's bully boys caught me on Whistler's Lane. He said Tozer doesn't want her taken right now. He said to be ready and someone would contact us on the day."

Talon threw his hands in the air. "Great. No way to get to her and now Tozer's got plans. Get out of here, Rat. Get out before I punch you in the face. I've got serious thinking to do."

Rat left without a word.

ᔕᴏ · ᴄ઼ᴈ

The next evening, Lindren sat with Arnir in front of the fireplace in his suite. Darsha, Shain and Kelwyn had gone into town with two of Mathyn's Elves, ostensibly visiting taverns; in reality they searched for Jonlan.

Arnir slouched in the stuffed chair, his feet stretched out to the warmth of the fire, a glass of wine resting in one hand. "It's been nine days since we removed Dayn's spell and I can finally say I think…think mind you…that I'm back to normal. I guess I should have waited longer after healing you. I didn't realize it had taken so much out of me."

"It was the same with me on the ship. I just hope we don't have to repeat it anytime soon."

All four of his sons shared his silver-grey eyes, brown hair, and oval face, yet each had their own touch of distinctiveness in the curve of their mouths, the shape of their noses. Arnir's difference was Rhianna's smile, the way his eyebrows swept up at the ends—a throw-back to Lindren's mother—and his remarkably gentle nature. Arnir had been trained for war, like all Lindren's sons, but although he wore a sword, he rarely used it.

A smug smile of satisfaction settled on Arnir's face. "We did something special here, didn't we?"

"We did. I don't know of anyone else who's had to remove one black spell on a person, let alone two." Lindren sipped his wine, a light, pleasant white. "I spoke to Jeral earlier. He translated the words on the back of the amulet. It was just as he thought, a mind control spell. When he wrote them down, the paper burst into flames." No Elf could use a spell like that, nor would one wish it. "Jeral also feels the magic wasn't released until Dayn put the amulet on and that might be why it slipped by the wards without detection."

Arnir raised an eyebrow. "That's powerful magic."

"It is. Which means this Tozer is no back alley hopeful. Jeral places him about the level of Wolfhame Ebon." Lindren hadn't lamented that one's death. Cat's uncle, Berenchaid, had done the deed and suffered incredible injuries as a result.

Now Arnir frowned. "The spell on Dayn was easier to deal with than the one on you, once we got rid of the amulet. If Tozer is on a level with Wolfhame Ebon, why would he use a weak spell of finding?"

Lindren shrugged. "Overconfidence perhaps? He had no idea we were coming to Tezerain. Possibly he felt it sufficient and his victim wouldn't travel far like I do."

"He's going to be tough to bring down."

"That he is. If he has more people in the castle, who knows what we could be facing?"

"At least Josef is gone. Fortunate that he wasn't another sorcerer." Arnir drained his glass and set it on the table. The man had only used a spell made for him by Tozer.

"Just a nasty man with too much ambition." The former kitchen servant had the trial Rodrin was required to give him by law. So many people came forward with proof of injustice at Josef's hands that the Elves weren't needed to testify, to Lindren's relief. The man choked out the last of his life at the end of a rope two days earlier.

One down, how many more to go?

Chapter Eleven

Rhone leaned against the hospital door and stifled a yawn, while Cat sat in the herb room with Wendyl discussing head lice. Not his favourite topic. Eight days had passed since the discovery of the passage into the sewer. Eight days of boredom and sore feet from standing all day. The nights, however, were sheer bliss. A smile crinkled the cloth mask over the lower half of his face. Rhone had sensed Cat would be exceptional in bed and he'd been right. She didn't just match his energy, she exceeded it. Every new thing he wanted to try, she did as well. *Never has a woman…*

"Fox."

Rhone almost hit the roof. Cat glanced in his direction, then smiled, though not at him. Kelwyn stood behind Rhone. *Have to stop daydreaming. Some bodyguard I am.*

"Sorry to startle you," the Elf said. "Come out into the hall. I have news."

"My lady," Rhone said to Cat. "I'll just be in the hall speaking with Lord Kelwyn if you need me."

Now she directed her dazzling smile at him. "I'm not going anywhere."

Out in the hall, Kelwyn leaned his head close. "Gattin and Trivan think they spotted Jonlan last night. They said the man they saw had a Y-shaped scar above his right eye."

"Where?" Rhone whispered. His heart skipped a beat. Did he dare hope? No one had seen him at the warehouse, so the Elves had kept watch on the inns and shops.

"At a tavern on White Smith Road, called the Sword and Crown."

Sword and Crown. The name sounded familiar. Rhone searched his memory. Then he had it. "Jonlan and I went there a few times six years ago. He fancied one of the serving girls." They stopped visiting after they'd caused a bar fight over the same girl.

"They're passing the news on to the rest of Mathyn's crew and our

Elves. They'll take turns strolling by the place in the evening to see how often he goes there."

Rhone took in a long breath, then let it out, steadying his heartbeat. "Let's hope this is it."

Kelwyn nodded and left. Rhone stepped back into the hospital.

Lindren leaned against the railing of Mathyn's ship, Arnir beside him, enjoying the cold winter breeze ruffling his hair. A cloth sack lay at his feet, the two crystals he'd kept from Jeral resting within. Talifir had done a fine job repairing the damage from the battle; he could now touch the wood and instead of pain a feeling of contentment rose from the living ship. A noise behind announced Mathyn. The captain joined Lindren and Arnir, and they watched the passing forests and farms.

"How are you making out with Charyn's new sail?" Lindren asked.

"Amazingly well. We went out a few days ago with some one-person rafts we built. The mages used no magic, just the wind, and travelled a remarkable distance, even allowing for the flow of the river. When they tried their spells, they fairly flew through the water. I'd like to practice with them on a lake before constructing one for the ship." Mathyn snorted. "Who would have thought a triangular sail could work so well?"

At least something good came out of the battle.

"I've picked a spot not far from the base of the foothills," Mathyn said. "We scouted it while we were out practicing with the sail. There's a small copse of trees close to the water, and far from people, that would suit your needs."

"Sounds fine."

In a short time, they arrived. The weather mage on duty directed the wind to bring them close to the rocky shore. Six other air mages sat in a circle on deck, chanting. One by one, Lindren, Arnir, Mathyn and Yira were lifted off the ship by magic, floated across the narrow expanse of water between ship and shore, and set gently down.

127

A few minutes' walk brought them to a clearing in a grove of elm and maple. The snow lay only a couple inches deep.

Lindren set the cloth sack on the ground and pulled out one of the crystals Cat found on Crescent Island. Six inches long and three wide, it resembled a large goose egg. "Let's sit in a circle," he suggested.

"I'll just stay under this tree, out of your way." Mathyn, one of the few Elven captains without Arvanion's power, rode the seas for the sheer enjoyment of it.

Once the three of them were comfortable, Lindren placed the crystal in the center. "Jeral said it took him a while to figure out how to use it." There'd been no point asking the wizard how he made the amplifier work; Human and Elven magic were too different. "I suggest we probe it first."

Arnir and Yira agreed, and the three began the chant to focus their magic. Their hands, hovering over the crystal, glowed white. Lindren's power flowed from the center of his being to the tips of his extremities. Once he secured control, he sent a thought to the crystal. His power touched it, and nothing happened. Lindren poured some of his magic into the heart of the crystal. A warmth flowed back to him, restful, soothing to the soul, like a peaceful melody from the time before Udath Kor and his army of death; not what he'd expected. The wizard had destroyed four trees in two seconds, with very little effort. Lindren got music.

He sat back, keeping hold of his power. "What do you feel?"

"It's like music," Yira said. "A song I remember my mother singing."

"Same here." Arnir sat with his eyes closed. When he opened them, they shone silver-grey. The music had the same on effect on the son as it did the father. It soothed, calmed. "That's not what it's supposed to do."

Lindren chewed the inside of his cheek. *A seed. I need a seed.* "I'm going to try something different." He held his hands out, palm down, over the ground. A quick search around him produced four viable seeds, one elm, two maple and a dandelion. He placed them near the crystal and sat down.

More ancient words sent his power through the crystal to the seeds. He chose the elm, pouring his magic into it. The shell burst. A small, pale green shoot dug its way into the soil, sprouting thin, white, roots—all to lovely background music. The little tree produced two bright green leaves before Lindren quit. The elm grew faster than nature allowed, yet normal for Lindren's magic on its own.

He stopped his spell, holding on to his power. "Jeral destroys trees. We get 'Arvanion's Summer Garden'."

Yira cocked her head. "I heard 'Whispers of the Wind.'"

They turned to Arnir, who let out a short cough. "Rabbits and Frogs."

Mathyn laughed. "A child's song?"

Arnir held his head up, though he bore a pained expression. "It was my favourite."

Lindren had to smile. He remembered his son parading around the house singing at the top of his lungs, Rhianna adding harmony. A wonderful memory, but one that didn't solve the problem at hand. "We all heard different tunes, interesting in itself and of no help whatsoever."

He refused to give up. An hour later, both maple seeds had grown to saplings, the dandelion's flower made a bright yellow sun against the snow and Yira had created a thunder storm, all at rates normal for their power. Arnir tried to use the spark of fire Arvanion had given the Elves to light their handfire and campfires. The best he could do was burn a few dead leaves, still wet from winter snow. The three of them sat, dejected, staring at the crystal.

Mathyn cleared his throat. "Perhaps we should leave it for another day."

With a mere thought, Lindren wrapped the four new plants in a spell to protect them until the sun shone warm again, then rose to his feet and brushed the snow off his trousers. "It isn't looking hopeful, is it." He let his power go, picked up the crystal and returned it to the sack. "I'll take them to Silverwood. Perhaps, with time, we'll figure out a way to use them."

They made their way back to the ship, and back to Tezerain.

Over the next five days, Elves had spotted Jonlan at the Sword and Crown twice, both times at sundown. On the sixth, Rhone asked Darsha and Shain to investigate and come get him if his former friend showed up. Not long after the sun set, the two brothers ran back to the castle and up to Cat's room, where Rhone waited with Kelwyn and Arnir.

"He's there," Darsha said. "Playing darts with three other men."

Rhone tied on his mask and pulled up his hood. "Let's go."

"Lindren's out visiting Duke Blaise Rilandon," Kelwyn said.

"We'll have to go without him." Rhone would have preferred his wisdom, but they couldn't wait.

"Am I coming?" Cat asked, hope all over her pretty face.

"Of course." Rhone strode into her bedroom and retrieved her cloak from the wardrobe. "Besides the fact that I'm not leaving you by yourself, I need you to tell me if he's lying."

Cat's face lit up and they headed out the door, Kelwyn, Darsha, and Arnir with them.

They hurried to the Shipper's Quarter and the Sword and Crown. By the time they arrived, Rhone was out of breath and struggling to keep up. The Elves and Cat waited for him just outside the tavern.

"His table is at the far right corner, in an alcove, by the dart board," Darsha said.

"Perfect," Rhone managed, while trying to catch his breath.

Shain folded his arms and leaned against the inn wall. "What would you like to do?"

Rhone tried to picture the inside of the tavern. His memory let him down and he risked a peek through a dirty window. No features could be made out, though four men still played darts in the back corner. "Arnir, I'd like you and Cat to go in. We'll watch from a place by the door. Get yourselves a drink and sit as close to them as you can. Strike up a conversation."

He drew in a deep breath and let it out with a whoosh. "If everything goes well, Darsha, Shain and Kelwyn will join you. If he tries to leave, find some excuse to keep him there. When his friends have gone,

130

I'll make my appearance."

Arnir nodded and held his arm out to Cat. Rhone joined Shain against the tavern wall, his heart pounding.

℘ • ℭ

As soon as Cat and her brother entered the tavern, all eyes turned to them and conversation ceased.

Arnir dipped his head close to hers. "Don't look at Jonlan. We don't want to alarm him." He pointed to an empty table along the right hand wall, not far from where Jonlan played his game.

They dodged their way through tight packed benches and smelly bodies. The fireplace, taking up most of the back wall, snapped and crackled, sending a light haze up to the broad rafters. A single wooden chandelier, scraped and gouged, lit the room with the help of a few wall sconces. The tables and benches appeared just as old. Dirty straw covered the floor and a hushed murmur filled the room. Like the tavern in Meat Town, in smelled like old food and stale beer.

Arnir directed Cat to a spot against the right wall, then took the seat opposite. She could see Jonlan out of the corner of her eye. He sat near a round board that looked like nothing more than a cross-section of a tree, his gaze fixed firmly on her and Arnir. She'd only caught a glimpse of him at the warehouse. He was just as Rhone said, lean and a little shorter than her.

Cat smiled at her brother and, speaking in Elven, said, "This place is similar to the tavern Rhone and I visited in Meat Town, except there's a lot more people in this one and it's cleaner."

"It looks like it's been around for a while. I imagine these folks' fathers and grandfathers did their drinking here. Speaking of drinking, would you like beer or wine?"

"Wine, please." Although she enjoyed the light ale Rodrin served at breakfast, Cat didn't like the beer she'd had in Meat Town. Who knew what it would be like here?

Arnir turned and waved to a young girl in a plain blue dress and white apron. Her bodice hung low and some of the men's eyes roamed

131

back and forth from her chest to Cat and Arnir.

The girl smiled, a nervous one, and gave them a short curtsy. "Can I help you, m'lord?"

"Two glasses of white wine, please, your finest," Arnir said.

"Certainly, m'lord." With another curtsy, she wove her way back through the crowd.

After a few minutes, Jonlan returned to his game, though he kept glancing in their direction. Cat tried to watch, without turning her head. She'd never seen the game before. Their wine arrived and Arnir paid the girl. Cat took a sip. It tasted fruity, though not as smooth as that served in the castle. The people in the tavern resumed their loud conversations, peppered with glances in their direction.

"I don't think they've seen many Elves," Cat said, continuing in Elven.

"I doubt they have. These people aren't soldiers, used to fighting with us, and we don't usually make a habit of wandering around town every day." After a few minutes, he said, "Our friend seems to have relaxed. Start watching the game, but only the board, not the players and especially not him."

Cat nodded and took another sip of wine. Three crates were laid on the floor, placed in a row perpendicular to the wall with the board. As she watched, a man about the same height as Jonlan, with grey in his light brown hair, stepped close to the last box, his right toe touching. He threw what looked like a short, thin arrow with green fletching. It stuck in the board halfway between the bottom and the pith. Hundreds of tiny holes pocked the surface.

The man groaned. "Had a bad day, it's put my aim off."

The others laughed and Jonlan said, "You're aim's always off. Have another beer."

The men laughed again. One of them took his place. He was a few years younger, and taller, with dark brown hair and blue eyes.

"What's this game called?" Cat asked Arnir, in Torian.

"Darts." He added in Elven, "Maybe you should ask them how it's played."

Cat sipped her wine, for courage, and slid off the bench. The man

132

threw his red fletched dart. It hit close to the center mark.

"Hah!" he said. "Beat that, my buckers."

"Excuse me," she said to the brown haired man. "I don't know this game. How do you play it?"

The man smiled, a pleasant smile in a pleasant face. "M'lady." He gave her a bow, as did the others, though Jonlan's eyes held only suspicion. "I'd be pleased to show you. If I may be so bold as to ask yer name?"

"Cat." She waved Arnir over. "This is my brother, Arnir."

"Pleased to meet you both, Lady Cat, Lord Arnir. My name is Coulan. These are my friends, Petery..." Coulan indicated the older man who'd played first. He gave her a bow.

"Jorge..." He pointed to Jonlan, proving Kelwyn correct in his assumption that he'd changed his name. Jonlan bowed also, his suspicion plain on his bearded face.

"Last is Manred, the boy of the group."

Manred, a full head shorter than Cat, glared at Coulan while he bowed. "M'lady, m'lord. And I'm not a boy. I'm almost twenty now."

Petery and Coulan laughed again and Petery clapped Manred on the back. "Oh, to be twenty again. The changes I'd make."

"If I may be so bold, my lady," Jonlan said, no smile on his face. "May I ask why you and your honoured brother are slumming tonight?"

Cat had no idea what slumming meant. Arnir answered for her. "This is my sister's first real visit to a Human city and she wishes to see all aspects of it."

"I'd be pleased to show you how to play darts, m'lady," Coulan said, with a gleam in his eye. "I've had my turn and now it's Jorge's." He stepped back so Jonlan could take his place. "The game's quite simple. We each take turns throwing the darts three times. Whoever is closest to the centre ring wins. The one who's dart lies farthest from the center has to buy the next round of drinks. Jorge, show the lady."

Jonlan lined up his shot and let the blue fletched dart fly. It landed just above Petery's. "That's how it's done." He returned to the table near the board and sat down, staring into his beer.

"It looks like fun," Cat said, making a point of not looking at him.

"I watched you and Petery take your turns, so it must be Manred's?"

"That's right. C'mon boy, show the lady what yer made of." Coulan grinned.

Manred smiled and ducked his head in a brief bow. He wiped his hands on his trousers, then picked up a yellow fletched dart from the table. He took a few minutes to aim, prompting ridicule from the older men, then let it fly. It missed the board and they all roared, even Jonlan.

"Put a pretty lady near you and you can't find your beer let alone hit the board," Petery chortled.

Manred's face burned and he almost fell back into his seat. They each took their turn twice more. The last two times Manred hit the board and Jonlan bested his first throw to win the game.

Cat clapped her hands. "Well done!"

Jonlan gave her bow. He seemed to have relaxed somewhat.

"If the loser has to buy beer, what does the winner get?" she asked.

Coulan answered. "To keep his money."

"But so do you," Cat pointed out.

Petery indicated they should sit with them and Arnir retrieved their wine. "We do, m'lady, but this is for practice. If Jorge keeps playing the way he is, he'll have the opportunity to play in a special game called a tournament and win money."

Cat smiled at Jonlan. "I hope you win."

He studied her a moment. Still no smile. "Thank you, my lady."

Coulan waved the serving girl over. "Another round for all, on Manred here."

Manred's face turned white. He fished in his pockets.

"I'll cover this one," Arnir said. "As a thank you."

Manred let out a breath of relief. "Thanks, m'lord. I seem to be a bit shy tonight."

"Yer always a bit shy." Petery ruffled the younger man's hair and Coulan laughed.

"If you don't mind my asking, why are you in town?" Jonlan asked, just before draining his mug.

Once again Arnir answered. "We've been invited to Prince

Gailen's wedding. I haven't been to Tezerain in many years. It's interesting to see what's changed."

Cat was impressed with how Arnir maneuvered around the question. The drinks arrived and talk drifted from one thing to another. Then Kelwyn and her brothers wandered over. Jonlan stiffened.

"There you are," Darsha said.

Cat smiled at Jonlan, hoping to put him at ease. "These two are also my brothers, Darsha and Shain, and this is Kelwyn, our cousin and my friend."

Greetings were made and the four Humans stood, offering their seats to the Elves.

"No, we don't mean to put you out," Darsha said. "We were looking for our brother and sister."

Not exactly true, but he couldn't tell what they really intended. Sometimes Cat wished she could lie.

"No trouble," Coulan said. "As much as I've enjoyed the unusual company, if I don't go home to my family I'll never hear the end of it."

Petery chuckled. "Same here. My wife's got a tongue on her like a magpie." He grabbed Manred by the collar. "C'mon, you don't need to be hanging around here drooling. Yer mother will tan yer hide."

"She will not! I'm a man now. I can stay out late."

"Except you have to be at work in the morning and I'm not covering for you if you've got a sore head." Petery pushed Manred in front of him and bowed to Cat and the Elves. "M'lady, m'lords, have a pleasant evening."

"Same to you," Arnir said.

Jonlan picked up his coat from a nearby hook. "I have to go."

"Do you have to? I haven't played this game yet and I was hoping someone could help me." Once again Cat smiled.

Jonlan paused. "I also have a family I must go home to."

"Just for a few minutes?" Cat wished Rhone would come soon.

Jonlan put his coat back, hesitant. "For a few minutes I suppose."

Darsha ordered beer for himself, Shain, Kelwyn and Jonlan, as well as more wine for Cat and Arnir. Cat didn't want it, her head felt light enough, but it kept up appearances. The serving girl placed their drinks

135

on the table—Darsha paid for them—and disappeared.

"May I go first?" Cat asked, picking up a green dart.

"Of course, my lady." Jonlan directed her to the spot in front of the boxes.

"I stand like this?" She positioned herself so she was almost half turned from the board, just as she'd seen the others do.

"Yes. Hold the dart lightly in your hand. If you hold it too firm, it won't go where you want." Jonlan showed her how to hold it. "Aim for the center. When you're ready, let it go."

Cat threw. It landed just under the center mark.

Jonlan blinked. "Well done, my lady. Though I shouldn't be surprised an Elf would have good aim."

Kelwyn grinned. "She's an archer, one of our best."

"That would explain it. Shall I go next?" Jonlan picked up a blue dart. His landed on the top half of the board, not as close as Cat's. He sat down on the bench against the wall while Kelwyn had a turn, then Shain. Both landed close to the center, beating Cat's. She improved on the second round, hitting the pith; so did Kelwyn and Shain. Jonlan bettered his shot, though not by much.

"Remind me not to play with Elves again," he said, retaking his seat after the third shot.

When Kelwyn placed his last shot beside his second, he sat next to Jonlan, trapping him in the corner. Just as Shain played his last dart, Rhone appeared behind Cat. Jonlan almost fell backwards off the bench.

Kelwyn grabbed his arm to steady him, and didn't let go. "It's all right. We just want to talk. No one wants to hurt you." Shain slid in beside him. Now Jonlan would have to go through two Elves if he wanted out.

"Besides," Darsha said, leaning against the wall, appearing quite relaxed and blocking most people's view of Jonlan. "We're in a room full of noisy people and can't hurt you without someone noticing. We truly mean no harm."

Rhone sat down between Cat and Arnir. She slipped her eyes out of focus to check Jonlan's light. Most of it was coloured with fear.

Chapter Twelve

Rhone stared across the table at the man he'd called friend for over five years. Besides the beard, he'd changed little; a few more lines crinkled his brow and the corners of his eyes. No sign of recognition gleamed in Jonlan's eyes; with the mask, the hood pulled close and the gloom of the tavern, Rhone would have been surprised if he recognized his own mother.

"If you mean no harm, then what's he doing here?" Jonlan used his chin to indicate Rhone.

Rhone laid his gloved hands on the table, palms down. "Asking questions. You get to answer them."

Jonlan frowned, his glare hard as ice. His personable features tended to fool people; the man could be a real son of a bitch if warranted. "What questions?"

"Did you have anything to do with Jornel Yarrow's murder?" Rhone leaned a little closer.

Jonlan tried to stand. Kelwyn's grip prevented it. "What's this? That murder's four years old! It's done with!"

"This is very important to us. Please?" Cat's wide golden eyes shimmered in the candlelight.

"Why do Elves care about a murdered Human? I thought you never stuck your immortal noses in our affairs."

Arnir folded his hands on the table. "Answer the questions and we might tell you."

Jonlan narrowed his eyes. "The answer is no. Now let me go."

Rhone glanced at Cat and her slightly crossed eyes. She nodded.

"Another question." Rhone sat back, making sure he kept his head lowered. "Do you know who did?"

"No."

Cat cocked her head and her eyebrows dipped in a frown. Keeping his face away from Jonlan, he leaned close to her. "Is there a

137

problem?"

"I think he is and isn't telling the truth," she whispered. "Purple flashed only briefly, there and gone. I've never seen that before." Though he couldn't possibly have heard the exchange over the noisy patrons, Jonlan cast her a strange look.

Is and isn't? Shouldn't it be one or the other? He sat back. Truth was a funny thing. Rhone was right when he told Cat you don't have to lie to deceive. "What do you know about the murder?"

"I don't have to tell you anything!" Jonlan struggled against Kelwyn's grip.

Shain rose and placed himself behind Jonlan, his hands resting on his shoulders, pushing him back into his seat. "Yes, you do."

"Please tell us," Cat said. "It's important and we really don't want to hurt you."

"I don't think being nice to him is going to help, my lady." Rhone's first temptation was to slip one of his knives out of its sheath and place it against Jonlan's throat. It would attract too much attention, however. People already stared.

Jonlan ceased his struggles and studied Rhone. "There's something familiar about you."

Rhone's heart skipped a beat. He lowered his already deep voice. "Just answer the question."

"And get myself killed?" A flash of fear crossed Jonlan's features.

He does know something! Rhone clenched his fists. "Tell us. Now."

"The sooner you do," Darsha said. "The sooner you can go home."

Arnir held out one hand, palm up. "I understand your fear. You have a family to worry about. If you tell us the truth, we can protect them, and you."

A family? Rhone hadn't thought of Jonlan with a family. He'd always talked of settling down one day. *The bastard actually did it.* "Is that it? You saw something and are too scared to say what?"

Now anger flashed in Jonlan's eyes. If he had a wife and kids, he'd do anything to protect them. Perhaps it was time to take a chance. "I've heard you're a man of your word," Rhone said. "I'll let you in on a secret,

138

if you swear you won't tell anyone."

Jonlan eyed him warily. "What secret?"

"Why we want to know who murdered Jornel Yarrow, Jonlan." Rhone folded his hands and rested them on the table.

The man tried once more to escape Kelwyn's and Shain's grip, with no more success than before.

Shain pushed harder. "Do you swear?"

Cat placed her hand on Rhone's arm. "Are you sure?" Fear now showed in her wide eyes.

"Yes. I think I can trust him."

"Why?" Jonlan demanded. "Why are you doing this? Why do you want to know?"

"Swear first," Kelwyn said.

"I swear I won't tell your dirty little secret to anyone. Satisfied?" Jonlan spat the word.

Rhone pushed back his hood, just enough to reveal his face, and pulled down the mask. Jonlan's mouth dropped open. Kelwyn covered it before he could blurt out Rhone's name. When the former captain pulled his eyes back into his head, he removed Kelwyn's hand.

"Great Ar!" Jonlan reached across the table and grabbed Rhone's hand. "You're real. You bastard. You bloody thrice damned bastard!" His shock turned into a grin and he clutched the hand, pumping it up and down. "That's why you sounded familiar. I thought you were dead!"

Rhone put a finger to his lips, hoping no one overheard. "So does most everyone else, including the king, and I'd like it to stay that way." He took his hand back and replaced his hood and mask, relieved Jonlan was glad to see him. "Now, what do you know of the murder?" *And why didn't you come forward to defend me?*

Jonlan glanced at Cat, and where her hand still rested. He sat back, his grin fading. "I got tired, that night. You took longer than I thought you would and I headed back to the barracks. When I got there it was really late. Two men were carrying Lord Jornel's body into your room. I pulled my sword, but someone behind me hit me on the head. I remember one of them said to toss me in the river. The next thing I remember we were near the docks. I had a bag over my head and my hands tied. There was a fight and someone knocked me out again. I woke up on the 'Sunset Queen' headed for the south Westren Sea. Never thought I'd be glad to see the pressmen. It took me two years to find my way home. By that time you were dead…or I thought you were."

Rhone leaned back and looked at Cat. She smiled. Jonlan told the truth. He couldn't come to his aid because he'd been pressed into service on a privateer. At a nod from him, Shain and Kelwyn released their grip.

Shain resumed his seat next to Kelwyn. "See? That didn't hurt at all, now did it?"

"Why the games? Why didn't you show me who you were at the start?" Though Jonlan's features radiated confusion and curiosity, his dark brown eyes sparkled.

Rhone held his breath a moment before releasing it. "You'll have to forgive me. These past four years…all kinds of scenarios passed through my mind, including one where you framed me. I should have known better, but…"

Jonlan held up his hand. "I'll forgive you if you tell me what happened."

Rhone gave him a brief rundown of his arrest and trial.

His friend glanced at Cat again. "Someone else didn't come forward to clear you."

"No. And that hurt for a long time."

Confusion now rested on Cat's sweet face and Rhone patted her hand. He'd have to put off her inevitable questions.

Anger flashed in Jonlan's eyes once more. "I can't believe it. I thought…" He shook his head. "So why are you still alive? I heard your ship sunk on the way to the mines of Ordran."

"It did. I was washed overboard and clung to the broken mast with two sailors. They both died and I ended up on Crescent Island alone for four years. Better than the mines, but not by much. A few weeks ago, Lady Cat and her family saved me and for some strange reason made my cause their own."

Cat smiled, her eyes shining.

Jonlan let out a soft whistle. "Vania's own luck followed you."

"It did." Rhone folded his arms across his chest, dislodging Cat's hand. "Is there anything else you can tell me about that night? Any little detail might help."

"Not much, but I can tell you the reason I hid. The fellow who said to toss me in the river? His exact words were, 'Throw him in the Dorrin. His Grace wants no loose ends'. I remember because it ran through my sore head for two days."

Rhone and the Elves perked up.

"His Grace? That's not good news for Rodrin," Darsha said.

Shain snorted. "Looks like he has more rats than he thought."

"Rats?" Jonlan looked to Rhone.

"We found secret tunnels in the castle the king knew nothing about. Thieves have been using them for years."

"Well, this rat is a big one, a bloody duke no less." Jonlan swigged his beer, draining half the mug. "The last thing I wanted to do was draw attention to myself. After all, as far as the army was concerned, I'd deserted. So when I found out you were dead, I picked up a new identity and laid low. I'd hoped something else would happen and your innocence would come to light. I'd planned on stepping forward then, but nothing's happened. The dukes have all played the narrow line to the best of my knowledge."

Rhone scratched his chin through the cloth on his face. "Why would a duke want Jornel killed? He didn't have the influence at court his brother does."

"Perhaps he also saw something he shouldn't have," Arnir said.

What the hell else is going on in Tezerain? And who's doing it? Rhone let out an exasterated breath. "We've found a few answers, not the ones we really want." He glanced at Jonlan, once again relieved his friend wasn't involved, at least not on the wrong end. "Would all of you mind if I spoke to him alone?" he said to Cat and the Elves.

"Of course not," Darsha said. "We'll be outside when you're done."

The Elves downed the rest of their drinks. Cat hadn't touched her wine. She put her hand on Rhone's arm again. "You'll be all right?"

He chuckled. "I think I can manage from here. Thank you, my lady."

When they'd left, Jonlan said, "I get the impression she might be more than just a jaw-dropping gorgeous Elf who rescued you."

Rhone smiled, though Jonlan wouldn't see it. *A whole lot more.* "I'm supposed to be her bodyguard. That way I can move around the castle without fear of finding the hangman's noose."

Jonlan's dark eyebrows rose. "Bodyguard? Why would an Elf need a bodyguard?"

"Someone tried to kidnap her. Almost succeeded. We think the idiot wants her for a brothel. He's one of the assholes using the tunnels. King Rodrin's ordered them bricked up, but it's going to take weeks to complete. So we're keeping a close watch." Time to get off that subject. "I hear you have a family?"

An instant smile appeared on Jonlan's bushy face. "I married a wonderful girl named Saysha just over a year ago and we have the most beautiful baby girl in the world, Kiria."

Rhone grinned. "That's a pretty name. I hope for her sake she looks like her mother." They both laughed. "I'm happy for you."

Jonlan lost his smile. "I still can't believe she didn't come forward. All she had to do was say you were with her."

"And ruin her precious reputation?" Rhone's good humour vaporized.

"She didn't have to say what you were doing."

"That late at night, it wouldn't be much of a stretch to the truth." Truth…a virtue Rhone had always tried to hold close to his heart. Now it eluded him, playing a deadly game. "No, she cared more about what others would say than she did about me." He couldn't keep the bitterness from his voice. "That's a road I won't travel again."

"I understand, but I'm sorry you feel that way. Saysha is a remarkable woman." Jonlan took a drink. "Have you run into her?"

Rhone shook his head. "She hasn't yet arrived for the wedding. If I do, I'll ignore her. She won't recognize me in this get up, anyway."

"Don't be too sure. She's a smart woman." He drained the last of his beer. "Lord Arnir mentioned something about protecting my family if this gets out?"

Rhone nodded. "If we find out more, and you want to stand up

142

for me, we'll move you and your family to the Elven ship at the docks. They're here while we're here. If we can't get to you, and you're at all concerned, go there. I'll have Darsha or Shain alert the captain."

Jonlan stuck his hand out. "Thank you."

Rhone gripped it. "Thank you for the information. I'm not sure how it'll help yet, but it certainly can't hurt. You take care of yourself, and that family."

"I will. And you keep in touch. I'm usually here in the evenings, and now that I know an assassin's not after me, I'll make sure I'm here more often." He shrugged. "Or as often as Saysha lets me get away with." They laughed, just like old times.

Rhone joined the Elves and Cat for the walk back to the castle. He had much to digest.

ℰ   ✦   ℛ

Lindren tapped his fingers on his leg. When he'd arrived back at the castle to find Rhone and his family gone, he guessed the reason. What he hadn't guessed was that a duke was involved in Jornel's murder.

Rodrin sat beside him in the king's study. "Well? Did you ask to see me this late at night just to stare at the fire? At least share some wine with me."

Lindren nodded and Rodrin poured a rich red. Fitting, for the blood that had been spilled…Jornel's blood…and for that yet to be shed. "What reason would a duke have to order the murder of another noble?"

Rodrin's brow creased. "Years ago it could have gained him lands or wealth. We have laws against that now. He'd get nothing but a noose around his neck. Jealousy perhaps? Why do you ask?"

Lindren shifted uncomfortably. "You're not going to like this. Apparently, one of your dukes had Jornel Yarrow killed."

Rodrin slowly set his wine down, all sense of humour gone. "And you know…how?"

"A witness told my sons what he saw. Beyond that, I can say no more. He fears for his life."

"Hmmm. A commoner?"

Lindren nodded.

"His word would never hold up against a duke's without a wagonload of proof." Rodrin picked up his wine and downed it in one gulp. "It sheds doubt on Rhone Arden's conviction. I wish he would have stepped forward four years ago. I wouldn't have lost a good commander."

"It wasn't possible."

Rodrin clenched his fist. "So there's a viper in my kingdom. One placed quite high. Perhaps I should borrow your Fox."

"There's nothing to say this was anything more than a quarrel, but one can't be positive. Increasing your personal guard might not be a bad idea." Lindren didn't like it, not any of it. They sat for a moment, both staring into the fire. "Speaking of dukes, any word from Raimon?"

"As a matter of fact, yes. A messenger arrived this afternoon. He says he's solved the problem with his barons and plans to be at his manor house day after tomorrow."

Finally. Though Lindren didn't expect to discover anything different than what the northern barons told him, he needed to hear it from Raimon Teale.

൞ • ഼

The Duke of Teale arrived as expected and two days later Lindren rode into town to meet him at his manor house with Darsha as company. They guided their Hrulka through the massive wrought iron gates to the doors of the stable and were met at the house by Crinon Teale, Raimon's chamberlain and third cousin.

"Well met, Lord Lindren, Lord Darsha." Crinon gave them each a bow.

"Thank you, Crinon," Lindren said, handing the chamberlain his cloak.

"His Grace is in his study. This way please." Crinon led them through a large room with little more in it than pictures and lanterns on the wall, and a large fireplace on the west side. A right turn at the end of the hall led to another, which took them to Raimon.

The duke sat in a leather padded wooden chair by the fire. "Welcome, Lindren. It's been too long. Crinon, bring more chairs and pour the wine." Warm words, with a cold smile to accompany them.

Crinon bowed. "Yes, Your Grace."

"Did Andros and Aura come with you?" Lindren asked, noting Raimon's lack of use of the traditional honorific granted the Elder of Silverwood. Not that Lindren cared much.

"No. They wanted to stay home for a couple more days. Visiting friends or some such. They arrive tomorrow but will stay at the castle." Raimon's son and daughter both inherited his colouring and their mother's disposition. Just as well, one Raimon was enough.

The chamberlain brought the chairs, plain wooden ones with no padding, and Raimon motioned them to sit. Crinon poured the wine and left.

"I hear Aura is to marry Brade Kerend," Lindren said.

The duke scowled. "Not because I want it."

"Then why did you agree?" Darsha asked, echoing Lindren's thoughts.

"Because they bloody well wore me down. Between Aura crying every time I walked into the room and Aris' brat begging, I had to give in to keep my sanity. I hope she likes barren rocks and cold wind. It's all she'll gain from that marriage."

And that explains that, sort of.

"Now then, Lindren. King Rodrin says you wish to speak with me over the Kerend matter."

"I do." Lindren sipped his wine, an amber from Thallan-Mar. "Nice. It never ceases to amaze me that two countries who are frequently at war can keep a healthy trade going."

Raimon laughed. So like, yet unlike Rodrin. The king had a warm, friendly laugh. Raimon's sounded like icicles falling. They were cousins, King Garven's sister had married Raimon's father. Of an age, they both had broad faces and blue eyes, and Lindren swore they had the same amount of grey in their once black hair. The real difference was Raimon's neatly trimmed, grey-streaked beard. Though the two had been friends in their youth, disagreements over the years had put a rift in the relationship.

"Isn't that what you're always saying? You don't understand us Humans?" the duke said. "Personally, I'm glad you don't. Life would be boring if you could predict everything."

"It would." *On the other hand, sometimes it would be nice to predict what goes on in your head.* One always knew where he stood with Rodrin, not so with Raimon. "So, why don't you tell me what happened in Broken Man Pass?"

Raimon gave him a humourless smile. "I'll tell you the same thing I told the king. There was nothing in Broken Man Pass that shouldn't be there." He sat back and sipped his wine.

"And...that's it?" Lindren discreetly tapped his thigh with one finger. The man hadn't changed over the past seven years. He glanced at Darsha. His oldest son sat straight in the uncomfortable chair, his wine glass resting in one hand, all his concentration on Raimon.

"What else do I need to say? Aris' man sent up an alarm for nothing. I took time out of my busy life to go up there, for nothing." The duke sat forward. "One small band and they were long gone. There's one thing I will tell you, Lindren. Those barons are in over their heads. That's what happens when you put commoners in positions only noblemen can handle."

And that would be why the northern baronies are so successful after only thirty-nine years. "You know why I need them there," Lindren said.

"I never argued that point." Raimon refilled his glass and offered Lindren and Darsha more. They both refused. "I just think second or third sons of dukes should have been sent up there instead of those... Well, you know what I mean." He reclined into the chair.

Yes, I do. All too well.

"Could have missed something?" Darsha asked.

Raimon lost what little smile he had. "Are you suggesting I may have been negligent in my duty?"

"No. Perhaps I should rephrase it," Darsha said, his voice as cold as Teale's. "You couldn't have personally searched every inch of the pass yourself. Could your men have missed something? I've been up there, it's craggy and pocked with caves. It would be easy to..."

146

"My men are well trained," Raimon said, his voice taut with anger. "They missed nothing."

Lindren chewed the inside of his cheek. The whole thing made no sense. Aris insisted both he and his man saw large numbers of tracks. Gethyn, Rais, Miklin and Teale all said there was little to be found. Based on sheer numbers for and against, Lindren should drop it. Something nagged at him, though, and he'd learned long ago to pay attention to his hunches.

"It may be nothing, but I've sent a company up to Kerend anyway to help Aris in case of trouble." Lindren had actually sent two, one to stay with Aris, the other roaming the hills. The second company needed to remain secret. He expected Raimon to oppose the decision. What he didn't expect was the man's reaction.

Raimon almost leapt out of his chair, spilling his wine. "Why in the nine hells would you do that? It's a waste of men who could be used elsewhere." He waved his finger at Lindren. "You coddle those barons far too much. One vaurok and they go running to you. It's pathetic!"

What in the nine hells is the matter with you? "I think that's my decision, don't you?"

Darsha's eyes turned dark. He set his glass on the table beside him. "I agree with the decision. It's better to be safe than sorry."

"Of course you'd agree with him! He's your bloody father!" Raimon tugged on his crimson tunic, remaining perched on the edge of his chair.

Lindren stood, motioning to Darsha. "If you have nothing else to say about Broken Man Pass, we should be going. It's almost dinnertime and Rodrin is expecting us."

"Crinon!" Raimon's bellow hurt Lindren's ears.

The chamberlain opened the door. "Yes, Your Grace?"

"Lindren and Darsha are leaving. See them out. Close the door, I don't want to be disturbed. After I've gone to dinner, send someone in to clean up this spilled wine."

"Yes, Your Grace." Crinon motioned them out the door.

"I'll see you at the wedding, if not before," Raimon said, refilling his glass.

Lindren nodded and walked out, keeping what he wished to say to himself.

80 • ଓ

Raimon waited until Lindren left the house before setting down his wine. He retrieved a round glass ball from a locked desk drawer. Dark green, with milky white clouds, the orb rested comfortably in the palm of his hand. He sat back in his chair. A few words, a name and a great deal of concentration produced a wavering form in front of the fireplace. The image settled into that of a man, seated in a large chair.

"You have news?" the image said.

"Lindren," Raimon hissed. "He's stuck his nose in our affairs a little too far. He sent a company up to Kerend to assist Aris."

The figure tensed. "Are they in the mountains?"

"He didn't say, just that they were there to help Aris in case of trouble."

"It was hard enough hiding the tracks that fool scouting party left behind," Tozer said, a snarl in his voice. "Now we have to avoid Elves." He made a rude noise. "That troll-turd has hindered us for the last time. You're going to have to take him sooner than planned, but be careful. The master doesn't want him killed. Understand?"

"Yes. When?"

"Day after tomorrow. Have him brought to Tanner Row. Third house on the left, second floor, first room on the right. Dump him there, just make sure he won't get free. Your men are to ignore anyone else they see in the house. Got it?"

"I understand." A chore Raimon anticipated with pleasure.

"Good."

"I'll need some of your wonderful little blue balls, just in case there's trouble."

"You'll get them tomorrow."

The image of Tozer vanished. Raimon Teale sat back with his wine, the orb warm in his hand, a smile on his face.

148

Chapter Thirteen

Tozer tapped the arm of his throne. *That damned Elf.* Lindren had forced him to move up his plans. The wedding would have been perfect, almost two hundred people were invited. Nabbing both Lindren and his daughter would have been easy in all the confusion of the celebration. Now he had to inform Delcarion, who waited on Fornoss, that the two had to be taken earlier.

He pulled a dark green orb from a pocket in his leather jerkin. "Bachra rocharag dracaena Delcarion."

An all too familiar cloaked and cowled figure shimmered into ghostly existence. "What do you want?" Delcarion folded his arms across his massive chest. "I'm busy."

"Just a small problem." Tozer examined his fingernails, then pulled a little dagger from his jerkin.

"I have enough problems here getting these idiot goblins through a portal."

"Well you're about to have more. Lindren's sent a company up to Kerend." *He also destroyed my spell on that ass of a prince and broke my amulet. Damn him to all nine hells!* Tozer picked a piece of dirt out from under his thumb nail. "We can't have him getting any more brilliant ideas, so I'm having Teale take him day after tomorrow, three days early."

"Why wait that long? Take him now."

Tozer shook his head. "I wanted to wait for Prince Gailen's wedding. Second best is the formal greeting ceremony. Hopefully we can hide what we're doing in the confusion. I need to coordinate Lindren's capture with his daughter's, otherwise we'll never get her. Which is another problem. The king found out about the tunnels in the castle. He's sealing them up. Grabbing her is going to be difficult."

Delcarion was silent a moment. "Perhaps not. You said there are over thirty Elves in the city?"

"I did. Except there's more now. That Elven ship hasn't left."

Delcarion dismissed the issue with a wave of his hand. "I'm not concerned with them. The Elves at the castle are from Silverwood. Chances are they're riding Hrulka."

"Those demon horses?" Tozer flicked more dirt from another nail. "Those things are the reason she wasn't taken the first time. There's now a plan in place for them." That runny nosed brat bought enough No-Kill from his dealers to put them down for an entire day.

"Good. There's a link between the Tiranen and their horses. If they're threatened, she'll know. She'll come running. Just be ready, I doubt she'll be alone." Delcarion's image shimmered against the stone wall. "Send them through as soon as you have them."

"Of course. What the hell else would I do with them?" *Idiot.* Tozer scratched the scar running from the corner of his mouth to his collar bone. The damnable thing always itched when his anger rose.

"No mistakes this time."

"Mardragh!" Tozer snarled, and the image vanished. *As if he's perfect.* He threw the knife at the wall. "Willet!" *Time to put things in motion.*

The thin old man opened the door to Tozer's dim underground chamber. "Yes, my lord?"

"Get Hamm and Basher. I have a job for them."

      ◆      

Talon lay on his pallet, his head resting on his arms. *What am I going to do?* He'd been stuck in Yait's hideout for almost three weeks. When the leader of the Pit Lords found out about the tunnels, he'd thrown a tantrum of gargantuan proportions. Talon still carried the bruises from that rampage. So did Rat. Nonetheless, he felt lucky; he lived and had a home where he could hide.

He sat up and scrubbed his hair. If only Rat hadn't gone to see the girl, they'd have a chance to get her. Talon racked his brain the entire time he'd been in hiding and still hadn't come up with a workable plan. All that money, floating away. He raised one leg and rested his chin on it.

A rapid series of knocks dragged him from his thoughts. "What is it?"

Rat opened the door and shut it as if a demon chased him. His normally dirty, worn clothes appeared even more disheveled.

Talon raised his head. "What happened to you?"

The little procurer threw himself on the pallet beside Talon. "Tozer's bully boys. They said we have to take the girl day after tomorrow and if we don't do it right we might as well slit our own throats 'cause it'd be a hellava lot faster than if Tozer gets us. Those guys scare me."

Talon groaned. "Day after tomorrow? I still haven't figured out how!" He fell back on the bed again. "We're dead."

"Maybe not."

He sat up. "Why?"

"They also said the girl can sort of talk to the horses and they can talk to her. If you do somethin' to them, she'll come runnin'."

"Really?" Maybe there was hope after all. Talon thought for a moment. "The No-Kill. If the horses are sick, that might get her attention."

"Yeah! That's what I thought too."

Right. You don't have a brain to think with. "I'll need your help and all the No-Kill we've got. We'll do it in the evening when the horses get their mash." *I knew hanging around the stables would prove useful.* "There's always two men to do the job in each stable. We get them with a dart first then load up the mash with the No-Kill. I'll take the stable in the courtyard, you take the one behind the castle. If you see her, dart her as fast as you can and anyone else who comes with her."

"Got it." Rat's excitement shone in his brown eyes. "I'll go tell Yait the good news. He can let the king's guards know where Tozer is hiding when the time comes."

That was the only advantage to Rat dealing with Tozer. He now knew where the turd hid. Talon smiled as an image of gold flowing back into his pockets flitted through his head.

Rhone drummed his fingers on his arm as he leaned against the door frame to the hospital. Cat helped Wendyl tend to a young boy who'd spilled scalding water over his hand. He sat on his mother's lap, his cries rattling the windows; another reason not to marry, kids were noisy, smelly things.

He sighed. Three days remained until the wedding. Three days to find out who killed Jornel Yarrow. The Elves couldn't remain in Tezerain forever and with Cat gone, his reason for staying in the castle would disappear. *I can't do it. I need more time.* Time he didn't have. He'd have to leave Kitring-Tor, find a new life elsewhere, never to see his family again.

"Get out of the way, you're blocking the door!"

Rhone jumped at the woman's voice. *Daydreaming again.* He turned and stared down into the green eyes of Calli Yarrow. He almost blurted out her name. She looked the same. Nothing had changed. Her honey-blonde hair fell in shimmering waves to her waist, the sides tied up with a green velvet ribbon. A matching dress hugged her slender waist, drawing the eye to her full bosom. He also noticed she wore no ring on the middle finger of her left hand. *Still unmarried.* Despite the annoyed frown, Calli was just as pretty, her lips just as full.

"I said, get out of my way! What do you think you are, a door?" She glared up at him.

And just as feisty. Rhone stepped aside.

Calli flounced over to Wendyl. "I have a headache that just won't go away." She ignored Cat and the crying boy. Rhone was surprised she hadn't sent a servant for the cure.

"I'll be with you in a moment, my lady," Wendyl said.

"Now. I swear I'll vomit if you don't give me something. Can't you shut that brat up?"

That was new. Calli usually treated other nobility with the respect they were due. Commoners were another matter. Wendyl wasn't just the king's healer, he was cousin to one duke and nephew of another. He deserved better.

Wendyl kept his features bland. "Lady Cat, would you continue to apply the honey?"

"Certainly." She gave Calli a disgusted glance and took the jar from the healer.

"This way, Lady Calli." Wendyl directed her to the herb room.

She passed near Rhone, cast him a strange look, then stood in the doorway, her back to him. No, she hadn't changed much. He had.

Four years ago his passion for her burned hot and fiery. He still held an image of her in his mind, from the night of Jornel's murder, the night they'd first made love, two weeks before they were to be married. She'd stood naked in the moonlight, shy, nervous, trying to cover herself with her hands, yet, her eyes said she wanted him, loud and clear. He found her innocence sensual and it heightened his passion further. Looking at her again, despite knowing what lay underneath, he felt nothing.

Rhone glanced at Cat; innocence of a different kind and far more sensual. Making love to Calli had been awkward, done in the dim light of one little candle. She'd been afraid and entirely inexperienced. He'd intended to change that once they were married. Because of her, it didn't happen. Cat, on the hand, was a girl made for love.

"I've crushed some willow bark, my lady," Wendyl said, handing her a packet. "Have someone make it into tea and drink it all."

Calli spun on her heel without a thank you. Rhone wondered where her rudeness came from. She strode by him. He made a point of not looking at her. Just as she left the room, she snagged his arm and pulled him into the hall. Rhone's heart pounded.

She couldn't have guessed!

Calli glanced around. No one was in sight. She pushed him against the wall and peered into his hood. "You and your sea-green eyes can't hide from me, Rhone Arden."

"Shhh! Do you want to get me killed?" Now his heart leapt from his chest. *Where to run? The ship. Lindren said to run to the ship.*

A coy smile curved Calli's lips. "Don't worry, I'm not stupid. I won't tell anyone."

His heart settled, a little. "How did you know it was me?"

"I saw you last night, with *her*, just after I arrived. I know your

153

walk, Rhone, the cat-like way you move. That's one of the things I love about you." She trailed her finger down his chest. "Among other things."

"Stop saying my name. If you have to say something, call me Fox."

"Fox. Right." Calli pressed herself against him. He pushed her back. "I don't really have a headache. I asked where the Elf was. I knew you'd be with her. Why?"

"Why what?"

Her smile disappeared. "Why are you with *her*?"

"I'm her bodyguard. It lets me move around the castle." Rhone pushed her farther away. "Someone's going to see us."

The smile returned. "Meet me in the Winter Garden. Tonight. Alone. Everyone will be in the the throne room formally greeting Gailen and Selesa. You can tell me how you survived."

"Calli…"

"Meet me…Fox…or I'll tell my uncle you're here." The smile turned sly.

You bitch. "Tonight, then."

She sashayed down the hall, her hips swinging like a pendulum. He'd thought that walk sexy once upon a time. Now it left him cold. Rhone leaned against the wall for support. *What the hell do I do?*

℘ · ℨ

Lindren shook Gailen's hand and kissed Selesa's. "I truly hope you two will find the happiness you deserve," he said.

The pair stood in front of Rodrin's throne, greeting those who'd attend the wedding.

Gailen's smile lit up the room. "I know we will. Thank you, Lord Lindren, although I'd be happier if I didn't have to stand here for hours greeting people I already know."

"I must admit," Selesa said, with a grimace. "My feet hurt already."

Lindren chuckled. "It will be over soon enough, and so will the wedding. Then your life together can truly begin."

"Thank you." Selesa leaned over and kissed his cheek. "We're lucky to have a friend such as you."

Lindren bowed and let the next person in line greet the pair. That formality done, he scanned the room for Cat. All his family had taken their turn before him and now wandered the throne and dining rooms. Rodrin had kept to his word about extra guards. Lindren could swear there were more dark blue uniforms in the throne room than nobles. He finally spotted a familiar silver-gold head near the doors to the dining hall.

Cat hung onto Kelwyn's arm, dressed in her green outfit, the twining leaves in the silky fabric shimmering in the candlelight. Rhone stood behind her, as still as a statue, studying the crowd.

"There you are." Lindren gave her a kiss on the brow.

Her eyes shone. "I've never heard of this custom before," she said. "Greeting all the people who are coming to your wedding three days before it actually takes place."

"You've never heard of most wedding customs," Kelwyn said, a twinkle in his eye.

"Not yet." She smiled. Kelwyn returned it.

Lindren still worried about those two and the love Kelwyn had for Cat, and shouldn't. At least his nephew wasn't interfering with Cat and Rhone's relationship. "As long as you're enjoying yourself."

"I am. I can't wait for the wedding. I've heard Selesa will be wearing a special dress and flowers will be thrown at her feet and Gailen will give her a beautiful ring..."

"I thought you didn't like dresses." Lindren said, with a smile.

"Not on me. Selesa's a very pretty girl. She looks good in them."

"So would you, if you'd just put one on," Kelwyn said. "I still think you should wear the crimson one. You'd knock every man to his knees."

Cat frowned. "Why would I want to do that?"

They laughed, so did Rhone.

"Well, have fun you two. There's people I need to talk to."

She wrinkled her nose. "There's always people you have to talk to."

155

Lindren chuckled and made his way back through the throne room. What he really wanted was some peace and the Winter Garden seemed the perfect place.

"There you are, Lord Lindren." Raimon Teale glided up beside him, white lace showing at the cuffs of his dark green tunic. "It's awfully stuffy in here." His already stern features turned even more serious. "I need to talk to you about something, but I'd like to speak to the king first. Would you meet me outside, by the smithy?" Sweat beaded Raimon's brow.

"Outside? Wouldn't the Winter Garden suffice?"

"No. It's quite important. I don't want to risk anyone overhearing and with all these extra guards around there's no privacy anywhere."

Important? I wonder if it has anything to do with Broken Man Pass? "All right. How long do you need to talk to Rodrin?"

"Just a few minutes, why don't you go ahead?" Raimon disappeared into the crowd.

Four soldiers guarded the hall between the outer and inner doors instead of the usual two. Lindren nodded to them and slipped out the door. Eight guards now stood outside, four by the doors, four at the bottom of the stairs. They all bowed to him, he smiled back, thinking how nice it would be to finally return to Silverwood and be done with all the formality.

The cold, fresh air came as a blessing. Lindren took a deep breath. Though the city maintained its usual winter odour, it was better than the sweaty bodies in the throne room. He stood by the smithy, listening to the night sounds, the whicker of horses in the stable, the cough of a guard on the wall. Then Raimon strode across the courtyard, not from the main doors, but from somewhere near the outside exit to the Winter Garden.

"What's so important?" Lindren asked, when the duke arrived.

Raimon continued walking around to the back. Clouds hid the moon. No one would hear them, and no one would see them.

Lindren tensed. "Why all the secrecy?"

Raimon sighed. "It's about Broken Man Pass. I did see something up there, but I couldn't tell anyone."

Lindren's tension turned to alarm. "Why not?" A scuffle sounded to his right. He turned and felt a sting in his neck. A man stood at the opposite corner of the building.

"What the...?" Lindren plucked a tiny dart out of his skin. His head swam. His legs felt like they wouldn't hold him up. "What have you done...Raimon." The words slurred. He sank to his knees.

Raimon crouched beside him. "Wouldn't you like to know."

Darkness descended. The last thing Lindren heard was, "Take him to the manor. I'll be along shortly."

Chapter Fourteen

Talon cracked open one of the back doors of the stable. Mattu whistled a tune while he and his teenage son, Lucan, prepared the mash they fed the horses twice a week. Both had their backs to him. Sneaking into the courtyard had been easy enough; he'd borrowed a horse and wagon from Yait. Disguised as an old man bringing hay for the royal stables, with Rat as his grandson, he simply drove through the gates that afternoon. Talon intended to go out the same way with the female Elf hidden under burlap bags in the back.

The darts sat in his coat pocket, ready to go, one for each of the stablemen and the Elf, along with a few extras in case of unwanted company. Talon crept through the door, staying to the shadows. A few yards away from Mattu, he placed the blow tube to his lips. Lucan turned and Talon sent the dart on its way.

"Hey!" Lucan pulled the dart out. "What's this?"

Mattu stopped stirring the mash. "What's what?"

A hard puff of breath and the second dart found its target. Talon slipped the blow tube into his pocket and waited for the inevitable.

"Someone stuck me!" Lucan cried, then stumbled, falling to his knees. A moment later, his father followed.

"Help!" Mattu tried to call out again. Nothing came out.

"What's wrong?" came a voice in the shadows. "Hey! Mattu?"

Talon's heart pounded. *There's someone else here!* Before he could retrieve the blow tube, a man stepped out from behind a broad beam, right in front of him. With no time to fish around in his pocket for the darts, Talon grabbed a nearby pitchfork and shoved it into the man's gut. He grunted, his eyes opening wide in shock. In a flash, Talon had his dagger in hand and slashed the stranger's throat.

He stood back, taking deep breaths to calm his suddenly jangling nerves. Talon hadn't intended murder, that wasn't the plan. Fate had other ideas. After hiding the dead man in a pile of straw, he pulled Mattu and Lucan into the shadows, propping them up against the back wall. There was nothing he could do about the blood sprayed across his jacket.

Talon dug into another pocket, brought out two small vials of yellow fluid, No-Kill, and dumped them into the prepared mash. After a good stir, he set about filling the feed bags for the Elves' horses.

ℰ ⋅ ℭ

Rhone leaned against the wall near the Art Gallery, keeping an eye on Calli Yarrow. Cat still clung to Kelwyn, especially now that Soran Rais had found her.

"My lady, I regret that I haven't been able to visit you since your return. Lord Wendyl is quite the drill sergeant when it comes to his patients resting and the times that I've been able to slip away, you were busy," the Baron of Rais said.

Cat flashed him a smile, there and gone, and Rhone knew where the baron sat with her. "I'm glad you're better. I just wish I could have done more."

"You did a remarkable job, considering the circumstances. I have a brutal scar down my chest, but, thankfully, none to add to the collection on my face." Soran had two scars, one on his chin and the other over his left eye; added to a broad, flat face and narrow eyes, it made for a rather ugly man.

Rhone thanked Ar the scar down the right side of his own face did little to mar his appearance, though he doubted that would have made a difference to Cat. He'd been in a pitiable state when she found him—half starved, with shaggy hair and beard—and yet, for some strange reason, she'd wanted him.

Calli motioned to the east doors of the throne room. It was time. He caught Kelwyn's eye. "I have to go to the Winter Garden. I'm hoping to find out something more about my little problem."

Kelwyn frowned. "Do you want us to come?"

"No. This is something I need to do myself."

"I'll stay with Cat, then."

"Thank you."

Rhone dodged through the crowd, enduring glares and rude comments when he accidently touched someone. *Ar and Vania, what a bunch of trumped up snots nobles are. I hate to admit I'm one of them.*

Once through the doors to the outer corridor, he had a clear walk to the Winter Garden.

Calli waited just inside. "What took you so long?"

"Nobles don't make way for mercenaries."

She smiled. He still felt nothing.

"Let's go farther in. I want to make sure we're not disturbed." Calli slipped her arm through his.

Rhone removed it, keeping his voice down. "I can't take any chances. If we're seen walking arm in arm, someone might guess."

Calli pouted, then turned away in a swirl of taffeta and silk. She took the lead, wandering the paths until they arrived at an arbour shrouded in wisteria. A heady scent filled the air. She turned to him, pulled down his mask and kissed him. He didn't dare stop her. He couldn't take the chance of offending her; she might tell her uncle, Jornel's brother, that he was alive.

When she finished, she put her arms around him and rested her head on his chest. "I missed you so much."

Rhone replaced the mask and set his hands on her shoulders. He couldn't bring himself to hug her back. "Then why didn't you come forward and tell the board where I was?" It was difficult keeping the bitterness out of his voice.

"I couldn't. I was a terrible liar when I was young and everyone in the castle knew it. They never would have believed me."

Flimsy excuse. You could have at least tried. Perhaps it was for the best. He'd had four years to think about what had attracted him to Calli. Her looks most definitely, and her flirtatious ways, though it took him two months to finally to get her into bed. Two months, not much time to get to know someone. He'd been so sure. This Calli was not the woman he'd planned to marry. That one wouldn't have lied, she wasn't rude to others of her station. That woman was a myth.

Cat was completely different, and not just in looks. She wouldn't lie, she wasn't rude to others, unless, perhaps, they deserved it. Cat also

160

wouldn't have let someone die for something he never did. Rhone had known Cat just over six weeks, and yet, he knew her better than Calli. Cat was open with her feelings, so honest. Not Calli.

"I suspected King Rodrin would step in somehow," Calli said, her arms still tight around him. "He thinks a lot of you."

"And if he hadn't?"

"If I saw you there, on the gallows, with a rope around your neck, I think would have come forward then."

You think? Rhone's heart turned cold. "Instead, you let them take me away to the mines."

She pulled back and smiled. "If something new was found out, you could come home."

Never mind the long hours of hard labour with bad food and worse supervisors. Thanks Calli. "I have to go."

"But..."

"I'm supposed to be guarding Lady Cat. I really do have to go."

She sighed and hugged him again. "I hope you're getting paid for this."

Rhone frowned. *Why would she care?* "Yes, I am."

"And so you should be." Calli pulled his mask down for another long kiss. "Meet me here again tomorrow night."

"I'll try. I can't promise any more than that. The official signing of the marriage documents is tomorrow night. I might be able to get away, but I don't know what Lady Cat will want to do." Rhone pushed her back; he couldn't push her far enough.

Calli pouted. "Lady Cat. I don't see what's so special about her. To hear the men talk, you'd think they'd never seen an Elf before."

Rhone fought back the urge to smack her. "I'll try to come see you tomorrow night. Let me leave first, you can follow after a few minutes." *Or never.*

Calli pulled him down for another kiss. Rhone adjusted his mask on the way out. Even if by some freak chance he could clear his name, he'd never consider marrying her.

Cat hugged Kelwyn's arm, wondering where Rhone went and when Soran would leave. At least Dayn hadn't found her—yet. Cat hadn't seen him since the Elves removed the spell. When Lindren asked about him one evening at dinner, Gailen said Jeral had him running up and down the stairs on errands several times a day. Dayn ate in his rooms and fell into bed right after. He was apparently in attendance tonight. Luck was with her, so far.

An itch formed in her brain, a faint scratching, like fingernails on skin; not quite the same as when someone watched her. Cat tried to shrug it off. It didn't go away. *It must be someone watching me.* Possibly Dayn, or one of any number of noblemen in attendance. She pushed it aside.

"It's been boring here to say the least," Soran said. "This is the most excitement I've had in two months. And you, my lady, are very exciting. You look spectacular tonight." He gave her a half bow, his gaze firmly on her chest. "I would be honoured if you'd come to the Winter Garden with me."

"I have already been, thank you." That was the last thing Cat wanted. "Have you heard from your wife?"

Soran frowned. "One letter. All's well in Rais."

"We should probably move on, then," Kelwyn said. "Lindren would like her to meet some of the dukes in attendance."

"If you insist." Soran sounded less than pleased. "Perhaps later."

Kelwyn led Cat away. "Thank you," she said in Elven. "I don't like him. He has a wife, he shouldn't be flirting with me."

"Apparently he doesn't care."

"Where did Rhone go?"

Kelwyn steered her around a small knot of people. "To the Winter Garden. He said he had to meet someone there."

"Who would he have to meet?" Rhone was supposed to be in disguise.

"I don't know, he didn't say."

"Let's head over there, then." *Maybe I can help with whoever it is.* "I actually wouldn't mind seeing the garden again. It's very beautiful and smells a lot better than in here."

"Oh, Lord Kelwyn." Arissa Kail grabbed his other arm, her simpering smile aimed at him. "I'm so pleased to see you."

Oh no, not her. Poor Kelwyn. Here we go again.

"I wanted to show you the Tapestry of Ages the last time you were here, but that awful man kidnapped your cousin." The plump girl turned to Cat, keeping a firm grip on Kelwyn. "I'm sorry for all that trouble. I hope it didn't tarnish your visit. Most of us aren't like that."

"I'm sure you're not," Cat said. "I am enjoying myself tonight."

"Oh, good." Arissa gazed up at Kelwyn, a ridiculous look of infatuation on her round face. "Then let's go the Art Gallery."

"I'm sorry, Lady Arissa. Cat's bodyguard is busy at the moment and I have to watch over her."

Arissa's smile faltered. "Who would dare take her in this crowded room?" The smile came back. "The Tapestry is quite fascinating."

"It's something, all right," Cat said. *A big chunk of worn out fabric with lies all over it. 'Ar' and 'Vania'. What a pile of manure.* "I want to go to the Winter Garden. It's not far. I think I can make it on my own." She wanted to see Rhone. If something went wrong with the person he was meeting, he'd need her help to get to the ship. The itch in her head grew worse, more like the buzzing of bees.

"No, Cat, wait for me." Kelwyn tried to brush Arissa off his arm. It would have been easier to remove his own ear.

"It's all right, Kelwyn," she said. "Really. If I run into trouble I'll scream. With all these guards, someone will hear me." It seemed every time she turned around she bumped into one. She slipped into the crowd.

"Cat!"

She ignored Kelwyn. Sometimes it was nice to be alone and she hadn't been since she found Rhone six weeks ago.

Four dukes, five barons and a variety of other nobles tried to speak with her on the way to the door. All had healthy doses of orange in their lights. Cat only wanted Rhone and he was in the Winter Garden.

When she reached the doors, she glanced around. No one followed her. *Perfect.* She slipped out of the throne room and let out a long breath. A short walk brought her to the garden. The guard outside gave her a bow and a smile when he opened the door.

Now where would he be?

Cat wandered the paths, concentrating on sounds. If he was meeting with someone, they'd be talking. After a few moments, she heard his voice and another's, a female.

"I'll try to come to you tomorrow night. Let me leave first, you can follow after a few minutes," Rhone said.

Around the next bend, Cat spotted them. A woman stood on her tiptoes, kissing Rhone. Her heart thumped, then sank to the pit of her stomach. The woman stepped back. *Calli Yarrow. That must be the girl he wanted to marry.* The blood rushed in her ears, her vision blurred. Cat spun, running back to the garden door, then stopped. Rhone couldn't stay with her forever; she knew he'd been betrothed. Why did she think he was hers alone? *Because I've let myself fall in love with him.*

Cat opened the door, ignoring the guard's bow, tears filling her eyes. Down the hall she walked until she arrived at the huge outer doors of the castle. The buzzing in her head grew stronger. So did the pain in her heart. She couldn't go back into the throne room, not with tears in her eyes. *The Hrulka.* The stable. She could find comfort there and a quiet place to cry out her pain.

A guard opened the door for her and she forced herself to walk. Two of the soldiers at the bottom of the stairs fell in behind her. Cat wished they'd go away. *It's my own fault. I shouldn't have let myself love him. I knew better.* She wiped away the tears, more followed.

Nausea overwhelmed her, the buzzing formed into blurry pictures—Hrulka down on their knees in pain. *The Hrulka!* Now Cat ran, dashing the last of her tears from her eyes. The Hrulka, her friends, were in trouble. *What could have happened?* She skidded to a stop at the big double doors, standing wide open. *Mattu. Where's Mattu?* The nausea and pain of the horses threatened to overwhelm her.

"Krir!" Her Hrulka was stabled closest to the door. She rushed to him and felt something prick her thigh.

The guards caught up to her and stood, confused, just inside the doorway. "My lady? What's wrong with your horses?" one of them asked.

She paid no attention to him and threw open the stall door. Krir knelt on his forelegs in the straw, the nose bag still on, his eyes dull. Sweat coated his neck. She pulled off the bag.

"Hey! Something bit me!" a guard cried out.

"Ow!" It was the other soldier.

Auri, in the next stall, kicked, causing the wall in between to shudder. He should have knocked it down with ease. Cat couldn't get clear images from any of them. *What's wrong?* Dizziness and nausea washed over her, her own this time. She grabbed the stall door for support. Her head swam. Another prick, this one to her arm.

"What's this?" Then, "I don't feel so good," came from behind her. The words were followed by a thump, then another. "Help...someone..."

Cat's legs wouldn't hold her up. She dropped to her knees. Her vision blurred. This time, tears had nothing to do with it.

"You're a tough wench, aren't you." A voice. A man. "Nice outfit, by the way."

Cat tried to find the source. She slid into a sitting position. Sweat dampened her face.

"Don't fight it," he said. "You won't win. Be a good girl and go to sleep."

She did try to fight it, whatever it was. Cat lost.

ॐ ⋆ ☙

"I don't understand why you don't want to see the Tapestry," Arissa said, in her annoying, breathy voice.

"I'm worried about Lady Cat." Kelwyn kept his eyes on the double doors leading to the outer hallway. *I should go after her.* A feeling of dread crept into his bones. He peeled Arissa's hand off his arm. "Please excuse me. I'll talk to you later, I have to find Cat."

Kelwyn made his way through the crowd and almost to the doors when Rhone walked through. Alone.

"Where's Cat?" Kelwyn asked. His heart clenched.

"I thought she was with you."

"I was trapped by Arissa Kail and she went to look for you. I told

165

her not to, but she didn't listen."

Rhone headed back out the door. "I must have missed her, she's probably wandering around the garden."

They didn't wait for the guard to open the door.

"You take the east side," Kelwyn said. "I'll take the west.

Kelwyn searched and called her name. No response. He met Rhone back at the door.

"Did you see Lady Cat?" Kelwyn asked the guard.

"The Elf with the silver hair? Yes, she headed back to the throne room."

So did they.

Kelwyn's heart raced. "I watched those doors, she didn't come through them." Where would she go? "The guards at the outer doors. They might know something."

They ran back down to the entrance and outside.

"Yes, she was here, my lord," one of the guards said. "She headed for the stable. Two soldiers went with her."

Thank Arvanion. At least she isn't alone. "Did she run?" Kelwyn asked, wondering if someone had said something to her. Cat usually ran from emotional upset.

"She walked about halfway, my lord, then ran."

He headed for the stables, Rhone trotting beside him. "Why would she come out here?" Rhone asked. "She was enjoying herself."

"I don't know. But I have a bad feeling in my gut." Moaning came from the stable. Kelwyn paused in the doorway. Two guards lay at his feet. Krir's stall door hung open. Cat's horse knelt in the straw, his neck glistening with sweat. "The Hrulka! They're down!"

Rhone checked the soldiers. "They're out cold. I can't find any wounds."

"Cat!" Kelwyn called. "She was here. I can smell her. Cat!" No answer. "That's why she came, the Hrulka needed her." *But why wouldn't she come get me first? Why are they sick?*

Rhone ran farther in. "Kelwyn! There's two more men here!"

Kelwyn crouched beside the older one. "It's Mattu. He's still alive."

166

Rhone checked the other. "His son's alive as well. I'm going to check outside."

Kelwyn nodded and searched the stalls, behind every barrel and trough, until he found a body under the hay. This one was definitely dead and Kelwyn knew Cat had been taken. He stood and cried his anguish to the rafters. "Cat!"

Chapter Fifteen

A thorough search outside the stable proved fruitless. Rhone strode back in, his heart sick. Kelwyn stared down at the unconscious guards, his face set in anger.

"I'm sorry, Kelwyn. I never should have left her."

"And I never should have let her go. There's little sign of a struggle, only the place where that man was killed. I don't understand. Cat would have put up a fight."

Rhone's blood turned cold. He knelt beside the guards. "Unless she was drugged, like these men. There's a nasty substance the thieves like to use called No-Kill. It renders the victim unconscious in a remarkably short time. I'll bet that's what wrong with the Hrulka too." Rhone turned one of the men over, ensuring both soldiers lay on their bellies, heads turned to the sides; he also remembered something about them throwing up when they woke.

"Thieves. Like Talon?"

Rhone nodded. "Gold to copper he's got her." How would he get Cat out? "He'd have to go through the gates. There's only one other door, near the archery range, and it's well guarded."

"The gates it is." Kelwyn beat him there. When Rhone caught up, the Elf said, "According to the guards, one cart came through almost half an hour ago driven by an old man with a kid." He thumped his fist against his thigh. "We'll never find her now."

"We'd better tell Lindren." That thought didn't please Rhone. He was supposed to guard Cat; he'd let her, and Lindren, down.

They ran back to the castle and into the throne room. Darsha stood near the doors talking to Duke Alain Randin, Selesa's father.

Kelwyn pulled his cousin away, his eyes dark as storm clouds. "Cat's missing. We think she's been kidnapped again. Two of Rodrin's soldiers are unconscious, as well as Mattu and his son. One man is dead."

"*What?* How in the nine hells did that happen?" Darsha looked to

168

Rhone for an answer.

It was one he didn't want to give. "It's my fault. I went to see someone in the Winter Garden, about the night Jornel died."

"It's my fault too," Kelwyn said, his voice tight. "Arissa Kail waylaid me and Cat went after Rhone alone. I told her not to, but she didn't listen."

Rhone continued. "For some reason, she went to the stables. One man is dead. The Hrulka, Mattu, Lucan and two guards are drugged, and we think Cat was as well. A single cart left through the gates half an hour ago. She had to have been in it."

Darsha's eyes changed from silver-grey to thunder clouds as the story unfolded. "With the Hrulka down, they can't help us find her."

Rhone's frown deepened. "Will they be able to help when they recover? If they react the same way as Humans to the drug, they should be better by tomorrow. If they've taken her to a brothel…"

"Or they might take her right out of the city. The Hrulka can only communicate with Cat for a distance of a few miles." Darsha grabbed Kelwyn by the sleeve. "We have to get Father."

They found Shain by the drink table and Arnir in the dining hall. A thorough search of the throne and dining rooms, the Winter Garden and Lindren's room proved fruitless. Cat's father was also missing.

"We're going to have to tell Rodrin," Shain said. "We need help."

When they found the king, Darsha explained what happened and that they couldn't find Lindren.

Rodrin could look positively fierce when he wanted. He glared at Rhone. "And what the hells were you doing? Not your job, obviously."

"It's not his fault," Kelwyn said. "He had to go to the garderobe and I was watching Cat."

Rhone raised an eyebrow, surprised Kelwyn would lie for him.

Darsha flashed him a strange look as well. "Fault is not important. We have to find Father and we have to get Cat back."

"You're right," the king said. "I'll send two full units into the city to search for any sign of an old man and a kid with a cart, or a silver haired Elf. They'll knock on every door if they have to. As for Lindren, I don't know where he could have gone, but I'll find out." Rodrin

169

scratched his chin, then said, "I'll send more men out to known criminal hideouts. Maybe we can get someone to talk. Besides, a good cleaning can't hurt." The king strode off to make the arrangements.

A thousand men. I hope it's enough. In a town of over forty thousand people, not all of them honest, it would take a while.

Rhone couldn't just stand by and do nothing. *Jonlan can get word to the dock workers.* He put his hand on Kelwyn's shoulder. "I'm going to the Sword and Crown to see if Jonlan's there. He might be able to help."

"I'll come with you. I have to do something."

Darsha nodded. "We'll keep looking for Father, he has to be around here somewhere."

"Let's take horses," Rhone suggested. Fortunately, whoever took Cat didn't drug the castle's horses. "We can get there faster." *And I can keep up.*

In no time, they rode down Dolphin Street, the horses' hooves clattering on the cobblestones, echoing in the stillness of the night.

Jonlan wasn't at the tavern.

"Where does Jorge live?" Rhone asked the bartender.

"I...I don't know."

Rhone grabbed him by the front of his tunic. "If you can't tell me then find out! Someone here has to know!"

"Please," Kelwyn begged. "The silver haired Elf who was in here last week, she's my cousin and her life is in danger. Jorge might be able to help. Please!"

Sweat formed on the bartender's brow. Another man at the bar said, "Two blocks down. In White Oak Close. Third house on the right, top floor."

They mounted up and galloped the short distance, reining in the horses out front of the house. Though old, it was better kept than most homes in the area. Rhone followed Kelwyn up the outside stairs to the third floor. Jonlan answered at Kelwyn's knock.

Rhone told the tale and Jonlan grabbed his coat.

"Jorge?" A blonde haired woman stepped out of a room, holding a small baby. "What's wrong? Who are those men?"

Jonlan strode to her and kissed her cheek. "It's all right, Saysha, they're friends. The Elf's cousin is missing and I need to get word to the dockers. I'll be back soon." He kissed her again and followed them out the door. At the bottom of the stairs, he said, "Let me borrow one of your horses, I can move faster." He rode off.

Rhone clenched his fists. *Cat! Where are you?*

Kelwyn mounted the remaining horse and held his hand out to Rhone. He took it and settled himself behind Kelwyn.

"I guess there's nothing we can do now but go back to the castle and wait," the Elf said.

Rhone hated to admit he was right.

ℴ   •   ℚ

Raimon Teale threw his cloak at Crinon. "Did Lindren arrive?"

"Yes, Your Grace. He's in the wine cellar, as you asked." The chamberlain bowed.

Raimon strode through the main hall and down the corridor to the kitchen. The staff had left for the night, except for Crinon and Ulic, the captain of his guard. He grabbed an old metal basin from a shelf, lit a torch and tugged open the basement door. Narrow stone steps, worn smooth by time and use, wound down to dirt walled storage rooms. The wine cellar lay near the back. A vaurok stuck it's head out, baring it's pointed yellow teeth in what passed for a grin. Its green-tinged skin glistened like wet grease in the torchlight.

When Raimon approached, the seven-foot tall monster gave him a mock bow. The vaurok's oily black hair, caught up in a metal band on the top of his head, dipped in front of his face. He flicked the hair back when he straightened. "Your prize awaits, Duke Raimon."

Raimon pulled a small vial from the pocket of his tunic. "Give him this. It'll revive him." Few knew of the antidote, not even the thieves who predominantly used No-Kill. He entered the wine cellar, lined on both sides with cubby holes containing vintages of various age and type.

The vaurok took the vial in his meaty fingers and glanced at Lindren lying against the far dirt wall, bound hand and foot. "Sure you want to? He has magic."

171

Raimon suppressed a shiver. He still couldn't get used to the vaurok's gravelly voice speaking Torian. "Don't argue with me, Mordach, just do it. You'll need this."

When he passed the vaurok the basin, Mordach raised one shoulder in a half-hearted shrug, a Human movement that seemed odd on the vaurok. He knelt by the Elf's side and dribbled the clear liquid under the tongue, then moved Lindren onto his side so he didn't choke. After a few minutes, the Elder coughed.

"Move the basin under his mouth," Raimon instructed.

Mordach slid the basin closer. The Elf coughed harder and threw up.

The vaurok's nostril slits closed shut and he breathed through his mouth. "And Elves call us disgusting."

"It's an unenviable side effect of No-Kill."

Once Lindren had emptied his stomach, his dark grey eyes tried to focus on Raimon. "Why?" The word came out as a hoarse whisper. The Elf panted, his brow damp with sweat.

"Because I've finally found a man who understands the way things should be. Someone who knows that some people are born to lead while others are…" Raimon glanced at Mordach, "…mere vaurok food."

He crouched near Lindren, keeping away from the foulness in the basin. "I have power, Lindren. More than you could dream of." Raimon concentrated on the dark words taught to him. "Gradagh lothoreg bachra." A small red flame came to life in the palm of his hand. "I can control fire. Your people can't."

"Tozer?" Lindren coughed again, bringing up bile. He spat the last of it out of his mouth.

"Very good. I imagine you got that information from Dayn. He'll be taken care of soon enough, along with his annoying father."

"How…long?"

"How long? You mean how long have I been planning this?"

Lindren shook his head, as much as he could.

"How long I've been a sorcerer?"

The Elder nodded.

"Over a year since I started training in earnest, though I've been

172

dealing with another sorcerer for almost five. When Tozer moved into town two years ago, matters progressed in proving my worth." Raimon blew out the tiny flame. "But that's not important. I have something else to show you."

He rose to his feet and spoke a few more harsh words. A soft cushion of air surrounded his hands. He turned to a shelf near Lindren and the small box sitting on it. Mordach opened it for him. Nine small blue balls, the size of a man's eye, rested in individual pockets of velvet. Raimon picked one of the blue balls from the box and held it in the palm of his hand. "Now this little gem is a real treasure."

Raimon nodded to Mordach, who retrieved a sack from the corner by the door. The vaurok dumped out its contents…one fat rat. The rodent scuttled away from Mordach, searching for a place to hide. When it stopped in a corner, Raimon threw the ball, hitting the rat in the side. A trail of blue-white light followed it; so did Lindren's eyes.

The rat squealed and thrashed as an eerie blue glow spread from its side to the entire body, dissolving the flesh. The creature's screams increased in both volume and intensity, then ended abruptly when the spell found its heart. In a few minutes, the rat was gone, neither bone nor scrap of flesh remained. The blue light faded. Mordach chuckled, a sound like boulders rolling over stones.

"Wasn't that enjoyable, Lindren?" Raimon spoke the words to remove the cushion of air from his hands and crouched by the Elf once more. He wished he could make them; Tozer guarded that secret well. "Just think, we'll be using those against your Elves when we take Silverwood. Let's see how well your healers deal with that."

Lindren coughed again. This time nothing came up. "I…don't…understand…"

"I have you to thank for my decision. You're always saying you don't like interfering with Humans, yet that's exactly what you do and those baronies are a fine example. Setting up commoners was a stupid idea. It undermines the authority of the nobles and causes the ordinary folk to think they're better than they are."

Lindren shook his head. "Not…my…idea."

"No, it was Rodrin's father who set them up, but he'd been

influenced by you since he was born, as have most of the Kitring-Tor kings. Taught to do what you want, not what's best for us. Tozer helped me see it. He's a smart man. Comes from somewhere far away. A noble of some sort."

"Broken Man...Pass..." The Elf's eyes narrowed.

"Not your problem anymore."

"You...fool." Lindren retched.

Raimon laughed. "Not a fool, Elf. A sorcerer. I'm still learning, but now I'll have the years to spend on it." He grabbed a fistful of brown hair, pulling Lindren's head back. "Plenty of years to enjoy the aftermath of Rodrin Talesar's downfall and the end of your Silverwood." He let Lindren's head fall to the floor and stood, easing the pressure on his knees. Too bad black magic couldn't heal. He'd still age, though at a slower rate.

Lindren tried to look up at Mordach. "Rodrin said...there were vauroks...in Willow Wood, in Randin."

"That would be Mordach and his band. They were testing a new temporary portal spell. Sometimes it works..." Raimon shrugged. "Sometimes it doesn't. We also tried it on a farm up by your lands. Worked quite well there."

The Elf laid his head on the dirt floor. "The missing caravan, people..."

"Vauroks need to eat too."

Lindren closed his eyes. "You were...in the Old Forest."

"Well, well, well. You do get around," Raimon said with a chuckle. "The Old Forest is a great place to play with these little blue balls. I thought it would be safer than around here, even though the vauroks don't like it." He shrugged. "It doesn't matter. All is set."

Raimon pulled out another vial, tiny, smaller than the first, less than half the size of his little finger. This one contained a pale yellow liquid.

"I don't know why Tozer wants you, nor do I care, just so long as my wishes are granted." Raimon picked a small dart out of another pocket and dipped it in the vial. "Time to say good night." Lindren tried to struggle. His bonds, and the lingering effects of the No-Kill, reduced

174

his struggles to that of a new born pup. Raimon stuck the dart into the main vein in the Elf's neck. In mere moments, Lindren closed his eyes and fell limp.

"Father! What are you doing! That's a vaurok!"

Raimon jerked his head up. His son stood in the doorway, his eyes wide in shock. Mordach snarled. Andros recovered quickly and fumbled at his belt for a sword that wasn't there. He grabbed his dagger instead.

"Why aren't you at the castle?" Raimon covered the distance between them in a few strides and twisted the knife out of Andros' hand.

His son's eyes burned with anger. "I saw you with Lindren and followed you. You've been acting so strange and when you insisted we stay at the castle instead of here, I had to know why. And now I do. You're a traitor!"

Raimon plunged the dagger into his son's chest.

Andros' eyes widened and his mouth opened. He looked down at the knife, up at Raimon, then slumped. "Father. Why?" Blood gushed from his mouth.

Raimon eased him to the floor. "Sorry, son. I'm sorry. I wish you'd listened to me, but I can't let you go running to Rodrin." He held Andros close in his arms, rocking him until the life left his eyes, then removed the dagger, dropping it on the dirt floor. *Why couldn't you just listen to me?* Raimon closed his son's eyes, hiding the shock and reproach they held.

Mordach's nostril slits flared. "His blood smells good."

"You don't touch him!" Raimon stood and picked up the body of his only son. "There's a large sack in the corner. Put Lindren in it. I'll send Crinon and Ulic for him."

The vaurok gave him another mocking bow.

Carrying Andros' lifeless body, Raimon trudged up the stairs and down the hall, determined to keep him away from the vaurok.

Crinon met him at the bottom of the stairway leading to the second floor. "Your Grace! What happened! I didn't see Lord Andros come in." The chamberlain frowned. "It's that vaurok! I knew you never should have let him into the house!"

"It wasn't the vaurok. I killed him. He found me with Lindren and Mordach."

Crinon clamped his mouth shut. Raimon hoped he kept it that way. Both Crinon and Ulic had been promised lucrative positions once Raimon gained the throne; promises he intended to keep, as long as they stuck to their part of the bargain.

Raimon ascended the stairs to Andros' room. Crinon followed. He laid his son's body on the bed. "I want this door locked until I give him a decent burial. No vaurok is going to have my son for lunch."

"I...of course...Your Grace."

Andros! Why couldn't you have stayed at the castle? Raimon smoothed down a lock of his son's black hair. Sixteen years old. Far too young to die, though he couldn't fault the boy's bravery. *He'd have made a fine prince.* Brade would be dead soon and a suitable husband found for Aura. *Soon. Soon the castle, and Kitring-Tor, will be mine. Then I'll have another son...like Andros.*

Raimon tugged at his tunic. Andros' blood soaked the front of it. "Crinon. I need a change of clothes. Is the wagon ready?"

"Yes...Your Grace. It's...it's waiting around back by the stable." Crinon hadn't stopped staring at dead Andros.

Raimon pushed him out of the room and into his own. "Once I've left for the castle, take Lindren out to the wagon and drive to Tanner Row, third house on the left. Take him to the second floor, first room on the right."

"Yes, Your Grace. Do you need Ulic to guard him?" Crinon pulled out another tunic and shirt from the large wardrobe, dark brown this time, with a cream shirt and lace showing at both the neck and sleeves. The chamberlain's hands shook.

"No. Lindren's daughter should be there by now and guards set in place." He dug two yellow orbs out of his pocket. "Take these. Open a portal when you arrive. They're spelled to Delcarion's stronghold on Fornoss. When the portal is established, someone will come through and take Lindren and his daughter off your hands. Make sure Ulic wears nothing to tie him to me. I don't need trouble before I'm ready." Raimon tossed his bloodied clothes in the corner. Crinon helped him into the clean ones. "I'll be late tonight. Once the throne room is clear, I have some preparations to make."

"Yes, Your Grace." Crinon's voice trembled.

"Don't fall apart on me now, Crinon. I need you and Ulic both." He put his hand on his cousin's shoulder. "Be strong, and one day soon all of Teale will be yours."

Crinon managed a small smile. "Yes, Your Grace. Thank you."

Raimon turned on his heel to return to the castle. Everything was falling into place.

Chapter Sixteen

Talon locked the last shackle on the Elf girl, then replaced the key on the nail by the door. She lay on her stomach, her hands and feet manacled to the floor. "Let's see you get out of that."

As Talon expected, sneaking the girl out of the castle proved ridiculously easy. The hard part had been convincing the six bullies at the house, two stationed outside, four in, that he was supposed to stay with the Elf. Everything was ready, right down to the wooden bowl he'd need when the girl puked. Now all he had to do was wait until she woke up.

Rat crouched and touched her hair. "I wonder how much Tozer will charge for her?"

"I don't know." Talon sat in a chair by the window, the only piece of furniture in the small room. "As soon as she wakes, and finishes throwing up, I'm going to take her. After that, I don't care. Speaking of Tozer, go get our money , then tell Yait and the guards at the castle where he's hiding. I'll wait here. She won't wake up 'til morning anyway."

"Yeah, I know."

Rat left and Talon rubbed his eyes. Perhaps some sleep was in order. A thumping came from the stairs. *It can't be Rat, not even he's that noisy. Maybe it's those idiot guards Tozer hired.* It sounded like two people carrying something heavy up the stairs. Talon stood, knife in hand, and held his breath. The footsteps came to a halt outside the door. It opened and two men, both with grey in their hair, struggled with something in a large burlap sack. One wore a plain cloak over a dark tunic, the other, a chubby man, had finer clothes.

"Are you supposed to be looking after Lindren's daughter?" the one wearing the expensive clothes asked.

"Yes."

"Well, here's Lindren." He dropped his end of the bag on the floor near the girl.

"You don't look like much of a guard," the other said, letting his end down gently.

"I can handle myself." Talon stood, fingering the dagger at his belt. "No one told me I was to watch him as well."

"You're not." Fancy Clothes turned to the plain dressed man. "Should we take him out of the bag?"

The other man shrugged. "I guess so. It must be hard to breathe in there and if he suffocates we're the ones who'll die for it."

It took them a few moments to do the job. Talon didn't bother offering to help. Fancy Clothes took something out of his pocket. It looked like a yellow glass ball.

"Do you know how to use that?" the plain man asked.

"I've seen it done. You just toss it and a portal opens."

Talon blinked. "A what?"

The plain man's eyes narrowed. "You work for Tozer, right?"

"For this job."

"Which explains why you don't know anything." Fancy Clothes threw the yellow orb against the wall. The thin glass shattered and smoke poured out. It stunk.

Plain Man scratched his head. "Didn't work. Try the other one."

Fancy Clothes pulled another orb out of his pocket and tossed that against the wall, with the same results. "Now what do we do? His Grace isn't going to like this."

"Go back for more. We've got no choice." The plain man turned his attention to Talon. "I guess you're watching over Lindren after all. If anything happens to him before we get back, you're a dead man."

Talon clenched his fist, thinking of a dozen retorts and saying none. When they left, he sheathed his knife and checked his new charge's eyes. *No-Kill. He'll be out for a while.* Then he examined the small shards of remarkably thin glass. Some of them had landed on the Elf the men called Lindren. *A portal?*

After a few minutes, Talon gave up trying to find out what the glass was for and opened the tall dirty windows to clear the air of the awful stink from the smoke. He turned his attention to the girl. When she woke, he'd have a fine time with her and once Rat brought their money Talon could do what he wanted—leave Tezerain.

179

Darsha stood with Shain, Arnir and Rodrin in the throne room. The few people who hadn't retired for the night milled around, talking and staring at the Elves.

"According to the guards at the main doors, Lindren left some time ago," Rodrin said. "Before Cat did."

"Why would he leave?" Shain stared at the doors, as if willing their father to walk through them.

Rodrin shook his head. "I have absolutely no idea."

A young guard approached, performed a parade stop and saluted the king, arm across his chest. "Your Majesty, I may have some information."

Darsha's ears perked up. The guard drew Shain's and Arnir's attention as well.

Rodrin glanced around. No one was close. "Go ahead."

"I don't know if it's important, Your Majesty," the guard said. "I just finished my shift at the east door of the Winter Garden and heard the news. I thought it would be quiet tonight, what with the celebrations. I didn't expect to see anyone, but Duke Raimon went out my door a couple of hours past. I thought it strange because I've never seen him use it."

"Did he come back in?"

"Yes, Your Majesty, about half an hour ago."

"Thank you, go get some rest."

The soldier saluted before turning on his heel and striding away.

Rodrin turned back to Darsha. "I don't know if it means anything either, but it's odd behavior for Raimon. He's proud of his position and makes a performance of his entries and exits."

"And there's a duke involved in Jornel's murder," Arnir said.

"Just so. I'd hate to think it was Raimon, though. He's family." Rodrin tapped his chin. "Vergel's in the dining hall. I'm going to talk to him, find out if Raimon came or went through the main doors. I haven't seen him for a few hours, but, apparently, he's here. If he is, we'll find him."

Darsha nodded and the king left. "It would be a fine thing if

180

Raimon was involved in the murder, he's the king's right hand."

"But what would that have to do with Father?" Shain asked.

Arnir let out a long breath. "Maybe Father discovered something else regarding the murder."

"It's a possibility," Darsha said. "I hate to say it, but we're going to have to wait until Rodrin gets back."

₮ • ‒

All thirty-four Silverwood Elves sat in the dining hall. Kelwyn looked like he wanted to punch someone. Rhone paced. Rodrin's commander-general, Vergel Mandearan, had questioned the guards at the door. They'd seen Raimon Teale come in once, at the beginning of the festivities. The duke was up to something, Rhone felt it in his bones. *I never did like that man.* The king, however, trusted him and respected his opinions, even if he didn't always listen to his ideas.

Darsha had suggested Rodrin go to bed, there was nothing that could be done until someone talked or Raimon was found. Rhone couldn't even think of sleep. Between his clenched jaw and tightening fists, he thought he might burst with anger. He wasn't alone, all of Lindren's family had dark eyes.

"We have to find Lindren," Talifir said. "If I knew he was dead, I think I could handle it, eventually." He spoke in Torian, for which Rhone was grateful. "It's the not knowing."

Darsha shook his head. "This is the work of the Black Lord. He still wants Father and now it looks like he's got him."

Kelwyn's hand clenched into a fist. "We can't just sit here. He's probably got Cat too."

Arnir placed a hand on his arm. "What can we do? Rodrin's soldiers are out searching, the gates to the city have been closed, Mathyn has his Elves searching the ships and watching the docks, guards have been sent to Raimon's home and the dock workers are putting the word out on the streets."

The guards had also returned from Raimon's home; he wasn't there.

The door to the throne room opened and a guard ran in. "My lords! A note!" He waved a piece of paper.

Darsha stood and motioned the man to him. He read it. "Where did it come from?"

"A guard at the outer gate said a kid ran up and threw it at him. He was gone before anyone could grab him."

"What does it say?" Shain asked, all sense of humour long gone.

"The handwriting is pretty bad, but I think it says, 'If you want Tozer, look for him under the old fuller's building on...' I think it's White Birch Lane."

"That's in the northeast corner of the city, not far from the outer gates," the guard said. "And there's an old fuller's building at the end of the street."

"Take this to the guard outside King Rodrin's suite." Darsha pressed the paper back into the man's hand. "We need his help."

The guard ran back through the double doors to the throne room.

"Let's go," Rhone said, his hand on his sword hilt. "The king's men can catch up."

Kelwyn jumped to his feet.

"No," Darsha said. "We'll wait for Rodrin."

Rhone froze. "Why?"

"It's what Father would do."

Kelwyn glared at his cousin, his jaw set tight in anger.

"We don't like killing Humans unless they're sorcerers," Darsha continued. "Tozer may be one, but I doubt any of the rest of his men are. And we have no idea how many of those men he has, or if Father and Cat are actually there. They may be innocent in this."

"They're thieves, procurers, murderers," Rhone said, his hand squeezing his sword hilt. "Not worth my spit. Do you plan to sit here? Wait for Rodrin's men to roust the rats?"

"No, we go with them, but we don't fight unless necessary, or if we know for sure about Father and Cat." Darsha sat down. "Rodrin will have his men up and out in a very short time."

"Well I have no qualms about separating a man's head from his shoulders if he deserves it." *And these men deserve it.*

182

"Then join the king's men," Darsha said. "We'll be right behind."

Kelwyn stood. "I'm going with him."

"No, you're not." Darsha said something in Elven. Kelwyn's hands opened and closed. He spoke back, obviously an argument. Darsha said something else, his tone firm and Kelwyn sat down, his hard gaze on the floor. With Lindren out of the picture, it looked like Darsha was in charge and Rhone wondered if leadership of Elven enclaves passed from father to son. He resumed his pacing, ready to split somebody in two.

It seemed ages before Rodrin's loud voice was heard in the throne room. "I want two squads. Fully armed."

Two hundred men. Rhone ran for the Hall doors and threw them open.

Vergel Mandearan, commander-general of Rodrin's forces, executed a perfect bow. "Immediately, Your Majesty." The uncle of the current Duke Mandearan, Vergel was at least fifty and looked a good ten years younger. Only a hint of grey speckled his brown hair and when he turned his blue eyes on a man they either sparkled like a mountain tarn or bored into him like icicles through powdered snow.

The commander-general spun on his heel and strode to the outer doors. Vergel must have been waiting for the call; he still wore his uniform, the gold braid of his rank bright against the dark blue of his tunic and trousers.

He must be headed for the short barracks. The long barracks, which held four times as many men, lay at the rear of the castle, up against the north wall. The short barracks, in the front courtyard, held more than enough men for his needs.

"What do you think you're doing?" Rodrin said, his features grim. It appeared he hadn't slept either and stood ready for war, right down to the plain hilt of his sword.

Rhone gave him a bow. "I wish to join your men, Your Majesty. Lady Cat is still my charge," he said, lowering his voice.

The king pointed to his sword. "You any good with that thing?"

"Those who find themselves on the pointed end tend to regret it."

Rodrin frowned, his gaze intense. "Your speech is unusual for a mercenary."

"Not all mercenaries are uneducated." Rhone gave him another bow, his heart pounding. If Rodrin caught sight of his eyes, chances were he'd recognize him.

Kelwyn appeared to Rhone's right, Darsha and the other Elves behind him.

"We're going as well," Darsha said.

Rodrin nodded. "Can't say as I blame you. Wish I could come, but Vergel would have my hide for it."

Darsha nodded and led the Elves out of the castle, Rhone hard on his heels. They waited in the courtyard, all eyes on the barracks against the south wall. Vergel stepped out and strode towards the Elves. Darsha and Kelwyn met him half way.

"The men will be ready in a few minutes, Lord Darsha," Vergel said, giving him a bow.

"Thank you, we appreciate it."

"We've been trying to get this piece of goat filth for two years. I just pray Lord Lindren and Lady Cat are there. And that it isn't a ruse."

"As do we."

Men poured from the door, forming up as they fastened cloaks and buckled belts. Within minutes they stood at attention in two groups, ten across and ten deep. Each arm of twenty men had its own lieutenant. Five arms comprised a squad, with a second-captain in charge. Their first-captain, in command of the entire unit—five squads—stopped in front of Vergel and bowed. "Commander-General, the men await your orders."

All three captains Rhone knew well. They'd been his men. Unwanted memories washed over him, from the days when he commanded this unit and its twin, comprising the twenty-first regiment. Rhone wondered where their commander was; probably at his family's home in the city. His hands curled into fists and he maneuvered his way closer to Vergel.

"Thank you, Captain Madoc. No horses." The commander-general's voice echoed in the cold, dark night. "I doubt we'll catch them by surprise, but I'd like to get as close as we can before they bolt. Captain Eladan, when we arrive, split to the right and surround that half of the building, leave me one arm." He pulled a pair of gloves out of his belt.

184

"Aye, sir."

"Captain Leydan, you will take care of the left, also leaving one arm." Vergel tugged on the gloves.

"Aye, sir."

"Captain Madoc, you're my shadow. Let's go."

Vergel broke into a trot, Rhone swung in beside him, the men behind. The Elves brought up the rear. The commander-general never was one to sit back and let others do the work, one thing Rhone had always admired.

"King Rodrin told me about you." Vergel's breath plumed in front of him. "Where do you think you're going?"

"My charge was kidnapped. My fight."

Vergel eyed him up. "You stay out of my way."

"You stay out of mine."

Vergel kept them running at a mile eating pace to a rundown section of the city. Not a soul moved in the pre-dawn light, though it didn't mean no one was there. Two blocks from the east wall, Vergel halted the troops with a hand signal passed from first-captain, to second-captain, to lieutenant. After a few minutes to catch their breath, the commander-general gave the sign to execute orders. Eladan's men moved right, Leydan's left.

The old building sat at the end of White Birch Lane. A wide dirt yard surrounded it, most of it hidden by a blanket of snow. Snow also lay heavy on the part of the roof that hadn't fallen in. Gaps showed in the grey planks framing the structure. Two large doors faced the street. It seemed a good place to hide a few rats. The well trodden path to the door showed they were big rats.

Vergel cracked open one of the doors and peered around it. He waved to the lieutenants in charge of the two arms left with him. Rhone beat them through, his sword and dagger at the ready. Nothing moved, though a lingering scent of torch smoke hung in the air.

"There must be a trap door here somewhere," Vergel said.

Darsha moved up beside him. "Our eyes are better in the dark. Let us look." Kelwyn stood at his elbow. Darsha said something to him in Elven. Kelwyn didn't answer back.

The commander-general nodded and the Elves went to work. Eladan opened a small door in the north wall. Vergel motioned for him to remain where he was. A moment later, Leydan did the same to the south. Then one of the Elves signaled Darsha and flipped up a large wooden trap door in the southeast corner.

"There are footprints all around here," the Elf said.

Arnir stepped forward. "I'll send my handfire down, in case there are any surprises."

"Good idea." Vergel signaled to the two second-captains and the men filed into the large, empty building.

"I found a ladder and a tunnel, " Arnir said. "But I can't see very far."

"There are torches here, sir," Captain Madoc said, motioning to a pile nearby.

"Perfect. Pass them around" Vergel said.

Arnir extinguished his light.

Once the torches were distributed, Arnir and Talifir lit them.

Rhone took one, then grabbed Arnir's arm. "Could you send that light back down there? I'd like to have a look myself."

Arnir nodded and his white handfire dipped down into the tunnel. The distance to the floor wasn't far. Rhone jumped into the hole, bypassing the ladder. He spun, searching in all directions. "No one's here."

"That was a stupid thing to do," Vergel said.

Rhone glanced up at the commander-general's face. "While we're wasting time, they're getting away." There was only one direction to go—west. Rhone took it.

Another trap door lay at the end. When Rhone flipped this one back, three swords stabbed up at him and he leapt backwards. "Found the rats." He crawled to the edge and shoved the torch down as far as he could reach. One man screamed.

Rhone tossed the torch to Vergel. "All yours." He jumped into the hole, sword swinging.

Dawn showed a barely discernable streak in the east before Raimon returned home. Tired, and grieving for his son, he only wanted sleep. Now that Lindren and his daughter were through the portal to Fornoss, he could concentrate on his plans to take over Kitring-Tor.

Keying the temporary portals to Rodrin's throne room had taken longer than planned. Some of the nobles didn't clue in when the party had ended, staying to chat with relatives and friends, and then the Elves refused to leave the dining hall. Raimon had to hide in the Art Gallery until everyone had gone, then tiptoe out to the throne room, praying none of the Elves noticed his spells. He was almost caught twice by guards.

Two of the king's men waited outside his gate. They both bowed. "Your Grace, we're sorry to bother you. King Rodrin requires your presence at the castle immediately."

"I've had a long night. I need to rest and change my clothes. Tell him I'll be there this afternoon." Raimon opened the gate.

"But Your Grace, His Majesty..."

"Get out of here! I said this afternoon!" Raimon shut and locked the gate before striding up the walkway. He slammed the manor house door. "Crinon! Come take my cloak!"

The chamberlain appeared in the far doorway, fully dressed. Raimon had expected him to be in his room, asleep.

"Your Grace! Thank Ar you're home!" Crinon took his cloak.

Raimon frowned. "What's the matter? You got Lindren to the house all right, didn't you?"

"Yes, Your Grace, but the orbs didn't work. Neither of them."

More failures. The sorcerer had given him two, just in case. He'd also mentioned the one who'd designed them and 'incompetent' in the same sentence. "Wonderful. Now we're several hours behind. I'll have to get more." He strode through the main hall. "I'll be in my study. Bring me some coffee."

"Yes, Your Grace."

The temporary portals were proving more trouble than they were worth. Raimon didn't know how to make them, yet, though he could key them to their destination. Unfortunately, you had to be at that location to tie them in. Tozer would have more keyed to Fornoss, he just had to ask.

When Raimon reached his study, he removed the green orb from his desk drawer. In moments Tozer's form took shape.

"What is it?" The sorcerer already appeared less than pleased.

"Lindren and his daughter are at the house, but the two portal orbs you gave me didn't work."

"Just what I need. I've got problems of my own here. I'll have to organize another way to get them."

"As you wish."

The image faded. It was no longer Raimon's problem. He smiled.

ᔕ • ᔐ

Tozer sat in his chair, listening to the battle noises. *Bloody Rodrin! How in the nine hells did he find me? That worm ridden carcass of a king couldn't have picked a worse time.*

He pulled out the green orb from his jerkin and spoke the words to contact Delcarion. The cowled creature's image wavered against the dirty bricks.

"What is it now, Tozer? Can't you do anything on your own?"

"Not with your thrice damned defective crap! Both temporary portals Raimon had didn't work. If you can't make them more reliable, then maybe you should…"

"Shut up, Tozer. I'd like to see you do better. You probably messed up the keying spell. Give your lackey a couple more. You bragged about how many you have."

"I can't. Rodrin found me. He's sent a pile of toy soldiers down here. My boys can't stop them."

Delcarion snarled. "We'll have to bring Lindren and the girl through from here. Do you have any orbs keyed to where they are?"

"Yes. Three." Tozer fingered the yellow orbs in his right pocket, the ones keyed to Fornoss.

"Bring them here."

188

Tozer spoke the word to end the conversation and Delcarion's image vanished. He rose, crouched in front of the throne and slid out the box that lay underneath. He opened the lid. Fifty-four diamonds, the largest the size of his thumbnail, rested inside; his reserve for just such an emergency. Another, smaller, box lay behind it. This one contained the four orbs keyed to the house on Tanner Row as well as several others to various locations. Tozer set the box with the orbs on the seat of the chair and picked one from his pocket. He tossed it against the far wall. It shattered into smoke.

"Delcarion, you demon-futterer!" He threw another. A circular portal shimmered into existence, it's grey surface shifting in a writhing mass of liquid smoke.

Tozer tucked the diamonds under one arm, the orbs under the other and stepped through the portal to Fornoss.

Chapter Seventeen

Jonlan pushed a lock of hair back from his brow. Once he'd told his friends about the Elves, he explained the situation to anyone he found out and about in the early hours of the morning. Dawn had broken and he'd hit all the warehouses, telling his story. No one had seen anything. He now leaned against a brick wall half way up Wharf Street, the reins of the horse dangling in his hands, wondering where he should go next. The situation between Rhone and Lady Cat was obviously more than that of a bodyguard and his charge, at least on the lady's part. *Strange for an Elf to find a Human attractive.* No matter the job, Rhone would do his utmost to see it completed, especially if it involved a girl as beautiful as Lady Cat.

"Hey, mister."

Jonlan looked down into the blue eyes of a boy, no more than eight years old. He wore a new wool coat, clean trousers and leather shoes—odd for this part of town. Perhaps some merchant's son who'd wandered off. "What do you want?"

"What's goin' on? There's soldiers everywhere, knockin' on doors an' stuff."

He didn't sound like a merchant's son. "We're looking for two missing Elves, one a man, the other a woman. It's very important we find them."

"Does she have pretty white hair?"

Jonlan straightened up and placed his hand on the boy's shoulder. "Yes, she does. Have you seen her?"

"Not for a while. She gave me some money a few weeks ago. My mommy bought me new clothes and shoes and we have good food to eat." His huge smile showed crooked teeth. "I have friends. Do you want me to ask if they seen anythin'?"

What could it hurt? "Please. I would appreciate it and so would her family. If you find out anything, go straight to the castle and talk to the guards at the gate."

190

"Okay." He ran off up the street.

Jonlan watched him a moment, then decided he should go to work. He was already late and hoped his boss would understand; he'd return the horse to the castle later.

℘ • ℘

Rhone swung his sword to deflect a blade, then stabbed up with his dagger, catching the bald, filthy man in the neck, glad he'd spent the time practicing with the Elves. He shoved the dying man away with his foot. Captain Madoc dispatched his opponent, then helped one of his men with another.

With the room clear, he paused to take stock of the situation. Four of Rodrin's men, and Rhone, had dispatched the seven criminals here. Two of them were little more than boys, yet they'd fought like demons, forcing the soldiers to kill them.

The corridors split again and again, until Vergel's men spread all through the complex maze. Rooms, small and large, lay off the stone and brick tunnels. The king said Tozer had been in the city only two years; he couldn't have built it in that time. It must have already existed.

"Let's carry on," Madoc said, and led the way out of the room.

Rhone checked a gash on his calf. It wasn't deep, so he followed. He'd been cut in a few places; fortunately, nothing serious. Kelwyn waited outside the door, his face unreadable. He held his unblooded sword in one hand, a torch in the other, obviously annoyed that Darsha hadn't allowed him to fight. They both followed Madoc to a door at the end of the tunnel. The first-captain stood to one side, his bloody sword held before him, and kicked the door open. No one met them. Madoc entered, cautious. Rhone pushed his way through. Three other doors exited the room.

One old man, little more than a scarecrow, sat huddled in a corner in a puddle of what could only be urine. "Please, my lords! I beg you! I'm not a fighter!"

Rhone beat Madoc to him and, with one hand, picked the man up by the front of his tunic. The old man's feet dangled several inches off the

191

floor. "Where's Tozer?"

The man's frightened eyes glanced at one of the doors, straight across from the one they'd entered. Rhone let him drop and the man curled up in his corner, sobbing. One solid kick opened the door. Rhone strode through, Kelwyn right behind.

A strange sight greeted his eyes. Grey smoke swirled against the right wall. Circular, about ten feet in diameter, it resembled nothing more than roiling clouds. Only a large chair, resting on a raised dais, occupied the room. "What in Ar's name is that?"

"A portal," Kelwyn answered. "But I've never seen one that colour. They're usually white and much bigger. And have a rim."

Madoc pushed his way through. "Great Ar!"

With sword in hand, Rhone strode to the portal, intending to follow the demon-futterer. In a swirl of grey clouds, it shrank to a point and disappeared. Rhone's shoulders sagged and his heart thudded with fear for Cat. He hit the wall with his gloved fist. "He got away."

Kelwyn nodded, his eyes black in the torchlight.

Rhone spun on his heel. In a moment he held the old man before him once again. "Did Tozer have an Elf and a silver-haired girl with him?"

"N...no, no. They're somewhere else. But I don't know where! Dear Vania, I swear I don't know where!" The man's jaw trembled as he sobbed out the words.

Rhone tossed him back in the corner. "If he's telling the truth, there's still hope."

Madoc sent men into the other two rooms. One held an incredible amount of gold, jewels and valuable objects, all sitting neatly on shelves or stacked in sacks. The other was a bedroom, nicely furnished with expensive woods and fabrics. A girl, clad only in a flimsy shift, huddled on the wide bed.

Kelwyn gripped Rhone's shoulder. "I'm going to find Darsha. Maybe someone else has found something."

Tozer's den had proved a dead end, so Rhone left the clean up to the king's men. It took a while for them to find the rest of Lindren's sons and warriors. Between them they'd searched all the other rooms. Just as the man said, Lindren and Cat weren't there. When Rhone and the Elves finally climbed the ladder up to the ramshackle building, the sun shone bright through the gaps in the walls. They jogged to the castle. No one spoke a word.

Rhone ached all over. The cut on his calf throbbed along with the pain in his heart. *Cat! Where are you?* He slowed, limping.

Darsha called a halt. "You're hurt."

"Yes, but we can't stop now."

"We can for a few minutes." Arnir pulled him into an alley.

Darsha sent the Silverwood Elves on ahead while the rest of Lindren's family blocked the entrance.

"Lift up the back of your shirt." Arnir whispered Elven words, then laid his hand on Rhone's back. "Prepare yourself. It will hurt a bit, but I don't think you want sleeproot right now."

Rhone clenched his teeth in preparation. A warm feeling spread through his entire body, then he hissed in pain as the torn flesh shifted back where it belonged. A few minutes later, it was done.

"You're tired," Arnir said. "I can't fix that."

Rhone nodded. "I've been tired before. I'll be fine. Thank you."

They carried on to the castle, the pain in Rhone's calf easing with every step until it vanished. When they approached the gate, two boys, waving their arms in excitement, were speaking with the guards. A soldier opened one of the gate doors and another ran through it towards the castle.

The guard talking with the boys looked up. "My lords! Thank Ar you're here. These boys say they might know where at least one of your missing family is."

Darsha fell to one knee in the slush, his arm resting on the other. "What's your name?"

"Timri, m'lord."

"Timri, please tell me what you know. It's very important."

The boy looked familiar, though Rhone couldn't place him.

"I heard the nice lady with the white hair is missing so I asked my friends." The lad's words came out in a rush and Rhone remembered the boy Cat gave money to the first day off the ship.

193

"Rikky here said he was out late last night. Sometimes he has to stay away from the house 'cause his dad gets all drunked up. He says he saw two men carryin' what looked like a body from a wagon into a house on Tanner Row and now two mean lookin' guys are standin' out front."

Darsha looked from one boy to the other. "Can you take us there?"

The other boy, Rikky, Rhone assumed, nodded, his hazel eyes wide.

"Will you fight now?" Rhone asked Darsha as they ran, much easier now that they only had to keep pace with the boys.

"Yes."

Kelwyn's dark eyes flashed.

ဢ • ଔ

Talon sat in the chair and drummed his fingers on the windowsill. People passed by on Tanner Row, two stories down, going about their miserable little lives. Soon, he'd no longer be one of them. He shivered and blew on his hands. The stinky smoke from the two shattered glass balls lingered, so he'd left the tall windows wide open. The sun shone in, right onto the Elf girl where she lay, face down, on the floor, though it didn't warm him much. She moaned and Talon jumped. He almost leapt the few steps to her side.

Talon brushed the hair back from her face and slid the wooden bowl under her mouth. He held her head, waiting for the inevitable. It arrived in a flood a moment later. The girl gagged and retched, rejecting whatever sat in her stomach.

Light footsteps ran up the stairs. *It must be Rat.* The door opened and the little procurer held up a small burlap sack. With a grin, he kicked the door shut and shook the bag. It clinked.

Talon's grin matched Rat's. "How much?" The girl retched, spewing more vomit into the bowl. She groaned. "Shhh. It's all right, pretty one. Not long now." He stroked her hair.

Rat spotted the male Elf where he lay, head near the door. "Where'd he come from? And what's that stink?"

194

"Two of Tozer's men brought him in the middle of the night. They threw a couple of glass balls at the wall and left. They haven't come back. Left a mess, and the smell, behind." He pointed at the male Elf and the thin glass shards on the floor. Fortunately none had come close to the girl.

"Glass balls?" Rat shook his head. "Anyway, we got five hundred gold royals. Five hundred!" Rat fell to his knees next to Talon, who lost his grin.

"You should have got twice that much, Rat! Tozer cheated you!"

Rat's joy turned to confusion. "But this is a lot of money, far more than I've ever heard of anyone payin' for a girl."

A groan came from the other side of the room. The other Elf stirred, then retched.

"Oh, great," Talon said. "Now he's throwing up and we don't have another bowl."

The Elf called Lindren only produced a bit of bile, though it didn't stop him from trying to puke.

"He ain't got nothin' in his stomach." Rat dumped some of the contents of the bag onto the floor. Shiny gold coins, an inch and half in diameter, spilled out. "This is lots of money, Talon. Remember what Yait said? He wouldn't get a thousan' gold royals for the queen herself. Besides, Tozer's man said this was all I was gettin' and be glad to get it."

Rat played with two of the coins. "Let's see. Yait gets fifty percent, so that's...one, no, um, two..."

"Two hundred and fifty, which means we get a hundred and twenty five each." Talon hoped it would be enough to buy his land in Thallan-Mar and support him until that land produced. Someday he'd be a nobleman or die trying.

The Elf girl retched again. Nothing came up, so Talon removed a cloth of dubious cleanliness from his pocket and wiped the girl's mouth. He passed it to Rat. "Here, clean him up."

"Me! Why do I have to do it?" He shoved the coins back into the bag and set it near the girl's feet.

"Because I said so. I think she's finished now. I can take her." He set the bowl in the far corner so any struggle she attempted wouldn't overturn it.

"You said I can watch. Blood and bones promise." Rat made a cursory wipe of the male Elf's mouth, then tossed the cloth on the burlap bag.

"Yes, you can watch."

"Who...who are...you?" Lindren's eyes tried to focus on them, his voice rough.

"None of your business," Rat said.

"Help me flip her." Talon retrieved the key from the nail by the door and unlocked her hands.

She tried to fight. Talon had to give her credit; it took the two of them to get her half twisted onto her back and her hands shackled once more. Her feet were harder, she kicked more than he thought possible; the drug wouldn't completely wear off for hours yet. The girl said something in what Talon assumed was Elven.

"Leave her...alone." Lindren squirmed, rolling onto his side.

"Sit on him," Talon said, slipping the key over the nail once more. "I don't want any interruptions." He knelt, straddling the girl, and pushed up her tunic. Leaves shimmered in the strange green fabric. It held his attention only a moment, her chest was much more interesting.

Rat shifted the male Elf onto his stomach and sat on his back. Air whuffed out and Lindren groaned.

"Did Tozer say when someone was coming to get her?" Talon asked, running his hands over the girl's breasts. She struggled. Her pretty amber eyes, though dull from the drug, displayed her outrage. The girl spoke more words. It sounded like threats.

"Nope. I don't know how long we got." Rat leaned forward, almost drooling. "It might be a while. The king sent men to Tozer's this morning an' routed them out. Word is Tozer escaped, but most of his boys got sliced to pieces. A few crawled into the sewers. One of them might come."

Talon turned to Rat and grinned. "And he might not. Maybe we can sell her again."

"Yeah!" Rat's eyes gleamed, his eyes glued to the girl's chest. "With that kind of money I can start my own gang. Yait'll be sorry for the way he treated me."

Right. As if anyone would follow a snotty nosed kid. The girl struggled harder. "Keep that up, pretty lady, you're only going to make it more enjoyable for me." Talon pulled his dagger out of his belt and cut her trousers, slicing the fine fabric all the way down the left side, then did the same on the right. The girl tried to knee him, but the chain prevented it.

"No...stop, don't..."

Rat smacked Lindren on the back of the head. "Shut up."

"You're...Talon..."

Talon's head whipped around. "How did you know?" His eyes narrowed. "Jewel talked, didn't she. Well, she'll get hers when I've finished with this one. Gag him with that cloth, Rat." He glanced from one Elf to the other. "She's your daughter? Doesn't look much like you."

"He doesn't look old enough to have a daughter that age," Rat said, retrieving the dirty cloth.

"Elves don't age, stupid." Talon removed the girl's trousers. *This was worth waiting for.* He ran his fingers through the dark gold curls between her legs and her struggles increased more.

"I'm not stupid. Are you going to take her or just touch her all day?" Rat jammed the cloth in Lindren's mouth and the Elf retched again.

"Shut up, Rat." Talon bent down to kiss the girl's sweaty cheek. She thrashed her head and he had to jerk back. He backhanded her. "Stop it! Behave yourself or you'll get hurt."

Talon tried kissing her again, burying his face in her neck. The girl twisted her head and a sharp pain erupted in his right ear. "Ow!" Talon put a hand to the injury. It came away wet with blood. This time he belted her hard. Bright red welled at the corner of her mouth. "Enough."

The female Elf jerked the chains, trying to get her hands on Talon. They pulled tight, stopping her before she could reach him, just as he'd planned. Her father mumbled something though the gag. Talon laughed and undid his belt. "This is going to be a whole lot of fun."

இ • ஐ

Rhone peered around the corner of the rundown house. Two armed men stood outside a narrow three storey building, three houses

197

away. Either man could block an entire doorway. He glanced back at Darsha and nodded.

"See?" Timri said. "Just like we said."

We? Timri had done all the talking. Rikky hadn't uttered one word.

"It's just as you said." Darsha reached into a pocket. "Hold out your hands."

Both boys' eyes widened. The Elf put a silver crown into each dirty palm. Their jaws dropped. To them it would be a small fortune.

"Wow! Thanks, m'lord!" Timri grinned. Rikky stared at the coin, his mouth still open.

"You're welcome. You earned it. Now, I want you to go back to the castle," Darsha said. "Tell the guards that the Elves need horses, fast, then tell them where we are."

"Okay, m'lord!" Timri gave him a sketchy bow and headed back up Tanner Row, dragging Rikky behind him.

"Let's hope we've got the right place this time," Rhone said.

"How should we do this?" Shain asked. "As soon as we show our faces, they're going to lock themselves inside."

"Then we break the door down." Kelwyn slid his sword out of its scabbard.

"We could go back to the castle and get help," Arnir said.

"No." Rhone and Kelwyn both spoke the word.

Rhone took out his blades, sword and dagger. "If you want to leave, that's fine, but I'm going in now."

Kelwyn tested the edge of his weapon. "So am I."

"It was only a suggestion." Arnir put a hand on his sword hilt.

"No, Arnir," Darsha said. "We might need you to heal Father. We have no idea what shape he's in or how many men are in that house." He tugged his sword out, so did Shain.

Darsha glanced at Rhone before checking the situation for himself. "Kelwyn, Shain and I are going first. We can run faster and have a better chance of catching them."

Rhone grudgingly admitted they were right. "I'll be right behind you."

The Elves startled several people. One woman screamed. Both men outside the house ran for the door. Neither made it. One fell to Kelwyn's sword, the other to Darsha's. Rhone ran past the Elves and slammed into the door. It flew open. He dashed in and a shadow appeared in front of him, too short for Lindren, too broad for Cat. A quick stab and the shadow bellowed.

Shain leapt up onto the stairs to tackle another man. Rhone charged into the figure before him, knocking him to the ground. His eyes adjusted to the dark interior and he thrust his sword into the man's throat. Kelwyn slipped past him to take on another thug in the narrow hall. Darsha and Arnir followed Shain up the stairs. Kelwyn removed his opponent's head with one well-aimed swing. The Elf seemed to have things in hand on the first level, so Rhone took the stairs two at a time, leaping over Shain's kill just in time to see Darsha dispatch another at the top of the stairs. By the time Rhone arrived, none of the bully boys remained.

Kelwyn appeared to his left. "The rooms downstairs are empty."

"Where do we start?" Shain asked. "There's two more floors."

"We're on this one, it's as good as any." Darsha glanced around. "Five doors, five of us. We each take one."

Kelwyn put a hand on his cousin's arm. "I hear noises from that one." He pointed to the first door on the right, the one closest to Rhone.

℘ • ℭ

Talon undid the buttons on his trousers, one by one, grinning at the look on the girl's face. She spit fire, all in Elven. Despite the drug, her thrashing increased. The brothel owner who finally ended up with her would have to keep her in manacles. "Better get used to it," he said to the girl. "This is your life from now on."

Something on the wall to the left caught his eye. A small circle of grey swirling smoke formed on the cracked plaster not far from Lindren's feet. "What in Ar's name is that?"

"What's what?" Rat's eyes followed his. "Whoa!" He fell off Lindren and scuttled back until he hit the door. The male Elf groaned.

The grey circle grew until it hit the ceiling. A cloaked and hooded shape, dressed in black, stepped through the smoke, carrying pieces of rope. His cowl brushed against the roof; he seemed to fill the entire room. Talon looked up, way up. His jaw dropped. The man had to be eight feet tall. Though Talon knelt mere feet away, nothing could be seen in the cowl. The giant studied the male Elf first, then the girl and Talon.

"What do you think you're doing?" The huge man's voice, deep as thunder, sounded hoarse, like he had a sore throat. "Get off her. You're not worthy to lick her spit off the floor."

Talon's jaw snapped shut. Lindren thrashed and tried to say something through the gag. The cloaked man crouched beside the Elf and picked his head up by the hair. "Be patient. I'll get to you soon." He let go of the hair and Lindren's head hit the floor.

"Take those manacles off her, but be careful, she's stronger than she looks." The man tossed Talon some rope, then took a cloth out of a pocket and threw him that too. "Tie and gag her, then bring her through the portal. When you're done, come back and get him." He indicated Lindren, turned and entered the roiling smoke.

Talon looked at Rat, sitting on the floor, his back plastered to the door. "Portal? Those men mentioned something about a portal."

"Wha…what was that?" Rat pointed at the circle of smoke. His hand shook.

"Him or that…thing on the wall?"

"Uh, both?" Rat's eyes still bugged out of his head. Lindren hadn't stop thrashing. He wiggled his wrists, trying to loosen the rope.

"I don't know, but he can wait until I'm finished." Talon undid another button.

The giant appeared once more. One long stride took him close to Talon. "I said get off her." One massive gloved hand picked Talon up by the throat.

Talon kicked his feet and tried to pull the man's thick fingers off his neck. His lungs labored to suck in air, his heart pounding. He tried to tell the man to stop; only gurgles and choking noises found their way out. Talon's unbelted, unbuttoned trousers slipped to his knees. The man didn't move, didn't react to the kicks. Talon's vision darkened and his

200

world reduced to the need to fill his starved lungs.

Then he hit something hard and fell to the floor. Gasping, he clutched his throat and coughed. Feeling with his hands, he found the wall he'd hit and leaned against it.

"Bring her or I'll toss you out the window. I'll make it easy for you." The man's words were followed by a loud smack, like a fist hitting flesh then, after a moment, another.

By the time Talon's vision cleared and his lungs received badly needed air, the giant had disappeared again. Rat fumbled with the manacle on the girl's left wrist, then attacked the right, his hands shaking. Blood dripped from a split on the girl's cheek. She moaned. The giant had pulled down her tunic, covering her beautiful breasts. He glanced at Lindren; red trickled down his face and he didn't move either.

Talon picked himself off the floor and jerked up his trousers. *Futtering asshole.* The tall stranger had remarkable strength. Talon and his little dagger had no hope.

"C'mon! Give me a hand," Rat said, holding the girl's wrists together. "If he comes back, we're dead!"

"I haven't had my chance with that Elf, yet." Talon clenched his fists.

"Face it, Talon, you're not goin' to. Now help me. Quick!" Rat fumbled with the rope.

"Maybe I could dart him, futter the girl and scram out of town before he wakes up." Talon shook his head. His vision wanted to blur.

"In this small room? He'd have plenty of time to smear you all over the wall before he passed out."

Talon kicked the chair, tipping it on its side in front of one of the windows. "Ar's balls! Why? I worked so hard for this!"

"We still got the money. Now help me!"

Sinking to his knees next to Rat, Talon grabbed the rope out of the little procurer's hands. He tugged it tight, too tight, but he didn't care. Rat skittered around to her feet and unshackled them. When they were free, Talon tied them as well. He wished he could punch that stupid giant right in his cowl.

The sounds of metal on metal came from the hall beyond the

single door and Talon wondered if the king's guards had found them. They had to hurry and take the girl through, then her father and get the hell out of there. While waiting for her to wake up, Talon had checked for a possible escape route and found one—the drainpipe outside the window. If there were soldiers on the ground, he could climb up and over the roof. Once the male Elf was gone, Talon planned to grab his money and run.

Rat picked up the girl's feet. Talon took her head and backed into the swirling grey clouds on the wall, his heart thumping. Wherever this strange hole in the wall took him, it couldn't be good.

Chapter Eighteen

Rhone kicked in the door, his sword held before him. A boy, carrying a pair of shapely bare legs, walked to a portal like the one in Tozer's lair, fear on his young face. Lindren lay nearby, tied hand and foot, not moving. Empty manacles were bolted to the floor with Cat's trousers lying in a puddle near them. Cold air blew in the open windows.

"That's Cat!" Kelwyn cried in his ear. The Elf dashed past him, reaching the portal just as the boy disappeared.

Kelwyn thrust his arm in the grey swirling mass. An instant later the boy reappeared, Kelwyn's hand on his thin arm. The Elf shoved the dirty urchin away and grabbed Cat's bound ankles.

The boy slammed into the wall by one of the windows. By that time, Darsha, Shain and Arnir had entered the room. Shain closed the door. All three of Lindren's sons crouched beside him.

Kelwyn gently pulled on Cat's legs. "Someone's got hold of her in there. He's tugging on her."

Rhone sheathed his sword and placed his hands above Kelwyn's. "How hard can we pull?

"I don't know. I've never done this before."

"Father's alive," Arnir said, removing the gag, while Darsha and Shain untied the ropes.

The person on the other end of Cat tugged hard. Rhone braced himself. "I'm ready when you are."

Darsha and Shain joined them, their swords ready to take out whoever came with her. Rhone and Kelwyn yanked on Cat's legs and the rest of her slid out of the grey smoke.

A young man with sandy brown hair stumbled after, holding onto her shoulders. "Rat! What are you…" His brown eyes widened.

Darsha pointed his sword at the man's throat. He dropped his burden and raised his hands. Kelwyn let go of Cat's legs and only just caught her before her head hit the floor. Shain grabbed the young man's arm and dagger before jerking him away from her and the portal.

Darsha positioned himself beside the circle of storm clouds, keeping his blade pointed at the grey mass. "In case someone else comes out."

Kelwyn picked Cat up and clutched her to him. She wore only her tunic, which did little to conceal her nether regions. Rhone's heart stopped for an instant. *She's been raped!*

Arnir joined Darsha at the portal, his sword ready. "Father's very sick and his left cheek is shattered, but he's in no danger."

A large, dark shape emerged from the swirling clouds. Very large. "What are you idiots…"

Darsha and Arnir plunged their swords into the giant's chest and he stumbled back through the portal. "Arnir, can you close this thing?" Darsha asked.

"I can try." In a moment, his hands glowed white and he laid them on the smoky edge of the portal.

Rhone hauled up the young man by the front of his coat and Shain let go.

"What did you do to her?" Rhone said through clenched teeth.

A vaurok charged through the portal. Darsha took its head off. Arnir gave up trying to close it and drew his sword. Another vaurok followed the first; both Darsha and Arnir stabbed its face while Shain skewered it through the neck. It fell forward onto the body of the first. A third stuck it's head through.

Before the Elves could react, the swirling grey clouds of the portal shrank to a dot and vanished, separating the vaurok's head from its body. The repulsive head hit the second vaurok and rolled into the corner where the boy had landed, spraying oily, dark green blood in stripes across the floor and walls. The boy wasn't there.

Rhone searched the room, it took only a moment. "Where's that kid?" He let go of the young man and ran to the left window, just as the boy dropped from the drainpipe to the ground, then dashed around the corner of the house. Rhone's fist hit the wall. "He's gone."

Shain rested the tip of his sword against the kidnapper's throat. "Don't even think of moving." The man gulped.

Kelwyn laid Cat on the floor near Lindren while Arnir helped the Elven Elder to sit. Rhone lost the battle with his pent-up anger and hit the young man in the jaw, sending him crashing into the wall close to the now vanished portal. Shain's sword tip left a red line across his neck. Rhone didn't give the kidnapper time to recover from the blow before he hauled him up once more, his fist ready to inflict more damage.

"Don't." Darsha's hand covered Rhone's. "We need information."

"What did you did you to the lady, you son of a demon-futterer!" Rhone shook off Darsha's hand and tightened his grip on the young man, lifting him off the floor. Somewhere in the background he heard Cat talking in Elven between her sobs.

"Nothing! Now put me down!" Blood dripped from the man's mouth.

"Horse shit!" Rhone slammed him against the wall. "You raped her!"

"No! I...I didn't get time before that giant came!" The young man tried once more to wriggle out of Rhone's grasp. "What is it with you big guys and dark concealing clothes? Do the women like it?"

Darsha gripped Rhone's arm before he could hit him again. "Let him go. Cat says he's telling the truth."

Rhone released him and the man stumbled before regaining his balance.

"Your name is Talon?" Darsha's voice was quiet, though his eyes were darker than the clouds in the portal.

Talon frowned. "Jewel told you. Well, I know a few things about her. She's from the Pit and has been lying about..."

"We know." Lindren's words stopped Talon's tirade.

The young man's gaze flitted from Lindren to Cat, then Kelwyn, before settling on Rhone. "Pretty good lay, isn't she? Wish I'd had my turn."

Once again, Darsha stopped Rhone's fist from making contact with Talon.

The thief turned kidnapper flashed him a lewd smile. "Bet you don't know she was futtering that dark haired Elf."

Rhone froze.

"No!" Kelwyn leapt from Cat's side, jumped over the vaurok bodies and smashed his fist into Talon's sneering face. The young man fell backwards, tripping on an overturned chair. His knees hit the windowsill and he disappeared.

Shain ran to the window. "He landed on the sidewalk. I think he's dead. That boy is back."

A young voice came from the street. "You killed him! Murdering Elves! You'll pay for this!"

"He's gone again. And now the guards show up." Shain waved to them.

Rhone still hadn't moved. *Kelwyn laid with Cat?* It was possible. Kelwyn had spent time alone with her the day the Elves removed Dayn's spell. He shifted his gaze from the window to Kelwyn and the anguish and rage on the Elf's face. "You…"

"It wasn't like that," Kelwyn snapped.

Cat's shock turned to a flood of tears and Kelwyn moved towards her. Lindren said something in Elven and he stopped, his hands clenching and unclenching.

Rhone gave in to fury of a different kind. "Then what was it! I was told you weren't lovers!"

Kelwyn opened his mouth to speak.

Lindren halted him. "The guards are coming. We'll have to discuss this later," the Elven Elder said, his voice bristling with anger. He looked like he'd been dragged through all nine hells.

Arnir chanted, his expression grim. His hands glowed with magic. Before the guards pounded on the door, Lindren's wound was gone and some of the colour returned to his face.

"Just a moment!" Darsha said, in response to the guards' knock. "We can't let them see Cat like this."

She huddled against the door, her face buried in her arms, shoulders shaking as she cried. Rhone no longer cared. He'd been lied to, again, though it appeared Kelwyn and Cat had lied to Lindren as well. *It doesn't matter. She gave me what I wanted.*

Arnir gathered Cat into his arms while Darsha removed his shirt and tunic. Between them, they tied the shirt around her waist. When

Darsha had slipped back into his tunic, Lindren gave the order to open the door. Arnir picked Cat up and stood back. Rhone ducked around the vauroks' bodies and strode to the door.

Lindren's voice stopped him "Wait."

Rhone gripped the doorknob. Something inside him made him listen.

"We have to talk. I know you're angry. So am I. You weren't the only one deceived. Please come to my room before you go. And, don't say anything to anyone about our rescue. It's important."

Rhone wanted to leave, now, put it all behind, his rank, both civil and military, his friends, his family, go some place where no one knew him, where he could hide in peace. Alone. He nodded, not sure why, and strode out the door.

∞ · ∞

Lindren let Darsha help him to his feet. With the headache gone and his smashed cheek repaired, he felt a little better. He wished Arnir could also heal the nausea and weakness. Those had to go away on their own.

"Lindren, I can explain…"

His gaze put an end to Kelwyn's words. "I said, not now."

Though angry with Cat as well, his heart hurt for her. Rhone was as good as gone. "Shain, if you could explain to the guards, I'd appreciate it. I'm just not up to talking to anyone."

Shain gave him a nod. "Of course, Father. I'll catch up."

Vergel stood in the open door. He took in the Elves, the vaurok bodies, the manacles, Cat and her sliced trousers.

"Shain will explain what happened here," Lindren said. "My daughter is understandably upset and we're both sick from that drug." Upset didn't begin to describe Cat. She'd buried her face against Arnir's chest, her sobbing completely out of control. Kelwyn stared at her, his face like stone, eyes black as Udath Kor's soul.

Vergel bowed. "Of course, my lord. Horses are waiting below to take you back to the castle."

207

"Is it possible to get us there without anyone seeing?" Lindren asked. "I don't want others to know we've been found. I think it's the only way to get a rat out of its hole."

Vergel frowned. "The men with me can be trusted, but we're going to have to hide you."

"There's a wagon around the back, sir, my lord," said a guard behind Vergel. "It has a bunch of burlap sacks in it."

"That will be fine." Lindren leaned against the wall, his stomach rebelling any movement. "It's probably how at least one of us was brought here."

The guard performed a half bow. "There's also a back door, so we can sneak you out, my lord."

"The men King Rodrin put to work sealing the tunnels haven't made much progress," Vergel said. "We can take you up that way."

Lindren thanked Arvanion for slow workers. "Put the tunnels to good use for a change?"

Vergel gave him a smile and a half bow. While Shain filled the commander-general in on the tale, improvising why Talon died, Lindren sat on the chair, hoping to regain some of his strength. When the tale and plans for sneaking into the castle were completed, Lindren struggled to his feet. Cat cried the entire time. Vergel and his men cast her strange glances.

One of the soldiers passed a clinking sack to Vergel.

"That's the kidnappers' ill-gotten gains," Lindren said. "It should go to the king."

Vergel agreed and took charge of the gold.

Sneaking out proved harder to do than it sounded. Cat cried all the way down the stairs and to the rear door, Arnir trying to soothe her. Lindren didn't have the strength to hold her himself, but he had to calm her down somehow. While Arnir held her, Lindren rubbed her back, his glare keeping Kelwyn at bay.

"You have to stop crying, Cat," Lindren said, in Elven. "We have to go back to the castle, but I don't want anyone seeing or hearing us. It's important."

Cat drew in a shuddering breath. "I...can't!" The crying

208

continued.

Lindren leaned against the wall. He couldn't wait an hour for her to stop. Exhaustion and nausea overwhelmed him, and he still had to speak with Rodrin and deal with Rhone and Kelwyn before he could rest.

"Cat, please. I know you're hurting." Lindren remembered a long ago day, shortly after Cat had awoken from wherever it was she went after her people were killed. She'd been embarrassed, humiliated and hurt. The last thing she wanted was to face people. "Cat, listen to me. No one else has to see you. We're both going to hide under sacks in the back of a wagon. Will that help?"

She nodded. It still took a few minutes for her to calm enough so Arnir could carry her out the door. He laid her on the wagon bed and she curled into a ball, still shaking. Her crying had subsided into shudders and sniffles. Darsha helped Lindren lie down; the effects of the drug had weakened his muscles to the point where he found walking difficult.

Once settled, his sons left with Kelwyn and all but one of the guards. The single soldier removed his uniform jerkin and huddled in his cloak, the insignia of Kitring-Tor hidden in the folds. Several minutes after the others left, he covered both Lindren and Cat with sacks, then drove the wagon out from behind the old house and onto Tanner Row.

Before he left, Vergel ordered his guards to patrol the streets to the dock and the path that lead to the tunnels. Under the watchful eyes of the soldiers, the wagon slowly made its way along Tanner Row and down Wharf Street. As they neared the docks, the sounds of sea gulls and men drifted on the late morning air.

Lindren wished the driver would move faster, the air under the sacks was stale and suffocating. The sacks themselves smelled of old sweat, rotten food and bad beer. He couldn't imagine what they'd been used for, nor did he want to.

Cat spent the entire trip quietly sobbing while Lindren held her and tried to find a way to tell Rodrin his most trusted duke, and cousin, was a vile traitor.

The wagon rolled over rough ground before coming to a stop. A whispered conversation confirmed Vergel had arrived, as had his sons and nephew. Darsha, Shain and Arnir uncovered Lindren and Cat, hiding

209

them in borrowed cloaks as they were helped off the wagon. Shain picked Cat up and they headed for the tunnel entrance concealed by bushes and strategically placed soldiers. Vergel strode ahead of them, a large sledge hammer in one hand. Where he got it, Lindren had no idea. Even with Arnir and Darsha's help, it took him much longer to walk the path than it should have. The snow lay thick here, every step a struggle.

When they arrived, three soldiers stood watch near a five and a half foot round stone. It plugged a cement conduit emerging from one of the low hills of the city. Another smaller rock lay nearby, a natural one, and Arnir helped Lindren sit. A tiny creek rushed through a narrow ravine near the sealing stone to the river. The water called to Lindren and he wished he had the strength to crouch down for a drink.

One of the guards reached a hand inside a hidden hole and a portion of the large stone slid back, revealing a four foot tall, three foot wide gap.

"Wait a few minutes, Father," Arnir said. "You need to rest."

Lindren shook his head. "Every minute we're out here is another chance for someone to see us."

He struggled to stand. Only five feet separated the floor and ceiling of the sewer. Everyone had to duck. Vergel led the way with a torch he'd picked up just inside the door, a lieutenant brought up the rear. The other guards took the easy, though longer, way back to the castle. The gentle incline of the sewer felt like a steep mountain and Lindren wondered how Shain was making out carrying Cat.

An eternity later, Vergel stood up straight. "This is how our thief turned kidnapper got into the castle." He pointed to the bottom of a garderobe, then passed the torch to Darsha and hauled himself up. "I'll help Lord Lindren through."

With Vergel pulling and Darsha shoving, Lindren made it through the broken seat. Though the odours were decades old, he hoped he never had to see the underside of a garderobe again, or the inside of a sewer. Vergel helped Lindren out of the little room and to the unused bed. While he caught his breath, Darsha climbed up, then took Cat so Shain could come through. Kelwyn and Arnir were next with the lieutenant last.

Not far now. "Arnir, run ahead and ask Talifir to sit with Cat. We need to talk and I don't want her alone."

Arnir nodded and left. The dusty bed demanded Lindren lay down and close his eyes. Instead, he forced himself to stand. Vergel opened the secret door, another bookcase, and led the way inside. A newly made brick wall blocked their path.

Rodrin's commander-general demolished it with a few blows. "That was too easy," he said. "I'll inform His Majesty that perhaps three rows of bricks are needed."

To be fair, the mortar was still damp; Lindren could smell it. They ran across two more walls, just as easily destroyed, then Vergel led them straight to Lindren's room. Shain helped Lindren to a chair. Cat, in Darsha's arms, had finally quieted, though she still sniffled and hid her face against his chest.

Vergel opened the sitting room door and stepped out. Lindren heard him speak to the guards. Soldiers were only posted outside Kelwyn's and the boys' rooms; no point in protecting someone who wasn't there. With their new orders, the guards now watched more than one door.

The commander-general stuck his head back in the room. "Lord Darsha, please follow me." They took Cat to her room.

Lindren sat back in his chair and closed his eyes. His suite had never looked so good.

℘   •   ℭ

The afternoon sun shone warm on the cobblestones of the courtyard as Rhone strode from the stable to the castle. No Elves were present in the throne room, for which he was grateful. He took the stairs two at a time and almost ran to Cat's room. When he flung the door open, he startled Jewel who sat in front of the fireplace.

She stiffened and stuck her nose in the air. "Did you find my lady?"

"Get out." Rhone reached under the cot for his pack.

"You're supposed to be…"

211

Rhone gripped her arm. "I said get out." He pulled her to the door, pushed her out, then slid the bolt home. One tug removed the mask and he took a deep breath.

Jewel pounded and threatened. He ignored her. One pair of trousers and one shirt rested in the pack. The only other set of spare clothes he had were off in the laundry. Rhone decided he could live with one change for now, then paid a quick visit to the garderobe.

His grooming supplies sat on the small table. He scooped them up and re-entered the bedroom. The big bed called to him and Rhone wished he could sleep before heading out. He doubted he'd find anything as comfortable on the road, then decided his anger was enough to keep him awake.

Another use for the bed rushed up from recent memories. He pushed them aside, strode into the sitting room and stuffed his supplies in the pack. A few minutes more and all the straps were tied. Rhone was ready to go.

He sat on the cot and undid the top fastenings of his jerkin; his money rested in the upper inside pocket. Rhone fished it out. Six gold royals, three silver royals, four gold crowns, six silver crowns and a number of coppers of various sizes sat on the palm of his hand. A tidy sum for any mercenary and more than enough to purchase a decent horse, riding equipment and cover his travel expenses to The Denfold.

Rhone wouldn't have to hide his face there. Though allies with Kitring-Tor, they always seemed to be embroiled in trouble with the eastern nomadic tribes. Finding work wouldn't be a problem. The fastest route lay east to Hunter's Bridge. A road led from there to The Denfold, skirting the southern edge of the Old Forest.

Jewel stopped pounding on the door. Rhone tucked the money back in his pocket. He'd earned it, though the job hadn't been an onerous one, watching Cat during the day and sleeping with her at night. He doubted his next job would be so cushy. The life of a mercenary was hard and dangerous, but he needed to kill something and anything would do.

Rhone stared at the carpet. The reds, blues and greens had muted over the years. Thousands of feet must have trod on it, though most of the edges were still good. The only truly worn place was in front of the door. Arden's keep had no large carpets like this until a couple years before Rhone left.

He thought of his room at home, perhaps half as big as Cat's sitting room. The only rooms this large in Arden were the baron's and two guest suites. Rhone's small room had faced west, towards Silverwood. The Elves' home couldn't be seen from Arden, it lay four days away.

Nonetheless, he spent hours staring out his window imagining life in Silverwood, how the Elves lived, fought and played. Some of his earliest memories were of Lindren visiting his father. He never imagined he'd grow close to the Elder and his family, or care about the last living Tiranen.

Rhone pushed that thought from his mind. Others took over. His family, home, his life before Jornel's death, the things he no longer had. Voices in the hall roused him. A glance at the balcony doors showed him the sun sitting low in the sky. He'd sat on the cot longer than he thought.

The door knob rattled. "Fox? It's Darsha. Could you let me in?"

Rhone jumped to his feet and unlocked the door. Darsha walked in, carrying Cat. The cloak covering her slipped down, exposing Darsha's shirt around her hips. Cat's face was buried against his chest. Just as well. Her shoulders shook; she was crying again, or still. Darsha took her into the bedroom. Rhone didn't follow. A few minutes later, someone else knocked on the door.

Talifir entered. "Lindren asked me to watch Cat."

Rhone pointed him in the direction of the bedroom. A few minutes later Darsha returned to the sitting room.

"Are you coming to Father's room?" he asked, his face sad.

"Yes, for a couple minutes."

Darsha nodded and left. Rhone picked up his pack and replaced his mask. He stared at the bedroom door, wishing events could have turned out different. His luck had left him again. After a last look around the sitting room, Rhone opened the door. A few steps took him to Lindren's. He almost kept walking. His head wished to leave; his heart wanted to stay and find out why it hurt. He rapped a knuckle on the door.

Chapter Nineteen

Rhone set his pack by the door and closed it. Lindren rested in his usual chair, Arnir and Shain on the floor, Darsha leaning against the stone of the fireplace. Kelwyn stood in front of the bookcase, his hands at his sides, curled into fists.

The chair beside Lindren was empty. He motioned for Rhone to take it. "Thank you for coming."

Rhone nodded and tugged down his mask. He settled himself into the chair, feeling anything but comfortable. Silence followed.

Lindren broke it, his gaze on Kelwyn. "You told me on the ship there was nothing to worry about."

"There isn't." Kelwyn's voice shook with emotion.

"I was under the assumption you and Cat weren't lovers." Lindren folded his hands on his lap, deceptively calm for someone who was not only sick, but angry as well.

"We're not. Not really. I...I help keep her ache away. You know I don't like seeing her in pain." Anguish twisted Kelwyn's normally cheerful features.

"Ache?" Rhone and Shain spoke the word together.

Darsha frowned. "What ache?"

Arnir looked to Lindren for an answer.

Linden glanced at Rhone, then stared at his hands. It took him a while to answer. "Cat isn't comfortable talking about her life with men."

Rhone already knew that.

"Neither am I. The entire subject was practically taboo amongst the Tiranen," Lindren continued, his dark grey eyes now resting on Rhone. "The year Cat awoke from the state she was in after her people died, she turned sixty, an important age for the Tiranen. She was sexually mature, but with no one to love her. Cat discovered shortly afterwards that if she's not with someone on a regular basis, she suffers pain, down...there."

All three of Lindren's sons frowned. It was obvious they hadn't known either. "Why?" Rhone asked.

Lindren shrugged. "I don't know. It might be normal for a Tiranen, but we have no way of finding out. Arlayva told her nothing before she died, Cat wasn't old enough. And ever since her people were killed, Cat's moon cycle has been horrific. She only has two a year. Perhaps it's related."

In the five weeks since he'd first lain with Cat, she hadn't had her moon cycle. The thought of it never occurred to him either, though Calli had been such a bitch during hers. "Why only two? Were all the Tiranen like that?"

Lindren shook his head. "Not at first. The Tiranen bred quickly, though not like Humans. Elves usually have two or three children, my four was unheard of. The Tiranen just kept having kids, one every couple hundred years, changing partners frequently. Then something went wrong. Over the last several millennia, the women's moon cycles slowed to two a year and they almost stopped having babies. Cat was the only Tiranen born in the last thousand years. Her people were dying long before the Black Lord finished them off."

Arnir sighed. "I only know of four Elves who've lain with Cat."

"Five," Darsha said. "If you count Cadwyn."

"Cadwyn doesn't count." Kelwyn's voice was tight with anger and Rhone figured he'd discovered the source of Cat's distress the first time they'd made love.

"Still," Arnir continued. "That's a lot of time in between for her to suffer."

"It's why I do what I can." Kelwyn's eyes glistened with unshed tears, something Rhone had never seen in an Elf.

He felt sorry for Cat, though the story didn't lift his heart much. "That's why Cat was so forward with me when we met. She only wanted me for what I could give her."

"No," Kelwyn said, his voice solid with conviction. "Cat would never lay with just anyone. She'd rather live in pain than be with someone she didn't care about. Yes, Cat was less than subtle, but she doesn't know your ways. She was only trying to get to know you." He

215

stood poker straight, his entire body screaming anger and anguish. "Yes, I laid with Cat the last time we were here, once and never since. There was no need. Besides, I consider you a friend. I wouldn't do that to you, or Cat. I won't lie with her again until you leave. Ask Cat. She'll tell you the truth."

"The truth is something that appears to be more than a little evasive with you people," Rhone said, tired of the secrets, the deceptions, even if he understood the need for them. "If Cat doesn't like talking about this subject, what makes you think she'd tell me the truth?"

All eyes turned to Lindren. He leaned forward. "Because she can't lie. It's part of her truth-seeing."

The news hit Rhone like a rock between the eyes. All he had to do was ask her. Everything she'd told him was the truth; not that he'd doubted her. She could be devious, her plan for him as her bodyguard showed him that. When speaking with her, however, the only impression he got was that she spoke the truth. Now he knew why.

Rhone looked at Kelwyn, his tight fists and angry, tear-filled eyes. "You love her."

"Yes. All my life. But we can only be occasional lovers. I'll find my soulmate one day. Cat deserves better. I help take her pain away, so she doesn't have to use so much sleeproot, and we look for other lovemates."

Rhone's brows dipped in a frown. "It's that bad?" It would explain why she knew the effects of the drug and didn't like it.

"Yes, and Tiranen can take a great deal of pain," Lindren said. "Running and keeping busy helps, but sometimes it's so fierce the only way she can find relief is with sleeproot. She tried to hide it from me and suffer in silence, but it's difficult to keep something like that a secret from those you live with."

Rhone sat back in the chair. Cat was a complicated girl. Her eyes, hair, fragile emotions, her truth-seeing and now all this. Then he realized she wasn't just a girl, she was a Tiranen girl. *I've been treating her like a Human and expecting her to act like one.* Rhone could have kicked himself.

Once again he was making assumptions before finding out all the facts. His father's words rang in his ears; *'Never assume anything.'* It had almost cost him his life. He'd assumed Calli would come forward and

216

state where Rhone was that night. When she didn't, his heart died. He didn't care if he swung from a rope. Rhone had been wrong in another assumption, his luck hadn't deserted him. He stood, readjusted his mask, and picked up his pack by the door.

"Is this goodbye?" Lindren asked. His eyes were rimmed with red, his face too pale. The Elven Elder needed sleep, badly.

"Not necessarily. I need to talk to Cat."

"If she's still crying," Kelwyn said. "Rub her back."

Rhone nodded.

℘ • ℭ

When Rhone closed the door, Lindren settled into his chair and clasped his hands tighter. They shook and if Arnir spotted it, he'd never allow Lindren to remain awake long enough to talk to Rodrin. At least Rhone might stay and that was good news for Cat.

"Is there nothing we can do about Cat's ache?" Arnir asked.

Lindren shook his head. "Other than the sleeproot, no." He glanced at Kelwyn. His nephew stared at the carpet, his anger finally receding. "I'm still concerned about you laying with Cat. I simply don't understand why you love her like you do."

Kelwyn's head snapped up. Judging by his eyes, his anger hadn't receded far enough. "There's nothing to worry about. We're both well aware it can't work. I don't stop her from having lovemates, I'd never do that to her." Two tears finally fell from his dark eyes. "Nor does she stop me from finding mine."

Cat showed no hesitation about latching onto Rhone. Maybe there was nothing to worry about. Nonetheless, Lindren hoped Kelwyn found his soulmate sooner rather than later. The only good thing about it was that Cat didn't hurt quite so much. His cousin Taurin helped her when he was home, though he usually stayed away for years in between.

Lindren sighed. "You do realize, Kelwyn, that if you hadn't reacted the way you did, I'd have assumed Talon lied."

"Me too," Shain said. Arnir and Darsha nodded.

Kelwyn returned his gaze to the carpet. "It came as such a shock, I

217

didn't think."

"Understandable." *In some ways, not in others.* As much as he wished otherwise, there was nothing Lindren could do. "Then let's put it behind us. Shain, would you mind asking Rodrin if he could come here to speak with me? After all we went through this afternoon, I don't want to risk someone spotting us."

"Of course." Shain dashed out the door.

"Poor Cat," Arnir said, with a sigh.

"What's amazing," Darsha added, "is that she's able to hide it so well."

Arnir frowned at Lindren. "And that, as sick as you are, you're able to stay vertical."

Lindren couldn't argue, he felt like he'd been run over by all three thousand Hrulka. It had been almost an entire day since he'd first been drugged and nausea continued to plague him. "I must speak with Rodrin and apologize for not attending the signing ceremony for Gailen and Selesa tonight. I know you're tired, but all of you must go. They consider us the royal family of Silverwood and some people would take it as a slight if no one put in an appearance."

"We can handle it, Father," Darsha said.

Arnir added more wood to the dying fire. "How about telling us why you wanted to sneak into the castle and how someone managed to kidnap you?"

"I'd rather wait until Rodrin arrives."

Lindren glanced at Kelwyn. Instead of standing like a stiff oak, he now leaned against the bookcase. They passed the time until Rodrin arrived in familial silence.

The king came wrapped in a plain brown robe, the hood concealing his face, Shain trailing behind. "I don't usually visit people like this," he said, once the door was closed. "People come to me."

Lindren waved him to the empty chair. "I appreciate it and I won't keep you. It wouldn't look good if the father of the groom was late for the signing ceremony."

Rodrin grimaced. "Which is why I came already dressed." He removed the robe and sat beside Lindren. The king wore a thigh length, long sleeved tunic of shimmering dark green silk. Embroidered gold stags chased each other around the hem. A white linen shirt peeked out at collar and cuff. Black, fine woolen trousers met ankle high boots of polished leather. Subdued, when compared to the crimson he'd worn the night before, though no less fashionable. Everyone in Tezerain expected their king to shine and he rarely disappointed them.

"So," Rodrin said. "Shain says you didn't just wander off last night."

"No, not quite." Lindren sunk deeper into the chair, resting his head on the wing. He kept his hands clasped, wishing he could sit on them to stop the shaking. "You're not going to like this."

"I didn't think I would."

Lindren decided the direct approach best. "It was Raimon Teale."

Rodrin's expression turned predatory. "He was acting strange last night, according to one of my guards. After you came up missing, he couldn't be found either here or at his house. I left a guard at the Teale manor with instructions that our errant duke was to report to me immediately. Raimon showed up this morning, but brushed the guard off. Told him he'd come this afternoon…and never put in an appearance. The guards I sent got no response when they knocked on his door."

"Tozer got to him as well as Dayn, only he succeeded with Raimon. He's spent the last year learning magic. The black variety." Lindren settled into the tale, explaining everything from Raimon's deception to the vaurok in the wine cellar and the rescue.

By the time Lindren finished the tale, Rodrin fumed. "So Teale's responsible for the vauroks in Willow Wood as well as the ones on Randin's land? No wonder he volunteered to take care of the matter."

Lindren nodded. "Said he was testing a new portal spell."

"That must be what we saw in the room where you and Cat were held," Darsha said. "It had grey clouds instead of white and was a lot smaller than the ones I've seen."

Kelwyn shifted his stance, leaning his back against the bookcase instead of his shoulder. "Fox and I saw one in Tozer's lair. We think it's how he escaped."

"Apparently it's a temporary portal, though what that means, I couldn't tell you." *But it can't be good.* "Raimon also showed me a spell built into a blue glass orb. When he threw it at a rat, it consumed the creature in a matter of moments. There was nothing left, no blood, no bones, no fur."

Rodrin rested his head in his right hand, rubbing his temples. "Bad news piled on bad news. Teale knows all the state secrets, troop locations, every advantage we have."

"Change it," Arnir said. "I know it will be difficult and take time, but it's your only choice."

The king nodded. "My mind reels. This couldn't have come at a worse time." He glanced over at Lindren. "He wouldn't tell you what's going on up north?"

"Unfortunately, no. Only his reasons. He feels I've compromised the leadership of Kitring-Tor and that your father made a huge mistake setting up commoners in the baronies."

Rodrin snorted. "Teale never hid his contempt for the lower classes. I can just picture how he'd have run the country. The merchants and peasants would have revolted before he could warm my throne with his futtering ass. As for you, your guidance has been invaluable."

"Thank you, Rodrin. I just wish I could have gleaned more from him before he put me out again. It wouldn't surprise me if he's the duke involved in Jornel's murder."

"What will you do now?" Shain asked the king.

Rodrin turned his attention to him. "As Arnir suggested, change the way things are done, order my men to keep an eye out for Teale and hang the bastard as soon as I get my hands on him."

"Which is why I felt keeping our escape a secret would be in order," Lindren said. "He might be more willing to show his face. It may not work. Talon is dead, but there's always the possibility the boy will talk. Nonetheless, I feel we should try."

Darsha's eyes darkened. "Talon called him Rat. He's the one from the Dolphin fountain. I recognized him."

Rodrin cast him a questioning glance.

"He tried to con Cat into going with him when we first arrived," Darsha explained. "I'd hoped I'd put the fear of Ar into him. I guess it didn't work."

"Rarely does with that kind." Rodrin placed both hands on the arm of the chair. "I don't know what Teale is up to, but I hope he comes out of hiding soon. I'd like both you and Cat to attend the wedding. I know she's looking forward to it." The king rose to his feet.

"We'll do what we can and I apologize for both Cat and myself about tonight." Lindren wanted to see Rodrin out, but doubted his legs would hold him up. "Neither of us is up to it."

"I understand. I hear that drug is brutal." Rodrin picked up his robe from the back of the chair and threw it over his shoulders. "You just worry about getting the sleep you need."

"I will."

Arnir stood. "We'll make sure he does."

Rodrin paused. "I just had a thought. Andros and Aura are both staying at the castle instead of the manor, which might mean they know nothing of what their father's done."

"Do you dare take that chance?" Lindren asked.

The king shook his head. "If I arrest them, questions will be asked and it might alert Teale."

"Can you put guards on them?" Arnir suggested. "Perhaps as a precaution because Father and Cat are missing, and now Raimon."

"That's a good idea. Cat didn't say why she went to the stables, did she?" the king asked, as he tied a thin rope around his waist. With the hood up he resembled one of Ar's monks who worked as clerics in the castle.

Darsha answered. "No, she was in no shape to talk. We only know that the Hrulka are sick and she probably felt it."

Rodrin nodded. He placed his hand on the door knob and paused a moment. "Teale said there was nothing in Broken Man Pass that shouldn't be there. What did he feel was supposed to be there?"

Lindren's hands curled into fists. They still shook. "I don't know, but the thought scares me."

"And I." The king left.

"I noticed you didn't say much about that giant that came through the portal," Arnir said.

Lindren forced his hands to relax. "Because I recognized him."

His sons all cast him confused looks. Kelwyn frowned. "Is he the same creature you saw on Morata?"

Lindren nodded. "Not exactly on Morata." Lindren had been caught in Udath Kor's place between worlds. "But yes, that's him."

"Well, he's dead now," Darsha said. "Arnir and I both skewered him in the heart."

"Perhaps not. I'd hoped he was already dead." Nausea watered Lindren's mouth. His stomach heaved and he forced it down. "Besides, if he's a demon, his heart might not even be in his chest." Demons were like that, you never knew where to strike.

Darsha's shoulders slumped. "I hadn't thought of a demon."

"Maybe there's two of them," Shain said. "Or more."

Nausea surged and Lindren retched. The shaking shifted from his hands to his entire body.

"No more discussions, no more explanations," Arnir said. "Anything else can wait for tomorrow. You are going to bed."

Lindren didn't argue.

⚯   •   ⚲

No sound came from Cat's bedroom and Rhone wondered if she slept. He set his pack on the floor, still not certain if he'd stay. It depended on her answers. Rhone rubbed his tired eyes and pushed the door to the bedroom open, tossing his cloak and mask on the foot of the bed.

Talifir sat beside Cat. He looked up at Rhone's approach. "I think she's asleep."

Rhone nodded. "I'll take over watching her. Thank you."

The lighted candle on the small table by the bed flickered, highlighting the Elf's cornflower blue eyes. "Pleased I could help. I'm glad you came now, though. The ceremony is due to start soon and I'd like to attend. My soulmate loves to hear about other traditions." He picked at his dark blue tunic. "I need to wash and change my clothes first, though."

"Have a good time."

Talifir nodded and left. Rhone took his place in the chair. Cat faced away from him, still in her green tunic. Darsha's shirt lay over the back of the chair. He touched her shoulder and she shuddered. *She's not asleep.*

"Cat, we need to talk."

She buried her head under the pillow and cried, her sobs shaking her body. "No!"

"Why? Because Lindren and your brothers know about you and Kelwyn?"

She said nothing, just cried under the pillows.

"It's not a crime, Cat." Not now that he knew the reason for it. "Kelwyn explained he only lay with you so you wouldn't hurt."

Her crying increased. Rhone pulled the blankets down to her waist and lifted her tunic enough to slide his hand underneath, intending to rub her back. She pulled away from his touch, scooting across the big bed. Tears still fell and her beautiful eyes blazed, not in desire, but anger.

What in Ar's name is the matter with her? "I just need some answers, Cat."

"Why?"

Rhone blinked. "Why? I need to know if…"

"Why do you act hurt and angry when you don't care about me!" Tears flowed down her golden cheeks. She clutched a pillow to her chest, her hands squeezing its softness.

"What are you talking about? I do care…"

"I saw you!"

Saw me? He thought a moment about all that had happened in the last couple days and what occurred the night before. "The Winter Garden. You saw me with Calli."

"Yes!"

Rhone sat back in the chair. *Another misunderstanding.* "I loved Calli, four years ago. Not anymore."

Cat wiped her tears with the back of one hand. "Then why did you kiss her?"

"I didn't. She kissed me and I had to play the part." He folded his

223

arms across his chest, wishing she'd let him hold her. "She recognized me and threatened to tell her uncle I was still alive if I didn't meet her last night. I couldn't risk anyone finding out, especially Greyson Yarrow."

Cat clutched the pillow, blinking away more tears. "You don't love her?"

"No. As a matter of fact, I don't even like her. She…" Rhone didn't want to say the words. "I was supposed to marry Calli. The night Jornel died, she and I…we were together. Jonlan was supposed to stand outside the door, keeping watch. My people aren't as understanding about that sort of thing as yours. When I was arrested, I thought Calli would come forward and clear my name. She didn't. My love for her died at that moment."

"Why…" Cat hiccupped. "Why didn't she say anything?"

"I asked her the same question. She said she used to lie when she was younger and that no one would believe her. I doubt that's the truth, but I can't confront her, not while she holds my life in her hands." It was nice to know Cat would believe him. "I don't care about her, Cat. I do care about you."

"I don't feel very good." Cat sank down on the bed, stuffing the pillow under her head.

Rhone tugged off his boots and climbed in, clothes and all. He pulled her to him and rubbed her back, up and down, Cat's soft skin warm under his fingers, the curve of her bottom enticing.

"I need some answers," he said. "Just nod or shake your head. You don't have to say a word if you don't want to."

"All right."

"Did you lay with Kelwyn since I met you?"

Cat drew in a shuddering breath and shook her head.

"Would you ever lay with anyone else if I'm still around?"

She responded with an emphatic no. Rhone relaxed as he realized that was the answer he not only hoped for, but expected.

"One more question. You don't have to answer if you don't want to." Rhone almost held his breath. "Do you…love me?"

Cat took a few moments to respond, a minute nod of her head. Now that Rhone had his answers, he could relax completely and exhaustion swept over him. He drew Cat closer and closed his eyes.

A knock startled him awake. Rhone wondered how long he'd slept. "Stay here," he said to Cat and threw on his cloak and mask.

He opened the door to find Arnir carrying a tray of food. Cat's brother entered and Rhone closed the door, then tugged down his mask.

"I thought you'd like something to eat," Arnir said, setting the tray on the desk. "This was for us, but we can eat downstairs."

Rhone's stomach growled. He hadn't eaten since the night before. The day had gone by so fast, he hadn't even thought of food. "I'm surprised Jewel didn't bring something."

"Rodrin's had her assigned to other duties for now. Officially, Father and Cat haven't been found, which is why there's no guard outside their doors." Arnir headed for the bedroom. Rhone followed with the tray.

When Cat saw her brother, she started sniffling again. He hugged her and kissed her forehead. "Do you still feel sick?" he asked, not quite touching the cut on her cheek.

Cat nodded. "I'm having trouble sleeping because I keep feeling like I'll throw up."

Arnir retrieved a small towel from the garderobe, poured some water in a basin and dipped the cloth in. He brushed her hair back from her face, dabbing at the blood on her cheek. "I can't stay, the signing ceremony is about to start. Listen to me, both of you. Raimon Teale is responsible for kidnapping Father." He turned to Rhone. "We think he's also the one who ordered Jornel murdered. No one can find him and we're hoping if he thinks Father and Cat are still missing he'll come out of hiding. Kelwyn can fill you both in tomorrow, if that's all right."

"Fine," Rhone said. He'd never liked Teale; he liked him less now. "We're both exhausted anyway."

Arnir finished cleaning the wound, hugged Cat again and strode to the sitting room door. He glanced at Cat, then at Rhone. "Is everything all right?"

"We're fine."

Arnir smiled. "I'm glad. Bolt the door, just in case Jewel tries to come in."

Rhone nodded and closed the door behind him. He bolted it and the one to the bedroom. Once again he removed the cloak and mask, then crawled back into bed, undressed this time. He pulled Cat close. "Arnir brought some food. Do you want any?"

Cat wiped the last of her tears away. "No. My stomach is still sick and I hurt all over."

"Then go to sleep. I promise I'll be here when you wake up."

Rhone picked at the bread, cheese and fruit on the tray while Cat tried to rest. When he settled down, holding her, he fell asleep in a moment.

Chapter Twenty

Raimon Teale stepped through the temporary portal to his wine cellar, relieved the damn thing had actually worked. His chamberlain and commander followed a moment later.

"Crinon, bring wine to my study. Ulic, I need the box on the shelf."

Raimon carried on up the stairs and through the empty kitchen; he'd given the staff the day off to avoid unwanted eyes. His soldiers had stayed at the castle in Teale, completely unaware of their duke's plans. His current forces consisted of several hundred vauroks hiding with Mordach in White Deer Wood. The past several hours had been spent organizing those troops and finalizing plans.

Raimon was extraordinarily pleased with himself and his scheme to gain the crown of Kitring-Tor. Eight temporary portals were now in Mordach's hands, keyed to four places in the throne room. He hoped at least two of them would function properly. That afternoon would see over four years of hard work come to its inevitable conclusion.

The study's fireplace had grown cold long before. It didn't matter, he'd only be here a few minutes. Raimon sat in his favourite chair in front of the non-existent fire. The first step was the message to Rodrin, one that would call the dukes to council. Those not living in the city should have already arrived for the wedding, along with most of the barons.

When all were settled, waiting for Raimon to reveal his big discovery, the portals would open. His vauroks would kill everyone in the Hall, then spread to the rest of the castle, slaughtering whomever they could find, except for Prince Dayn. That weakling would be held hostage, ensuring the cooperation of the surviving nobility and commanders.

The deaths of the dukes and barons would throw the country in turmoil, open to invasion. Delcarion gathered those forces north of the Barriers to avoid detection; his portals seemed to stay open longer when entrance and exit were on the same world.

When Raimon gave the word, the vauroks, goblins, mountain trolls and hell wolves would pour into the country. He'd held an important piece of information from Lindren—the reason behind his many absences from both the city manor and his dukedom. Long hours had been spent keying temporary portals to strategic locations in Kitring-Tor.

Unfortunately, two of his barons discovered him with Mordach and were killed for their curiosity. Their widows mounted searches for them after Raimon pretended to respond to their requests for assistance. No matter, they'd find nothing.

Crinon and Ulic arrived. The chamberlain poured Raimon's wine, passing him the glass, adding a hasty bow, while the commander set the box on the desk. Both waited by the door.

Morning sunlight filtered through the sheer curtains on the glass doors, highlighting the rich, red liquid. He took a sip of his wine and wondered where Lindren was; languishing in one of the Black Lord's cells, no doubt. Apparently Delcarion wanted the daughter. Neither were Raimon's problem.

In all likelihood, the Silverwood Elves would find themselves at a disadvantage without their Elder and that suited him fine, all the easier to overrun the forest when the time came. The Elves currently in the castle were doomed, reducing their number further.

The end of Silverwood was for another day, though. Now, he had to concentrate on the task at hand. He removed a piece of paper from his desk, composing the message in his head before writing it down. When done, he set it aside to dry and turned his attention to the box.

Eight little blue balls remained. After a couple hours sleep, Raimon planned to tuck the orbs in his pocket, cushioned in an air spell, ready to use at the castle. The first one had Rodrin's name on it. He closed the lid and tossed back the wine.

"I'm going to get some sleep. Wake me in two hours, Crinon." Raimon strode out of the study and up the stairs.

He paused at Andros' door. His son's body would have to be buried soon, before it turned rank. A moment's regret, then he opened the door to his suite.

228

Cat awoke to bright sunlight and a familiar face. "Kelwyn?" She looked around the bedroom. Her heart leapt to her throat and her gut twisted. "Where's Rhone?" *He promised! He said he'd be here when I woke up!*

Kelwyn didn't appear upset, though his eyes weren't as bright as usual. "Running an errand. He'd hoped to be back before you woke."

Relief, then anguish washed over her. She threw herself in Kelwyn's arms, tears blurring her vision. "How could that man have said such a terrible thing? Lindren and the others know!"

He held her tight and kissed her forehead. "It's all right, Cat. I told them I lay with you to help your ache."

"That's what Rhone said." She sniffed. "I didn't want anyone finding out."

"Neither did I. It happened and we can't change it. Dwelling on it doesn't help either. Time to set it aside." Kelwyn wiped her tears with his sleeve. "None of them are upset anymore."

She let him hold her for a few minutes, calming her torn nerves, breathing in his light musky scent. "I want to go home."

Kelwyn rubbed her back. "What about Rhone?"

"He's the only reason I'd want to stay." She sighed. "I tried so hard to escape those chains and when I couldn't it scared me, and then I was so angry. I said some things Lindren won't like, but that man was going to take me. Right in front of Lindren!"

He stopped the massage and held her tighter. "I didn't think we'd get you back." His voice broke and tears misted Cat's eyes.

Images, some clear, some not, rampaged through her head—the sick Hrulka, the leering face of the young man who'd kidnapped her, Lindren tied up and a huge man in a cloak.

"Who was that man who hit me?" She touched her now healed cheek. "I haven't seen anyone that big since my people died."

"Lindren says he's the same one he saw when Udath Kor put that spell on him on Morata."

Cat pulled away enough to gaze up at him. "I thought Lindren

229

killed him."

"He wasn't sure he did. Shain thought there might more than one of them."

"That's frightening." She cuddled into him again. "Are the Hrulka all right? They were pretty sick." Cat resisted connecting to them. Her stomach churned and if the horses still felt nauseous she might throw up.

"Arnir checked on them last night and again this morning. They're much better and eating. Are they why you went to the stables instead of finding Rhone?"

Cat stiffened.

Kelwyn pushed her back. "Cat, what happened?"

She looked down. It all seemed so foolish now. "I felt something, a strange itch and then a buzzing. I thought it was just because people were watching me. When I went to the Winter Garden...I..." She hugged him. "I saw Rhone kissing Calli Yarrow."

"*What?*" Kelwyn held her at arm's length, his eyes dark. "He's upset because I'd been with you before we even met him and..."

Cat put her hand over his mouth. "He explained. She guessed who he was and told him he had to meet her in the garden or she'd tell her uncle he was still alive."

Kelwyn removed her hand. "So that's who he had to meet."

She nodded. "Rhone said he had to pretend to still like Calli so he had to let her kiss him." She snuggled back into Kelwyn's arms. "He says he has to keep pretending, too. She's a terrible person. Rhone says they were together the night her father was killed and she didn't come forward and say it, so he was blamed for something he didn't do."

"It's not acceptable here to lay with someone you're not bonded to," Kelwyn said. "Besides, you don't like talking about those things, maybe she doesn't either."

Cat pulled away. "If it meant someone's life, I'd talk. I couldn't let someone die for something like that, especially if I loved him."

"I know you wouldn't. She obviously would." His eyes had lightened, though still not the normal bright silver.

"I'm worried, Kel. Rhone's running out of time. He won't be able to prove he's innocent unless she talks."

"Maybe he can convince her to come forward," he said. "Which means he's going to have to spend more time with her." Kelwyn held her chin in his hand and kissed her nose. "So, I'm assuming after you saw Rhone and Calli, you ran."

"Only to the door of the garden. Then I decided to walk to the stables. I needed to cry, but didn't want everyone seeing me, so I thought I'd go to the Hrulka, except, as I got closer, I realized what the buzzing in my head was. It was them, trying to tell me they were sick. When I got there, Krir was down on his knees and the Hrulka were moaning and I didn't know what to do. I felt something hit my thigh, then my arm, and the guards who followed me went down. After that, everything's kind of hazy. I remember that man, though. The one who tried to…"

Kelwyn crushed her to him. "It's over now. He's dead. He can't hurt you anymore."

"I know, but I still see his face." She was afraid she'd see him for quite awhile in her nightmares.

Cat's stomach growled and Kelwyn let her go. "Nausea's gone?" he asked.

"Most of it. I think I can eat now. Arnir said I'm not allowed out of my rooms."

Kelwyn stood. "No, not until Raimon Teale shows his face. It's not a problem, though. Wait here." He disappeared into the sitting room and came back a moment later with a tray. "It's part of our breakfasts. We did the same thing for Lindren."

Cat scrunched back into the pillows and stretched out her legs. Kelwyn set the tray on her lap. "Did you get enough to eat?" she asked, taking a tentative nibble off a slice of brown bread.

"Yes. There was plenty of food last night and the king has asked for more generous portions for us."

The bread paused half way to her mouth. "Last night. I missed the ceremony. I really wanted to see it."

"You didn't miss much," Kelwyn said. "The king and Selesa's father signed a bunch of papers and then everyone stood around eating and drinking. I think it's just another excuse for a party."

"What about tomorrow? I might miss that too if Raimon doesn't

231

come out of hiding." Her heart sank at the thought.

"You can't worry about that right now. What happens, happens." Kelwyn motioned to the food she held in her hand. "Eat."

Cat ate, relieved her stomach let her, though she still felt sad about possibly missing the wedding. When she finished, Kelwyn set the tray on the bedside table. "If I do have to miss it, will you tell me everything? Especially all about Selesa's dress."

"I'll do that." Kelwyn smiled, his eyes now their usual shade. "I still think you should wear one of yours."

A knock sounded at the bedroom door. Kelwyn unbolted and opened it. Rhone came in, holding something under his cloak. "I'd hoped I'd get back before you woke," he said to Cat. "I brought you something." He pulled out a squirming, furry, little bundle. It hissed and spat. "Careful, its claws are sharp. Took a demon's time to catch it."

"What is it?' Cat asked, tentatively probing the creature's mind. Anger, frustration and fear poured through her head. She sent a calming thought to it...no, him.

Rhone cast her an odd look. "A cat. Kitten actually. This one looks about three months old. You don't have them in Silverwood?"

She shook her head and took the squirming kitten from Rhone, soothing it with her mind. "I've never seen one this close." The animal responded quickly to her comfort, settling into her arms.

"I found it in the stable," Rhone explained. "There's always plenty of them around to control the rats and mice."

"It's a male," Cat said, smiling up at Rhone and Kelwyn. "He's beautiful. And so soft."

The cat wasn't much like the one she'd seen when they'd first arrived in Tezerain. That one was fluffy with black and white fur. The little creature she held in her hands had short fur, a brownish grey with dark stripes. The tips of his ears and tail were black, the belly and feet white.

He screwed up his little face. "Mwah."

Cat's heart floated in her chest. "He's so sweet!" She stroked his fur smooth and he made a funny rumbling sound. Worried now, she looked up at Rhone. "He's making a strange noise. Is he snoring, like you

232

do? He doesn't look asleep."

Rhone laughed, so did Kelwyn. "He's purring. It means he's happy."

She confirmed it with a touch of her mind. Cat smiled again, her heart warm from more than the gift.

"You could be stuck here for a few days, so I thought you'd like company of a different sort." Rhone pulled a piece of twine out of his pocket. "Got this from the stable too. Watch." He dangled it in front of the kitten who batted it with his paws, rolling over on Cat's lap as he tried to snag the string. When he did, his claw stuck and Rhone tugged his paw up and down. The little cat tried to bite the twine and everyone laughed.

Rhone passed the string to Cat and she played with the kitten. "What are you going to call him?" he asked.

Cat stopped moving the twine and the kitten grabbed it, stuffing it in his mouth. "He needs a name?"

"Most people name their pets." Rhone reached down to stroke the little animal. The kitten dug its claws into his glove and rabbit-kicked his hand. He chuckled and picked the kitten off him. It dashed to the other side of the bed, then crouched, watching as Cat moved the twine, it's eyes darting everywhere, examining any movement.

"I'll have to think about it," she said. Letting the kitten play with the twine by itself, she pulled Rhone's head down and kissed his cheek. "Thank you."

Rhone smiled, his sea-green eyes sparkling. "You're welcome. A box of dirt for him will be arriving soon."

"Dirt?" Cat jerked the string and the kitten pounced.

"His own personal garderobe."

"I'm going to Lindren's room," Kelwyn said, an odd catch to his voice. "He wasn't awake when I checked earlier."

"All right," Cat said, flashing him a smile. "Thank you for the food."

"You're welcome." Kelwyn left.

Rhone sat on the bed and gathered Cat in his arms. "Would you like a better kiss?"

He leaned over and Cat put her hand over his mouth. "I would,"

233

she said. "But my mouth tastes terrible. And I really need a bath."

"So do I. The guards in the hall know you're here. I'll have them ask for a bath for me." Rhone kissed her forehead and strode to the outer door, pulling up his mask.

While waiting for the water and tub to arrive, Cat amused herself with the kitten, wondering what she could call him. She'd never had a pet before, not a real one. Spiders, flies, toads and frogs didn't really count. The kitten fell asleep just before the bath showed up, curled in a little ball in the middle of the bed.

When the men setting up the bath left, Cat shed her dirty tunic and wondered if Rhianna could obtain any more of the cloth to replace the trousers. She slipped into the bath, the water hot and wonderfully soothing. While waiting for the bath, Rhone had built a fire and the snapping and crackling helped calm her. He shed his cloak and armoured jerkin, rolled up his sleeves and helped Cat wash her hair. When she was done, he had his turn while she towel-dried her hair in the comfy chair by the fire. It took several rinses with water and two mint sticks before her mouth felt clean again.

She helped Rhone dry off and they headed for the bedroom. He settled himself on top of her and treated her to a long, delicious kiss.

"I'm glad you stayed," Cat said.

"So am I." He nuzzled her neck.

A rapid series of knocks sounded at the outer door. Rhone cursed and pulled on various items of clothing. When he answered the door, Darsha and Shain burst in. Cat scooted out of bed and grabbed a shirt from the wardrobe. It was the one the seamstresses had made.

"Raimon's sent a message," Darsha said, holding a brown robe in his hands. "He claims to have important information and wants all the dukes to meet for council with Rodrin."

Shain grinned. "Get dressed, Cat. It looks like the ruse worked."

�’ · ꞔ

Lindren awoke to see Kelwyn sitting by the bed.

"I was starting to worry about you," his nephew said. "Cat's been awake for a while." He stood. "I'll wait for you in the sitting room so you can get dressed. Mathyn's here by the way."

It wasn't just Mathyn. Yira waited for him as well.

"You gave us quite a scare," the captain said. "We scoured several dozen ships before Darsha sent word you'd been found." He chuckled. "Discovered a couple smugglers and several people who'd been pressed. We're less than popular on the docks right now."

"I appreciate it, Mathyn. I just wish I hadn't been so foolish as to step into Raimon's trap." Lindren sat in his chair by the fire, next to Yira, and ran his fingers through his hair to force it to lay down properly. Kelwyn set a covered tray on the table between them.

"Don't be so hard on yourself." Yira patted his arm. "You couldn't possibly have known what Raimon was up to."

"He was acting strange. I should have suspected something." Lindren removed the cloth from the tray.

"The cheese is a little dried around the edges," Kelwyn said. "It's a collection of food from our breakfasts."

"It's just fine, Kelwyn, thank you." Any food looked good.

Lindren ate everything on the tray, relating events of the last couple days with Mathyn and his soulmate. He'd just finished the last bite when Arnir came in, carrying a brown robe similar to the one Rodrin had worn the day before.

"Raimon Teale sent a message," Arnir said. "Apparently he has some information and wants Rodrin to gather the dukes for a council. He'll be here soon."

Lindren gripped the arms of the chair. "Whatever it is he wants, we can't trust him. What are Rodrin's plans?"

"He doesn't trust him either. Raimon's son can't be found. No one has seen him for over two days and the king figures he's in league with his father. Only a handful of dukes will be there with as many soldiers as Rodrin feels he can use and not scare off Teale. He also wants us there, all of us." Arnir pointed to the robe. "You and Cat are to wear these. She can let him know when Raimon is lying. There will be several other monks in attendance so you don't stick out."

"That worries me," Lindren said, taking the robe from the back of

235

his chair.

"Are you expecting a fight?" Kelwyn asked.

Lindren set the robe on his lap, glad he'd had a good sleep and something in his stomach. "With those new portals, anything is possible."

"Hadn't thought of it." Mathyn stood and held his hand out to Yira. "Need more help? I can have forty Elves here within the hour, along with Ardamin and Hanrish."

Lindren stood. "It would be appreciated. Arnir, Kelwyn, I suggest you put your mail on under your tunics so Raimon doesn't see it."

Everyone left. Lindren dug his mail out of the wardrobe and put it on, slipping his tunic overtop. His sword belt came next, then the robe. He listened at the door for any wandering servants, opened it and risked a peek. Only the guards were visible. Lindren crossed to Cat's room and gave a knock.

Darsha answered it. "I think we're all ready here."

Cat stood near the fire, swathed in a robe like his.

Lindren closed the door. "No, you're not."

At the questioning glances, he said, "There's every chance we could be facing a fight. With those small portals, Teale could have a sizable force here in no time. Hide your mail."

Shain and Darsha ducked back to their rooms.

Rhone helped Cat into her mail, stuffing the edges of her still damp hair into the coif, then helped her back into the robe.

Lindren set a hand on her shoulder. "I need you to stick close to me. Rodrin wants you to let him know when Raimon is lying. Don't say anything, we don't want him to guess who you are until the right time."

Cat nodded, her eyes bright with excitement. When Darsha and Shain returned, Arnir and Kelwyn in tow, they left for the throne room. Rodrin waited for them, Gailen and Dayn flanking him, all armed. Just behind Rodrin stood Dukes Alain Randin, Greyson Yarrow, Denys Bearne, Blaise Rilandon and Tyrol Corsin, the brother of Tomis, Rodrin's chamberlain. Two dozen guards stood alert at the entrance and exit to the Hall as well as at the stairs and door to the Art Gallery. Another dozen men in the brown robes of Ar's monks were scattered around the room. At least the king had the sense not to use real monks.

Rodrin motioned Lindren over to the throne. "I'll let him sink himself first. When I tap my fingers on the arm of my chair three times, reveal yourself."

Lindren agreed. As the rest of the Silverwood Elves entered the Hall, he bent down close to Cat's ear. "Check to see if anyone has black lights. We don't need any more surprises."

She scanned the room and shook her head. He smiled, pleased she remembered not to speak. Now all they had to do was wait. It seemed an eternity before word came that Raimon had arrived. Mathyn's Elves hadn't showed yet, which worried him.

The duke strode into the hall as if he owned the world, his normal attitude, then stopped when he saw who waited for him. Four guards moved in front of the closed door, preventing his escape in that direction.

Raimon frowned. "Your Majesty, I thought we were holding a council meeting, not an Elven festival."

Rodrin set the base of his scepter on the floor in front of him. "Lord Lindren's and Lady Cat's lives may depend on what you have to say."

The Duke of Teale walked the blue carpet towards Rodrin's throne, his eyes darting everywhere.

He'd almost reached the throne when Rodrin held his hand up. "You can report from there. What is this information you bring?"

Raimon frowned again and put a hand in one of his pockets. He bowed, stiff and formal. "I must first apologize for my lack of attendance yesterday, Your Majesty. I was called away to a meeting with an old friend of mine who said he had important information."

Cat shook her head. Lindren wasn't surprised. Raimon had no friends who weren't nobility. If the man was of the upper classes, he'd have mentioned the fellow's name.

Rodrin glanced in Cat's direction then set his steel blue eyes back on Duke Raimon. "I ask you again, what is this information?"

Raimon paused a moment, his brows dipped in a fierce frown. "He says he just came back from a trip to the Barriers, visiting a cousin or some such. There's been increased activity in the mountains, so much so, that the barons have sent to Silverwood for help."

Lindren's heart thumped, then eased when Cat shook her head.

"That's bad news, with Lindren missing," the king said.

Raimon bowed his head. "Just so. Which is why I felt it important to tell you as soon as I could."

"I have also recently found out news of my own," the king said. "Apparently one of my dukes was responsible for Jornel Yarrow's death four years ago."

Raimon stiffened. "The board decided Rhone Arden was guilty of the murder."

"It turns out the board was wrong and you proclaimed Rhone's guilt the loudest." Rodrin leaned forward, gripping his upright scepter in his left hand. "Did you order Jornel Yarrow killed?"

Lindren turned a quick eye to Rhone, who stood behind Cat, ramrod straight. He had his hand on his sword hilt, the other on the dagger at his waist.

Teale's cold blue eyes flew open. "Your Majesty! Of course not!"

Rodrin glanced at Cat, who shook her head once more. He tapped his fingers on the arm of the throne three times.

Lindren lowered his hood. "We believe you did."

Raimon snarled. "How did you escape?"

"Two little boys. You'd call them street urchins." Lindren shed his robe and set his hand on his sword. "I am officially accusing Duke Raimon Teale of murdering Jornel Yarrow, black sorcery, drugging me, tying me up and plotting, with a vaurok, to turn me over to the Black Lord. He's also harbouring vauroks and hiding information as to what really happened in the Barriers last summer."

The princes' jaws dropped. Four of the dukes gasped and muttered amongst themselves. Greyson Yarrow pulled his sword. "You killed my brother?" he roared. "*Why?*"

Now that the truth was out Raimon appeared relaxed. "He caught me using black magic. I realize now I should have been more careful, but..." He shrugged.

Rhone stepped closer to the duke. "Why did you put him in Rhone Arden's room?"

Raimon frowned. "I don't know you. I don't have to answer your questions."

The king thumped his scepter. "Yes, you do. I want to know the answer."

Raimon shrugged again. "Quite brilliant that. Young Arden was a real fireball. Energetic, smart, brave, cocky, just the sort of commander who'd achieve great things. I saw an opportunity to deal your kingdom a blow and took it."

With a growl, Rhone launched himself at Teale.

Lindren grabbed him around the waist. "Don't kill him. Yet."

Now they had Rodrin's attention. The king's eyes narrowed. "What's going on?"

"There are five dukes in attendance," Lindren said. "Not counting Teale. Enough to call a board of peers to clear Rhone Arden's name. Do you all agree that the case should be re-opened?"

One by one, the dukes nodded. Greyson was emphatic. "Yes."

Lindren released Rhone and gave him a nod. Arden's youngest son lowered his hood and pulled off his mask, for good.

Rodrin stared. "Well, I'll be..."

Raimon took a step back. "You were supposed to have died on that ship!"

Rhone's jaw clenched. "You sent that storm? I thought there was something strange about it." He stepped towards the traitorous duke.

Raimon pulled his hand out of his pocket. "I can honestly say it wasn't me. But it does mean I can kill you now!" Quicker than Lindren thought possible for a Human, Teale threw three small blue balls, one at the king, another at Rhone, the third at Lindren, who recognized them. Blue-white trails of light followed the orbs.

Time seemed to slow. Duke Blaise, a lean man, well into his seventies, caught the ball meant for Rodrin; Cat, the one for Rhone. Talifir leapt in front of Lindren, taking the glowing orb on his chest. It burrowed quickly through his tunic and the tiny gaps in his mail. Screams erupted from three mouths – Blaise, Talifir and Cat.

Chapter Twenty-One

The smell of burning flesh singed the air as Cat's screams echoed in the rafters. Kelwyn drew his sword and ran towards Teale. Dayn beat him. The prince dove off the dais, striking Raimon's head from his shoulders before the duke could pull anything else out of his pocket. Kelwyn changed direction mid-stride and headed for Cat. He knelt by her side, Rhone opposite him. She screamed and writhed, keeping her hand as far from her as possible. Rhone tried to hold her down, with little success. Dayn appeared, sword smeared with Teale's blood, his eyes wide, face pale.

"Don't touch those orbs!" Lindren cried over the screams of the victims.

The little ball had burrowed into Cat's hand. No blood escaped the wound. Kelwyn stared as the flesh around it dissolved, lit by a blue fire, spreading in an ever widening pattern. Dragon magic glowed blue; this was different, softer, pretty in a sickening sort of way. The deep sapphire radiance of Cat's dragon bones exuded comfort, not horror.

Nearby, Arnir knelt over screaming Talifir, his hands glowing white as he chanted to center his magic. Lindren knelt beside him while Arilan and Therrin tried to hold Talifir still. Two of the dukes and one of the guards attended Duke Blaise. Rodrin sat on his throne, his face steaming with anger.

Kelwyn laid his sword on the floor and lifted Cat so she leaned against him. Every muscle in her body was taut, the veins in her neck stood out like roots. She kicked and shook her hand, trying to dislodge the thing. Her fingers disappeared. The terrible glow crawled up her wrist, disappearing into the sleeve of her mail and worry crept into Kelwyn's heart.

"What can we do?" Rhone asked, his features dark.

"I don't know. I thought she could fight it, but it's eating her." *She's Tiranen! She should be able to fight it.* Kelwyn pushed up the mail sleeve, taking care not to touch her skin. The blue light ate more of her arm, her shirt with it. *Arvanion! Help us!*

Talifir gave one last shriek and fell silent.

"I can't stop it!" Arnir cried. Talifir was his childhood friend.

Lindren rose and turned to Cat. "Hold her arm out," he said. "Keep it steady."

Kelwyn slid back and gently lowered Cat to the floor. He stretched out her arm and pushed up the sleeves of her mail and shirt, while Rhone practically lay on top of her. Dayn held her legs. With one swing of his sword, Lindren removed her arm, just below the elbow. She screamed again as blood spurted.

Lindren grabbed the robe he'd worn and wrapped it around the stump. "Now she can heal," he said in Elven. He strode off to attend Duke Blaise.

Cat's severed arm slowly vanished in a flurry of blue sparks. Kelwyn wanted, needed, to hold her. He couldn't as Rhone now had her clutched to his chest. Dayn crouched nearby, his hand reaching for her as if he, too, wanted to comfort her. She sobbed, gradually regaining a measure of control. The first part of her healing kicked in, dulling the pain, readying her for healing sleep. This was a pain she understood. Kelwyn clenched his fist, wishing he could have beat Dayn to Raimon Teale. The bastard wouldn't have died so quickly.

He glanced in the traitor's direction. His body lay on the right side, the same side as the pocket that held the balls. A blue glow lit the underside where it touched the floor. As Kelwyn watched, the body of Raimon Teale began to disappear. He left Cat with Rhone and stood over the dead duke. Lindren joined him.

"Greyson removed Blaise's arm," his uncle said.

"Why is it happening to him?" Kelwyn pointed at what remained of Teale.

"I'd say he had more of those balls in his pocket. When I was tied up in his wine cellar, he demonstrated one of them. He put a spell on his hands. I think it was air. I'd say he did a similar thing here, but the spell died with him."

Perhaps it was best Teale died fast.

Arnir still knelt over Talifir, his hands glowing white, deep in concentration. He let out a long breath. "I can't find the source," he said. His voice broke and he took a moment to control himself. "I'm going to have to study one of the balls to figure out how to stop it."

"I don't know where we can get one, son," Lindren said. He pointed to Teale's body. "I think the others are broken."

Arnir nodded and sat beside Talifir, who's body slowly vanished as they watched. The soldiers disguised as monks, their hoods now down, huddled in a group near the fireplace, murmuring amongst themselves. The Silverwood Elves quietly grieved for the loss of one of their own. Kelwyn thought of Elyria, Talifir's soulmate. There was now one more *qira* in Silverwood. He wondered if she'd still be there when they returned home; the two had no children, there'd be no reason for her not to *fade*.

Then he thought of Talifir's parents. They'd know something was wrong when Elyria turned *qira* and he had no way to tell Rhianna that he was all right. Kelwyn's fist clenched and he wished he could kill something, anything.

Rodrin sat up straight and pointed to a spot on the north wall. "What the hells is that?"

A grey mass swirled against the oak on the east side of the massive stone fireplace.

"It's a portal!" Kelwyn's yell was taken up by the other Elves, who drew their swords. In seconds, the portal opened and vauroks poured out.

A vaurok grabbed one of the disguised soldiers and tore his head off, bellowing in triumph. He lost his own head a moment later to one of the fake monk's blades.

"There's another over here!" Darsha's voice came from somewhere near the Art Gallery. "And another!"

Kelwyn balanced his sword and ran for the nearest vaurok. Death rode in his heart.

Metal on metal rang throughout the room. Lindren pulled his sword and turned to Rodrin, who stared wide eyed at the invasion in his throne room. "Get out of here! Take Blaise, Cat and your sons with you!" Several guards had already swarmed to their king, weapons raised in protection.

Rodrin almost jumped off his throne. "Gailen get the door! Dayn, help with Lady Cat! Greyson, Denys, get Blaise out of here!"

Everyone snapped into action. Gailen ran for the doors to the dining hall, the others following. He tugged on them several times. "They won't open!"

Lindren dashed to his side, centering his magic. The sickly taint of a black spell washed over him. "They're spelled shut!"

Someone pounded on the other side. It sounded like Vergel. Rodrin must have had more men in the dining hall, just in case. They'd do little good now.

"That futtering bastard!" Rodrin unsheathed his sword. Not the ceremonial one he usually wore, this one was meant to kill. Gailen followed suit.

Lindren pushed them under the stone stairs. "Stay here! It's easier to protect you."

Greyson Yarrow and Denys Bearne carried an unconscious Blaise and laid him behind Rodrin. Dayn and Rhone tried to do the same with Cat. She fought them.

"I have to fight!" she cried, unclipping her tchiru with her left hand, tears still dampening her cheeks.

Rhone grabbed her shoulders. "You're in no shape. You've got no right hand!"

"I can use my left." She shed the cumbersome robe. "It doesn't hurt that much anymore, not like that blue thing."

The stump of her arm had almost stopped bleeding. The Tiranen healing process would have dulled the pain and now Cat's natural fighting instincts took control. In this instant, she was pure Tiranen. The mail sleeve slid down, covering the stump. Her eyes glazed, possibly from pain, perhaps from the strange state she fought in.

Lindren sliced a chunk out of his robe with his boot dagger, then folded and wrapped it around her stump, tying off the remains of the shirt sleeve to help hold it in place.

"Let her go," Lindren said to Rhone. "We can't stop her when she's like this. Just stay close to her right side."

Rhone nodded. He removed his cloak, tossed it near the stairs and followed Cat into the fray.

Dayn watched her go, his eyes wide. "I wish I could use my magic, but it's too crowded to throw fire."

"You proved you can use that sword at your waist. Use it now to protect your father and Duke Blaise." Lindren didn't wait for his response. He turned his attention to the maelstrom of Elves, Humans and vauroks, each fighting for their lives.

Over the din of battle, he heard another sound, yelling and thumps coming from the east doors to the throne room. Raimon had spelled both sets of doors closed and the Ringwood Elves were trying to get in. A quick search showed Darsha and Shain fighting near the Art Gallery, protecting Arnir who tried to close one of the four portals. Lindren headed in that direction, engaging a vaurok before he took half a dozen steps.

ℂ · ℛ

Steel ground against bone as Kelwyn dug his long sword further into the vaurok's chest, giving it a vicious twist before pulling it out. He kicked the body aside, into another vaurok. The second vaurok lost his balance and Kelwyn released his pent-up anger. One mighty, well-aimed swing cut the vaurok almost in half, hitting between two bands of thin iron girding its leather cuirass. Its nostril slits flared and it screeched, stretching thin lips over dagger sharp teeth. Kelwyn dragged his sword out of the vaurok and slammed it into the thing's head, spraying blood and bone over Rodrin's carpet. He didn't much care.

Raimon must not have sat high in Udath Kor's favour. These vauroks were the smaller variety, only six to six-and-a-half feet tall,

244

except for one who fought nearby. That one stood a full seven feet. The big vaurok caught Zain on the shoulder, sending the Silverwood Elf stumbling to the ground. Two strides took Kelwyn close enough to thrust his bloody sword into its back. The vaurok grunted as the blade hit a band on the front of the cuirass.

The creature spun, yanking Kelwyn's sword from his grip. He dodged the vaurok's hastily swung short sword, then stepped behind it and, with a sickening crunch, twisted its neck. The vaurok dropped to the floor. Kelwyn pulled his sword out of its back and searched for another.

℘ • ℭ

A now familiar nausea washed over Lindren as he tried to locate the thread that tied the portal to its location. Darsha and Shain cut down any vaurok who tried to come through while two of his Elves, Therrin and Arilan, protected him and Arnir from those already in the room.

Lindren searched the bottom of the portal where the thread on its larger cousin would be...it wasn't there. He sent his quest farther up. Mathyn and his Elves pounded on the outer doors, while others did the same on the ones leading to the dining room. A splintering of wood was almost drowned in the clamour of the battle, the screams of the dying.

Lindren couldn't check it's source, he had to concentrate on the thread. Then he found it in the center, a band of thick, black magic spanning the minute distance between the portal and the wall. Lindren focused his power and peeled the fabric of the thread apart, strand by strand. It took only a few moments, though it seemed forever. The portal shrunk to a dot, then vanished.

Another crack sounded from the outer doors. Lindren turned in that direction. The silvery shine of metal appeared in the door, accompanied by another crack. An axe. Mathyn was hacking his way through.

"On to the next," Lindren said. His sons, Arilan and Therrin followed him.

245

ଔ · ଔ

Rhone jammed his foot against a dead vaurok and took a shattering blow on the flat of his sword. He pushed, keeping the new enemy at bay while Cat leapt and danced beside him, her tchiru removing the head of another vaurok. It had taken her a few minutes to find her balance, but now she fought like a whirlwind of destruction. Rhone tried to duck inside the guard of the vaurok he faced and take it with his dagger. The creature dodged. Cat spun, taking advantage of the vaurok's preoccupation with Rhone, and stabbed her magical sword through its neck. Her mail had been damaged in the battle on the ship and she now bled from two wounds, one in her side, the other on her right leg. She appeared to take no more notice of it than she did her severed arm. Rhone couldn't even imagine such a thing.

Three more of the damned creatures came at them. He parried a blow from the one on the right. Cat did the same on the left. The middle one, with a howl of glee, stabbed him through his jerkin, despite Rhone's attempt to block it with his dagger. His belly erupted in pain.

He stumbled backwards, pulling himself off the filthy blade, and tripped over a body. Rhone landed with a grunt, his vision a blur. He lost hold of his dagger and it flew into the air. *Cat!* He promised Lindren he'd protect her, just as he'd promised to keep her safe from the kidnapper. Rhone had failed at one, he couldn't fail at the other.

Struggling to his feet, he watched Cat slice through the chest of the vaurok who'd struck him. Holding his gut with his left hand, he stopped a blow from the vaurok on the right, one intended to strike her neck. He twisted his sword, yanking the weapon out of the vaurok's hand, then skewered the ugly thing. The vaurok on the left had fallen to Cat. A crash and a bellow came from the outer doors. Rhone prayed it wasn't more vauroks.

ଔ · ଔ

One of Rodrin's soldiers fought a vaurok near the fireplace. He was losing. Kelwyn dashed to his side, too late to save the man's life, just two steps away when the creature ripped the man's throat with a jagged

246

dagger. Kelwyn swung down, splitting the vaurok's head. Part of it spun away to fall into the fire. Now burning flesh added to the aroma of filthy vaurok, blood, sweat, fear and death. Bile surged, burning his throat.

Raimon's features appeared, attached to a vaurok's body. Kelwyn thrust his blade into it. Blood sprayed in a geyser of gore. Then Talon's smirking face materialized and he hacked it. Words echoed in his head, 'Bet you don't know she was futtering that dark haired Elf.' With a cry of rage, Kelwyn struck again and again, his spelled sword slicing skin and iron bands. Green blood splattered his face, his mail, adding to that already there.

Kelwyn had taken three injuries, a shallow stab to the upper right side of his chest, another to his left arm, above his elbow, the third to the left thigh. The pain was a dim second to the anger coursing through him. Dairon's distorted face swam up from his memories and he swung again and again. He hit nothing.

Wiping blood from his eyes, he glanced around a room piled with bodies—vaurok, Elven and Human. Kelwyn panted, absorbing the sight before him. No one alive was nearby. All four portals had vanished.

Rodrin still stood under the staircase, his sons in front of him, both with bloodied swords. Blood also smeared the king's blade. Several guards lay at their feet entwined in a grisly embrace with dead vauroks.

Arnir crouched with Lindren near a fallen Elf, close to the Art Gallery, his cousin's hands bright with the white glow of healing. Darsha, Shain, Therrin and Arilan stood over them, their swords at the ready. Mathyn fought near the outer doors, his men surrounding the healers working on injured Elves. Rodrin's guards filled in the gaps behind them. No vaurok remained except those near Mathyn. It was almost over.

Near the stairs, he caught sight of a coifed head leaking strands of silver hair, a familiar head that lay too close to the ground. "Cat!"

Kelwyn leapt over bodies, some writhing in pain, others still. The wound in his thigh reminded him of its presence. He ignored it. Cat sat on the floor, cradling someone in her good arm, tears in her dull eyes.

Those beautiful eyes widened. "You're hurt!" she cried in Elven. She struggled just to remain sitting.

"I'm fine for now." He dragged his gaze from her sweet, blood covered face to the body she held. It was Rhone. He lay still, his skin pale and slick with sweat. "Is he…alive?"

"Yes, but not for long. He's got too many wounds. Get Arnir! Please!"

Kelwyn spun and almost lost his balance as pain lanced up his left thigh. He reached out and caught the end of the wooden banister, sending more agony shooting up his wounded arm.

"You're not all right!" Cat cried.

His vision wavered and he struggled to regain control. "I can find Arnir."

Kelwyn stumbled in the direction he'd last seen his cousins and uncle. *The Art Gallery.* Bodies piled on bodies, mostly vauroks, hindered his movement.

When he drew close, Lindren looked up at him. "What got into you? I've never seen you fight so brutal."

He spoke in Elven. Kelwyn answered in kind. "No one hurts my family." He fought to stand up straight.

Arnir stood, then frowned when he saw Kelwyn. "You look terrible. What did you do? Bath in vaurok blood?" His eyes took in the wounds. "You'd better lay down before you fall down. Do you want me to put you out?"

Kelwyn grabbed his arm, more for balance than attention. "I can wait. Rhone's dying. He's with Cat by the stairs."

"Chew some raw sleeproot while I'm gone," Arnir said.

Kelwyn just nodded and watched his cousin walk away.

₨   •   ₲

Arnir strode towards Cat, his father and brothers following.

"Arnir!" his sister cried, her tear-filled eyes searching the room.

"I'm here," he answered and knelt at Rhone's right side. The man was in bad shape. Arnir didn't need his magic to see it. Elven custom dictated he should leave him to die; Arnir couldn't do that to Cat. A quick glance confirmed no Human stood close by. Rodrin and his sons remained under the stairs while Rhone lay by the bottom of the steps.

Everyone else was busy caring for the wounded.

Arnir tugged the glove off Rhone's left hand and pulled it onto his own. Rolling the Human over onto his side, he slid his right hand under the man's jerkin and shirt where it couldn't be seen, laying it flat against the skin of his back. Lindren didn't say a word, just set his hand on Arnir's arm and leaned over, as if to confer with him, hiding the glow of his magic and lending him his magical strength.

Arnir whispered the chant to centre his power. Rhone lay near death, bleeding heavily from wounds in his belly, leg and right arm. He had several other cuts, not serious, including one on his scalp.

Pulling the sides of the damaged stomach together with his magic, Arnir built tissue and veins until they were whole once more, though he left the slice in the skin. With that done, he concentrated on the leg wound, borrowing some of Lindren's power to repair it, then worked on the injured arm.

Now that the worst of Rhone's wounds were dealt with, Arnir had to coax the man's system to work harder than usual; Rhone's blood needed to be replaced. The man would be terribly thirsty when he woke.

"I can't heal him all the way, Cat," Arnir explained. "People have noticed he's down and if he has no wound, they'll be suspicious. The head wound will suffice to explain why he's unconscious. Rhone's out of danger. You need to sleep."

Cat nodded and wiped her tears. She almost fell over onto Rhone.

Lindren helped ease her down so her head rested on Rhone's chest, then glanced around them. "It looks like the fight is over. Darsha, carry Cat upstairs. Shain, get someone to help you with Rhone."

Arnir's brothers nodded and he stood. Kelwyn sat near the Art Gallery, his head resting on his chest. He headed there, worried about his cousin. As he checked him over, Kelwyn raised his head, not saying a word. His thigh wound still bled and needed immediate attention. Though he'd also lost a lot of blood, the other two injuries could wait.

Several minutes later, Arnir and Lindren left him. Therrin waved to get his attention. Zain was down, his next patient. Before he reached the Elf, he already had control of his magic and tried to force aside the memory of the screams of poor dead Talifir.

Chapter Twenty-Two

The gentle murmur of Arnir's healing lent a subtle backdrop to Lindren's wandering thoughts. He rubbed his eyes with his free hand, wondering when this mess would finally end. Never had a trip to Tezerain been as stressful as this one, and not much of it could be blamed on Cat. *Strange,* he thought, *if I hadn't brought her, we wouldn't have discovered Raimon's treachery in time.* If not for the prophecies, he'd have attended Gailen's wedding celebrations alone and probably been captured while Kitring-Tor fell to the duke's deceit.

What made him decide to search for those prophecies when he did remained a mystery. He'd waited all those years, why now? All he could come up with was that it felt right. The prophecies could only have come from Arvanion. Was this his way of countering a move by Udath Kor?

A sigh from Arnir brought Lindren out of his thoughts. The whole affair had to be doubly hard on his third son. Not only did he help close the portals and heal the wounded, he grieved for Talifir. Nothing of Arnir's childhood friend remained except his mail and a few bits of metal—his dagger, sword, some coins, buttons and a belt buckle—now buried somewhere in the blood and bodies. Lindren would have died if not for his bravery. He'd have to think of an appropriate line to add to Cyrun's Song of Remembering.

As soon as Arnir finished healing Zain, another mage would have to take over lending him power; there was something else that needed Lindren's attention. Fortunately, Mathyn had brought along fourteen weather mages. The healers would have plenty of support.

Arnir finished with Zain and sat back. "You've done enough, Father. Time for a break."

"I was just thinking the same thing." Lindren scanned the busy room. Elves and Humans bent over bodies, separating the dead from the living. A quick count showed most of his Elves standing or sitting; he hoped they'd only lost Talifir. Tywyn glanced in his direction and he waved the Ringwood weather mage over. "I can't rest though," he said to Arnir, "I need to find someone who can help with the dining room doors. Vergel is behind them."

"Why didn't he go around and come down the stairs?" Arnir asked.

"That's what I'd like to know." Rodrin's guards poured through the smashed doors, lending assistance where needed. Among them he spotted Wendyl Banren and several of the priestesses of Vania who assisted him.

When Tywyn had picked his way through the dead and injured, he said, "There's two near the fireplace who need your help."

"I'll head there now," Arnir said, rising to his feet. "Father's tired, I'll need your assistance if you're available."

"I am." Tywyn led him to the wounded Elves.

Lindren rose from his crouch and headed for the stairs. Cat and Rhone had been taken to her rooms, though Darsha and Shain had yet to return. Rodrin's carpet was ruined. Blood — vaurok, Elf and Human — had soaked into the fabric. The room stunk with the aftermath of the battle and Lindren's stomach heaved from the odour of cooked flesh. He forced down his rising gorge. Blaise Rilandon lay under the staircase, protected by Dayn who held his bloodied sword in one hand, shock plain on his young face as he stared at the bodies around him.

The king stood with Gailen near the dining hall doors. His commander-general still tried to pound his way through.

"Wendyl is going to have his hands full." Rodrin said. "I've sent for healers from the town. We've got too many injured and dying men."

"Our healers are doing what they can for the worst injuries," Lindren said. Fortunately all Elven healers knew the ways Humans cared for their wounded.

Rodrin shook his head. "I don't understand why Vergel didn't come by the stairs when he found the doors shut."

"Neither do I." Lindren scanned the room once more and caught the attention of two of Mathyn's weather mages, Zeric and Vron. He motioned them over. "We're going to try to remove the spell on the

251

doors," he told the king. Tired though he was, it needed to be done.

He explained his plan to the Elves. Zeric rested one hand on Vron's, while Vron did the same for Lindren. All three chanted the words to focus their power. Rodrin and Gailen stood back.

Lindren cast a tentative touch to the spell on the doors expecting a rush of nausea. He wasn't disappointed. Added to the smell of burning flesh, it was hard to keep from throwing up. He wasn't alone, the two weather mages had the same problem. Lindren located the spell, at the bolts that held the door closed. It was a complex weaving of water, air and earth. He doubted Raimon could have done it by himself, not with only a year of covert training. The traitorous duke had help. One name came to mind...Tozer.

There was one advantage; the spell didn't need to be contained, as with Dayn's taint. This one couldn't spread, though it was folded in upon itself in a series of tangled threads of elements, twisted and entwined, making it difficult to sort out. Lindren set to work unfolding it, making generous use of Vron's and Zeric's power.

Now he understood why Mathyn's mages didn't unravel the spell. It was much faster to just break down the doors. Lindren was already tired from assisting Arnir. Not wanting a repeat of the pain and frustration he'd suffered on the ship, he pulled power from Vron and Zeric and settled in for a long working.

℘   •   ℘

Kelwyn sat on the floor near the Art Gallery, watching the activity around him; Arnir forbade him to do anything else. Cat had been taken to her rooms, so he saw no point in arguing. Guards had come through the shattered outer doors, too late to do anything but clean up and help with the wounded.

Lindren worked at the dining hall doors. Others sorted the dead from the living, as well as dispatching any vaurok that still breathed. More carried the Human injured to the hospital, under Wendyl's direction. The air still stunk of burned flesh, sweat and blood.

His wounds hurt, his abused muscles ached. Kelwyn's rage had

252

flared higher than he'd thought possible. Now he felt nothing and realized he'd done exactly what Lindren had told him not to do—let his anger control his fighting. Sorting through the images of the battle, he realized the thigh wound he'd taken could have been avoided if he'd just used his head instead of charging in like an enraged bull. He knew better; he also had to admit that releasing his pent-up anguish helped. He'd worked out his anger against Raimon, Talon, Tozer and those responsible for poor Dairon's condition. However, they weren't the only sources of his distress.

Darsha, Shain and Teryl had taken Cat and Rhone upstairs. They would have laid them in the same bed. In a strange way, Kelwyn was glad Arnir had healed the Human. Cat would be devastated if anything happened to him. She loved Rhone, there was no doubt of it, and when he left, either willingly or by death, she'd need Kelwyn again. He tried to take comfort from that thought.

This time, he wouldn't let her down; he wouldn't leave her the way he had in Tiralan. Kelwyn would do anything in his power to keep her from going back to wherever she'd hid for eight long years. Although he couldn't be with her the way he wanted right now, his time would come again. Eventually.

℅   •   ℆

Lindren pulled the last strand of black magic from the bolt and opened the door to the dining room. A fuming Vergel waited on the other side. The rest of his men, sitting at the tables, jumped to their feet.

"Thank Ar! We were going crazy in here." The commander-general strode through the door, sword in hand, scanning the carnage. "Both sets of doors were locked, but there's no lock on them!"

"Both?" Lindren cast his magic to the doors opposite him, the ones leading to the kitchens. Black magic flared back. *No wonder Vergel didn't go around.* Those ones would have to wait, however. "Teale spelled them shut."

Vergil's bushy eyebrows flew up. "Teale? When did he learn magic?"

"Long story. Talk to Rodrin about it."

Vergel tucked his weapon in its sheath and moved to Rodrin's position.

Zeric put his hand on Lindren's shoulder. "I'll see if I can find someone else to help undo the other spell. You are far too tired."

Lindren nodded and rubbed his eyes. The headache had returned. Fortuantely, he had accessed his magic easily. "Also, have someone check the other doors leading to the second floor. There's no reason Mathyn couldn't have gone around unless they were also spelled shut."

He lifted his head to see Shain's normally cheerful features set in stone. "I think we've done what we can, Father. Cat and Rhone are as comfortable as we can make them. The guards are removing the bodies and Rodrin's sent for servants to clean up the rest of this disaster."

Darsha helped Kelwyn to the stairs. Lindren and Shain met them at the foot. "You look as bad as Kelwyn, Father," his oldest son said. "You need sleep more than Rodrin needs you. It's going to take several hours to clean all this up. By that time, we might be able to figure out what in the nine hells happened."

Lindren couldn't argue and when Rodrin joined them a moment later, the king agreed. Despite the amount of time he'd spent in his bed over the last couple days, sleep sounded far too good to resist. Once he arrived at his room, however, he discovered Jewel hovering near Cat's door.

"Oh, my lord!" she cried. "You're safe! I heard there was fighting! Right here in the castle! Is...Lady Cat...?"

"She was rescued as well and is asleep in her bed," Lindren said. "Come into my rooms, we need to talk. Darsha, take Kelwyn into his room."

His son frowned. "You're supposed to be getting some rest."

"As soon as I've talked to Jewel." Lindren motioned the maid through the door and directed her to one of the chairs. Shain leaned against the cold fireplace.

Lindren's chair felt almost as good as home. "Much has happened since the greeting ceremony, but all you really need to worry about is two things. First, you were right about Talon. He and a boy named Rat

254

kidnapped Cat. He's dead, so your secret is safe."

Jewel stared at the floor, her hands worrying her apron. "I know why he did it. He was as desperate as I to get out of the life we were born to. Back when…he was just a thief, he talked about saving enough money to leave Tezerain and buy some land of his own." Her shoulders sagged and she choked back a sob. "Talon used to be a nice boy, when I knew him two years ago. He was funny and kind to me." Jewel relaxed her hands and returned her gaze to Lindren, her eyes shining with unspilt tears. "He changed. I guess he let greed and his dreams lead him down the wrong path."

"He already walked the wrong path," Shain said. "You got out by hard work and determination, not by stealing from others."

Jewel shook her head. "No. I was lucky. If not for Lady Deana…who knows where I'd be." Her pale blue eyes flashed. "You have no idea how hard it is growing up in the Pit. Usually the only way out is by joining one of the gangs or dying. It's worse for women; starvation, the brothels or, at best, marriage to a drunken, abusive, lout."

"You're right," Lindren said. "We don't know. Our lives are very different from yours. Regardless, we cannot allow anyone to hurt one of our own. What Talon did was inexcusable."

Jewel hung her head, the fire gone as quick as it had come. "I can't argue the point, my lord. My poor lady never should have suffered what she has. There was something else you wished to talk about?"

Lindren was just as glad to get off that topic. "Fox. He's more than just a mercenary."

The little maid turned a curious gaze his way. "What do you mean, my lord?"

"The news will be all over the castle in a very short time. Fox is really Lord Rhone Arden."

Jewel frowned. "I know Baron Corbin Arden, but I've never heard of a Lord Rhone Arden."

"You weren't here when he served as a commander for King Rodrin. He's Corbin's brother and was convicted of a murder he didn't commit. Rhone was with us not only as Cat's bodyguard, but also to find out who was really responsible. Duke Raimon Teale confessed to the

255

murder this afternoon. A formal court will be held to clear Rhone's name, soon, I hope. In the meantime, he'll be staying in Cat's room as her bodyguard."

Jewel sat with her mouth open, then snapped it shut. The normal blush of her cheeks faded to pale white. "I...I'm afraid I didn't treat him very well. I didn't know he was a lord."

"Don't worry about it. He knew he'd be treated like a mercenary and not a nobleman." Lindren sat forward in the chair. "Both Cat and Rhone were wounded in the battle downstairs. They're sleeping in Cat's bed right now and I'll hear no arguments or comments against it. Is that clear?"

The maid nodded. "Is...is she hurt bad?"

No concern for Rhone. Lindren wasn't surprised. "She lost part of one arm."

Jewel's hand flew to her mouth. "Dearest Vania! No!"

"She'll be fine in a few days," Shain said. "Her arm will be as good as new."

She lowered her hand and used it to scrunch her apron. "Oh, that's right. You Elves can heal each other."

Lindren smiled. "Not quite. Only some of us have that power. My son Arnir is one of them. He will look after her." Not exactly the truth. He imagined Kelwyn would help watch over Cat while she healed. "In the meantime, I'd like you to ensure Lord Rhone receives his meals. Cat will wake from time to time until she's healed. Beef broth will be sufficient for her."

"Of course, my lord. I have some of Lord Rhone's laundry to put away as soon as the guards will let me in the room."

Lindren stood. So did Jewel. "I'll let the guards know, but please wait until tomorrow. They both need sleep."

Jewel ducked her head and Lindren dismissed her.

"Think there'll be any more problems?" Shain asked. His face still held no hint of his usual humour.

"I hope not. You should get some rest-*. I'm going to check on Cat."

"Make it fast," his son said. "Or Darsha will be breathing down

256

your neck."

A smile tugged the corner of Lindren's mouth. "I will."

After giving their guards a brief rundown of the events of the afternoon, and Rhone's real identity, Lindren entered Cat's bedroom and stood at the foot of the massive bed. Rhone lay near the edge, his face pale. The boys had removed his bloodied jerkin and shirt, cleaned and bandaged his wounds and cared for the cut on his head. Cat slept beside him, her truncated arm wrapped in a clean piece of cloth.

An extra little body caught his eye. A tabby kitten slept on the pillow above Cat's head. "Now where did you come from?"

The kitten cracked one eye, then stretched, yawned and rolled over onto its back, four legs askew. Lindren smiled as a strong suspicion came to mind over who gave Cat the little creature. Reassured all was well, Lindren sought his bed.

ఴ • ౿

Rhone awoke to cold air, blurred memories, a headache and raging thirst. He sat up and winced. Pain shot through his belly as the memories rushed back. A candle fought off some of the darkness in the room and he glanced at Cat, relieved she'd survive. How she managed to fight after losing her arm, he had no idea. Her bravery, stamina and just plain stubbornness rivaled that of the bravest warrior in any army. With a shake of his head, he turned his attention to the bandage on his stomach.

Gingerly, he peeled back the cloth, then winced again as dried blood pulled on tender skin. Bruises marred the area around a narrow slice in his belly. Careful prodding showed it to be much shallower than he remembered. Rhone had felt the vaurok blade pierce him and was sure it had gone deeper. He remembered extreme pain, and panic that he couldn't protect Cat.

"Arnir."

Once again mixed feelings ran through him; relief he was still alive and irritation that the Elves couldn't heal everyone. Rhone replaced the cloth and shifted his feet to the floor while other injuries made their presence known; a gash on his left thigh and another on his upper right arm, both bandaged. He touched a gentle finger to the lump on the side of his head, an explanation for the pain there.

Rhone felt like he'd been dragged through all nine hells and back. A pitcher of water sat on the table beside the bed. He didn't bother with the cup and half the pitcher was gone before he lowered it, gasping in air, then groaning as his stomach muscles protested the movement.

One good thing had come from the frightful events of that afternoon. The king and, more important, Greyson Yarrow knew he was innocent of Jornel's murder. Two days before, he'd almost given up hope. Now the sun shone bright and clear on his future, though just what that future would be, he didn't know.

He had no job here now, though he was sure King Rodrin would take him back into the army, at a lower rank. After performing the duties of a commander, could he take orders from just anyone? The answer flowed swiftly behind the question. No. He drained the rest of the pitcher.

Regardless of a job or not, Rhone wanted to go home, he *needed* to go home. He hadn't seen his family since he'd left at sixteen, ten years before. Corbin, his oldest brother and baron of Arden, had come once or twice a year so he kept up on the news and, for a time, that sufficed. Until he'd found himself stranded on an island in the Westren Sea. Strange how family suddenly became more important. Was his mother still alive?

A violent shiver reminded him he only wore a pair of trousers. Using the bedside table for support, Rhone stood, sucking in breath at the agony shooting through him. He hurt everywhere. If it wasn't bumps, bruises or injuries, it was abused muscles. He straightened up and set his sights on the garderobe. That was one discomfort he could ease. His bloody shirt and jerkin hung on the back of the nearby chair, prompting him to check his trousers. They fared no better. Despite the severity of his belly wound, all that blood couldn't be his. It had to be Cat's.

Moving like an old man, Rhone made his way to the sitting room and his pack, which still lay where he'd placed it when he thought he was leaving. He pulled his last pair of clean trousers and shirt from it and shuffled to the garderobe.

Removing the bloody trousers proved harder than he'd thought and, when the job was done, he snorted in disgust at the mess left behind on his skin. A wash was in order. After relieving himself, he emptied most of the pitcher into the basin and drank the rest. He proceeded to wash off what he could of the blood, then tugged on the clean trousers. The cut on his leg had stopped bleeding. Rhone had no clean bandage, so just left it. His hair would have to wait for a proper bath. He picked up a clean wash cloth and dipped it in the basin. Another shiver ripped through him as he removed the residual blood from his chest and face.

Just as Rhone wiped away the last of it, a strange yowl sounded from the bedroom. He opened the door expecting to see the kitten playing with something. Instead, a boy straddled Cat, a bloody knife held in one hand. The other was occupied with a hissing, spitting kitten. The little creature had attached itself to the boy's face, a familiar face. Though Rhone had only seen him for a few moments, he recognized the brat who'd helped kidnap Cat.

"Get off me!" the boy cried. He tossed the kitten against the wall. It yowled, then lay still.

A groggy Cat belted the boy with her left fist and he flew off the bed.

Before Rhone could take two steps, Rat recovered and launched himself at him. "You futtering bastard! You killed Talon!"

Instinctively, Rhone reached for a sword that wasn't there. At the last moment, he turned and took the blade on his left shoulder. Rat fell to the floor, yanking out the knife. Hissing at the new pain, Rhone grabbed the gutter snipe by the throat. "What did you do, you little shit!"

One look at Cat confirmed his worst nightmare. Red blood seeped through her shirt, right above her heart. Heated rage replaced the cold shivers.

Rhone slammed Rat against the wall and the knife slid from the boy's fingers. "What have you done!" Rat's head hit the stone, his mouth open, brown eyes wide. *Cat!*

How could she survive such a wound? Bone thunked against the wall. Rat kicked and thrashed. Rhone barely noticed. All he could see was Rat's bulging eyes. All he could think about was Cat, her warm breath, soft touch and the blood pouring from her chest. He bashed the little monster against the wall, squeezing the vaurok-futterer's throat with every hit. The walls, the bed, everything vanished as his vision shrank to one sight—a small, brown-haired head and the blood-smeared stone.

A voice penetrated his darkness. "My lord! Stop!" A hand pulled at his arm. "He's dead!"

Rhone shook his head, clearing his vision. A guard's face blurred into view. The boy no longer moved, held up only by Rhone's hand at his throat. Brown eyes, now lifeless, stared back at him. He dropped the body and dashed to Cat, who lay partly on her side.

Her eyes were closed. No pulse. Rhone jerked the guard close to him. "Get Lindren!"

The guard ran. Rhone yanked his shirt off the chair and climbed on the bed beside Cat. *It's too late!* He pressed the cloth against the wound anyway. *Please don't die! Dearest Vania! Don't let her die!*

It seemed an eternity passed before Lindren arrived. He spoke to the guard, then quietly closed the door behind him.

"She's not breathing!" Rhone set his fingers against her throat. He felt nothing.

Lindren put a hand on his arm. "She'll be fine. She's Tiranen, remember."

"But the knife went straight into her heart. There's no pulse!" Rhone kept pressure on the wound, even though he knew it was useless.

"There is," Lindren said. "You just can't feel it. She's in a sort of hibernation, deeper than that of a bear or squirrel. It slows her system so her heart doesn't beat while it's repaired."

Rhone sat back, his bloody shirt in one hand. "She's not dead?"

Lindren shook his head. "Cat will be fine. In less than an hour she'll start breathing normal again."

After giving Lindren a brief rundown of the events, he said. "I'm sorry." His heart sat in a tub of clay, his pride somewhere underneath. "I'm a lousy bodyguard."

"You did your best. No one expected him to come back." Lindren stared down at Rat. "I know he's only a child, but it's hard to feel sorry for him. I assume he used the tunnels, which means the guards are either drugged or dead. I'll opt for drugged."

Arnir opened the door. "I assume she's fine." His features were pale and drawn, and Rhone remembered he'd lost a friend.

"She is. I just needed you for appearances," Lindren said. "To most people, Cat is still an Elf." He indicated the furry bundle near Rat's body. "Is that Cat's cat?"

Arnir's brow rose. "Cat has a cat?"

"I gave it to her this morning." Rhone slid off the bed and crouched by the kitten. "He attacked the boy, brave little thing."

Arnir touched the animal and a moment later his hand glowed white. "He's still alive, though not for long. His skull is fractured along with some bones in his spine and some internal injuries."

"Cat will be devastated." Rhone could find another. She'd still cry. He didn't like to see her cry.

"This is a small job compared to a person," Arnir said and his words changed to an Elven chant. A few minutes later, he picked the kitten up and placed it beside Cat. "He'll be fine. He just needs sleep now."

Lindren eyed up Rhone's shoulder. "As if you didn't have enough injuries, you managed to find yourself another. Too bad the guard saw it."

Rhone grunted. "I'll live." The damn thing throbbed worse than the one in his belly.

Arnir disappeared out the bedroom door for a moment. When he returned, he said, "I've sent for some water and bandages. I can at least clean and stitch it for you. Wendyl's far too busy with this afternoon's casualties."

"Thank you. And for this." Rhone pointed to his now oozing belly wound. "I owe you Elves a great deal."

Arnir gave him a nod. Lindren said, "Don't worry about it. Glad we could help."

Rhone returned to Cat's side and sat heavily in the chair. "She tried to fight him off. I thought she was supposed to be in a deep sleep."

"Instinct." Lindren's quiet voice sounded behind him. "Tiranen know when they're threatened, even in healing sleep."

"Should I tell Kelwyn?" Arnir asked, wiping blood off Rhone's

261

arm with a towel.

"Not until morning." Lindren's tone took a hard turn and he walked to the bedroom door. "I'll ask the guards to send someone to remove the boy's body and clean up."

Perhaps he was still angry with his nephew over Cat. Elven deceit, Elven lies, Elven tricks. Humans were far more devious. It meant nothing. Not really. The only one that mattered lay on the bed, not breathing, yet apparently alive.

Chapter Twenty-Three

Dawn had arrived a couple hours before in a flurry of puffy snowflakes. Somewhere out there the sun shone, just where Rhone couldn't say. It wasn't Tezerain.

He stepped away from the bedroom window, wishing he could have slept more. His injuries had kept him awake most of the night and he ached from head to toe. Just walking to the garderobe seemed a chore. His torn, bloody jerkin still hung from the back of the chair. He fingered it, wishing it was wearable. The cold seeped through his shirt to his wounds and into his bones. A shiver disrupted all his injuries. A quick search showed no sign of his cloak. It was probably still downstairs in the throne room where he'd tossed it before the battle.

No fire had been lit, no point for someone who wasn't supposed to be in the room. Now that Cat's escape was known, it would be a simple matter to correct. Rhone made his way to the sitting room and laid down kindling, groaning as he knelt. A knock interrupted him.

Jewel stood on the other side of the door, a full tray in her hands. She ducked her head, staring at the floor. "My...my lord. I'm...so sorry...for the things I said."

"Forget it. Just don't repeat it." Rhone took the tray. "Is the food hot?"

"Yes, my lord. Just made. Audney will be bringing a pot of coffee and your clean laundry shortly." Jewel entered the room and quietly closed the door, a far cry from her usual flounce and sneer. "There's broth there for my lady as well. Is...is she awake?"

Rhone shook his head as he examined the tray. A half loaf of still warm bread, three fried eggs swimming in the grease from half a dozen thick slices of bacon, two slabs of ham and a winter apple. He didn't wait for it to turn cold. Sitting at the desk, he shoveled in one egg whole.

Another shiver reminded him he was still chilly. "You can finish building the fire. And start one in the bedroom as well."

"Yes, my lord."

There had been times Rhone detested his title. Not now. He dug into his breakfast, taking more than a little pleasure from Jewel's subdued attitude. The bacon was done to perfection and the ham almost melted in his mouth. Before long, only Cat's broth remained. Maybe he should wake her. She hadn't eaten since lunch the day before.

A knock at the door announced Audney and the promised coffee, as well as his last set of clothes. It didn't matter. Now he was free to shop to his heart's content and, with Lindren's money, he could purchase more than just one outfit. His heart lifted at the thought. Should he go today? Or wait for Cat? Stiff and achy though he was, he decided today.

Rhone poured his coffee, took it and Cat's broth into the bedroom and set them on the little table. Jewel finished the fire and the snap and crackle of dried wood helped him feel warmer. A glance at the window showed him the snow hadn't stopped and didn't appear to have intentions of doing so any time soon.

"It's too bad about the snow, my lord," Jewel said as she stood and straightened her apron.

"Why? It often snows this time of year."

"I mean the wedding this afternoon, my lord. Lady Selesa will have to have a covered coach take her to the temple if it doesn't clear."

With a start, Rhone realized he'd forgotten all about the wedding. "Is that mess cleaned up in the throne room?" The reception was to be held there and in the dining hall. Blood smeared all over the carpet and walls would offend the ladies and some of the more squeamish noblemen. Duke Ethond Lyria, with his insipid smile and brace of catamites, came to mind.

She nodded. "Even the carpet's been pulled up. There's no time to replace it, of course, but at least all the blood is gone. King Rodrin also ordered fragrant candles lit all night to help remove the odour. I haven't been in there myself yet, but Quint says the Hall looks cleaner than it has in years."

Jewel couldn't keep her eyes off Cat's bandaged stump. "My lady is so...lively. It's strange to see her this still."

"A few days and she'll be back to normal." Rhone watched the slow, steady, rise and fall of her chest while he sipped his coffee.

True to Lindren's word, less than an hour after the attack Cat's eyes had flown open and she dragged in a deep breath before coughing her lungs out. Lindren gave her some water. Casting a bleary gaze in Rhone's direction, she drifted off to sleep and hadn't moved since. He still felt she needed something in her stomach and waved the bowl of broth under her nose.

Cat stirred and, with a moan, opened her eyes, their bright amber now dull and unfocused. After a moment, they settled on him and she managed a small smile. "You're alive."

"Just a few scratches, nothing serious." He needed to get her off that topic; Jewel stood at the foot of the bed. "You look hungry. Want some broth?"

He helped Cat sit up, while Jewel hovered nearby, and held the bowl while she drank. Once it was finished, Rhone tucked her back under the covers and her eyes drooped.

"Where's my kitten?" she asked.

"Sleeping beside you." Rhone kissed her forehead and her eyes closed.

"When did she get the kitten?" Jewel spoke almost in a whisper.

"I gave it to her yesterday morning." Rhone glanced over at the box of dirt a guard had brought up. Beside it sat two dishes, both empty. "The kitten's bowls need refilling. And bring up more water. We're out."

"Yes, my lord."

After Jewel left, Rhone kissed Cat's cheek and headed for the door. His aches and pains had settled down to a dull throb and as long as he didn't work his shoulder too much, he should be able to visit a tailor. Walking through the castle without a mask would be a joy. Another shiver briefly yanked his injuries to the foreground. He'd ask about his cloak on the way out. His dagger was out there somewhere as well.

Rhone opened the door to find an extra guard on the other side. The dark, unruly hair, sparkling brown eyes and innocent, boyish face hadn't changed one whit in four years. "Padrig!"

The soldier bowed. "Lord Rhone, it's good to see you. I couldn't believe it when Commander-General Mandearan said you were alive."

None of the guards on duty for the past six weeks had been familiar. This, however, was a face he knew. Here was a man anyone would be proud to command. Almost as tall as Rhone, he was the only soldier who'd beaten him in hand to hand combat—once. "Still with the Twenty-First?" His regiment, once upon a time.

A flicker darkened Padrig's eyes briefly and Rhone wondered what bothered him. "Yes, my lord." The guard turned his shoulder. "I even managed to make sergeant."

Rhone laughed. "Again? And how long will it take to lose that badge this time?"

A wounded look crossed the man's features, then he grinned. "I've kept it a whole year now."

"Good for you. I'd love to stand around and talk, but I was just on my way out."

Padrig lost his smile. "Going to the hospital?"

Rhone's brows dipped in a frown. He probably should see Wendyl. Maybe later. "No. Why? Is there a problem?"

"I'm sorry, my lord. I wish it was anyone but me. Commander Robrai has assigned me to you. You are allowed to go to the hospital, in my company, but that's all. Until your trial."

It took a moment for the full weight of what Padrig said to sink in. Rhone blinked, then clenched his fist. There was no one he could hit and not feel guilty afterwards. "I'm under arrest? I'm innocent! Teale admitted he murdered Lord Jornel."

Padrig's expression showed only sympathy. "I know, my lord. And if it was me I'd let you go wherever you want. I have to follow orders." His right shoulder lifted in a half-hearted shrug. "At least you're not in the dungeon."

Rhone leaned back and thumped his head against the closed door. It didn't help him feel any better. "There go my new clothes." He pushed himself away from the door and opened it. Cat shouldn't be left alone anyway. His aches and pains throbbed in time with his anger. Maybe he should see Wendyl sooner than planned. "Any chance of someone locating my cloak…and my dagger?"

Lindren sipped his tea and watched the thick snowflakes fall outside Rodrin's study window. The fire snapped and crackled, adding a warmth to the room he didn't really feel. He could have lost Cat again and the thought chilled him to the bone. "I shouldn't have counted Rat out just because he was a child."

Rodrin snorted. "Don't twist yourself inside out over it. I've got a city rife with kids just like him. If Cat's injury is on anyone's head, it's mine for pulling my engineers off rebuilding those brick walls in the tunnels."

With a wry smile, Lindren said, "Now who's twisting himself inside out. Between combing the city for Cat and myself, ensuring you and the rest of the people in the castle were safe, preparing for the wedding and cleaning up after yesterday's disaster, you needed all the men you could get."

"Thanks for trying to cheer me up. It isn't working." Rodrin's gaze shifted to the window. "I had six men clean and polish the open carriage that took my mother to Vania's temple for her wedding. Looks like all that time was wasted."

"Not necessarily." Lindren set his empty cup on the table between them. "I'll send Darsha to the docks to talk to Mathyn. A couple of his weather mages can have the sun shining in no time."

Rodrin turned back to Lindren, a slight frown on his face. "They'd do that for me?"

Lindren nodded. "If I ask them. I'd hate to see Selesa disappointed just because of some snow. It's the least I can do for all the trouble we've caused."

Rodrin's surprise shifted to a glare. "The trouble goes both ways. If it wasn't for you and Cat, I'd have found out about Teale far too late to stop his attempt at my throne. I'll hear none of that nonsense."

"As you wish," Lindren said, with a chuckle. He poured himself another cup of tea from the gilded pot. His thoughts kept returning to another discussion they'd held the night before—what to do about the Barriers. Both of them felt sure something was up that needed serious investigating. Preparations were already underway.

Rodrin polished off his coffee before helping himself to more from a pot that matched the one holding Lindren's tea. "I still think it would have been nice to know Rhone was alive. I swear my heart almost stopped when he dropped his mask."

Lindren sighed. He'd spent most of an hour discussing it with the king last evening.

Before he could say a word, Rodrin raised his hand. "I understand your reasons. I was just wishing. I also wish I could put him back in charge of his old regiment, but Tolbert Robrai would start his own revolt. He was pissed enough when I gave it to Rhone in the first place." The king sat back, his coffee cradled in his hands. "I didn't sleep last night. Too much to think about. Like Rhone and Cat. Judging by his actions yesterday, I'd say he's more than just a bodyguard to her."

"You'd be right."

A sly smile crossed Rodrin's face. "I guess this means I get to keep Cat with me. I can't offer Rhone his old job, but I'm sure I can find a place for him somewhere."

"That's up to them, I suppose. I doubt he'll stay with her long, a couple years maybe, then find himself a wife."

"His reputation with the ladies points to that. Even a couple years would be an advantage." Rodrin sipped his coffee. "She could teach my archers a thing or two. First we need to hold a new trial and declare him officially innocent. How long will Cat be out? I'd like her there, just to make sure things stay on the up end."

Lindren paused with his cup half way to his mouth. "A few more days. You think something else might happen?"

"I can't take any chances. I'm finding it hard to trust any of my dukes. Yarrow is in full agreement that Rhone is innocent, but I heard some mutters last night that didn't sound promising. I won't mention names. One of the complaints was that Rhone was working with Teale. I know it's not true. However, I need to convince the board of that."

Rodrin set his cup on the table and leaned closer to the fire. "I doubt Aura was involved in her father's double dealings, especially since we found Andros dead." He shook his head. "Never could I have imagined Teale would betray me. Far more than that, how could he kill his own son?"

Lindren had felt sick when Vergel brought the news after conducting a thorough search of Teale's house. Crinon and Raimon's commander had been found and arrested. It didn't take much coercion to convince Crinon to talk. The man babbled for over an hour, actually shedding tears when he told of Andros' death.

"I'd like Cat to check Aura when I question her as well as everyone involved in Rhone's retrial," Rodrin continued. "Just to be on the safe side."

Lindren nodded in complete agreement.

₭ • ℓ

Kelwyn drank the last of his pitcher of water, his second that morning. Breakfast had gone down equally quick. Only his movements were slow. Arnir hadn't healed him all the way and his injuries protested any incautious move. Dressing had been agonizing and he didn't bother with a tunic. He needed to see Cat, then Arnir.

An extra guard stood outside Cat's door. Kelwyn wondered if something else had happened and didn't knock before entering. He found Rhone sitting next to the fireplace in Cat's bedroom, his expression darker than storm clouds. A quick check showed Cat's chest rising and falling in the rhythm of sleep.

"Why does Cat need an extra guard?" Kelwyn asked.

"He's not for her. I'm under arrest."

"But you're innocent."

"You don't have to tell me." Rhone cast his gaze at Cat. "Have you talked to Lindren this morning?"

Kelwyn shook his head. "I came right here after I ate."

Rhone told him of Rat's visit the night before and Kelwyn's fists clenched tight. He strode to Cat's side and sat on the edge of the bed. His need for her flooded his senses; her sweet face, tantalizing musky scent, the memory of her touch, her delicious kisses all threatened to overwhelm him. How many times had he almost lost her since they came to Tezerain? *Too many.*

Kelwyn jerked his thoughts away from the one person who held his heart firmly in her grip and scanned the room. No sign of blood anywhere. Whoever cleaned up did a good job. Even the sheets had been changed. The kitten stirred and took a few wobbly steps. He picked the little fellow up and carried him to his dishes. If he was half as thirsty as Kelwyn had been, he'd need more than his small dish of water.

He knelt on one knee next to the kitten and stroked him while he drank. "I'm sure the board will find you innocent."

Rhone just grunted.

"What will you do once you're free?" How long will you stay with Cat? How badly will you hurt her when you leave?

"Go home. Tolbert Robrai has my old command, though Ar only knows why the king put him in charge. The man is a weak-chinned fool. It explains why he wasn't with his men the night we searched for Cat and Lindren. That lazy sod wouldn't bother climbing out of bed to find his prick."

Go home. Cat would be crushed. Despite the fact that she'd tried to keep her love for Rhone quiet, Kelwyn knew the signs. His heart thumped. It thumped louder, then he realized it was a knock on the door.

"I'll get it," Kelwyn said, though his body protested when he rose to his feet.

Jewel walked in. "Good morning, my lords. I have Lord Rhone's bath waiting outside. One will be arriving for you soon as well, Lord Kelwyn."

Something was different about the little maid, though Kelwyn couldn't put his finger on it. Rhone dragged himself out of the bedroom. He had to feel at least as bad as Kelwyn, who had to admit a hot bath sounded very good.

"At least I've got a set of clean clothes to change into," Rhone said. "I'd be a lot happier if I could have gone shopping this morning, like I'd planned." The man's expression grew darker.

"My lord?" Jewel held her hands clasped in front of her, her gaze on the floor. "I could have the seamstresses come and measure you. I'm sure they could make some nice clothes in a very short time. All the wedding outfits have been completed and they won't have much to do. Although, I guess you're stuck with what you've got for this afternoon."

Her attitude had changed. Kelwyn almost laughed out loud.

Rhone's expression lightened. "That would be fine. Please send them up after I've had my bath. And no weird colours. I've seen some of the clothes the nobles are wearing these days and I'd prefer not to embarrass myself. No lace, no frills. As a matter of fact, stick to black, brown, blue or dark green. Understood?"

Jewel gulped and Kelwyn choked back another laugh. "Y…yes, my lord." She curtseyed and hurried out the door.

A slow chuckle rumbled in Rhone's throat and Kelwyn gave in to his laughter. "Changed her tune somewhat, hasn't she?"

A small smile slid across Rhone's face. "Just a bit."

℘   •   ℘

Kelwyn refilled his cup from the punch bowl, taking in the splendor before him. He wore the same outfit he'd worn to the banquet on their first visit, a sky blue tunic with white shirt and black trousers. If anyone noticed, they didn't say anything.

If he didn't know better, he'd never tell a brutal battle had taken place in the room the day before. The single hint was the stone floor, now covered with scented sawdust. Between that and the beeswax candles, even Kelwyn couldn't smell the blood and burnt flesh that had permeated the room. Garlands of pine and evergreen, festooned with coloured ribbons and paper balls, adorned the walls and doorways adding their own scent.

The lords and ladies wore their brightest outfits, glittering with gold, silver and jewels of every colour. Gailen and Selesa stood out above them all, him in a form fitting tunic of royal blue decorated with gold buttons and trim, the double stag crest of Kitring-Tor picked out on his left breast in shimmering thread of the same colour. White trousers tucked into high black boots finished the ensemble.

His bride wore a dress of gold cloth, split up the front to the waist, and embroidered with red roses at the hem, for luck apparently. An ivory silk underdress showed through the split and a silver belt, studded with rubies, hung from her hips. The dress showed off both her narrow waist and high bosom.

Selesa's thick black hair was piled on her head, covered with fine lace dotted with more tiny rubies. They danced together near the middle of the room, eyes only for each other. Kelwyn memorized every detail of what he saw, as he had during the ceremony. Cat would have a thousand questions for him when she woke.

Music filled the air while dancers dipped and twirled in time. Others stood near the fireplace or against the walls, chatting, laughing and flirting. Mathyn's and Lindren's Elves gathered in groups or pairs, some conversing with one noble or another. None of them danced, so far. All seemed at peace. For one day, Tezerain set aside its woes and pretended all was right with their world.

Even Aura Teale had put in an appearance, though her red rimmed blue eyes contrasted with her pale skin. Despite her sorrow, she shone in a dark blue dress, trimmed with white and gold, setting off her waves of black hair. Kelwyn wondered if a dance or two would help cheer her up, though he was sad comfort for a traitorous father and a murdered brother.

Tossing back the punch, he set down the cup and headed in her direction. She stood by the stairs, no one else around her except her constant companion, one of Rodrin's guards, and Kelwyn figured the others shunned her because of Raimon's deceit.

He gave her a bow. "Would you like to dance, Lady Aura?"

She looked startled. "I...I don't..."

Kelwyn smiled and held out his hand. "A beautiful girl shouldn't be standing in the shadows on a night such as this."

A light blush coloured her cheeks. "Thank you, I would like to dance." Aura turned to the guard. "If...that's all right?"

The guard nodded and Aura braved a tiny smile. She proved as light on her feet as any human could be and they enjoyed first a waltz, a circle dance called a branle that involved changing partners, and then The Morning Rose, a stately group dance that resembled a rose opening its petals.

They finished with a flourish, a bow and curtsey. Shain stepped between them, his ever-present grin in fine form. "You're hogging all the lady's time," his cousin said.

Kelwyn relinquished Aura's hand and sought the solitude of the outer hallway. Dancing with Aura had only reminded him how much he missed Cat, though with luck Rhone would be on his way north soon and he could have her to himself.

Rhone hadn't bothered coming to the wedding, citing Cat's need of a bodyguard as an excuse to stay close to her. Just as well. If Rat had found his way in, someone else might.

A fancy-dressed porter closed the doors behind him. Kelwyn decided against going outside for fresh air. Mathyn's mages had cleared the skies for the wedding. Once all were ensconced in the castle they'd relinquished control and the storm continued, unabated. He wondered how buried the city would be if the snow had fallen normally.

He sauntered down the hall, his gaze wandering from one picture to another, then a suit of armour, and a gold rimmed vase on an oak stand. How much simpler life was in Silverwood. There, a Celebration of Life, the Elven equivalent of a wedding, was held with joy and laughter, and none of the long, drawn out ceremony and pomp of Tezerain's court.

A quiet sound broke through his thoughts. It came from a room just ahead on the left. It sounded like a girl crying. Kelwyn's jaw clenched. Some humans could be horrid brutes. He opened the door.

Arissa Kail sat in a crumpled heap of yellow brocade in front of a cold fireplace, her face buried in the back of the stuffed chair. Having second thoughts, Kelwyn almost closed the door. He'd managed to avoid her so far.

A shudder ran through the girl, the result of a stifled sob. Against his better judgment, Kelwyn approached her. "Lady Arissa?"

She sat up with a start, then wiped tears from her eyes. "Lord...Lord Kelwyn! I..."

"What's wrong? Did someone hurt you?" Kelwyn crouched beside the plump girl, his hand on the arm of the chair.

Arissa straightened and produced a lacy handkerchief from somewhere in the folds of her dress. She dabbed her eyes. "No, nothing

273

like that. It…it's nothing, really. Just silly girl nonsense." Her eyes said otherwise.

"Tell me what happened, Arissa," Kelwyn said. "Someone hurt you. Please. You can confide in me. I won't tell anyone else."

"I…I'm sorry, my lord. I've been a nuisance. Pestering you to see the Tapestry of Ages and…"

"Is that what's bothering you?" Human girls could let some strange things upset them, but then, so could Cat.

Two tears leaked from her eyes. She wiped them with the handkerchief. "I'm just, sort of lonely, I guess. I know I'm not pretty or have a nice figure like the other girls. I try to be like them, but…"

"Don't."

"P…pardon, my lord?" Her hazel eyes blinked.

"Don't try to be like them. You're not. You are you and that's who you should be." Arissa reminded him of Cat, in a peculiar way. Cat didn't like her body either because it didn't conform to what her people had seen as normal.

Kelwyn almost jerked as he realized he'd done what everyone else did to Arissa, judge her by others' standards. He'd spent his life trying to convince Cat she was beautiful and her body perfect..for her. He loved her for more than her physical beauty. She was smart, sometimes too smart, and made him laugh even if she didn't intend it.

He sat back on his heels to take a better look at Arissa. Underneath the fat, behind the fleshy face, was a person. Someone who laughed, cried and needed to be…needed. Kelwyn stood and held out his hand. "Come with me. We'll go see the Tapestry of Ages. Just you and I. I don't have to worry about Cat tonight. Lord Rhone is watching over her." It sounded like an excuse. *That's because it is.*

"My lord?" Her eyes widened further and Kelwyn realized they were pretty eyes, brown with emerald green flecks, ringed with dark grey. Arissa tended to look at people with half open eyes. She should let them be seen.

If she wore her hair back, lessened the face paint and dressed in darker colours, it would help considerably. Perhaps he should talk to Selesa or Queen Lisha.

Kelwyn spent the next hour in the Gallery with Arissa as she explained the history behind the Tapestry of Ages, wrong though it was. She also showed him the other items and pictures on display, talking at ease about each one. He realized not only was she more attractive than he'd thought, she was intelligent and when she used her proper voice, instead of that annoying breathy whisper, pleasant to listen to.

Afterwards, he asked her to dance and, with subtle gestures and hints, Arissa improved. All in all, Kelwyn had a pleasant evening.

Chapter Twenty-Four

A perpetual rusty haze lent the sky of Fornoss a blood hue. Barren hills rose in the distance, muted in the strange light, while eddies of red dust twirled and danced over the ground. Corralled horses neighed their discomfort to the pale sun. After two hundred years, something in their blood still yearned for the blue skies and moist earth of Arvanion's other worlds.

Delcarion drummed his fingers on the stone window sill. He hadn't been born when Balphegor took Fornoss and ruined it, though he suspected it would be similar to those he knew.

Few of the wildlife survived. Only hardy vegetation and crops grew, and that for only a couple hundred miles on either side of the equator. Beyond that lay cold, frozen waste.

Most food was brought from the other worlds, taken as spoils of war. Not that he or the vauroks cared much for grains, chicken or pork, but the Humans who lived here did.

Closer to the keep, hundreds of dusty tents sat in huddled disarray, home to both vaurok and Human warriors, their allegiance owed to him, and through him, to Balphegor. Vauroks, on orders from the master, brought the Humans' ancestors with the horses. Even so, Delcarion couldn't trust their allegiance. Not yet.

Too many rumours abounded about the capture of their great-great-grandparents and what was done to them to ensure their loyalty. Now vauroks trained their descendents to serve Balphegor. Still, the Humans whispered amongst themselves, cast suspicious glances at the vauroks and goblins, and kept their thoughts closed. Perhaps in another two hundred years they'd be ready.

Heaving a sigh, Delcarion turned from the window in one of the two towers in his keep, a three storied square building, simple but adequate for his needs. He sat in front of the fireplace on an intricately carved oak chair, its mate across a table made from the same tree.

A soft, comfy mattress, covered in fine sheets and a thick down coverlet, perched on a frame also of dark oak. A matching wardrobe filled with outfits of the finest Human fabrics stood tall against one wall. Empty shelves, ready for gifts, adorned other walls. Plush carpeting kept the floor warm.

Soon. Soon, this would be her home. Delcarion's first glimpse of her had been in Balphegor's pool. He'd had a better look in the house in Tezerain. The last Tiranen. Short, but beautiful. His fist tightened. She should be here now. She should be his. Now.

"Fools." Delcarion rubbed his chest, the places where the Elves' swords had pierced him. The injuries were healed and, yet, a memory of pain lingered. It should be gone, nor should there be scars. He traced the lines left by the swords through his heavy, armoured jerkin. "Stupid troll-futtering sorcerers."

Tozer and Teale were supposed to have captured Lindren and the girl, then brought them here to his keep. After too many blunders, they'd managed the first part. Somehow, Lindren's sons had found him and the Tiranen.

Delcarion pulled a yellow orb of thin glass from a pocket in his cloak. He hated to admit it, but it wasn't all Tozer's fault. If Tozer's orbs had worked properly, Lindren and the girl would have been brought through long before the others arrived. He blamed the sorcerer's inability to key them, but Delcarion knew the fault was his. Elements of the keying spell were erratic, unpredictable, and despite his best efforts he couldn't correct the problem nor make them last longer. Still, they were an advantage the Elves didn't have. He put the orb back in his pocket.

Casting a glance at the pale sun, Delcarion rose from the chair. He'd spent a great deal of time preparing the room for the girl. Vauroks had stolen every item, including the material for her outfits, from a captured town. He hoped she'd appreciate it. She wasn't his, yet, but would be someday. For now, however, other problems plagued him.

Teale should have sent his signal twenty-four hours ago. Over fifty thousand vauroks and other creatures, camped on the plains north of the Barriers on Urdran, waited for a war that had not come. Delcarion could only surmise one thing—someone had learned of Teale's activities and stopped him.

Without the assurances that the king and dukes of Kitring-Tor lay dead, their duchies in disarray, he couldn't order the temporary portals opened, couldn't risk the chance of attacking blind.

Fortunately, he had a backup plan. Delcarion descended the steps of the keep tower, then strode through the throne room and outside. A shimmering portal, thirty-five feet tall, sat several yards from the door. No temporary portal, this one had stood since Balphegor took Fornoss, ages upon ages ago. A wyvern in full flight could use this portal; they had to walk through his, wings folded, heads ducked. Half a dozen vauroks guarded this side of the big portal, they couldn't risk the Human warriors finding their way through to Balphegor.

A great vaurok stepped forward. "The signal has come?"

Delcarion shook his head. "Plans have changed. I go to speak with the master."

The vaurok signaled to the sorcerer on duty to open the portal and, a couple minutes later, Delcarion stepped into the white clouds. In less than a moment, he left the red dust of Fornoss and entered the endless grey of Balphegor's place between worlds. Long strides brought him quickly to his master's castle and up the long steps to the room at the top of the tallest tower. He knocked, then waited for a response; and waited.

"Enter, Delcarion." The oily voice slid through his thoughts like a snake through water.

No one attended the master. Balphegor had ignored him for a reason. Delcarion grit his teeth and covered the distance between the door and the throne, then prostrated himself before the Human-lion shape the god had assumed.

"My master, Raimon Teale's signal never came and Tozer had to escape Tezerain." The Human sorcerer stayed only briefly at Delcarion's keep, long enough to rail about one supposed offense or other.

"You may kneel."

"Thank you, master." Delcarion rose to his knees, suppressing a shudder at the horrid glare in Balphegor's good eye.

"Raimon Teale is dead. The other dukes of Kitring-Tor still live. I am not

pleased."

Which explained Balphegor's ire. "I suspected as much, my master. I have another plan."

"Speak it."

Delcarion rested back on his heels, organizing his thoughts. "Your army waits beyond the Barriers. They could still take Kitring-Tor, but at a slower pace. I could have your sorcerers key temporary portals to positions in the foothills of Kerend, below Broken Man Pass. The baronies are Kitring-Tor's weakest point. We attack there. It would take at least a week for word to reach Tezerain by horse and another three or four weeks for Rodrin to bring up troops.

"By that time," Delcarion continued, "we will have wiped out all seven of the baronies. Each only have a couple thousand trained soldiers at best. Most of their people herd animals and work what land they can. Once those baronies are secure, you could open a permanent portal." It would take months, but would be well worth the effort.

"From there," Delcarion said, "it would be easy to overrun first Silverwood, then Kitring-Tor. Thallan-Mar has broken relations with Rodrin again, so no help would come from there. The Denfold is too far, the single road too narrow to bring in troops effectively." They wouldn't dare travel through the Old Forest.

Once the Elven enclave fell, the girl would be his. As far as Delcarion was concerned, Kitring-Tor didn't really matter. Balphegor's single good eye, black with malice and corruption, bored into Delcarion's brain. What was left of his soul shivered and shrank to hide deep within him.

"See to it. But you are not to lead the army. Tozer is already there looking after another matter. Make sure those portals of yours work this time or your blood will cover my table." Balphegor's usual oily smooth voice took on a hard edge.

Delcarion bowed, forehead to the floor, and, despite the threat, he smiled.

279

A bitter wind, cold enough to freeze a man's balls to his lance, blew across the frozen wastes north of the Barrier Mountains. Atax Daemonica sat on a small hillock two hundred feet above Balphegor's army, wrapped tight in a cloak of white seal skin. An invisibility spell, one of his devising and jealously guarded, ensured his concealment.

Below him, chaos erupted in the vaurok camp. A stolen item, a few words here and there, and a fight he'd started between two lesser vauroks grew into a major confrontation as a crèche-brother came to the defense of one of the combatants, then another and another. Before long, a hundred lesser vauroks pounded and stabbed each other.

Atax chuckled. Dark green blood, glistening in the pale sun, spattered the trampled snow. Several bodies lay still. Now the Firsts and Seconds intervened, delivering clouts as easily as they issued orders. No lesser vaurok was allowed those positions anymore, not since the great vauroks made their appearance half a century before, long after Atax had broken away from Balphegor's control.

Larger and smarter, the great vauroks caused more problems for the Elves than he could ever have imagined. Where had they come from? Atax doubted Balphegor had much to do with it; he'd never shown any inclination to improve those he'd created. *Perhaps the Mothers have taken a hand.* They laid eggs time and time again. Then those eggs were taken from them, the little vauroks inside rarely to be seen again, unless by some chance the egg was white. A female. It had to be hard on them. Another conundrum. How could the male and female of the same species look, and act, so different?

A puzzle Atax had pondered more than once. He set it aside. Something else needed to be done. Now that the Firsts and Seconds had interfered, the fun was over. Atax rose and tossed a silver armlet onto a rock—the object of the vaurok dispute. He descended the backside of the hill, whispering a transportation spell as he walked; a spell of his own construction, also one he kept to himself. The snowy wastes north of the Barriers changed to the low, snow-covered hills of the barony of Gethyn.

An hour's walk took him to the current training area for Gethyn's tiny army. Fifty thousand vauroks, goblins and hell wolves waited over the barriers. Here, barely two thousand scruffy men practiced with dull swords, wooden maces and stick pikes. Bales of hay provided a backdrop for the archers' practice arrows.

Atax ignored them, heading instead for a stack of boxes and crates. Naron sat there with five other young soldiers near the trampled ground of the training area. Under the concealment of his spell, Atax listened in.

"I don't understand your obsession with the Elves," one young man said. Blond hair hung over his forehead in a greasy lock.

"They let Rayson die!" Naron's venomous words hissed out of clenched teeth.

A lad with shiny black hair rolled his dark brown eyes. "But they can't heal Humans. Everyone knows that."

"I told you already. It's a lie meant to make us suffer." Naron's once quiet voice had attainted an icy edge. His blue eyes burned with conviction. "We're fodder for the Elves' war!"

"You're crazier than a squirrel in a cage," said the blond haired youth.

Another man with a broad, flat nose snorted. "You've told us the same garbage over and over, but you have no proof. Only what that guy...Atar...Ajax..."

Naron lowered his head, but not his eyes. "Atax."

The broad nosed man waved a hand in the air. "Whatever. What makes you think he's telling the truth? He's one man, probably with a grudge. Like you."

Time to step in. Another spell turned Atax's cloak to ordinary brown wool, his clothes to those of a peasant. He ducked back amongst a stack of boxes holding arrows and allowed his invisibility spell to fade. A quick check of an inside pocket ensured the presence of a full canteen of his special brandy. Whistling a quiet tune, he approached the young men.

Naron's angry eyes stabbed Atax, then widened in surprise. "You! I thought you went to Tezerain." He stood and held out a gloved hand in greeting.

Atax shook it. "I did, and didn't like it. The entire city is a pit of

281

sick vipers. Women parading half naked in the streets. Men drunk with wine pawing them. It's disgusting. I decided to come back north. People know how to live the good life here, honest, trustworthy, straight as arrows."

"You were in the wrong part of Tezerain, then," mumbled one young man.

"How did you find me?" Naron asked.

"I followed the tracks of two thousand men," Atax said, with a chuckle. "It wasn't hard."

Naron introduced him to his companions and directed Atax to sit on his recently vacated crate. Atax took it. "Are you going to rejoin the Kerend army?" Naron asked.

"No." Atax sat forward, leaning on his arms, obviously no threat, and the young men relaxed. "Remember I told you about my dead cousin? I'm going to spend at least a few months at his home. His widow will need help planting the fields, caring for her garden and looking after the animals. Her children are still quite young."

One of the men nudged his neighbour. "Bet she's got another garden that needs sowing." His guffaw split the cold air.

Atax sat up and artfully lost his smile. "What a disgusting thing to say. My cousin's wife is a sweet woman, but my intentions are strictly honourable. I only wish to help."

Naron fixed his icy gaze on the rude man. "Apologize, Kalda."

Kalda's mouth opened and closed faster than a whore's legs in a roomful of rich, horny men. "I...I, uh...I didn't mean...uh. Sorry." He stared at the ground, properly chastised.

Atax struggled to keep up his indignation, and to not break out laughing. "No harm done. Just don't misunderstand my intentions again."

The blonde haired man kept his eyes solidly on Atax, not blinking for several moments. "Naron, here, says you've seen and heard some things about the Elves."

Atax sighed and slowly shook his head. "Sad to say, I have." He reached inside his cloak for the canteen. "I have far too many stories, all true. Listen closely, my friends."

Chapter Twenty-Five

The day after the wedding, Lindren and the male portion of his family attended a special breakfast in honour of Gailen and Selesa, then stood around talking while the newlyweds opened their gifts. They'd all chosen trinkets to give the happy couple—a jewelry box, candlesticks and the like—except for Cat, who'd picked out an ornate trio of matching gilded vases, glazed with blue and orange, all different sizes. Lindren had no idea why she chose them, but Selesa said she loved them and told him to thank Cat for her. He suspected she was being diplomatic.

Gailen gave his bride an intricately carved dressing table, an expensive gift. Lindren remembered from past Kitring-Tor weddings that grooms traditionally gave their new wives a gift on the morning after as a thank-you for giving up their maidenhood. In his opinion, Humans made far too much of a perfectly natural act, but it wasn't his place to say. After the gifts had been opened, Gailen and Selesa departed for the royal estate in White Deer Wood where they'd spend the next month. He wished them well on his and Cat's behalf.

The next few days were spent in discussions with Rodrin, Jeral and Vergel, organizing the mechanics of moving five thousand men to Kerend in as short a time as possible. Most of the dukes opted to remain in Tezerain for Rhone's retrial, sending messengers to make the arrangements for their levies to meet where the North Road crossed the border. Rodrin set up Finan Alaryn, brother of Duke Valter Alaryn, as temporary lord of Teale's lands. Much depended on Aura's guilt or innocence.

Lindren needed to go home and arrange the Elven forces, but first Cat had to wake up.

ဆ • ၛ

Rhone spent the first three days of his confinement recovering

283

from the worst of his wounds. The next three took forever to pass while he stared out the window, read books Jewel brought him, played with the kitten, visited the hospital and watched Cat's arm grow back.

Lindren and his sons came from time to time, especially Arnir, who had to keep the pretense that he was the one healing Cat. Kelwyn kept him company occasionally, but Cat's best friend divided the rest of his time visiting either Aura or Arissa. Rhone could understand his attraction to Teale's daughter, though what he found interesting in Arissa Kail was beyond him.

Cat's room had grown smaller. It seemed whenever he turned around he ran into a wall. If she'd been awake, he could have at least passed some of the time in her arms.

Calli Yarrow tried to see him on several occasions. He used the excuse of his arrest as a reason to avoid her and spent some of his free time imagining what he'd say to her when the time came.

Six days after the royal wedding, Rhone sat by Cat's side, studying the ends of her fingers. The new skin on her arm appeared pale next to the old with more of a pink tinge than the usual tan. Lindren assured him it was normal and would change shortly after the healing process had finished. In anticipation of Cat's awakening, a tray loaded with food, mostly meat, sat on the table next to the bed. Kelwyn waited with him, though he stood near the door.

"How much longer?" Rhone asked. Everything appeared back to normal.

"Very soon." Kelwyn opened the door. "I'll get Lindren."

Not two minutes after he left, Cat's unique amber eyes fluttered open. Rhone had a cup of water waiting and held it for her while she drank.

"You have new clothes." Cat took another deep drink.

"I do. Queen Lisha's seamstresses made them. Three tunics, three shirts and two pairs of trousers." All in colours he'd requested and no lace or frills. He currently wore a dark green tunic over a white shirt with black trousers.

"They look nice."

"Thank you. How's your arm?"

Cat flexed her fingers. "Stiff, and everything tingles."

"Is that normal?" Rhone fluffed the pillows, then placed the tray on her lap.

"I think so. I've never lost a limb before." Cat used her left hand to spear a thick chunk of cheese. "Would you mind cutting my meat for me? I think I should wait a while longer before using my hand."

Rhone complied. Just as he finished, Lindren, his sons and Kelwyn entered the room.

"How long have I been out?" Cat asked, shoving another piece of cheese into her mouth.

Lindren answered. "Six days."

Cat blinked. "That's a long time, isn't it?"

"Not necessarily." Lindren stayed near the door with the other Elves. "It varied between your people. And there were extenuating circumstances."

At Cat's curious expression, Lindren told her about Rat's visit and subsequent death, including the kitten's part.

"If he hadn't attacked the kid, I might not have heard anything," Rhone explained. "He's a proper little hero."

"I don't remember any of it." The kitten slept beside her. She waved a small piece of meat under his nose, waking him. The little creature snatched the morsel from her fingers. Before long it had disappeared and he sought another. Cat indulged him. "You said he needs a name. How about Hero?"

Kelwyn laughed. "It fits."

Rhone smiled. "Hero is a good name."

"I wish I hadn't missed the wedding," Cat said, around a mouthful of beef.

While she ate, Kelwyn told her the events of that special day with Lindren and his sons adding their own comments and opinions. Then Lindren told her of the plans made to head to the Barriers.

"Rodrin's contingent of two thousand men left this morning with Vergel in command," he said. "Jeral went with them, along with his crystals. I think he's eager to fry a few vauroks."

"Is Dayn coming too?" Cat asked.

Darsha shook his head. "Jeral still has him running up and down the tower with chores. He's leaving him several books to study."

"Now that you're awake," Lindren said. "Rodrin can hold Rhone's retrial, probably tomorrow. He wants you there to ensure only the truth is told. Depending on how long it takes, we might be able to leave right after."

Cat had finished her tray and sat petting the kitten, who lay on her lap, his eyes half closed in contentment. "Tezerain is an interesting place, but I think I'm ready to go home."

Shain chuckled. "I never thought I'd hear you say that."

The Elves approached the bed. Lindren sat at the end of it and Rhone realized it had been the meat keeping them away.

"I also want to go home," Rhone said. "If everything goes as it should tomorrow, I'd like to travel with you until we catch up to Vergel."

Lindren nodded his agreement.

"Have you decided if you're coming with us to Broken Man Pass?" Kelwyn asked. "There's still the matter of the prophecy."

"And you're an important part of it," Arnir said.

Rhone almost groaned. He'd shoved the prophecy to the back of his mind and left it there. "It makes me more than a little uncomfortable. I can't see how whoever wrote those words would know I'd take the nickname Fox. Or that I'd wear black."

Cat's delicately arched brows dipped in a frown. "But if you don't come, I might not be able to wake the dragons."

"If that's what it means," Shain put in.

It would give Rhone more time with Cat and he wasn't ready to give her up. "I'll think about it."

Cat yawned. "You said that last time."

Lindren stood and motioned to Kelwyn and his sons. "Looks like it's time to leave. You need sleep, daughter of mine. This can be discussed tomorrow."

Each of them gave Cat a kiss and said goodnight. Rhone wondered just how tired Cat was. "I'd hoped to spend a little private time with you tonight. How can you be tired? You've been sleeping for six days."

Cat yawned again, then carefully picked up Hero and laid him beside her. "Healing sleep isn't really restful. Once I get a good night's rest I'll be fine. Can you wait until morning? Or are you too uncomfortable?"

Rhone kissed her lips. "Yes. Before you nod off, can you answer a couple questions?"

She snuggled down into the covers and nodded.

"Do you love me?"

"You asked me that already. Yes."

"Why?"

"Why what?"

"Why do you love me?" He'd asked Calli the same question four years ago. She'd given him a mischievous smile and said, 'Because you're handsome and I love kissing you'. It took him two of those four lost years to realize it meant nothing.

Cat's sleepy eyes drooped further. A moment passed before she answered. "You're brave, a good fighter. Despite your persistent anger, you're a good man. Honest. I can trust you. I like talking with you, though it seems I do most of the talking." She rolled onto her side, facing him. Her arm must not bother her much anymore since she now lay on it. "You're smart and you have a nice laugh when you want to use it. I really enjoy spending time with you. And, I was right." A coy smile curved her full lips.

"About what?"

"When we first met, I just knew you'd be handsome under all that hair."

Rhone laughed, his heart lighter than a cloud for the first time in years. He tucked her in and kissed her again, then took up his position at the window. The sun set in a spectacular display of gold, red and orange while he thought about how the trial would play out, that damnable prophecy and his future with Cat.

The night sky began its slow retreat, fading from black to grey. Rhone lay on his side watching Cat, wishing she'd wake up. One of Ar's good spirits must have granted his wish, for no sooner had he thought it than she opened her eyes.

"Morning," he said. "Still tired?"

Hero stretched, yawned, then bounced off to his dishes. Cat pulled Rhone down for a long, sweet, kiss. "Does that answer your question?"

Rhone laughed. "Yes, it does. And I have another question for you."

"What is it?"

"Marry me?"

Cat jerked away and sat up, her golden eyes wide. "Rhone, I can't!"

Rhone's heart, so light a moment ago, crashed to the ground. "Why not?"

"I can't give you children! You'll want children one day."

His heavy heart rose a little. "I don't want children."

"Everybody wants children."

"No, Cat." He traced a line down her nose. "Not everyone. Including me. I don't really like children. They're noisy, they smell and cause a lot of problems. While I was growing up, my older brothers and sisters had kids. Some of them are my age, the others younger. Trust me. I know what children are like and I don't want any."

"But…" She blinked once, then twice. "But what if you change your mind?"

"I doubt it will happen."

"It might. You told me marriage is for life, it's not like bonding."

"It is and I want to spend my life with you." Rhone still shook his head over the Tiranen form of marriage. If you fell out of love, you simply changed partners, no hassles, no anger, no hurt feelings.

"But…" Cat let out a heavy breath. "Rhone, please. Think about it."

"I did. For half the night. I know you want children and I wish to Ar I could give you one. Not for me, for you. But I can't. I don't want anyone but you and I don't want children. How can I make you understand?"

"Rhone, I...I never imagined you, or anyone, would give up the chance to have children for me. You're right, I don't understand."

He motioned her back into his arms, hoping he was wearing her down. "I've thought about it, now you need to. Nothing has to be decided right now." A long kiss silenced her next protest. "Besides, I have other plans for you."

Rhone pulled her on top of him and unleashed his pent-up passion, touching, kissing, caressing, until her eyes shone with the glow he'd come to love. He helped her shed the shirt she'd worn for six days. Sharp raps sounded on the door, startling Hero, who ran under the bed.

"Ar's balls! It's barely dawn!" Rhone reluctantly pushed Cat aside and tugged on his trousers while she slipped her shirt back on.

"My eyes!" Cat said, in a loud whisper.

"Hide in the garderobe. Think about what Rat did to you and Hero."

When he opened the door, Jewel flounced in. "Good morning, my lord."

"What in the hells are you doing here at this hour?" Rhone demanded.

"King Rodrin's orders, my lord. Your trial is set for two and a half hours from now and Lady Cat needs a bath. Her hair takes a long time to dry. Breakfast will be here shortly."

Jewel motioned to someone behind her and two men entered with a wooden bath tub. More followed with hot water. "Is my lady awake?"

"She's in the garderobe. I'll get her." Rhone slammed the bedroom door and opened the one to the garderobe. "It's Jewel. She's here with your bath."

Cat's eyes had calmed. Perhaps the fright of Jewel seeing them made it happen sooner. That, or she was remarkably angry at Rat. She tugged on a strand of hair. "Well, I guess I really do need one. I wish it could have waited awhile."

"So do I." Rhone grabbed his shirt and tunic from the chair and put them on.

"Do you need a bath?"

He shook his head. "I had one yesterday." With a wave of his hand, he motioned her out the bedroom door. "My breakfast had better arrive soon or someone's going to hear about it."

₲ • –

Hero played with the piece of string while Jewel brushed out the last of Cat's hair. It fell in damp waves down her back. Rhone sat in front of the fire, his expression as dark as the clouds adorning the morning sky. Cat wasn't sure if it was because of his impending retrial or anger at their interrupted lovemaking session. Or both. A quiet knock roused them from their thoughts.

Jewel answered it. Lindren entered and dismissed the maid.

"It's already been an interesting morning," he said to Rhone. "Tolbert Robrai demanded to know why you aren't in the dungeon and feels you should be brought to trial in chains."

Rhone muttered something unintelligible under his breath, then said, "That vaurok-lover has been a pain in my side for years. I can just imagine how much he gloated when King Rodrin gave him my old command."

"Don't worry about the chains. Rodrin refused his request." Lindren looked to Cat. "How are you feeling this morning, Little One?"

He hadn't used her nickname for quite awhile. *It must mean he's finally back to normal. And not mad at me.* She smiled. "Much better, thank you."

"Rodrin would like you to wear your cloak, with the hood up. You'll be sitting with me in the front row so he can easily see when you shake or nod your head."

"Did Jonlan get my message?" Rhone asked Lindren.

"Yes. He's waiting downstairs with his wife."

Rhone let out a slow breath. "His testimony will go a long way to prove my innocence."

290

"Then let's get this over with." Lindren opened the door.

Rhone collected Cat's cloak, helped her into it and they headed for the stairs. A soldier she'd never seen before fell in beside Rhone. Cat was surprised to find she had butterflies in her stomach and wasn't sure if it was the impending trial or Rhone's shocking question. She still couldn't believe he'd asked her to marry him. *How can he not want children?*

She had to force those thoughts aside, however, and concentrate on the task at hand. They descended the wide staircase to the throne room. Benches sat in rows for most of the length of the hall, filled with the nobles of the court, dukes, barons, lords and a few ladies; including Calli Yarrow sitting beside her uncle. Cat's jaw clenched. She was one person Cat hadn't liked from the moment she met her. How Calli could hurt Rhone lay well beyond her comprehension.

Several Elves attended the trial, including Mathyn and Yira. A low murmur echoed in the room as people talked, whispered and shuffled to find a more a comfortable position on the wooden benches.

King Rodrin sat on his throne, wearing the same crimson, fur-lined robes he'd worn when they first arrived in Tezerain almost three months before. He cradled his scepter, the jewels on the knob glittering in the light of the hundreds of candles burning in the chandeliers overhead. Six dukes sat beside him; Samsin Kail, Valtar Alaryn and Randyl Kantin on his left; Hayden Dorbrook, Lanton Banren and Goran Robrai, brother of Tolbert, on his right. Tomis, the king's chancellor, stood behind him, holding a long staff, the end set with a brilliant sapphire.

Lindren directed her to the centermost bench. Kelwyn, Darsha, Shain and Arnir were already there. She sat beside Kelwyn, Lindren on her other side. The soldier who accompanied them downstairs led Rhone to a chair against the wall near the Gallery. Aura sat there with another guard, clasping her hands tightly in her lap.

Cat shifted her eyes out of focus. Aura's light showed blue awash with dark blue-green and a yellowish blue-green—worry and anxiety—swirling with an agonizing blend of green, yellow and reddish blue, the colour of fear. Rhone's showed some of those colours with red predominate. He was angry, just as he had been most of the morning.

Rodrin crooked a finger at Tomis, who leaned down to hear what his king had to say. A moment later he straightened and rapped his staff on the floor three times. "Attention. King Rodrin will now speak."

The murmurs quieted. "My people," Rodrin said. "These past few days have seen events both happy and tragic. A man I trusted with my life, nay, my kingdom, has been exposed a traitor. By his own words, witnessed by five of my dukes, Raimon Teale admitted to using black sorcery. In an attempt to take my throne, he used said sorcery and Blaise Rilandon lost his life while saving mine. Talifir, a brave Elf of Silverwood, was also killed in like manner protecting Lord Lindren, his Elder."

A murmur rippled through the crowd. Cat sat in shock. She tried to remember what had occurred that day. Blurred images of a pale blue ball flying through the air at Rhone mixed with a terrible pain and scenes of vaurok faces, blood and Rhone dying. She found no image of Talifir.

Lindren squeezed her hand. "My apologies, Little One. I should have told you."

Kelwyn clutched her other hand, his quiet presence a calming reassurance. Cat could say nothing and forced herself to concentrate on Rodrin's words, blinking back the inevitable tears. At least they made it easier to see Aura's light.

Rodrin's features held none of his usual humour. He sat as if he were carved in stone. "We have recently discovered two of Teale's barons are missing and possibly dead by his hand. Besides these crimes, he is responsible for the murder of Andros Teale, his own son, as claimed by Crinon Teale. We have every reason to believe him."

The king then asked each of the remaining dukes who were present that day to swear to what they had seen and heard regarding Teale's heinous crimes. Then, one by one, the board agreed the dead duke was guilty.

"If Raimon Teale was still alive," the king continued. "He would hang for what he's done. My son, Prince Dayn, granted him a swift death, and, I believe, that was for the best. Who knows what other black deeds he might have accomplished. Raimon Teale is hereby stripped of all honours accorded to his name. There is no body left to bury. Even so, there will be no memorial, no official ceremony, as befits a traitor to Kitring-Tor."

Aura broke down in tears. Rhone patted her shoulder, small comfort for the girl.

Rodrin motioned to Tomis once again.

The chancellor rapped his staff on the floor three times, allowing Rodrin to speak again. "Andros Teal died in defense of his country and will be accorded all honours. The state funeral will take place two days from now. Aura Teale, present yourself before your king and the board of peers."

Aura made her way to a spot halfway between Cat and King Rodrin, her eyes rimmed with red. She gave the king a less than graceful curtsy. When she folded her hands behind her back, Cat could see them shaking. She felt sorry for her and sincerely hoped she was innocent. There'd been so sign of black in her light, which was promising.

Rodrin studied her a moment while the girl stood before him, trembling. "Aura Teale, the charges before you are suspicion of treason and use of black sorcery. A declaration was sent out six days ago asking if anyone had information on your possible involvement in your father's treachery. No one stepped forward. Crinon Teale and Ulic Gardeson were interrogated in this and other matters. Both spoke of your innocence. We believe this to be true, but we need to hear it from you. Aura Teale, were you involved, in any way, in treasonous acts or in the use of black sorcery?"

Aura shook her head emphatically. "No, Your Majesty. I knew nothing of what my father had done or intended. And, I deeply regret any harm that has come from his actions. I am willing to pay reparation, though it will not substitute for a life."

The girl's aura showed a flash of many colours, none purple. Cat felt Rodrin's eyes on her and nodded.

Rodrin looked to the dukes on his right. "What say you?"

Hayden Dorbrook spoke. "I believe Aura Teale to be innocent of the charges before her."

The other two answered likewise and when Rodrin turned to those on his left all three agreed. Cat wondered what would have happened if one of them disagreed. Lindren was reluctant to tell anyone else of her truth-seeing.

The king held his scepter lengthwise in front of him. "Aura Teale. The board of peers declares you innocent of the charges brought before you. You are free. There is no need to pay reparation, for, as you say, money cannot replace a life. Finan Alaryn is caring for your father's lands until you marry Brade Kerend, at which time he will become the new duke of Teale. When the army leaves for the Barriers, I will send word notifying him. You are dismissed."

Aura curtseyed once more, this one steadier. "Thank you, Your Majesty. You are most gracious." She found her way to her former seat beside Rhone. He gave her a smile; she managed a small one back, dabbing at her eyes with a handkerchief.

Rodrin laid the scepter on his lap and spoke to Tomis.

The chancellor tapped the staff on the floor three times.

"Rhone Arden, present yourself before your king and the board of peers," Rodrin said.

Cat forced herself to breathe.

Chapter Twenty-Six

Rhone took a deep breath before he stood.

"I believe in you," Aura said. Her genuine smile reminded him not all nobles were vain, pompous, self-indulgent, overbearing asses; only most of them.

He gave her a nod and strode to the same spot as Aura, with a quick glance in Cat's direction. She also had a smile for him. Rhone bowed to Rodrin.

The king's expression gave no hint as to what he believed regarding Rhone's guilt or innocence. "Rhone Arden, the charge previously brought before you was suspicion of the murder of Jornel Yarrow. You were found guilty of that charge and sentenced to spend the rest of your life working in the mines of Ordran. The charge still holds, though we now have evidence to believe you are innocent. This is one of the reasons you are here before us today. The other is a charge brought forward this morning by Duke Goran Robrai, the failure to present yourself to the proper authorities upon your return."

Lindren had said nothing of the new charge. Rhone glanced back at him. The Elven Elder' s face revealed some of the shock reflected on Cat's. Three rows behind him, Tolbert Robrai sat wearing a smug smile and he knew who was really responsible for the charge. His right hand curled into a fist. He could do nothing, say nothing. Rhone forced his hand open and turned his attention back to the king.

"A declaration was sent out six days ago asking if anyone had information on both the old charge and the new. One man stepped forward."

Rodrin raised his hand and Tomis spoke. "Jonlan of Tezerain, also known as Jorge of White Birch Lane, come forward and present yourself to your king and this board."

A few moments and Jonlan stood beside him, bowing to the king.

"Please explain to the board the events regarding the murder of

Jornel Yarrow, as you remember them," the king said.

Jonlan looked first at Rhone, then back at the crowd behind, not at his wife, at Calli Yarrow; a mere moment, yet long enough to let Rhone know of Jonlan's uncertainty as to whether to reveal all.

"Your Majesty, Your Graces, the night in question I was returning to my barracks room when I saw two men carry a body into Lord Rhone's quarters." Jonlan went on to explain all he had seen and heard, as well as why he couldn't report it four years earlier. "After two years at sea, I saw little point in coming forward. I thought Lord Rhone dead and I feared for my life. I'm a commoner and I have no evidence other than what I just related to you."

Duke Goran leaned forward. "Do you know where Rhone Arden was that night?"

Jonlan paused before answering. "I do, Your Grace." He glanced sideways at Rhone, who nodded once. "He was with a girl. I was watching outside their door to ensure they weren't interrupted. I left before…they were finished…because I was tired and had duty early the next day."

"Who's the girl?" Samsin Kail asked.

Now Jonlan looked more than a little uncomfortable. "Is it necessary to reveal her, Your Majesty? It would ruin her reputation."

Duke Samsin snorted. "A nobleman's daughter, then. Calli Yarrow might want to know who she is."

The king cast him a glare. "That has no bearing on Rhone's guilt or innocence, not at this point." He turned back to Jonlan. "Do you have anything further to add?"

"No, Your Majesty."

Rodrin dismissed him and, with a bow to the king, Jonlan walked back to his wife. The king then asked the four surviving dukes who'd heard Raimon's confession to report, one at a time. Each said the same thing—Teale had admitted killing Jornel because he saw him using black magic and that he'd framed Rhone Arden.

When all were done, the king once again turned to the board for their judgment. Dukes Hayden and Lanton both responded quickly with declarations of innocence. Goran Robrai looked first to his brother before giving a reluctant verdict of innocent. The three remaining dukes all adamantly agreed.

"Rhone Arden, the board of peers declares you innocent of the charge of murder." Good news, though the king didn't appear pleased. Rhone wasn't either. "There is still the matter of the second charge. Please explain yourself."

Rhone bowed. "Your Majesty, Your Graces. After my rescue from the island, Lord Lindren gave me the choice of leaving the ship at Meat Town and going my own way or returning to Tezerain. If I left at Meat Town, I would never see my home or family again, never prove my innocence, so I chose the latter. If I presented myself to the authorities, I would have no opportunity to investigate the truth. Because I was free, and with the help of the Elves, I was able to find Jonlan. Unfortunately, because he is a commoner, his testimony alone would not be enough, so I continued my disguise."

Goran Robrai sat forward, his features set in a deep frown. "Is this an attack on the structure of our society?"

Pompous vaurok-lover. He's as bad as his brother. "No, Your Grace. I merely state a fact."

"Were you able to discover anything else while you were running around the castle, free as air?" Goran asked.

Rhone struggled to keep his hands relaxed. "No. Not until I found out Lindren suspected Raimon Teale."

Goran sat back. "Then it was a waste of time. Time you should have been spending in the dungeon."

"Enough," Rodrin said. "We have a confession, with extenuating circumstances. Consider your decision, gentlemen. What say you?"

To a man, they said 'guilty'.

Rhone's jaw clenched. Anger tightened his muscles, churned his gut. Despite everything he'd done to clear his name, he'd still end up a criminal. He tried to take consolation from the fact that he'd at least be alive. Angry murmurs rumbled through the crowd. He glanced back at Cat, and saw the fear on her sweet face.

The king motioned to Tomis, who rapped his staff three more times. "Rhone Arden, the board finds you guilty of the charge brought

297

before you. This is a minor transgression, one that has not occurred for quite a while. I had my clerics search the records and they found a case from a hundred-and-forty-two years ago. The board at that time decided three years in prison a suitable penance. Does this board agree?" They did.

Three years. Just for trying to find proof of his innocence. So much for his marriage to Cat. Would she wait for him? Would she want a criminal for a husband?

Rodrin glanced at the dukes to his right, then those to his left. "There are few advantages to having this crown stuck on my head. One of them is my privilege to commute a sentence if it is deserved. Based on Rhone Arden's past service to our kingdom, his proven loyalty and integrity, and the fact that none of it would have been necessary if not for Teale's deceit, I declare the time spent trapped on Crescent Island sufficient penance. Rhone Arden, you've served your sentence. You are a free man."

Rhone's mouth dropped open. He found himself and bowed to Rodrin. "Thank you, Your Majesty. You are most gracious and kind."

The room erupted in cheers, except for Goron Robrai, who shouted something Rhone couldn't hear. He suspected he'd find Tolbert in an equal frame of mind. Relief replaced anger. Instead of returning to his seat, as Aura had done, Rhone strode to Cat and pulled her to her feet, enveloping her in a tight hug.

Rodrin laughed. "Rhone!" the king shouted over the noise. "When are you going to marry that girl?" The room fell silent.

Cat gasped and tried to pull away. "Rhone..."

He clamped his hand over her mouth. "Shush." He released her and bowed to Rodrin. "Your Majesty, if you would be so kind, would you excuse us for a few moments?"

"Granted. Just don't take too long. I'd like to get out of this robe."

"Thank you, Sire." After giving the king another bow, Rhone grabbed Cat's hand and almost dragged her into the Gallery. When he closed the door, he gathered her in his arms once more.

"Rhone! I thought you said we didn't have to decide right away. I thought you were going to think about it." Cat wriggled out of his grip.

He snatched her hand back, keeping her close. "No, you were. I told you, I've already thought about it and I want to marry you."

"But...your children!"

He pulled her to him once again. "How many times do I have to tell you? I...do...*not*...want...children. I'm not going to change my mind. Do you love me?"

"You know I do."

"Then marry me." Rhone cupped her cheek with one hand. "I love you, Cat. I need you. I want you. What more do I have to say?" He kissed her, not as long as he wanted; he couldn't risk her eyes glowing. Not right now.

Tears moistened Cat's eyes. "You love me?"

Rhone tried hard not to laugh at the expression on her face. "Yes, I do. Very much. If I didn't, I wouldn't have asked you to spend the rest of my life together. You told me last night you trust me. Well, you are the only one I can trust with my heart. I know you won't hurt me. Do I need to get on my knees? Do I need to beg?" He dropped to one knee.

Cat pulled him up. "No! Rhone, no."

"Then say yes."

Her mouth worked a moment. Then she said the one word, the only word, he wanted to hear. "Yes."

Rhone crushed her to him, burying his face in her neck, overwhelmed by the flood of relief coursing through him. He wanted, *needed*, to hold her, caress her, make love to her...it would have to wait. If he had his way, he wouldn't wait long.

Grabbing her hand once more, he pulled her back to the throne room, back to his former place in front of the king. "Your Majesty, would this afternoon be too soon?"

A rumble of laughter came from the throne and the crowd burst into cheers once more.

"Not at all," the king said. "Not at all."

"Rhone Arden! How dare you!" A shrill voice pierced the noise. It took Rhone a moment to realize it was Calli. Stiff as a board, she forced her way through the throng. Her chest heaved in anger, shown quite clearly by her low cut gown. "How dare you! You are betrothed to *me*!"

Rhone slipped one arm around Cat's waist. "Calli, don't. Just back off and walk away."

She set her hands on her hips, her emerald eyes hard as the stones they resembled. "I will not walk away! You made a promise to me! You can't marry that...that Elf!"

"Your Majesty," Goron said, a snide curl to his lip, "you just spoke of Rhone's loyalty and integrity. It appears you were wrong."

"I trusted you!" Tears formed in Calli's eyes, though not enough to fall. "I believed you loved me. You told me you were only her bodyguard!"

Cat opened her mouth to speak.

Rhone had no idea what might come out and put a finger on her lips. "One chance, Calli. Walk away."

With a low snarl, Calli tried to push Cat from Rhone's side. Not only did he hold her too tight, Cat could easily brush her off.

"That's it." Still holding Cat, Rhone turned to the king. "Your Majesty, I have one more piece of information about the night Jornel Yarrow was murdered that I'd like to reveal."

Calli's face paled. "You wouldn't!"

"You've given me no choice." Rhone snapped the words and Calli's expression turned to one of fear.

Tomis tapped his staff again so the king could speak. "Let's hear this information." The room fell silent.

Rhone removed his arm from around Cat and held her hand. "Jonlan reported I was with a girl the night Lord Jornel was murdered. Duke Samsin deduced that girl was a nobleman's daughter."

"Rhone, no!" Calli cried. "You can't!"

"Silence!" Rodrin's bellow stunned the girl quiet. "I am hearing testimony. You are not permitted to speak."

Calli clamped her jaw shut. Real tears now leaked from her eyes.

Rhone continued. "Duke Samsin was right. The girl I was with was Calli Yarrow."

The room burst into noise. Calli threw herself at Rhone, fists flying. "How could you! You promised! You promised me!" She crumpled into a sobbing heap at his feet.

300

Rhone stepped away. "Your Majesty, I didn't say anything at my first trial because, at that time, I loved Calli and didn't want to mar her reputation. We were young and impatient. It was two weeks before the wedding and we didn't think it would matter. We were wrong. I'd hoped Calli would do the right thing and step forward for me at my trial. She chose not to and I was sentenced to spend the rest of my life in the Ordran Mines. I pondered her choice for a long time while I was stranded on that island and decided she loved her reputation more than me. She doesn't deserve my love."

"There's more to it than that." Greyson Yarrow, Calli's uncle, stepped out of the crowd. "When Calli was younger, she displayed less than lady-like desires in regard to men. Her mother had passed on by that time and left her a large trust. In an effort to curb those desires, Jornel decided to hold the trust back until Calli married and was proven a virgin on her wedding night."

"Don't bother looking at my light," Rhone whispered to Cat. She'd see only red. He turned back to Calli, his jaw tight. "This was about money. You wanted money more than me."

"I...I didn't think it would matter if we were together that close to the wedding," Calli sobbed. "I was going to tell you on our wedding night so you could tell Daddy I was a virgin. I didn't think it would matter! How was I supposed to know what was going to happen?"

"You wanted me to *lie* for you?" Rhone cried. "You disgust me."

Greyson yanked Calli to her feet. "As her guardian, I release you from your betrothal vow, Rhone. You're right. She doesn't deserve you."

Calli screamed "No! You love me! You kissed me in the garden!"

Rhone stepped back, away from the woman he once cherished. "No. You kissed me. I played along to try to get you to come forward."

Greyson shoved his niece in the direction of the outer doors. "Calli, go back to the town house immediately and pack your things. You're going home."

Calli ran off in a flood of tears.

Greyson rubbed his forehead. "I apologize for all this. She's caused you pain and suffering you never should have endured. How I'll marry her off now, I'll never know."

That was Calli's problem. "Apology accepted." Rhone pulled Cat to him once more, safe in the knowledge that she'd never do anything like that to him.

Jonlan appeared beside him, holding his wife's hand, his face split in a grin. "I guess that means the wedding's on again. I'm glad you changed your mind."

Rhone gripped his friend's shoulder. "Me too. Stand with me?"

The grin widened. "I was hoping you'd ask."

Goron jumped to his feet. "This is outrageous! Elves don't marry Humans!"

"First time for everything." Rodrin stood and passed his scepter to Tomis. He shed his robe.

Tolbert Robrai pushed his way through the crowd, his fleshy face florid. "Goron is right. This Elven witch must have put a spell on Rhone!"

The crowd quieted, curious to see what further entertainment lay in store. Rhone just wanted to hit something, preferably the Robrai brothers.

Lindren rose from his seat and approached Tolbert, his grey eyes dark. Rhone had learned that was not a good sign. At least, not for Tolbert. "My daughter is not a witch. No Elf can use magic like that, nor can Cat, and I resent your accusation."

That remark brought a puzzled frown from more than one person.

"Are you sure you want to do this?" Rodrin asked.

Lindren nodded. "It doesn't matter anymore. The people I was trying to protect her from know who she is. I believe it would now be to her benefit for others to know the truth."

"Lord Lindren, what are you talking about?" Goron demanded.

"Cat is my daughter only because I adopted her."

Gasps and murmurs filled the room once more.

Rodrin motioned to Tomis. It took several raps of his staff to restore order.

"Her real parents are Thelaru and Arlayva," Lindren continued, his hard gaze fixed firmly on Tolbert. "She is the last living Tiranen."

A split-second of silence preceded a burst of pandemonium. Cat leaned into Rhone. He wrapped her cloak around her and held her close,

302

shielding her from curious onlookers. Tomis thumped his staff continuously until order prevailed.

Lindren still glared at Tolbert. "Would you deny Cat this shred of happiness simply because you hold a grudge against Rhone?"

Tolbert's eyes flew open. "What makes you think I have a grudge against him?"

"All this nonsense about the petty charge brought against him. The ridiculous questions and accusations...unless you have something against me or my daughter."

"No, my lord! I..."

Rhone added his own steel gaze to Lindren's. "Is this about the trouble in the barracks?"

Tolbert's cheeks burned.

"What trouble?" Rodrin asked. He sat once more on his throne.

This story had waited a long time to see the light of day. "Not long after you gave me the command of the Twenty-First, Your Majesty, problems began arising in various squads. Stolen items, bullying, petty blackmail; nothing big on its own. Put together, however, it caused ripples in groups of men who were supposed to be brothers-in-arms."

Cat pulled away from him enough to get a good look at Tolbert.

"I asked around and discovered very little of this sort of thing had occurred before I'd taken over, so I dug a little deeper. It took me quite a while," Rhone continued, "until I found the men responsible and explained my position to them. Either they told me what was up or I'd bypass the standard punishment and kick them out with a dishonourable discharge. Most of them talked. A man had come to them offering money to cause disruption in the regiment. That man I traced back to the employ of Tolbert Robrai."

"It was just a prank!" Tolbert retorted.

Tolbert jumped at Rodrin's bellow. "Not when it disrupts one of my regiments! I need my men to work together for the safety of this country. That act could be considered treason!"

"So what did you do?" Shain asked.

Rhone allowed himself a small smile at the memory. "I cornered him here in the castle and broke his nose. I also told him if he caused any more trouble I'd make a formal report to King Rodrin."

"Which is what you should have done in the first place," Rodrin put in.

Rhone released Cat long enough to give him a bow. "You have plenty to worry about as it is, Your Majesty, and this was simply a matter of petty jealousy."

"Petty jealousy or not, a formal investigation into the state of the Twenty-first will begin tomorrow." Rodrin stood once more. "Now enough of this nonsense. We have a wedding to celebrate and the room needs to be cleared. Everyone out, proceedings are over."

Rhone found himself surrounded by both noise from a dispersing crowd and Cat's family. They appeared more puzzled than pleased. "I suppose I should have asked your permission first," he said to Lindren.

"That's not our way, but I must admit to some surprise and confusion. You're aware of the consequences?"

"I am. Cat made me think about it and I made her. This was our decision."

Lindren smiled and held his hand out. "Welcome to the family."

Rhone shook his hand as well as those of the rest of the Elves. When he took Kelwyn's hand, he pulled him close enough to whisper in his ear. "I'll never hurt her. And when I'm gone, promise me you'll be there for her."

Kelwyn nodded and gripped Rhone's shoulder in friendship and he knew he'd done it right.

"Well, this has been an interesting morning," Rodrin said, moving in beside Lindren.

Rhone bowed. "Thank you again, Sire, for all you've done."

"You're more than welcome. Now we have preparations to make. The kitchen needs to be notified of an impromptu wedding feast and I'll send a messenger to the priests of Ar. I'm sorry we don't have time to decorate the hall."

"We don't need anything fancy, Your Majesty," Rhone said, his grip still firmly on Cat. "And don't worry about gifts either. They're not necessary."

"Nonsense. I'll bet most of that rabble is off to the shops. It's good

304

for business."

They all laughed, then Rodrin rubbed his hands together. "We have plenty to do, and so do you. Kelwyn, would you escort the bride upstairs? Rhone's not permitted to see her again until the wedding."

Rhone gave Cat a quick kiss on the cheek before Kelwyn whisked her away.

"Lord Rhone," Jonlan said. "If you have a moment, I'd like to introduce you to my wife. Saysha, this is Lord Rhone Arden, the best friend anyone could ask for."

Rhone took Saysha's hand and kissed it. He stole the opportunity to examine the woman he'd only seen briefly the night Cat disappeared. Jonlan had chosen well. Saysha's pretty face was framed by long blonde hair, pulled back at the nape of her neck. Her warm blue eyes sparkled.

"Pleased to meet you," Rhone said. "I don't know how you put up with this reprobate, but I'm glad he's got someone to take care of him."

Jonlan laughed. "You haven't changed."

Saysha ducked her head. "I'm pleased to meet the man my husband refuses to stop talking about, my lord. He never said you were nobility." She cast her husband an annoyed glance.

"We've taken up enough of your time." Jonlan said. "And we need to arrange for Saysha's mother to keep Kiria for the rest of the day. I guess we'll have to find something new to wear. Neither of us own anything suitable."

Rhone reached into a pocket and pulled out two gold coins. "This should cover it."

Jonlan's eyes popped out of his head. "I can't take that!"

"Of course you can. You can't make much working at the warehouse and you have a wife and child to support. Besides, I don't need it. Once all this is done, I'm taking Cat and going home."

Jonlan stared at the coins in his hand.

"I guess this means we both lose," Rodrin said to Lindren.

Rhone cast him a questioning look and Lindren chuckled. "A private joke."

Perhaps Lindren would tell him later. "Darsha, Shain, would you mind accompanying me into town? I have an errand to run."

Chapter Twenty-Seven

Cat sat on her bed while Kelwyn occupied the chair, holding her hand. Hero played with something under the bed. She took a deep breath in an attempt to calm her whirling head.

Jewel rummaged through the wardrobe. "It's a good thing you had your bath this morning, my lady. Your hair is mostly dry, but you have so much of it I don't know how we're going to put it up properly."

"So don't put it up it," Kelwyn said.

"But it's my lady's wedding." Jewel straightened and held up Cat's silver and gold hairclip. "This will have to do, I suppose."

Cat didn't really care. She was still trying to absorb all that had happened that morning. *I'm getting bonded?* Every time she thought about it, her heart thumped. She loved the idea of spending a lot of years with Rhone instead of just a couple. Now that the reasons for his anger were resolved, he should be a more pleasant person to live with.

"Now then," Jewel said. "Which outfit would you like to wear? If you want my opinion, the gold one would look really nice with this."

The first time Cat wore the hairclip she'd worn it with that outfit, then something Rhone said popped into her head and wouldn't leave. *'I really like the red one.'* "I can't believe I'm saying this. I want to wear the red one."

"But you don't have a red outfit, my lady."

"No. The red dress."

Cat almost laughed at the expression on Kelwyn's face.

Jewel clapped her hands. "Oh, my lady! What a wonderful choice. Red is such a lucky colour." She scampered back to the wardrobe.

"Are you sure?" Kelwyn asked.

"I'm sure. Rhone said he liked it. I can wear it this once, for him."

Kelwyn leaned close, speaking in Elven. "Why did you agree to bond with him? What about children?"

"He keeps insisting he doesn't want any," she replied in kind. "I

306

tried arguing with him but he wouldn't listen."

"I suppose it's up to him. I hope he doesn't regret it." Kelwyn took her chin in his hand. "Are you happy, Cat?"

She smiled. "Yes, I am."

"Good. That's the most important thing."

Jewel carried a pile of clothing over to the bed. None of it was red.

"What's all this?" Cat asked.

"Your under clothes, my lady. There's a chemise, breast band, an underdress, stockings…" She pointed to each item. "Oh. You have no shoes."

"I don't need any. I haven't been wearing anything on my feet most of the time I've been here so I don't think people will notice."

Jewel frowned. "I suppose so. You could wear your ankle bracelet I guess, but…"

A knock interrupted her. Audney came in with another woman.

"Oh, good," Jewel said. "I'm glad you're here. I need help getting Lady Cat ready. She wants to wear the red dress."

She shooshed Kelwyn into the other room and Cat shed her clothes. The breast band came first, a strip of shaped cloth, tied up at the back, made of something stiff that held her breasts in place. It was surprisingly comfortable.

"You should wear one all the time, my lady," Jewel said. "Otherwise you might sag as you grow older."

"Sag!" Cat couldn't remember any of the Tiranen women sagging.

Jewel slipped the strapless chemise over her head, tied it to the breast band, then turned back to the pile of clothes. Cat took that opportunity to make a dash for the door.

"Kelwyn! Jewel says my breasts might sag as I get older," she said in Elven.

Kelwyn rolled his eyes. "How old was your mother when she died?"

"Three thousand-two hundred-and twenty-four."

"Did she sag?"

"No."

Kelwyn gently pushed her towards the bedroom. "Then don't

worry about it."

Amid multiple tsks, oohs and aahs, the ladies helped Cat into the ivory underdress, then finally the red one. It fastened at the front and showed off the fine material of the underdress. A snug fit, the gown hung just off her shoulders, the tight sleeves reaching below her elbow.

Once the women were done, she wasn't allowed to sit. Jewel said it might wrinkle her dress and sitting in the carriage would be bad enough, so she stood near the fireplace with Kelwyn, waiting for Lindren. Her friend wore the only dress outfit he'd brought, the sky blue tunic and white shirt over black trousers. She didn't care, so long as he was with her.

Audney and the other woman left leaving Jewel to fuss over last minute details. She stood on a chair, arranging Cat's hair. "I wish we had time to curl this."

A quiet knock sounded on the door and Kelwyn let Lindren in.

Her father's jaw almost dropped to the floor. "A dress?"

Now Cat felt a little sheepish. "Rhone liked it."

Lindren kissed her forehead. "You look absolutely gorgeous. It suits you perfectly. Rhone will be pleased."

Cat stared down at the open expanse of her bosom. "I just hope I don't fall out. I doubt King Rodrin would appreciate it."

"You won't fall out, my lady." Jewel patted down the back of her hair and climbed off the chair. "The breast band will make sure you don't."

Lindren held his arm out. "We have to leave now, Little One. The people will want to see you before and after the ceremony, which means we need the light."

"Why do they want to see me?"

"The citizens of Tezerain love royal weddings, but there are few of them and many aren't invited, so the only opportunity for them to see the bride and groom is on the ride to and from the temple."

"But I'm not royalty."

"You are to them. They think of me as the king of Silverwood, though I don't let them call me king. So, that makes you a princess in their eyes. And the fact that you're Tiranen is going to fly through the city faster than an eagle. Everyone will want a glimpse of you.

"Rhone has already left." Lindren opened the door and motioned her out, Kelwyn following. His sons waited in the hall. Shain whistled. Darsha's mouth hung open.

"Never in my life would I have thought I'd see you in a dress," Arnir said. He took her hand and kissed it, like a Kitring-Tor noble. "You look fabulous."

"Why?" Darsha asked, when he found his voice.

Cat smiled, enjoying the shocked expressions on her brothers' faces. "I'll tell you on the way."

The ride to the temple proved more of an experience than Cat could have imagined. Rodrin lent her the same open coach Selesa had used. Lindren helped her in, then climbed up beside her. Cat tried to arrange her dress to keep down the wrinkles. Kelwyn, Lindren's sons and the royal family all followed in closed coaches with other nobles trailing behind them. Lindren's and Mathyn's Elves walked alongside.

Rhone said the sun had shone for the past several days and what remained of the snow clung to the shadowy parts of the roads and alleys. Throngs of people, all lining the streets, barely allowed room for them to pass. Guards tried to control the cheering, waving crowd with little effect. Lindren told her to wave back while he did the same. Cat wanted to crawl under the leather-lined bench.

Vania's Temple lay north of the corner of Wharf and Dolphin streets, nestled amongst large, fancy houses. The white, rectangular structure was mounted with a simple roof, topped with a bell tower and fronted by a large courtyard. Two thick columns with fluted sides flanked a brace of large, oak doors. Ar's Temple, across the street, appeared identical, yet seemed to have a more masculine feel to it.

The carriage stopped at the bottom of the broad, shallow stairs. Lindren helped Cat down. Her bare feet touched the cold, wet cobblestones and she lifted her skirts, trying to keep the dress reasonably clean. A sense of detachment let her see everything; the cheering crowds, the following carriages discharging their occupants—Kelwyn, her brothers, the king, queen, Dayn—yet it all seemed a dream.

Queen Lisha's smiling face appeared and she took Cat's other arm. She and Lindren guided her to a door on the north side of the temple while the others entered through the huge doors. It took a moment for Cat to remember why Lisha was with her. She was the only woman in Tezerain, besides Selesa, whom she could call friend. The queen was to stand with her as a witness.

"Cat, are you all right?" Lindren pulled a chair over for her.

She sat on a nearby bench, not caring about a few wrinkles. "Yes, I think. I...I don't know what to do." Jewel had chattered about this and that. Not a lot of it made sense.

Lisha set a comforting hand on her shoulder. "You don't have to do much. When the time comes, walk with Lindren to Rhone's side, at a slow pace. Then just follow his lead."

"I can do that."

Lindren crouched beside her. "Are you sure you want this? Really sure?" he said in Elven.

Her heart gave a thump and everything snapped back into place. She found her smile. "Yes. Rhone knows I can't give him children. He says he doesn't want them and I believe him."

"All right, Little One. I trust you to do what is right, for both of you."

While Cat sat waiting for everyone else to take their seats, a warm glow washed over her and she wondered if Selesa, if every female, felt the same way before their bonding. The bells tolled and her heart thumped again.

"It's time," Lisha said. "You and Lindren go first. I will follow."

Lindren took her hand and tucked it under his arm. Someone opened the door. Then all she could see, all she wanted to see, was Rhone, standing next to Jonlan. A man and a woman, in identical robes, stood near them. Her love wore a deep blue velvet tunic over a bright white shirt, with black trousers and boots up to his knees. The look in his eyes only confirmed what her heart already knew.

Rhone tried not to look like an idiot as he watched Cat approach him. *A dress. She actually wore a dress.* Not just any dress, she wore the deep crimson one, lined with cream silk. It hung so it left her shoulders bare. The tops of her perfect breasts formed two, barely constrained, half moons. The top portion of her hair was pulled back from her face, held by something he couldn't see. The rest cascaded in gold-tinted silver clouds around her. Rhone fell in love with Cat, all over again.

The bells stopped when she reached his side, her smile as bright as the sun shining outside. Lindren turned her to face the high priest and high priestess, whose robes of blue, green, yellow and red stripes stood in sharp contrast to the bland, austere atmosphere of the temple. Behind the clergy stood two statues, one a man, one a woman, both with their robed arms held out to him and the five hundred Humans and Elves crowding the temple nave. Ar and Vania. God and goddess. Man and woman.

"Your Majesties, Your Highness, Your Graces, my lords and ladies," the priest began. "Lord Rhone Arden, Lady Cat. We stand in the presence of our blessed Ar, our beloved Vania, to join these two in life, to live and love together. A woman is beloved first by her father who protects and provides for her while she grows. Lord Lindren, do you approve of, and grant your blessing to, this union?"

"In the eyes of Ar and Vania and before these honoured witnesses, I do." Lindren took Cat's hand and placed it in Rhone's, bowed to the two statues, then took his place on the first velvet covered bench, beside his family and Rodrin's.

Cat's warm hand fit comfortably in Rhone's. He gave her a smile, she returned it and he gazed into her magnificent amber eyes while the clergy intoned prayers to Ar and Vania.

The priestess looked to Rhone. "A woman is beloved second by her husband, who takes over the duty of protecting and providing for her. Lord Rhone Arden, do you swear to love, honour and protect Lady Cat, who will be your lawful wife for the rest of your life?"

Rhone squeezed Cat's hand. "In the eyes of Ar and Vania and before these honoured witnesses, I do." He meant it with every fibre of his being.

More prayers followed and a choir of boys, high up on a balcony above the nave, sang praises to god and goddess. Rhone passed the time staring into Cat's eyes. He sincerely hoped the priest remembered to skip the part about children. No point in causing Cat anguish.

The priest turned to Cat. "When a woman is joined by Ar and Vania to the man who will be her husband, it is her sworn duty to make herself his in all ways, to honour and obey him…in return for his protection and provision."

Nice recovery.

The man's eyes flashed to Rhone for a moment before settling on Cat. " Lady Cat, do you swear to love, honour and obey Lord Rhone Arden, who will be your lawful husband for the rest of your life?"

Cat blinked her eyes. Her smile vanished. "Obey? What if he tells me to do something wrong and he doesn't know it's wrong?"

Twitters of laughter broke through the crowd. Lindren and his family tried hard not to laugh. Shain failed and Rhone thought he might fall off the bench. The priestess put a hand over her mouth, though it couldn't hide her smile and Rhone had trouble keeping a straight face.

Rhone took both Cat's hands in his. "Do you promise to love me for the rest of my life?"

Her smile returned. "Yes."

"That's all that matters. Drop the obey part," he told the priest, turning to face him.

The man looked from Cat, to Rhone, then back to Cat. "Uh, I suppose…uh, Lady Cat, do you swear to love and, uh, honour Lord Rhone Arden, who will be your lawful husband for the rest of…his…life?"

"In the eyes of Ar and Vania and before these honoured witnesses, I do." Cat lifted her eyes, and her smile, to Rhone. His heart stopped beating. With a thump, it started again.

The priestess pulled the ring Rhone purchased earlier out of a vestment pocket. "This ring has been properly blessed by Ar and Vania. Lord Rhone, please place it on the middle finger of Lady Cat's left hand as a sign to all of your love and commitment."

Rhone did so, pleased he'd made a reasonable guess at the fit. Cat stared at it in wonder.

The high priest and high priestess raised their arms. "With the powers and rights granted to us by the great god Ar, and the powers and rights granted to us by the goddess Vania," the priest intoned. "I hereby declare, on their behalf, that Lord Rhone Arden and Lady Cat are formally, and officially, in the eyes of our honoured deities and in the eyes of the witnesses, truly joined as man and wife."

Rhone leaned down to whisper in Cat's ear. "I'm supposed to kiss you now. Can you handle it?"

Her eyes widened. "I think so."

He took both her hands and pulled her close, giving her a short, sweet kiss on the lips. Cat's cheeks reddened, though she held her head high and proud. The crowd erupted in cheers and clapping. Tucking her hand in his, Rhone walked her down the aisle, followed by Jonlan and Queen Lisha, to the tolling of the bells and loud congratulations of the crowd. Despite the sun, a cold blast of air greeted them when the doors were opened. Priestesses stood on either side of the staircase, ready to throw flower petals gathered from the Winter Garden.

"Do you have a cloak?" Rhone asked, taking his from the monk who held it.

"No. I didn't need one."

They descended the stairs amid a rainbow shower of petals. The carriage and throngs of cheering people awaited them at the bottom. Rhone helped her in. That's when he spotted her bare feet. "Aren't you cold?"

"No."

Rhone shook his head and settled in beside her, waving to the people. The trip back to the castle seemed to take forever as it wound its way through the crowd, the sun just starting to dip behind the White Mountains to the west. When the carriage stopped, Rhone helped Cat down and led her through both sets of doors to the throne room, then the dining hall. The servants had been busy. Tables set with linens, china and silverware crowded the rooms. No garlands or paper balls decorated the doors and windows, though vases with bright, colourful flowers from the

Winter Garden sat on the tables. He stopped at the head table, waiting for the king and Cat's family. No one was visible, so he took a moment to kiss Cat again, though not long enough to start her eyes glowing.

"Are you happy?" he asked.

"Very." She fingered her ring. "When did you get this?"

"Right after the trial. Darsha, Shain and I picked it out." Rhone held her close. "You've made me the happiest man alive."

Voices told him the others had arrived and he released Cat. Congratulations were offered with hugs and a shake of hands. The king and queen sat in the centre of the head table with Rhone and Cat to Rodrin's right and the rest of Cat's family, along with Prince Dayn, arranged around them. The rest of the Elves sat in the same room. Somehow, the cooks managed to provide a mountain of food, none of it containing meat.

The king gave a speech, mercifully short, as did Lindren and Jonlan. There'd been no time to hold a formal signing ceremony, so Rodrin presided over a truncated version. Lindren signed as Cat's father. Since Rhone's father was dead, he signed the papers himself.

The tables were cleared and whisked away. The first dance belonged to Rhone and Cat. He requested a waltz and led Cat around the throne room, glad he didn't stumble. Cat was so light on her feet, it almost felt like he danced by himself. When they finished, everyone wanted their turn with the bride and groom and it was several dances later before he found Cat again.

Rhone took her hand, tugging her under the staircase. He reached into his pocket and pulled out a small box. "I'm supposed to give you this tomorrow morning at the gift opening. Unfortunately, Lindren wants to leave right away. The king's planned a formal announcement about it later, but I wanted you to have this now."

"You already gave me this nice ring. It has pretty leaves and everything."

It also had their names engraved on the inside. "This is different," he said. "It's traditional."

Cat took the box and opened it. Inside, on a piece of red velvet, lay a silver mountain cat in mid leap, a tiny topaz set as its eye. "Oh. This is beautiful."

"It's a broach."

"There's not much room on this dress for it."

"Wear it tomorrow, then, to hold your cloak closed." Rhone took the box back and tucked it in his pocket.

"I don't have anything for you."

"You don't need to. Lindren is supposed to provide a dowry, but I don't care about that. I have you, that's all I need."

Cat's smile grew. "What's a dowry?"

"It's nothing important."

"There you are," Shain said. He took Cat's hand. "I wanted to show you something."

He led Cat to the Gallery door, Rhone following, then pointed to the opposite side of the room, near the fireplace. Kelwyn danced there with Arissa Kail.

"Oh dear," Cat said. "She found him again."

Shain grinned. "Actually, Kelwyn's been spending time with her over the past several days."

Rhone leaned against the wall, his arms folded. "I wonder why."

"He says she's a nice person, when she's not pretending to be someone else, and very smart, but that's not the interesting part. Look over there." Shain pointed to a spot near the doors to the outer hallway. A slender young man with a long thin face stood there staring at Kelwyn and Arissa. It was Baron Pel Arnos. "I've been watching him. Every time they dance, he glares at them."

"Why would he do that?" Cat asked.

Rhone glanced at the baron, then Kelwyn and back to Pel. The look on the young man's face could only mean one thing. "He's jealous."

Cat's brow dipped and her head tilted slightly. "Then why in all the worlds doesn't he ask her to dance?"

Worlds? "In all the what?"

"World," Shain said. "She meant world. I think I'm going to tell Kelwyn about Pel."

"Shain," Cat warned. "Don't you cause any trouble."

"No trouble this time. We're leaving tomorrow and if we can

match up Arissa and Pel, she'll take Kelwyn's absence better."

Rhone had to agree. "Then we'll work on the baron."

Shain headed for Kelwyn, Rhone led Cat to Pel. It took only a few minutes to talk enough courage into him. They escorted Pel to Arissa. The plan was for Cat to dance with Kelwyn so Pel could make his move. It worked perfectly. The Baron of Arnos whisked the young lady out onto the floor. Rhone stood by the fireplace with Arnir and Darsha while Cat and Kelwyn danced.

"That was sneaky, but nice," Arnir said, when Rhone explained the plan.

"It was actually Shain's idea."

"Does this mean he's finally growing up?" Darsha asked.

Arnir laughed. "We can hope, though I sincerely doubt it."

After several more dances, Lindren halted the music, gaining everyone's attention. "At the Elven equivalent of a wedding, we traditionally perform a magical dance called 'Stepping Through The Forest'. It involves a strict set of dance steps blended with illusions. To honour my daughter, I would like to ask her to dance it with me."

With guidance from the Elves, amid hushed whispers and murmurs, the crowd moved to the edges of the hall, onto the staircase and the balcony above. Several of Mathyn's crew had brought their instruments and now took the place of the Human musicians.

Rhone walked Cat to her father, who waited by the outer doors, then stood with Darsha. "What does he mean by illusions?"

Darsha's eyes sparkled. "Wait and see. Only mages can perform this dance and Father's very good at it."

Lindren began in one corner of the hall, Cat the other. At the first strains of the melodic Elven music, they stepped out at an angle towards each other. On one beat Lindren held out his hand to her, on the next, she took it. His lips moved, though Rhone couldn't hear the words. As father and daughter twirled and danced slowly up the hall, images formed in front of the audience.

Flowers of many colours and varieties sprang from the floor; roses, peonies, tall graceful gladioli, rhododendrons. Rhone swore he could smell them. Trellises covered in vines and bright blooms arched

316

between the rows of flowers on either side of the hall as the dancers made their graceful way across the floor. The arrangement looked familiar. Then Rhone remembered where he'd seen it. The Winter Garden. He reached out to touch a lily.

Darsha pulled his hand back. "It will ruin the illusion."

Other Elves prevented various lords and ladies from trying the same thing. Lindren and Cat danced, dipped and twirled, oblivious to the watchers. Rhone had never seen a more graceful dance, nor heard more beautiful music. It warmed him to his soul, bringing him a peace he hadn't felt since…possibly never. By the time Cat and her father reached the throne, bushes and trellises, thick with flowers, lined the path the dancers had taken. They didn't stop there.

A small, silver cloud formed just a few inches off the floor. The crowd gasped in amazement as first Lindren, then Cat, stepped onto the cloud. Another formed, then another, each one slightly higher than the last. Father and daughter made their way back down the Hall, dancing from cloud to cloud, sometimes forward, sometimes back, each step perfect, eyes only on each other.

Every person in the crowd gaped at the pair and, as they danced, the flowers slowly sank into the floor and the clouds rose, just a few inches each time, and it seemed the dancers made their way into the sky. The room grew darker. Tiny pinpoints of white light appeared, until the flowers were gone and the dancers danced amidst stars in a nighttime sky. As the pair approached the end of the hall, the clouds descended and the garden rose, bringing the dancers down from the heavens.

Near the doors, Lindren bowed to Cat, who returned it with a curtsy. He held her hand, stepping gracefully to the point where they began. By the time they reached the doors, the garden had faded and the myriad stars flitted to the floor as snowflakes before vanishing. The strains of the music faded as a dream. Cat and Lindren turned to face the audience. The Elves clapped and cheered while the Humans stood in mute silence. Once they found their voices however, they outshone the Elves. Rhone added his appreciation, his heart filled to bursting.

All his life he'd read anything written about the Elves, listened in for as long as he was allowed when Lindren came to visit. The magical,

317

enigmatic, Elves. His own illusion had been shattered by their lies and deceit, though he understood the reasons. This incredible experience washed all that away. The magic, the wonder, flooded back to him. Most wondrous of all, these magnificent people were now his family.

Thunderous applause boomed through the old rafters, none as loud as Rhone's. As soon as Lindren released Cat, he strode to her and picked her up, twirling her in a circle.

She laughed and hugged his neck. "Did you like it?"

"How could I not? That was the most incredible thing I've ever seen."

Lindren chuckled. "Actually, it wasn't my best. I didn't have much time to think it out."

Rodrin reached them and pumped Lindren's hand. "Marvelous! I've never seen the like. Don't suppose you'd be willing to show us a few other Elven dances?"

"That's our most elaborate dance," Arnir said, "but I'll ask the musicians if they wouldn't mind playing a couple more. Cat, are you up to it?"

"I am. After all, it's my wedding."

Rhone set her down, then watched as Cat danced with first Arnir, then Darsha. Her feet seemed to barely touch the ground as they stepped in time to a lilting song that reminded Rhone of a summer breeze playing in long grasses, then a faster paced one that sent Cat's skirts in a whirl, the dancers' feet almost a blur.

Afterwards, Cat found Rhone and took his arm. "This next one is for males only."

Sixteen Elves lined up, including Kelwyn and Shain. They faced each other in two rows of eight and performed the most intricate, mind-boggling steps Rhone had ever seen. Each Elf danced with his arms folded across his chest, almost touching his partner. Their feet tapped and thumped in time to the quick music, intertwining with those of their partners. They turned and twisted first one way, then another, exchanging places with the pair next to them. Why no one was kicked or tripped, Rhone had no idea. The music sped up, faster and faster, until he couldn't tell one set of feet from another. It ended suddenly with each dancer standing exactly where he'd started. Once again the room thundered with approval. The Elven musicians bowed, then left the stage.

Rodrin took that moment to make an announcement. "Dear ladies and fine lords. Lord Lindren would like to leave at dawn tomorrow, so your gifts to Lord Rhone and Lady Cat will be packed up and sent to Arden. For now, we must bid our newlyweds a fair goodnight." Applause, hoots and whistles greeted his words. "Ladies of the single persuasion, if you please."

Servants poured through the dining room doors, each one with a basket of flower petals. The unmarried women scooped up a handful each and spread them on the stairs.

When they were done, Rodrin said, "No rain nor cold nor loneliness shall you feel, for you are shelter, warmth and companion to each other. Two lives have become one. We wish you well for all the future holds." He raised his cup and took a drink, as did everyone else.

Rhone bowed. "We thank you, Your Majesty."

Rodrin waved them away. "Off with you. You've got better things to do than lolly around here."

Laughter following, Rhone led Cat up the stairs to the balcony. He held his hand up for silence. "I would like to thank each and every one you for sharing this special day with us. I also thank you in advance for your wonderful gifts. Now, if you don't mind, I'll say goodnight."

He scooped Cat up in his arms and strode down the hall to their suite, more laughter following them. The guard opened the door for him, a grin plastered on his face. Rhone set Cat down and leaned against the door, holding it closed against all intruders. He kissed Cat, slow, sweet, sensual, until his lips, and his groin, burned. After ensuring Cat's amber eyes lit up the room, he bolted first the outer door, then the one to the bedroom.

"No one will dare interrupt us tonight, my beautiful wife." Cat smiled. Rhone lived for that smile, those brilliant eyes and her gentle heart. Now she was all his. "Did you wear that dress for me?"

"Yes."

"You didn't have to, but I'm glad you did. How do I get you out of it?"

"I don't know," Cat said. "I'm not sure how they got me into it."

Rhone laughed and kissed her again, just as a knock sounded at the door.

"I don't believe it." Rhone opened it, ready to punch whoever stood on the other side.

Jewel curtsied. "I'm here to help my lady…"

"I'll do it myself!" He slammed the door and bolted it. "Enough is enough." After kissing Cat again, he undid the fastenings of the red dress.

It would be fun unwrapping this wonderful package, the greatest gift anyone had ever given him.

Chapter Twenty-Eight

Morning came too soon for Cat. Life was tearing her in so many directions. She liked Tezerain and its royal family. Now that Dayn had committed himself to Jeral's training, he'd become more likable, less of a pest. Nonetheless, Cat wanted to go home. She missed Rhianna, Robbi, Lowren, Tarine, sitting in the oak tree with Kelwyn, spending time alone at her camp. The prophecy called to her, enigmatic as it was, which meant they'd head for Broken Man Pass very soon. Then there was her new life with Rhone.

He also wanted to go home and where he went, Cat would follow. Yesterday had rushed by in a blur and she hadn't discussed with Rhone where they'd live, for she felt sure Lindren would let him stay in Silverwood despite the fact no Human had ever visited an enclave, let alone lived there. King Rodrin offered to find some position for Rhone. All her new bondmate wanted was to return to Arden and his family. She needed to talk with both Rhone and Lindren, and decided to wait until they were on the road.

Jewel had spent the evening before packing their belongings. She even remembered to include Cat's beach treasures. One set of clothes had been set out for each of them and while they had a very early breakfast with the king and queen she packed the rest of their things.

Cat gave Jewel her dresses. She had no need of them and though they didn't fit Jewel she could either cut them down or sell them, whichever the little maid preferred. It was one of those rare moments when Jewel found no words to say. Cat gave her a hug, thanked her for all her help and wished her luck. Rhone just said goodbye.

Taking their leave of the royal family tugged harder at Cat's heart. She couldn't help wondering if she'd ever see them again and she deeply regretted that she hadn't had the opportunity to say a proper goodbye to Gailen and Selesa.

Just before they left, Rodrin gave Rhone a piece of paper, a declaration proclaiming his innocence in case anyone tried to arrest him.

After several rounds of hugs, mostly on Cat's part, Lindren and his family headed for the stables where the rest of the Elves waited. Mathyn and his crew planned to sail at sunrise, leaving only the Silverwood Elves to ride home. Lindren suggested Rhone could use Talifir's Hrulka. Cat took a few moments to explain to the mare that Talifir wasn't coming back. Despite her grief, the horse agreed. Cat thanked Arvanion Talifir was the only one they lost.

Cat asked Hero if he wanted to go back to his mother. To her surprise, the kitten chose to come with her, so she tucked him inside her tunic to keep him warm and mounted Krir.

Just outside the stable, someone waited for Rhone.

"You're up early," Rhone said, dismounting to shake Jonlan's hand.

"A little." Jonlan bowed to the Elves and Cat before continuing. "I just wanted to say goodbye and to let you know the king spoke to me last night after you and Lady Cat left. He's forgiven my desertion, quoting understandable circumstances, and offered me a place in the palace guard. Lieutenant, not captain, but I can work my way up again. And it's more money than the warehouse."

"Congratulations, you deserve it." Rhone pumped Jonlan's hand again. "King Rodrin knows a good man when he sees one."

"Don't be a stranger."

Cat's heart almost broke at the look in Jonlan's eyes. Circumstances hadn't allowed the two to be together for very long.

"It'll probably be a year or two, but I will be back to visit," Rhone said. "Meanwhile, write. Let me know how that beautiful little girl of yours is doing."

"I will."

After a heartfelt embrace, Rhone mounted Duon. Before long, thirty-five Elves, one Tiranen, one Human and one kitten, set off down Dolphin Street. The sun had yet to rise.

Lindren and his sons lead the group, with Rhone, Cat and Kelwyn following. It didn't take long for Rhone to realize he had a problem. He hadn't ridden in four years and his muscles let him know it. When they stopped for lunch by the side of the road, he took the opportunity to stretch and walk out the stiffness.

To his chagrin, Cat noticed. "Are you hurting?"

"Stiff. I haven't ridden for a while." It was only the first day of many.

"Maybe Arnir can help."

Rhone hated asking him. "I'll think about it."

"That's what you always say." Cat kissed his cheek. "Can I talk to you and Lindren?"

"Sure."

Rodrin had provided food for them. Cat dug into Rhone's saddlebags and came up with some bread, cheese and a couple apples. She set Hero on a stump, gave him a few small bits of cheese, then stood with Rhone and Lindren to eat her share.

"What's on your mind, Little One?" Lindren asked.

"First of all…" Cat turned to Lindren. "I meant to apologize sooner, but I couldn't find the right time. I'm really sorry for the words I used back at that house, when Talon was…" She looked at the ground and Rhone knew exactly what she meant.

"Excusable this time," Lindren said, his eyes darkening a shade. Rhone doubted it was because of Cat's language. "Talon deserved every word of it. Just don't make a habit of it."

"I won't."

Lindren kissed her forehead and Cat found her smile. "Second, everything happened so fast yesterday. I have no idea where we're going, Silverwood or Arden."

"Arden," Rhone said. Now that he'd cleared his name, had a beautiful wife who loved him and was free of his commitment to Rodrin, all he wanted was to go home and find a quiet life for himself and Cat.

"Not quite yet, if you don't mind." Lindren folded a piece of bread around a thick slice of yellow cheese. "Cat's moon cycle is due shortly and I think she'd be more comfortable at home this time. I also need to organize more forces before we head for the Barriers. I have a bad feeling about what's happening up there and I'd like a solid army in place before the thaw hits. Besides, I want you to meet Rhianna and the rest of our family."

Rhone's food halted half way to his mouth. "You want me to come to Silverwood? But no one…no Human has ever seen it except from a distance."

"You'd be the first Human in any enclave," Cat said, with a smile.

Lindren swallowed his food. "Not quite. Taurin's mercenaries come through there all the time." He turned to Rhone. "Taurin is my cousin. He runs a mercenary band of mostly Humans. They need to be able to travel quickly, so they come to the enclaves, but they're bound and blindfolded. It was the only way the other Elders would permit it. So, while you're not the first Human to enter an enclave, you will be the first to actually see one."

Rhone's need to return to Arden could wait. Never in all his dreams as a child could he have predicted he'd see Silverwood, though one thing peaked his interest. Why would Taurin's band need to enter the enclave to travel faster?

When he asked Lindren, the Elder only smiled and said, "You'll see."

With the meal done, they mounted and carried on. By the time they stopped for dinner, Rhone could hardly move. Cat spoke to Arnir. The Elven magic helped immensely and he realized it would be far too easy to get used to it.

They stopped for the night in a copse of poplar and birch only just beginning to bud. A small clearing allowed Rhone to set up the tent Rodrin provided for him and Cat. The rest of the Elves slept on the ground, wrapped in blankets. Cat assured him they weren't cold though Rhone still felt guilt over his modest comfort, then annoyance when Cat balked at making love; the Elves were too close. The thought of spending more nights beside her, unable to touch her the way he preferred, annoyed him.

324

Late the next morning, they caught up to the army waiting at the border for stragglers and the few dukes who'd accompany Vergel. Between Rodrin's and the dukes' men, the Kitring-Tor army would number five thousand. Snow still covered the ground here, though it wasn't deep, and the supply wagons had been outfitted with runners to make the journey easier. When the weather turned warmer, they could be removed with little trouble. Spring always came late in the Barriers and snow often hung around for a few weeks past the equinox.

Lindren passed on the news regarding the trial and wedding, as well as the letter for Brade. He also explained their plans and that the Elves would catch up to them in Kerend.

While Lindren spoke to Vergel, Cat dragged Rhone around the camps looking for Harrol. She found him with the rest of the northern men who'd hadn't completed the journey home three months earlier. The one armed soldier congratulated her on her marriage to Rhone as did all the men, except Soran Rais.

"Why would an Elf marry a Human?" Soran demanded. "Especially since you ignored my company. If I'm not good enough to take you for a walk in the Winter Garden, why is *he* good enough to marry?"

"You have a wife," Cat said, before Rhone could say a word. "And you made it plain to me that you wanted more than a walk."

"Then you misunderstood my intentions." Soran took a step towards her.

Rhone intervened. "Stay away from my wife, Rais."

Soran stiffened. "That's Baron to you! I don't care if you've been found innocent. Show respect for your betters!"

"Actually, as Lindren's son-in-law, I outrank you."

With a snarl, Soran motioned to his handful of men and stalked off. The others laughed. So did Rhone. He pulled Cat close to him while she spoke with Harrol; they'd become friends over the past few weeks. For a simple soldier he showed great promise as a cleric. With more training, he'd have no trouble finding a position in Aris' keep. They said their goodbyes, Cat giving Harrol a hug and kiss on the cheek, rejoined Lindren, then headed for Silverwood.

Just past the border, Lindren led them west, off the North Road, cutting across the empty plains, following the Silver River west and north. He slowed his usual pace, taking a total of six days to reach the northeast corner of Silverwood. Cat said the trip usually took four from Tezerain. Still, they rode long hours and by the time night came, Rhone was glad to fall into bed. He clung to Cat for warmth, the kitten wedged between them.

Their last night was spent by the pool at the foot of Silverwood Falls. Rhone had caught a glimpse of them before night fell, though their true beauty and majesty didn't become evident until morning. Far above, water thundered over a massive plateau to crash into the pool. He had to crane his neck to see the distant top. A smaller waterfall, lower and to the right, spilled from a cave.

"How high are those?" he asked Cat, as they ate breakfast.

"Over three hundred feet."

"There's nothing like them in the Barriers."

Cat hugged his arm. "There's lots more I want to show you too."

Kelwyn nudged him in the ribs. "You should ask Cat about her experience with the falls."

The tips of Lindren's ears twitched.

"Kelwyn! You weren't supposed to say anything," Cat complained.

"What experience?" Darsha asked, as puzzled as his brothers.

"I didn't want anyone to know," Cat said, her pretty brow dipped in a frown.

Shain snorted. "Too late for that."

It took a moment for her to respond. "On my one hundredth birthday...I jumped off the top of the falls."

Rhone almost dropped his bowl of porridge. Arnir coughed before he could swallow what was in his mouth.

Even Lindren appeared stunned. "Is that why you were late to your party?"

Cat nodded, her cheeks blossoming. "I broke a few ribs."

"It must have been terrifying!" Rhone exclaimed. "Why on Ar's world would you jump off the falls?"

"I thought it would be fun. And it was, with the wind and spray in my face, the sensation of falling...right up until I hit the water. It hurt more than I thought it would. It's just water!"

Lindren shook his head. "Sometimes I think I'll never understand you."

So did Rhone.

All that day they travelled at the base of the plateau. Part way along they reached what Cat called the Steps, a literal name. The ground rose in a series of long, shallow, snow-covered steps. Cat explained how Lindren's earth mages had gently reshaped the land, altering the natural rises so horse and rider could make the trip up the high slopes easily. Farther to the east, the North Road ran over flatter ground.

By dusk, they reached the northeast corner of Silverwood. Rhone held his breath as the Hrulka carried him off the Steps and into the forest. They were immediately greeted by two armed, and curious, Elves; part of Lindren's border patrol. The Elven Elder introduced Rhone, then spoke to them in Elven. One didn't appear pleased, making Rhone uncomfortable. As they travelled farther into the woods, he set it aside.

A skiff of snow lay on the ground inside the enclave. The trees, ones Rhone knew and others he didn't, rose to impossible heights. Cat named the unknowns. Dacia, with broad, dark green leaves and biren bearing long, slender leaves remained green all year long, continually shedding and producing new foliage. The avalar, a massive tree with a trunk thicker than two men, shed its blue-green leaves in the fall. Lindren explained that the trees required Elven magic to survive, so weren't found outside the enclaves.

"Just wait until the avalar trees blossom next month," Cat said. "They're so beautiful. The blooms are bigger than the palm of my hand."

Rhone caught himself looking everywhere at once, reminding him of Cat in Meat Town, while his wife chattered on about one thing or another. They followed a well-travelled path before arriving at a large meadow Cat called the Commons. A fountain sat at the eastern end, while several benches stretched along part of its length.

"I'll bring you here later," Cat said, almost bouncing out of her saddle in excitement. "I love the fountain."

They ran across several startled Elves on the way. Lindren spoke to each of them, explaining who Rhone was, following it with something said in Elven. Some of the Elves who travelled with them split off at various paths. Then Lindren left the main path. His family followed and, before long, they arrived at Lindren's. The house was nothing like what Rhone had expected. Ever since he was a boy, he'd pictured the Elves living in houses built in the trees. It couldn't have been further from the truth.

Lindren's cottage-like home sat firmly on the ground in a clearing. The rounded roof looked exactly like the bark of a tree, though none of it overlapped and Rhone could see no seams where it had been nailed together.

A curtained window, next to the door, overlooked various bushes still winter bare. Log benches surrounded a cold fire pit in the front yard. A large tree, green when it should have been bare-branched, sat close behind and to the right of the house, the bark the same shade of dark brown as the roof.

Rhone leaned over to Cat. "Why is the house right in front of a tree?"

"Because the house is grown from it."

Rhone blinked. He couldn't see the join from where he sat on Duon. "Like the ship?"

"Yes, but it's not the same kind of tree. This is a shirren."

That was all the time Rhone had to examine the exterior of Lindren's home. The door slammed open and a brown-haired Elf ran out, skidding to a stop in the snow when he saw Rhone. His eyes, the same colour as Lindren's, flew open. Rhone assumed this had to be the Elder's fourth son, Robbi.

It was confirmed a moment later when Cat called his name and jumped down from Krir. She hugged the Elf, who looked about eighteen. He stood a little shorter than Lindren and his face wasn't as lean, as if he hadn't lost all his baby fat. Robbi spoke to Cat in an excited voice; he also kept staring at Rhone, who decided he'd have to get used to it.

A woman followed Robbi. Lindren dismounted and strode to her, gathering her in his arms and speaking to her in Elven; it seemed he had no qualms about kissing in front of others. It had to be Rhianna.

Rhone's mother-in-law was a beautiful, slender woman with pale blue eyes. Delicate pointed ears peaked out of honey-blonde hair falling in a silken sheet to her waist. She stood a foot shorter than Lindren. The name Elyria was mentioned and Rhone realized they were talking about Talifir's wife. No, soulmate.

Somewhere in the sadness, nestled snug in her soulmate's arms, Rhianna found her smile. "Welcome, Rhone. To our home and our family."

Cat's eyes widened. "You speak Torian?"

Rhianna laughed, a pure sound, like golden bells; quite different from Cat's throaty laugh. "Lindren thought it might be necessary one day. It turns out he was right."

Rhone climbed off the Hrulka, stiff from the day's ride, his head reeling in wonder.

℘ • ℰ

Cat had been home less than two minutes and already wanted to cuff Robbi. Hero squirmed and she pulled him of her tunic.

"He's a real Human? How come you bonded with a Human? Why did Father let him in Silverwood? I thought no Humans were allowed here. He's got strange eyes. Does he speak Elven? I want to talk to him. It's not fair Mother knows Torian and I don't." Robbi spotted Hero. "Hey, what's that?"

"Shut up, Robbi." She put Hero on a log by the fire, instructing him to stay put. The kitten crouched, eyes darting in every direction.

Kelwyn laughed and slid off Joar's back. "He's Cat's kitten. A gift from Rhone."

Robbi made a move for Hero. Cat cut him off. "Leave him alone. He's scared. I'll show you how to play with him later."

"But I want to play now."

"I brought you back some things from the beach," she said. "If you don't behave I won't give them to you."

Her youngest brother grimaced, then turned his attention back to

329

Rhone, staring as if he might disappear any moment. Lindren's older sons each greeted their mother and brother. Cat waited until they were finished before she gave Rhianna a hug, then showed off the ring and broach Rhone had given her. She thought she knew everything about the Elf who'd become her mother. It seemed Rhianna still had a surprise or two hidden somewhere.

"I'm so happy for you, Cat." Rhianna gave her a kiss and hug. "I told you a special man would fall in love with you one day."

"I never expected him to bond with me."

Rhianna laughed. Rhone held his hand out to Robbi, who acted like it was a poisonous snake.

"You're supposed to shake his hand," Cat said, in Elven. "It's a Torian custom for greeting people."

Robbi took the offered hand and shook it, from side to side.

Rhone gave him a lop-sided smile. "He doesn't speak my language, I assume?" It took him a moment to get his hand back.

Cat shook her head. "He wants to, though."

Rhone then turned to Lindren's soulmate. "I'm pleased to meet you, Lady Rhianna." He bowed.

"No one bows in Silverwood," she said, giving him a hug and a quick kiss on the cheek, "and it's just Rhianna."

Rhone appeared lost, so Cat took his arm. "We need to get our things."

Robbi followed, picking up a handful of snow. "What's this in Torian?"

Cat told him. Her brother pointed to the house. "What's that?"

"Not now." She undid the straps on her bow case and quivers. A wet snowball smacked her in the back of the head. "Robbi!" She scooped up a ball of her own and tossed it.

Robbi ducked and the snowball hit Shain. The fight was on. It only took a couple hits for Rhone to join in. Snowballs flew through the air, everyone laughing, until Robbi tried to dodge a ball from Darsha and tripped over one of the logs, scaring Hero. The kitten yowled and ran off into the bushes.

The boy's youthful clumsiness had put a tear in his trousers and a cut on his knee. His crying put an end to the fight. Arnir fixed him up, then ruffled his hair while Cat searched for Hero, finally using a piece of dried beef from Rodrin's supplies to coax him out of the bush.

"Dinner will be ready soon and we need to change," Lindren said. "No time for baths, I'm afraid. We're having company. Let's get everything inside. I'm sure Rhone must be frozen."

"Who's coming?" Cat asked, cradling Hero and slinging her pack over her shoulder.

"Lowren, Tarine, Cerinna, Tiree, Tanvir, Biera and Faelen."

Cat raised an eyebrow. "It's going to be crowded around the table."

Darsha, Shain and Arnir all perked up. "I gather we're staying for dinner," Arnir said.

Rhianna smiled. "Daelyn's patrol spotted you last night, so we've had plenty of time to prepare."

"How's Tarine?" Cat asked, then turned to Rhone. "She's pregnant."

"You already told me."

"Tarine's fine." Rhianna's eyes sparkled and she had a mischievous cast to her smile. Cat wondered what was up.

Lindren pulled the last of his belongings off Auri. "Robbi, take the Hrulka to the pasture and unsaddle them. Ask Andren and Tarkin to give them rub downs. We won't have time."

"But I want to talk to Rhone." Robbi stuck his bottom lip out in a pout.

Rhone gave him a peculiar look, then chuckled when Cat rolled her eyes.

Lindren glared. "If you argue, you can do the rub downs yourself and miss dinner."

Robbi let out a quick, heavy breath and gathered the reins. Grumbling, he led the Hrulka out of the clearing. Darsha, Shain and Arnir placed their belongings on the logs by the fire pit, then everyone went inside.

Rhone tugged Cat back. "Robbi looks almost the same age as everyone else, but he acts like a child."

"That's because he is a child. He's only thirty-eight."

Rhone blinked. "He's older than me."

"I think he'd be about ten or so if he was Human."

Rhone shook his head. "This is going to take some getting used to."

Cat gave him a hug and a quick kiss, wondering when they'd find time for something more. She'd have to take him to her shelter to find any kind of privacy. "Faelen is Arnir's son. You'll meet him at dinner tonight. He's younger than Robbi, but looks the same age. I'll warn you now, Robbi's probably going to pester you to help him learn Torian. Faelen too."

Rhone laughed. "I think I can handle it."

"You don't know Robbi."

Chapter Twenty-Nine

Rhone's beautiful wife proved right, the table was crowded. Lindren told Robbi and Faelen they'd have to sit on the floor by the fireplace. In what Cat called the common room, six chairs surrounded a table that could be made larger by pulling it apart and adding planks. The fireplace, wide enough to hold a cooking cauldron, took up part of the north wall with two elegantly carved, wooden chairs in front of it.

The kitchen and pantry extended off the back of the room, to the west, with one closed door on the same wall to the right, Robbi's room according to Cat. The back door sat to the left of the kitchen while Lindren's and Cat's rooms exited on the south wall. Another room, on the north wall, showed a large wooden bathtub and washstand. Apparently the privy was out back.

The other guests arrived, bringing chairs with them, and the party was on. The evening with Cat's family provided an interesting insight to Elves at home. Again, it was far from what Rhone expected. He ate a delicious meal of bean soup, vegetable pie, fresh green and yellow beans with carrots, three types of bread he'd never tasted before and a variety of cheeses. Bowls of berries with cream finished the meal. Where had all the fresh food come from? The first day of spring had only just passed. Rhone wanted to talk to Cat. In a roomful of Elves, however, it would have to wait.

When the meal was done, everyone pitched in to clean up. No servants here, no pretensions that one was better than another. Rhone helped clear the table and distributed tea when it was made, and didn't mind in the least. Halfway through cleanup, the rest of Lindren's family arrived—Darsha's sons Kethyn and Dairath, their soulmates and Kethyn's son Celarin. The party moved outside. In moments, Lindren had a fire roaring in the pit and Rhone huddled next to Cat, wrapped in his cloak. Hero played with bushes, fallen leaves, snow, Robbi, Faelen, whatever he could find.

Conversations took a while. Not everyone spoke Torian. Questions were asked, and answered, through others. The entire story, from the time the Elves left Silverwood to their return, took most of the evening. All the women, Robbi and Faelen cried when they heard about Lindren and Cat's kidnapping, then again when they found out how Talifir died. Rhianna had news of her own, that poor Elyria had *faded* only two days after her soulmate's death. More hugs and kisses were dished out, and the love and respect this family had for each other, and their race, smacked Rhone in the face.

He wondered how some members of his family would receive him. One in particular. As the evening wore on, Rhone found it increasingly difficult to stay awake until finally he couldn't stifle his yawn.

"That's enough for tonight," Rhianna said. "Rhone needs rest and so do our other weary travelers."

"Before everyone leaves," Tarine said. "I have an announcement to make." Lowren held her hand. She placed the other over the small bulge of her unborn child. "We wanted to wait until everyone was together again. This is…the most amazing news. I'm carrying two babies."

Pandemonium erupted as everyone leapt to their feet, talking at once, all in Elven. Rhone sat, now alone, staying out of the way. Cat hugged Tarine, Lowren, Kelwyn, then Tarine again, chatting non-stop. Each face bore a mixture of shock and wonder, none more thrilled than Cat. A unexpected pull tugged his heart. Tarine glowed, surrounded by a loving, excited family.

Finally, Cat returned to his side, clinging to his arm. "This is the most wonderful, unbelievable news."

"Twins don't happen every day." Rhone pulled his arm out of her grip and placed it around her.

"You don't understand." Cat's eyes shone. "No Elf, or Tiranen, has ever given birth to two babies at once. Not ever."

Rhone started. "Then why now?"

"Lindren says he doesn't know. He's never heard of such a thing. And it's not the only thing strange. Ever since Robbi was born, there's been more babies than the Elves have ever seen at one time. Lindren and Rhianna are no longer the only ones with four children. It's all so puzzling, but he says it's better for the enclaves. We'll have more warriors."

Rhone held Cat close while he watched Lindren's loving, happy family. *More warriors.* They might be excited, to him it seemed wrong that these people should raise their children just to fight the Black Lord. Though most Humans did the same, his people also fought each other for stupid, petty reasons. The Elves only wanted to protect their world, their peaceful, wonderful, way of life.

Rhianna came to sit beside her daughter.

"You knew, didn't you," Cat said, her eyes shining bright.

"Yes, I did."

Cat talked Rhianna's ear off while Rhone watched the rest of Lindren's family. A pang tightened his chest and once again he wondered how he'd be received at home.

When everyone calmed down, Rhianna stood and announced again it was time for the gathering to end. In moments, the tea cups vanished and Lindren's older sons and their families said goodnight, taking their chairs with them. Then Lowren, Tarine and Kelwyn left, after more hugs and kisses. It seemed a mere blink and he was left with Cat, Lindren, Rhianna and Robbi.

Rhianna spoke to Lindren, then her son, in Elven. The young Elf countered with something that sounded like a protest in any language. One glare from Lindren put an end to it.

"Lindren, Robbi and I are going for a walk," Rhianna said, taking her soulmate's hand. "We'll probably be a couple of hours."

Cat had a good hold on his arm and hugged it, a smile growing on her pretty face.

"I'll say goodnight, then." Rhone started a bow, then caught himself. "Thank you for a wonderful dinner and great company."

Rhianna's smile, though different from Cat's, was just as dazzling. "You're welcome. We'll see you in the morning."

Cat waited until they left the clearing, then pulled him into the house, and her room. Hero followed them, making himself comfortable in a basket of rags Rhianna put together for him.

Rhone's exhaustion melted away before his sudden, burning, passion. Cat made short work of his cloak, armoured jerkin, tunic, shirt and boots. When she broke off kissing him, she said, "I thought we'd have to go to my place for privacy."

He held her close, her now naked chest warm and delicious.

"How long to get there?"

"For me, an hour's run."

"Too long." Rhone buried his face in her neck. "Two hours is all I need." His trousers fell, then hers. He backed her towards the bed, barely big enough for two. "Rhianna is a very smart woman."

ℰ · ℭ

Rhone awoke to Cat stroking the fine pelt of hair on his chest. He placed his hands on either side of her face and pulled her down for a kiss. She quit far too soon.

"Why'd you stop?"

"Everyone's awake. Can't you smell breakfast?"

That's when he noticed she was dressed.

"How long have you been up?" he asked.

"Two hours or so. I had something to do."

Rhone sniffed and found the enticing scent of cinnamon. His stomach growled. Cat rolled off and tossed him his trousers. "I want to take you to Tiralan today."

"Tiralan? Where's that?" Rhone slid out from under the blankets and shivered. The heat from the fireplace didn't make it through to the bedroom. He dressed quickly.

"It's where I was born, the home of my people." Excitement lent a gleam to Cat's amber eyes, reminiscent of the glow they made when she wanted him, though not anywhere near as intense.

"Cat, we've spent six long days traveling. The last thing I want is to get back on a horse."

"It'll only be for a couple hours or so. Please? I really want to show it to you."

336

"Can't it wait a day or two?" Rhone tugged his boots on.

"Not really." Her voice grew quiet.

"What's wrong?"

She plunked herself on the bed beside him. "It's my moon cycle. I've been having pains for a couple days. It could start any time."

Great.

"Lindren wants to leave as soon as it's over."

"All right." Rhone stood and held his hand out to Cat. "We'll go today."

Rhianna served large bowls of cinnamon flavoured porridge, thick with chunks of apple and nuts sprinkled on top. Lindren and Robbi both plopped a dollop of honey on theirs, so Rhone did as well. It was the best porridge he'd ever eaten, though it would have been more enjoyable if Robbi hadn't wanted to know the Torian word for everything in the house. Afterwards, Lindren invited him to sit by the fire while Cat and Rhianna puttered in the kitchen.

Cat came out a short while later with a small sack. "Time to go."

"I'll walk with you," Lindren said.

They opened the door and Hero dashed in. Cat scooped him up. She pet him and held him up to look into his eyes. "He wants to come, too." She tucked him inside her shirt, then took her cloak off the hook by the door, fastening it with the mountain lion brooch he'd given her.

Rhone grabbed his cloak and they headed out the door and down a path leading more or less south. They stopped by the pasture to pick up Duon, Talifir's mare, and Krir. Lindren talked about various aspects of the enclave until after they'd left the pastures.

"You're going to see something no Human has ever seen and very few knew about," the Elder said.

A short walk brought them to a clearing close to the grey cliffs of the White Mountains. The entire meadow was taken up with three long rows of flat stones, each about two feet in diameter. A path, wide enough to walk a horse, separated them. A single rune was etched into each stone, pale against the darker grey of the rock.

"What's this?" Rhone asked. He'd learned some Elven runes while playing Rune Stones on Mathyn's ship and recognized none of these.

"The gates." Lindren directed him to the farthest row. "Urdran is only one of six worlds."

Rhone stared at him, not sure he'd heard right. "I don't understand."

"There are six worlds," the Elder said. "Urdran is only one and there are enclaves on five worlds. In order to travel between enclaves, and worlds, we need these gates."

Cat took his arm. "Tiralan, the place where I was born, is on the world of Tiru."

"Six...worlds?" Rhone knew there was more than one enclave. Several times Elves had come to the aid of Kitring-Tor, both in the country proper and the northern baronies, far more than could live in one forest. Mathyn and his crew came from an enclave called Ringwood that lay far to the south. There were many places Rhone had heard about in his studies, countries to the east, south and across the sea. But...*worlds*? "Why?"

"Because that's the way Ar wanted it," Lindren explained. "Before the coming of the Black Lord, there were thousands of enclaves on all the worlds. When he first attacked us, he took one of those worlds for his own, Fornoss. All gates to it were destroyed to stop him from using them. That move gave us a short break while he figured out how to make portals. During that time, Ar taught us what he could of warfare. Still, thousands, millions of us died. That's why Ar created the Tiranen. It's also why he brought your people here and to the other worlds."

Rhone's head reeled. "There's Humans on other worlds?"

"Yes. Three others, Tiru, Morata and Cathras. Darda is home only to Elves."

"Morata." Rhone had heard that word. Cat said it. He thought it might be an island. It wasn't. "So, why don't my people know about this?"

Lindren leaned against a nearby tree. "Most of your people rarely travel more than a day from their homes, nor do they want to. You have everything you need with your agriculture, mining and trade. Each of the worlds has many different countries and cultures, as does Urdran. I hate

338

to say it, but your people have problems with other cultures and beliefs. It's bad enough that you argue amongst yourselves on Urdran, the last thing we need is wars conducted between one world and another."

Rhone hated to admit he was right. "How do these stones work?"

The Elven Elder pushed himself off the tree and pointed at the first stone. "Each one is spelled to a particular stone elsewhere. This one, for example, will take you to Gold Moon, where Shain lives. That's the enclave where I and my three older sons were born. It lies to the west, on the other side of the White Mountains."

Lindren indicated the second stone in line. "This one leads to Blue Hills, Arnir's home on Tiru, the same world where Cat was born. The third goes to Tiralan. Most of the others lead to enclaves on Urdran. There are more enclaves than there are stones, a lot more. To get to some places we need to step on a stone here, then another in say, Blue Hills, then another to end up where we want to be. They were originally created to help us find our soulmates who could be born in any enclave on any world. After the Black Lord attacked, they've proved most valuable for transporting our warriors to where they need to be."

Rhone's gaze wandered over the slabs of slate filling the clearing. "And you don't think it would be handy to have Rodrin's troops in Kerend right now?"

"Yes, it would. But as I said, we don't need wars between worlds, or even between cultures half a world away. And I'm not sure your people have the kind of magic it takes to make one."

Cat remained silent, clinging to his arm, Hero peeking out of her shirt.

"What do you think of all this?" Rhone asked her.

"I haven't really thought about it. I grew up with them. They've always been here."

Secrets and more secrets. Did it ever end? "I understand," Rhone said. "I really wish my people weren't so...predictable." Give them something nice and someone would ruin it. Then a thought hit him. "You said these stones also lead to other places on Urdran?"

Lindren nodded.

"So that's where the fresh fruit and vegetables came from."

"Yes. Each of the enclaves produces more than they need of whatever it is they grow," Cat explained. "They trade with the other enclaves for what they want, especially in winter. Some even raise sheep, cows and goats for our cheese, cream and butter."

"We also have caves that are spelled to preserve food," Lindren added. "The berries we ate last night came from Greenwood, on Cathras. It's summer there."

Rhone glanced around the forest-rimmed clearing, trying to absorb all the new information. "What do you grow to help the cause?"

A little smile turned up a corner of Lindren's mouth. "We harvest oats, wheat, barley, corn and hay from the plains. There are also orchards in the middle of the enclave, with apples, pears, peaches and cherries. We do our part. If you have no more questions, I'll leave you. I have arrangements to make before we head to Kerend. Cat will explain exactly how to use the gates." With that, Lindren stepped on the nearest stone and vanished.

Rhone almost jumped out of his boots. "Where'd he go?"

Cat tried to hide her laugh. "To Gold Moon." She tugged on his arm, leading him and the Hrulka to the third stone Lindren had pointed out. "Each one has a rune saying where it leads. If it's glowing, stand back, because that means someone's coming through and they might have a Hrulka with them."

"What happens if you try to use it when someone else is?"

"It can't happen. It's spelled so it won't work if a person's standing on it and you can tell if someone is because it's lit up. Do you want to go first?"

Panic turned his palms sweaty. Lindren had just...disappeared. "No. You go first."

Cat shrugged and, holding Krir's head close to hers, stepped on the stone. Just like Lindren, she and the horse vanished. Rhone took a deep breath and clutched Duon's reins, holding the horse's head close to his, as Cat had done. "I assume you've done this before," he said to the horse.

Duon snorted and gave him a look that Rhone could swear meant 'Of course I have, idiot'. Rhone closed his eyes, placed his foot on the

340

slate and held his breath. Nothing happened.

When he opened his eyes, however, he was in a different clearing. The snow was deeper, the meadow much larger. A cold wind blew. There'd been barely a breeze in Silverwood. Cat waited a short distance away and he led Duon to her.

"It's colder here," Rhone said, tugging his cloak around him.

"Tiru is a month behind Silverwood. It's still winter." Cat mounted Krir.

Rhone swung himself into Duon's saddle. The trees were similar to those in Silverwood, far bigger than the ones he knew. Cat led him along a path wide enough for the Hrulka to canter, her braid bouncing up and down on her back. They travelled due east, through a forest shrouded in snow, the trees so tall Rhone could see little of the sky. Every now and then, other paths branched off the one they took. He passed the time thinking about the gates and the fact that, apparently, he was on a completely different world, a concept he had a difficult time grasping.

After an indeterminate amount of time, Cat slowed and exited the forest near a lake so big he couldn't see the far shore. It had to be deep, ice only crusted the edges. She dismounted and stretched. So did he.

Cat scanned the blue-grey water. "This is Lake Havrin."

Once out of the forest, Rhone could see mountains rising to the north and south.

"That's the Spine Mountains," Cat said, pointing north. "An enclave sits in a valley about a hundred and fifty miles from here." She turned south. "Those are the Blue Hills. Arnir's home is sixty miles south, also in a valley."

Taking his hand, she led him along the shore. Then she stopped. Rhone could see no reason why. Cat let go of Krir's reins, took Hero out of her shirt and placed him on Krir's saddle. The kitten stayed put while Cat stared across the endless snow, her expression lost.

"This is where my people are buried," she finally said. "Leave Duon here. Follow in my steps."

Rhone did as she asked. Eventually Cat stopped, crouched and brushed away the snow from something. Closer examination showed it to be a sword hilt.

341

"The first time I came here the mounds could still be seen," she said, her voice quiet and solemn. "This is my father's tchiru. It shows where he's buried."

Her mother and brother lay on either side of her father. Cat spoke, though not in Torian. Rhone had heard enough Elven lately to realize it wasn't that language either and he wondered if she spoke Tiranen. She took in a shuddering breath and tears fell.

Rhone put a hand on her shoulder. "What are you doing?"

Despite her tears, she smiled. "Telling them about you."

Pulling her to her feet, he wrapped her in his arms. "You don't have to. Not if it upsets you."

"I'm all right." Cat sniffed back her tears. "I don't come here that often. When I do I like to talk to them."

She wiped her face and led him farther south. The Hrulka shadowed them half a mile away. After a time, Cat stopped and the horses turned in their direction.

"We're at the end of the graves," she said. "Duon wants to go back to the herd. She's still grieving for Talifir, but I'm sure we can find another for you."

"It's not necessary."

"It is. You need to be able to keep up on the ride to the baronies. Only a Hrulka or an Elven horse can do that." She pointed due south. "There."

Rhone could see nothing for several minutes. Then the white snow changed to a black smudge. Before long he could make out individual animals. The herd was massive. "How many are there?" he asked.

"Over a thousand here. A couple thousand more are elsewhere, ridden by Elves." She let go of Rhone's hand, tucked Hero back in her shirt and undid the straps on Duon's saddle.

By the time they finished removing the Hrulka's equipment, the others were there, surrounding them, nosing Cat, seeking her attention. They ignored him, until one animal shoved his nose into Rhone's shoulder, almost knocking him over.

Cat laughed, her tears forgotten. "I've told them who you are. He wants to go with you."

Speechless, Rhone patted the horse's nose. Others shoved in then, seeking attention.

"His name is Shuar." Cat stroked one nose, then patted a neck.

"How do you know?"

"He told me."

Rhone's hand faltered mid-pet. "Is this like the dolphins?"

"Yes. They speak to me in images and feelings. The name just comes to me."

As one, the herd turned and headed back south. They saddled Shuar, Rhone still trying to digest everything that had happened that morning. Then he realized the horse took the saddle surprisingly well.

"Who trains all these horses?"

Cat flashed him a cheeky smile. "No one. They train each other. Though Shuar has never worn a saddle or tack, he knows what to expect and what's expected of him. Now that Duon has been released, she'll help teach the young."

Mounting once more, Cat took the lead heading back into the forest. Rhone followed, wondering what was next. Sometime later she slowed, turning down a side path. They walked their Hrulka until they came to another clearing, this one the same size as Lindren's. It also held a house surprisingly similar to the Elder's.

It was an easy guess. "Your home."

Cat nodded. They left the Hrulka to nibble on the few stalks of dried grasses poking their heads above the snow near the edge of the clearing and entered the house. It was almost the same as Lindren's, but in reverse, with the door facing west, not east, the fireplace on the left instead of the right. Two extra-long swords hung crossed over the mantle, round shields flanking them. Just like Lindren's, two chairs faced the cold fireplace. The room had simple furnishings, larger than Lindren's. One chair at the table had longer legs than the other three.

"How tall was your father?"

"He and Mordru were both over eight feet. Mother was seven. Father had that chair made for me so I didn't feel so short." Cat placed her sack on the table and sat in her chair.

She tugged out several items, all wrapped in green leaves. Soon, cheese, bread and fruit lay on the table. Rhone sat in one of the other chairs, feeling like a kid again. Cat's shirt moved and the kitten stuck its head out.

"All right, Wiggles," Cat said, pulling Hero out of her shirt. She reached into the sack again and brought out some dried meat for the kitten, placing it on the other end of the table.

When they'd eaten their fill, Cat wrapped everything back up while Hero played with a dust ball under the table. Two items, besides the sack, remained—a small golden dragon pendant and a knife.

"What's this?" he asked, picking up the dragon. The work was incredibly detailed.

"I think it was supposed to be a gift for me. The day everyone died was a Festival day."

"Why haven't you taken it? It's a beautiful piece of work."

"It didn't feel right." A strange answer. Cat slipped off her chair and opened the door to the south. "This is…was…my parent's room."

It contained a bed, a wardrobe and a table with a mirror, brush, comb and a box. The bed was huge, which made sense if her father was over eight feet. Rhone picked up the box. Another work of art, with carved hummingbirds flitting around the top and sides. He opened it. A small fortune in jewelry lay inside.

"Why don't you wear these?" He pulled out a necklace of golden leaves joined tip to tip by diamonds set in tiny flowers.

"They were my mother's." Cat took the box from him, placed the necklace back inside and closed the lid. "I don't want to. Not…yet."

Rhone took the hint and let it be. She showed him her room, with a much smaller bed under the window, a clothes chest on the right and a shelf with an old doll and some other items on the left. The kitchen was smaller than Rhianna's, the washing room was the same. He suspected the privy was several yards outside the back door, just like Lindren's.

Cat sat in one of the chairs by the fireplace, her expression sad. Rhone watched her a moment, then pulled her to her feet and kissed her.

"We're alone here," he said, hoping some attention would perk her up.

It did, though she took him to her room, not the larger bed belonging to her parents. The sheets, surprisingly clean and unworn, felt like ice and Rhone clung to Cat for more than just passion. Afterwards, she lay on top of him, talking about her dead family.

Then it was time to go. Rhone took a last look at Cat's simple home before noticing a door she'd missed. "What's in here?"

Cat grimaced. "That's Mordru's room. I don't go in there."

"Mind if I do?" He opened the door. Her dead brother had similar furnishings to Cat, which meant not much. A few things of interest sat on his shelf, a jade carving, a crystal horse, and several rocks with streaks of gold in them. Hero dashed in, almost tripping him. The kitten poked around the corners, found something to play with, then skidded under the bed.

"We should go," Cat said, from the doorway. "Hero, come out from under there."

The kitten hissed and growled.

"What's his problem?" Rhone asked.

"He smells something funny. Mordru died here. We should leave."

Rhone crouched and peered under the bed. The only thing there, besides Hero, was a small black box. He pulled it out. "I wonder what's in here?"

"We probably don't want to know. Hero, come out, we have to go home." Cat sounded afraid.

This time the kitten obeyed, running almost sideways into the common room. Rhone opened the box to find a small dagger and some dried up pieces of…something. "What's this?"

"As I said, we probably don't want to know." Cat scooped the kitten up and placed him back in her shirt.

"It looks like dried fungus."

He took the box to Cat, who stiffened. "I remember that awful stink. Mordru smelled like that sometimes."

"You can smell something?" He held it up to his nose. All he could detect was the faint odour of wood, dust and perhaps a bit of old mould. "Maybe we should take it to Lindren." Rhone put the box in the top of Cat's sack and refastened the ties. He also picked up the dragon pendant and knife. "You should take these, especially the dragon. If your parents meant for you to have it, wouldn't it be honouring them to wear it?"

"I didn't really think of it that way. It was another reminder that they're gone."

"Maybe you should think of it as a reminder of their love." He tucked them into the sack as well. Taking her hand, he led her out the door and closed it. "You didn't have to bring me here, Cat. You've been upset most of the day."

"I wanted to show you my home. I think...I needed to show you."

He held her tight a moment and kissed the top of her head. They mounted their Hrulka and rode back to the gates.

Chapter Thirty

"So what do you think it is?" Cat asked. Sitting in Lindren's common room erased her silly fears over what Rhone found under Mordru's bed.

Rhianna had taken Robbi out for a walk, promising to teach him more Torian words. Lindren wanted him well away, which perked Cat's curiosity even more.

Lindren turned the small black box in his hands. "Thelaru made this when Mordru was little. It was for holding *sharlas*. Mordru had quite the collection."

"Sharlas?" Rhone asked.

"Small coloured glass balls. They're used to play games." Lindren set the box on the table.

Cat rose and picked a red and orange alley off the mantle. Her brother had a habit of leaving things lying around. "This is one of Robbi's."

Rhone took it from her, rolling it in the palm of his hand. "We have something like these. Marbles. The poor folk use rounded stones. Usually played in a circle?" He gave it back.

Lindren nodded and flipped open the catch on the box. Cat sat beside him, leaning over so she could see. The sour, pungent, smell, with a trace of mould, wafted up to her nose and she jerked back. Eight small, dark pieces of…something…sat in the bottom of the box along with the little dagger Rhone mentioned. Lindren closed the lid and sat back, his expression grim.

"What is it?" Cat asked.

"Something I'd hoped never to see connected to someone I'd known and cared about." Lindren rubbed his forehead. "It's hatterith. The fungus throk is made from."

"That drug those vauroks on the ship used?" Cat asked. "Why would Mordru have it?"

Lindren remained quiet a moment, then took in a breath and sat straighter. "I can only surmise that he was eating it."

"That stuff is disgusting." Cat had sampled almost everything in the forest when a child. There were a lot of things she never ate again, including hatterith.

Rhone took the box and opened it, sniffing the contents. "I still can't smell anything."

"What happened when you ate it?" Lindren asked Cat.

"I felt funny. Sort of lightheaded, but it also made me feel like I could do anything."

"Ale and wine will do that," Rhone put in.

"The taste was so bad I didn't eat anymore," she added.

"Probably a good thing, Little One. Humans have eaten this fungus and, over time, were unable to stop eating it. It made them act crazy, more so than ale or wine," Lindren said. "They didn't care about anything but getting more of it, any way they could. It's worse with the Throkdogs. It's reduced to a concentrate, making the effects more powerful. They rarely feel pain and have little clue as to where they are or what they're doing. It's why they're so hard to kill. Too unpredictable."

He studied Cat's face, as if deciding if he should say what was on his mind, peaking her curiosity. "Thelaru told me, not long after you were born, that Mordru's behavior had changed. It was gradual, but noticeable. He said Mordru exhibited mood swings and would disappear for days at a time. When he confronted him, Mordru said he was angry over a lovemate who'd left him for another and was having trouble getting over it. That rarely happened with your people and Thelaru didn't believe him. Mordru was an adult and performed well in battle, so he let it go."

Rhone opened the box and studied its contents. "I don't think I've ever seen a fungus like this."

"It doesn't grow on Urdran," Lindren told him.

His behavior changed. "How long after I was born?" Cat asked.

Lindren turned back to her. "You were about seven or eight."

"Could this have had anything to do with how he treated me?" Rhone closed the box.

"It's very possible, Little One." Lindren put his hand over hers.

348

"This fungus changes behavior in Humans. I can see where it could have the same effect on a Tiranen, though it wouldn't have done any permanent damage."

"Perhaps that's where he was going the night you caught him in a lie," Rhone said. "To chew more of this stuff."

Lindren nodded. "A possibility."

Cat stared at the table. Did it make her feel any better that it might not just be her that made Mordru change? Would that night have been different if he hadn't ever eaten hatterith? Would the following forty-two years have been different? "Why would he start eating it?"

"Who knows why anyone does anything," Lindren said. "It may have been on a dare. Your brother was famous for taking any dare, any time." He picked up the box and stood. "Regardless of the how's and why's, I'll dispose of this. I don't need Robbi finding it. Sitting under a bed all these years has dried the fungus. I suspect it's as concentrated as throk."

Rhone also rose and held his hand out to Cat. "I think we'll go for a walk."

As soon as Cat stood, a sharp pain cut across her lower belly. *Stupid moon cycle.* Maybe she should take Rhone to her shelter. It might be the last night they could spend some time together for the next week, provided it didn't start too soon.

$$\text{\scriptsize ℁} \quad \bullet \quad \text{\scriptsize ℞}$$

Rhone walked a wide path amidst giant trees, the stars winking in and out with the movement of the branches. Cat led him south and east. She didn't say much and he left her to her thoughts. Dealing with a pain-in-the-ass older brother was something Rhone understood quite well. After a long walk, he heard the sounds of a river gurgling and a muted rush of water.

They entered a clearing. A small shed stood on the near bank, the river rushing past a few yards away. A cold fire pit, flanked by logs, lay nearby. Rhone sincerely hoped it wasn't what he suspected.

Cat found her smile. "Welcome to my camp."

His heart sunk. "This is your home?"

"Yes, when I'm not at Lindren's."

"This is a shack. A shed. Something you put wood in or store tools. This isn't a house." Rhone opened the door.

A long bed, wide enough for two, took up most of the space. Shelves lined the end walls, littered with objects. No fireplace. No washing room. He stepped around the back. No privy to be seen. "You expect me to spend the night here? What if I have to relive myself? I'll freeze my...privates...off." He didn't need to see Cat's face to know he'd made a mistake. A big one.

With a sob, she ran into the dark. Rhone followed, but she scampered up a massive oak before he could catch her.

"Cat!" he cried, then remembered Kelwyn told him he didn't need to shout. She'd hear him. "Cat, come down. Please. I'm sorry. It's a nice shed. Really well made. Cat!"

୫ᴏ   •   ଓଃ

Lindren trotted down the trail to Cat's place. He found Rhone sitting on a log, his hands tucked under his armpits. "Trouble?"

"How did you know?"

"The border patrol heard you and I was at Darsha's, not far away." Lindren gathered some of the kindling and wood stacked beside the shelter. He placed it in the fire pit and lit it with his handfire.

Rhone huddled further into his cloak. "I said something I shouldn't have. Again."

Lindren chuckled. "Sometimes it doesn't take much, especially this close to her moon cycle. Shall I take a guess? You don't like her shelter."

"You'd be right. I have to admit, I'd expected something more along the lines of your house, maybe a little smaller. Cat seemed so proud of it."

"She is. You should have seen what she had before we built that one. I was surprised a good wind hadn't blown it down. Took an earthshake to do it in."

350

Rhone glanced up from the fire. "Earthshake? Does it happen often around here?"

"No. It occurred before the baronies were set up, when Cat found the dead dragon." Lindren cast his gaze to the oak tree. She was there, though well hidden. "I'll see if I can get her down. When I do, wait until she comes to you."

It took him almost half an hour. Once she touched the ground, Lindren gathered her in his arms. "You wanted to spend some private time with him?"

She nodded, her head on his chest, then sniffled.

He kissed the top of her head. "Didn't you think he'd get cold? You don't have any way to heat your shelter."

"He was all right in Tiralan," was the muffled response.

"I'm sure he was cold there too. Let him apologize, he really is sorry." There couldn't be much time left before her moon cycle started. "Are you in pain?"

She nodded. "I have been for a couple days."

"Then come home. Rhianna, Robbi and I will go for another walk. If it starts before we get home, just tell Rhone where everything is."

Cat pulled away from him. "I don't think he'd want to help. Taurin doesn't."

"Rhone's not Taurin. Just come home. We'll deal with it when it happens."

Lindren held her hand and took her to Rhone, who clutched her to his chest, apologizing with every breath. They found other things to talk about on the walk home.

ⅎ • ‣

By morning, Cat was in agony. Rhianna decided to give her a healthy dose of sleeproot before her cycle started. Lindren took Rhone on a walking tour of Silverwood. There was no point in him sitting by the bed staring at her.

He took him south past Lowren's to Rainbow Lake and the twelve ice-encrusted waterfalls tumbling from the White Mountains, the warming sun casting rainbows willy-nilly. Though a mere shadow of their summer grandeur, the falls splashed in misty plumes into the blue-green waters of the lake, still mostly frozen over.

A walk along the Silver River took them to the flour mill, it's wooden wheel creaking with the current. They passed Cat's shelter, chuckling over the episode of the night before, then walked to the edge of the plateau to look out over the snowy expanse of the plains and Steps. After Lindren described more of Cat's adventure under Silverwood, they headed northwest, past Darsha's house and the orchards before arriving back at home.

Lindren left Rhone with Rhianna while he paid a visit to Blue Hills and Brightwood. He wanted to gather an army of three thousand to add to Kitring-Tor's five thousand and the two hundred he already had in Kerend. Part of the day before had been spent speaking with Lowren about events in the enclave and news from the baronies. Two messengers had come, the last one three weeks before. Nothing had been found. It didn't mean nothing was there. Teale had hinted at something in the Barriers and Lindren wasn't about to ignore it.

SO • CR

While Cat was confined to a drugged sleep, Rhone spent the time visiting with various members of her family, at least those who understood him. Rhianna insisted on taking his measurements and, with the help of the other women in the family, presented him with Elven style clothes; a cloak, cream shirt, dark brown tunic and matching trousers. All of them were made from material Rhone considered suitable for summer. When he put them on, along with the cloak, he was surprised by how warm they kept him.

He thanked her and kissed her cheek. Rhianna's smile lit up the room. When Rhone mentioned it to Lindren, a soft gleam came to the Elder's eyes and he said, "Rhianna loves to sew for people, especially those she cares about. You've made her very happy by accepting her gifts."

Those she cares about.' She'd known him only a few days, yet she'd

352

opened her home, and her heart, to him. Lindren and his entire family had accepted him on Cat's word. This was the way a family should be and Rhone intended to help them as much as he could; and, despite the annoyance, that included Robbi.

The young Elf sought him out at every opportunity, pestering Rhone to tell him the Torian word for everything in the forest. After a few days, Robbi could almost hold a conversation. He tended to mix Torian and Elven words, just randomly filling in what he didn't know. The entire situation amused his parents immensely.

Rhone spent the rest of the time helping out where he could, playing with Hero, sitting by Cat's side, ensuring she ate something when the sleeproot wore off and administering more of the drug as needed. On the morning of the seventh day, he awoke to Cat's amber eyes.

"Do you need more sleeproot?" he asked, reluctant to come out from under the warm covers, not to mention that Hero slept on top of him.

"No. I still have lingering aches, but it's over." Cat's eyes didn't shine the way they should and Rhone wondered if it was the pain or the drug causing it.

He shifted the kitten, then forced himself out of bed and into his clothes. "You must be hungry."

"A little. I usually feel this way afterwards. I should be fine by tonight." Cat motioned him into an embrace. "I've missed you."

"I've slept next to you every night. Sat beside you for hours. But I missed you too." Rhone kissed her, deep, long, passionate, not caring if her eyes glowed. He couldn't make love to her now; later would do.

When he broke off, there was no glow, though her eyes seemed clearer.

"I really need a bath," she said.

A knock sounded at the door. It was Rhianna with their breakfast, followed by Lindren. The Elder whispered something in Cat's ear and she instantly perked up.

"Oh, yes!" she exclaimed. "Now would be perfect."

Lindren chuckled. "Let me know when I should bring it in."

"You will eat first." Rhianna set the tray over Cat's lap and put the spoon for her porridge in her hand. They both left.

The tray held food for two. Cat ate her porridge and a piece of cheese. Rhone sat on the end of her bed and finished off everything else.

When Rhianna removed the tray, Cat said, "I've told you about my dragon bones."

Rhone had heard the story of the dead dragon only Cat could see, the source of her bow and the boot knives she, Kelwyn and Lindren carried.

"I have…had, two more that I didn't know what to do with," she continued. "When we were married, I knew exactly what to do."

She nodded at Lindren, who left the room returning momentarily with a long object wrapped in cloth. Cat's smile, the love in her eyes, overwhelmed Rhone. It took him a moment to realize Lindren offered the item to him.

"What's this?" he asked.

"My gift to you." Cat waved for him to open it.

"You didn't have to give me a gift." In Kitring-Tor it was up to the father of the bride to provide a dowry. Rhone hadn't asked for anything. That wasn't why he'd married Cat.

"I know." She nudged him with her toe. "I wanted to do this."

"Don't argue with her," Lindren said, his eyes silver-bright. "We tried when she gave us the daggers. We lost."

With a sigh of resignation, Rhone unwrapped the gift. It was a wooden scabbard, covered in soft black leather beautifully decorated with gold inlaid oak leaves intertwined with intricate knots and Elven runes. More interesting than the scabbard was what stuck out of it. Now Rhone knew what Cat meant when she talked of dragon bones. He had no idea what they originally looked like; now they were shaped into the hilt of a sword.

A single rune rose a half inch from the flat top of a large, round pommel. Creamy bone protrusions extended from the bottom of the pommel to provide protection for the hand. More runes were engraved on the sides, then disappeared under the black leather wrapped grip.

They reemerged to decorate the guard, a stylized dragon head carved on each end, curved for more protection. With all the reverence this piece of art was due, Rhone slid the sword from the scabbard. Three feet of gleaming metal greeted his eye. Still more runes danced and whirled their way down the blade, matching the long length of the fuller. He hefted it, feeling it's weight, or lack of it.

Rhone shivered. "Why does it suddenly feel colder in here?"

"It's the sword," Lindren said. "Several mages and craftsmen have put a great deal of time and effort into that blade. A combination of air, spirit, water and the remaining dragon magic make the metal like ice. Not only will it do what a normal sword does, it should both burn and freeze any vaurok and their ilk. But if you accidently scratch yourself, it won't hurt you."

"I thought Elves couldn't work fire magic," Cat said.

"We can't. That's the dragon magic at work," Lindren said.

Speechless, Rhone held his hand an inch above the blade. It felt like he dipped it in ice water. He touched the sword. Cold seeped through his skin, though it didn't stick like frozen metal should. "This is...an incredible weapon. I don't understand. Why would they make it for me?" he asked Lindren.

"Because Cat asked."

She beamed. "I wanted a special sword for you. The first morning we were here, while you slept, I took the two dragon bones to Corfindin. He's the one who made my bow and the hilts for the daggers. I told him I wanted something unique, but I didn't know what he'd come up with until now."

"The blade is stronger than any Human weapon. It's built so the tang runs the full width, through the grip, to the pommel," Lindren explained. "I've never helped make a weapon before. It was quite interesting."

"You helped?" Cat asked. "I thought you were busy gathering your army."

"Arnir and I supplied the spirit magic. Arnir's contribution was the rune on the pommel. He thinks it will affect your opponent if you hit him with it, but we didn't have time for tests." Lindren turned back to Rhone. "This is a unique weapon. Unless we find more dragon bones, there'll never be another." Lindren stood and kissed Cat's forehead."You should get some rest. After lunch I'll heat water for your bath."

Rhone stared at the blade resting on his lap. The cold leaked through his trousers. "I don't know how to thank you, both of you...all of you."

Lindren strode to the door. "You're welcome. The blade will need to be cared for as any other and will wear out, though not for a very long time." He and Rhianna left, closing the door behind them.

Judging by the way Lindren said those words, Rhone knew the sword would outlast him. Turning it one way, then another, he admired the craftsmanship. The sword could be used single or two-handed, which suited him perfectly. He replaced it in the scabbard and leaned it against the chair. One push and he had Cat lying on the bed underneath him, nuzzling her.

"I didn't need the sword, Cat. I only need you." He pulled back. "But thank you. It's the most incredible weapon I've ever seen."

She ran a finger down the scar on his face. "I want you safe. This sword will help keep you that way. So will my father's dagger. I want you to have it. I love you, Rhone, so much my heart wants to burst."

Rhone's almost did. "I love you too, heart of my life."

₭ • Ⅎ

The evening didn't turn out quite the way Rhone had expected. Instead of the usual quiet family dinner, he and Cat were taken to the clearing with the remarkable wooden fountain in the shape of a girl—the Commmons. This was where Lindren's war councils were held, where the warriors gathered before heading to battle, a place for young Elves to sit and talk. It was also where large celebrations were held, like their Mid-Winter Festival. Tonight, Lindren explained, was one of the latter, a Celebration of Life for him and Cat.

Rhone leaned down close to Cat's ear. "Did you know about this?"

She blinked, staring at the tables, food, decorations and the gifts wrapped in brightly coloured cloth tied with ribbon. "No."

Coloured lights of a type Rhone had never seen before hung from the trees surrounding the meadow. He could swear they were made of paper. A profusion of flowers decorated garlands of pine and fir, strung from limb to limb in the trees; another contribution from a distant enclave and an odd contrast to the patchy snow on the ground.

He estimated two hundred people filled the clearing. Everyone sat on benches or logs, if they chose to sit. Lindren gave a short speech welcoming Rhone to the family and wishing them the best for their life together. Then everyone lined up to help themselves to food.

Several of the guests were other Elven Elders, whom Lindren introduced as the evening wore on. If they had a problem with a Human in an enclave they hid it well. Then again, Lindren may have invited only those he knew would have no issues.

Cat made sure he had plenty of rhura and tarva. The first was a drink he'd never had before, a delicious mix of apple cider, Elven mead and cinnamon. Drunk hot, it warmed Rhone from head to toe. The second was the tastiest treat he'd ever eaten, a honey-flavoured loaf loaded with nuts, seeds and dried fruit that he'd eaten on Mathyn's ship.

Instruments came out after the meal and when the music started, so did the dancing. There was no formality here, no ceremony, no special dance for the happy couple, just plenty of friendship, love and laughter. Rhone danced with several of the women, apologizing to each for his lack of Elven agility. None seemed to care, least of all Cat.

As at the wedding in Tezerain, Lindren danced 'Stepping Through The Forest' with his daughter. Instead of part of Queen Lisha's Winter Garden, Lindren's illusion consisted of blue and silver pine trees, all different sizes, surrounded by deep purple bushes and dotted with tiny lights of red, green, yellow and white.

As they danced the length of the Commons, multi-coloured hummingbirds flitted by deer-like animals with impossibly long antlers. Black and yellow striped forest cats lay on branches, their golden eyes reminiscent of Cat's. On their return down the Commons, the two dancers didn't rise into the air as they had before; they sunk into a chasm, past golden mice scurrying through the bushes and silver beetles with glowing green runes on their backs.

Instead of cloud steps, they entered the depths of the earth on

357

floating slabs of gold-veined white quartz. They stepped and twirled past layers of different coloured rock littered with incredibly large bones and veins of ruby, sapphire, emerald and amethyst. At the bottom of the chasm lay a still pool, rippled only by the feather touches of Lindren's and Cat's feet. Rhone hadn't moved an inch. He didn't have to look down at the dancers; nonetheless, Lindren took him on a fantastical journey underground. Then back up they came, the chasm slowly closing behind them. They ended where they'd begun.

Cheers and applause followed the last strains of music. Rhone's senses reeled, even more so when Cat returned to his side and kissed his cheek, her clean, musky scent adding to the delightful whirl of unreality commanding him.

Shortly after, Lindren appeared at his side. "I hate to cut short your celebration, but we have to leave at first light. And, once again, your gifts will have to wait. Everyone knows and understands."

Rhone took Cat by the hand. "Do I have to make a speech?"

"No," Lindren said. "Just make your way to the west end of the Commons saying goodnight to whomever you meet. Then leave."

That was simple enough to say, harder to do. Everyone they passed congratulated the pair with kisses and hugs. The last person they spoke to was Kelwyn.

He gave Cat a kiss on the forehead. "You look so happy, both of you. I wish we didn't have to leave and you two could spend the time alone you're supposed to."

Cat kissed him back, then gave him a long hug. "I wish that too. But we can't ignore the prophecy or what Teale said, and Rhone wants to spend a couple days at his home before we continue."

That stupid prophecy again. He'd have to talk to Cat about it. Later.

One of the many things he'd learned over the past week was that male Elves didn't shake hands, they clasped forearms. Kelwyn offered his, palm up. Rhone took it, with genuine affection for the Elf.

Cat's best friend rested his other hand on Rhone's shoulder and gave it a gentle squeeze. As Kelwyn turned away, a beautiful blonde-haired girl took his arm and dragged him to the dance area, leaving Rhone and Cat finally alone. They almost ran back to Lindren's.

358

Chapter Thirty-One

Cat scooped Hero off the bed. "You can't come. Not this time."

During her confinement, the kitten had become adept at stalking small winter birds. Rhianna also fed him yogurt mixed with cooked, mashed vegetables.

Cat cuddled the little bundle of fur. "Rhianna will take good care of you." Holding Hero up so she could look him in the eyes, she added, "And you will behave for her. Understood?"

The kitten purred and rubbed her nose. She kissed the top of his head and put him on the floor so she could make the bed. Once done, she hoisted her belongings and headed out the door. Rhone stood with their Hrulka, strapping on her bow case.

When they were ready, they said goodbye to Rhianna and Robbi and walked the horses to the Commons. The plan was for the army to leave first with their supply wagons following. Several pack horses would carry enough food until those wagons reached Kerend.

When they arrived at the Commons, Lindren was at the centre of two hundred anxious Elves, arguing with Lowren. Kelwyn stood beside his father, his face a mask of worry. Darsha, Shain and Arnir, behind Lindren, all showed the same concern.

"Why would you risk your life like that?" Lindren said in Elven, his voice and expression hard with anger, his eyes stormy-dark.

"You do it all the time," Lowren countered. His eyes matched Lindren's.

Lindren took a step forward. "Not when Rhianna's pregnant!"

Cat had never seen them argue. She sidled up next to Kelwyn. "What's going on?"

"Father wants to come." He choked out the words.

"No!" She grabbed Lowren's arm. "What are you thinking? What if something happens to you? Tarine will be *qira* and trying to raise two babies. You can't come!"

Lowren gently removed her hand. "I have to, Cat. I'm just as certain as Lindren that something is happening in the Barriers. We may already be too late. If we lose there, it's only a matter of time before Silverwood falls and I won't let that happen."

"Did you know about this?" Cat asked Kelwyn.

"No. Not until this morning when he and Mother said goodbye."

"This is my home," Lowren continued. "I've spent the last thousand years protecting it and I'm not about to stop now." He clutched Lindren's shoulders. "I fight for the same reasons as you. Don't deny me my right to defend my family."

Lowren rarely left the enclave, staying behind to take charge when Lindren was away. He did odd jobs here and there, repairing things that didn't require magic, overseeing the training of the young, taking charge at harvest time and just being there when he was needed. Cat couldn't understand why he'd want to go now.

Rhone took her arm and pulled her back. "What's going on?" She explained.

"I can see both sides," he said. "We Humans don't have the luxury of waiting for our children to be born before going to battle. If we did, chances are no one would survive."

"One more person isn't going to make a difference," Lindren said. "Stay here. Spend the time with Tarine. Feel your children move in her belly. There'll be plenty of other battles if you need to get out."

"No." Lowren removed his hands and stepped back. "If the baronies fall, I'll never forgive myself. I have to go. If you leave without me, I'll follow. You're my Elder, but I have to stand firm in this."

Lindren unclenched his fists, then tightened them again. "There's nothing I can say, is there."

"No. I'm coming."

"Once we leave this forest," Lindren said. "You will obey every word I say. Is that clear?"

"Yes, sir." Lowren won, though no one looked happy.

Cat tried once more. "You can't! Your babies! What about Tarine? What if..."

Lowren put his fingers over her lips. "Please have some faith in my fighting abilities. Tarine and I have discussed almost nothing else all week. She agrees with me. She wants our babies born here, nowhere else." He removed his fingers.

"Of course she'd agree," Cat countered. "She's your soulmate."

"Then it's our decision." Lowren turned back to Lindren. "Which company would you like me in?"

"Ride with me."

Darsha tugged on Huar's reins, bringing the Hrulka closer to him. "I'll stay here. Someone needs to watch over the place."

"Thank you." Lindren, his eyes still dark, embraced his oldest son. "I'll send word as soon as I know something." He slipped his foot into Auri's stirrup and hoisted himself into the saddle, indicating everyone else should mount up.

"I gather he's coming," Rhone said. "I have to admire his bravery."

"I have a bad feeling." Cat didn't feel fear often; now it sat like a rock in her gut.

"It's his decision." Rhone settled himself into Shuar's saddle. "A man has to follow his heart, no matter where it leads." He gave Cat a pointed look, then took his place in line behind her. The long string of Hrulka made their way to the forest edge.

₭ • ℜ

Rhone rode out of Silverwood into a world slightly different from when he'd entered. The spring sun had shone steady over the past several days, melting a good portion of the snow. A wide trail of muddy heath led straight to where Lindren's army waited, half a mile away. Some rode Hrulka, most rode the grey or white Elven horses. The Elder had wanted three thousand warriors. A rough count showed he'd come up short. As they approached the waiting Elves, Rhone asked why.

"It seems we're not the only ones having problems," Lindren answered. "Twenty-five hundred was the best I could do on short notice, but with Rodrin's five thousand and whatever the baronies can give us it should be enough."

Lindren took the lead with two other Elders beside him, Sandrin of Blue Hills and Rendir of Greenwood; Rhone got the impression from last night's party that they were friends. Lindren's sons and brother rode behind them with Rhone, Cat and Kelwyn next in line. Once all were in some semblance of order, the Elder pointed them east and a little north, increasing his speed to a canter. The ground thundered with the pounding of hooves.

ঙ০ • ୦৪

Once again they traveled from dawn to dusk and three days later they arrived at the southern border of Arden. Memories ran rampant through Rhone's mind, a mixture of places, emotions, people and events. Patches of brown grass showed through the disappearing snow on hills dotted with sheep and goats. Stone fences marked off the few places grain would grow. Scrubland and stunted forests, a sad parody of those in Silverwood, spread over land not yet cleared or that not worth clearing.

When they reached the point where the North Road bent east to the remainder of the baronies, Lindren called a halt. Deep ruts and churned mud showed Rodrin's army had passed several days before. After a brief consultation with Sandrin, Rendir and Lowren, the main body of the army broke away, leaving Lindren, his sons, Kelwyn, Rhone, Cat and one hundred Silverwood Elves to carry on north.

The late afternoon sun peered between a wispy layer of cloud and the distant peaks of the White Mountains. Just a day's ride remained to the keep and Rhone found himself growing anxious, a tumbled mess of mixed emotions. They'd almost reached the sheltered dale where Lindren planned to spend the night when Cat reached over and touched Rhone's arm.

"Are you all right?" she asked.

"Why wouldn't I be?"

"The colours in your light are all crazy."

He'd forgotten about Cat's truth-seeing. "I'm just a little nervous. It's been ten years since I've been home. I'll be fine." He urged Shuar forward in an attempt to avoid further questions. It worked. For now.

362

By dusk the next day, they stood on a hill, the keep, and the village surrounding it, in plain view. *Keep.* It was a fortress perched on a sloped, man-made plateau circled with overlapping layers of thick flat rock to stop sappers. The top of the hill was encompassed by a double curtain wall, the inner sitting higher than the outer.

The first, twenty feet thick, housed horses and storerooms of arrows, crossbow bolts and barrels of oil. It also allowed men and horses to move inside. In between was a moat with two drawbridges, one to the south of the keep, the other to the north. The second curtain wall, just as wide, housed soldiers with families. The massive gates, north and south, complete with double portcullis and murder holes, were accessed by a switchback road. Each barony had the same style of keep protecting it. Lindren had wanted the best.

The village—a pile of stone houses, shops, a tavern and an inn— was cut with roads comprised of mud and slush winding around the base of the hill. Chickens, dogs and cats shared the alleys, roads and yards with their owners. More than one house had a pigsty attached.

Ten years had changed nothing, not in the village, not at the keep; at least on the outside. Guards, dressed in the dark green of the barony of Arden, walked the outer curtain wall. Behind the inner, in the middle of the courtyard, stood the keep itself; the place where Rhone was born.

The three storey square tower seemed as sturdy as it ever had. A rectangular, two storey building—the residences—had been added on the left side after the keep population grew too large. The baron, now Rhone's eldest brother, along with his wife and heir, slept on the third floor.

All other members of the family, as well as guests, occupied the top floor of the residences, with the servants, Corbin's study and the library on the bottom. Another one level building hung off the right side of the keep—the kitchens and storerooms. Other buildings lined the walls, a smith, barracks, an outdoor kitchen, more storage rooms, stable and a small temple to Ar and Vania.

Rhone pulled up beside Lindren and asked him to stop. He reached into a pocket in his jerkin and removed the declaration of innocence King Rodrin had given him. Passing it to Lindren, he said,

363

"Give this to whoever greets us. I'd like to see their reaction before I reveal myself."

Lindren cast him a quizzical eye as he took the folded piece of paper. Rhone tugged his new Elven cloak close around him, pulling the hood down to shade his face. The Elder then directed the bulk of the Elves to remain outside the village.

They made their way up the main road. People stared from windows and shop fronts, some waved. It wasn't the first time they'd seen Elves. The guards at the base of the keep popped out of their huts to wave them on to the winding road leading up. More guards greeted them at both gates. Hrulka hooves clattered on the cobblestones under the portcullis and they entered the main courtyard.

It hadn't changed either. Chickens squawked as they flurried to get out of the Hrulka's way. Pigs rooted along the east wall, a pen of goats near them. The stable, a long, low building, stretched across the west wall. Rhone turned Shuar's head in that direction, then stopped as a figure hobbled out of the front door, leaning heavily on a cane.

With a start, Rhone realized it was Corbin. The last time he'd seen his brother had been three weeks before Jornel's murder. Corbin hadn't made it back in time for the trial. Four years ago, his brother had a smattering of grey at the temples. Now, hardly any of the original brown remained. Nor had he needed a cane. Rhone hadn't been the only one to suffer tough times.

Corbin limped towards them. "Lord Lindren! It's good to see you. Been too long."

Lindren slid off Auri with the grace of a mountain cat. "I apologize for that. Keeping well?" They shook hands.

"As well as possible." Corbin tapped his cane. "Commander-General Vergel sent a messenger on his way by with news of possible trouble in Kerend."

"I believe it's more than just a possibility. Did he tell you the news about Rhone?" Lindren removed the declaration from somewhere inside his cloak.

"What news?" Corbin's brows dipped in a frown. The lines on his face showed concern visted far too often in his life. "I thought that was all

364

over and done with."

Lindren passed him the document. "Raimon Teale confessed to Jornel's murder. Rhone was innocent."

Corbin read the document, then stared at the ground. After a few moments, he took a deep breath and let it out slow. "I never believed he was guilty. Rhone was a lot of things, but not a murderer." He looked up at Lindren. "Thank you for bringing this. It will ease Ellica's heart."

A rush of unexpected emotion surged through Rhone. For the first time in years, tears misted his eyes. *Damn me for a childish idiot.* He forced them back, urged Shuar forward and dismounted. Corbin watched him, his frown returning.

"That's more than I'd hoped for." Rhone lowered his hood.

Corbin stared, his mouth working. No sound came out. The declaration slipped out of his fingers. A breeze scooped it up and Kelwyn jumped off his Hrulka, running after it.

Then, in a rush, Corbin hobbled to Rhone, throwing his arms around him, slapping his back. "Great Ar! I don't believe it! We were told you were dead!" He pushed Rhone back, tears watering his eyes, then put his hands on Rhone's face. "It's you. It's really you. Blessed Ar, I don't believe what I'm seeing."

"Believe it," Rhone said, his heart lifting high in his chest. He pulled his brother to him. "I'm home. I'm finally home."

"How? What happened? Your ship sunk!"

"I'll tell the story inside." Best to tell it once.

After too short a time, Corbin broke the embrace. "The rest of the family is going to want to see you." He grabbed Rhone's arm, dragging him towards the keep. "Come on, everyone," he said to the Elves. "You're all welcome. There are food and hot drinks waiting." He waved to a boy to take the Hrulka to the stable.

It took a moment for Rhone's eyes to adjust to the dim light of the guardhouse occupying the entire lower floor. Quarters for the officers were here, along with two offices and another armoury. The basement housed more of the keep's guard and, on odd occasions, prisoners.

Corbin took the steps to the second level one at a time, unable, or unwilling, to bend his right leg. "Rika! Dev!" he hollered up the stairs.

"Gather everyone! Wonderful news!"

Corbin's wife and oldest son stood near the long table in the baron's hall. A much larger equivalent of Lindren's common room, it served as a dining area, family gathering room and council chambers. Little had changed here either, right down to the tapestries on the wall and the carpet on the floor. Except for the people.

Rika had aged almost as much as Corbin, her once slender figure now plump. Rhone barely recognized his nephew Dev, just a year older than him. Where there'd been a mischievous youth, Rhone stared at a grown man. They'd played and ridden together many times as boys. The confusion appeared to be mutual. Not even Rika recognized him.

"It's Rhone!"Corbin limped to his wife and grabbed her hand. "I swear to Ar! It's Rhone! He's innocent!" He motioned to Kelwyn for the pardon. With a shake of the paper, Corbin said, "This proves it. It's a writ from King Rodrin declaring him innocent. Raimon Teale killed Jornel Yarrow."

Rika recovered first, rushing to Rhone. Then Dev dashed over to pump his hand. Before he knew it, men, women and children arrived, heard the news and clamoured to welcome him home, though the younger children hung back in a small crowd, staring at the Elves. Rhone hardly dared believe the reception, but accepted it all with an open, and full, heart.

Then the crowd parted, now almost silent, revealing a tall, regal woman with streaks of grey at the temples of her nut brown hair. She almost collapsed when she saw him. Rhone shrugged off the others and gathered her in his arms. "I'm here, Mother. I'm home."

He held her gently, afraid he'd hurt her, though he wanted nothing more than to crush her to him, drink in her familiar, perfumed scent. A foolish wish crossed his mind, then disappeared—the desire to sit on her lap, one more time, as she rocked and sang him to sleep. Those days were gone. Long gone.

When Ellica pulled away and placed her hand on his scarred cheek, he noticed the unfamiliar fine lines around her eyes, her mouth. Ten long years had passed. She was now forty-eight, a year older than Corbin, yet she held on to her youth better than Rhone's oldest brother.

She touched the scar as a flash of sadness briefly overcame her joy. "Corbin said you'd grown. I had no idea just how much." She gazed up into his eyes, her own wet with the tears flowing freely down her face. "Oh, Rhone." Her voice broke and she hugged him tight once more.

No one bothered them. No one said a word for long minutes. Then she pulled back once more. Rhone didn't want to let her go. "I knew you were innocent," she said, a catch in her voice. "I knew no son of mine could commit murder. Welcome back, Rhone." She hugged him again.

Another voice, from the door leading to the residences, broke the silence. A man's voice; one Rhone remembered all too well. "So. You're alive. What a shame. I guess it means I can arrest you. I don't know why Corbin hasn't done his duty and thrown you in a cell."

Ellica spun around. "Iyan! That's enough."

Rhone gave his brother a mock bow. "Thank you for such a warm welcome."

Corbin placed himself in front of Iyan. "Don't be an arrogant son of a..." He glanced back at Ellica before turning a hard gaze on Iyan. "Rhone's been proven innocent. I have word from the king."

Iyan shrugged, a haughty smile plastered on his face. "Too bad. I would have liked to have seen what he looks like behind bars." His gaze ran from Rhone's face to feet and back again. "Been standing in horse shit?"

"Iyan!" Ellica's sharp voice split the air.

"My apologies, Mother." Iyan gave her a half bow. "I meant manure. Our Rhone has grown quite large, like a fungus in the dark. Must have been that time spent in prison."

Ellica moved beside Corbin, blocking Iyan's path to Rhone. "That is enough. If you can't be civil, leave."

Someone took Rhone's arm. He glanced over to see Cat, her eyes blazing anger. Her hood lay flat against her back, the long silver-gold braid hanging over her shoulder.

Iyan's tone changed in an instant. "Well, well. What have we here?" He ducked around Corbin and took Cat's hand to kiss it. She snatched it away. Iyan frowned. Rhone chuckled.

Recovering his composure in an instant, Iyan said, "Aren't you going to introduce us, brother dear? Oh, by the way. Welcome back. I guess."

Rhone took Cat's hand and stepped back. "How rude of me. I'm sure you remember Lord Lindren, his sons, Lords Shain and Arnir, and Lord Kelwyn."

Greetings and handshakes were passed around.

"And this spirited treasure?" Iyan tried taking Cat's hand again, with no more success than before.

Rhone put his arm around her. "This is Cat, my wife."

Rika's hands flew to her mouth. "Oh, my! More wonderful news!"She hugged Cat and welcomed her into the family.

The others were quick to follow except for Iyan, who was shoved to the back of the group, and Ellica, now staring at Cat and examining every inch of her.

Iyan forced his way back through the crowd. "So," he said.

Rhone kept a good grip on Cat's hand. The other curled into a fist.

"Which family are you from?" Iyan asked Cat, wearing a condescending smile Rhone knew all too well. "My dear brother didn't say your father's last name."

The Elves kept their eyes on Rhone, except for Kelwyn, who glared at Iyan. Tension, tauter than a bowstring, thickened the air in all directions.

"She doesn't have one," Rhone said, waiting for the right moment to deliver the truth.

Ellica's eyes hardened. "A commoner?"

Iyan laughed. "What happened? Did Lady Calli drop you for the cad you are?"

"No. I dropped her." That shut him up. "Cat doesn't need a last name. She's Lord Lindren's daughter."

Now it was Rhone's turn to laugh, particularily at the stunned expression on Iyan's face. Then he sobered when he saw his mother. Her eyes, the same shade of sea-green as his, bored into Cat, who shrank behind him. No one said a word.

This time, Ellica's voice pierced the silence. "*Why*? What were you thinking?"

Rhone put Cat's hand on his arm, pulling her close to him. "What do you mean, Mother? I thought you'd be happy for me." All eyes turned to Ellica.

"She's an Elf! She can't give you children!"

"I don't want any."

"That's ridiculous! Of course you want children. It's obvious you weren't using your head. At least not the one on your shoulders!"

"Mother!" Rhone never imagined she'd receive Cat so poorly. The Elves, especially Lindren, were respected, honoured.

Ellica rounded on Lindren. "You *know* they can't have children. How could you let them marry?"

Lindren folded his arms across his chest, a picture of calm. "Because they are in love."

"What happened to her ears?" Dev asked.

Lindren glanced at him before returning his darkening eyes to Ellica. "Cat is not an Elf, she's adopted."

Ellica relaxed and closed her eyes a moment. "You scared me grey."

Rhone held his finger up. "Something you should know. Cat's not Human, either. She's Tiranen. And before you go off on another rampage, it was *my* decision not to have children. Cat tried to talk me out of it, but I..."

All eyes swung back to Cat.

"She's *Tiranen*?" Corbin hobbled his way through to Rhone. "That's impossible."

"Not impossible," Lindren said. "There's much to tell. Perhaps we should sit at the table and discuss this like civilized people."

The children were hustled off and food and drink brought for the travelers.

"We've already eaten," Corbin said. "Help yourselves. Please."

Kelwyn made a point of sitting on the other side of Cat from Rhone. Long used to visits from Lindren, Corbin served dishes suitable to their taste. As they ate, Rhone introduced his brothers and their wives to Cat, then the tales were told, both hers and his. Ellica remained silent, sharing her glare equally between Rhone, Cat and Lindren, until Rhone's story of the shipwreck, his time on the island and the rescue. She cried and hugged him again and again. When the stories were finished, Corbin declared an end to the night.

Rhone took Cat's hand, then kissed the top of Ellica's head. "Don't worry about it, Mother. We're happy. Isn't that what counts?"

Despite her earlier emotion, Ellica remained aloof. "We'll discuss this further in the morning."

"I'm afraid your old room is taken, Rhone," Corbin said. "The family has grown and we needed it."

A twinge of disappointment washed through Rhone. "That's all right. Guest suite?"

Corbin nodded. "The one on the right. Lord Lindren's is on the left."

"Don't worry about the rest of us," Arnir said. "We'll stay with the others outside the village. We know you don't have much room."

"Thank you."

Kelwyn said goodnight to Cat, then followed Shain and Arnir to the staircase.

"That was an entertaining evening," Shain said to Darsha as they headed down the stairs. "I think I'll make sure I'm here for breakfast."

Cat rolled her eyes. Rhone led her out of the hall, his emotions in turmoil. He hadn't expected such a warm welcome, nor had he expected his mother's vehement opposition to his marriage.

When they entered the hallway to their rooms, Cat leaned close to him. "Your mother doesn't like me."

Rhone patted her hand. "It isn't you she doesn't like, just the fact that you can't give her grandchildren."

"It's not something I can change."

"Don't worry about her. She'll get over it once she gets to know you."

"Why does Corbin look older than your mother?" Cat asked.

Rhone sighed. He didn't feel like answering questions, then decided he should just get it over with. "My mother isn't his mother. My father's first wife died after giving him eight children. He married my mother who was much younger than him. She gave him two more, Iyan

370

and myself. There's twenty-one years between Corbin and I. Only one between Corbin and my mother."

"Why don't you look like your brothers? Iyan is the only one who looks even a little like you."

Rhone shrugged. "Mother said I take after an uncle of hers. It happens sometimes."

"Lindren said the same thing. I don't look like my parents either."

"Iyan is my only full-blooded sibling. The others are half-brothers or sisters. They have a different mother, so there's more chance I won't look like them."

Rhone opened the door to their rooms, a similar set-up to Cat's suite in Tezerain, though not as large or as fancy. A woven carpet covered most of the floor. Their belongings sat in a pile in the corner near a small desk and chair, the only other furnishings besides two plain wooden chairs in front of the fireplace. Rhone silently thanked the servant who'd lit the fire.

Cat slipped into his arms. "I don't think I like Iyan. I checked his light. He has some strange colours."

"Such as?" He kissed her cheek, then moved to her neck. He hadn't made love to her since the night of their Celebration of Life.

"Sort of a dark red mixed with green. I've never seen it before. And..."

"And?" Rhone pulled back.

"Orange."

Lust. "Cat, stay away from him." He took her by the shoulders. "You hear me?"

She nodded and undid the laces of his trousers. Thoughts of his mother, his brother and every other worry vanished with the touch of her fingers, her heady, musky scent and a rush of sweet desire.

Chapter Thirty-Two

Cat lay on her side, listening to Rhone snore. He sprawled over most the bed, as he usually did. At least this one was bigger than her bed at Lindren's.

The evening had turned out nothing like what she'd expected. She was glad Rhone's family was happy to see him alive. Although he hadn't said anything, he'd seemed concerned about it. He had so much family, meeting them all was fascinating. Besides Corbin, there was Gavan, Jerran, Leath, and Iyan. His sisters, Alera, Kyah, Sary, and Danessa were married and lived outside the keep. Alera and Danessa both had homes in Arden and Corbin would send for them tomorrow. All of them had children. Thirty-six in all, and two of those children had children.

It would take hundreds, if not thousands, of years for Elves or Tiranen to have that much family, and then it would be mostly cousins. Taurin told her Humans bred quickly. She hadn't realized just how fast it could happen.

Rhone called Corbin his half-brother. She understood people having the same father and a different mother. It didn't happen with the Elves, though it did with the Tiranen who changed mates often. Her mother's brother was what Rhone called full-blooded, though her father's sister had a different mother. They didn't make the distinction of half-brother or sister, though.

She lay down, hoping she could sleep, and snuggled up to Rhone. He stopped snoring and rolled towards her, flinging his arm around her. Cat smiled. It didn't matter what his mother thought. Every time Rhone said he didn't want children, he meant it. She loved this man. Nothing, and no one, would take him away from her. Not before his time.

Rhone stood at the window of the sitting room while Cat had a wash in the garderobe. The Barriers filled almost the entire view and he wished he had his old room back. It looked towards Silverwood. Though too far away to be seen, he could place himself there much easier now than when he was a boy. All sorts of fanciful imaginings had wandered his young mind. He knew the truth now and it was both more, and less, fantastic than he'd imagined.

He wished he was back in Silverwood. Cat's family accepted him right at the outset, just as he was. During the week Cat slept away her moon cycle, he grew more acquainted with them and, despite Cat's absence, they spoke with him as if he'd been living there for years.

Why can't it be like that here? Why can't Mother accept Cat? There had to be more to it than just the fact Cat couldn't give him children. He loved his mother, but sometimes…

A knock came at the door. He opened it to find Jerran on the other side.

"Good morning, little brother." Though thirteen years older, Jerran stood half a head shorter than Rhone. "I hate to be the bearer of bad news, but Ellica wants to see Lady Cat right after breakfast."

Before Rhone could say a word, Cat exited the bedroom wearing only her trousers and carrying the belt with her tchiru. "Have you seen my pack? Oh, here it is." She headed for the corner where their belongings were piled.

Jerran's eyes followed her every inch of the way. "Lucky bastard."

"Cat," Rhone said, trying to block his brother's view. "Didn't you see Jerran standing here?"

She smiled and pulled out a shirt. "Good morning. I hope you had a good sleep." Cat slipped into the shirt, then did up the belt.

Jerran laughed. "Yes, I did. Thank you." He leaned towards Rhone. "I guess those stories we heard as children are true."

Rhone sighed. "They are. Just don't say anything to Mother. Please."

"I'm ready," Cat said.

"I'm not. I still have to shave." Rhone said it a little more gruff than he'd intended; Cat's parade had caught him off guard.

"I'll escort her if you like," Jerran said, holding his arm for her to take.

Cat smiled and took it. "It's nice to see you're not cranky in the morning."

Jerran laughed again and the two headed for the hall.

Rhone almost slammed the door behind them, then made short work of shaving. Throwing on his tunic, he dashed for the Hall, relieved to see Iyan nowhere in sight. Cat sat beside Kelwyn, eating porridge. Rhone filled his bowl from a large pot on the sideboard and sat next to her. For some reason, the porridge didn't taste the same. Perhaps Rhianna's delicious recipe had something to do with it.

"Excuse me, Lord Kelwyn. I'd like to sit here." Iyan had arrived.

Kelwyn moved over, reluctantly. Rhone's fist tightened around his spoon. Shain, Arnir and Lindren sat across from him. Though they said nothing, all their eyes darkened.

"Good morning, lovely lady," Iyan said to Cat. "When we're done breakfast, Rhone will want to visit with Mother so I thought I could show you around the place. Perhaps we could go for a short ride."

The spoon dug into Rhone's hand. "Mother wants to see Cat right after we eat."

Cat's eyes widened. "She does?"

"That's too bad." Iyan snatched a piece of bread off a platter. "We can go afterwards. I'd really like to show you this lovely spot I know..."

"She's busy," Rhone said, his breakfast forgotten.

"Where's your wife?" Cat asked. "I don't think I've met her."

"Having breakfast with the children. She rarely comes out of our room for meals." Iyan cut a thick chunk of yellow cheese and placed it on his bread.

Cat took another bite of her porridge, keeping a wary eye on Iyan. "Why aren't you eating with them?"

"I prefer to eat out here." He rested his elbows on the table and took a big bite of the bread and cheese.

When Cat finished swallowing, she said, "I think your wife would prefer you go riding with her."

Iyan laughed. "I doubt it."

He continued to make light conversation with Cat. She didn't answer most of the time. When she was finished eating, Rhone took her away from Iyan, though where he took her worried him just as much.

Kelwyn followed them out the door. "I think we're going to have a problem with Iyan."

"I know we are," Rhone said. "He did this to me all the time. I'd find a girl and he'd do everything he could to take her away. What really makes me angry is that he usually succeeded. That one was born with a silver tongue." He'd also steal Rhone's things, then sell them for a copper bit to some kid in town regardless of the value. His father always sided with Iyan because Rhone had no proof. The kids were too afraid to tell the truth or refuse to buy the item. Iyan was the baron's son and a bully.

"I don't want to be taken away from you." Cat clung tighter to his arm.

"I know and I trust you. Just be careful around him."

"Let me know if you can't be with her," Kelwyn said. "I'll make sure I am."

"Thank you." Nothing had changed with Iyan. It was starting all over again.

Kelwyn returned to the Hall. Rhone walked with Cat to Ellica's rooms. For most of the first sixteen years of Rhone's life, his mother shared the largest suite on the third floor of the keep with his father. When he died, Corbin took over those rooms as the new baron and Ellica moved to another room farther down the hall from the rooms he now occupied.

When they reached her door, he stopped, taking Cat in his arms. "Just remember, it isn't you she doesn't like. Mother can be gruff, but a lot of it's posturing."

"What's that?"

"She thinks she's impressing people by acting that way. Don't worry, I'll be with you." Rhone opened the door.

Ellica sat like a queen in a rocking chair by the fire, wearing a morning robe of crimson velvet lined with fur. Why did it remind him of blood?

Her bed, already made, sat on the opposite side of the room. The only other furnishings were a wardrobe against the wall at the foot of the bed and a desk by the window with a wooden chair behind it with another in front. Quill and ink sat primly on the desk.

"Thank you, Rhone. Corbin is waiting for you in the study. We won't be long."

"I'm staying, Mother."

"No. You're not." Ellica rose and sat in the chair behind the desk. "Lady Cat, you can sit here." She pointed to the wooden chair across from her.

"Mother, whatever you have to say to Cat, you can say to me."

"And how am I supposed to get to know her if you're standing here scowling? This is a woman to woman talk and you're not invited." Ellica's silky voice held a sharp edge to it Rhone found all too familiar.

Cat put a hand on his arm. "I'll be all right. I don't want to cause trouble between you and your mother."

Ellica gave her a single nod. "I see she has somewhat more sense than you. Now be off, Corbin's waiting."

"Are you sure, Cat?" Rhone had a feeling Ellica intended more than just a friendly chat.

"I'm sure." She sat in the chair.

Rhone felt like he was leaving a child with a hungry she-wolf.

                                                          ജ · **ര**

Cat sat with her hands folded tight in her lap; they didn't shake that way. She wondered if Lisha and Selesa had a talk like this. Did every Human female have to go through it?

"You're not playing fair." Ellica's eyes, identical to Rhone's, drilled into Cat's skull. "You made a mistake marrying my son. I understand there's no one of your kind, but you shouldn't have married one of us. Humans don't live long lives like your people and Rhone deserves to have children of his own." Ellica leaned forward, resting her hands on the table.

376

Cat tried to keep her heart from pounding. "I told Rhone that, several times. He still…"

"It's Rhone's duty to provide sons for Arden."

Now that was a ridiculous statement. Cat had met twenty-one of the children, big and small, and that didn't include any that belonged to Iyan or Rhone's sisters.

"Rhone's father would have been disappointed with this thoughtless action, and very angry. He never would have approved."

Though she fought against it, Cat's eyes misted and she caught a flash of washed-out purple in Ellica's light, slashed through with a pale blue-green she didn't know and a healthy dose of red. Did that mean Arden wouldn't have been disappointed and angry?

"Arden knew his duty. He wouldn't have considered marrying someone who couldn't give him children." Now there was no purple.

What's going on?

Ellica sat back, her hands flat on the desk. "By the time I married him, he had eight children and he wanted more. Life is harsh in the north and it's only by Ar and Vania's Grace that none of Arden's sons have lost their lives in battle. We need sons to help protect this land and daughters to provide more sons."

Cat's hands tightened. She remembered Kendrick's father, on Morata, wouldn't allow them to be together even for a short time. "It's Rhone's decision. I made him think about it before I accepted."

Ellica didn't listen. She ranted on about Rhone's father and what he'd think. Oddly, sometimes when she mentioned him purple glimmered in her light, other times it didn't. She'd only seen purple washed out the same way once, when Rhone questioned Jonlan. Always there, however, was the strange pale blue-green Dayn had exhibited the day they removed the spell.

Cat slid forward, perched on the edge of the chair. "Is it up to you who Rhone marries?"

"It's normal to acquire approval before marrying." Every muscle in Ellica's neck stood out like cords. "Rhone should have brought you here first. And I can tell you that if he had, I would not have given my blessing. Not only are you barren to him, you aren't a proper lady. Just look at the way you dress. You're not even wearing shoes! My son deserves better."

Her scorn cut as deep as Mordru's cruel teasing. Cat blinked away her tears and stood, fighting the urge to run. "I was under the impression people in Kitring-Tor could choose their own mate."

Ellica pushed her chair back. It almost fell. She leaned over the desk. "Within reason. A lord wouldn't marry a tramp and Rhone should *not* have wed one not of his own race!"

Gellen had refused to let her spend time with Kendrick. Now this woman wanted to take Rhone from her. Her head whirling with Ellica's anger, contempt and her confusing lies, Cat ran for the door and ripped it open. She headed first for her rooms. Rhone wasn't there. He was with Corbin in the study and she had no idea where it was located.

Kelwyn. He'd be with the rest of the Elves outside the village. Cat ran down the stairs and out the door.

ഌ • ඊ

Rhone swallowed the last of his coffee, a rare treat in the north.

"I killed the vaurok," Corbin said, patting his leg. "But not before he split my leg open and shattered my knee. Now I can't bend it properly. I'm no good in a fight anymore so Jerran leads the men now. He has a better head for it than Gavan. But I can still run the barony and no one else wants to deal with the petty details, so they put up with me." He laughed, still the same Corbin despite the injury.

Rhone could find no humour in anything. Cat had been closeted with his mother for a while and it worried him.

Corbin watched him a moment. "She'll be fine."

"You don't know Cat. I've never met anyone like her." Rhone set his cup on the table between them. "She's stronger than anyone I've ever known. She fights like a demon, can tolerate pain that would drop an enraged bear, but her emotions are made of the thinnest, most fragile glass." He stood. "I'm sorry, Corbin. I have to see how she is."

Corbin pulled himself out of the chair and gripped Rhone's shoulder. "I understand. If I had a treasure like that, I'd worry about her

378

too."

"You do have a treasure. Rika is an amazing woman." Besides running the domestic side of the keep and raising her children, she kept the accounts, smoothed ruffled feathers and helped in the village during times of need.

"She has to be to put up with me." Corbin laughed again and pushed Rhone towards the door. "We can talk later."

Rhone covered the distance to his mother's room in long strides, up the stairs and down the hall. He knocked on the door and entered at Ellica's bidding. She sat once more by the fire, Cat nowhere in sight.

"Where is she?" he demanded.

Ellica rose and kissed his cheek "I don't know, dear, she left."

"What did you say to her?"

She held her head high. "The same thing I said last night. I don't endorse this marriage. You should go see a priest of Ar and have it annulled. Lady Faralyn is looking for a husband. You could marry her and become baron of Jayme."

"I will not! I love Cat and she loves me. Nothing you say will make me change my mind." Why was his life one long argument?

"Your father..."

"My father wouldn't have cared! He never cared about anything I did. I tried everything I could think of to make him notice me. I worked hard at weapons practice, harder than anyone, hoping to make him proud, but it didn't matter. The only things he noticed were the things I did wrong." It took years, and time spent alone on Crescent Island, for Rhone to realize he'd found ways to get in trouble just so his father would pay him some kind of attention.

"Rhone! That's not true." Ellica rested her hand against his cheek. He almost pulled away. "I've never told you this, but you are my favourite. I've missed you terribly. My heart broke the day they told me you died. I'm overjoyed you're alive, but you shouldn't throw your life away on someone who can't give you children, someone who won't grow old with you. Please. Think about this."

"I have. I'm staying married to Cat whether you like it or not." Rhone turned on his heel and opened the door.

"Rhone!"

He slammed it, then headed out to find Cat.

₭ · ₲

"Why are Humans so mean?" Cat mumbled into Kelwyn's shoulder. They sat behind a small barn not far from the Elven camp.

Kelwyn rubbed her back. "Not all of them are. Most of Rhone's family welcomed you with open arms." He had a point.

"Sit up." Kelwyn wiped her tears with his shirt sleeve. "You and Rhone are bonded. I doubt there's anything Ellica can do except complain."

Cat sighed. "I suppose. I just wish she liked me. I think Rhone wants to live here. It'll be difficult if she hates me."

"Rhone is the only one you need to worry about keeping happy."

Another good point. She leaned into his embrace. "I wonder what the strange purple in Ellica's light is supposed to mean. First Rhone's father wouldn't be disappointed and angry, and then he would? What did she mean? And I have no idea what that other colour was."

"I wish I could help you." Kelwyn kissed the top of her head. "Feeling better?"

She nodded.

"Then we should find Rhone. We've been here a while and he's probably worried."

Kelwyn helped her to her feet and they headed for the stone fence near the barn. He hopped up first, then she did and they walked the top back to the Elven camp; less mud that way. Her feet were dirty enough.

Rhone stood near Arnir's tent, talking with her brother. He strode to meet them, his new cloak swirling around him. "How are you doing that?" He stared at her feet and the narrow fence they walked.

"Doing what?" Cat jumped off the fence.

"Never mind." He took her chin in his hand. "You've been crying. I'm sorry, Cat. If I'd known Mother would act like that, I'd have carried on to Kerend."

"You couldn't have known." She leaned against his chest,

380

listening to his heartbeat. "Any chance of having a bath?"

Rhone chuckled. "A bath for two sounds like a wonderful idea. And it'll be a good excuse to avoid Iyan. We should have lunch first, though." He reached his hand out to Kelwyn and clasped his forearm, Elven style. "Thank you for looking after her. I appreciate it."

"Never a problem."

Kelwyn strode towards the Elven camp, while Rhone took Cat back to the keep.

ℴ · ‘’

Drying Cat's hair was a chore and a half. Baths weren't brought to individual rooms as in Tezerain. Instead, Arden Keep had a special room set aside just for bathing and they decided to return to their rooms to dry her hair. Rhone finished one side, then started on the back amazed by how much it relaxed him. Once her hair was reasonably dry, there'd be plenty of time before dinner for...

"Have you decided about the prophecy, yet?" Cat asked. "You said you'd think about it."

Rhone closed his eyes a moment. *That stupid prophecy.* "I did think about it and I'm still having a problem with it."

Cat craned her head to look at him, pulling the hair out of the towel. "But it really happened. I saw the dragon and he told me..."

"I don't doubt it." He turned her head back and resumed the drying. "I just can't help thinking it's a trap. The Barriers are dangerous. There are caverns with heated pools that are perfect for crèches. We're always chasing vauroks out of there. It's obvious that the Black Lord wants both you and Lindren, and that prophecy is sending you straight into his arms."

"But I was told about the prophecy by a dragon and Lindren said the dragons didn't like the Black Lord. And Lindren's not supposed to go, so the trap wouldn't work on him."

Rhone moved in front of her, leaning on the arms of the chair she sat in. "The Black Lord could have fooled you into thinking you saw a real dead dragon." *Real dead dragon?* Cat's crooked thinking must have rubbed off on him. "This trap might be meant for you alone."

"Then why are you and Kelwyn supposed to come?"

"To throw you off, perhaps. Make you think you're safe. There is that part about 'all will fall'." Rhone hadn't liked that line from the moment he'd heard it.

"Why warn us that all will fall? Wouldn't that make us think twice?"

"You're not thinking twice, now are you?" He stood straight, folding his arms across his chest. "The entire notion is ridiculous. You, Lindren and Kelwyn have accepted that prophecy at face value. So has the rest of your family. You're all prepared to go off into vaurok-ridden mountains to supposedly wake Sleepers. Maybe those Sleepers aren't dragons. Maybe they're demons. Did you think of that?"

Her eyes shone with unshed tears. Rhone strode to the door, blocking it. She wasn't running this time.

Cat jumped up from the chair. "They are dragons! Lindren thinks so and so do I. I don't know how to explain it, but it feels right. And if it is dragons, they might be able to help us fight the Black Lord in exchange for waking them!"

"And if it isn't dragons? What if waking whatever these things are makes us all fall? I don't want to die yet, Cat. I want to spend the rest of a long life in Arden, with you, helping my brothers with the barony. Fighting to protect my home is one thing, but I no longer want to fight for a living and that includes going on some hair-brained, prophecy-chasing, mad mission to find dragons!"

Cat's eyes blazed. "Fine. Don't come! I'm going and so is Kelwyn."

"No, you're not. You are my wife and…"

"I didn't promise to obey you because you might tell me to do something that's wrong. And that's exactly what you're doing now!"

Rhone threw his hands in the air. "Ar's balls, Cat!"

"It's Arvanion! Not Ar! Your people have it wrong!"

Where did that come from? "What do my people have wrong?"

Cat moved her gaze to the floor, as if sorry she'd said anything. "It doesn't matter."

"Yes, it does. What do we have wrong? Is this more Elven secrets?"

Her shoulders sagged and she walked to the window. "I don't know. But your god is our Creator and his name is Arvanion. I have no idea where Vania came from. There is no goddess."

Rhone needed to sit. He didn't dare leave his post at the door, though; she'd be gone faster than a jack rabbit down it's hole. How could there be no goddess? Lindren bowed to her at the wedding ceremony. Rhone wasn't an overly religious man, but he knew the story of how his people came to Urdran. "Ar and Vania brought us here from our dying world. You've seen the tapestry. It tells the story."

"I don't know where that story came from. Lindren might. I do know that Arvanion created both the Elves and my people, and brought yours from a world we've never heard of. Arvanion is real. Lindren has seen him, but just after your people came he disappeared."

"Disappeared? How does a god disappear?" Rhone risked the few steps to grab the chair, taking it back with him to the door. He fell into it.

"I don't know. Neither does Lindren. All he knows is that Arvanion used to visit his people, and mine, and no one has seen him since your people came."

Not Ar? No goddess? It was impossible, wasn't it? Ar. Vania. Arvanion? Did his people really have it wrong? Why didn't it surprise him more than it did? *Because the Elves have to have it right. They live for thousands of years. And Cat said Lindren met him.* "Why didn't the Elves say something when my people first arrived?"

She shrugged. "I don't know. I hope you're not too upset. I didn't mean to say anything."

"I don't know what I am." Numb. Confused.

"Lindren thinks the prophecy is from Arvanion. That's why he trusts it. And that's why I have to go, whether you come or not."

Rhone tried to push the thoughts of Ar, Vania and Arvanion to the back of his mind. He'd have to sort it out later. "Lindren feels it's right. I think it's wrong. I can't let you go."

Her jaw tightened. Tears formed in her eyes and he realized she wouldn't give up. Cat would go without him. He'd lost. Part of his marriage vow included protecting her, but how could he if he wasn't with her? He threw his hands up in defeat. "Fine. But you're not going alone. I'll come."

Cat blinked back her tears. "You…you mean it?"

Rhone moved the chair from in front of the door. "I mean it. You're my wife. I can't let you go without me." He motioned her into his arms. To his relief, she came. "I love you, Cat. If I didn't go, I'd worry myself sick."

"Thank you."

She hugged him tight, the clean scent of her making his head light. Or was that her revelation concerning Ar? When she let him go, Rhone kissed her, then said, "Sit down. I'll finish your hair." He picked up the towel, shifting his thoughts to Ar and Vania, and the being called Arvanion that Cat said was the true god. One more thing to weigh on his his already over-burdened shoulders.

Chapter Thirty-Three

Dinner that night was awkward. Not between Rhone and Cat, however; they'd resolved their differences. He sat his wife away from his mother, at the far end of the long table, which had grown to accommodate the expanding family. Now other tables had to be set up to allow room for all the children as well as Alera, Danessa, their families and Lindren's portion of the visiting Elves.

Iyan's wife and children were in attendance and introductions made. She was a pretty, blonde haired woman, soft spoken, with little to say. Perfect for Iyan, as far as Rhone was concerned. His brother preferred to do all the talking and far too much of that. She hardly looked at Rhone and seemed to be afraid of him. He wondered what stories Iyan had told her about him.

Rhone's sisters wept at the sight of him, then welcomed Cat to the family. No one but his mother seemed to find their marriage a problem. He took heart from their approval.

With dinner done, the youngsters were sent off with nannies so the family could discuss various events. Only the adult children were allowed to stay. Rhone's trial and experiences on the island, Teale's treason and the kidnappings were rehashed, as well as what Teale may have hinted at in Kerend.

"I still don't understand Gethyn's, Rais' and Miklin's behavior," Corbin said. "They swore on their honour that their men saw nothing in Broken Man Pass and now it looks like they were wrong, or lying."

"Arden would never have made that mistake," Ellica said, sitting primly near the head of the table.

"You mean swearing on his honour when he didn't see for himself?" Rhone asked. "He could be just as blind as the others. I've seen it."

Ellica's cold gaze settled firmly on him. "Your father wouldn't have sent someone else. He would have investigated himself and the

385

truth would have been discovered."

Cat tilted her head, her pretty brow dipped in a frown, her eyes on Ellica.

Rhone leaned close to her. "What's the matter?"

"She's lying. "

Lindren's head whipped towards her. "Cat!"

Shain sat up from his slouch. "What's she lying about?"

Cat's puzzled expression remained. "I'm not sure, but it's the same kind of lie she told me told this morning."

Ellica's eyes moved from Cat to Rhone and back again. "How dare you! I don't lie!"

"You just did." Cat clutched Rhone's hand under the table.

"Lindren!" Ellica turned her icy gaze to the Elder. "What kind of trouble-making brat did you raise?"

He sighed, the long weary one of an exasperated father. "The kind who can tell when someone is lying."

Trusting Cat's truth-seeing, Rhone stared Ellica straight in the eye. "Are you saying my father wouldn't have gone himself? Or that the truth wouldn't be discovered?"

His mother stood, sliding her chair backwards. "I'm saying Arden knew his responsibility and if he was still alive, he would have gone himself, despite his ill health. And I resent being called a liar!"

Rhone looked to Cat, who said, "Now she's telling the truth."

He ran both his mother's statements over in his mind while everyone else stared at one combatant or another. "First you said my father wouldn't have sent someone else and Cat said that was a lie."

"It was not!" Ellica appeared ready to spit fire.

Rhone held his hand up. "Let me finish. Then you said Arden would have gone himself and that wasn't a lie. What are you trying to say?"

"I've told you. Twice."

"According to Cat, one of those was a lie. The first one." Rhone's mind whirled. "My father would have sent someone else, but Arden wouldn't? What does that mean, Mother?"

"She's the one who's lying!" Ellica's body radiated anger and indignation.

Lindren stood, holding up one hand. "I don't know what's going on here, but there's one thing I can tell you. Cat has a talent that is rare among the Elves and unheard of in Tiranen. She knows who is, and who isn't, telling the truth. We don't know why she has this ability, but she does and we trust it completely. Which means only one thing, Ellica. When you said Rhone's father wouldn't have been fooled, it was a lie."

"More a half-lie," Cat said. "It's very confusing."

"What does it mean, Mother?" Rhone demanded.

Ellica's eyes blazed. "Did you know about this when you married her?"

"Yes. I did." Rhone pushed his chair back and stood. *"What does it mean?"*

His mother's eyes darted from him, to Cat, to Lindren and back to him. Everyone else sat in mute shock, except the Elves; especially Shain who sat back in his chair with his arms folded, wearing a smirk. He appeared to be enjoying the show.

"I..." The blood drained from Ellica's face. She set her hand on the table to steady herself. Dev retrieved her chair and she sat, heavily.

An unwanted thought occurred to Rhone. "The truth, Mother. If it means nothing, why is it so hard for you to say?" He needed to hear her words, yet dreaded them at the same time.

All the fight left Ellica. Her shoulders slumped, her eyes dropped to the table. "Arden...Arden is not your father."

"What?" Corbin voiced the word Rhone couldn't.

He sat back in his chair, his mind numb. 'Not your father.' It rang in his ears, echoed off the high ceiling, bounced from the walls. Other voices said words he didn't understand. One stood out too well—Iyan's laugh.

Corbin thumped his cane on the table. "I think we deserve an explanation, Ellica."

Rhone tried hard to listen, tried to sort his rushing, running thoughts, remembering when Arden seemed to enjoy beating him, the times Rhone had caught him with loathing in his eyes.

Tears now washed his mother's face. "Not...not long after Iyan was born, Arden grew ill. He was old when I married him. I only did so

387

because my father wanted me to. It would raise our station, make a better name for the family. I was young and my father was a demanding man. I realized shortly after that I'd made a mistake." She pulled a handkerchief from her sleeve and dabbed her eyes. "Pardon me. This is a story I thought I'd never tell.

"A young woman needs a man and when Arden's health failed, he couldn't... Well, one of the guards caught my eye. He was tall, strong and very handsome. I fell in love. The inevitable happened and the next thing I knew...I was pregnant."

Ellica still stared at the table. Rhone closed his eyes, covering his face with his hands, his life falling apart like shards of glass from a broken goblet.

"I was so afraid to tell Arden," Ellica continued. "He'd know the babe wasn't his, but the time came when I couldn't hide it anymore. He was so angry. It was the one and only time he ever hit me. Once he calmed down, he told me to say nothing to anyone, which surprised me. His next words didn't. Arden said he'd claim the child as his own, but only because he didn't want the embarrassment. The nobles in Tezerain were disdainful of the northern barons as it was. A scandal would only make it worse."

It explained much of the torment in Rhone's life; why his father...Arden...never showed him love as he did Iyan and the others. *I'm not a son of Arden.* He'd worn the name with pride, the son of a war hero. It was something no one could take away, even when he sat in Rodrin's prison, endured the beatings on the ship.

I'm a bastard. A nothing. A nobody. *I have no last name.* Corbin, the brother he looked up to as the father he should have had, was not his brother. Not even a half-brother. The only one he could claim relation to was Ellica and Iyan, the despised Iyan. As a bastard, he wasn't even entitled to his mother's maiden name.

Rhone shoved back his chair, took the stairs two at time and grabbed his cloak from a peg by the door. Voices called after him. He ignored them. At the stable, he mounted the nearest horse, bareback. It wasn't a Hrulka. He kicked the animal into action, waving for a guard to open the southern gate, thundered across the drawbridge, through the outer gates and into town, the cold night air slapping him in the face. A quick stop at a tavern for a bottle of brandy and he was off across the fields to the east.

ℰ · ℭ

Cat tried to follow Rhone.

Corbin stopped her at the top of the stairs. "Let him go," he said. "He needs to be alone right now."

Ellica's tears flowed freely. "This never would have happened if you'd kept your mouth shut!"

"This never would have happened if you'd been honest with him in the first place," Cat countered, sick of the lies and Ellica's unreasonable anger.

"That's enough." Lindren's glare put an end to her outburst. "Sit down. I think you've caused enough trouble for one night."

"The fault's not entirely hers," Corbin said, with a pointed look in Ellica's direction.

"Yes, it is." Ellica held her head up, full of pride once more. "Arden swore me to secrecy. I couldn't disobey him."

But you could lay with someone else while married to him. Cat didn't take her seat. She needed to leave. As if reading her mind, Kelwyn came to her side, his eyes dark.

"Why didn't you tell us about your daughter?" Ellica demanded of Lindren. "We didn't even know you had one, let alone this…this ability of hers. Look at the trouble it's caused!"

"I explained yesterday why I had to keep her secret." Lindren's eyes were shadowed as well. "As for her truth-seeing, it's something best kept quiet. It works better that way and protects her from people who'd abuse it."

It was the first time Cat had heard that excuse. *How can people abuse it?* Her stomach felt sick; dinner churned. "I don't feel well. I'd like to go to our rooms."

Lindren nodded and Cat almost ran to the door leading to the residences. Kelwyn followed. Neither said a word until they were in the

389

bedroom, with both doors closed.

Cat collapsed in a heap on the bed. "I've ruined everything for Rhone," she sobbed. Kelwyn gathered her in his arms. "Why can't I keep my mouth shut?"

ℰ • ℭ

Rhone didn't travel far, just two miles east of town to a small graveyard. He slid off the horse and stumbled to one grave in particular. Disregarding the half-frozen mud, he plunked himself down and ripped the cork out of the bottle. He threw it somewhere behind him and took a long drink. The brandy burned his throat. Old snow covered the small stone indentifying who lay under it. Rhone brushed it away.

A long time he sat, taking drinks from the bottle. When it was more than half gone, he poured a measure onto the grave. "Some for you, Varek, old friend."

Laughing eyes and a playful grin surged up from Rhone's memories. "You shouldn't have died. My life might have been very different."

His friend, his only true best friend as a child, had been a commoner, son of the blacksmith who worked in the keep smithy. There were times when Rhone liked to rub in that he was noble. It never bothered Varek. He'd just laugh and say he had more freedom, none of the restrictions and expectations of a nobleman.

They'd met when a young Rhone needed to escape the keep after yet another beating from Arden. Varek found him in the stable, crying, and took him to the smithy where he became a regular visitor. Varek's father never judged him, though he didn't let Rhone get away with lording his title over him either. The big man treated Rhone the same as he had Varek and Rhone loved him for it. Right up until the day a horse kicked the blacksmith in the head. He lived for two days and Rhone had stayed by his side with Varek the entire time. Arden hadn't even known he was gone.

"I finally found out why Arden hated me," Rhone told the body lying in the grave. "I'm not his son. I'm as common as you. No, lower. I'm

390

a bastard." Varek wouldn't have cared. Rhone swallowed more of the brandy, letting it warm him to his toes. "I wouldn't have known if not for my wife. And I wouldn't have met her if you hadn't died." What a convoluted mess.

Rhone wouldn't have felt the need to leave Arden, to find peace elsewhere. No trial, no four years spent on a deserted island and no Cat. "You'd like my wife. She's so beautiful…eyes like the sun, hair like the moon and she puts the stars to shame. She also talks too much."

If Cat hadn't spoken up, however, Rhone would still be living a lie. More brandy slid down his throat and another measure dripped onto the cold ground covering his friend. "Here's to you. To your honesty. Your laugh. Your ability to find us girls when I was too shy."

They'd been fourteen and it was more that the girls found them. Varek had the easy manner and smooth talking that led to them both discovering the truth between man and woman, even if the man was only a boy. After that, they spent a large amount of their time trying to find other willing girls.

When Arden died, Rhone was fifteen. For some reason he felt the loss and Varek spent the entire day with him. Then Varek died six months later on patrol in the Barriers, the first real patrol for both of them. Rhone gulped back more brandy. He'd held Varek while he choked out his last breath, an arrow buried deep in his chest. Rhone left for Tezerain shortly after his sixteenth birthday, sick with the loss of his friend and Iyan's continual torment. Trouble came easily, so Corbin recommended the king's army.

Rhone had found fame and a nice promotion after saving Rodrin's life in battle. After that, his life took a giant swing upwards. Then came Jornel's murder and the hard fall from grace. Meeting, and marrying, Cat was a high point. Now it had all come crashing down around his ears again. "My life has more ups and downs than these hills."

He traced the entwined symbols of Ar and Vania on the small, flat, gravestone. "Here's another lie, apparently. But I suppose you'd know that by now. What's like in Ar's…Arvanion's…Hall? Are you happy?" Did he have a Hall? "Is it a place I'd like? I suppose it doesn't matter now. I'm a bastard. Bastards don't go to the Hall." They went to

Nakara, the first hell; punishment for something that wasn't their fault. Or was that a lie as well?

Another drink, a small one, and the bottle was empty. "Time to say goodbye, Varek. I'm out of brandy." Rhone stood and threw the bottle somewhere in the direction of the Arden family plot, farther north than Varek's resting place. "That's for you, Arden. May you travel all nine hells for the rest of your unnatural life. Bastard." He frowned. "No, I'm the bastard."

Rhone staggered to the horse and, after some effort, clambered on its back. Using his hands, he steered the beast back to town.

℘ • ℀

The swirls in the knots of the wooden ceiling hadn't changed since the last time Cat looked at them. She lay half on the bed, her legs hanging over the side. "Why doesn't he come back?"

"He was really upset," Kelwyn said. He stood at the bedroom window, staring out at the dark mountains. "If you were upset like that, would you come back so soon?"

A sharp rap sounded at the outer door. It was Lindren. Cat's heart sank. Lecture time.

"Cat," Lindren said. "What am I going to do with you?"

"She lied. And it was all so confusing because the purple was washed out and there was another colour there I haven't seen before." She sat up.

"Couldn't you have come to me about it? We could have talked with Rhone to see if he wanted to deal with it and how."

Cat fell back onto the bed again. "I wasn't going to say anything, but then she lied again and she made me so mad when she said I wasn't good enough for Rhone, and..." She sighed. "I just didn't think."

"Again." Lindren held his hand out. Cat took it and he pulled her up. "Is there no way I can get you to think before you do something?"

Cat hung her head. What could she say?

"Well, the damage has been done," Lindren said. "Corbin and his brothers are organizing a search for Rhone. The boys and I are going with

392

them."

"I want to come too."

"No. You stay here with Kelwyn. I think it best if laid you low for a while." Lindren left.

Cat joined Kelwyn at the window. "Why do I always have to mess things up?"

"Because you don't like lies." Kelwyn held her shoulders and kissed her forehead. "Neither does Rhone. Once he's over the shock, he'll probably thank you."

Another knock came at the door. Iyan shoved his way in and Cat groaned.

"I thought you went to look for Rhone," Kelwyn said, his eyes darkening.

"I came out of concern for Lady Cat." Iyan gave her a bow. "It's only fair she knows what her new husband is really like. A couple months isn't enough time to get to know someone."

"She knows what Rhone's like." Kelwyn stepped in front of Cat, forcing Iyan to keep his distance. "He's an angry man and you're responsible for a large portion of it."

"Why don't you go get us something to eat?" Iyan asked Kelwyn. "It's been a while since dinner and I'm sure my lady is hungry."

"I'm not going anywhere."

"Have it your way. I was only thinking of Lady Cat." Iyan sat on the bed. Cat wished he'd get off. "Rhone is actually a spoiled brat," he said. "Father pretty much ignored him when he wasn't yelling at him. Now I know why. Mother made up for it. Rhone got more toys, more love and more attention than I did."

"From her only. Is that why you hate him?" Kelwyn asked.

Iyan laughed. "I don't hate him." Cat let her eyes slip out of focus. Purple flared in his light. "I sort of feel sorry for him, bastard-born that he is. As you said, Rhone has a lot of anger in him. It builds up and then he has to let it out. I'm just concerned that when he does…well, it might not be good for Lady Cat."

Cat frowned. "I don't know what you mean."

"Come with me into town." Iyan stood and held out his hand.

393

"There's a couple people you should meet who know all about Rhone's anger."

Purple, and a healthy dose of orange, rimmed Iyan's light. "You're lying."

Rhone's strange brother laughed. "So it wasn't a fluke that you caught Mother. I'm not like Rhone. I don't let my anger take control. And I'm not like Mother. I don't care one whit if you can have children or not."

Every muscle in Cat's body tensed.

"All I care about is that you have what you need." Again, Iyan held his hand out. "Come with me to town. We can go look for Rhone together. I think I know where he might have gone."

"Cat's not going anywhere with you," Kelwyn said.

Iyan lost his smile. "I think it's up to the lady to decide."

"Get out," Cat said, fighting not to punch him in the face. "I know what you're trying to do. You've got a wife. You shouldn't be here."

The smile returned. "The children tire my wife easily. She understands I have needs."

"You're disgusting. A cad, a boor and a dishonorable lout." Cat's eyes narrowed. "Get out before I do something Lindren will regret."

Kelwyn grabbed Iyan by the arm, hustling him out of the bedroom and through the outer door. "If you know what's good for you, you'll stay away from Cat. She's Tiranen. She'll never cheat on Rhone."

He tossed him out the door, slammed it, then turned to Cat, a little smile creeping in. "I'm proud of you."

She tilted her head. "Why?"

"You handled him quite well and didn't use the words you did on Dayn."

The tension drained from her body in an instant. She smiled, glad to have her best friend by her side.

Chapter Thirty-Four

Rhone fell off his horse in front of the Potter's Wheel, the most ridiculous name he'd ever heard for a tavern. The owner's wife liked to make pots. She wasn't very good. He picked himself up off the now frozen ground and tripped up to the sidewalk. Catching his balance on a nearby post, he aimed for the door.

"We're closing," Yano, the barkeep, said. He looked the same. A little more grey maybe.

Rhone squinted, sorting out his vision. No, a lot more grey. "I just want an ale." No point in using his non-existent title. He was a nobody.

The barkeep poured a tankard. "Make it fast."

Rhone swallowed it in one draft. He set the tankard back on the counter, harder than intended. "Another."

"I said I'm closing." Yano reached for the mug.

Rhone grabbed him around the wrist. "Another. You can keep this for your trouble." With his other hand he reached into a pocket in his jerkin and pulled out a gold crown.

Yano's eyes popped out of his head. "You can have another. I have some cleaning up to do anyway." The half coin disappeared. He poured the ale so fast he almost spilled it.

Rhone found a dark corner, sitting with his back to the wall. "I'll want more."

"No trouble at all, sir." The barkeep proceeded to wipe down the counter. Slowly.

The décor had changed little. Slightly misshapen pots of various sizes sat on tables, the counter, the floor, all with gaudy glazes applied with a less than steady hand. It was a place to drink, however, and that was all Rhone wanted, to drink until he couldn't think. He'd downed three and a half tankards when the door opened. His fingers curled into fists.

Yano gave the newcomer a nod. "Evenin', Lord Iyan."

"Evening, Yano." It didn't take long for him to find Rhone. He took the bench across the table.

"Well, here you are," Iyan said, his condescending smile firmly in place. "Judging by those eyes I'd say you're pissed. Everyone's out looking for you. Mother's worried sick."

"Leave me alone."

Iyan snapped his fingers and Yano came running. "Your best ale. Make it a large one."

"Of course, my lord."

"You left your beautiful wife wondering what happened to you."

Rhone leapt to his feet, spilling his ale. "Stay away from Cat!" He tried to reach for Iyan, but only succeeded in falling back to the bench.

"Oh, yes. Good and pissed." Iyan examined his nails. "She's a gem that one. Got a scent to her that brings the blood to a man's pintle. I paid her a visit tonight."

This time Rhone's fist connected, square on Iyan's jaw. His brother flew backwards to sprawl on the floor, just missing the barkeep bringing his ale.

"Lord Iyan!" Yano cried. "I'll get the guard!"

Iyan held a hand up. "No! I'll handle it." He wiped blood from his mouth. "Not bad, for a drunk. You really should find another way to deal with your anger. This one's getting old."

Yano retreated behind the counter. Through the fog of brandy and ale Rhone could see one thing, a brother who'd tormented him for sixteen years. He found his way around the table. Iyan leapt up, catching him with a hard right to the cheek. Rhone's head jerked to the side.

Ignoring the pain, he dodged Iyan's fist, then hit him on the shoulder, then again on the side. Iyan fought back. Rhone managed to avoid most of it while landing two more blows to Iyan's body and another to the side of his head. Then he connected with a jab to his brother's gut.

Iyan doubled over, gasping for breath, and Rhone clipped him on the jaw. With a crash, Iyan fell into a bench, knocking over the table behind it. The table landed on a large blue and yellow vase, and pottery shards flew everywhere. Small loss. Rhone reached for his life-long antagonist. Iyan kicked him in the knee and it buckled. Rhone rolled with it and staggered upright, avoiding another kick. An attempt to connect his boot with Iyan's genitals caused Rhone to lose his balance and he only hit a thigh. His brother cried out in pain. Rhone grabbed the edge of a nearby table for support, preparing for another round.

Panting, his brother clambered to his feet and raised his fists, hopping on one leg, trying to keep his distance. "You've improved. Something tells me I shouldn't pick a fight when you're sober."

"Come closer and I'll show you what I've learned." Rhone had found himself involved in more than one drunken bar fight in Tezerain. Keeping up his guard, he took a step forward. The room wavered and he had to concentrate to stay vertical.

Iyan stepped back. "A halt. You win." Blood dripped from the cut on his mouth. Rising red marks on his jaw and cheek showed the result of two of Rhone's punches.

"Stay away from Cat or I'll kill you. I swear it."

A blurred Iyan held his hands up in surrender. "Between you and that bulldog Elf, I can't get within five feet of her."

Bulldog Elf? It had to be Kelwyn. He'd promised to stay with Cat. A surge of guilt forced its way through the alcohol. Rhone shouldn't have left her. He needed to get back to her. He needed to…sit.

Somehow, he found a bench. Iyan sat several feet away, wiping blood from his face. "You've definitely grown, little brother."

Yano handed him a cloth. "Little brother?"

Iyan took the offered cloth and used it to clean his face. "I'm not surprised you didn't recognize Rhone."

"Lord Rhone? My apologies, my lord! I thought you a traveler. You've changed."

Rhone waved a hand in his direction. "Doesn't matter."

"Bring ale, Yano," Iyan said. "We both need a drink. Well, I do. Rhone looks like he's had enough."

"I'll have one." Rhone struggled to his feet and found his way back to his original seat, not quite avoiding the spilled ale.

His brother joined him. "That's one hell of a wife you've got. Didn't fall for a single one of my lines. Mind you, I didn't try very hard.

With Lord Kelwyn guarding her like a dragon with its hoard, there wasn't much point." The ale arrived. "Here's to you. Congratulations on your marriage. You finally found someone good enough." He tipped the tankard and didn't put it down until it was half gone.

Rhone sipped his. What was the bastard up to now? "What do you mean?"

"What I mean, brother of mine, is that if I could talk a girl away from you she wasn't good enough."

Those words didn't make sense and Rhone doubted it was the alcohol. "Not good enough for what?"

"For you." Iyan pointed a finger at himself. "I am the only one who's allowed to hurt you. It's my job as older brother to make sure you're tough enough for life and judging by the way you are now, I've done an excellent job." He took another drink.

What in the nine hells? "I thought you beat me up and took my girls away because you hated me."

"Don't get me wrong, I do. But I had a responsibility as your brother, your only one now, to make sure you were tough enough to survive life up here. It should have been Father's duty, but..." He shrugged.

"You're full of shit. If having the crap beaten out of a person qualifies him for life in Arden, then Father...your father, more than did his job."

Iyan laughed. The door opened again, admitting Lindren and his sons.

The Elven Elder glanced around the room, taking in the broken pottery, the fallen table and chairs, then studied Rhone. "Did you settle your differences?"

"No," Rhone said.

Iyan said, "Yes."

Shain peered into Rhone's eyes. "You're drunk. Ale and brandy by the smell." He took one arm, hauling Rhone to his feet. "Cat's worried. Time to go home."

"Cat." Her sweet face flashed before his eyes. His need for her returned tenfold.

Rhone took two steps, then had to use the table to support himself. Arnir put a shoulder under his other arm. He didn't remember reaching the door.

ℰ　·　ℭ

Cat sat on the bed and sighed. "I wish I could go look for Rhone myself."

"And make Lindren even angrier than he already is?" Kelwyn asked, brushing out the last of her braid.

The outer door banged open and both sprang to their feet. Cat flung open the bedroom door. Shain and Arnir carried Rhone between them. He looked unconscious, had a red lump on his left cheek and stunk like alcohol.

Cat took over for Shain. "What happened? Is he all right?"

Lindren and Corbin entered.

"He's passed out drunk," Corbin said. "Put him to bed. He'll be sick in the morning, but he'll survive."

Shain helped them remove Rhone's cloak and they laid him on the bed.

Cat tugged his boots off. "What happened to his face?"

"He and Iyan had a bit of a brawl in a tavern," Shain said. "Apparently Rhone won."

Corbin gave him a wry smile. "First time, from my recollection."

Cat pulled a small towel from a drawer and soaked it in a basin of water. "Why don't they like each other?" she asked, dabbing at the cut below Rhone's eye.

"They've hated one other for years," Corbin said. "Ellica always favoured Rhone, making Iyan jealous, while Father made a point of spoiling Iyan, which made Rhone jealous. I never understood it until now."

Jealousy. Perhaps that was the red-green colour she saw in Iyan's light.

Corbin moved to the outer room. "He needs sleep. It's late, so I'll bid you goodnight."

Once he'd left, Cat set the cloth on the bedside table. "Arnir, will he really be all right?"

Her brother set his fingers on Rhone's injured cheek and murmured the words to call his magic. After a moment, he said, "He'll be fine, though I suspect he'll regret drinking the amount he did. When he wakes, get some water into him."

"Consequences, Cat." Lindren leaned against the door frame. "If you hadn't said anything, Rhone wouldn't be in this state, nor would the family be in turmoil."

"But he wouldn't know the truth, either. Which is better?"

Her father shrugged. "It's a hard call. I suppose if I asked you one more time to think before you did something, it wouldn't do any good." He shook his head and pushed himself away from the wall. "Time we said goodnight as well."

The Elves left, Kelwyn giving her a hug and kiss, leaving Cat with Rhone. She held him all night, making sure he stayed breathing. Corbin came to check on him in the morning, offering to sit with him while Cat had breakfast. She declined and he had something sent up for her.

When the sun had almost reached its zenith, Rhone stirred, groaning. His left eye had swollen shut, the purple and black matching that of the raised bruise on his cheek and a couple other places on his body. There were more marks, and dried blood, on his knuckles.

When Cat tried to hug him he put a pillow over his head.

"Close the curtains." His voice came out like a croak.

She did as he asked, then poured some water.

"I feel like I've been trampled by a herd of cattle." Rhone tried to sit up and failed. "I'm sorry, Cat. I shouldn't have left you last night."

"I don't blame you for being upset." She tried to give him the water; he wouldn't take it. "I was worried, though. And I'm sorry too. I shouldn't have said anything."

"I'm glad you did. At least now I'm not living a lie. It explains...much." He put the pillow back over his head. "I feel awful. Somebody's pounding an anvil in my head."

"Do you want me to get Arnir?"

"I doubt he can cure stupidity."

"I don't understand."

"Never mind. One thing I did decide last night. I don't belong here. I'm not a son of Arden and I shouldn't live in his keep. I'm just a bastard who doesn't even know his father's name."

"What's a bastard?"

"It means my parents weren't married. A great sin in Kitring-Tor."

"I don't care. I love you just the way you are."

Rhone raised the pillow enough to peer out at her through one bloodshot eye. "Thank you." He groaned. "I hope you've got an empty basin handy. My stomach's churning."

"I'll get Arnir. Wait here." Cat set the water on the table.

"Trust me. I'm not going anywhere."

Cat found her brother in the hall, talking with Gavan. After checking Rhone over, Arnir said, "I've taken care of the headache and nausea, but you need food and water. Corbin and Iyan have seen your face, so I'm afraid I can't do anything there."

"I'll live." Rhone sat up. "I don't remember much of the fight. There's a few things about last night I don't remember."

Cat's heart skipped a beat. "Is that normal?"

Arnir chuckled. "After the amount he drank? Yes. It's time for lunch, do you feel like coming to the hall or do you want something brought here?"

"I'll come. At least now I think I can walk. Thank you."

Cat helped Rhone dress and by the time they reached the hall Rhone's family was there, except Iyan. Also missing were Lindren, his sons and Kelwyn; they chose to eat with the others waiting outside the village.

Rhone directed Cat to the opposite end of the table from his mother, her glare following them every step of the way. Lunch was eaten in painful silence. Slices of mutton accompanied winter vegetables, a bread loaded with different grains, and various cheeses. Cat would have enjoyed it if the air in the room hadn't felt so tense that the hairs on the back of her neck stood up.

The servants cleared the table, the children were dismissed and tea poured.

"Nice you could join us for lunch," Ellica said to Rhone, her tone that of a scolding mother. "Your face is slightly better than Iyan's."

"I'm feeling better, thank you."

"I heard Lord Lindren and his sons had to carry you home last night." Ellica's features remained as cold as marble. "A fine example you're showing our Elven friends."

Matching sea-green eyes glared at each other up and down the table. Cat doubted it was the first time. The rest of the family appeared used to it. They sat quietly watching one opponent, then the other. She just wanted to hide.

"If you'd told me the truth after Arden died," Rhone said, through clenched teeth, "I wouldn't have felt it necessary to drown my sorrows last night."

She studied him a moment before turning her icy gaze on Cat. "I hope you're happy. No one needed to know. Ever since you arrived, you've caused nothing but trouble."

Cat's guilt turned to anger. She wasn't the one who'd started the whole mess.

"No, Mother," Rhone said, before Cat could open her mouth. "You're the one causing trouble. No one else here has a problem with Cat as my wife. Only you. And it's not Cat's fault you chose to keep a lie secret, even after Arden died. I'm glad the truth is out." He stood, pulling Cat up with him. "Now if you will excuse me, I'm tired."

Cold eyes and tense silence followed them out of the hall.

୨୦ • ଓ

Rhone chose to have dinner brought to their rooms, it would be easier on Cat. Lindren stopped by to tell them they had to leave in the morning. Just as well. The situation with his mother was rougher than expected.

Corbin also paid a visit. "Rather than upset Ellica further," he said, "I thought I'd talk to you here. Father claimed you as his own, even if he only did it to save face. As far as I'm concerned, you are my brother.

402

I watched you grow with my Dev. You'll always have a home here."

Gripping Corbin's shoulder, Rhone said, "Thank you. It means much to me, now that I'm a bastard."

"According to Iyan, you always were," Corbin said, with a chuckle. "Truth tell, bastard or not, you now outrank me."

"I won't hold it over your head." They both laughed, easing Rhone's wounded heart. A bastard wasn't entitled to rank, except through marriage. The thing was, the Elves' rank was only imagined, put on by the people of Kitring-Tor. They had no king, no nobles. The rank had already proved useful in dealing with Soran Rais, however, and might come in handy again.

Despite Corbin's words, sleep didn't come easily that night. Even time spent with Cat didn't alleviate Rhone's distress. A deep sorrow lay on him. Arden had been his home. Through the years in Tezerain it supported him, knowing there was always someplace to return to if he chose, if he felt the need to come home to a proper family. While on the island, it was a paradise, out of reach yet something that might be achieved, with luck and a passing ship. Corbin said he was still welcome. Would the others look at him differently now? How would they have treated him if they'd known all along?

For the first time since the revelation, he thought about his real father. He was a soldier. Where had he been born? What had he looked like? Rhone's mother always told him he resembled an uncle of hers. Was that another lie? Did he actually look like his father? Could that be the reason she loved him more than Iyan? The reason she smothered him and tried to control his life? Perhaps his father was still alive, though he doubted Arden would have let him remain within reach of Ellica. He might even have been transferred to Tezerain. Had he met him?

Questions. Too many questions. Perhaps one day he could sit down with his mother and hold a proper conversation about his father.

Chapter Thirty-Five

Rhone left Arden Keep with Cat and the Elves, right on schedule, accompanied by Gavan, Jerran, Iyan, two hundred cavalry and eight hundred foot soldiers. The rest stayed behind in case of an attack there instead of Kerend. Saying goodbye to his mother had been strained and short. She'd tried one more time to convince him to leave Cat. While saying goodbye to the rest of his former siblings, each one indicated they still considered him a brother.

The band of Elves and men took eight days to make the journey to the rolling hills below Broken Man Pass in northern Kerend, passing the Elven supply wagons on the way. Lindren stopped to speak to the Elf in charge and they filled their saddlebags for the rest of the trip. The events of the past few days continued to plague Rhone. By the time they arrived, he decided he'd just have to live with it.

Iyan listened to Rhone's threat, at least for now, and stayed away from Cat, riding with the Arden men. Just as well. With the mood Rhone was in, he might actually have followed through with the threat.

They arrived to find Vergel's army spread across the scrub-covered low hills in a sea of tents, dotted with islands of campfires and weapon caches, the supply wagons in a ragged line to the south. The Barriers stood stark against the early spring sky, a drab combination of dark, rocky shadows and old snow.

Commander-General Vergel Mandearan, under the king's banner, was positioned in the middle of the army with a small hill all to himself. The dukes who'd chosen to come spread around the command centre, each flying the colours of their houses, their banners flapping in a cold breeze, adding a splash of colour to the predominantly brown, grey and white landscape.

Jerran and Gavan wished Rhone luck, took their leave of Lindren and headed for Vergel's tent for instructions. The Elves carried on to where Sandrin and Rendir had set up camp on the eastern flank.

When they drew near, Cat moved Krir closer to Rhone and tugged on his arm. "I wonder if Lindren would let us put our tent on that little hill?" She pointed to a small rise at the farthest extent of the Elven camp, a good quarter mile to the east of the nearest campfire. A scant few Elven tents were set up and Rhone shivered at the thought of sleeping the way the Elves did, out in the rain and snow.

Still he chuckled, glad to have his humour back. He knew what Cat was after. How could he argue? "I doubt he'd let you be off by yourself like that, but you could ask him."

"I won't be by myself. You'll be with me." She stood up in her stirrups. "Oh look! It's Taurin." Her finger directed him to a black banner on the western edge of the Elven camp. When the wind blew right, it showed a red sword dripping blood, an unusual banner for Elves.

"If he's here, you can bet on trouble," Kelwyn said. "He's got an uncanny instinct for it."

Shain nudged his Hrulka closer. "He hates to miss a good fight."

Taurin. Lindren's *qirand* cousin, if Rhone remembered correctly. Kelwyn gave Shain an odd look, then moved up to where Lindren rode with Arnir. A few minutes later, they arrived at the outskirts of the Elven encampment. One of the patrol directed them to where the rest of the Silverwood contingent had set up, near the centre of the Elves. That would put a wrinkle in Cat's plans.

Rhone shifted his gaze to her. Cat wasn't paying attention to where they rode, she had her eyes on Broken Man Pass, several miles to the north; probably had the prophecy on her mind. He still didn't believe in it the way she did. She tilted her head, her eyebrows dipped in a frown. The expression he'd learned meant her curiosity took control.

"What's the matter?" he asked her.

"I feel something."

"Like someone watching you?" There were certainly enough people around.

She shook her head. "When someone's watching me, it's like an itch. This is a kind of throb, like a heartbeat, in the back of my head. And I know exactly where it's coming from."

He didn't need to ask. *Broken Man Pass.*

Tiny winter birds clung to dried bushes beside Lindren's tent. Their trill reminded him of home, as did something else he stared at...Cat's wide, innocent eyes. "These hills can hide any number of vauroks or goblins and you want to camp a quarter mile away?"

"There are patrols, aren't there?"

Once again, Cat hadn't thought things through. "Yes, but don't they defeat the purpose of you being out there?" he asked.

Her shoulders slumped. "I hadn't thought of that. What can I do?"

Lindren scanned the encampment. Only one spot came to mind. "How about near the Torian supply wagons? They're a good distance from the tents as well as the southern patrols."

Cat perked up. "That would work." She gave him a light kiss on the lips. "Thank you."

He chuckled as she bounced off to find Rhone.

"Looks like Lady Cat is happy."

Lindren recognized the voice. "Aris. It's good to see you again."

Kerend's baron shook his hand. "I heard you'd arrived, so I thought I'd come say hello. I'm afraid I'm unable to offer you the usual hospitality."

"Understandable."

Aris' keep lay too far to the south to make it a good command centre for the pass. All the people had been moved out of the area, evacuated to Kerend keep and the town surrounding it.

"However, I can offer you mulled wine in my tent," the baron said.

"Sounds good."

"Vergel filled me in on the doings in Tezerain," Aris said, as they walked. "You and Lady Cat have had quite a time of it. Bad business that. I have to admit, though, I'm surprised your daughter married Rhone, even if she is Tiranen." He laughed at Lindren's surprise. "Vergel informed me of that as well."

"I apologize for not telling you when you were in the city."

"I understand. It wouldn't have mattered. I still couldn't have given her what she needs. I hope Rhone can. At least he doesn't have the responsibilities I do."

"He appears to be doing a good job so far."

They both laughed.

"Ever since he read the letter from King Rodrin," Aris said, "Brade's been up and down my back about outranking me once he's married."

"I'm glad Aura had nothing to do with Teale's treachery."

"So is Brade. He says he's up to the job. I'm not so sure, he's only twenty. He'll have his work cut out for him restoring the Teale name."

Lindren had to agree. When they arrived, Aris nodded to the guards outside his tent. One of them opened the flap. Just before entering, Lindren glanced at the open expanse of Broken Man Pass, wondering just what Teale had done.

ဢ · ဣ

Cat pounded the last peg into the ground. She chose a spot at the Elven end of the train of Human wagons, twelve yards from the nearest tent. Not ideal, but better than nothing.

Kelwyn looped the rope around the peg and tied it off. "That's got it."

"I'll be glad when Lindren's wagons arrive," Rhone said, bringing over Cat's saddlebags. "A pallet would be nice." He'd made it clear the first night out of Tezerain that he hated sleeping on the ground. Rhone ducked into the tent.

"He complains a lot," Kelwyn said, in Elven.

Cat shrugged. "I think I'm getting used to it."

Kelwyn pointed over her shoulder, a smile sliding up his face. "We've got company."

Two figures sauntered in their direction. It took Cat only an instant to recognize them. "Orrin! Arufin!"

Kelwyn's brother reached them first, catching Cat in a hug. He kissed her lightly on the lips before putting her down. "I hear congratulations are in order. You're an old married lady now." Orrin

407

used the Torian word though he spoke Elven.

"That was fast," Cat said. "We haven't been here long."

"We saw Lindren," Orrin said.

"My turn." Arufin bent her over backwards before kissing her.

"Excuse me. That's my wife." Rhone's deep voice had a hard tone to it.

Arufin almost dropped her. He put his hands in the air. "I only kissed her cheek. Honest," he said, switching to Torian.

Rhone still didn't appear happy. A quick check of his light showed red along with the same red-green mixture Iyan had; definitely jealousy.

Cat took his arm, hoping it would calm him. "This is Orrin, Kelwyn's brother, and Arufin, his friend."

Relaxing, Rhone gripped Orrin's forearm. "I should have known, you look like the rest of Lindren's family. Kelwyn and Cat have talked about you."

"I'm innocent."

Rhone laughed, then held his hand out to Arufin. "Cat's talked about both of you."

"I'm innocent too." Arufin accepted his friendship grip.

Orrin held up a finger. "But not as innocent as I am."

They all laughed.

Kelwyn pushed his brother. "You're not going to say hello to me?"

"I was getting around to it. You're not as cute as Cat." He gripped Kelwyn in a bear hug, lifting him off the ground. "That better?"

Then it was Arufin's turn. He added a kiss to the cheek.

When he let Kelwyn down, her friend wiped it off. "I really didn't need that."

Rhone shook his head. "I think those stories are true."

They talked for a few minutes, then Orrin said it was time to go.

"So soon?" Cat asked. She'd missed the pair of them, especially Arufin; she'd reserved a spot in her heart just for him.

"Now that the army's here we have to behave ourselves." Orrin kissed her cheek again.

408

Arufin copied him. " We've got patrol, but we can stop by later."

They said their goodbyes. Rhone watched them leave, an intent expression on his face. The red-green mixture in his light remained and Cat wondered just what was going through his mind.

ಐ · ೞ

Morning arrived with a thunderous crash as a rainstorm passed overhead, adding to the mud problem. At least it appeared the snowstorms had left for the year. Lindren sat just inside his tent with the flap pulled back, eating his breakfast and staring through the rain at Broken Man Pass, wishing Vergel had placed the army closer to it.

He ate alone. Though Lowren visited the previous day, he hadn't seen him since. Firinn, the captain of the company he'd sent three and a half months before, reported in shortly after his arrival. He'd stayed with Aris, helping the baron run patrols. Officially, they'd seen no sign of vauroks, goblins or any other dark creatures. Unofficially, Cainfir's company, hidden in the mountains, killed two bands of fifty vauroks each.

Nothing. Those numbers are nothing. But what are they doing here this time of year?

Firinn had no answer, neither did Lindren. Something was there; he felt it in his bones. Cainfir was still out in the mountains and due to report back any day. Lindren couldn't help wondering if they'd find something this time.

The sun came out later that morning and with it came Taurin. Lindren was sitting on a camp stool outside the tent when he came by; bad timing as far as Lindren was concerned. Cat and Rhone were due any minute. They'd all been invited to Aris' tent for lunch.

"Good to see you, cousin," Lindren said, clasping his forearm. "Been busy?"

"Yes. There's quite a bit of activity out there. We just finished a job in the badlands on the small continent of southern Tiru." Taurin's grey eyes were as dark as Lindren had ever seen them.

"Again? It seems we clear them out and they're right back there."

409

Taurin shrugged. "Plenty of caves for crèches." His dead *qirand* voice hadn't changed either.

"Taurin!" Cat appeared from nowhere, flinging her arms around Taurin's neck.

A light appeared in his cousin's eyes, two candles burning in the impenetrable darkness of his *qirand* state. Impenetrable, that is, until Cat came into his life.

Rhone rounded the corner of the tent, his half-smile vanishing in an instant. Lindren silently groaned; Taurin had his face buried in Cat's neck. When she kissed him, lightly on the lips as she would any other member of the family, Taurin frowned.

"Don't I deserve a better kiss than that?" Thankfully, he spoke in Elven.

"I can't," Cat said, wriggling out his grasp, her excitement adding a lightning charge to the already tense situation. "I have a bondmate. You were right, someone did want me." Switching to Torian, she said, "I'd like you to meet him."

She took Taurin's hand and pulled him closer to her bondmate. "This is Rhone. I met him on Crescent Island." Her eyes sparkled.

Taurin's, on the other hand, lost their light, shadowing to deep wells of despair. "Pleased to meet you." He didn't offer his hand.

"Same here." Rhone didn't either.

The air thickened. Time to get them away from Taurin. "Cat," Lindren said. "Why don't you head over to Aris' tent? I'll be along in a few minutes. I want to talk to Taurin."

"All right." She kissed Taurin's cheek, then clutched Rhone's arm, chatting as she left.

Rhone gave Taurin a backward glance. It wasn't hard to guess what ran through his mind. Taurin watched them go.

"It's what you wanted for her, isn't it?"

Taurin turned his black gaze on him. "Yes. It is." He didn't look like he believed it. Instead, it appeared another part of him died. "What did you want to talk about?"

"We found a prophecy concerning Sleepers." Lindren related the visit to Jeral's tower, though he only told him of the first prophecy.

"Dark Elf." Taurin glanced in the direction Cat had gone. "That would be me. Who's the Black Fox?"

"Rhone. Fox is the name he took when he was Cat's bodyguard and he wore black then." Lindren held a hand up. "It's a long story. I'll tell you later. Jeral and I feel the Dark Elf is Kelwyn, because of his black hair."

Taurin had the same brown hair and grey eyes as Lindren, except his eyes never lightened to silver-grey, not since his soulmate, Katrin, died in battle over two hundred years ago.

"I don't agree. I hear what people say, that my nature is dark. You've said it yourself." Taurin's entire body tensed. "I'm going. She needs me. Who knows what's hiding in there."

"You're not going. Kelwyn is. Jeral feels it's right and so do I. We need you here. You may have a mercenary company of your own, but you're still a Silverwood Elf and I'm telling you, you're not going."

Taurin flexed his fingers. Lindren hoped he wasn't in for a fight. His cousin had a healer alter him, making him larger than any other Elf. He now stood eight inches over six feet and was as broad across the chest as Rhone. Lindren would lose.

"There's nothing happening here." Taurin's normally cold voice rasped ice.

"Not yet. I have a feeling that will change. Trust me. I need you."

Taurin's dark gaze bored into Lindren.

He returned it, glare for glare. "Have you sunk to such a low level as to dishonor yourself by defying your Elder?"

His cousin didn't move a muscle, the only reaction to Lindren's words was a slight widening of his hard eyes. Taurin's hand flexed, moved towards the hilt of the dagger at his waist. Was he truly capable of attacking his Elder? His cousin?

Black, soul-lost eyes bored into Lindren. No one knew what went on in the mind of *qirand* and Taurin was one of a kind, a *qirand* who'd survived the *moraren*, the horrible wrenching of one soulmate from another. With his father's help, he'd defied the overwhelming urge to *fade*, to join his dead love on the Other Side. Three other *qirand* still lived, Taurin's lieutenants, though they acted like Taurin used to before he met

411

Cat.

A *qirand* couldn't feel love, nor much in the way of any emotion except extreme anger and loss, yet Taurin felt something for Cat. Just what, Lindren had no idea. Even Taurin couldn't explain it. He needed her in a way no one truly understood. Somehow, when she was with him, she eased the pain of his lost soulmate. Taurin made love to Cat, though he should have been impotent. Was his cousin now capable of murder? If so, he'd be the first.

Taurin's left eye twitched. So did the hand hovering over his dagger.

Lindren folded his arms across his chest and glared back. "You wanted this for her. At least that's what you said. How do you think Cat would react? What would she think of your behavior?"

Taurin snatched his hand away from the dagger. His eyes opened wider. Without a word, he spun on his heel and strode away.

Lindren let out the breath he'd held. His hands shook. He hoped Taurin stayed on his side of the camp and left Cat alone.

ഞ · ൙

After a pleasant lunch with Aris, Rhone sent Cat back to their tent with Kelwyn. He wanted to speak to Lindren. After relating Cat's view on Ar and Vania, Rhone said, "Is this another Elven secret?"

Lindren couldn't hide his exasperated sigh. "I really wish she could keep her mouth closed for once. It's not a secret. As a matter of fact, my father and several Elders tried to tell your people, and the others who came through with them, that it was Arvanion who'd freed them from inevitable death." He indicated the stools sitting outside his tent. "Have a seat."

Once settled, Rhone said, "Cat told me he disappeared right afterwards."

"He did. Your people, who first settled in Thallan-Mar, believed in a god and goddess on their world and refused to change that belief. They felt Arvanion was simply another incarnation of their deities and called him Ar. The last part of his name became your goddess, Vania."

412

Lindren shrugged. "We tried to tell them otherwise, but it upset them and we decided we didn't need a religious war on top of everything else."

"Perfectly understandable." Why were his people so stupidly stubborn? Although, if they weren't, carving a life for themselves on this world, and the others, would have been much harder. "So why does it bother Cat?"

"I'd have to say she's so obsessed with the truth, and how to avoid it, she's letting it control her."

Rhone raised an eyebrow. "How to avoid it?"

Now a smile turned up Lindren's mouth. "As proved by her plan for you as her bodyguard, Cat can be a sneaky, devious person."

Rhone aleady knew it.

"She'll never lie outright, but my daughter has become adept at finding ways of skipping around the truth without ever saying a lie."

With a chuckle, Rhone said, "Like my scars. She only said I had them, not where they were, and everyone assumed they were on my face because I wore a mask."

"Exactly."

Rhone gave him a sidelong glance. "If my people have different gods than you, is the Black Lord different as well?"

Lindren shook his head. "Only the name. Udath Kor. It means Dark Lord, pretty much the same thing. Arvanion called him Balphegor. Regardless of names, he is who he is in all cultures. And as far as I'm concerned, it only means one thing. Death for too many souls."

Rhone had to agree. "These other people, the ones who came through with mine. Do they believe in Arvanion?" Were his people the only idiots?

"Some. Others don't. They still worship their old gods or come up with new ones."

That halted Rhone's thoughts. "How can you come up with new ones? The gods are always there, aren't they?"

"Arvanion has been, from long before he created my people. But with Humans, views change. Some old gods no longer fit their perspective of life, so they reinvent them."

"Reinvent. Does that mean you don't believe these other gods exist?"

Lindren clasped his hands and stared at a spot on the ground for a moment. "No, I don't. It's possible they stayed behind when your people arrived. There's no evidence to show me otherwise. Arvanion is the only one I've ever seen and we don't think of him as a god in the same sense your people know one. He created us and we honour and love him for it. But we don't worship him. We don't kill, make offerings or build temples in his name. Nor do we sacrifice others to appease him."

Rhone jerked straight. "Sacrifice? Who does that?" The priests and priestesses of Ar and Vania preached only benevolence. Far too few paid attention to them.

"Several cultures to start with. We convinced most of them to stop. Five remain. Two on Cathras, two on Tiru and one on Morata. When we tried to force them to change their views, they turned on us. So we don't have anything to do with them."

"And they survived?" Kitring-Tor had relied on Lindren's aid many times in its thousand year history. Without it, Rhone doubted life would be as comfortable as it was, especially in the baronies.

"They have, but only because they're all on islands of little interest to vauroks."

Lindren's words tugged a curiosity in Rhone, one that had remained buried for many years. As a child, he'd loved reading about the peoples of other lands, those to the east, south and far across the sea. He pressed the Elder for information.

By the time Cat came looking for him, the afternoon sun sat low to the west and Rhone had his head filled with images of new lands and different cultures. Perhaps Cat could take him to some of those places. It struck Rhone that regardless of the shock of his true parentage, he was a very lucky man.

Chapter Thirty-Six

A myriad of stars shone in the night sky. Cat had her eyes on one particular grouping, that of the Torian constellation the Bashful Lady.

> *'Silver Cat, Black Fox, Dark Elf,*
> *All will ride, all will fall,*
> *Under the gaze of the Bashful Lady,*
> *All will bring the Sleepers home.'*

The words of the prophecy had run through her mind over and over for the last two and a half months. Now she'd been here for three days. Cat had wanted to leave for the pass the day after they arrived; Lindren said no, he needed to know the situation first.

'All will ride, all will fall'. What did it mean? Would they fall down a cliff while looking for the Sleepers? Fall also meant dying in battle. If that happened, they couldn't all bring the Sleepers home. Did it mean they'd bring the Sleepers home and then fall? That wasn't the order of the prophecy, however. Or did it have an order? Where were they supposed to bring the Sleepers? Where was home? The whole thing made Cat's head ache.

Regardless of what it meant, something pulled her to the pass. She'd felt it as soon as they'd arrived in Kerend, a strange sensation in her head, thrumming in time with her heartbeat, urging her to come. Tomorrow. Lindren said they would go tomorrow. *'All will fall.'*

Rhone opened the tent flap, huddled in the cloak Rhianna had given him. "Worried about tomorrow?" He moved in behind and wrapped his arms around her.

She nodded. "I'm excited. I've waited so long for this. But I'm afraid too."

"You'll do just fine."

"I'm not afraid for me. I'm worried about you and Kelwyn."

"Don't be. We can take care of ourselves," Rhone said. They stared up at the sky, silent for a few moments. "You really like dragons, don't you."

"I have all my life."

He pointed northeast. "See that bright star? The one above that peak, over there?"

"Yes."

"If you follow that down and to the left, to that other bright star, it forms the tail of the constellation we call The Dragon. Those stars, there, there, there and there, are the wings."

It didn't make sense to Cat; it was just a bunch of stars. What she did see was that the tail pointed to a spur on the side of a mountain bordering the pass. A shiver ran down her spine and the pulsing increased. *That's where I need to go.*

She turned at a nearby sound.

Lindren strode out of the darkness, a package tucked under one arm. "Beautiful night."

"It's cold," Rhone said. "But at least we're on the good side of cold now. It'll warm up eventually."

Lindren chuckled. "That it will. I have something for you." He handed him the package.

"Another gift? You've already spoiled me with the clothes and sword."

"The clothes were from Rhianna. The sword was Cat's gift. This is mine."

When Rhone removed the cloth wrapping, metal rings shone like silver. "A set of mail?"

Lindren nodded. "When I took Cat's to be repaired, I had the maker alter a set to fit you. I just finished putting the spells on it."

Rhone lifted the shirt. Delicate rings of various sizes, artfully woven, formed a fine pattern of leaves across the neckline while the rest spilled like liquid from his hand. "I don't know what to say. Thank you doesn't seem enough."

Lindren smiled. "You're welcome. It's a two part gift. The rest will take longer. I've also ordered a set of full plate mail for you."

416

"Full...Elven plate mail?" Rhone's voice reflected his shock.

"You're part of the family and we need to keep you as safe as we can," Lindren said.

Rhone stared at the mail in his hands, then at Lindren. "I'm speechless." He tucked the mail under his arm and held out his hand to Lindren.

A warm rush filled Cat from head to toe.

"I doubt your expedition tomorrow will take one day," Lindren said. "Make sure you have enough food."

"We've already been to the supply wagons," Cat said. "Our bags are stuffed."

Lindren gave her a kiss. "I'd like to see you before you go." He took his leave.

"We should go inside," Rhone said, nuzzling her neck. "If this is going to take a few days, I'd like to make love to you tonight."

That idea fit perfect with Cat's intentions; Rhone slept deeper after laying with her. He pulled her into the tent. She paid him particular attention, keeping him warm under the blankets. Afterwards, she lay with her head on his chest, listening to his heartbeat, so strong, rhythmic. Her love wanted to burst from her heart, wash over him, keep him safe.

Cat waited until the deep of night. The moon hadn't risen yet, which was good. There were no clouds, which wasn't, and the starlight shone bright. Slipping quietly from the bed, she dressed in shirt, vest, trousers, boots, mail shirt, long tunic and cloak.

She strapped on her boot knife and fastened the belt holding the tchiru. Her bow and two quivers lay in a corner, ready to go. She slipped them and her full pack over her shoulder. Krir sent her a worried thought. Cat soothed him, then instructed her Hrulka to wander away from the herd and meet her in a copse of small trees to the east.

Keeping a careful watch for sentries, she made her way to the Hrulka herd, urging them to keep quiet, and slipped through to the other side. Ducking behind trees, crouching low to the ground between the hills, Cat made her way to the copse. When she judged herself far enough from the sentry lines, she mounted Krir bareback. It wasn't the first time she'd crept past Elven sentries; this time, however, she left Kelwyn behind.

Cat had wanted Rhone to come, needed him to see it was true. Now the line, 'all will fall' wouldn't leave her thoughts. She couldn't take the chance of losing Kelwyn or Rhone, perhaps both. Urging Krir into a canter, she headed for Broken Man Pass.

The quarter moon rose in the clear sky, casting a pale gleam to the mounds of remaining snow and added a muted sparkle to every little rivulet running from the mountains. Night birds, just recently returned from the south, sang to each other from groves of stunted trees. It was a pleasant ride, if Cat didn't think about what she'd done. Lindren would be angry, so would Rhone and Kelwyn. It didn't matter; she couldn't risk the lives of two very important people.

When she entered the pass itself, Cat slowed Krir to a walk keeping her eye on the spur she'd spotted while with Rhone. The snow lay deeper in the shadow of the mountains, sometimes past Krir's knees. In the sliver of moonlight, the dark recess of a cave grew visible, right under the spur.

Cat dismounted, excitement coursing through her. The cave entrance was just large enough to allow Krir inside. However, it quickly became apparent that she'd have to send him back to camp. The wide opening narrowed to a tunnel too low for the Hrulka.

Resting her head on Krir's neck, she told him the bad news. The horse didn't want to leave. "You'll be safer if you do," she said. "Go back to camp. I'll worry about you otherwise."

The Hrulka nosed her shoulder and she hugged him goodbye. When Krir left, Cat took a deep breath, lit her handfire and headed for the tunnel. Not long after, the passage split, one tunnel angling off to the right, the other to the left. A blue glow mingled with the light from her handfire. It took a moment for her to realize it was the dragon bone bow over her shoulder and the dagger tucked into her boot.

When Black Wing, the dead dragon, had first given her the bones, they'd shone a deep sapphire when she touched them. After they'd been worked, the dagger hilts only glowed when reacting to the blood of one of Udath Kor's creatures. The bow hadn't shone since she'd given it to Corfindin.

Cat pulled the magic weapon off her shoulder, wondering what would cause it to start shining now. She headed to the right tunnel and the glow dimmed. Changing to the left, the light from the bow brightened. It had to be a sign she was on the right track. She chose the tunnel the dragon bones indicated.

ᔒ · ᘓ

Rhone rolled over, searching for Cat, and fell off the pallet, the cold shocking him awake. No Cat. He crawled back under the covers, wondering if she was bringing him breakfast. After a while, he decided she wasn't. Cursing the frigid air, he threw on cold clothes, then wrapped his cloak tight around him and strode out of the tent in search of his wife. Kelwyn hadn't seen her, nor had her brothers or uncle. Rhone almost ran to Lindren's tent, most of Cat's family with him. No sign of Cat.

"She wouldn't," Lindren said, his eyes turning dark.

"She would." Shain appeared just as worried, so did Arnir and Lowren.

A sinking feeling crept into Rhone's gut just as Kelwyn entered Lindren's tent. "Cat's bow and pack are gone."

Rhone kicked himself for an ass. He should have noticed. "I can guess where she is."

"That little fool." Lindren ran a hand through his hair. "You're going to have to catch up." He unhooked a lantern hanging from the roof of the tent and lit it with his magic.

"She's worried about us," Kelwyn said. "And that line about 'all will fall'."

"That's no excuse for heading off on her own, especially when she knows Udath Kor is after her." Lindren threw back the flap. "Shain, Arnir, help me saddle their Hrulka. You two get your things. And Rhone, don't forget your mail."

Lowren gripped his son's shoulder. "You be careful. Who knows what's awaiting you."

Kelwyn nodded. "You too. There are two babies who'll want to meet their father."

419

They embraced and Kelwyn left at a dead run. Rhone ran back to the tent and glanced at the empty place where Cat's pack and bow belonged. Cursing, he put on the new mail, strapped the ice sword on his back, threw on the cloak and tossed the pack over his shoulder. He headed straight for the pasture. Kelwyn was mounted and ready to go when he arrived.

"She took Krir," Lindren said to Kelwyn. "One of the patrol found him heading back. Following her path should be easy. Once you get to your destination, you'll just have to do your best." He passed him the lantern.

Kelwyn gave him a nod and they were off. Krir's tracks through the mud and snow led straight to a cave a quarter mile into the pass. Once it was determined the Hrulka could go no farther, they removed their packs and sent them on their way.

It would have to be a cave. Rhone hesitated at the entrance as memories, long pushed back to a corner of his mind, shoved their way forward. Dark, crawling with insects, stinking like the dirt of graves.

"What's the matter?" Kelwyn asked, pausing several feet in, the Elven lantern held in front of him.

"I hate caves." Rhone moved past the Elf, forcing the memories at least part way back to their hole.

"Didn't you use the ones on the island?" Kelwyn asked.

"Only when I had to."

With the light of the lantern guiding their way, they left the wide entrance behind and entered a narrow tunnel, only a few inches taller than them. Kelwyn crouched just inside and inspected the ground. "She definitely came this way. There's a track, here in the dirt. Looks like the toe of her boot." He ran his hand along the wall. "This is worrisome. It doesn't look natural, but it's not smooth enough for one of ours."

Wonderful. Rhone fingered the reassuring hilt of the new long sword under the cloth of his cloak. Lindren also had a harness made for the sword and the weapon now hung down his back. He tugged the cloak closer around him. Ice lined the tunnel walls and his breath rose in a cloud. *If it had to be a cave, couldn't it at least be a warm one?*

Farther in, the tunnel split and the Elf searched for a clue as to

420

which way Cat had gone. He checked the right tunnel, then the left and back to the right. "It's all rock here," Kelwyn said. "And Cat's very good at hiding her tracks when she wants to." He thought a moment, glancing from one tunnel to the other. "Right. I think she'd go right."

"Why right?"

The white glow from the lantern, reminiscent of intense moonlight, cast soft shadows on Kelwyn's face. "When we were young, we scoured caves searching for dragon eggs. If we came upon a split, we always took a right turn, then a left if it split again, then a right and so on. I'm hoping Cat follows the same configuration." He glanced at the tunnel. "We'll have to eat while walking, I don't want her to get any farther ahead."

They pulled out some food for breakfast and walked to the right. After what seemed a couple hours, they hit a dead end. Cobwebs stuck to Rhone's hair. The oppressive darkness, weighing on him like the End of Days, receded reluctantly before the Elven light. "What happens if the lantern goes out?"

Kelwyn squeezed past him, heading back to the intersection. "It shouldn't for a long time yet. Let's hope we find Cat first. I can't conjure handfire. We'll be walking in the dark."

Great.

They turned back and entered the opposite tunnel. As they walked, the walls closed in on Rhone like a coffin, the only sounds the scuff of feet, mostly his, and the thudding of his heart.

He had to break the grave-like silence. "I need to ask you something."

Kelwyn glanced back. "Sure."

"That friend of your brother's...were he and Cat...?"

"Yes. But that was over twenty years ago. They're just friends now."

"And Taurin?" That Elf had been far too familiar with Cat for his comfort. The biggest Elf Rhone had ever seen, Taurin had the same brown hair and shape of face as the rest of Lindren's family. He also had the same eyes, though the look in those black pits when Cat introduced them had turned Rhone's blood to ice.

Kelwyn was silent a moment. "They have a special kind of relationship."

"Like you?"

"No. Taurin was the one who brought her back after her people died."

Rhone hated to ask the question. "Are...were they lovers?"

Again the answer was slow in coming. "They have been. But he's away a lot, usually years at a time." He stopped. Rhone almost ran into him. "Don't worry. Cat will never lie with anyone else while you're alive. She wouldn't even consider it."

"I'm not worried about her. It's everyone else I don't trust," Rhone grumbled.

Kelwyn motioned him forward. "No Elf would ask and even if one did, Cat can take care of herself when it comes to unwanted attention. She handled Iyan quite well the night...you got drunk."

That's what had started the fight, Iyan admitting he'd tried to take Cat away. "According to him, I have you to thank for that as well."

"Glad to help."

Rhone kept the terror of the ever-present dark at bay with other subjects, picking Kelwyn's brain about Arvanion and his worlds. The tunnel they followed led to another split. Kelwyn took the left, then a right, then another left. All of them slanted down.

The last one opened up into a small cavern, the echoes of any little noise bouncing from one wall to another and back before fading. Dark lumps littered the floor. Acrid smoke tinged the stale air. When the light of the lantern reached lumps, Kelwyn dashed forward, crouching by the closest. He turned it over, revealing a grisly mess.

It was a vaurok. Fresh green blood oozed dark and oily from a hole where its left eye should have been. All the black shapes proved to be dead vauroks killed by arrows, though no arrows were to be found. Three torches, still smouldering, lay with the bodies.

"It has to be Cat," Kelwyn said. "We're getting close."

"Why are there vauroks in here? I thought Lindren said your people didn't find anything significant." Rhone spoke quietly, keeping his voice to the same level as Kelwyn.

"There are only a dozen vauroks. That's not significant." Kelwyn's eyes matched the darkness of the tunnels. It might be the lack of proper light, or it might be worry. "I'm afraid the reason they haven't been found is because they're hiding down here."

"Cat, what have you gotten yourself into?" Three tunnels led off the cavern. "Which way?"

"If she's following our pattern, it should be the middle one." Kelwyn lowered the lantern to the floor of the tunnel. "No tracks, but by the way the bodies have fallen, it looks like she was standing here when she fired. I don't see any red blood."

A good sign. Kelwyn checked the other tunnels, just to be sure, then waved Rhone to the one in the middle.

ℒ · ℛ

Yellow handfire bobbed in a brilliant ball in front of Cat. Not even pushing it to its brightest and highest revealed the ceiling of the cavern or the bottom of the chasm before her. A narrow strip of rock bridged it. Without hesitation, she walked the length, wondering what lay on the other side.

The vauroks had come as a surprise. Fortunately they weren't quiet and Cat had plenty of time to extinguish her handfire and hide in the tunnel. The stupid creatures didn't even know what hit them. Reaching the end of the bridge, she stepped off, sending her handfire ahead. Two more tunnels greeted her.

"Cat!" Echoes rang in crazy circles.

She spun on her heel, her hand reaching for her tchiru. Kelwyn and Rhone ran from the tunnel she'd come from, stopping at the edge of the chasm. Kelwyn held a lantern, his face a mask of anger. Rhone fumed.

Her heart sank. "You weren't supposed to follow."

"What did you think we were going to do?" Rhone's words followed the echoes of the first shout. "How could you possibly think we'd stay at camp and let you do this on your own?"

"I didn't want you hurt." Cat sent her handfire closer to them. She wasn't sure if Rhone could make it across the bridge. The way he stared

423

at it, he didn't think so either.

"Thank you for the thought," Kelwyn said, his sarcastic tone not lost on her. "This was supposed to be the three of us, just the way the prophecy said."

"How do we get across?" Rhone asked. "There's not much room on that thing."

Kelwyn stepped on the narrow bridge. "Hold my shoulder. Use me to balance yourself."

Taking slow steps, more like a shuffle-slide, they made it across with only one scare, Rhone's foot slipped two-thirds of the way.

Once on solid ground, Kelwyn gripped Cat's arm. "Don't you ever do anything so foolish again. We are in this together."

Cat pulled out of his grasp, her heart a confusing conflict of emotions.

Then Rhone took over, his face only inches from hers. He oozed anger. "What happened to you wanting me to come? What was that argument about if you intended to leave me behind?"

She took a step back. "I didn't think about coming alone until yesterday. I was afraid you'd die." Rhone didn't look like he'd let it go. Time to change the subject. "How did you find me?"

"We followed Krir's tracks then used the same method you did to get here," Kelwyn said. "Our old pattern."

Cat hadn't thought of their pattern. "I didn't do it that way. I used my bow."

Kelwyn frowned. "How did you use your bow?"

"Whenever there was a choice of paths to take, it glowed."

They both froze. Rhone's sword was covered by his cloak, though Kelwyn's boot knife stuck out of its sheath. "With the lantern shining, I never noticed," Kelwyn said.

Rhone tugged the hilt out from under the cloak. "I didn't know I was supposed to notice. I thought it only glowed when it was stuck in a vaurok."

"I think it's guiding me," Cat said. "Which way did you come?"

"The first right was a dead end." Kelwyn shifted his pack. "So we took a left, a right and another left. We came across the vauroks you killed, then took the middle."

That was a puzzle. "I took a left, two rights, a left, another right, and a long left that curved to the right. It came out at the small cavern where I heard the vauroks."

"Did you stop?" Rhone asked.

"Twice, but only a few minutes." Cat didn't want to think about what it meant.

Kelwyn glanced back at the tunnel they'd come from. "That must be why we caught up. It's hard to tell for sure, but I'll bet our path was shorter than yours. It looks like we were meant to find you. There's another hand involved in this and it could well be Black Wing."

"How can a dead dragon take a hand in anything?" Rhone asked, his expression a mixture of angry puzzlement.

"How could he give Cat the bones in the first place?" Kelwyn countered. "Lindren said the dragons were capable of amazing things, when they bothered." He rounded on Cat. "And that means you are not doing this alone."

It was hard to argue. Cat tried anyway. "But I..."

Rhone waved his finger in her face. "I have no idea how to explain what's happening, but we're coming. And that's final."

Cat gave up. "I guess I have no choice."

"No, you don't. Let's carry on. I'll lead." Kelwyn pulled his boot knife and walked towards the right tunnel. It glowed. So did the hilt of Rhone's sword, Cat's dagger and her bow. Cat extinguished her handfire so it didn't drain her and they carried on together.

℘ • ℆

Kelwyn held the lantern as far in front of him as his arm would reach. The tunnel stretched endlessly onward, turning first one way, then the other, angling down, then up, like walking in circles up, down and around a hill. He peered into the darkness, hoping to find an end.

"Does it seem a little lighter?" Cat asked, walking behind him.

A sharp grunt echoed from Rhone's direction. "How can you tell?"

Pulling his concentration back, Kelwyn scanned the walls around him. Cat was right. He blew the lantern out.

"Hey! Why did you do that?" Rhone's voice rattled off the stone walls.

"There's light coming from somewhere. Don't worry, Cat can relight it."

She touched his arm. "Do you see it?"

As Kelwyn's eyes adjusted, a gentle green glow emanated from the wall. "I do now." He scraped the wall with his fingernail, removing some of the strange stuff. "I've heard about this."

"What is it?" Rhone asked.

"Some sort of fungus or very small creatures that produce their own light. It's rare. I've only heard of a few places where it happens."

Cat removed her hand and shifted her pack. "Interesting, but we should move on." She used her handfire to light the lantern and they continued.

ℰ · ℛ

Rhone followed Cat and Kelwyn, his fingers brushing the odd fungus on the walls. It had taken a couple minutes to see it; now he knew what to look for. Pale green covered most of the walls, only visible away from Kelwyn's lantern. Even the light from the dragon bones subdued the strange substance.

"Shhhh!"

Cat stopped at Kelwyn's hush. Rhone almost ran into her. She slipped the bow from her shoulder. With concentration, he could just make out sounds coming from somewhere ahead. Kelwyn extinguished the lantern and set it on the ground.

The dead weight of the mountain pressed on Rhone. A dim light appeared much farther down the tunnel and the Elf slid the sword from the scabbard on his waist. Without a moment's hesitation, Rhone flipped back his cloak and his new weapon left its sheath. He hefted it, testing the balance. They shed their packs.

"Wait here," Kelwyn whispered.

426

Cat started to protest. Kelwyn put his hand over her mouth and shook his head. Rhone gathered Cat in one arm, keeping her with him while Kelwyn scouted ahead. When the Elf re-appeared, silent as a thought, Rhone heart leapt into his throat.

"Small cavern, no room for a bow," Kelwyn reported, in a whisper. "Eight big vauroks, two goblins, all sitting on the floor. Some are repairing weapons. They'll react fast, but we have surprise on our side."

"They'll feel safe under this mountain." Rhone adjusted his cloak, giving his sword arm more room. "Another point in our favour." He pulled his new dagger, Thelaru's dagger, from the sheath at his waist.

Cat laid her bow on the ground and unclipped her tchiru. The double edged weapon flashed into existence, soundless, deadly. Her boot knife appeared in her left hand. They crept forward. Rhone pushed Cat back when they approached the cavern. Torches cast dancing shadows on the walls and the creatures. Guttural, barking laughter and the distinct, irritating language of the Black Lord's creatures echoed in the chamber. Just as Kelwyn said, they sat in a circle, some repairing weapons, others eating Ar—Arvanion—only knew what.

The torches lit up Cat's slightly glazed eyes, a look he'd come to recognize as her need to slice into the creatures. If glares could kill, those things in the cavern would already be dead and cremated, their ashes floating on the wind.

Kelwyn gave the signal and they leapt from the tunnel. The Elf took the right, Rhone the left, leaving Cat the middle. With a roar, the vaurok closest to him jumped to its feet, brandishing the short sword used by most of its kind. Rhone ducked, then slashed. The ice sword whipped across the beast's throat as if passing through air. He wasn't sure he'd hit it until the vaurok dropped to its knees, spurting blood.

Another vaurok took its place, a third coming at him from the left. Rhone dodged to the right, nailed the second vaurok on the forehead with the pommel, curious what it would do, then blocked a blow from the third. The second staggered back, its eyes crossing, while the vaurok on the left caught Rhone's side with a swipe of its dagger. The blade slid off the Elven mail. He slammed his blade into the creature's skull, splitting it, then turned his attention back to the stunned vaurok. It

427

swayed, the sword slipping from slack fingers, yet it remained upright, the eyes glazing. The imprint of the Elven rune on its forehead glowed a soft white.

Rhone took up a defensive stance; the vaurok paid him no attention. He put the point of the weapon against a gap in the iron bands on its chest. It ignored him. With a simple push, the sword slid through hardened leather and Rhone pierced the heart of the vaurok. A breath of fetid air escaped its thin lips. Like a slow motion dream it collapsed, the wound sizzling and spitting as fire warred with ice. The hilt of the sword glowed a deep, comforting blue.

"Anyone hurt?" Kelwyn checked a body to ensure it was dead.

Rhone said, "No." So did Cat, though all of them were spattered with vaurok blood.

"You should see this." Rhone pointed his sword at the vaurok with the cut throat.

Bubbling, sizzling blood poured from a wound rimed with tiny white feathers of frost. The creature's skin turned from a pale green to ice blue, spreading out from the gash in its neck. Blood boiled, yet skin froze. When it stopped, frost covered the vaurok's head and half its torso. The blood on the blade sizzled and spat, alternately freezing and burning until the metal was clean. An acrid, foul stench stung his nose. The hilt's glow increased.

Rhone tapped the end of the magic blade on the frozen vaurok skin. It cracked like thin ice and he let out a slow whistle. "If I just wound a vaurok, it should die."

"The daggers only burn and it doesn't spread as far," Cat said.

Rhone touched the blade. Nothing happened. "I am utterly speechless."

In subdued silence, they made sure every one of the creatures had met its demise, then returned for their packs, Cat's bow and the lantern. Kelwyn urged them on.

Chapter Thirty-Seven

The evening sun slid towards the White Mountains, far to the west, casting Broken Man Pass in shadow. Hints of stars played with fingers of light cloud in the gloom to the east. Lindren sat outside his tent with Lowren, fingers drumming his knee.

"They've probably caught up to her by now," Lowren said.

"I hope so." He let out a heavy sigh. Something he seemed to do too often when dealing with Cat. "I'm somewhere between deep anger and total fear. When will she learn a little responsibility?"

"Probably never." Lowren cocked his head and his ears twitched. "Hear that?"

Excited voices rose above the usual noise of an armed camp waiting for something to happen. Elven voices. Following the sound, Lindren and Lowren arrived at Rendir's tent to find three of Cainfir's company, still winded from their run. A crowd had gathered.

"What news?" Lindren asked Rendir.

The Greenwood Elder's expression reflected more than concern, fear flashed in his eyes. "The worst kind. Cainfir's company discovered the trouble we've been searching for. They found an army where there was none six weeks ago."

There was no room in the Barriers for an entire army, not camped in one area. If they were in several different places, Cainfir should have spotted something long ago. Lindren grabbed Rendir's arm. "Where?"

"On the tundra, north of the mountains."

Plenty of room. Lindren released his grip. "They'll have to traverse the entire pass to attack and it will be blocked for another couple weeks at least." It allowed time to make plans.

"How many?" Lowren asked.

"That's the really bad news," Rendir said. "Cainfir estimated over fifty thousand."

Lindren's heart almost stopped. "They've never gathered in

numbers that large." His mind raced with the implications, and the uneven odds. Twenty-seven hundred Elves, five thousand men from Rodrin and another seventy-five hundred contributed by the baronies amounted to one of the largest armies he'd ever seen. "I need details."

One of Cainfir's Elves stepped forward. "Mostly vauroks, Elder. A quarter of them those large ones. Five hundred Throkdogs and a thousand each of goblins and hell wolves. We saw no wyverns, but there are over two hundred mountain trolls."

Just what they needed. "There won't be any wyverns. They don't do well in the cold." Lindren had heard of wyverns in the snow just once, when the men from the baronies were attacked. Even without them, that was a hell of an army. "We don't have time to send for reinforcements from Kitring-Tor before the snow in the pass melts. Silverwood might be an option. If we tell other Elders of the trouble we're in, we should get more companies."

"Make it archers," Lowren said. "We can pick off a good number of them through the pass. Even the odds."

"Are you volunteering to get them?" Lindren didn't hold his breath.

"Nice try. No. I'll let Vergel know what's happening." Lowren left at a trot.

Rendir sent Cainfir's Elves to rest. "I don't understand why Lowren's here."

"I don't either." Lindren knew, however, that he had to find a way to keep his brother out of trouble.

"There's one more problem," Rendir said. "They're building a permanent portal."

"Wonderful. Why not throw in a shadow demon or two?" Lindren wanted to hit something, an odd sensation for him. "How far along?"

Rendir set his hand on Lindren's shoulder, giving him a gentle squeeze. "Not far. Cainfir says they're having trouble digging the foundations in the frozen ground."

Lindren's mind whirled with possibilities. "We have time, then. It'll be a couple of months at least. The reinforcements will come, we'll wipe out thousands in the pass, then destroy the portal."

It sounded simple enough. Too simple.

℘ • ℞

Kelwyn crept towards the dim light at the end of the passage. They'd run across three more groups of vauroks since meeting up with Cat, every band larger than the last. Rhone's new sword proved a remarkable asset.

A discreet check of the cavern showed no vauroks or goblins. For the past several hours, the tunnels had led upwards and now they'd come to an unusual sight. He waved Cat and Rhone forward into a massive, almost roofless chamber.

The dawning sky shone through a hole on the right, the size of the clearing in front of his parent's house. The feeble morning sun spread fingers of red and gold onto boulders of various sizes, some covered with ice and snow. Shattered, misshapen chunks of rock littered the floor like a giant child's toys, though it appeared most of the caved-in ceiling had fallen into the chasm splitting the cavern.

Old snow drifts piled against the boulders, trailing wisps of themselves behind. As in the chamber where they'd found Cat, a narrow rock bridge spanned the darkness below, thankfully away from the snow and ice glinting under the sun of a new day.

"Not again," Rhone said.

Another check showed no tunnels on their side of the chasm. "I'm afraid so. We'll give our packs and the lantern to Cat. Hold my shoulder and we'll go slow."

He motioned Cat to cross. When she reached the other side, Kelwyn took his first, careful, steps, Rhone keeping a firm grip on his shoulder. With the same slide-shuffle motion, they made it just over halfway when high pitched squeaks echoed above. Kelwyn looked up to see a rush of dark, squealing shapes pour through the roof opening.

They flew straight for them, like arrows. Kelwyn couldn't run; Rhone would be left on the bridge with no support. Before he could think of some way to avoid the creatures, the hard bodies struck them both. He

431

flung one arm up to shelter his face. Rhone cried out, clutching Kelwyn who lost his footing. Cat screamed.

Kelwyn caught the edge of the bridge with one arm, smacking the side of his face against the rock of the thin bridge. With the other hand he reached to grab Rhone. All he clutched was cloth.

Using his swaying body as leverage, Kelwyn hooked both legs around the narrow span. His free hand held Rhone's cloak, waving in a gust of wind from the open ceiling. Rhone's cry reverberated from the black abyss below. The last of the bats disappeared into the chasm with a series of ear shattering chirps. Then silence.

ࠍ · ʘ

Naron rubbed polish on the heel of his lieutenant's boot. A few more buffs and he'd be done. Two Elves passed by, chatting as if they had no concern in the world. *Of course they don't. It's we Humans who die for them.* He attacked the boot with a few angry swipes, then held it up to the sun.

"Lady Faralyn had better make up her mind soon." The voice of his lieutenant came from the tent behind Naron. "If she doesn't find a husband, King Rodrin will do it for her. It's been months since her father died."

"Pity he only left daughters. He was far too young to die. The old Baron Jayme only passed on three years ago and now this. Tragedy's running rampant in that family right now." The other voice belonged to the lieutenant's brother, a captain in another unit.

That's the least of their worries. Far more important than a woman in control of a barony was the conspiracy of the Elves. Naron set the boot down, then rubbed sleep from his eyes, careful not to transfer boot polish. He and his friends had crept out in the dark of night to the Elven supply wagons. He'd managed to break the arrows in four boxes before slipping away, fearing discovery. His friends damaged more. Loss of sleep was a small price to pay. Tonight they'd hit the food wagons, destroy some rations. *That'll hit them hard. They should eat sheep and pigs like normal people.*

"Naron!" The lieutenant's voice jerked him alert. "Are my boots

432

done yet?"

"Yes, sir. Just finished, sir."

The officer stuck his head out of the tent and Naron passed him the boots. A moment later he exited, followed by his brother. "I'll want my breakfast when I get back."

"Of course, sir." Naron added a bow; after all, the man was a nobleman's' son.

As he headed for the cook fires, Naron thought about the plans for tonight. Though satisfying, in a small way, what he really needed was for the Elves to suffer much more.

୪ · ଓ

Still clutching Rhone's cloak, Kelwyn scrambled back to his feet and ran along the strip of rock to Cat.

"Rhone! No!" She had dropped their belongings and now stood on the bridge, tears flowing down her face. "We have to get him!"

"Off the bridge, Cat. We have to get off the bridge." He had to push her, force her off before she dragged them both down.

"NO! Rhone! I have to find him!"

He picked her up and threw her over his shoulder. Once on solid ground, Cat collapsed, calling for Rhone, though she still tried to crawl out onto the bridge. Her words, mangled by her need to follow him into the chasm, jumbled with sobs until the crying took complete control.

Kelwyn sat and scooped her into his arms, keeping her from the edge. It took every bit of strength he could muster. "Stay with me, Cat! Please! You have to stay with me!"

Fear and guilt guided Kelwyn. He talked to Cat, soothed her, rocked her back and forth. He wouldn't leave her. Not this time. Not like he did in Tiralan when they found the bones of her dead people. "I'm here, dear heart. I'm here. I'll always be here, but you have to stay with me."

Kelwyn used his entire body to clutch her tight while she cried, struggled, died inside. A long time he held her before her words grew intelligible once more. He didn't quit talking, keeping her with him both

433

physically and emotionally.

"I have to find him," Cat sobbed.

"We can't, Cat. I'm sorry. I'm so sorry." *I wanted you back, but not like this. Never like this.* "I tried to save him. I almost caught his arm." Kelwyn lifted his hand, the one still holding Rhone's cloak. He had to look at it through blurred eyes. He hurt for Cat. He hurt for Rhone.

"We have to go back for rope. He might still be alive." Cat reached out to the abyss, as if she could drag Rhone back from its clutches.

"That chasm is deep. I never heard him hit bottom. We have to carry on, Cat. If we stay in one place, vauroks might find us."

"But what if we're supposed to follow him? Rhone fell! That was part of the prophecy. It says we're all supposed to fall."

Kelwyn doubted it. She wasn't thinking straight. "Where does your bow lead?"

Cat scrambled to her feet, wiping her bloodshot, swollen eyes and picked up the bow, holding it over the chasm edge. It didn't glow. "No. This has to be the way." She shook it.

Tugging his boot knife from the sheath, Kelwyn pointed it towards the three tunnels. It glowed for the one on the far left. "I'm sorry. It's this way."

Cat's shoulders slumped. Kelwyn thought she'd fall, so close to the edge, and pulled her back into his arms. "We have to continue. You've got to concentrate on the Sleepers. Lindren thinks it's important and so do I. There's nothing we can do here."

He picked up Cat's pack and helped her into it, then slung her bow and quivers over her shoulders while he carried his and Rhone's packs as well as the extra cloak. One never knew what would be needed.

Kelwyn kept Cat walking and talking, pulling her behind him. He couldn't take the chance that she'd fall back into the hiding place she'd gone to after her people died. Cat alternated between crying and trying to figure out a way to go back for Rhone. Kelwyn decided they'd have to come back, with help and a lot of rope. Rhone's sword was too special to leave lying at the bottom of a mountain. Perhaps if they could bring Rhone to Arden for burial, it would help Cat find a lessening to her heartache.

The trail led steadily upwards through tunnel after tunnel, until voices sounded from ahead. Kelwyn turned a corner to find the dim light of torches at the end of the passage.

"Stay here, Cat, and you have to keep quiet." He drew his sword.

She nodded, sniffling back her grief. Kelwyn hadn't learned the language of the vauroks, as Lindren had. He didn't need that skill, however. Not this time. This one spoke in Torian.

The vaurok's voice sounded like gravel rubbing on stone. "Someone else is here, Sorcerer Tozer. There are horse tracks and footprints in the snow at the southern entrance to the mountain. Three sets, two Elven, one Human."

Tozer! Keeping flat against the tunnel wall, Kelwyn sidled closer to the light.

"Did anyone bother to track them?" The rough voice dripped scorn. "You know what's hidden here. It's our responsibility to see none of those damned Elves find it."

Kelwyn slid close enough to see the face of the man who'd almost succeeded in kidnapping Cat and Lindren. Lean, with tanned skin the consistency of leather, the most prominent aspect of Tozer's angular features was the scar pulling the left side of his mouth into a permanent frown. He looked more a back alley hoodlum than a skilled sorcerer.

"Too much rock," the big vaurok said, folding its thick arms in a stance reeking of defiance. "Can't track in rock."

Tozer's eyes narrowed. "Find them. I don't need problems right now. We attack soon and this has to be a surprise."

Surprise? Kelwyn's heart thumped. *Attack from where?*

Fifteen other vauroks waited in the cavern, all of them wearing their version of a scowl, thin lipped mouths baring half their yellowed, pointed teeth. Kelwyn made his way back to Cat. "Sixteen vauroks. One Human. It's Tozer."

Cat took two deep breaths, her body tensing, and unclipped her tchiru.

Kelwyn grasped her wrist. "Can you do this?" He hoped so. Taking on that number of vauroks by himself, even with full armour instead of the mail he wore, would be stupid. He wasn't Tiranen.

435

She nodded, her eyes now determined, tears gone, her anger at Tozer overshadowing the grief for Rhone. For now. Cat pulled her tchiru and dagger free and they leapt into the cavern, weapons flashing.

Tozer had left through one of the two tunnels exiting the cavern. Still, without Rhone they had a fight on their hands. If not for Cat's graceful, meticulous, dance of death, he wouldn't have risked it. She performed as expected, leaping, ducking, twirling, delivering devastating blows with grisly efficiency. Kelwyn tried to save the vaurok that had spoken to Tozer for last, hoping to just wound it, force it to talk. Cat beat him, removing the creature's head with one swipe of her magical tchiru.

When it was over, Kelwyn steadied her as she came out of her unique fighting style. "They're dead," he said. "Tozer got away." She was unhurt. He wasn't so lucky.

"You're bleeding!" Cat brushed the errant lock of hair back from his forehead, revealing the deep gash flowing freely. "Sit down. I have bandages."

Kelwyn groaned as he sat, his ribs injured from a side blow of a vaurok sword. His mail had stopped the penetration, not the force behind it. "I think my right ribs might be broken."

Cat ran back for the packs. She wrapped Rhone's cloak around him.

"What are you doing?" he asked.

"Making sure you're warm. Wendyl says it can help wounded men."

Somewhere, Kelwyn found a smile. Cat cleaned and dressed his head wound, then bound his ribs. There was nothing she could do for the smack he'd taken on his cheek when Rhone fell other than keep it clean. Once he was back into clothes, mail and cloak, Cat made him eat, drink and rest. "Does this count as you falling?"

"I don't know, but I hope it does." Kelwyn leaned on Cat as they followed the path the dragon bones showed them, the tunnel to the right.

෴ • ଓଃ

With a heart of lead, Cat helped Kelwyn sit in another open

436

chamber, its ceiling lost to some past cataclysm. Moonlight streamed in the gaping hole, the chunks of former roof casting weak shadows on the rock strewn floor. Tiny bits of minerals glinted where snow hadn't settled. No chasm split this floor. No bridge waited to take another part of her soul.

Ensuring Kelwyn had easy access to food and water, she climbed the rocks to the open air, hoping to find a little solitude to try to deal with her aching sorrow. What she found sent all thoughts of grief to the back of her mind.

Endless campfires stretched across the flat land below the mountains. This wasn't Rodrin's army. His men slept in tents perched on the rolling hills of the south. This was north, the land stretching far away in an unbroken plain of snow-covered scrub, and these weren't men.

"Kelwyn!" She scrambled down the rock pile. "There are vauroks out there! Thousands of them!"

"I've lost my direction. Which way?" He struggled to stand.

Cat pushed him back down. "North. The other side of the pass. What do we do?" They hadn't wandered just one mountain, but several.

"Nothing. It'll be a couple weeks or so before the snow melts. We should be out of here long before then and we can let Lindren know, if Cainfir hasn't already. Go back and estimate how many you think there are." With a gentle shove, he urged her back to the pile of rocks.

At the top, Cat counted campfires, the easiest way to estimate the size of an army. On Morata, at the battle of the Wall, she'd linked with a kestrel to spy on the enemy behind the hundred foot doors. Campfires had burned there, too, with eight to ten creatures to each fire. It took much longer to count these ones.

"About forty-eight thousand, maybe fifty," she reported to Kelwyn. "Vauroks, goblins, hell wolves and mountain trolls."

Kelwyn closed his eyes and leaned his head against the wall. "Pray for us, Cat. Never in my life have I seen an army that big."

"Can't Lindren send to Silverwood for reinforcements?"

Kelwyn's dark grey eyes opened. "If he's going to do that, we have to tell him, which means we have to find the Sleepers."

She helped him to his feet. "Maybe that's why we found the

437

prophecy now, so the dragons can help us."

"Arvanion, let it be so."

Kelwyn shouldered his pack, keeping the extra cloak around him, while Cat took hers and Rhone's packs, as well as the bow and quivers. She left the lantern behind; with her handfire, they didn't really need it and it was one extra thing to carry.

The single tunnel exiting the chamber wound downwards to another cavern, this one with a large boulder resting against the right wall. A trickle of water ran near, disappearing into a small hole.

"Is it getting warmer?" Cat asked.

"Could be. I need to rest. Maybe we can refill the canteens with some of that water."

"Let me get rid of these packs and I'll help you." Cat set them against the wall.

"Time to die, Elf," a gravelly voice said.

Cat whipped her head around just in time to see a small ball fly towards Kelwyn. It shone blue.

"NO!" She leapt, reached for it. Too late. It hit him in the abdomen.

An instant later, Kelwyn's boot knife flew at the man who'd thrown the ball, burying itself in his chest, knocking him to the ground. It had to be Tozer.

Kelwyn screamed, the horror of it ripping through Cat's soul. She tore off his mail and shirt. The tiny blue ball had seeped through the rings of his mail, ate away part of his shirt and now burrowed its way into her best friend's belly. Sweat broke out on his brow and he writhed and screamed his agony to the dark ceiling above.

"Kelwyn! No! You can't leave me!"

He grabbed her arm, pulling her close, pain lending him strength he didn't normally possess. "Kill me! Now! Don't let me die like Talifir!"

"I can't! You're my best friend. Dearest Arvanion, I can't kill you!" Tears flooded her eyes. Where the ball glowed blue in real vision, her truth-seeing showed pure black and it covered Kelwyn's stomach.

"Please Cat! It hurts! Arvanion it hurts! If you love me, make it go away!" He cried out again, screaming, writhing, his back arching in

438

agony. "Kill me! Please!"

There was nothing she could do. Arnir wasn't here. A healer couldn't help anyway. Cat slid her boot knife out of the sheath. Kelwyn's arms flailed, his fists pounded the floor as he writhed in agony. Cat had to kneel on his right arm as she held the knife over his chest, above the heart she loved so deeply. Tears streamed down her face, blurring her vision. She couldn't do it. How could she live without him?

"Please Cat! Now!" Kelwyn's voice turned hoarse with the torture of the blue ball. "I love you, Cat. But I can't take it. Do it! Please! It's eating me! Make it stop!"

She wiped her tears away; she had to do it right. With a swift plunge, Cat buried her dagger in Kelwyn's chest, stilling the heart that was her life. Kelwyn's eyes, black from agony, dulled. She kissed him, one last time. With a shudder, he breathed his last.

Cat bellowed her grief and pain, her screams echoing back and forth, up and down the cavern and tunnels. She leapt to her feet, then spotted the man who'd tossed the ball.

He lay near the rock, laughing and coughing up blood."That was entertaining. You ended it too soon, though. Far too soon." His light pulsed a sickening miasma of pale yellow, dark reddish purple and other colours, black the most predominant. "My master wants you, bitch, or you'd be screaming beside him."

Kelwyn's dagger had missed the vaurok-lover's heart. She wouldn't. With a cry, Cat leapt too fast for Tozer to react. Straddling him, she yanked the dagger out, then stabbed him again and again, tearing great gashes in his chest. Blood poured, spattering her clothes, the rock, wall and floor. She yelled, screamed, cursed and hacked at the man who'd killed her friend, her love, her life.

Tozer's chest was a bloody ruin, his eyes long dead, before she ran from that chamber of horror, running through one tunnel, then another, ever upward, leaving her best friend's body to vanish in the darkness.

Barely aware, Cat followed the blue glow of Kelwyn's dagger, the blood coating it and her hands dark in the light of the dragon bone knife and the bow across her back. Lost in her overwhelming grief, she ran into a huge cavern. The bones glowed brighter than ever, revealing a shape surrounded by a shield, shimmering in the magic light. A black shape. There was no exit.

Cat dropped the dagger, let her bow and quivers fall to the floor. She approached the object, tears running in rivers down her cheeks, and hit it with her fists. Once. Then again and again, pounding her anger, her despair.

"It's your fault! They're gone! They're both gone! And it's your fault!" She sank to her knees, still pounding the shield. "It's your fault!"

Sobbing, Cat collapsed to the floor, weeping for her lost loves.

Chapter Thirty-Eight

Utter darkness greeted his eyes. Fear stabbed at his gut. He had a headache. Gradually, a soft blue glow from over his shoulder broke the stygian gloom. His new sword. The gift from Cat, still strapped on his back.

Rhone lay on something soft. *A bed?* He moved. It was bouncy and clung to him. *Not a bed.* Then his full memory returned.

"Cat! Kelwyn!" Only the echo of his voice answered.

Things flapped all around him, sending vibrations through whatever it was that had stopped his fall. Rhone tried to sit up; something restricted his movement. A quick test showed no chains. *Not a captive then.* With only a little resistance, he yanked his right arm free.

Gingerly, he touched a finger to the spot where his head hurt. It came away wet. Something dark glistened in the pale light of the dragon bone hilt. *Blood. I must have hit something on the way down.* This wasn't the bottom of the chasm, however. Rock didn't bounce. Rhone yanked his other arm free.

Whatever he lay on ripped, shifting him, arse down, into a hole. He grabbed the edges, soft and sticky. Then the whole thing let go, yanking hairs from his head. Rhone cursed and tried to right himself, and was caught again. A careful testing showed it was the same stuff. More of it clung to his jerkin, his hair. It shone back the blue of the sword hilt. Did that mean this was the right way to go? Down a deep abyss?

Rhone looked up. No light could be seen. If Cat was up there, the lantern's glow didn't reach him. Neither did the morning light. "Kelwyn! Cat!"

No sound could be heard except the flapping punctuated with high pitched squeaks. The weak light of the dragon bones showed what he'd fallen through; a woven net of a fine white substance, similar to a spider web. The threads of the web were much wider, the holes bigger, and formed a criss-cross pattern, not the complex designs a spider would

441

make. Dark shapes nearby struggled to free themselves.

The web tore again. First a little, then more, and Rhone fell through to the next layer. This time when he landed, it was on a slant and he rolled despite the sticky substance of the web trying to hold him back. Something sharp scraped on the mail shirt and leggings, snagged the skin on his hands. He rolled into air. Grabbing at darkness, Rhone found the edge of the web. He held on, praying he could swing himself back up. Perhaps the layers went high enough that he could climb out.

That thought left his head as the webbing tore again, lowering him further into the chasm. He could see nothing below him. With a final rip, it let go. Rhone cried out and hit something hard. His right ankle buckled under him, shooting knives of pain up his leg, and he fell onto his side. Stars lit up the darkness as he cursed the air blue.

When they faded, Rhone tested his ankle. It hurt whenever he moved it and he prayed it wasn't broken. The flapping of the trapped creatures continued, though now he heard another sound, a chittering and clicking blended with something that sounded like words. *The thing that made these webs?*

Rhone sincerely hoped not. To make webbing that size, the creature would have to be huge. Childhood nightmares of giant spiders and creepy crawlers seeking his blood rooted Rhone to the spot, his heart pounding in his ears, despite his urge to run.

He closed his eyes, forcing his breathing to calm, then listened to the scrabble and, more important, the words. Creepy crawlers didn't speak words. Listening, he changed his original perception; it wasn't one thing, it was many, coming from the left. A soft pattering of small, bare feet added to the mumbling and clicks. He searched the darkness, afraid to move. Worried, he sat on the ledge. Then he noticed a pale green glow, the same green on the walls they'd passed not long after finding Cat.

Forcing his eyes to adjust, Rhone made out other shapes, the size of children, leaping up to grab the webbing. They scrambled skillfully along the lines, like squirrels in a tree. When they came to one of the trapped creatures, they clubbed it still, then plucked it like fruit, stuffing it in a bag before carrying on to the next.

Rhone squeezed his eyes shut, then had another look. The

flapping creatures were bats, caught in the webbing after knocking him off the bridge, their fragile wings torn from the tiny spikes woven into the snare. Kelwyn must have fallen with him. Rhone found no sign of him on what webbing he could see.

Not all the pale, child-like creatures harvested the fruit of their trap. Others pulled something out of a pouch hanging from their waists and stuffed it in their mouths. They chewed it, then used it to repair the torn webbing. Some spotted him, creeping cautiously nearer, their clubs held before them. Rhone struggled to his feet, keeping the weight off his injured ankle. The double glows of his sword and the green fungus showed he stood on a wide ledge, only blackness past it, and he hobbled to the wall, pulling his sword.

Never had he seen anything like the little creatures. Huge, round, luminous eyes shone in the light of the fungus and sword. Dark, greasy hair, caught up in a horsetail on the top of the head, like a vaurok's, cascaded down around pale, gaunt faces. These weren't vauroks, however. They had noses. Yet they weren't Human, either. Thick lips covered pointed teeth. Not a one of them stood over three feet tall. Their ears stuck up like a fox's, complete with tiny tufts of hair at the ends, similar to a goblin's. Their hands resembled claws, with long, sharp, fingernails. Though barefoot, they wore rags on their skinny bodies.

One of the strange people leapt at Rhone, its spiked club held before it, the wide mouth stretched back in a high-pitched shriek of rage. A single swipe of the Elven sword removed the creature's head, abruptly cutting off the screeching battle cry. The small head flew to the left while the club skidded to the right and off the ledge. The body dropped near Rhone's feet, dark, red blood pumping from the neck. Low growls boiled from the throats of the remaining creatures. Those gathering food and repairing the web stopped their activities, their attention now on him.

Rhone moved out to the center of the ledge to gain room to swing his sword. He tried to keep his eyes on all of them at once, the weapon held in front. The dragon bone hilt glowed brighter, causing a stir amongst the little beasts. They crept forward, cautious, chanting something in their clicking language, their clubs ready to inflict damage, hatred twisting their already hideous faces.

"Keep back and no one else will have to die." Rhone swung the sword in a practice pattern, hoping to intimidate them. Every eye watched it, their expressions changing from hate to wonder.

He moved the weapon to the right, the left, then hilt up. The creatures ignored him, hypnotized by the dragon bones. They shone brighter still, pulsing with a rhythm of their own. Gasps of wonder echoed in the cavern and the creatures laid their clubs on the ground. Holding their hands in the air, they knelt and bowed deep from the waist, their horse-tails washing the dust. Again and again they bowed, their chanting reverberating up the chasm.

"Good. That's good. Just stay like that for a while."

Rhone backed away, careful not to put too much weight on his ankle. Using the wall for support, he left the creatures, still on their knees, bowing. The glow of the hilt remained strong and he hoped that meant he was headed in the right direction. The cavern narrowed to a single tunnel. No ice coated it. Just as well, he'd lost the wonderfully warm cloak Rhianna had given him.

He backed into the tunnel, then, reassured no one followed, removed the sheath from his back and put the sword in it. Using the weapon as a crutch, its light as a guide, he hobbled in the direction the tunnel led; upwards, his only hope of finding his beloved wife.

☙ · ❧

Cat lay on her side at the base of the shielded shape, her fingers tracing the outline of the brooch Rhone had given her. Silent tears fell, splashing in the thin layer of dust covering the rock floor. She'd cried herself to sleep and when she woke, cried again. Now she felt dead inside.

She forced back the last moments with Kelwyn and Rhone, concentrating instead on other memories, happy ones. It didn't work and she felt like throwing up. Then she thought of Lindren and Lowren, and how to break the news. How could she tell them it was her hand that ended her best friend's life? Would they understand that he begged her? That she had to end his misery? More tears fell, adding to those already on the floor.

When she could cry no more, Cat sat up. The only light shone from Kelwyn's boot knife and her bow, yet something glittered in the gloom. She lit her handfire and the room came to life. Two boulders, big enough to sit on, rested on the floor, one across from the tunnel, the other near her and the object. Something else drew her attention.

Emeralds, diamonds and rubies, the size of her fist, decorated the circular walls. They weren't trapped in veins, but roughly worked jewels, sparkling in the light of her handfire, set in simple patterns. Upon examination, she discovered they were glued on with a hard white substance. Someone had gone to a lot of trouble to decorate the chamber, the place where the dragon bones had led her. The chamber had to be the end of the journey, but who had done the decorating?

Cat turned her attention to the strange object in the middle of the cavern, possibly their only hope against the army waiting north of the Barriers. It resembled an odd sort of table, triangular in shape and roughly thirteen feet long on all sides. Milky in colour, it bulged slightly on the top and narrowed down to eight feet at the base.

It was a shield. Unlike an Elven shield, the shape behind it couldn't be seen clearly. It was indistinct, muted. Cat could have sworn she'd seen black when she first came in. A quick check of her truth-seeing showed not the white of Elven magic, but total black. She hadn't imagined it. Udath Kor had trapped the dragons.

The shield was smooth, cold and shivered with dark magic. Cat jerked her hand away. Peering through it, she made out two forms, large, though not as massive as Black Wing, the dead dragon. She could determine no distinct wings or tails. What could be two elongated heads rested one against the other as if in an embrace.

She unclipped her tchiru and poked at the hard, unyielding shield. When she hit it, the weapon bounced. Kelwyn's dagger lay on the floor. Cat picked it up and tapped the bone hilt on the shield. A shimmer of blue spread out a few inches from the point of contact. *Dragon bones reacting to dragons?*

A strike to one of the three rounded corners produced a much brighter reaction. This time, the ripples of blue spread almost halfway to the next corner. She hit it harder, with exactly the same effect. Kicking the thing, hitting it with both her fists and the tchiru did nothing. The only reaction came with the boot knife and it wasn't enough. She needed Kelwyn and Rhone.

"You stupid dragons! I need them! But you killed them both!" Cat kicked the shield, beat it with her fists. "Stupid prophecy! Stupid, stupid, dragons!" With a final kick, she retreated to the wall near the tunnel and slid down to a crouch.

Cat twisted the ring on her left hand, the one Rhone had given her at their wedding. Did she have take it off now that...? Her shoulders sagged. She wanted to cry again; for some reason, the tears wouldn't come.

Maybe I should go back. I really can't do this on my own. That meant returning to the chamber with Kelwyn's remains. *But the prophecy said nothing about anyone else, just the three of us.* Maybe part of the prophecy was missing.

A sound from the tunnel jerked Cat upright. It came again, a strange chunk-shuffle. Then again. Fearing a vaurok, Cat drew her tchiru, retrieved Kelwyn's dagger, then hid behind the shielded dragons. A quick thought extinguished her handfire. The sound grew louder, came closer, the same slow chunk-shuffle echoing off the rock until Cat thought she'd scream.

A lone figure exited the tunnel, accompanied by a deep blue glow. It took her a moment to recognize the shining mail and the strong features partly covered by a two-day growth of beard. She had to be dreaming. Cat lit her handfire.

"Rhone!" She jumped out from behind the sheild. He unsheathed his sword in a moment, crouching in a fighter's stance.

"Rhone."The tears she couldn't find a moment ago misted her eyes. His light showed the pale yellow of pain. "You're hurt."

Blood matted his hair. He lowered his weapon and opened his arms to her. "Mostly my ankle. Don't lean on me, heart of my love. I'm so tired I can barely support myself, but I couldn't be happier to see you."

His deep voice, his touch, his distinctive scent, mixed with sweat, dirt and blood, washed over Cat's senses, alleviating part of her grief. She

446

held him, not too tight, and let him lean on her. His kisses tasted like he smelled, but she'd never had better.

Rhone wiped a tear from her cheek with his thumb. It came away dirty. "You're a mess." Then he pushed her back. "That's red blood!"

Cat scraped a fingernail over one of the red smears on her long tunic. "It's not mine." She touched his face, ran a finger down the scar on his left cheek. "I thought you were dead."

Still holding her hand, Rhone limped to the boulder across from the tunnel. "You won't believe me. I don't think I believe it." He related a tale of giant webs and peculiar little people who ate cave bats and bowed down to his sword. "It was a long walk to get here, mostly uphill. I thought I'd freeze to death, but as I walked, the air grew warmer. It's stifling in here."

"I hadn't noticed." Cat stood beside him, picking pieces of webbing off him.

"Cat." Rhone took one of her hands in both of his. "I owe you an apology. I didn't believe your prophecy, but those bones led me here, straight to you and...whatever that is." He indicated the shapes behind the shield. "That story I told you, I didn't really believe it. Now I have to believe. It's obvious I was supposed to be here."

He glanced around the cavern, his gaze settling on the shielded shapes. "I assume those are the dragons?" Cat nodded. "This must be their treasure." He indicated the rough jewels glued to the walls. Then he frowned. "Where's Kelwyn? I thought he fell with me, but I didn't find him. I hope he's all right."

Cat's heart almost stopped cold. Her ever-present tears poured as she told him the horrible tale, one she didn't want to tell, didn't want to believe. What would she do without Kelwyn? He'd been her best friend all her life, the other half of her soul.

"How are we supposed to wake these things?" Rhone asked, his voice gentle, his touch loving, obvious in his desire to get her mind on something else.

Cat showed him what she'd discovered. The blue ripples expanded outward to the same point as before.

"Help me to that other boulder." The second rock sat close to one of the corners of the dragons' prison. He held his sword and scabbard like a club. "You hit one at the same time I hit this one."

Two waves of blue rippled out from the corners. Where they met, the shield bubbled, then subsided. A second test produced the same results.

Rhone laid his sword on his lap. "We need Kelwyn. At the very least, the other knife."

Dread ran through Cat, head to toe. "I...could go back and get it." *I don't want to!*

Motioning her to his side, he took her hand. "I hate to ask you, but I don't know where it is. I didn't pass through any cavern that had...a dead Human in it."

"You couldn't anyway, not with your ankle." Cat let his hand fall from hers. "I'll go."

"If it's any consolation, all that should remain is metal."

It didn't help. Gathering the fragments of her courage, she kissed Rhone and followed the route back to the place where Kelwyn had died.

§ · ℞

Lindren stood on a hill near his tent, watching the snow melt in Broken Man Pass and waiting. He'd sent three of his Elves to Silverwood the day before, praying the reinforcements made it back in time.

"Here you are." Lowren trotted up beside him. "We've got a problem. Someone's urinated on sacks of oats and flour in every one of our wagons."

"*What*? Who would do that? Why?"

"No one knows, but it didn't happen to any of the Torian's stores." Lowren looked angry enough to bite someone's head off.

Lindren's blood turned cold. "This is a deliberate attack against us. I want guards on those wagons at all times. Have the all the other supplies checked." His right hand curled into a fist. "This has never happened in Kitring-Tor." In the past, other Humans felt threatened by the Elves, some sabotaging or outright attacking them, but it hadn't happened in centuries.

448

"Always a first time, I guess."

"How much do we have left?" One couldn't just pick food off the ground in the northern baronies, especially this early in spring.

"We've enough for two weeks, though porridge and bread will be a little thin. After that, we'll have to rely on Aris' generosity."

"It might suffice." Lindren wished he could send word to the Elves who'd left for Silverwood.

"I'll go organize the guards." His brother jogged back the way he'd come.

Lindren strode to Rendir's tent and told him the news.

"It's a sad day when you have to protect yourself from your allies as well as your enemies," Rendir said. "I'll let Sandrin and the others know. We should co-ordinate the guards."

Lindren's next stop was to Vergel, who almost blew the roof off his tent.

Once he cooled down, he said, "We'll get to the bottom of it, you can be sure of that. I will *not* have any of my men compromising our alliance."

"Thank you, Vergel. I'll admit, I'm more comfortable leaving it your hands."

Later that day, Lowren had more bad news. The arrows in three dozen boxes had been snapped in half. Between the waiting enemy, the sabotage and the unknown progress of Cat's excursion to the pass, Lindren wanted to scream.

ɞ · ᇰ

Rhone spent part of the time waiting for Cat digging at an emerald by the light of the sword hilt and trying not to think about the dark pressing in on him. The jewels, rough as they were, would set him and Cat up for life. The substance gluing the gem to the wall appeared similar to that of the webbing, though much tougher. Scraping with his dagger produced little result and without Cat's handfire, he couldn't get a really good look at what he did. Rhone finally gave up and played with the corner of the shield. Depending on where it was hit, he could make the ripples go up, down or off to the side.

The arduous journey through the tunnels had proved both painful and frightening. When the fungus disappeared, Rhone thought he'd go mad in the darkness, if not for the reassuring light of the dragon bones. The light of Cat's handfire, visible for a distance down the last tunnel, drew him like a beacon in a snow storm. Though his heart had almost stopped when she'd extinguished it, he understood why she'd done it.

His thoughts wandered to how his wife had forever changed his life. Different worlds, strange peoples, larger than life trees, horses that trained themselves. That was only in Silverwood. Once they'd arrived in Arden, she'd turned his life upside down one more time. Yet, he loved her all the more; her honesty, her innocence, the way she smiled at him as if he were the only one in the world that mattered. It wasn't true, painfully so, but somehow, when she smiled, when she kissed him, everything was good.

A rumble from his gut turned his attention elsewhere. He'd walked for Ar only knew how long. Arvanion. It was Arvanion. Rhone hoped Cat remembered the packs. He removed his sword from the scabbard and ran a finger along the blade. No nicks that he could see in the dim light. It's reassuring, yet icy touch helped drive back the darkness. He set it across his lap, ready if someone other than Cat showed up. A short while later, she reappeared, empty handed, all in a panic, her handfire bobbing before her.

"There's nothing there!" she cried. "The packs, the knife, the mail...it's all gone!"

There went dinner. Or maybe it was breakfast. "The metal should have remained. It did in Tezerain. Is Tozer's body still there?"

"Yes. Just all our things are gone." Cat appeared close to tears again. "Even Kelwyn's sword."

"I wonder if vauroks took them." If true, it didn't bode well for them. Rhone was in poor shape for a fight. "Mind you, vauroks wouldn't leave fresh meat behind. We've got your bow. Let's try that."

Cat pulled her bow from the case and leaned it against the third corner. They struck their points. No ripple expanded from where the bow rested. Again they tried, with no success.

450

"I think it has to be hit," Cat said, a picture of dejection.

Rhone stood, leaning on the shield for support. "Give me the bow. Between it and the sword I can reach two corners." Balancing on his uninjured foot in the middle of one side, holding the blade of his sword, he tried to hit both corners at the same time while Cat hit hers.

The bubbling covered the top of the shield, then after a moment it stopped with no visible damage. They tried again. Rhone hit harder and the blade slipped, cutting his hand. He dropped both sword and bow, hissing in pain.

"Rhone!" Cat flew to his side in a heartbeat.

A long, shallow cut sliced across his left hand. Blood dripped to the floor, onto the sword. Cat undid her long tunic and tore two strips off her shirt. She folded one into a thick pad and held it against the wound to slow the bleeding, then wrapped the other around his hand and tied it off.

"That was stupid of me," Rhone said. Pain and hunger muddled his common sense. "I should have used the scabbard. Let's try again."

Cat retrieved the scabbard from where it rested against the boulder facing the entrance. "It didn't make any difference when you hit it the second time."

"Once more. For good luck." For Cat.

This time the top of the shield erupted into waves of boiling bubbles where Rhone's sword hilt hit it, yet he felt no heat. Cat's corner and where the bow struck showed no change.

Cat's eyes widened as the boiling subsided. "What caused that?"

"Something's different." Rhone examined the sword. Some of his blood had hit the hilt. "Blood. It must be the blood."

With a quick cut, Cat sliced the palm of her left hand, then smeared blood on the hilt of the dagger and the end of her bow. Once she'd wrapped the wound in another piece of her shirt, she said, "Let's try again."

When they struck, the top of the shield burst into a boiling cauldron of shimmering bubbles, except where the bow hit. When it subsided, Cat smeared more blood on her bow. Another test fared no better. She collapsed to the ground in tears.

451

Rhone sat on the rock. "We need another person." That meant a long walk out of the mountain, if they could find their way. The bones led to the cavern, not away from it.

"Lindren and Taurin both have dragon bone knives. Maybe we could do it with one of them," Cat said, through her sniffles.

Or both. With more Elves to fight off the vauroks. "I can't go now, Cat. I need rest."

She scrambled to her feet. "Take off your boot and I'll check your ankle."

He stayed her hand. "I might not get it back on. If I have to walk out of here, I'll need it."

"What if your ankle is broken?"

Rhone tested it. "I don't think it is. It hurts like hell, but I can put some weight on it. Just leave it for now. What I need more is sleep." And food.

Cat laid her cloak on the ground for him, then helped him lie down. "I'll keep watch."

She held Rhone while he fell asleep.

ℰ   ✦   ℭ

Silence could be oppressive when sitting under tons of rock. Especially in almost total darkness. Only one sound broke the silence— the rumble of Rhone's belly. He'd slept for an indeterminate amount of time, then it was Cat's turn. She was a silent sleeper, unlike him…apparently. Though she cried too much, her tears were also quiet, not the full blown, screaming, blubbering collapse of other women he'd known.

Rhone rested his head against the shielded forms of the dragons. Cat lay near him and he kept his hand on her arm, reassured by her presence. When she'd fallen asleep, her handfire had faded, much to his chagrin. He'd grown used to the magic orb and resented its loss.

Soft glowing dragon bones provided the only light. When his eyes adjusted to the lower light level, he could make out objects and that helped, quite unlike the time Iyan had left him in a cave. A five-year-old

452

with a healthy imagination could see and hear all kinds of things in the dark. He'd hated caves ever since. Cat's breathing deepened and he wondered if she was ready to wake up.

She'd been a sight when he entered the cavern; disheveled clothes, red rimmed eyes, pieces of vaurok and dried blood in her hair, the braid a tangled mess and Tozer's blood splattered on her tunic, her face.

Who had she grieved for more? Him or Kelwyn? Did it really matter? After a moment's thought...no. How she'd been able to carry on after losing both of them, he couldn't even imagine.

"You must be hungry."

Rhone looked down into Cat's amber eyes. "So must you."

"Not really." She sat up and leaned against him. The handfire reappeared, temporarily blinding him. "I'm too upset."

He put an arm around her and kissed her forehead. "Feeling any better?" he asked.

Cat shrugged. "I don't think I'll ever get over it. It's hard to lose someone you've known all your life."

"It's not easy for my people, either."

"I wish we'd found one of those heated pools you told me about. A bath would be nice." Cat picked up her matted braid, then let it fall.

An instant later, she jerked upright. "What's that?"

"What's what?" Rhone heard nothing.

"Vauroks!" Cat leapt to her feet and Rhone was left holding air. She helped him up.

"Sit on that rock." Cat pointed to the one opposite the tunnel. She gave him her bow and quivers. "Shoot anything that comes through. I'll try to stay out of your way."

"It's been a while since I shot a bow. I'm not as good as you."

"You don't have to be." Her tchiru flashed into existence, the narrow blade catching the yellow light of her handfire. "This close, you should hit just about anything."

"I hope it isn't you." Rhone removed his sword from the scabbard, keeping it close. He could hear them now, their grunts and scuffing feet echoing up the tunnel. "Douse your handfire. It'll give us the advantage."

The light vanished and his eyes had to readjust to the blue glows. Cat kissed him, her lips so sweet he hoped she'd never stop.

She did, all too soon. "I love you."

"I love you too. Now go get ready to kill some vauroks." Rhone set the first quiver so pulling arrows would be quick, then notched one and aimed it at the doorway.

Cat positioned herself to the right side of the entrance, balancing on the balls of her feet, tchiru in her right hand, dagger in her left. When the vauroks arrived, Rhone could only see the torch, so he aimed for that. A scream sent a rush of satisfaction through him. The torch fell to the ground, providing him with more light. He pumped arrows at the tunnel as fast as he could. Cat danced somewhere to the right, taking care of the ones who slipped through. Rhone wished he could sit back and watch. He'd caught glimpses of her during their earlier fights in the tunnels, on the island and the ship. She had an amazing style he'd never seen.

Arden insisted all his sons learn to use a bow, even Rhone; warriors were needed, regardless of their birth. It paid off now as he dropped one vaurok after another until they came too close. Rhone switched to his sword. He stood, putting most of his weight on his good leg, and caught a vaurok sword on his. It gave him a moment to pull his belt dagger. The cut on his hand stung. He ignored it.

Pain shot up Rhone's leg and his ankle gave out. That he couldn't ignore. He fell back on the rock, his sword sliding off the vaurok's. The odd movement surprised the creature and put it off balance. Rhone stuck his knife between two of the iron bands girding its leather jerkin.

Pushing himself off the rock, he used his elbow to smash the vaurok's face, then ran his dagger across the thing's throat. Sitting back on the boulder, he kicked the vaurok out of the way with his good leg. Standing once more, Rhone blocked a swing from another vaurok, then stabbed with his dagger at the creature's face. He missed. It bellowed and jumped back just as another appeared to Rhone's left. Before he could react, the second one slammed a mace into his gut with the force of a rock thrown from a catapult.

Rhone doubled over, his breath gone. A boot kicked him in the face and he sprawled backwards over the boulder. He landed on his injured ankle and would have cried out if he'd had breath in his lungs.

The vaurok grinned, showing off its sharpened teeth. The nostril slits opened and closed like a fish's gills gasping for breath on the shore. A golden earring hung from one thick ear. Rhone struggled to his feet, sucking in air. His ankle let go once more and he sprawled on the floor of the cavern, his grip on the ice sword lost. *I'm going to die.*

The mace rose in the air for the final blow. It didn't fall. The vaurok, wearing an ugly expression of surprise, looked down at the gleaming steel sticking out of its chest.

Cat! Bless you!

When the vaurok fell, however, it wasn't Cat's face he saw.

Chapter Thirty-Nine

"Attack! We're under attack!" The cry came down the line to Lindren's tent. He dropped his breakfast and ran out, followed by Lowren, Shain and Arnir.

Orrin skidded to a stop. "They're using small portals! Thousands are coming through!"

They had to be the same ones used in Rodrin's Hall. Lindren cursed himself a fool for not counting them in. "How far away?"

"Three miles and they're running fast."

Lindren sent him on to the next camp. "We've got to hurry. Lowren, help me with my armour. I'll help with yours."

Shain and Arnir ran for their tents. Lindren wasn't quite ready when Firann stuck his head in. "What are your orders?"

"Get arrows to the archers. We'll take as many of them out as we can before they hit us." Lindren buckled on his sword belt. The loss of those arrows would hurt now. "I want swordsmen guarding them. We don't have time to co-ordinate with Vergel. If Rendir or Sandrin gives you an order, obey it. Pass that on to my other captains."

"Yes, sir." Firinn's face vanished.

Lindren scooped up his dragon helmet and pushed Lowren out of the tent. "You're with me. Stick to my left."

Shain and Arnir met them at Lowren's camp and between the three of them, they had him in his plate mail in record time.

Arnir gripped each of their arms in turn. "Good luck. I hope I don't see you until the end of the battle." Wearing only mail, he left for the place designated for the healers.

Donning his helmet, Lindren motioned Shain to his right and they ran for the battle lines. Tarkin met them with their saddled Hrulka. Flashes atop distant hills showed where temporary portals vanished, then opened a few feet away, spewing more vauroks. Lindren could see no sign of mountain trolls, though hell wolves bounded in front of the leaders, their red tongues hanging from their mouths. Standing four feet tall at the shoulder, they could bite through Human mail and tear a warrior's face off in seconds.

The cool air sang with arrows, dropping a third of the front runners, wolf and vaurok alike. When they drew close to the archers, the swordsmen took over, allowing the archers to send shafts farther back. Lindren motioned to Firann, who ordered the attack, and they crashed into the enemy line, swords swinging. Then the mountain trolls appeared, lumbering their way up and down the hills.

ᔥ · ᔢ

A slash to one vaurok's neck followed a stab to another's eye. Cat ducked and spun, avoiding the swing of a mace from yet another. She jerked upward with the dagger, landing a direct hit to the gap between the iron bands crossing the vaurok's massive chest. Crouching to avoid another swing, she lashed the tip of her blade, opening the creature's neck. She moved to another.

A face appeared. One that shouldn't be there. "No! You're not real! You died!"

Kelwyn's image spoke words, distorted, unnatural. Through the tears, she saw a remarkably blue light. It couldn't be. It had to be a sorcerer's trick, yet no black showed in his light. Cat dropped her weapons, used her fists to attack, pounding his chest. The fake Kelwyn fended her off. It couldn't be him.

"I killed you! You're dead!" Sobbing, her heart breaking, she sank to her knees. "You're dead."

"It's me, Cat. It's really me." Now the voice was clear. It spoke Elven.

Could sorcerers speak Elven? She hit him again. "It can't be you! I watched you die! I killed you." Cat wanted to die. Her sobs wracked her body. "I killed you."

Kelwyn gathered her in his arms. "It's me, dear heart. I don't know why, but I'm not dead. It's really me." The green of concern shaded his blue light.

457

Dear heart? A sorcerer wouldn't know the endearment used by soulmates. Kelwyn didn't look like a ghost. More important, he didn't feel like one. The voice, the scent, the familiar touch of his arms… It was him. "Kelwyn? Why aren't you dead?" she sobbed.

"I don't know. When you've calmed down, I'll tell you about it." He held her, rocked her, rubbed her back even though she couldn't feel it through the mail.

This was Kelwyn, her best friend, sometime lover, the soul of her life. Cat clung to him, crying out her relief, washing the pain, the hurt, the grief away. She had them back. Both of them. "Rhone!"

"Right here." He leaned against the rock where she'd left him before the fight, bleeding from a cut near his mouth. It had already begun to swell. Sweat beaded his brow.

With an odd sense of detached reality, she pulled away from Kelwyn, took his hand and led him to Rhone. Still holding Kelwyn's hand, Cat took Rhone's, bent down and kissed him gently on the lips. "I love you," she whispered in his ear. "You're hurt."

"I'm all right. My gut's a little sore, but I'll be fine."

A quick check of his light showed otherwise. "You can't lie to me, remember?"

"Guilty. Yes, I'm in pain. Got hit with a mace. I just didn't want you worrying."

Cat's perception snapped back into focus. She helped Rhone out of his mail shirt, jerkin, tunic and lifted up his wool shirt. A red mark covered most of his belly, already bruising. She tested his ribs. They didn't seem to be broken. "There's nothing I can do until we get you to a healer."

"I'll be fine. I've had bruises before."

Her finger hovered above the cut on his chin. "You'll have one here too." The bruises Iyan gave him had only just faded. Now he had another. She helped Rhone dress, then turned to Kelwyn and kissed his cheek. In Elven, Cat said, "I love you too." She switched to Torian. "I'm not complaining, but why are you alive?"

Kelwyn squeezed her hand. "I've never come close to dying before so I have no idea what to expect. Somehow I doubt it's what

458

happened. When you stabbed me, Cat..." He gave her hand another squeeze, easing her distress. "...the pain went away. I couldn't move, not even open my eyes. I could hear you screaming, then there was silence and I found myself on a green plain. The sky was blue, but there was no sun."

He pulled Cat down to sit on the floor between him and Rhone. "I wandered the plain for a while, until I saw a white light tinged with blue. It was circular, like a portal, but it had no rim or clouds. It was just white light." Kelwyn paused, playing with Cat's hand. "Then I heard a deep voice. It told me to take the gift of life and walk into the light. I didn't know what else to do, so that's what I did. The light blinded me and...I must have passed out. When I woke up, I was wandering the tunnels.

"I should have been laying on the ground," Kelwyn said, his expression a cross between puzzlement and anguish, "but I wasn't. I was upright, holding your boot knife. It took me a few minutes to organize my thoughts, then I followed the glow of the dragon bone. It led me back to Tozer's body. I picked up our things and followed the bone until I found you. When I heard the sounds of battle, I dropped everything and ran. Not only am I not dead, my injuries are gone. I'm not even tired."

"I went back for the packs and my knife. I didn't run into you on the way," Cat said.

Rhone took a short breath. "I don't believe I'm saying this, but maybe he wasn't meant to find you until now. There's a lot of tunnels out there."

Kelwyn looked at Rhone. "So, why aren't you dead? You fell in an abyss."

"My adventure wasn't...quite...as unusual as yours, but I think I run a close second. I got caught in a web." Rhone repeated the story of his adventure. "It looks like we were all meant to be here, death or not."

Cat held both their hands tightly in hers. "Rhone, you fell. Kelwyn fell to that blue ball. But I didn't fall. We're all supposed to fall."

"It's not over yet," Rhone said.

Not much of an answer. "Then I suppose we should try to wake the Sleepers." Cat explained to Kelwyn everything they'd tried to break the shield. "We were going to go back for Lindren, but the vauroks attacked." She smiled, the last of her grief, and confusion, gone. "Now we don't have to."

Cat and Kelwyn helped Rhone to his feet and sat him on the other boulder, the one nearest the dragons. She took the corner to his left. Kelwyn took the right. His boot knife had Cat's blood, so he kept her dagger, pricked a finger and smeared blood on the hilt.

"I didn't think of that," Cat said. She shrugged. It didn't matter, the long wound she'd made had healed while she slept.

Rhone raised his sword, once again in the scabbard, above his corner. "On the count of three. One...two...three!"

Blue, shimmering waves radiated outward from all three corners. When they met in the middle, the entire top of the shield bubbled and boiled like stew in a cauldron. Cat took a step back. With one last surge, it settled.

"It's supposed to work!" she cried.

"It is." Kelwyn indicated a series of long cracks covering the entire shield. "Hit it again. If it stops, keep hitting it."

After four hits of the dragon bones, the shield turned a dark blue, then black. The bubbles grew larger, popping with a snap. Cat ran to Rhone, concerned the droplets flying from the bubbles might hit him. With Kelwyn's help, she moved him back to the other boulder.

The boiling shield surged, rising six feet above the top, licking towards the ceiling like a flame. Pulsing blue rose from the bottom. All the dragon bones, even the bow, glowed the familiar sapphire blue, though much brighter than Cat had ever seen.

She let her eyes shift out of focus. Tiny blue shapes fought with others; miniature dragons attacking impossibly small, black wyverns. They flew and dodged, nipped, bit and gradually defeated the wyverns, one by one.

The dragons didn't have Black Wing's shape, however. Instead of the massive head, wide body, leathery wings, thick tail and legs, these dragons were long and slender, with elongated heads, whip-like tails and no legs or wings. In a final, bright, pulse, the black wyverns disappeared and Cat snapped her eyes back into focus.

The blue flame soared to the ceiling, high above, lighting up the entire cavern. The jewels in the walls sent back an irregular gleam. A rumble sounded overhead and small rocks fell on the fiery shield and the ground around it. Cat moved Rhone farther from the dragons, next to the far wall near the tunnel, avoiding vaurok bodies and puddles of blood. He slid to the floor, groaning.

With a roar, the flame burst through the rock above it. Daylight shone in. The pyre brightened to pure white, then vanished, leaving spots in front of her eyes. A crack, followed by the sound of falling glass, told her the shield had finally shattered.

Cat blinked her eyes clear. Surrounded by the broken remains of the shield, two creatures rested, their long, pale grey bodies entwined, heads leaning together. They didn't move. Cat took a step closer, her hand outstretched. Had they died? If so, there went their hope for stopping the army threatening from the north.

She almost reached them when another bright light appeared, this one shining down from the shattered ceiling, straight onto the dragons. Once again, Cat unfocused her eyes. Two misty, indistinct shapes travelled down the beam into the dragons. The light disappeared.

The beasts' hides came to life, shining a deep, iridescent brown shot through with rainbow colours shimmering in the light of her handfire and the now open cavern roof. Simultaneously, two serpentine heads rose and the dragons opened their jeweled eyes. Each one flashed white, blue, green, and yellow-orange, then repeated the pattern.

"Their eyes are like Black Wing's!" Cat took a step closer. Kelwyn and Rhone didn't move a muscle.

The dragons paid no attention to them, only to each other, rubbing noses, caressing with their heads. An odd rumbling, like Hero's purr, thrummed in the cavern. After several long minutes, the dragons disentangled themselves, rearing up like earthworms from a hole, taking in their surroundings.

One of them, with a narrow golden crest running between the eyes to the back of the head, stretched towards her. :*You are intruders. Leave.*:

Cat jumped at the deep, male voice. She glanced back at Kelwyn and Rhone. They still hadn't moved. "Did you hear that?"

461

"Hear what?" Rhone's gaze remained fixed on the dragons.

With a quick shake of his head, Kelwyn said, "I didn't hear anything."

Black Wing's voice had sounded in her head. This was the same. Exactly the same. It had to be Black Wing in a different body.

:Leave. Now. You are not wanted here.:

"You arrogant...!" All that work, all the grief and anguish. "After everything we did for you! We saved you. You were trapped in that shield and we saved you! A thank you would be nice." She stomped her foot. "You wouldn't be awake if not for us!"

"Uh, Cat..." Kelwyn said, warning in his voice.

Her tirade came to an abrupt halt when, quick as a heartbeat, the male dragon lowered his head, staring her right in the face. His jeweled eyes glittered their pattern of radiant colour, holding her trapped with his intense gaze. Deeper and deeper those eyes penetrated, peeling back the layers of her soul, baring her very being to his scrutiny. Then he pulled back, nuzzling his mate once more.

:You speak the truth.:

:It is good you have done this.: Now the voice was distinctly female. *:We can grow. We will mate.:* She swung her elegant head, scanning the cavern, then hovered over one of the vaurok bodies. *:These things are offensive. We do not want them here.:*

"They attacked us," Cat explained. "We had to kill them so we could save you."

:What is this!: The male's head whipped towards Cat's bow. *:These are the bones of one of our kind!:* The massive head flashed back to her. *:Why do you have them? Why have you desecrated them?:*

How does one deal with an angry dragon? Cat spoke fast. "Don't you remember, Black Wing? I was in your cave under Silverwood. You talked to me, in my head, like you are now. You told me to take them."

The dragon's eyes whirled. *:You have the gift of truth, from the one who made you. We cannot remember the between time. I am not Black Wing. This much I know.:* Mollified, he resumed cuddling the female.

"Between time? What's the between time?"

The female responded. *:It is where we go when we do not breathe. We*

462

roam the stars and see all, but it is not permitted to remember when we are reborn. We must live our mortal lives not knowing, for the knowing would be too painful. It would be agony to know the beauty of beyond and not be permitted access.:

Now that was confusing. "If you're not supposed to remember, how do you know there's a between time?"

:This we remember,: the male said. *:It is why we are not afraid to die. We know there is more and it is good.:*

"Cat!" A note in Kelwyn's voice dragged her away from the creatures she'd waited all her life to see. "It's Rhone!"

The dragons could wait. Cat turned her back on them, left them to their caresses. Rhone's face shone with sweat. His light showed a predominance of the pale yellow of pain.

Cat touched the back of her hand to his forehead. No fever. "Lay down."

Rhone almost fell over. He tried to curl into a ball. With Kelwyn's help, she once again removed his mail, jerkin and shirt. Her gentle fingers probed the bruising on his belly. When Cat pushed, it took a moment for his belly to give, like standing on wet sand.

"His stomach is hard." A sure sign of blood where it didn't belong. She looked at Kelwyn, worry overshadowing the discovery of the dragons. "He's bleeding inside. We've got to get him to a healer."

Kelwyn crouched beside her. "How? It's taken us a couple days at least to get here."

"I'll walk out," Rhone said, his breathing shallow. "But I'm tired. Give me a few minutes."

"You can't walk. You can't even sit." Maybe the dragons could help. Cat turned back to them. "My bondmate was badly hurt saving you. Is there anything you can do?"

The male answered. *:No. We are of earth, not of spirit.:* He didn't even stop nuzzling the female.

Tears moistened Cat's eyes. The dragons had lights, a radiant sapphire, deeper than that of Elf, Tiranen or Human. "Is there nothing you can do?" *I lost you once. I can't lose you again!*

The female nudged her mate's head away. The two shook

463

themselves, then stretched, unfolding their bodies from the tangle they'd laid in for only Arvanion knew how long. Though smaller than Black Wing, they were still impressive, the male had to be thirty feet from his nose to the tip of his tail and five feet at his widest girth. Apparently he hadn't finished growing.

The female was only slightly smaller. :*You have helped us. We can help you. Above is a way out. We can lift you there. But then you must leave. We wish to be alone.*:

"The dragons can help," Cat told Kelwyn. "They said they'll lift us up to that hole."

"It's better than nothing." Kelwyn slung Rhone's sword over his shoulder, helped Rhone back into his shirt, wrapped him in his and Cat's cloaks, then picked him up in his arms. "Get our packs, Cat. They're just down the tunnel. Rhone's cloak is there as well."

She retrieved the packs, then dashed back to the cavern. "I've got them." After gathering Rhone's mail, jerkin and her quivers, she said, "We're ready to go."

The male dragon rose up, balancing on his tail. With a leap, he crashed into the edge of the gap, widening it. Small rocks rained down and Kelwyn shielded Rhone from them. The big rocks never hit; the dragons gulped them down like food.

When he was done, the male said, :*I must take you in my mouth. I will not hurt you. You have made it possible for us to live. We owe you this.*:

Before anyone could move, a strange noise echoed in the tunnel. Cat unclipped her tchiru.

"I know that sound," Rhone said, pain heavy in his voice. "It's those creatures I told you about."

He proved right. Little people with fox-like ears and wide eyes poured into the cavern, chanting something in their weird language. Strangest of all, they had mostly blue lights. Without a glance in their direction, some of them removed broken arrows and picked up the vaurok bodies, one taking the head, another the feet and hustled them out of the room.

"Those vauroks are heavy," Kelwyn commented, a puzzled expression on his handsome face. "How can those little folk carry them?"

464

Cat shrugged.

The rest of the creatures lined up in front of the dragons and bowed to them, over and over. Others gathered up the vauroks' weapons and any other bits and pieces they'd left behind when they died. In moments, they, and all trace of the vauroks, were gone.

"What are those creatures?" Cat asked the dragons.

:*Darani. They serve us, watch over us while we sleep.*:

"They didn't do a very good job," she said.

The dragon had no comment.

"They must be the ones who stuck the jewels on the wall," Kelwyn said. "Do I want to know what they're going to do with those vauroks?"

"Probably not." The Darani were the least of their problems. Cat glanced around the cavern, ensuring they had all their belongings, then took a deep breath. "I'm ready."

The dragon opened his jaws impossibly wide. Three rows of sharp teeth glistened in the light. As gentle as a mother wolf with a cub, he placed his mouth around her middle, packs, bow, quivers and all. Sharp as the teeth were, Cat didn't feel a single one. He lifted her up and, with an undulating motion, climbed the wall to the hole in the ceiling. How he stuck to the rock, Cat had no idea.

The dragon set her just as gently on the ground, clear of the hole. The bright sunshine blinded her and it took a moment for her eyes to adjust. The sun shone spring warm, turning the snow she stood in to slush. The dragon's head popped out, holding an almost unconscious Rhone. She held him, waiting for Kelwyn.

Once her friend stood on solid ground, Cat said, "Thank you. I wish I could talk to you more. What are your names?"

:*I am Rockbiter. My mate is Sandfang. We go now.*: With that, the dragon vanished.

"South is that way." Kelwyn pointed in the right direction. "But we'd better give Rhone another cloak."

They wrapped Rhone as snug as they could, then Kelwyn picked him up again. "We're not far from where we started." He kept his eyes on the ground as he walked, taking care with every step. "We've still got a

465

long way to go. I'd love to hear what the dragons said to you, but I think you should run ahead. You can bring back a healer faster that way."

Cat set her hand on his arm. "You'll be all right?"

"I'll be fine. Hurry."

Fear lent wings to Cat's feet. She leapt from rock, to outcrop, to rushing stream, downward, ever downward, then almost stumbled as she came to a sudden halt.

Dark figures swarmed across the hills below. They didn't come from anywhere, they just appeared. Cat sank to her knees. "Portals. Arvanion. No."

It had to be Udath Kor's army, the one she'd spotted north of the mountains. Fire erupted from various points deep behind enemy lines. Jeral responded as best he could. Even as she watched, a sorcerer's fire spell landed near the line of battle, scattering or killing the combantants, enemy, Elf or Human. More vauroks and hell wolves poured from the portals.

How could she get through to Arnir? "Rhone's going to die."

"Cat?"

She whipped her head in the direction of the voice. It was an Elf. "Cainfir?"

"What are you doing here?" He held his hand out and she stood. Other Elves appeared from the rocks.

"A long story. I need help. I...I have a bondmate now. A Human. He's badly hurt." Cat's voice broke. "I think he's dying. Please help him."

"Cat, I can't."

She grabbed his arm. "You have a healer, don't you?"

"Yes, but..."

"Rhone knows. He knows. Hanrish has healed him, so has Arnir." She clung to the captain's arm. "He understands. He won't talk. I promise! Please!"

Cainfir's deep blue eyes bored into hers. "All right. Gaelwyn."

A slender Elf with violet eyes stepped forward.

"Go with Cat. Your patient is Human. Cat says he won't talk." Cainfir motioned to two other Elves to accompany him.

Gaelwyn cast him a skeptical glance, then indicated to Cat she

466

should lead the way. Back she went, guiding the Elves to Rhone and Kelwyn. By the time they reached them, Rhone appeared worse. Despite the cold, his face shone with sweat.

"It's our missing swordsman," one of the Elves said to Kelwyn. "I thought you were in Tezerain."

Kelwyn laid Rhone on a flat rock. "It's been a long four months." He stepped back to allow Gaelwyn room to work. "I'll tell you around the campfire when this is over."

The healer's chant was identical to Lindren's and Arnir's. In moments, the white glow of Elven magic lit his hands. "The *talien* has ruptured. It's leaking into his belly. I can fix it, but he'll need rest and plenty of water afterwards."

Cat nodded.

"*Talien*," Kelwyn said. "I don't think I've heard that term."

Cat glanced up at him. "The blood reservoir. Wendyl called it a spleen. If it's damaged, it keeps on bleeding until there's no blood left."

"Leave him with us," Gaelwyn said. "We'll get him to safety. Cainfir could use your help."

Cat touched Rhone's cheek. "When did they attack?"

"Half an hour ago," one of the Elves said. "Cainfir's not sure what to do. There's only a hundred of us. If we attack from behind, we'll be wiped out."

Someone tugged on her arm. It was Rhone. "Give Kelwyn...my sword. It will help. I wish..."

Cat kissed his damp, cool lips. "You just listen to Gaelwyn. He'll make you better."

She checked her quivers. Between the two of them, she had twenty-eight arrows. Even if she had all four quivers completely full, they'd have no effect on the horde south of the pass. *What can I do?*

Chapter Forty

Naron kept his sword in hand, though he hadn't blooded it yet. Edan Gethyn, the new baron, had commanded his squad to guard Jeral, the king's wizard. Despite the old man's spells, it would only be a matter of time before they were overrun. Never in his worst nightmares could Naron have imagined the numbers of vauroks pouring from the portals.

Worse yet, an undetermined number of sorcerers sent fireballs into Elven and Human lines, killing or wounding warriors of both races. Several of the burning orbs had landed in the camps, setting fire to tents and boxes of supplies.

Jeral, several feet to Naron's left, stood straighter than someone his age had a right to, tossing fire and sheets of lightning whenever one of the enemy sorcerers poked his head up from behind a hill.

"Look to the sky!" one soldier cried, running for cover behind a small tree.

A blazing ball arced towards them. Naron held his shield over his head. It would provide the same amount of cover as the tree, which was none. As it drew closer, Jeral mumbled something unintelligible.

Mumble faster, old man! Jeral had a magic shield covering them. Nonetheless, Naron swore he felt the heat of that infernal fire penetrate his mail and leather clothing.

With a cry, the wizard completed his spell and the fireball shattered, dispersing into the cool air without touching a single man. A few gobbets fell harmlessly on the shield. The old fellow was good. No denying it. Naron lowered his shield and groaned. Two more fireballs headed their way. By the looks of it, from the same hill as the first.

"Enough is enough," said the wizard. He pulled something heavy from a deep pocket in his thick robe. Oblong, like a big glass goose egg, it scattered the colours of the sun, casting rainbows on the dead grass of the hill. He pulled a leather sling from somewhere else in the robe and cradled the crystal in it.

Mumbling more magic words, Jeral caressed the crystal like a newborn babe, pointing it at the sorcerers. Without warning, a red-gold blaze of fiery light shot out the end, tossing the wizard flat on his ass.

The bolt of fire slipped through the shield with nary a thought and, widening into a wave, streaked towards the sorcerer's hill, slamming into first one fireball, then the other, smashing them apart. Pieces showered down onto the black creatures below. Shrieks of pain and outrage were met with laughter and cheers from Naron's squad. When the sheet of fire struck the sorcerer's hill, however, the laughter turned to silent awe.

Jeral's spell didn't hit the sorcerers themselves, not directly; those cowards had taken cover right after releasing their fire. The searing wave from the crystal sheared off the top of the hill in an explosion of dirt, rock and splintered trees, tossing bodies in all directions, goblin, vaurok, troll and sorcerer. Nothing could have survived the devastation. Jeral chose another spot, clear of Human and Elf, and cut loose again, this time to the cheers of the squad.

Naron had no idea how long either man or crystal could hold out, but until one or the other fell, the damage they dealt was tremendous. Deep in his heart, for the first time in his life, Naron wished he could use magic. A force like that would work as well against Elf as vaurok.

৪০ · ৫৪

Screams of dying Elves, men and vauroks floated up the mountainside. Atax Daemonica sat on an outcrop he'd carefully cleaned of slush, eating walnuts from a small cloth bag. Nothing could be nicer than a pleasant spring day, the breeze rattling the still bare branches of the small trees. A few brave mice and ground squirrels searched for any scraps winter may have left, while the first birds back from the south picked at winter dried berries. He tossed a nut to a squirrel.

He'd found a nice place to watch the battle, not far from the eastern edge of Broken Man Pass; a great view, wildlife, even entertainment. No excursion was complete without it. A mountain troll tore a Human soldier's head off, then tossed the body behind him, hitting

469

a vaurok. The vaurok bellowed, whirled its mace over its head and let fly at the troll's head, producing a howl from the troll. The stupid creature turned its back on the Humans trying to kill it and hit the vaurok with the head it had ripped off.

Atax laughed, almost spilling his walnuts. "This is too funny," he said to the squirrel and threw it another nut. "It would be nice to have some companionship while watching the show, but it's difficult to find someone who appreciates the finer points of life. And death."

In the middle of the free-for-all, an Elven warrior stood out, swinging a sword larger than Elves usually wielded. Atax had watched this one before. Unlike any other Elf he'd seen, he was built more like an oversized Human. Not only did he fight different from his people, he didn't even fight with them, but at the head of his own mercenary company. Atax found him fascinating. His black armour was a weapon in itself. As the Elf struck down a vaurok with his sword, he slammed a spiked vambrace into another, destroying the creature's face.

Few vauroks survived a confrontation with that Elf, and those few, every one, had managed to run away. Reports came back of a demon with eyes blacker than Balphegor's soul. What had happened to make him that way, Atax couldn't imagine. Elven magic couldn't be responsible or there'd be more like him. Three others similar to him fought nearby, though they couldn't match his strength, skill or sheer savagery.

He watched the strange Elf for a while as he hacked and slashed his way through a rabble of disorganized lesser vauroks. Not far behind them, the great vauroks waited. The first line held their rectangular shields before them like a wall, their pikes sticking out as thorns on a vine. The ones behind placed their shields over the heads of those in front, a solid barrier to all but the most persistent, or suicidal, warriors.

Atax itched to see how the odd Elf would handle the bigger, smarter, great vauroks now advancing up one low hill then down. He had to marvel at their discipline, not usually seen in vauroks of any kind. Whoever trained them must have had remarkable patience. Or a very big stick.

On the western flank, a Human wizard destroyed a fireball sent

470

by a sorcerer. Two more followed it. "Let's see you take on both," Atax said, with a chuckle.

Instead of the expected counter spell, the wizard sent out a sheet of fire unlike anything Atax had ever seen. After blowing apart the two fireballs, it blasted through the hill the sorcerers hid behind, killing all in a quarter mile radius. Atax slapped his knee, his chortle scattering the birds and animals around him. "I must find out how he did that! That's incredible!"

Another wave struck, then another. Powerful and deadly in its own right, yet still a bare scrape on the table compared with what remained north of the Barriers.

A hell wolf bit a man's face off. A Human split a vaurok's skull, then died with an axe in his back. An Elf fell to a troll, his plate mail little good against the massive spiked club it carried. Another fireball slammed into a crowd, killing Elf, Human and vaurok. Yes, this was entertainment. The best show he'd enjoyed in years.

ဢ · လ

Elven arrows pierced the air above Lindren's head, bound for a group of vauroks over one hundred yards in front of him. A few more shafts followed. Then they stopped, the archers out of arrows. Lindren fended off a vaurok's sword. He kicked it on the chin and the creature stumbled backwards. Auri grabbed its arm in his strong teeth, tossing the vaurok further off balance. Lindren swung down with his sword and slit the creature's throat. Beside him, Lowren removed a vaurok's head. On his right, Shain's Hrulka reared, lashing out with his hooves at another vaurok, turning its face to pulp and clearing their area.

Lindren took advantage of the temporary lull to scan the field. The Elven and Human lines had been forced back to the edge of Vergel's camp, too close to burning tents and supplies. No reinforcements waited in the wings, not with over three to one odds. Aris Kerend's banner had flown near Lindren. It was nowhere to be seen. Other Torian banners were also missing.

Mountain trolls fought a half mile ahead of him, devastating

471

Elven and Human forces alike, tearing up small trees to use as weapons if they lost their clubs. He had to do something. Another battle came to mind, one on Morata, at the Wall.

"Come with me." Motioning to Lowren and Shain, he sheathed his sword, wheeled Auri around and rode back to the middle of the Elven camp.

"What are you doing?" Lowren asked.

"Guard me. I'm going to try something I used on Morata." Lindren whispered the chant to centre his magic. He sent a thought out to a tree on a hill. One with trolls on it. "If this works, pass the word."

The trees appeared dead. The life merely lay hidden, dormant from winter sleep, and Lindren concentrated his power on it. The branches grew, extending farther than the rugged northern terrain allowed, reaching for the nearest troll.

Wood expanded under Elven magic, curling around the troll's legs, tripping it. The Humans battling it pounced, stabbing the thing in the eyes. While the troll thrashed in its death throes, the soldiers backed away to attack another. Lindren removed the branches, then sought a different opponent. The flow of dark creatures continued from the portals, providing him with plenty of targets.

Two hell wolves skidded around a tent and leapt towards Shain, red tongues hanging out of slathering jaws. Lowren shifted his Hrulka, slashing at the one on the left. Shain took the other. One of the wolves, already dying from a deep gash to its chest, slammed into Lindren, sending him backwards off Auri. The wolf landed on top of him, long teeth snapping an inch from his face, red eyes, rimmed with black, gleaming like burning coals in the night. Claws from its broad feet scraped on his armour. Auri clamped his teeth on one of the wolf's back legs and pulled, with little effect.

Muscles straining, both hands deep in the fur ruff around its neck, Lindren held the wolf at bay. Despite the beast's wound and the Hrulka tearing into it's leg, it fought with an unbelievable strength. Hot breath, reeking of dead flesh and fresh blood, hit his face, churning his gut. Lindren jabbed his knee into the beast's belly.

It hardly noticed and latched its teeth onto his helm's cheek guards, the edges of the metal digging into his flesh. Another bite and Lindren's jaw erupted in pain. Then the wolf was gone. A short, painful bark signaled its end.

Lowren stood over the black body, blood dripping from his sword. He held his hand out. "You need to see a healer," he said.

Once he regained his feet, Lindren probed the bite to his jaw. The tooth had only scraped bone, not broken it. Blood dripped down his breastplate; fire burned in his jaw. "I'll be fine. Help me back up." He settled on Auri's back and picked up his interrupted chant.

Lindren wrapped branches from a different tree around the legs of another troll. Other mages had joined in the effort. *It isn't enough. Dear Arvanion. It isn't enough.*

જી · ભ

Cat crouched beside Kelwyn on a wide plateau facing south, Cainfir standing behind them. Her fingers itched. The need to kill the creatures below threatened to take control.

"I hate sitting here watching," Kelwyn said.

Cainfir blew out a breath. "You think I enjoy it?"

The Elves and Humans below had no chance. They hacked and slashed, stabbed and killed, yet more creatures poured out of the portals.

What do I do? I can't just sit here! A thought brushed her mind. Then another. It was the dragons, slipping through a tunnel right under her feet. Did she dare? Would they listen?

:Rockbiter! Sandfang! Can you hear me?:

Rockbiter's voice pounded in her head. *:We do not wish to be bothered.:*

Stupid arrogant dragons! Cat tried to calm her nerves. *:You're going to be really bothered if you don't help us! The Elves and Humans need you. Don't forget an Elf and a Human helped save you. If you don't help us, thousands of vauroks, goblins and mountain trolls are going to be crawling all over your mountains and those little creatures who worship you won't be able to stop them!:*

The silence stretched into an eternity. *:There is something you can do*

473

for us,: Sandfang said. *:Help the others.:*

:Others?: Did she mean Black Wing?

A rumble sounded from under her feet and the ground shook. Kelwyn grabbed her hand and tugged her back just as Rockbiter broke through the rock in front of her. The Elves scattered.

The dragon stared her in the face. *:The other dragons. There are two of us for each world. We are the first to awaken. The others will come in their time. Chances are, they are trapped also. You need to help them.:*

"I don't know of any other dragons, but when I find out I'll help them. I promise!" The prophecies mentioned nothing about more Sleepers. Maybe others would come to light.

:Then we will do what we can.: Rockbiter disappeared, the rock closing over him as if it had never been disturbed.

"They're going to help." Cat climbed to a higher location for a better view, Kelwyn beside her.

Several minutes later, another rumble shook the mountain. On the battlefield below, right under the portals spitting out more vauroks, the ground split in an explosion of dirt and rock. A serpentine shape appeared in the chasm, then vanished, followed by a second.

The screams of vauroks and deep howls of the mountain trolls and hell wolves disappeared with their owners into the newly formed abyss. Some clung to the ragged cliff edges before the power of the dragons shook them loose. Other portals opened in mid-air, ejecting more creatures into the void.

Cat and the Elves cheered. When the dragons reached the end of the battlefield, they turned and widened the gap. The ground under Cat's feet shook, as did the hilly battlefield below, knocking vauroks and soldiers alike to the ground. Only the nimble Elves managed to keep their balance. The thunder of grating rock reminded Cat of the earthshake under Silverwood when she first saw Blackwing and she wondered if the dead dragon had anything to do with the destruction of the cavern.

Though dust and falling dirt obscured her view, Cat could still make out the lay of things. It hadn't taken the Elves long to figure out what was happening. Keeping clear of the widening abyss, they took advantage of the confusion. Vauroks ran straight into the waiting swords

474

of the Elves. Trolls stared around them, confused, as the ground gave way, swallowing them into the darkness below. Hell wolves scrabbled with all four paws to gain purchase at the edge. Some succeeded only to fall to swords, pikes and maces as the Humans followed the Elven example, finally finding their senses and their legs. Plant mages used trees to grab vauroks, who thought themselves in the clear, and toss them in with their vanishing comrades.

The dragons continued in a zigzag pattern, covering the distance to the Elven and Human lines. Then they stopped, disappearing into the massive abyss they'd created.

:We cannot continue. If we do, we will harm Arvanion's children,: Sandfang said.

Arvanion's children? The Elves. *:Do you know Arvanion?:*

:We know of him.: Rockbiter's voice resonated deeper, more powerful, than his mate's.

:Do you know where he is?: It was a question Lindren had been asking for two thousand years. If Cat could get the answer…

:We know of him. We do not remember the between time, nor do we remember our lost lives or what became of those we knew then.:

It was worth a try. *:Thank you for your help. I will free the others when I find them.:*

:We go.:

Cat turned to Kelwyn and Cainfir. "They've done what they can."

Kelwyn put his hand on Cat's shoulder, his eyes on the remaining creatures. "How do we get down there? They need us." Portals still opened over the chasm, spitting out startled vauroks, goblins, trolls, hell wolves and even the odd sorcerer, though those still on the battlefield had to be dealt with.

"Simple," Cainfir said. "We go around the chasm, punch in on their right flank. The field is narrow now. We might even have a chance of surviving. Cat, hide your bow and quivers here. They're no good where we're going." With a wave of his hand, they were off.

"What in the nine hells are those vauroks doing?"

Taurin glanced at Gedren, one of his lieutenants. Blood smeared his armour, his face. Taurin doubted he looked much different. "Prolonging their death."

Well over a hundred vauroks hid behind a wall formed of rectangular shields, those behind guarding the heads of those in front, the shields of those in front helping to protect those beside. Long pikes poked out from between small gaps in the forward line, the only passage through.

Lady Jayme's commander had sent two waves against them, to no avail. When one vaurok fell, another moved in to take its place. Not enough vauroks died, not to Taurin's liking. The commander had recalled the few survivors and now conferred with his officers atop a small hill.

Taurin also held back, studying the situation. Horses, even Hrulka, would be useless. They'd shy away from the long pikes. Arrows only bounced off the broad shields held above. Throwing men against them also proved devastating.

The dragons had helped by destroying thousands and rendering their portals useless, but these vauroks had found a way to put a thorn in their side. A deep one. Despite his hatred of the creatures, he held a modicum of respect for whomever had devised the formation. That it came from Udath Kor's forces was surprising indeed and quite worrisome.

He glanced up as another of Jeryl's waves of fire roasted a hill dotted with vauroks and goblins. Perhaps magic was the only way to defeat them and, perhaps, the dragons had it right. They were not the only ones with the power of earth. Taurin preferred cutting down vauroks face to face, watching them bleed and die. Sometimes, however, magic was useful.

"Get the men ready for a charge," Taurin said to Gedren.

The lieutenant's features remained set in stone, just as cold and emotionless as Taurin's. "You saw how well that worked with Jayme's men."

"Our men will have help." Taurin removed the bloody, spiked gauntlet from his right hand. Crouching, he laid his palm flat against the cold ground. Calling up the words of magic, so familiar, yet so rarely used since Katrin died, he centered his power. A quick probe of the earth below him showed no natural faults; this part of Urdran had been stable for eons. What he did find were weaknesses caused by the disruption of the dragons. Perfect.

"Now."

Gedren snapped off a command and the band of mostly Human mercenaries took off at a run, bellowing an assortment of battle cries, while Taurin took advantage of the weaknesses, sending his power into the earth in carefully directed waves. A series of tremors hit the vauroks, enough to toss them to the ground, yet not disrupt any Human or Elf fighting nearby. He caught the vauroks completely by surprise.

Their shield wall collapsed as they lost their balance, struggled to stay upright. Taurin's men leapt in for the kill. Jayme's commander, quick to respond to the sudden advantage, sent the remainder of his men to take the vauroks on the right.

Faster than Taurin thought possible, the vauroks regained their feet and met his mercenaries, pike to sword. Though the shield wall was in tatters, destroying them would be no easy job. He slipped on his gauntlet and gripped his sturdy sword in both hands, striding to add his own effort to the destruction.

ℬ • ℛ

The ice sword sat light in Kelwyn's hand, its balance perfect. The magical weapon sliced through vaurok armour and troll hide with ease. The dust of the dragon's devastation covered the battlefield, hung in the air like a brown fog, clogging his nose; yet he hardly noticed.

Kelwyn leapt at the creatures with gleeful abandon, enjoying the screams and the sizzling/freezing of dark flesh. When he'd charged into battle, he'd wished he had his armour, the mail he wore seemed inadequate. The ice sword, however, with its light weight and wondrous properties, made it easy to keep the creatures at bay.

477

Cat fought close to him, her tchiru and dagger flashing in the muted light of the sun. Fresh, dark green blood spattered her hair, her face and her mail, adding to his elation.

Rarely did he feel joy in battle; today he did, fighting beside Cat, banishing his pent-up frustration over Dairon, Tozer and all those who sought to hurt the ones he loved. This battle wasn't like the one in the castle in Tezerain, however. There, he'd let his anger take control, followed his emotions instead of his skill and knowledge. With the help of Rhone's ice sword, Kelwyn put that skill to work, cutting down all those who stood before him like an avenging spirit.

When they'd fought their way through to the Kitring-Tor left flank, Cainfir appeared at Kelwyn's side. "There are mountain trolls just to the north, near the edge of that big hole. We're headed there."

Kelwyn shook Cat out of her fighting state and dragged her with him. Cainfir called together the rest of the company and they trotted north. Of the original ninety-eight who'd entered the battle, including Kelwyn and Cat, ninety-five remained.

Four large shapes loomed out of the dusty air. Mountain trolls; twenty feet of muscle, sinew and stupidity. Most arrows barely penetrated the thick, grayish brown, bark-like skin. To fight a mountain troll, an archer had to be lucky enough to hit an eye or leave it to the warriors who'd stab at it with swords and pikes, hoping to pierce something vital before it hit them. Once again the ice sword was up to the task.

Kelwyn darted in from the right, stabbing its lower back. A gush of thick, red blood rewarded his effort. The wound sizzled and spat with the conflict of fire and ice. Cat ducked under the club, then thrust her tchiru into the tree-trunk thigh while the dagger sliced higher up, through the loin cloth, into the genitals. It let out a strangled grunt. She had the troll's attention now and it swung the spiked club back and forth, bellowing its distress to the world. Kelwyn grinned and waited for his opportunity to strike again.

ઍ · ભ

Lindren sat astride Auri near the trampled ruins of an Elven camp. The surviving forces had the remnants of Udath Kor's massive army trapped against the edge of the chasm. In such close quarters, his magic could easily cause damage to Elves and Humans. Three air mages had come by and lent him their power allowing him to keep up his arcane battle with the trolls. The mages had now retreated to find somewhere safe to rest. Using their power had allowed Lindren to remain reasonably fresh.

He took the respite to scan the battlefield, or what remained of it. Bodies lay sprawled everywhere. Far too many. Members of both allied races searched for those still living and slit the throats of any black creatures still moving.

Not long before, a Kerend runner had informed him of Aris' death. The baron's men had stood near the centre, the brunt of the attack. Apparently he'd fallen while defending his injured son, Markus. Brade had also taken injuries, though both brothers would survive, one the new baron of Kerend, the other the next Duke of Teale. The news of Aris' death would upset Cat. Who else had they lost?

A check to the west showed that Jeral had also taken a well-deserved rest. Some of the men guarding him were sent forward to aid in the clean up. Though Lindren hadn't spoken with him, the crystal's power had been obvious and welcome. If he couldn't find a use for the two he kept, he'd have to turn them over to trusted wizards. They were needed in battle, as proven today.

Taurin's banner still flew not far from the edge of the dragon-made abyss. *Trust him to be in the middle of it.* True to his ways, he'd stay until the last vaurok had fallen.

"Shouldn't we go help?" Lowren asked. His mount, Zyar, pawed the ground, as impatient as her rider.

Lindren gave him a wry smile. "Is there much point? It's almost over."

His brother set his bloody sword across his lap. "There's always a point."

479

With a half-hearted chuckle, Lindren waved them forward. They managed to kill a vaurok each, with Lowren and Shain adding another hell wolf to their credit. The press of man and Elf grew too thick to penetrate safely on horseback and they backed off to the top of a nearby hill. Amidst cheers and shouts, the last of the dark army were killed or simply pushed back into the chasm. The victors celebrated, their weapons and fists raised in the air.

Lindren found little to celebrate. Between Vergel's army and his, they'd had fifteen thousand men. He estimated less than half remained. He'd heard no word from Firann for most of the battle and Lindren feared the worst. Silverwood had contributed three hundred warriors, less than a third of the entire population of the enclave, yet still a significant number. He prayed to Arvanion that they hadn't lost too many.

Lowren pulled a cloth from a saddlebag and cleaned his sword before sheathing it. "I'm going to help with the wounded. I can't just sit here." He slid off Zyar, set his helm and breast plate over the saddle, then put his hand on Lindren's thigh. "I told you not worry about me."

"You did."

Lowren trotted to the nearest body.

His brother's survival was the only high point of the day in Lindren's eyes. He dismounted and led Auri to a fallen soldier while Shain checked another.

$\wp \cdot \wp$

Cheering men surrounded Naron on all sides. Once released from protecting the king's wizard, his squad had torn into the remaining vauroks with a vengeance. He hadn't realized how hard it would be to stand back and watch his people die. While fighting, a soldier didn't think about those around him, only that he had to survive from one moment to the next.

Some of the men looted bodies, Human, vaurok or Elven, they didn't care. If they were caught, they'd care soon enough. Naron turned his back on them and knelt next to a fallen comrade. He still breathed, though he bled heavily from a wound to his thigh. "Here!" Naron waved to a healer's contingent searching nearby.

Once the man had been taken into their custody, Naron moved on. Back towards the encampment he worked, calling for aid when needed, closing eyes or folding lifeless limbs over silent chests when there was nothing he could do. All the while he raged. Most of the bodies were Human. Living Elves seemed to be everywhere, picking up their own scarce dead and wounded. Naron would bet a year's pay the odds would be uneven again, just as Atax said. More Humans died than Elves every time.

With his teeth clenched, he turned over another body, a man from Jayme. This one was long gone, his belly torn open. Naron retched at the sight, at the stink of ruptured entrails. If the man had proper armour he might have lived. He set the man back on his stomach, then stood, gasping for fresh air. The battlefield was a mess. At least the chasm provided them with an easy way to dispose of vaurok and troll bodies. Even now details worked to clear the low hills.

It was the first chance Naron had to survey the damage done by the dragons. At least, that's what Jeral said had caused them; when the earth tore open, he couldn't see a thing for flying dirt, rock and dust. He'd had no idea dragons existed any more. They were the stuff of stories. It would be something for him to tell his children and his grandchildren, when he had them.

The chasm spread from one end of the battlefield to the other, a distance of some three miles, east to west. The western edge almost cut off access to Broken Man Pass, only a narrow strip remained. If there were still creatures on the other side of the Barriers, they'd have a demon's time passing through. Just as well. They could all freeze in the eighth hell as far as he was concerned.

Naron turned his gaze from the shattered hills to find he stood close to the Elven lines. They moved everywhere, examining bodies, carrying wounded, talking to each other in their own language. If they fought with Torians, they could at least speak the tongue.

His eyes settled on a familiar head. This one he'd seen before, in reality and in his dreams. The build, the colour of hair, the way he

481

moved; it could only be Lindren. *Damn his hide! Rayson didn't have to die! You lied to me!* His brother's face swam before his eyes, demanding revenge, begging Naron to appease his tortured soul.

Without thought, Naron's hand found the dagger at his waist. The distance between them narrowed. Atax's words rang in his head. How to kill an Elf, 'Come from behind and go for the face. A quick stab to the eye and there you are.' *You could have saved my brother. You* can *heal my people!*

Naron hid the knife, moving closer to Lindren. The Elf half turned, enough to see and dismiss him. *It is Lindren!* Now certain of his target, Naron walked right up behind him, slightly to the Elf's right. "Will he live?"

Just as Lindren turned to answer, Naron grabbed his head and thrust the blade home, straight into the hated Elf's eye. Lindren fell without a sound.

Chapter Forty-One

Kelwyn scanned the battlefield. The combined Elven and Human army still fought in isolated pockets. Though all the trolls and hell wolves were dead, the few remaining vauroks and goblins defended themselves with a fierce determination unusual for their kind. They usually ran, now they had no choice with the abyss at their backs and Vergel's and the Elven armies to their fore.

The battle was over for Kelwyn and Cat, though. No enemies remained near them. Kelwyn crouched over the body of Cainfir, his captain, and closed the dead eyes. A hand rested on his shoulder and a small breeze sent Cat's familiar scent his way. She'd returned from the strange place she fought from with hardly a scratch.

"I'm sorry, Kel. I know you liked him."

Kelwyn just nodded, the peculiar joy he'd felt killing vauroks long gone, replaced by sadness, grief and a bone-weary ache. Six more of Kelwyn's comrades had fallen and twelve wounded, all of whom would survive until their healer returned. Thinking of Gaelwyn reminded him of Rhone and he looked up from his dead captain to the pass. Three shapes moved around the west end of the chasm, two with what looked like a makeshift litter. They appeared at the top of one hill, vanished, then reappeared atop the one closer.

"It's Gaelwyn," Cat said. "The other two are carrying Rhone. I'm going to meet them. I need to retrieve my bow and quivers too."

Rising from his crouch, Kelwyn said, "You're not going alone."

"If you insist." She turned away from him, towards the encampment. "I've called Krir and Joar. We can reach them faster."

Both Hrulka arrived with no tack or saddle. Kelwyn anchored his hands in Joar's mane and leapt to his back. Cat did the same on Krir and they galloped off to meet Gaelwyn, an impatient Cat riding several yards ahead.

Images of Cainfir's dead face plagued Kelwyn on the ride. Tough

483

on his Elves, the captain was just as hard on himself and it had resulted in a company who worked well together, trusted each other's abilities and defeated every enemy they'd fought. They lost members, it happened, but Cainfir had always been there to bring new members up to their level. Now he was gone.

Hoof beats sounded behind him. Before Kelwyn could turn to see who it was, a flash not far ahead of Cat and a little to the right, caught his eye. Only when the first vaurok came out, bearing a long spear, did he realize it was a side view of a temporary portal. Four other vauroks followed, three with short swords, one with an axe.

The first exited in front of Cat, now even further ahead of Kelwyn, its spear aimed at Krir's chest. The Hrulka tried to veer away from the weapon. At a full gallop, he lost his footing and crashed to the ground, throwing Cat off his back. With a wide, evil grin, the vaurok plunged the spear into the Hrulka. Krir screamed and kicked out, caving in the vaurok's face. Even in his death throes, the Hrulka protected his rider.

Cat lay on the ground, not moving. Another vaurok threw her over his shoulder and sprinted for the portal as Krir crashed to the ground. Kelwyn's heart thumped in his chest and he pulled Rhone's sword from its harness across his back. Another moment was all he needed to catch up. He didn't have it.

With a cry of victory, the vaurok carrying Cat made a dash for the portal. It didn't make it either. An arrow sprouted from its throat and it tumbled to the ground just a scant few feet from its target. Cat fell to one side.

Kelwyn didn't take the time to find out who'd fired the arrow. He praised the archer's talent and lashed out with the ice sword at another vaurok who tried to retrieve its prize. A sizzling wound opened on the creature's chest and it fell back. Kelwyn leapt off Joar and straddled Cat, the ice sword held before him, the open portal at his back. Not a good position. The two remaining vauroks bared their teeth and separated, one approaching from the right, the other the left.

Hoof beats still sounded to the south and Kelwyn silently thanked whoever it was for the assistance. Just as the rider brought his horse to a dancing halt, sunlight glittering off his sword, Kelwyn engaged the vaurok on the right, trusting the rider could handle the other. Joar didn't give him a chance. The Hrulka lashed out with his hooves, knocking the second vaurok to the ground. The rider finished him off with a sword thrust to the neck.

A wayward breeze brought the putrid scent of vaurok to Kelwyn—from behind. He spun, whipping the sword in front of him just in time to slice the gut of a smaller vaurok. In moments, all the creatures lay dead.

Kelwyn faced the portal, waiting for another vaurok to stick its head out. "Thank you for your help. That was nice shooting." He glanced over at the rider, then started in surprise.

"You're welcome. I'm always glad to help a lady in distress, Lord Kelwyn." Still holding his sword at the ready, Rhone's brother, Iyan, executed a perfect bow.

"What are you doing here?" Kelwyn demanded. He indicated Iyan should take up a position by the portal while he crouched next to Cat. She was out cold. A cut on the back on her head bled profusely. He stood, prepared to engage whatever else came through.

"I noticed Rhone wasn't with you. Did something happen to him?" A vaurok appeared. Iyan slashed its throat and kicked it back where it had come from.

Kelwyn had to think fast. Had Gaelwyn healed all Rhone's wounds? "He took a fall and knocked his head." He glanced in the direction they'd been riding. Gaelwyn and the Elves were less than a mile away.

Iyan snorted. "A bump on the head. What a kitten."

Kelwyn's grip tightened around Rhone's sword. "He fought valiantly with us until he fell. There's no reason to insult him."

Iyan laughed. "There's always a reason. Though it's not as much fun when he can't hear."

The pale, swirling clouds in the portal flickered, then faded, narrowing down to a point. With an audible pop, the portal vanished. Cat moaned and Kelwyn set aside the ice sword. He sat on the ground and pulled her into his arms.

"Interesting sword," Iyan commented, leaning closer to have a better look.

"It's Rhone's. A gift from Cat."

Iyan whistled. "Nice gift. I don't suppose she has another hanging around?"

Kelwyn almost bit his tongue trying to remain civil.

Cat blinked her eyes. "Kel. What happened?" she asked in Elven.

He answered in kind. "A portal opened in front of you. You fell off Krir and banged your head, probably on a rock. I…I'm sorry, Cat. Krir's dead." Tears formed in her beautiful amber eyes. "Rhone's despised brother is here. I hate to say it, but he's responsible for saving you. You were so far ahead of me I couldn't get to you in time. If he hadn't had a bow, you'd have been taken."

With Kelwyn's help, she sat up, then leaned into him, tears leaking down her cheeks over the lost Hrulka. He held her for a few minutes, Iyan standing over them with a cynical half smile.

Finally, she sat up straight. "My head hurts." She tried to touch the wound.

Kelwyn stopped her. "It's almost quit bleeding. Best to leave it alone."

Iyan crouched next to her, a handkerchief in his hand. "Here, my lady. Allow me." He dabbed at the wound.

Cat cringed closer to Kelwyn, unnoticeable to Iyan. "You should thank him," he said, still in Elven.

She let out a sigh and switched to Torian. "Thank you, Iyan. I owe you my life."

Iyan's smile grew. "You're very welcome, my lady. I'm glad to assist."

Kelwyn tried hard not to scowl; the man seemed inordinately proud of himself. A few minutes more and Gaelwyn reached them, Rhone laid out on a makeshift stretcher, buried under cloaks.

With a shake of her head, Cat clamboured to her feet. On wobbly legs, and with Kelwyn's assistance, she made her way to Rhone's side. Iyan tagged along.

"How is he?" she asked, again in Elven.

"I've repaired the *talien*, but left his ankle and the bump on his head," Gaelwyn said. "I thought he might need an excuse for not accompanying you to battle." The healer cast a sidelong glance at Iyan. "Who's he?"

"Rhone's brother," Kelwyn answered. "They don't exactly get along. Cat and I don't like him either. I'm not quite sure why he's here. He said he was curious about what happened to Rhone, but he saved Cat's life just now. I suppose it would be impolite to ask him to leave."

"We saw." Gaelwyn set the back of his hand against Rhone's cheek. "Wish we could have reached you in time."

"I hate to break up what's obviously an intense conversation, but how's my brother?" Iyan asked, staring at Rhone over Cat's shoulder.

Gaelwyn threw him a disapproving glance. "He has a cut on his head and a lump that causes me some concern. Your brother also has an injured ankle. I gave him something for the pain and it's put him out. I'd like him to stay that way for a while."

Iyan grunted. "My lady, here, is hurt. Can you help her?"

Kelwyn took over. "No. She's Tiranen. She doesn't need his help."

Gaelwyn started.

"I'm not a secret anymore," Cat said, in Elven.

"Is anything a secret anymore?" the healer muttered in kind. He stood. "Can I leave him with you? I'm needed elsewhere."

"Of course," Kelwyn said, switching to Torian. The Elves set the litter on the ground. "Iyan and I can carry him back to his tent." He pulled Gaelwyn aside. "Cainfir's gone. I thought I should let you know."

A pained expression crossed the healer's face and he nodded.

"Thank you for your help," Kelwyn said. "And both of you too." He nodded to the other Elves, then they and Gaelwyn set off at a trot to the Elven camps.

After helping Cat up on Joar's back, Kelwyn said to Iyan, "You take one end, I'll take the other. Cat can lead your horse."

With a shrug, Iyan passed over his horse's reins to Cat and picked up one end of the litter. Kelwyn took the other, wondering if Iyan really hated Rhone as much he let on. Cat stared at Krir's body as they passed and two tears trickled down her cheeks. With an unexpected dread in his heart, Kelwyn wondered who else they'd lost.

Naron stepped back from Lindren's body, his anger, and a strange sort of joy, rushing through his blood like hot lava. "Now you know how Rayson felt! Let's see you heal that!"

Someone grabbed his arm. It was a man, an officer from Rais. He appeared angry. Why?

"They're liars! Don't you see?" Naron clutched at the man. "They can heal us, but they choose not to because they want us dead!"

"What have you done!" Someone else gripped his arm, spun him around.

It was Lindren. His jaw had a long gash, swollen red surrounded by black and blue bruising, but his strange dark grey eyes were fine.

"I killed you," Naron cried, disbelief drowning his joy. "You're dead!"

"You killed my brother!" Lindren shook him so hard his teeth rattled. Grabbing a handful of hair, he dragged Naron back to the dead Elf and tossed him on the ground, shoving his face closer to the one he'd stabbed.

Naron took a good look. Someone had removed the dagger, leaving a bloody pulp where the eye had been. Another Elf held the dead one in his arms, his face hard with anger. This one had features like Lindren's, as did the dead Elf, yet not quite the same. Naron had made a mistake. "Your...brother?"

"Yes! Why? Why did you kill him? You don't even *know* him! What did he do to you?" The quiet voice that had spoken to him after Rayson died had changed, tinged with ice, hatred and overwhelming grief. His brother. Naron had killed Lindren's brother. Wasn't it justice? Wasn't it better than killing Lindren?

"Good!" Naron tried to struggle out of Lindren's grip. He only succeeded in pulling out some of his own hair. "Now you know how I feel! Do you like losing a brother? How does it feel?"

The next thing he knew, Naron sat on the ground, holding his jaw. A different Elf held Lindren back. Naron had never seen one with murder in his eyes. He did now. Others had gathered, of both races.

"You see?" Naron said to the men. "They mean us no good! The Elves are trying to get us killed!"

"You don't know what you're talking about." The Rais officer hauled him to his feet. "I thank Ar you're not one of mine. You should too, because if you were, you'd already be hanging from a gibbet!"

"You don't understand!" How could Naron make them understand? He needed Atax. He could explain it better. "The Elves can heal us, but they don't! They want us dead!" Mumbles proclaiming his insanity sounded all around. "You have to believe me! Why do you think they have better armour? Why fewer of them die compared to us? They want us dead!"

The officer pushed him at two men, both with their swords drawn. "Make sure he's carrying no weapons." He pointed his finger at Naron. "And I don't want to hear another word out of you!"

The officer turned his back on Naron, speaking instead with the hated Elf. "My sincerest apologies, Lord Lindren. I thought he was going to help your brother. If I'd had any idea…"

The soldiers removed Naron's sword, then poked and prodded him, treating him none too careful in their search.

"I want to know why he did it," Lindren said. "Why he thinks we can heal your people when I told him otherwise. If your baron can't make him talk, give him to us."

"Of course, my lord." The officer gave Lindren a bow. "Take him to Baron Edan," he said to the soldiers. "This one is his to deal with."

Fingers of iron encircled Naron's arms and the men dragged him away. *I have to make them understand!* Maybe the baron would listen. *Someone has to listen!*

℘ • ℭ

A bloody sunset highlighted the walls of Lowren's tent. Lindren sat at his brother's side, the body shrouded in a blanket. His jaw ached, it seemed nothing compared to his heart. *How could it have come to this?* When he'd talked to Naron three months before, the man had seemed to listen to his words. What had happened to cause Naron's rage to return?

489

No word had come yet from Baron Edan's camp as to the reason. Naron may be proving resistant to questioning. If that was the case, Lindren had a problem. He'd essentially told the Rais officer he'd get the information out of Naron if the baron couldn't. Truth was, Lindren had little knowledge of and no stomach for torture. No Elf did. Except, perhaps, Taurin. Who knew what he was capable of these days? If Naron refused to talk, turning him over to Taurin was at least a possibility.

The tent flap flew open. Kelwyn stood there, his face white.

Lindren leapt to his feet. "I'm sorry. I'm so sorry." No need to ask if they'd succeeded in their quest.

"Father..." Kelwyn dropped to his knees beside the cot, tears now running freely.

Lindren crouched beside him, gathered him in his arms and let him cry. Though sometimes annoying, Cat had it right, tears were the best way to heal from grief. When Kelwyn could cry no more, Lindren asked, "Who told you?"

"Arufin."

"I'd hoped it was Orrin. He was here for a while, then left. Was he with Aru?"

Kelwyn reached out a hesitant hand to his father and shook his head.

Lindren let out a heavy sigh. "I'm worried about him. He didn't handle it well."

"Who does?" Kelwyn started to remove the blanket from his father's face.

Lindren stopped him. "Don't. It's not a pretty sight."

Kelwyn's shoulders sagged. "I miss him."

"So do I. At least your mother will be around for a while. She has the twins."

"Mother." A little sob escaped his lips. "She won't be the same. She'll be like Taurin."

"Not quite like Taurin but, no, she won't be herself."

Tarine would already have lost her smile, most of her will to live. The effect of the *moraren* was instantaneous. Silverwood had lost too many, fifty-six at last count. The screams of the *qira* as their soulmates

490

died would have alerted the enclave. All Silverwood would be in turmoil.

Lindren could only hope Rhianna had been near Tarine when Lowren died. At the thought of his own soulmate, a pang clenched his heart. Although Rhianna knew he was alive, she'd worry. As much as he wished he could comfort her, there was nothing he could do right now. He sent a quiet wish to Arvanion to give her a little peace of mind.

"Why?" Kelwyn asked, fresh tears adding a sad shine to his eyes. "Why did that man kill him?"

"We don't know…yet."

The tent flap rustled and Arufin stuck his head in. "Tarkin says to tell you Firann has been found…under a dead troll. He's…" Arufin glanced at the body under the blanket. "I'm sorry. He's…also gone."

Lindren's heart sunk. His brother, his best captain, Aris, Janar Miklin….who else?

As if reading his thoughts, Kelwyn said, "Cainfir is dead too." His voice held no emotion and a shiver ran down Lindren's spine. He sounded almost exactly like Taurin.

Arufin sat beside Kelwyn and placed a hand on his shoulder. "I can't tell you how sorry I am." The blond Elf understood; he'd lost his father several years ago, and, as a result, his mother.

Lindren sat back in his chair. "Do you know where Orrin is?"

Arufin nodded. "He's with the Hrulka. He doesn't want to talk to anyone."

"Not even you?" Lindren asked. Orrin and Arufin were usually inseparable.

"Not even me. I'm worried about him, but I have to respect his wishes."

As long as he hasn't gone too far away. "Keep an eye on him."

With a final squeeze to Kelwyn's shoulder, Arufin nodded and took his leave.

"I gather your mission was successful," Lindren said. "If not for the dragons, I hate to think how many more would have died. Cat and Rhone are all right? I thought she'd be with you."

"She doesn't know yet. They're both injured, but will be fine. They're sleeping. It's…a long story."

491

"I understand. It can wait."

"Part of it can't." Kelwyn finally forced his dark grey eyes from the body of his father. "I have to tell you something. I think...I think Cat would find it difficult. She..." He cast his gaze to the floor. "Tozer was there, under the mountain. He surprised us and threw one of those horrible blue balls at me."

Lindren almost jumped off the chair, his heart thudding. "I'm relieved you avoided it."

Once more, Kelwyn turned his black gaze on Lindren. "I didn't. It hit me in the belly. It seeped through my mail and started eating me."

Lindren sat back, his eyes wide. "How in the nine hells did you beat it?" If there was a way, everyone had to know.

"I didn't beat it. I remember more pain than I ever thought possible. Never have I experienced anything like it. Nor do I want to ever again. I don't remember much, other than the agony, but I know I begged Cat to kill me. I saw Talifir die. I didn't want to go the same way. She..." Kelwyn's voice caught. "Cat cried, refused, but I begged and begged..."

A small sob halted his words. Lindren leaned over and gripped his shoulder, more to confirm he was really alive, that the blue ball hadn't taken his nephew, than to comfort him.

After a moment, Kelwyn continued. "It seemed like forever until Cat finally did...kill me."

"That's impossible." Could Kelwyn have been dreaming? Or perhaps injured to the point of delirium?

"It's true. Through the pain, the torture of that blue ball, I felt the dagger pierce my heart. That's the one part I will never forget." Kelwyn's eyes, dark from grief, held only truth.

Impossible though it sounded, Lindren had to believe. Or, at the very least, believe Kelwyn believed. "Then why are you sitting here now?"

"That part's even weirder." Kelwyn touched Lowren's arm, hidden under the blanket. "I...I wish he was alive to hear this." He lowered his hand.

The tale Kelwyn told was stranger than anything Lindren had ever heard, a tale of a green plain and blue sky, white light and a portal that didn't appear to belong to Udath Kor; and a voice, one telling him to follow the light.

Lindren thought long and hard on Kelwyn's experience while his nephew sat beside his father, buried in quiet grief.

℘ · ℭ

Spring birds chirped a greeting to the morning sun as Atax made his way around the east side of the chasm to the rear of the victor's lines, avoiding the Elven encampment. Curiosity drove him. Naron held great promise and he had to know how the young man fared.

The battle had proved most interesting. *Dragons. I wonder where they came from?* Atax had heard about the dragons, though they'd died long before his birth. They'd lifted the entertainment level of yesterday's free-for-all considerably. Too bad he couldn't see the looks on the vauroks and sorcerer's faces as they stepped out of the frozen north into a pit leading straight to the ninth hell. He'd sat on his rock, laughing until his gut hurt.

The dragons had turned the tide of the battle, without a doubt, yet another surprise awaited after the two giant reptiles had done their part. If Atax hadn't been looking to the west, he'd have missed it. A small band of Elves ran from the pass, around the edge of the chasm and attacked the vauroks' right flank. Not remarkable in itself; the girl he'd spotted, however, now there was a sight to see, silver hair shining in the sun, despite the dust. That one he'd spotted before, when he'd first found Naron.

Atax had never seen anyone fight the way she did — a short, narrow sword in one hand, dagger in the other, leaping, twisting, dodging like a leaf in a hurricane. Another Elf who diverged from the normal. Elven women never fought that close, always with the archers. Risking detection, he'd conjured a scry-spell, using the flat surface of the rock he used as a chair.

She was pretty, with the most unusual amber eyes, reminiscent of the Tiranen, except she was far too short. Six feet was an acceptable height for an Elf, not a Tiranen. The Elf who fought beside her, and

493

guarded her after the Hrulka had been killed, had to be her soulmate. Atax had never had the opportunity to play with an Elf. There was always a first time, soulmate or not.

Approaching from the south, he strolled towards Vergel's army as if he belonged there. Once again Atax wore a uniform of Kerend, though it was to Gethyn's camp he walked. After a long search, he ran across some familiar faces in a small copse south of the supply wagons, none of them Naron's. A modicum of concern crept into his breast.

Kalda and the others he'd met with Naron that day at the training camp were crouched in a circle, speaking in hushed tones. Each of them took turns glancing in all directions, as if afraid they'd be caught.

"Good morning, gentlemen."

To a man, they leapt to their feet, weapons drawn. Atax held his hands out, to show he bore no weapon. "Easy friends, it's only me."

The one called Kalda was the first to recover. "Atax! Are we glad to see you!"

Atax made a show of looking around. "Where's my friend, Naron? And why aren't you fellows with your unit?"

"We can't go back," the broad-nosed man said, dejected. "Naron convinced us you were right, about the Elves. He also talked us into helping him sabotage their supplies."

The tree appeared to be bearing fruit. *How nice.* "Naron always did show initiative." Atax gave them each a gentle smile, a teacher proud of an enterprising student.

"He took it one step further," Kalda said, just as miserable. "Naron…killed an Elf yesterday."

Atax couldn't help it, he laughed. "He killed an Elf! Marvelous! I knew he could do it."

"He got caught!" The broad-nosed man took a step closer to Atax, his fists clenched. "Baron Edan's soldiers have been torturing him all night. We *had* to leave in case he talked!"

"And we have nowhere to go!" cried another man, the blond haired one. "When our families find out, they won't want anything to do with us."

Atax sobered. He preferred to keep his existence quiet from those

494

in authority. He studied the young men before him, all strong with the intellect of a mosquito. Perhaps he should take advantage of the opportunity and cultivate them. These few would grow, maybe even into his own army. That could be quite entertaining.

"I understand your problem," Atax said with false sympathy. "Such is the way with revolutions. No one truly understands the way things are and they won't unless we tell them. That, however, will take time and a great deal of work. Sacrifices must be made as for any noble cause. Do you men feel, in spite of Naron's predicament, that I am right? Have you seen the way things are?"

"Well," Kalda said, his attitude that of a child who suddenly realized that perhaps the teacher was right after all. "I did get a good look at the Elves' armour and you're right, theirs is much better than ours."

"I didn't see anywhere near the number of Elven dead as Human," said another. "And there's that whole business with Naron's brother."

"That's right." The anger had left the broad-nosed man. "And the Elves walk around like they own the whole world. They even give advice to the Commander-General."

"I've seen that too," Kalda said. Another man agreed.

"Perhaps…" Atax played at mulling over a difficult decision. "Perhaps it's time I let intelligent, forward moving men such as yourselves into my confidence." Despite their fear, their lingering anger, he had the attention of each and every one of them. "I'm not a soldier of Kerend, as I led Naron to believe. I'm sorry for the deception, but it was necessary for my safety. You see, I'm a wizard who used to work for a king quite a distance from here. He fell under the spell of the Elves and, making a long, horrible, story short, it led to my country's destruction."

Mumbles and mutters followed the lie, all in Atax's favour. Emboldened, he pushed on. "Ever since, I've been trying to help people see the light, see the error of allowing Elves to run their lives. Naron did a fine and noble deed yesterday. He'll probably pay for it, but those in charge here are blind. It'll be difficult to change their minds. However, if you come with me, we can make a start elsewhere, so you can move freely without fear of capture."

"You...you want us to leave our homes? Our families?" Kalda asked. It was obvious the idea didn't sit well with him.

Typical country bumpkin. Atax spread his hands out, palms up. "You have no life here anymore. Your own baron will turn you over to the Elves for what you've done, if he doesn't hang you himself."

"Hang us!" The broad-nosed man put his hand on the hilt of his sword.

"You've committed treason in his eyes. You sabotaged the supplies of an ally." Atax had to calm them or his spur-of-the-moment plan would find itself at the bottom of the garderobe. "If you come with me, I can provide you with high quality armour, a good place to stay, better food than you've had in your lives, fine horses to ride and money to spend. You will be the start of my army, a righteous army, with the purpose of exposing the truth behind the Elves."

Atax had to chuckle inside. Truth was an elusive item, something believed only when one wanted to believe it. It had been so easy conning Naron, dressing the lie about the Elves' ability to heal Humans with the truth of their better armour and lesser numbers in battle. Of course, the drug in the brandy didn't hurt.

"You can be my generals, leaders of men," Atax said, wearing his most gentle, most trusting smile.

It only took moments for the men to decide, to a man, that they liked the idea. Atax gathered them into a circle and, using his very own transportation spell, took them...elsewhere.

Chapter Forty-Two

Cat rose from the hazy confines of sleep. A blanket was wrapped around her and her head rested on a soft pillow. Voices murmured in the background. Male voices. Two of them. One she recognized instantly. Rhone. With a smile, she sat up and rubbed sleep from her eyes.

Instead of lying beside her, Rhone sat on a chair near the flap of their tent, his bandaged right foot propped on a camp stool, a water canteen in one hand. His brother Iyan stood near him. Neither appeared happy and Cat wondered if they'd been arguing again.

Iyan's head turned towards her. He bowed, then gave her a strained smile. "My lady. I'm pleased to see you're awake."

Cat was pleased she hadn't bothered to take her shirt off before climbing in beside Rhone. She stayed on the pallet, most of her covered by blankets. "Good morning. I think. It is morning, isn't it?"

"Yes," Rhone said. His expression resembled the darkest thunder cloud Cat could remember. "Thank you for the news, Iyan. I'll try to see Jerran later."

"With that ankle?" Iyan gave a little snort. "You'll be lucky if you can make it to the campfire out front." He bowed once more to Cat. "I'll take my leave and, my lady, may I say how glorious you look when first awake?"

"Out!"

Cat started at Rhone's bellow. With a chuckle, Iyan left. She tossed back the covers and leapt out of bed. After giving Rhone a kiss and hug, she crouched beside him, placing her hand on his thigh. "Why was he here?"

Rhone took a long drink from the canteen before answering. "Rubbing in the fact that he saved your life yesterday, for one." His expression grew darker. "He also brought bad news. Gavan...is dead."

"Oh, Rhone. I'm so sorry." Cat rose from her crouch to hold him. He pushed her away. "Don't, Cat. Not right now."

Cat had only spoken with Gavan briefly during their stay at Arden's Keep. He struck her as a gentle, quiet man. The second oldest of Arden's brood, he had a wife, five children and two grandchildren who'd miss him deeply. Rhone's grief was understandable; why he refused her comfort was not. She resumed her crouch, unsure what to do.

A sound came from outside. "Cat? It's Lindren."

Just the person she needed to see. She jumped to her feet once more. "Come in."

One look at him and Cat lost the words she'd wanted to say. Lindren's clothes were rumpled and stained with blood, his hair uncombed and his normally silver-grey eyes were almost as black as Taurin's.

"What happened? You look terrible," she asked, her heart suddenly pounding.

Lindren took her by the shoulders. He stood with his jaw clenched, his grip tight. "Remember Naron?"

"The man who thought I could save his brother when I couldn't?"

"Yes. It seems…someone, a man called Atax, has been telling him…certain things. About us. The Elves."

"What things?" Cat asked. Her heart hadn't stopped pounding and now her gut wanted to sink straight to her toes.

"That we can heal Humans, but don't want to because we really want them dead."

"What?" Rhone removed his injured foot from the stool. "That's ridiculous. Why does he think your people want us dead?"

"Apparently we want Urdran to ourselves. That's why we have better armour that we won't share with the Humans and why we don't put as many warriors into battle." Lindren's grip on Cat tightened more. "This Atax has been feeding Naron's anger over the death of his brother and Naron soaked it up like sunshine on a winter day." He shifted his dark gaze to Rhone. "In case you're wondering, there are more Humans on this one world than there are Elves on all five. We *can't* bring any more warriors to battle."

Rhone said nothing.

Cat frowned. "That's not good, but what does it have to do with why you look like this?"

Lindren closed his eyes a moment before answering. "Naron tried to kill me. He...he thought he did."

Cat's heart pounded faster. 'You're all right?" He didn't appear hurt.

"Yes." The look in Lindren's eyes still said something was very wrong.

"If he didn't kill you," Rhone said, his deep voice as hard as ice. "Then who did he kill?"

Pain flashed across Lindren's handsome features. "Lowren." His voice broke.

The air turned cold. "No." Cat shook her head. "I told him to be careful," she sobbed. "I told him not to come!"

Cat's world crashed.

℘ • ℭ

Despite Lindren's firm grip, Cat collapsed in a heap at his feet. He joined her on the ground, his arms wrapped securely around her while she cried.

"I don't understand," Rhone said. "Why would this man spread that garbage?"

"I wish I knew. The battle was over. Lowren fought well, he even saved my life. He was helping with the wounded and Naron just..." Lindren couldn't say it. He stroked Cat's hair in an attempt to bring her, and him, a little comfort. "Five of Naron's friends are involved as well. They're responsible for destroying some of our supplies."

Rhone relaxed his fists, though he still looked like he wanted to hit something, or someone. "Naron I can sort of half understand, because of his brother. But what do the others care?"

Lindren shook his head. "This Atax must be well versed in the arts of persuasion. I desperately wish we could find him. And how he found out about our healing."

"What's going to happen to Naron? I know what he deserves."

"Edan will hang him tomorrow, just after dawn." Lindren

499

attempted to shush Cat's crying, whispering to her in Elven. It didn't work. "He wants a clear message sent that we are allies and you don't kill friends. Naron's cohorts have vanished and the baron has put word out with their descriptions. They had nothing to do with Lowren's death. Nonetheless, they're guilty of treason."

Rhone snorted. "They should be thrown in the abyss along with the rest of the trash. Did...did someone tell you about Gavan?"

Lindren nodded. "My deepest condolences. I know exactly how you feel."

"And I return them."

They sat in silence until Cat brought her crying under control. Lindren suggested she see Kelwyn, he needed her. Rhone told her to put her trousers on first.

"Do you want to come with us?" Lindren asked Rhone.

He shook his head. "I need to be alone for awhile."

"I understand." He guided Cat out of the tent.

೫ • ೪

Under a baleful spring sky, covered with pregnant rain clouds, thousands of Humans and Elves waited for a man to lose his life. Perched on a hill, so all could see, a newly made gibbet waited for its victim.

Cat insisted on coming to see Naron die, then regretted it. It was the first execution she'd ever attended and hoped it was her last. Two guards dragged Lowren's murderer to the top of the hill as he kicked and screamed curses to those who held him and most especially to the Elves. His face was battered and bruised.

Lindren said he'd been tortured and a shudder ran through Cat. Somewhere, deep inside, past the grief and anger, she felt sorry for him. Perhaps it really was her fault. She could have tried to save Naron's brother, even though she knew it was useless. Would that have helped? There was no way to know now.

She and her family stood with Vergel and the dukes who'd come to Kerend. Each of them had ungracious comments to make about Naron's conduct. According to them, a man should go to his punishment

500

with grace and civility. Naron showed neither. Cat had to admit, she'd kick and scream too.

Edan denied Naron a hood, the young man's agony on display for all to see as a warning; the baron wanted no further treasonous acts in his army. Nor was Naron given a long rope. Apparently a short one was a harder, longer way to die. According to Vergel, Naron's body would be buried in salted earth with no memorial stone. Raimon Teale would have received the same if his body hadn't dissolved.

Cat had no idea hanging a man was so disturbing. She almost lost what little she had in her stomach and had to turn away at the protruding eyes and tongue, the horrid colour of his skin. Kelwyn didn't. He watched with stony features and dark, stormy eyes. So did Orrin, who'd finally joined them on the walk to the hill.

Rhone didn't want Cat's comfort, at least not right now. Kelwyn did and she'd held and comforted him in Lowren's tent most of the previous day. Lindren explained some people, Humans in particular, grieved in their own way and she should respect Rhone's desire to mourn alone. Her bondmate stood beside her during the hanging, saying not a word, then made his slow way back to their tent with the help of a crutch Arnir had fashioned for him. Cat let him go, an ache in her heart.

After the hanging, Lindren led his family back to his tent minus Orrin, who disappeared somewhere with Arufin. They sat around the campfire, though little was said, each deep in their thoughts.

Finally, Lindren picked up a stick and poked the fire. When the end caught, he let it burn, then blew it out. "Judging by Cainfir's reports," he said, "there should still be a fair sized army across the Barriers. I've talked with Rendir and we both feel Cainfir's and Firann's companies should join as one under Tarkin and do some scouting."

"Good idea," Arnir said. He turned to Cat. "Is there any way the dragons would help us?"

She shrugged. "I can ask. It's hard to say. They don't like being bothered, but they don't like vauroks either."

After a moment, she located them deep under the mountains, their words distant, yet understandable. Once again they were reticent and annoyed at the interruption. After a brief, tense conversation, Cat passed on their decision. "They're willing to let Elves into the mountains, but not Humans. They also won't let any of Udath Kor's creatures through the pass, though they won't touch any who remain on the northern plains." She wrinkled her nose in disgust. "They say they're not their problem unless they enter the mountains or the pass."

Lindren nodded, reluctantly. "That will have to do. Once Tarkin's company returns, we'll have a better idea. At least Markus shouldn't have to worry about attack from the north, which is good. He needs the time to adjust to his new role and recover from this disaster."

They fell back into silence until footsteps approached the camp. Taurin, his features as dark and stony as ever, led his three lieutenants towards them. A fresh cut ran in a ragged line down the right side of his face. His left arm rested in a sling. It seemed the healers hadn't had time to get to him, though Arnir had healed Lindren before he came to her tent.

Lindren stood, blocking Taurin's path to Cat, his expression grim. "You heard the news?"

"Yes. I watched the hanging from farther back. He deserved a worse death than that. I imagine we've already lost Tarine."

Lindren frowned a moment, then said, "I suppose you wouldn't have heard."

"Heard what." Taurin's cold, dark expression didn't change one bit.

"Tarine's pregnant. And...she's carrying two babies."

The news penetrated even Taurin's perpetual gloom. "*Two*?"

"Another in a long line of strange occurrences lately," Lindren said. "So I doubt very much she will allow herself to *fade.*"

When it looked like Taurin had no more to say on the subject, Shain asked, "How did your men fare?"

Taurin's dead eyes turned in his direction. "I lost seventy-eight of my hundred. The battle did not...go well. Some vauroks formed up a wall of shields. That's where most of my men died." A lump rose in Cat's throat. Taurin didn't say hello to her, he didn't even glance in her direction. "I hear Cat killed Kelwyn," he said, eyeing up Kelwyn. "But he came back to life?"

A very much alive Kelwyn sat next to Cat, holding her hand in a death grip, breathing, whole, yet still her heart lurched at the memory.

"It seems that way." Lindren didn't offer him a seat or a cup of the tea keeping warm by the fire.

Tension hung in the air as taut as a drawn bowstring, far more than usual between them and Cat wondered what had happened.

Taurin kept his gaze on Kelwyn. "Tell me."

After the tale was related again, much to Cat's agony, Taurin drew his dragon bone knife and held it in his hand like a treasure of incalculable value. "It must have been this. The power of the dragon defeated the power of the blue ball."

"Perhaps," Lindren said. "But we won't know for sure until the matter is investigated further."

Gedren shoved his way in between the cousins. "Do it. As we discussed. I can't take it anymore."

A flicker appeared in Taurin's dark eyes. He plunged the dagger into Gedren's chest so fast no one had a clue to his intention. Soundless, Gedren clutched at Taurin's jerkin, sinking to the ground. The camp erupted in cries of outrage. Arnir pushed his way through, his magic already lighting his hands.

Cat leapt to her feet. "Taurin! Why? He's your friend!"

The reply was made in a voice as monotone and dead as she'd ever heard it. "He wanted me to. We'd discussed the matter and this was what he decided. It will either heal him or kill him. Either way, he'll be free of the pain." With one yank, he pulled Arnir away from Gedren. "We have to know if this will heal us or not. Don't interfere."

"I can't just let him die!" Arnir freed himself and resumed his chant.

Blood seeped around the knife in Gedren's chest, bright red against the grey the world had become. The metallic tang of it stung Cat's nose. Blood. Too much blood.

Another of Taurin's lieutenants checked for a pulse. "He's dead."

Despite the horror of the situation, Cat couldn't take her eyes off Gedren. Neither could the others. Would he come back to life? Did the dragon bones have the power to resurrect the dead? To heal *qirand* as

503

Taurin seemed to believe?

Arnir crouched by Gedren, examining him. When he stood, his fists were clenched, his eyes dark. "He didn't have to die! Hasn't there been enough killing?"

Lindren gripped Taurin's arm. "You've gone too far! As your Elder..."

"You don't understand. There's no way in Arvanion's worlds that you could." Taurin removed Lindren's hand. "This was Gedren's decision. He was talking about *fading* anyway. If these daggers can cure the *qirand* state, then it was worth it."

"Nothing is worth taking a life," Lindren said. He turned his back on Taurin and stared at the body. "Kelwyn was struck by a black spell. *Qirand* are not. Why would you think it would work the same way?"

Taurin shrugged. "Who knows what dragon magic is capable of? These daggers are strange." He leaned over Gedren's body. "It might still work. Kelwyn, do you have any idea how long it took?"

"No." The icy tone in Kelwyn's voice spoke volumes about his stand on the situation.

"Then we'll take him back to our camp and keep watch." Taurin signaled for the other two lieutenants to pick up the body, the dagger still deep in Gedren's chest. He seemed so matter-of-fact about the horrible incident.

Cat couldn't figure out how Taurin could just kill someone like that. Kelwyn had once told her the *qirand* was mean, though she'd never really believed it. What she did know was that she wasn't, nor ever could be, a *qira*, though with her truth-seeing she could see his endless pain and suffering. How horrible it must be to live like that day after day. At least Taurin knew some relief when he was with her, though why she didn't know. Gedren didn't have that advantage. If Gedren was in that much pain, why hadn't he *faded* long ago?

Lindren gripped his cousin's arm. "I don't understand you. Nor do I understand what you've become. You're unlike any *qirand* I've ever known."

"You have my father to thank for that."

"How can I trust you now? How can I let you in Silverwood?"

504

Once again Cat's heart thumped. She reached out to Taurin. Kelwyn held her back.

"I will come to pay my respects to Tarine. Don't worry, I have no intention of hurting her or anyone else. After that, I doubt I'll be in Silverwood much." Now Taurin did glance in Cat's direction, briefly. "Not for a very long time. Maybe not ever." He spun on his heel and strode away.

Cat shook off Kelwyn's grip and ran after Taurin, pulling him to a stop. Terror filled her heart. Would he ask one of the *qirand* to try the dagger on him? Was he finally ready to join Katrin?

On her tiptoes, she kissed his cheek, then whispered in his ear. "I don't understand how you could just kill Gedren like that, but I think I understand why. I...I still love you. Please. Wait for me?"

A flicker of light glimmered in Taurin's black eyes, a brief moment of life, there, then gone like the sparkle of sunlight on dark waters. After a moment, he gave a little nod and walked away. The sky chose that moment to open up and pour.

ം • ക

Cat spent the rest of the day in Lindren's tent with Kelwyn hiding from the rain and leaving Rhone to grieve in peace. Just past dusk, after the rain stopped, she said goodnight to Kelwyn and entered her tent. Rhone had been asleep when she'd returned the night before and had said little at breakfast.

He now lay on the bed, his foot propped up on a folded blanket. "There you are," he said, sitting up. He still had his clothes on. "I thought you'd forgotten about me."

Cat sat beside him, then kissed his cheek. "I thought you wanted to be left alone."

"I did, but not all day."

The sharp tone in his voice stung. Despite that, she wanted to hit him. "How am I supposed to know when you do and don't want to be left alone?"

He sighed and pulled her into his arms. "I'm sorry, heart of my love. I've been behaving badly. Mother would have my hide if she knew. A result of four years alone, I suppose." He kissed the top of her head. "Gavan's death hit me hard. It drove home just how much I still thought of him as my brother. I care about all of them. Even Iyan, to a certain extent. I suppose. Nonetheless, I've come to a decision. If Lindren will let me, I'd like to live with you in Silverwood."

Cat sat up. "Are you sure? Your family will miss you."

"Most of them, I guess," Rhone said, with a wry smile. "Fact is, I always seem to be arguing with either Mother or Iyan, or both. And we're not so far away that we can't visit from time to time. I think living in Silverwood would be more…peaceful."

More boring. However, Cat could easily envision life at Arden Keep with Iyan hounding her every step and Ellica rebuking her for one thing or another. Perhaps living in Silverwood would be best. "I'm sure Lindren wouldn't mind in the least. He likes you."

Rhone chuckled and pulled her close once more. "I like him too. And the rest of your family. Even Robbi."

After the loss of so many, both family and friends, Cat was surprised she could smile. "Robbi will grow up in another fifteen years."

"I think I can wait. Though there is one thing." He paused for a moment, as if measuring the words he'd say. "Is there any chance of us living in a proper house? With a fireplace? Or two?"

"For you…" She kissed him. "…I will live in a house. Lindren might even build it for us."

"That would be nice."

"Did you get your dinner?"

"Yes, I did. As a matter of fact, Arufin brought it. I like him too. He possesses a peculiar sense of humour."

That was an understatement.

Rhone lifted her chin, his wonderful sea-green eyes sparkling with a familiar fire. "My ankle still hurts. Would you mind taking the top position tonight?"

Cat's smile grew. "I'd love to." With a gentle push, she persuaded Rhone to lie back on the pallet. This was the kind of comfort they both needed.

Just south of the battlefield lay a flat heath covered in hardy grasses, small shrubs and heather. Not good for much. Markus Kerend donated the land for a cemetery with plans for a memorial, though he took his father's body home to the keep to lie in the family crypt beside his beloved Rhayna.

He invited the Elves to bury their fallen. They declined, preferring instead to take their dead family and friends home. The journey would take only a week for them and with spells put on the bodies there was no fear of decomposition. Rendir and Sandrin took the bulk of the Elven army and headed for Silverwood the day after Naron's hanging. Taurin left as well.

Lindren and his family attended the burial of Rhone's brother, Gavan. Iyan, unusually quiet and reserved, spoke not a word to Cat, though he and Rhone went off together for a time afterwards. Later, Rhone told Cat it was first time he could remember Iyan speaking to him in a civil manner and was surprised to find he enjoyed the reminiscence about Gavan.

Vergel and his army left five days after the battle, one since the burials were completed. Brade rode with him, after saying goodbye to Cat, on his way to his wedding and his new dukedom.

Lindren waited until he had word from Tarkin as to the numbers of creatures left on the other side of the Barriers. Either more of them had vanished into the abyss than they'd guessed or the remainder had left through the temporary portals that had caused Lindren so many problems.

Tarkin and his warriors found the remains of campfires, battered tents, old food, open latrines and a partially built permanent portal which they destroyed. The new captain also reported hundreds of enemy bodies littering the mountain pass. The dragons had kept to their word.

Reassured he could leave Kerend in Markus' hands, Lindren set out with his family and Tarkin's company, taking Lowren's body with them. He'd keep a closer eye on the barony as well as Miklin, now that both had new, young barons. When they arrived at the road leading to

Arden Keep, Lindren called a halt.

"Are you sure this is what you want?" he asked Rhone.

"It is. I've thought about it since before the battle and, if you don't mind having me, I'd like to live with Cat in Silverwood."

"I must admit, I prefer having my daughter near me. Of course you're welcome. How long do you think you'll be in Arden?"

Rhone glanced in the direction of the keep, still over a day away. "By the time I get there, visit and come back here...a week."

Lindren nodded. "Then I'll have some of my warriors meet you here in one week. I don't want Cat travelling without protection, not when Udath Kor is after her."

"I understand and agree." Rhone held his hand out. Lindren took it, then gave Cat a hug.

Once she'd said goodbye to Kelwyn, Arnir, Shain, Orrin and Arufin, Lindren guided his Hrulka to the head of the group. He stopped and turned in the saddle. "Don't worry about a place to live. With help, I'll have a new house for you two by winter."

A warmth spread through Rhone, a feeling he rarely felt. He decided he'd have to get used to it. "Thank you. I...we....appreciate it."

After turning Shuar's head towards Arden, Rhone kissed Cat's cheek. With Krir gone and all the other mounts carrying Elves, alive or dead, she had to share Rhone's horse. The loss of her Hrulka, Lowren, the other Elves she knew and Aris had hit her hard. She still tended to cry in the night. Rhone held her, stroking her back, until she settled. He had a feeling it would be a while before the tears stopped completely.

The ride to Arden was an enjoyable one, quiet with just the two of them. They spent the night in an inn, something Cat had never done and, despite her grief, her spirits picked up. Their arrival at the Keep was met with a mixture of tears and joy. Even Ellica was subdued and made not one rude comment to Cat. The day after they arrived, she invited them to her room. An invitation, not a demand, which surprised Rhone.

After a pleasant cup of tea accompanied by biscuits and preserves, Ellica smoothed her dress, then her hair. "Although I'm still not happy about this marriage, I understand that you are in love. I won't cause any more trouble. And...I give you my blessing."

It was as close to an apology Rhone had ever heard from his mother. He hadn't expected even that much.

Ellica stared at her hands a moment before continuing. "After thinking about everything that happened before you left for Kerend, I realized I wasn't happy in my marriage to Arden because I didn't love him. I only married him to please my father. And it was a rise in station for me." Her shoulders sagged. "Not much of a reason, is it."

Rhone agreed, though he said nothing. Cat just sat in her chair, wearing a puzzled expression.

"I also realized that I wanted you to have children because I needed to see your father in them," Ellica continued. "Also not much of a reason, I suppose. When I thought you dead, that dream was gone. Seeing you alive...it was all I could think about. I still wish you could have children, but..." She stood and turned to Cat, squaring her shoulders, holding her head high once more. "I would like to formally welcome you to the family, Lady Cat. And though I'm sorry you won't be living with us, I understand. I look forward to your visits, as a mother-in-law should."

Cat rose from her chair and gave Ellica a hug, surprising her. She returned it, with an awkward pat to Cat's back. Perhaps visiting wouldn't be quite as onerous as Rhone thought.

He also gave her a hug, then kissed her cheek. "Thank you, Mother." Once they'd retaken their seats, he said, "Would you tell me about my father?"

Ellica nodded. "I've kept him to myself far too long. You deserve to know." She poured another cup of tea for each of them. "His name was Kylun, and, yes, he was a commoner, but that didn't matter to me. Not then. The barony was still struggling and when Arden wasn't too sick, his duties frequently required his absence. Kylun was one of the keep guards. He was always around, helping with one thing or another. It just seemed...natural that we found each other. He was a very special man, tall and handsome. So much like you it hurts. I could see him in your face before you left for Tezerain, but now... Just look at you." She smiled, genuine, warm, lost in her memories.

"Is he still alive?" Rhone hoped so, he'd like to meet him.

A shadow crossed Ellica's face. "No. After I told Arden of my pregnancy, he sent Kylun on patrol. He never returned. I...I don't think Arden had him killed. I confronted him when I found out. He said he only wanted Kylun out of the keep and I believed him. I still do." A wistful expression replaced the shadow. "Kylun never knew I was pregnant. I think he would have loved you, though. He had a kind and generous heart. I also think if he'd raised you, you'd have his disposition as well as his looks."

Rhone wished that as well. A loving father would have made his life completely different. He reached over and clasped Cat's hand. They couldn't have children. He'd made his decision and didn't regret it, though he wondered, just for a moment, what kind of father he would have made. He'd told the truth when he said he didn't like children. Perhaps his own might have been different. Ellica talked about Kylun until a servant arrived to announce dinner. Rhone couldn't remember spending a more pleasant afternoon with his mother.

Before leaving Arden, Rhone took Cat to the family burial ground to visit the memorial set up for Gavan. Though his body lay in Kerend, the monument offered the family a remembrance of him. Rhone ignored Arden's grave and Cat didn't ask about it. On their way back, he stopped at a simpler cemetery and took her to Varak's resting place. She listened patiently as he told her all about him. He'd never talked to anyone about his childhood friend; it seemed right to tell her.

After a short search, they found Kylun's headstone in the same cemetery as Varak. The stone, fancier than the others around it, bore an engraved bouquet of flowers. Rhone suspected it was Ellica's doing and wished he could reach out to the man lying under it.

He took Cat's hand, another decision made. "When my time comes, Cat, I want to be buried here, beside my father. Perhaps in death I can get to know the man I never knew in life."

Though she said nothing, moisture brightened her eyes. His death would be the last thing she'd want to think about. Rhone pulled her close and wondered just how long he'd have to spend with her. However many years it was, it wouldn't be long enough.

510

Chapter Forty-Three

Tiny green shoots sprung from bushes littering the scrubland east of Silverwood. Five Hrulka galloped along a well-worn path through country too cold and too wind-blown to grow the abundant grains farther south, yet even here spring arrived.

Rhone led the group, Cat sitting in front of him, holding onto Shuar's mane. Four of Lindren's Elves followed, ones Rhone had never met. Like most of the others he knew in the enclave, they were friendly and good-natured. The trip from Arden had been swift and companionable, the goodbyes long and tearful.

The wagon carrying their wedding gifts from Tezerain travelled a few days behind. They'd opened them at the keep, to the delight of the women. The nobles had given them an odd assortment of trinkets, vases, crystal, dishes and things Rhone could see little use for. Other than the crystal, dishes and a vase or two, Cat felt the same way.

As they drew closer, Rhone picked out individual trees—oak, alder, and dacia. They slowed to a canter, then a walk. He shifted Shuar's reins to one hand, the other encircled Cat. He didn't guide the big horse, Shuar knew where to go. With every step, Cat's body grew stiffer.

"What's the matter, love?" Rhone asked.

"I want to go home, but I don't. It will be different, without..."

Rhone gave her a squeeze. "Lowren was very important to you, wasn't he."

Cat nodded. "He was like another father. My parents were away a lot and they left me with Lowren and Tarine. He helped raise me as much as they did. He was important to the whole enclave. When odd jobs needed doing, Lowren did them. He watched over the enclave when Lindren was away and organized the training of the young ones. I don't know what Lindren will do without him."

"I imagine Darsha will do some of it." Rhone intended to help out as well.

"He will. Darsha's good that way, but…it still won't be the same."
Rhone squeezed her tighter. "It never is."

Lindren met them at the forest edge along with Darsha and Robbi.
Even Lindren's youngest had trouble finding a smile. It was a solemn ride
back to the house.

Once Robbie left for the pastures with Shuar, Cat put her hand on
Lindren's arm. "Is he…did you…"

"Yes," Lindren said. "We buried him in a meadow near the gates,
the sunny one." With a nod, he indicated the house. "Tarine is inside.
Rhianna made her stay in your room until Kelwyn and Orrin arrived. She
still spends the days here. Rhianna won't have it any other way, not until
the babies are born."

Hero bounded into the clearing from the bushes near the house.
Cat scooped the kitten up, cuddling him while he rubbed his face against
hers. "I've missed you," she said, finally finding a smile. "Look how
you've grown."

A month and a half had passed since they were last in the enclave,
four months since the rescue from Crescent Island. A great deal had
happened in that time. Rhone looked forward to a little peace and quiet in
the Elven forest.

He took Cat's hand and they entered the house. Rhianna gave
both of them a kiss and hug, then vanished into the kitchen. Tarine sat in
a chair by the fire. The change in her was remarkable. When they'd left,
Tarine had been a smiling, intelligent, delightful woman with a
wonderful sense of humour and a deep understanding of people, even
Humans. Rhone's heart gave a jerk to see her now.

No smile graced her pretty face. Her shining black hair had turned
dull. She sat with her hands clasped tight over her swollen belly as if to
protect the tiny lives within. Every muscle screamed grief and pain,
though it was her eyes that disturbed Rhone the most. Deep blue, like
Arufin's, they had sparkled with life; now they resembled the cold icy
waters of a half frozen lake devoid of life. Though not black like Taurin's,
they were just as dead. Rhone shivered, glad, for once, that he wasn't an
Elf. He wouldn't ever have to suffer like that.

Cat put Hero down, knelt beside Tarine and took her hand,

speaking to her quietly in Elven. The only response she received was a tightening of Tarine's grip. Cat gave her a kiss on the forehead, her eyes moist, then rose to slide her arms around Rhone. He held her while Rhianna placed food and dishes on the table. Robbi arrived home, bringing Kelwyn and Orrin with him and quietly gave her a hand.

Tarine didn't join them for the meal, she just stared at the fireplace. Lindren kept the conversation up by asking Cat to describe her various experiences in both Arden and the mountains, with Rhone and Kelwyn filling in.

When she finished telling her tale, Cat said, "I don't understand why the prophecy was wrong."

"Wrong in what way?" Lindren asked.

"Rhone fell, literally. Kelwyn fell to that blue ball, but I didn't fall at all."

"I believe you did," Rhianna put in. At Cat's questioning look, she said, "From what Kelwyn and Rhone have said, it sounds to me like you fell into despair after you thought they'd died."

Cat's head jerked back and Rhone realized she was right. When he'd found her, Cat had been lost in a deep depression that only truly eased after Kelwyn returned.

Rhianna smiled and reached across the table for Cat's hand. "I'm very proud of you."

"Why?" Cat's head tilted slightly to one side and a brow dipped down in a frown.

"You lost the two most important people in your life. You grieved, which is understandable, but you didn't fall back into that place you went after your people died. You've proved to us that you're past that stage. You were able to push on and try to find a way to free the dragons." Rhianna's smile grew. "Cat, you used to say you were nothing but a nuisance and a bother. Not only did you free two trapped dragons, thereby saving thousands of lives, you proved you are a capable, intelligent and highly skilled grownup Tiranen."

Cat's eyes widened. Her mouth opened, though she said nothing.

Rhone put his arm around her and kissed her cheek. "I'm proud of you too."

"As we all are," Lindren said.

Despite the grief, the loss and the poor Elven woman sitting nearby, everyone at the table smiled and offered their congratulations.

"And that's not all," Rhianna said. "Rhone, you have grown as well."

"Me? How?"

"I hope you don't mind, Kelwyn told me you don't like caves. Yet, after you fell, you faced those little creatures and despite your injury made your way through the tunnels with nothing but the light from your sword."

Rhone realized the truth of Rhianna's words. Were all Elven women so insightful? There was more, however. He'd also come to fully accept Cat and Kelwyn's relationship as well as the fact that Cat's capacity for love was immense and that she had loved, and would love, others besides him. Rhone had also opened his eyes to the fact that there was far more in this old world than he'd thought possible. The prophecy and the dragons proved it.

"As far as Kelwyn's experience is concerned," Rhianna continued. "I believe there is more to be learned. What happened is nothing less than a miracle. That was a remarkable thing you did, Cat. Another sign of your maturity. It must have been extremely difficult. You fought past your need for Kelwyn and did right by taking his pain away. I don't know if dragon magic had anything to do with it or not, but there's one thing I can tell you. It's not over yet. You have more dragons to find, more adventures to experience. You may think you are a small and weak Tiranen. I feel you will have an impact on the future of all Arvanion's worlds."

Heavy words that reeked of another prophecy. Silence circled the table as everyone absorbed the import of what she said. Rhone felt only a deep sadness. He doubted he'd be a part of much of it. These people lived remarkably long lives. Whatever it was that Cat was destined to do, it would be done without him.

"There's just one problem," Kelwyn said.

Lindren shifted his gaze from Rhianna to him. "What's that?"

"Cat and I promised we'd never grow up."

Somewhere beyond the sadness, Lindren's family found their humour. It started small, quickly building into tension-relieving laughter. Rhone joined in, then took a mental step back. This was his family now. His and Cat's and, though he doubted he'd be a part of Cat's special destiny, he looked forward to a life no Human had ever lived, one based in a magical forest with an extraordinary wife.

ॐ · ଓ

As the summer days passed, Cat and Rhone's house took shape. Lindren tore down her shelter to make room for the shirren tree and the home that would be grown from it. A little smaller than the Elder's house, it included a kitchen, washing room, pantry, common room with a large fireplace and one bedroom—with a fireplace, at Rhone's request. Also added was a storage room, mostly to hold many of the gifts they'd received from both Tezerain and their Celebration of Life.

Some of the things they'd received from the Kitring-Tor nobles had no purpose as far as Cat was concerned; neither did she want to part with them and Rhone just shook his head. The gifts from the Elves, however, were needed. They gave things like towels, bedding, dishes and other items required for a home.

Lindren found the task of building the house relaxing and a good way to work through his grief over Lowren's death. It also gave him time to think about the events of those days, particularly Kelwyn's death. As he predicted, Gedren didn't come back to life. After hours of thought and debate with some of the other Elders, he decided Taurin was right in one thing, it had to be the magic imbued by Black Wing in the dragon bones and it only affected black magic. That thought confused him, however. Black Wing had been a fire dragon, not spirit. Healing wasn't his ability. Why would the bones of a fire dragon heal Kelwyn? By mid-summer, he still had no answer.

Another item the Elders agreed upon was the possibility of others carrying black spells like Lindren's. Every healer in each enclave made it a priority to check for evidence of a black spell.

Lindren also asked if anyone had heard of a small people, the

515

Darani, who lived under mountains. Each of the Elders stared at him as if he'd gone mad, the same reaction Lindren received when he told them of Kelwyn's death and resurrection. After a short discussion, it was decided to leave the Darani alone. Cat said their lights were blue and that was good enough for the Elders, though they'd warn anyone searching for crèches in mountain ranges to watch for them.

Three other plant mages worked with Lindren on the new house so it would be ready when the cold weather came. Rhone assisted where he could, performing tasks requiring no magic. Arden, born a commoner, had insisted all his sons help out in the barony and not just on the administration side. Rhone knew the basics of carpentry and how to use tools. Though not as experienced as Lowren, Rhone's abilities came in handy in other parts of the enclave. With Cat's and Robbi's help, by summer he'd picked up much of the Elven language.

One hot day in late summer, while Lindren worked with Rhone and the other mages on forming the bedroom, Cat ran breathless into the clearing.

"Tarine's in labour!" She ran out of the clearing just as fast.

Lindren had to chuckle. Cat loved babies and it would never change. The other mages waved him away and he and Rhone followed her, though a fair distance behind and at a much slower pace. These things rarely happened quickly. They arrived at Tarine's house to find most of the family there, including Arnir with his soulmate and son.

Tarine had become a little more communicative over the past two months, unusual since she hadn't been *qira* for long. Lindren didn't question it; it was better than the complete silence he'd expected. She'd asked for Arnir to assist with the birthing, just as he had with both Orrin and Kelwyn. Lindren stayed in the common room with the rest of the males, Rhone included, while the females busied themselves making tea, warming water and taking turns comforting Tarine.

The babies arrived with little trouble. The first to see the world was a boy, much to Cat's disappointment, then he was followed fifteen minutes later by his sister.

Cat whooped in delight. "It's about time! Finally! The curse has been lifted."

"Curse?" Rhone asked, casting her a skeptical eye.

"This family must be cursed. No girls have been born in it since I don't know when."

Lindren chuckled. "Come to think of it, I don't know the last time there was a girl in the family. My father had one brother and his father had two."

Rhianna finished cleaning and wrapping the little girl, then placed her in Cat's arms. "You can hold her for a few minutes while Tarine feeds Joryan."

Cat rocked the tiny babe, her pretty face glowing. "Joryan. I like that name. What did she call this little one?"

"Awyn. It's a very old Elven name." Rhianna ran her slender finger down the babe's face. She'd wanted a daughter. Lindren wished he could have given her one. Fate decided otherwise. They had Cat now, had watched her grow and considered her one of their own.

When both babies had fed, Tarine fell asleep, allowing the entire family to take turns holding the twins, even Rhone, though Cat had to show him how. Over the next while, these two tiny people, unique among Elves, would draw much attention. For now, though, they had Joryan and Awyn all to themselves.

ₔ • ₓ

That fall, after Cat and Rhone settled into their new home, Lindren packed his saddlebags with two sets of clothes, one used, one new, along with more food than he could eat in two weeks. With hope, and trepidation, in his heart, he set out for the Old Forest. He'd told the family he had some business in the baronies and he did intend to visit Miklin and Kerend. Only Rhianna knew the whole truth.

His soulmate's words, the evening of Cat's homecoming, struck a sour note within him. Cat had found the bravery to release Kelwyn from his pain. Lindren hadn't found himself capable of dealing with a similar situation. Dairon lived in just as much agony, though it was mental as well as physical.

For centuries, Lindren had hidden his elder brother from the

517

world, locked behind a shield in the southern part of the Old Forest. Though Dairon didn't face certain death like Kelwyn, the torture had to be as great simply because it had lasted so long.

After checking up on the new barons of Miklin and Kerend, Lindren followed the old trail down the middle of the autumn forest, dragonets swirling in a colourful array around him, though they didn't land on him or Auri the way they had with Cat. He preferred it that way.

Lindren passed through the gloom of the ancient trees where Cat thought she'd seen one try to grab her and he had to chuckle at the memory.

His daughter had a remarkably overactive imagination. Perhaps it's just what she needed to deal with life. It helped her believe the prophecy and see it through to its eventful end. Other prophecies promised more for her in the future and he prayed to Arvanion it all worked out well. He came to the fork where Cat had ridden off on her own and spotted a Human with vauroks. Lindren realized that the Human she'd seen had been Raimon Teale, the traitor. He wished now that he'd listened to her.

The trip through the Old Forest with Cat, Kelwyn, Darsha and Shain had taken four days, mostly because Lindren wanted Cat and Kelwyn to absorb everything the forest had to offer in winter, as well as learn its dangers. Lindren rode it in two and a half. He made a quick stop at the bridge over the Running River to make sure the shirren tree constructing it remained healthy, then travelled the final miles to the end of the wide path.

Lindren dismounted from Auri, gave him a reassuring pat and removed the saddle bags. Brushing aside hanging branches, he followed the debris-littered, narrow trail that led to a meadow. The shimmering shield disappeared left and right into the trees, surrounding a ten acre circle Dairon had called home for centuries, since shortly after he'd found his way out of Udath Kor's prison.

Udath Kor had ruined Dairon, both physically and mentally. The entire left side of his body was hideously malformed, though it was his mind that bothered Lindren the most. The kind, gentle, fun-loving brother he'd known had vanished, replaced by a tormented demon who insulted and threatened those who sought to help him.

The Elders wanted to put him out of his misery, send his tortured soul back to Arvanion. Lindren couldn't accept their solution and locked Dairon behind the shield, as much to protect him as those he might hurt, while he searched for a cure. With the aid of a weather mage, Lindren constructed the enclosure so it would always be warm enough to sustain the trees and plants he'd altered, ensuring Dairon would have food and shelter.

After setting the saddlebags on the ground, Lindren formed a hole in the shield as he always did. Normally, however, it was much smaller, enough to pass through the bag of clothing, breads and cheeses he brought every three months. This time, he made the hole large enough to allow him entry, the first time he'd done so in years. He brought in the saddlebags, closed the hole, then sat on the ground, waiting for Dairon's arrival.

He didn't wait long. A rustling, and Dairon's strange breathing, announced his brother's presence. He hadn't changed, though Lindren hadn't expected it, not after this long a time. The left side of his brother's face sagged, his once pale features twisted into distorted, dark leather-like skin. His mouth bent up in a repulsive grin, showing most of the teeth on that side. He walked with a limp, the result of a deformed leg. Dairon's right side showed what he had been, handsome, well-formed. Udath Kor had turned the other half into a thing that looked like it had crawled from the grave.

Dairon stopped halfway across the meadow, his left arm hanging useless, his right hand pointing at Lindren. "You're early."

"A little bit." Lindren rose to meet him, standing a pace away.

"To what do I owe the honour of your early presence?" Dairon tried to bow, but his ruined body forbade it. "Has Rhianna whelped yet another son?"

"No."

A moment passed. Dairon sucked an audible breath through his malformed mouth. "Did you bring that pretty Little Cat with you?"

"No." Lindren stepped closer.

"Why not? I think I'd prefer her company over yours. I'd have much more fun with her. Have you tried her out yet? But no, you can't, can you. You have Rhianna. You have a soulmate. Something I was denied. Give me Little Cat and maybe I might feel better."

This is not the way he is. This is only the result of Udath Kor's tampering. Lindren took a deep breath and pulled his dragon bone dagger, a gift from Cat. A very special dagger, if Lindren's hopes proved true.

He gazed into Dairon's single good eye, the other dead, blind and dark as the abyss the dragons had formed. Pus oozed from a sore on his left cheek, one of many on that side of his body. Always the left. The right was perfect, a horrid reminder of what Dairon once was.

His brother's eye travelled down to the dagger in Lindren's hand, then up to his face. "Do I dare hope?"

Cat had the courage; Lindren had to dig deep to find his. Lowren was gone. Could he live without Dairon as well? He took another step closer, the stink of Dairon's sores and filthy clothes an offense to Lindren's nose. "It ends here, now, one way or the other."

A quick thrust up, aimed sure and true, and the dagger found Dairon's heart. The mutilated Elf gasped, poised for a moment as if nothing had happened. Lindren let the dagger go, caught Dairon as he finally collapsed.

The breath came harder now through the distorted mouth. "Thank you. Lindren. My brother." The eyes closed. The tormented heart stopped beating.

"Arvanion. Please. Hear me." Lindren took in a shuddering breath. "By all you hold dear, please, bring him back to me."

Nothing happened. Tears washed Lindren's face. He cried his agony to the sky...until a blue glow penetrated his blurred vision. Intense sapphire radiated from the dragon bone hilt of the dagger, spread to Dairon's body in a powerful surge. Slowly, almost imperceptible, the damage to Dairon's face retreated. A sore healed over. The skin smoothed. His lips re-formed, as did the mass of flesh that had been his ear. Faster now, the power of the dagger defeated the black spell that had destroyed Dairon's life. His arm healed, his leg. The patches of dry, brittle hair on the left side of his head thickened, smoothed, shone with health.

Lindren's tears were forgotten as he stared at the restoration of his brother. The dagger remained in Dairon's chest, red blood surrounding it. He dared not touch it; he had to leave the dragon magic to complete its work, just as it had with Kelwyn. Then Dairon was whole again, lying on the leaf-strewn grass as if nothing had ever happened, except for the dagger, the blood and the fact he still didn't breathe.

Hope rose in Lindren's breast, and fell as long moments passed with no change. Then, so slow it was barely noticeable, the dagger shifted. It rose a quarter of an inch out of Dairon's chest, then another, pushed out by some force of power from the dragon bone. Cautious, Lindren sent a tendril of his magic to the dagger. A warm, comforting power greeted him, just as it had on Morata.

The dagger tilted and fell to the ground. The last of Dairon's chest wound, visible through his tattered shirt, closed, leaving not a scar. Lindren held his breath until it burned in his lungs. When he had to let it go, he touched a finger to the main vein in Dairon's neck. It pulsed, ever so slight.

With a gasp, Dairon sucked in a breath, a normal sound, then sat up, gulping in air. Lindren clutched him to his breast, his face raised to the sky. "Thank you," he whispered, tears falling from his eyes once more. Tears of joy.

When Dairon caught his breath, he scrambled to his feet, staring around him as if he'd never seen the meadow. "What happened? How did we get here?" He held a hand to his head. "I feel like I've been living a very long, very terrible nightmare. I...I remember a white light."

"It's over now," Lindren said as he stood. "I'll explain on the way home. I have clean clothes for you. And food."

With a joy in his heart he hadn't felt since before Lowren died, Lindren collapsed the shield and led Dairon to Auri, and home.

Epilogue

Two little babies slept peacefully, dreaming the dreams of the innocent. Tarine touched a finger to Awyn's cheek. Her daughter. She loved her as much as she was capable these days, as she loved Joryan, Awyn's twin brother. Yet that love was muted, reduced to a mother's need to take care of her children, to see them grown. They'd never know their father, as Orrin and Kelwyn had, never know his gentle teaching, his wonderful smile. People said she had amazing insights into others; few knew, however, that she'd learned much of it from Lowren. Pain and anguish, far past what she could have imagined, darkened her vision.

Tarine choked back a sob, struggling to regain some measure of control over her shattered emotions. Kissing each perfect brow, she centered her magic, whispering words of power. She placed a small spell on each child, just enough to ensure they slept for the next few hours.

On silent feet, Tarine slipped out of her room, grabbed her cloak from the hook by the door and crept out of the house, determined not to wake the two older sons sleeping nearby. Snow fell in soft, puffy flakes from a dark sky, adding to that already there. Her feet left almost no mark as she trod the path to the west, the same path she'd walked with Lowren on many occasions. All their children's names had been chosen on this path.

Tarine's knees buckled. She had to lean on a tree to keep upright. Her life consisted of pain and an aching lonliness, even in her dreams. She wanted to die, to join Lowren on the Other Side. Tarine had to stay, had to see the babies grown. When she recovered, she carried on.

Orrin and Kelwyn had given up their positions in their companies, staying at home to help her with the twins. She loved them too. *I know I do.* That love was also muted. She should be grateful, a warm feeling should come to her when she thought of them. All she felt was the wretched, soul-searing agony of loneliness and loss.

Lowren! I need you! Tarine held her empty arms out to the love that would never fill them again. Sobs, unbidden, racked her body as she stumbled down the path. When she reached her destination, she collapsed.

Strong arms lifted her up, carried her to a log near a fire. Rough, scarred hands forced something into hers, wrapped her fingers around it.

"Feel it, Tarine. Feel the wood, the pattern of the grain under your skin. Feel its power. Picture it in your mind. Raise the bow, nock an arrow. Raise it, Tarine." On and on the cold, dead voice spoke, pushing images into her head. "See the vaurok. It's grinning at you, mocking. Aim for it. You want to kill it, Tarine. You want to take your revenge."

Other words came to her, as they had come earlier that day. A single true, coherent, thought. "It wasn't a vaurok who killed...him." Her breath caught in her throat.

"Stay with me, Tarine. Feel the wood." He ran her hands over the bow, pushing with his words, shoving his way into her disjointed thoughts. "Concentrate on it."

Gradually, her vision returned. The bow came into focus. She had no idea where it had come from, she'd never seen it before he'd come to her. She looked up into dead, dark eyes. Though a different colour, her eyes were the same now.

"Good girl, Tarine. I knew you could do it," Taurin said. "I'm proud of you. This is the first night you've made it here on your own."

Here. A clearing south of the gates. Not the one sheltering Lowren. Not that one. She'd met Taurin here many times since the babies were born.

Taurin kept her hands on the bow, continued rubbing them over the wood. "The man responsible for your loss was coerced by a sorcerer named Atax Daemonica, trained by Udath Kor. Somehow he broke away. I've never heard of such a thing. He wanders the worlds now, doing only Arvanion knows what."

"Did you find him?" Her voice sounded just as cold and dead as his, even to her ears.

"No, but I will not stop searching." Taurin's hands shifted hers around the bow. "Udath Kor trained him. The vauroks serve Udath Kor. Feel the wood. See the vaurok. Aim. You want to kill the vaurok. You

523

need to kill it to exact your revenge."

Taurin's voice droned on, penetrating Tarine's grief. One day, when the twins were grown, fifty-five years from now, she'd find this Atax. She'd have her revenge.

ဆာ • ଔ

Fine spring rain misted the cloudy windows of the old keep. It sat on a rocky outcrop in the middle of a lake. Surrounded by a thick forest of pine, beech, alder, poplar and fir, the lake filled a good portion of a valley only two days away from the Elven enclave of Greenwood on the world of Cathras.

Atax Daemonica sipped his rich, red wine and fingered the small boxes containing the gifts he'd prepared for his new followers, completely unconcerned about his lair's proximity to the enclave. He performed little in the way of magic here, kept an extremely low profile. The Elves hadn't caught him even after almost a hundred years. Atax planned for it to stay that way. There were other places he used for developing his spells, but this place, this old Human holding, held a special interest for him.

Once known as Watercrest Keep, this was where he'd been born two hundred and thirteen years ago. He should have been its master when his father died, if not for a usurper cousin who'd killed the keep's lord and lady, and forced a young Atax to flee. No matter. Revenge was sought, and found, though it took one hundred and eighteen years to accomplish and Atax's conversion to Balphegor. Long dead, the cousin's descendents still resided in chains in the dungeon, next to the cousin's exhumed body, while Atax's parents rested in an elaborate mausoleum built into a small hill near the keep. All was now as it should be.

"A toast, to Master Atax." Kalda lifted his glass to Atax, who sat at the head of a long oak table in the main hall of the keep, the remains of a sumptuous meal before them.

The rest of the little troop clinked glasses, returning the toast. Only five, for now.

Atax smiled, like a father to his children. "Thank you one and all.

I'm extremely pleased with how quickly you have adapted to life here at Watercrest. Though the terrain is different from what you knew in Kitring-Tor, the true difficulty lay in leaving your families to follow, and fight for, the truth. As a reward, I have a gift for each of you."

Smiles greeted his words. Atax rose from his high-backed chair and distributed the gifts. The men opened them, holding up the newly made amulets. Blood gold shone with a reddish tinge in the candlelight. A bat-like face, conceived in hell, grinned back at them, complete with horns and pointed teeth; a demon from the second hell, one bound to each amulet. The men didn't need to know, however.

"My master," Kalda said, with fear in his eyes. "This...gift...it smacks of evil."

Mutters and murmured oaths showed the others' agreement.

Atax resumed his seat, taking another sip of wine before answering. "Not evil, gentlemen. Just as true evil can be disguised as good, good can also bear a less than appetizing countenance. These amulets are meant to protect you from evil. The face is gruesome, true, but it's purpose is to frighten evil away. Wear them and trust me, no harm will befall you.

"You've followed me here, to my home." Atax spread his arms to indicate the keep. "Have I not kept my promises? Have you not slept in comfortable beds? Bedded beautiful women? Eaten your fill of food so fine your lord couldn't even imagine? Do you not wear luxurious clothes? Possess the finest armour imaginable? I have opened my keep and my trust to you. I hold no evil in my heart. Believe in me, my friends, and you will go far."

A moment, then another, passed. With guilty glances at each other, and Atax, Kalda and the others donned the amulets.

Perfect. Atax set his glass down. "Just wearing them is not sufficient. The amulet must touch your skin."

Each man unbuttoned his fine silk shirt and let the amulet fall to his breast. The power hidden in the blood gold surged, melding skin to metal. Each man hissed in surprise and jumped to his feet.

"It's cold!" Kalda tried to pull the amulet away from him. "It...it's stuck!" Once again, fear whitened his eyes.

So entertaining to watch. "Don't panic, my friends, that is as it should be," Atax said. "The amulet needs to be a part of you or the magic will not work. You can't take it off, I'm afraid, and I do apologize for that, but it will protect you for the rest of your lives." What they actually did was allow Atax to know exactly where each man was at any given moment. An adjustment to the original design, one of his own devising, would allow more. "This is also an aid in our fight. I will teach you words of magic that, when spoken, will allow me to see what you see, hear what you hear and let us speak, though we are miles apart. That way, I will always be with you, the better to offer you my aid and protection." The better to keep an eye on exactly what they did.

More mutters sounded as each man did up his shirt and sat down.

Atax held up his glass. "This time, a toast to you, my faithful followers. May you find all that your hearts' desire."

"Hear, hear!" The five men clinked their glasses once again and downed the wine.

"And now, gentlemen, the entertainment." Atax clapped his hands.

Ten beautiful girls, dressed in little more than diaphanous rags, flowed into the room. From a door on the opposite side, five musicians entered. When the music started, so did the dancing, every man's eye on the women's perfect, undulating forms.

"When they have finished entertaining you this way, you may do with them what you wish. Enjoy yourselves, my friends, for you have earned it."

Smiles and leers replaced the fear and anxiety of only moments ago. These men now belonged to Atax for the rest of their lives. Though free to move about the worlds as Atax's desires required, they were bound to him just as much as every other soul in the keep; his, all his to play with as he wished.

Atax signaled a waiting servant for more wine, then reclined in his chair. Could life get any better than this?

Hammers pounding on metal and saws rasping through wood blended with the shouts of vauroks and goblins. Looking up from the long sheets of parchment displaying his blueprints, Khadag glanced at the pale sun hanging in a red sky. Fornoss never changed. It hardly mattered, the construction of his new ship progressed well.

A goblin ran up to him, out of breath. "First Khadag!" The little creature saluted him fist to forehead. "The last shipment of bronze has arrived."

"Excellent. Get it to the smiths as quickly as possible."

"Yes, First." The goblin ran back the way it had come.

The rest of the bronze had already been formed into sheets for the prow. They waited inside the warehouse where goblins shaped the mast. Others worked in another building near it, forging the ram that would see the end of the Elves on the sea. Made in the shape of a wyvern's head, in memory of his beloved *Wyvern Queen*, the ram would have something no wyvern ever did—a long iron spike protruding from its lower chest. This is what would stab a hole, one foot in diameter, below the waterline of Elven and Human ships.

Instead of forty oarsmen, this ship would hold fifty to a side. He had learned an important lesson from the loss of the *Wyvern Queen*; attacking Elven ships was one thing, ramming another. A vessel needed speed and protection at the bow to deal the damage to sink them.

Khadag rolled his shoulders, easing cramped muscles. He worked his crew from sunrise to sunset, guiding them every step of the way. No one complained. No one dared. He rubbed the stump of his truncated arm and turned his attention to the ship taking form by the shore. The ribbing, made from soft pine, as the rest of the ship would be, stood up from the cradle like a giant skeleton. Still months from completion, Khadag was confident this one would rule the seas. The original plans had called for wood from Tiralan. Delcarion had squashed the idea by reminding him of the wards around the forest. Too bad. They would have been perfect.

"Khadag." The voice came from behind him.

A red band encircled the upper arm of the vaurok who called his name. "Yadich. It's good to see you. What brings you here?" Khadag touched his right fist to his friend's, a salute only used between Firsts.

Yadich's nostril slits flared. "It seems the master prefers to use my skills for running messages rather than as a warrior."

A surreptitious glance showed no one near. Still, Khadag kept his voice low. "It seems the master has little regard for the skills of many."

"Truth. And we are not the only ones who are not happy."

That news didn't surprise Khadag. "What can we do? He is the master."

"Nothing, not as long as the mothers are held captive."

The mothers, the females of the vaurok race, were kept in enclosures, locked behind stone walls and thick gates, denied the rights that should be their privilege. Kept continually pregnant, they were treated worse than brood sows. Despite that, the mothers banded together to breed smarter, larger and stronger vauroks. Khadag and Yadich were both products of that plan. Balphegor's response was to take some of the great vauroks, feed them throk and send them into destruction.

Khadag's right fist clenched with an anger older than him. "One day, things will change."

"Or not," Yadich said, his dark eyes flashing. "There are also those who believe the master will win, that there can be no other outcome."

"There is that chance and I will strive for it. Perhaps once the master has all the worlds, he will release the mothers."

Yadich touched his fist to Khadag's, in a show of agreement. "There is that chance. I have wasted enough time. The master wishes to see you."

Khadag let out a snort. "Does he plan on taking my other hand?"

With a shrug, Yadich turned to the path leading to the portal. "Who knows? It wasn't right he took the one he did. I'll walk to the portal with you."

Yadich left him at the gate to Balphegor's castle; he had other errands to run now that the white egg had hatched and the occupant safely ensconced with the mothers.

Khadag passed through the massive gate, waving to the great vauroks manning the battlements, then ran across the empty courtyard. It never paid to keep the master waiting any longer than necessary. Dodging throngs of goblins and vauroks traversing the halls, he made for the long staircase leading to the throne room.

Once at the top, Khadag knocked, then waited several minutes.

Finally, the master's oily-smooth voice sounded in his head. *"Enter."*

Balphegor wasn't the only one in the room. Khadag recognized the concealing cloak and cowl of Delcarion who knelt before the master along with a dark-skinned human, a sorcerer by the name of Mandigo. Khadag sneered and covered the distance to the blue marble throne in long strides. He prostrated himself before the feline figure seated there and waited to be recognized.

"Explain yourself, Mandigo." Balphegor now chose to speak aloud.

"We almost had her, Master. The silver-haired girl." Mandigo's voice shook. "I spotted her and I happened to have a temporary portal spelled to a position nearby. I waited until she reached the place and opened the portal, but I only had a very few vauroks with me. They weren't sufficient. Perhaps if I'd had more. She had help and, I regret to say, escaped."

"Again. There are always excuses. Never results."

"But, my master…"

"Silence." Balphegor spoke the word no louder than the others, nonetheless the command in that voice had to be obeyed. The sorcerer shut up. "Delcarion. I am also displeased with you."

Khadag smirked. With his face a mere inch from the floor, no one would see it.

"My master," Delcarion said. "How have I displeased you? I beg of you to tell me so I may correct the problem."

"You have been attempting to correct the problem for some time now. And that…is….the problem." The tip of Balphegor's tawny tail, just visible in Khadag's line of sight, flipped in agitation. "These temporary portals are proving troublesome."

"My master, I have had some new success. I expanded the opening time to fourteen minutes. I'm now working on making it larger." Delcarion's rough voice held no hint of the fear he must be feeling.

"A paltry improvement. Khadag, you may kneel."

Khadag pushed himself into a kneeling position and bowed his head. "My master, I await your pleasure."

"I have received reports on the progress of your ship."

Suppressing a shudder of alarm, Khadag forced himself to remain still. *Who has been spying on me?*

"We are pleased. Every day the ship grows. At least some are good, loyal workers."

"Thank you, my master." Khadag's mind whirled with ways to expose the ones who spied. Although, if they continued to report the speed at which the ship was constructed, it might not be something to worry over.

"I punish. I also reward." Balphegor waved his hand and an object appeared in the air in front of him.

A stifled gasp sounded from behind. *Delcarion.* The object Balphegor conjured appeared to be a sword hilt made of a dark metal etched with runes, possibly Elven.

Balphegor plucked it from the air. "Khadag. Approach."

With a bow of his head, Khadag rose and strode to the throne. Never had he stood so close to the master.

"Hold out your left arm."

Khadag did as instructed. Balphegor gripped it, just above the stump. His touch, even through the leather Khadag wore, felt like ice tinged with dread and it sent a shiver down his spine. The master placed the pommel of the hilt against the scarred stump, then spoke words in a language Khadag had never heard. A sharp pain shot up his arm and he bit his tongue to keep from crying out.

The hilt buried itself in Khadag's arm, right down to the cross guard. Balphegor moved his grip to the end of the stump, his hand closing over flesh and metal. He spoke more words and Khadag felt his arm bones move as if to grasp the hilt on their own. He felt little pain now, though the sensation rose gooseflesh up and down his body.

Moving his hand from the arm to Khadag's forehead, Balphegor spoke more strange words. Strangling noises came from Delcarion's position and Khadag wondered if the master was responsible.

When finished, Balphegor lowered his arm to his lap. "Step back. What I have given you is a tchiru, a Tiranen sword. You now have control of it. A suitable replacement for your hand."

Khadag returned to his place. With a thought, he brought the sword to life. Gleaming steel flashed into existence, the crossguard sitting snug against the blunt end of his arm. After a few practice swings, he decided he could get used to it. Much better than the hook he had considered. He took a closer look. The runes had changed, though he still couldn't read them.

He bowed to Balphegor. "My master, this is a wondrous gift you have given me. I can't possibly thank you enough."

"Build me ships, Khadag. Ships to command the seas. You may go. Take this offal with you." An imperious wave of Balphegor's hand indicated Mandigo. "Escort him to the Black Masks. They may do to him what they will, but he is not to be killed. I may yet have a use for him."

A trip to the Black Masks, the vaurok torturers, would only mean pain and suffering. Mandigo's face paled. "My master! Please! I beg of you! Give me another chance!"

"I am. If you don't go quietly, I will change my mind."

Mandigo shut up. Once they'd left the master's presence, he gibbered under his breath like a fool, trembling like an vaurokling awaiting his first kill trial.

Khadag took the sorcerer to the Black Masks deep under the castle. Vauroks who'd been given specialized training, they wore the full leather masks that gave them their name so any surviving victims wouldn't be able to take revenge.

"The master wishes him to live. Unfortunately," he said to the closest Black Mask.

The vaurok just nodded as two others fastened manacles around the wrists and ankles of the now screaming sorcerer. One picked up a hot iron from a nearby brazier. Khadag didn't stay to watch the fun, he returned to the portal eager to finish his ship and play with his new toy.

Delcarion's entire body trembled. He'd lived without the tchiru for five hundred years. He'd thought it safe in the master's hands, that one day he'd have it again. The severing of the magical connection had hurt more than he'd thought possible. It was like losing his son, all over again.

"Delcarion. I have another job for you. Do not disappoint me." Balphegor leaned towards him, his tail flipping faster, his voice now silent, only sounding in Delcarion's head.

Forcing the words from his throat, Delcarion said, "I...await your pleasure, my master."

"I wish you to go to Tiralan. To the Pool of Memories you told me about. Use it. I want to know all there is about this silver-haired girl. Perhaps if we know more about her, capturing her will be easier."

Feasible, in theory. "Master, there are many Elven wards on the forest. They will know I have come. I have too much black magic in me."

"You will have my help. Once you arrive at the border, open the door to my power. I will let you through."

"Yes, my master." To go to Tiralan...could he handle it? The memories? Delcarion's heart pounded. Since his capture, the master had never permitted him to travel to any world except Fornoss. He had to do this right or he'd never be allowed out again. "Once we have the information, Master, may I take command of the search?"

"No. There is still rebellion in your heart. Until I have rid you of it, I cannot allow you full access to the worlds Arvanion's spawn still hold."

"I understand, my master." With a sinking heart, Delcarion bowed, then strode to the door, down the stairs and to the portal that would take him to Tiru.

The closest portal to Tiralan lay several days away. No horse would tolerate his black magic, even if he could find one big enough to carry him. He walked the distance, travelling by night and avoiding the towns and villages, and memories too painful to remember.

Snow lay all around the ancient forest, thick and white, not like the thin skiff that fell on most of Fornoss, tinged red by the sick sky. He breathed deep of the clean, fresh air and closed his eyes. Far back in his mind, a door waited. He removed the glove from his right hand and held it out to the wardings. Palpable, though invisible, the Elven spells rose up to attack his dark magic. If any Elves were in the forest, they'd know something was wrong even though he hadn't actually touched the wards.

"*Adrach tok raghad.*" Delcarion opened the door in his mind and reached for the thread connecting his power to his master's, the thread only selected sorcerers were permitted to use.

Balphegor allowed him the use of his power, which meant he had to trust him to some degree, yet he refused him free rein of the worlds like the other sorcerers. Delcarion hated Balphegor to the depths of his being. Despite his hatred, he could no more disobey him than he could kill himself. He wished it were otherwise, on both counts.

"*Tokara sharidig choll.*" He spoke the words that would allow Balphegor to use him as a vessel.

Power pulsated in his head to the point of agony. Delcarion raised his arms to the wards. Black strings of light shot from his fingertips, grabbed hold of the Elven warding spell and shredded a portion of it, just enough to allow Delcarion through. A hint of pain crossed the thread.

Destroying even a portion of the Elven spell was not as easy for Balphegor as he pretended. It had to be the strain of the oak tree Lindren created. The damn thing still sat not far from the entrance to the castle, disrupting the energies of the master's place between worlds. The tree had finally begun to shrink, but it would be a long time before it vanished.

Delcarion stared at the woods he hadn't seen for too long, praying no Elves were close, that none had decided to visit the forest that day. Chastising himself for a fool, he slipped through the hole, taking care not to touch the sides. Snow crunched under foot and, despite himself, memories rushed in. He forced them away. An hour's walk, then he stood before the Pool of Memories.

The forest hadn't changed. Delcarion couldn't say the same for the pool. Where there had once been a carefully maintained bright profusion of flowering bushes and plants, little but dead twigs remained. It was winter, yes, still, there should have been a scrap of life. Most of the overgrown plants had died years before.

Fragile leaves, winter brown, floated on the silvery, viscous liquid. Similar to the liquid in Balphegor's Pool of Seeing, it felt different. Not oily. Not tainted with the black magic Delcarion now held within himself.

After scooping out the leaves, twigs and refuse with a gloved hand, he paused, desperately needing to gaze into the memories in the pool, memories he'd put there of his bondmates, his son. Without his tchiru, he could no longer put in memories. He could see them, however, and he removed his glove.

To the nine hells with Balphegor. I need to see my son. One last time.

Delcarion dipped his hand in the liquid, one name ringing silently in his ears. *Oberain.* Images of his son flooded his head. His birth, the little boy who loved the Hrulka so much he'd learned to ride before the age of two; at age twenty, as Delcarion taught him to use weapons; his sixtieth birthday, when he could begin courting; the warrior he became, tall, skilled, strong and proud. Delcarion reveled in each and every reminiscence, watching some twice, three times, before moving on to his beloved bondmates, his parents and grandparents.

Time passed. The sun fell below the trees before Delcarion pulled his emotions back in line. Instead of the people important to him in his past, he concentrated on the one he wanted for the future.

Images flowed of people he remembered, their voices alive once again. Fifty-three years had passed since the end of the Tiranen, far more years since Delcarion had last spoken with Thelaru and Arlayva. He saw them again in the pool as they marveled over their newborn daughter, a tiny little thing with incredible lungs. No wonder she was so small now, she'd started life that way.

Tenaya. They called her Tenaya. Little Cat. Now he had a name to attach to the face. Delcarion watched her grow, play, learn to ride. What he didn't see was her training, how well she performed with sword, axe or mace. Delcarion remembered the one time he'd seen her, out with the Elves. She used a bow, a weapon not used by Tiranen. For some odd reason, it seemed to suit her.

Then he found memories no one ever put in the pool, ones he doubted she'd intended anyone to see—those of people close to her now, especially a young Elf named Kelwyn. Delcarion's brow raised as he watched her teach him how to love. He should have turned away, he should have been embarrassed by her display. Instead, Delcarion kept his eyes on all of it while feelings and urges long suppressed sent lightning storms straight through to his soul and he actually thanked Balphegor that he'd suppressed the intense ache that should have accompanied them. He watched that scene four times.

She put memories of others not of her race in the pool; Lindren and Rhianna, Lowren and Tarine, Taurin, two young Elves he didn't know by the names of Arufin and Kardrin, and three Humans, all of whom she held affection for, particularly the last one. Rhone Arden. This was a recent memory.

Delcarion yanked his hand out of the pool. "You shouldn't have turned to Humans for love. They're worthless. Useless. The Elves are bad enough. It's not natural."

He glanced at the winter dark sky. "Enough time spent on memories." Even those not his own. Delcarion spun on his heel and headed back to the hole in the wardings. "I will have you one day, Tenaya. Then you will see the way it is supposed to be."

As he walked, he thought about one of Tenaya's memories in particular, one involving the dragon Black Wing and the mission he'd set her on...to wake the Sleepers. *The Master will be very interested.*

Snow began falling, filling his tracks. Soon no trace of his passage would remain.

Cat's Tales continues with In The Company of Elves, coming in May of 2015!

Character Guide

I'm not including the names of every person in the book, only those who matter. There's so many who are mentioned only once or twice.

The 'au' sound is pronounced like 'ow', so vaurok is 'vow-rock'.

Arvanion— (ar-**van**-yun) – Creator of the Elves
Balphegor—(**bal**-fuh-gor) – Enemy of Arvanion, the Elves, the Tiranen and Humans

Tiranen

Cat – full name is Little Cat, Tenaya (ten-**ay**-ya) in the Tiranen language and Anshaia (an-**shy**-a) in Elven
Thelaru – (thel-**are**-oo) - War Chief of the Tiranen, Cat's father and Arlayva's bond-mate
Arlayva – (ar-**lay**-va) Cat's mother and bond-mate to Thelaru
Mordru – (**more**-dru) Cat's brother

Elves

Silverwood
> Kelwyn – (**kel**-win) Cat's best friend and Lindren's nephew
> Lindren – Elder of Silverwood enclave
> Rhianna – Lindren's soul-mate
> Tarine – (tar-**een**) Kelwyn's mother and Lowren's soul-mate
> Lowren – Lindren's younger brother, Tarine's soul-mate and
>> Kelwyn's father
> Taurin – (**tao**-rin) Lindren's cousin, a *qirand*
> Orrin – Kelwyn's older brother

Arufin – (**ar**-oo-fin) Orrin's best friend
Farin – (**fare**-in) a Silverwood warrior
Gilfalan – (**gill**-fa-lan) Silverwood's sword master
Denefir – (**den-** eh-fear) Silverwood's archery master
Darsha – Lindren's oldest son
Robilan (Robbi) – (**rob**-i-lan) Lindren's fourth son

Greenwood

Rendir – (ren-**dear**) Elder of Greenwood and Lindren's
friend
Cainfir – (**cane**-fear) captain of a company of mixed Elves,
Kelwyn's captain

Gold Moon

Terafin – (**tear**-a fin) Elder, Lindren's cousin
Shain – Lindren's second son

Blue Hills

Arnir – Lindren's third son
Sandrin – Elder of Blue Hills

Whitewood

Forcin – Elder
Cadwyn – Kelwyn's cousin on his mother's side

Humans

Tezerain

Rodrin Tallesar – King of Tezerain
Lisha – Queen of Tezerain
Gailen – Rodrin and Lisha's oldest son
Dayn – Rodrin and Lisha's second son

Raimon Teale – Duke of Teale and Rodrin's cousin
Talon – a member of the Pit Lords, a thief
Rat – a member of the Pit Lords, a procurer
Yait – leader of the Pit Lords
Rhone Arden – youngest brother of Baron Corbin Arden
Tozer – a sorcerer and leader of the Bloody Hands
Aris Kerend – Baron of Kerend
Brade Kerend – Aris' second son
Jewel – Cat's maid in Tezerain
Mattu – Rodrin's stable master
Crinon Teale – Raimon Teale's chamberlain and cousin

Balphegor's Creatures

Delcarion – a giant of unknown species
Khadag – a vaurok First
Yadich – a vaurok First

Arvanion's Worlds

Tiru
Enclaves
    Tiralan (home of the Tiranen)
    Blue Hills
    Spine Mountain
    Mistwood
    Eagle River

Human countries
    Daranor

Urdran
Enclaves
    Silverwood
    Gold Moon
    Ringwood

Human countries
    Kitring-Tor
    Thallan-Mar
    The Denfold

Morata

Enclaves
- Northwood (abandoned)
- Southwood
- Ravenwood

Human Countries
- Armatia

Darda

Enclaves
- Whitewood
- Swiftwater
- Summerwood

Cathras

Enclaves
- Greenwood
- Brightwood
- Moon Falls

Human Countries
- Greymount

Fornoss

Lost to Balphegor

About the Author

Sandie Bergen lives on an island in the Pacific; Vancouver Island to be exact, idyllic and perfect in its own way. She lives with Charlie, her husband of thirty-six years, and one muse, her cat Molly. She has two grown children, Amanda and Aaron. Sandie has been writing for years, mostly for personal enjoyment. The Jada-Drau is her first published novel followed by its sequels, Tyrsa's Choice and The Angry Sword. Also published are th first two books of Cat's Tales, Arvanion's Gift and Silver Cat Black Fox. She's also had two ghost stories with Whispering Spirits Digital Magazine, as well as stories published with Worlds of Wonder Magazine and Flash Me Magazine.

Visit her at:

www.sandiebergen.com
www.sandiebergen.ca

On Facebook at: Sandie Bergen, Author
On Twitter: @SandieBergen

About the Cover Artist

Ilsie Om creates beautiful book covers with passion and integrity and is an artist we find enjoyable to work with. To learn more about her visit her website at http://wonderburg.4ormat.com/home

Find more to read from Marion Margaret Press

http://www.marionmargaretpress.com

Book reviews are welcome. If you would like to tell us what you thought of this book, please send your comments to publisher@marionmargaretpress.com

You can also post a few sentences of what you thought and rate the book at various places around the internet.
Amazon.com encourages comments when you buy through their site and the comments help us with our ratings.
Join Goodreads.com to post your comments and rate the book.
Make a library at http://books.google.com/ and leave comments on any books you add in.

Or feel free to drop us a note via snail mail to:
Marion Margaret Press
Headquarters:
PO Box 245
Hebron, NE 68370

Be sure to visit our website and sign up for our newsletter so you get all the updates and the free goodies we'll give subscribers.

You can also find us on Facebook as Marion Margaret Press (page) and at Twitter as marionmbooks.

CPSIA information can be obtained at www.ICGtesting.com
Printed in the USA
LVOW07s0352081114

412584LV00002B/13/P